The MADONNA SECRET

"Sophie Strand's wrist is a time machine, not the sort composed of cogs, gears, and wheels but the kind that entrances: the fungal brew that slips into your cup and melts all of history. To read this book is to travel to a simmering world sensuously realized, the heat of which might force you to fall to your knees—in worship."

BÁYÒ AKÓMOLÁFÉ, PH.D., AUTHOR OF
*THESE WILDS BEYOND OUR FENCES:
LETTERS TO MY DAUGHTER ON HUMANITY'S
SEARCH FOR HOME*

"There are stories that define our lives and retellings of those stories that transform our lives. As I read Sophie Strand's *The Madonna Secret* I could feel the old, brittle bricks of a foundational story dissolving in my being. In its place rooted a reconnection to the healing of soil and place, a reweaving into the underground networks of women and ancestral wisdom, and a flowering expansion into possibilities beyond patriarchal myths. I wept as I finished the book, feeling how Sophie's deep scholarship and bright-burning heart rewrites the story of Magdalene and Jesus; it is riveting, revealing, and revelatory. I honestly can't recommend this book highly enough. It is one I will revisit over and over again. Be ready for a cellular shift that will not only change each individual who reads it but also transform the very paradigm beneath our feet."

HEATHERASH AMARA, AUTHOR OF
WARRIOR GODDESS TRAINING

The MADONNA SECRET

A Sacred Planet Book

SOPHIE STRAND

Bear & Company
Rochester, Vermont

Bear & Company
One Park Street
Rochester, Vermont 05767
www.BearandCompanyBooks.com

Text stock is SFI certified

Bear & Company is a division of Inner Traditions International

Sacred Planet Books are curated by Richard Grossinger, Inner Traditions editorial board member and cofounder and former publisher of North Atlantic Books. The Sacred Planet collection, published under the umbrella of the Inner Traditions family of imprints, includes works on the themes of consciousness, cosmology, alternative medicine, dreams, climate, permaculture, alchemy, shamanic studies, oracles, astrology, crystals, hyperobjects, locutions, and subtle bodies.

Cataloging-in-Publication Data for this title is available from the Library of Congress

ISBN 978-1-59143-467-2 (print)
ISBN 978-1-59143-468-9 (ebook)

Printed and bound in the United States by Lake Book Manufacturing, LLC
The text stock is SFI certified. The Sustainable Forestry Initiative® program promotes sustainable forest management.

10 9 8 7 6 5 4 3 2 1

Text design and layout by Virginia Scott Bowman
This book was typeset in Garamond Premier Pro with Americanus used as the display typeface

Cover illustration: *The Mystic Mary Magdalene, Patron Saint of Contemplatives* by Sue Ellen Parkinson, www.sueellenparkinson.com

To send correspondence to the author of this book, mail a first-class letter to the author c/o Inner Traditions • Bear & Company, One Park Street, Rochester, VT 05767, and we will forward the communication, or contact the author directly at **www.sophiestrand.com**.

• • •

For all mothers and grandmothers.

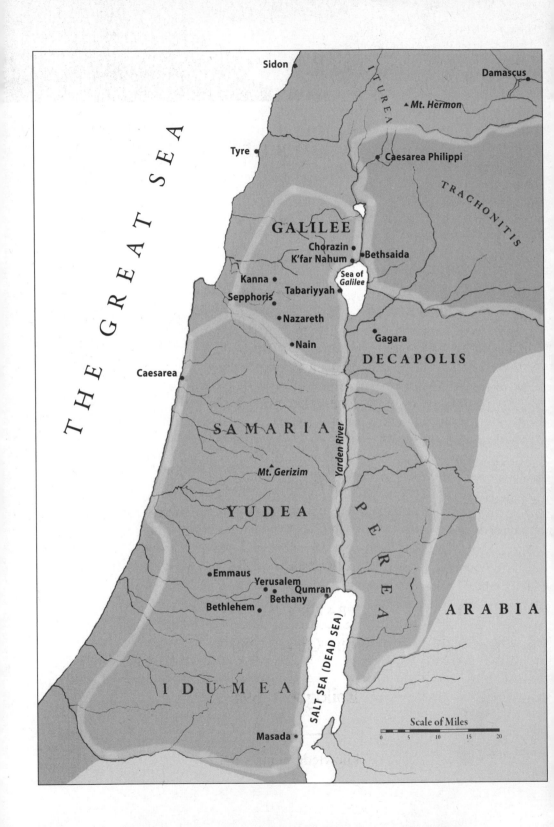

Contents

Author's Note

While *The Madonna Secret* is fictional, it is based on serious study of the primary documents available from first-century Palestine: canonical, gnostic, and apocryphal. In the tradition of my historical-fiction predecessors Mary Renault and Mary Stewart, I have sought to ground my characters, my setting, and my plot in textured, rigorous research.

Who was the historical Jesus? Who was Mary Magdalene? Why do folk traditions and recently unearthed gnostic texts put her at the center of the ministry? Why do the canonical Gospels marginalize her? Why is Luke's the only Gospel that includes the Nativity?

Judea and Galilee were under Roman imperial rule during the time Jesus is said to have lived. But the Gospels were composed in Greek many years after his death. Jesus and his followers would have spoken Aramaic, the language of the day in Palestine. What does it mean that his teachings come to us, not in his own words, but through—what was for them—the language of oppression? In the writing of this book, I have attempted to use the people and place-names that would have been used by the Aramaic-speaking Jewish people of first-century Palestine. Let us replant these characters in their proper social, spiritual, and ecological context.

Jesus would have been called something close to "Yeshua." Mary is Greek for the Jewish "Miriam." Peter, the well-known disciple who founded the church, is derived from the words *petros* and *cephas,* respectively Greek and Latin for "rock." Peter's real Aramaic name would have been "Shimon." And Lazarus would have been "Lazaros."

Likewise, I have attempted to locate versions of place-names closest to their Aramaic original. The Jordan River becomes the "Yarden River." Capernaum becomes "K'far Nahum." The letter *J* did not appear in Aramaic and Hebrew during this time period, so all *J* names have been returned to their original pronunciation. Thus, Jerusalem becomes "Yerusalem," James becomes "Yakov," and Jesus becomes "Yeshua."

It is important to remember that Jesus was a Jewish teacher, born to a people responding to years of imperial oppression. He was deeply informed by Jewish tradition, in particular the practice of Targums: spoken translations and interpretations of scripture that were the primary way of transmitting spiritual wisdom in the first century. Not only have many of his teachings been lost in translation, but the ecological texture of his stories and his lived, sensual reality have been lost across the millennia. I have attempted to tell a story that is deeply rooted in the flowers, the trees, the animals, the birdsong, and the human complexity of Bethany and Galilee as they existed at that time. I have tried to do what I so admire in other works of historical fiction: I have attempted to recreate a living, breathing ecosystem that shapes my characters.

Nevertheless, this book makes no claims to represent an authoritative interpretation of Jesus's teachings or the meaning of his life. It is the story of one woman. And because women are so often written *out* of stories, it attempts to understand the diversity of female experiences during the Second Temple Period.

The Madonna Secret is a work of fiction that takes seriously Jesus's love of storytelling. What does it mean to tell a story that threatens an empire? What does it mean to tell a story that heals? What does it mean to tell a story of love?

Some say it never happened,
Some say it happens over and over.
"The Flowering of the Rod,"
from *Trilogy* by H. D.

Preface

Gallia Comata 72 CE

The further north Leukas traveled, the harder it was to feel his god and to say the holy words. The prayers had barely left his mouth when they chilled in the cold air and turned to blue ash. Yet every morning he knelt in the frosty soil, bowing before the dawn light between the pines, and tried to kindle the faith that had so recently set his whole life aflame.

Your kingdom will come, your will be done . . .

Was this dark, thorn-encrusted country the kingdom? *This?* This land seemed to care little for men or for their ideas of beauty and well-being.

Leukas had come to find her. The one no one spoke of anymore. The one who had disappeared from the stories. But along the way he had lost touch with the very conviction that had sent him across the sea, into the land of the Celts, up into the wilderness of Gaul. When had his confidence finally crumbled? Perhaps it was the night he'd taken shelter in a cave, startled to light his candle and discover a nest of yellow bones topped with a bleached human skull. Still, he had forced himself to spend the night in that strange crypt, listening to the muttering of the invisible creatures above him, bat wings brushing the stone ceiling, sending flakes of ancient dust down into his eyes.

He was a trained scribe, traveling by way of storytelling. Certainly this would all make for a good story when he returned to Alexandria. But he was increasingly worried that he might *not* return.

He traveled faster these days, peering anxiously over his shoulder, even when the road was long and straight and he could see for miles in both directions.

Leukas missed his room near the harbors of Alexandria. What he would give for one slow day spent studying, uncurling scrolls so soft and well-used that they felt like a woman's skin in his hands. Later there would be a sumptuous dinner with the other Christians. Thick aromatic wine served in metal cups. Fresh fish that flaked apart at the slightest touch. Moist fig cakes. Rich, good food with flavor! The Gauls used no spices. They seemed to think that temperature was a flavor itself. The soup he was served at each inn was piping hot and he never failed to scald his mouth. He longed for the press of people in the streets; strangers arriving from every corner of the world, all the time.

What surprised him most was that he missed the sensual pagan gods, their statues smiling down on him from the front of every rich man's house. Leukas missed beauty that had been made by human hands. Even now, a convert to the new faith, Leukas's Christ was a son of man. Leukas pictured the Christ's body: his thin hands laced with blue, delicate veins. Wide, almost feminine eyes peered out from a stern, starved face. He pictured his god most often late at night, when he was shivering in the dark.

Our Father, who is above. Give me my bread today and tomorrow. Help me, help me . . .

God help him! Here the shrines and temples had not been arranged by the hands of men. Who had piled up those bullhorns? Who had placed those wreaths of dried roses on the branch of a tree? Leukas struggled to imagine men creating such displays. More and more, he imagined the winds, the tall, rain-blackened trees, and the bone-white cliffs as gods themselves. Surely it was the gray, muscular thunder that had shifted these huge boulders across the landscape. One night he found himself praying, not to his god, but to the wolf he'd seen watching him from a distant outcropping of rock, its fur rippling like water, eyes of molten amber.

It had been months of travel, stopping in every village. At each local inn he bought a cup of ale, which entitled him to be privy to the local gossip, rumors, and news from Rome. "The bard is dreaming again. He's in his cups."

"No!" Leukas was startled back into awareness.

The rotund innkeeper was eyeing him from across the table, his beetle-black eyes narrowing suspiciously. "You asked about her?"

"Yes," Leukas insisted, belching and trying to swallow back the sour taste of the ale. "Any rumors of her?"

"I have more than rumors. I have met her. She gave me back my eye."

"I don't believe it." Leukas gave a nervous laugh.

The woman beside him gripped her cup with such force that her swollen knuckles turned white.

"I don't need you to believe me," the innkeeper said. "Romans like you gouged it out. She touched me once in the market near Avaricum, and I had an eye again. Just like that I could see."

It was stories like this that kept him traveling past the last reaches of the empire. Leukas stopped in every inn, searching for tales. But time was running out. She would be very old by now. One of the last alive. If she *was* alive.

"She has grown fur over her entire body—like the animals she dwells with," a man told Leukas, his fingers stroking the long blade at his hip. Leukas repressed a shiver. He could imagine such a man tracking him through the forest.

"No!" said another man. "It's not fur. She goes naked except for her own hair. But it is long enough to serve as a dress."

"Yes. But it matters not that she is naked if she is hardly ever seen," a sallow-skinned woman countered, her green eyes swimming in a face as transparent as a tidal pool. "She spends all her time mourning the Christos in her cave up in the old country."

A pretty girl with chestnut curls nodded emphatically, her mouth puckering around the word Christos.

Yes, Leukas thought. *Tell me more about the Christos. Tell me what no one else has heard about him. Tell me anything.*

"She mourns him? Why does she mourn him while the other disciples spread the good news of his resurrection? Why is she sorrowful?" Leukas asked.

The men and women gathered around the table glanced at each other nervously.

"We are not followers of Christos here," the innkeeper answered. "We don't care about that story."

"But you care about her. Even though she lives like a hermit in a cave . . ." Leukas mused. He had heard this all before. *Where* was that cave where she lived like an animal, he wanted to know?

"She is no recluse!" a boy interjected. His pale hands fluttered anxiously on the table. "My mother saw her last month! She laid hands on a boy with withered legs and he walked again. She does not hide. She travels and heals."

"She tries to atone for her sins, her whoring . . ." slurred a bald man.

The pretty girl scowled, clearly angry.

"Shu . . . shu . . . shut up, Attalus. She is no whore!" croaked the nervous boy, his voice cracking. "She is a healer."

"A healer? A whore? A wild animal? What is she?" Leukas scoffed.

"Why do you want to know?" The pretty girl was suddenly suspicious.

"I'm a bard," he explained simply. "I've heard she has the best story of all. I've come to ask her for it."

"A bard, aye?" The old woman at his side jabbed him with her elbow. "Well, let me tell you the truth as I heard it from my sister. She came to Gaul by boat. And the boat had no oars. My sister was there on the beach, she was. Saw it all herself. Storm clouds a'chasin' the lady. And when the lady's foot touched the shore, there sprang forth a blue rose. Birds flew up from a chalice she carried with her. It was carved from a man's bone. And she came with a dark girl, a tall man, and another man who had died and come back to life . . ."

The chestnut-haired girl gasped. She'd never heard this version of events.

Leukas, though, was not surprised. He had heard this story before. She had arrived by sea with her brother, Lazaros.

"Children's tales," he said dismissively. "The fever dream of a madman!"

Leukas always played the good-natured cynic, knowing that his seeming disbelief would bring forth even more stories in attempts to convince him of her power. Everyone wanted to prove that they were an authority.

"She is in Upper Gallia," the Twin had told Leukas the night before he set out. "Of that I am sure. She has the secret teachings. But I doubt she will give them up easily."

At first everyone he met had a story about her. But as he went further north, they said less and less. The further he traveled up into Gaul the more people distrusted the Romans.

One rainy night, with winter's teeth still speared deep into the frozen ground, Leukas came to a squat stone inn. The door was barred by an old crone. "We've paid our due," she growled. "We won't abide by any Roman pretenders who want to milk us dry." Raindrops ran down the slanted thatch roof, dividing him from her, inside from outside. Leukas could see a large room behind her, lit by several candles, and a couple of men hunched over their cups. Women gathered in the corner, whispering.

It was late and he was drenched, his hair plastered to his forehead. He would have given the cloak off his back for a seat near a fire and a warm bowl of soup. The old woman narrowed her yellowed eyes. "Cheldric had his entire crop burned when he refused your lot. And the necks of his goats were slit. So we paid up. But I will not pay again. Not even if those fiends come on horseback and demand it."

"I will pay you!" Leukas insisted. "Trust me. I have come a long way. I am a storyteller, and will offer both coin and tales if you give me a bed."

He knew that she would not turn him away. He might be foreign, but he had stories from distant countries. Only a woman who enjoyed a gossip would run an inn for travelers. She fed off news.

"Not a *filli*? Not a magician?" she questioned, leaning closer to him. Was the woman sniffing him?

"*Ne*," he shook his head, water cascading from his hair back under his cloak. He wished she would speed up her interrogation. "I come from the south."

"Aye. I'll host a bard, but none of those filli from the west. They scare the animals and then none of the sheep will breed. You look too dark for one of them, though. They are fair and icy."

"I have no spells. No magic."

At last the woman reluctantly ushered him in. She took his coat from him and draped it over a stool near a fire that exhaled its smoke up a small open shaft. Rain fell in from the opening, crackling and spitting in the flame likes drips of animal fat.

The Twin had warned him about these people. The two of them had sat up until the morning hours, speaking about his journey. "They are said to be unpredictable," he told Leukas. "Keep your wits about you for I wouldn't be surprised if they cut your throat and bled you out into one of their fields. She would seek out such people. See them as her own. Of that I am certain. They follow the instructions of the trees. And trees care little for men like us."

"If I die, then my blood will spill for Our Father," Leukas had responded confidently.

The Twin had slammed his fist down on the table at that, almost upsetting their cups. His upper lip twitched with displeasure. "Never say that again! Such words are dangerous. He died for nobody. And nobody should die because of him!"

There were men and women in the inn, drinking ale at a flat table and sharing stringy stew that looked like boiled reeds from a pond. Leukas joined in quietly, listening to the strange blend of Gallic and Latin. When he saw that the men were reaching the bottom of their cups, he launched into his favorite story—the one about the woman who had turned her terrible husband into an ass. It usually roused laughter, but as he spoke, the words felt as threadbare as his cloak.

"I'll pay for all if someone tells me the news," he said after his story was done. "More ale! Please!" Those gathered watched him stonily.

A man with a purple scar along his flat nose eyed Leukas with distrust, but sipped deeply when his cup was refilled. "What kind of news?" he asked in a gravelly voice.

"I am searching for the woman they call Miriam," Leukas stated boldly. Sometimes he hedged, but his intuition this night was to ask directly. "She would be dark like me. A Jew."

"A lover?" asked an old woman who was bald except for a thin thatching of gray hair on the very top of her head. "She run away from you?"

Leukas snorted, placing his hand on his thigh beneath the table, gripping his own flesh in an attempt to steady himself. He was surprised he couldt get anyone to speak of her. He sensed that where the legends disappeared, the living woman might be hiding.

"There is no woman by that name here," the scarred man muttered.

"Yes, there is!" piped up a girl. "You lie, Talus! He must be speaking about Mother."

"Mother?" Leukas asked lightly. There was a pressure between his eyes, as if someone had pressed a finger into his forehead. Was it a headache? Or the sense that danger was close at hand?

"Be quiet, you stupid girl!" roared Talus.

The arrival of the old innkeeper silenced everyone. "You!" she screeched, pointing at Leukas with a crooked, arthritic finger. "Out! I want you gone by tomorrow. You may sleep here. But only until sunrise!"

He nodded deferentially, hiding the tingle of anticipation that was spreading from his aching temples into the rest of his body. Never had he come up against such secrecy and anger! It could only mean one thing.

He was close.

As he got up from the table to find his bed, someone tapped his shoulder.

"Do you want to speak to her because she was a follower of Christos?" asked a husky voice. He turned to see a woman with a golden complexion, which marked her as a foreigner. Egyptian, Leukas guessed.

"I want the truth," he answered breathlessly. The woman was close enough that he could smell her. Cinnamon. Balsam. The perfumes of a warmer country.

"You have the stories already. From Saul. From the disciples. They have all shared the good news. Leave her be." She held his gaze.

"Do not take me for a fool," he said softly so that no one would overhear. "I make my way by collecting stories, and I have heard enough from the men who knew him. There are things that no one dares to say. Why do they pretend she was not with them? What do they hide? She is the only one who might still know the truth."

Her eyes narrowed. He could see her left hand moving strangely, as if feeling for an invisible thread in the air.

"Come," she said at last.

"Follow you?" he asked stupidly.

"Yes. Now."

She swept from the inn and, coming to his senses, he hurried after her.

The woman led him through the village into the forest. The rain had stopped but the air was glittering. She slipped through the night like water into water, but his greater heft and height worked against him. He stumbled and tore his cloak on a branch.

In truth, he was afraid. He did not know this woman. Was it possible that he had violated some custom and was being led to a dark, anonymous ending?

Still, the fear was interesting. Leukas was always searching for those uncanny moments where the body and the spirit collided. The tension was better than drink. He always came out of the other side of fear with a better sense of his limits—or his lack of them.

At last they emerged from the forest into a meadow, and Leukas noted a small round house in the distance. There was a fire burning outside. One window glowed yellow.

The woman paused. He heard the whisper of parting grasses. "Nephthys!" she whispered, before leaning down and scooping up a black cat that then squirmed in her arms. The animal blinked at him with indifference.

"Did you find the cat?" called someone from within as they approached the house. "She's already brought me three voles tonight."

"Yes," the Egyptian woman answered. "And I found someone else, too." She beckoned Leukas through the low door.

The room was simple, almost bare, with a straw pallet at the far side, which was covered with a blue-and-white striped blanket. Leukas recognized it as an old Jewish prayer shawl. Had it belonged to someone from her past?

Immediately he was assaulted by smells—wet roots wrenched from the earth, the pollen of wildflowers, a musk as smooth and sensuous as water that has been used to bathe a lover's body. Roses. Above all, he smelled roses. He glanced up and saw clusters of dried plants. Grecian pots lined the edge of the room—elegant, refined objects that were out of place in such a rustic hut. On the side of an urn, Leukas thought he saw an etched image of the nymph Daphne turning into a tree.

On a large wooden table were three candles molded of unrendered fat, their pale, flickering light illuminating the face of an old woman.

She had been beautiful and was still beautiful in the way that an oak tree, clean of leaves in winter, stands stark and clear against the sky. Her skin was dark, and her white hair tumbled down into her lap. She stared at him, her full lips parted slightly. He could feel her eyes like blades of winter sleet against his face. They traced his every feature. The ice of her gaze traveled his spine and flowed down through the marrow of his leg bones. He could feel the life within him seeping into the very dirt beneath his feet.

The cat struggled and leapt out of the younger woman's arms, running to her mistress. The old woman released Leukas from her gaze and picked up the cat, settling the animal into her generous lap.

"What is your name?"

The voice was not unkind, but it *was* sharp and direct. *Masculine,* he thought, but not in actual tenor. It was high and fluid as music, and yet she spoke with the confidence of a man.

"My name is Leukas," he answered, the pressure between his eyes telling him to hide his Alexandrian ties. "I hail from Antioch."

"Leukas from Antioch," she said slowly. "You are a long way from home."

His mouth was dry. He had been a fool to come here.

"I have come to ask you for the truth . . ." he said hesitantly.

"I know why you're here," she interrupted. "Sera! Tell the sisters that I will not come tonight. This will not be done till morning."

Sera nodded, "I'll return to stoke the fire."

He was alone in the room with the woman he had been looking for all these months. Yes, her hair was long. But she was fully clothed. This was not the wild beast or the naked ascetic of the tales. Sparks did not fly from her. But Leukas sensed a vibration in the room that could only come from within her. It was a power that needed no proof, no display. He looked at her more closely, searching for a sign that she had known *him,* the Christ. Would it show on her? Like a sunburn? Or a scar?

Leukas was light-headed. His legs felt unsteady beneath him, like they did the first day of an ocean voyage.

"Sit," she commanded, pointing to a low, wooden stool by the door.

It's a stool for women, he thought sourly. His knees came up comically. But what did it matter if he looked ridiculous?

Her gaze unnerved him, so he made to examine the contents of the table: a hawk's feather, some tangled red string, an unfurled scroll covered in sun-faded characters.

"Do you read?" he asked, surprised.

"No," she said flatly, her eyes glinting dangerously. "I do not read."

He was at a loss. He had said something wrong. But he did not yet understand his error.

• • •

Had an hour passed? Leukas felt disoriented and ungrounded, uncertain of what was happening to him and around him. It was as though he had become unstuck from time, frozen in the crystal of his anxiety. He wondered when the woman Sera would return.

At last, outside, an animal screamed and an owl sounded a series of congratulatory hoots.

Miriam nodded as if she had received confirmation of something.

"A sacrifice has been made," he said wryly, thinking of that holy temple she must have spent time in when she was younger. It would have been full of the cries of dying animals. She was used to such things. "Do you require more blood? My own?" He laughed nervously.

To his surprise, she smiled. "I need nothing but your ears. Are you ready to listen? It is a long story. But in some ways much too short."

His body relaxed. Yes. The Father had answered his prayers. His faith had led him through dangers and deprivation to get here. "Yes, I have come for your story." The words he had carried for so long tumbled out eagerly. "It is said that you knew him better than most, knew him well."

"Knew him *well?*" Her nostrils flared.

Something beyond mere anger bloomed in her eyes.

In her pupils he saw sorrow. A sorrow that reminded him of the windswept, colorless skies over those white cliffs he had passed on his journey. It was a desolate space, void of sun and moon.

"You were his disciple . . ." he ventured. But the words died in his mouth.

"I was *not* his disciple," she said dryly.

Leukas found his voice and tried again. "I have come for the story of the Christos, the Son of God named Jesus, and to hear his teachings, which you heard firsthand." He paused, clearing his throat. "I believe you received his secret teachings."

"But *he* is not here to tell them to you," she said firmly. "Do you still want to listen?"

"I do," he whispered.

"Then you will get *my* story. But be warned, there are no gods in it."

He nodded.

"Good." She shifted in her seat, getting comfortable. "And remember. He was no messiah, no Christos. His name was Yeshua. Yeshua of Nazareth."

PART ONE

The Tower

One

I am too close to see him.

Instead I smell him, cedarwood, and sea salt. Grapes burst underfoot. Musk. The sharp tang of a lightning strike. I grip his muscled arms, press my face into his neck. He sighs into my hair. I feel his breath, hot and insistent, shiver against my scalp. I lick the sweat from his shoulder and his hands curl around my waist.

"Miriam."

I try to pull back in order to look up into his face and find I cannot. My arms betray me, tightening their clutch, knowing that to release him is to lose him. And he, too, presses me into his broad chest, our lungs paired like twin butterflies, buoyed by wind, flown through with a common spirit.

Ah. I see. You are confused.

You do not understand what I am telling you. I see in your eyes a desire I have come to distrust. You want the teachings. You want to understand how to do extraordinary things. Impossible things. Miracles. Do you think I will teach you how to transform water into wine, wine into blood? Do you think I will teach you how to raise the dead? Do you think I will teach you the secret of eternal life?

Forget everything you have heard.

Here is the first teaching.

The teachings do not matter to me anymore. The only thing I care about is whether or not I can tell the story with enough honesty that he returns to me. Maybe then I will see him again as he was. Maybe if I approach carefully, and do not leave anything out, I will again be able to see the face of my beloved.

• • •

I can still see Bethany so clearly—my home, perched high atop a grassy slope. Behind every white house is a garden. The children are running along the narrow, winding streets, calling to each other, playing a game. Smoke wafts away from the courtyards as women prepare for the evening meal. A group of young women are traveling to the baths together, their long cloaks a swirl of green and yellow in the springtime breeze.

I knew everyone in Bethany when I was a child, but now I remember so few of their names. Yet Ester I will never forget. Ester is burned into my mind forever.

Huddled in the dirt, down at the bottom of the cliff, her shawl splattered with blood, she was wailing, producing sounds so ragged I was surprised the air didn't rip apart around them. Her hands scraped the dry earth. She screamed with the agony of someone who knew she was about to die.

"What are they going to do to her?" I asked my sister, Marta. Already frightened, I clutched at her shawl.

"Be quiet, Miriam," she scolded. Her mouth twitched as her eyes stared up at the rocky ledge above Ester.

Old stone steps led down from the town gate, cracked by the roots of olive trees. After its descent down the slope, the path wound through the fields toward Yerusalem. To the right was a steep ledge overlooking a barren, rocky patch of earth. It was steep enough that whenever my family went into the city, my mother pulled me tightly to her side as if worried I might accidentally slip out of her grasp and fall to my death.

Ester was sprawled on the unforgiving stones below that ledge, her knees bloodied, her hands torn apart. Had she tripped? Looking down on her was a crowd of men.

Had they pushed her over the ledge, down into the gravel below? I could not believe they would do such a thing. These were not strangers to me. They were my father's friends—the men I saw every day in the marketplace. Friendly men. Good men.

There was Achan, the silver-bearded rabbi who read scripture in a reedy voice every Sabbath in the town synagogue. Caleb, a scholar, who argued endlessly about the Law with my father over a cup of wine and a loaf of my mother's seediest bread. Caleb, who greeted me with a grin when he stopped by, revealing his missing front teeth. *"Shelama,*

Miriam," he would say. "You are already more beautiful than your mother!"

Efraim, my friend Yohanna's father, spat down on the woman's head.

Yes, they were familiar. But their faces were transformed by rage.

Huddled in the dust the woman wept and shook.

"Oh, God! What has she done?" my sister whispered.

"It's Ester!" my little brother Lazaros cried. The cloth doll he had brought for our games hung limply in his hands. His face was flushed with emotion.

"And that's her husband, Gad," whispered Marta, almost too softly for me to hear. She pointed at a handsome man with a short beard, the angriest of them all. A vein in his forehead bulged with the force of his wrath.

"Why is Gad angry at his wife?" I whispered back. But Marta ignored me.

I remembered Gad from Ester's wedding the previous spring. He had worn an embroidered vest, his hair oiled back so that his high, broad forehead was more visible. He was beautiful to me.

Gad screamed at his wretched wife and her fear reached into my own body. Something tight and stone-like dropped into my stomach.

It was early spring outside of Yerusalem. The fields turned muddy by a long, cold rainy season were firming up under the steady sunlight. Cyclamen purpled the roadside, and the hillsides reddened with anemones. I'd overheard my mother and her friend Bithiah whispering about their relief that the bad weather was finished and the children could finally be sent outside somewhere where they wouldn't be underfoot.

We always headed straight for the fields to play. We liked to have enough space to run, sliding through the tall grasses as we chased each other. We returned striped with green stains. "How do you get so dirty?" my mother would chastise us as she inspected the damage. She had woven the clothes we wore and despaired that we undid her handiwork so quickly.

I looked down on Ester, then turned to my older sister for a sign of what to do. Marta always had a plan. But her lower lip quivered with uncertainty, as if a word was trapped there. Marta understood what was happening. She grasped my brother and me firmly by the hand. "Come!" she said finally. "We should not be here for this."

"Ester!" Lazaros called out, squirming away from Marta. "Ester! What is wrong?"

"Lazaros! No!" Marta shrieked, lunging forward and grabbing him around his waist. He was five, only a year younger than me, but he was spindly and small.

The path that led to the ledge was lined with gnarled sycamore figs and wild roses. I hid behind a bush, swallowing a cry when a thorn pierced my thigh.

My eyes were on Ester. She moaned.

I resisted clamping my hands over my ears, shutting my eyes tight. Something in me knew I had to witness this. I had to listen to her pain.

Ester was sixteen, and I saw her every time my family went to the synagogue. She would stand with us, pressed against the walls with the other women.

I loved to watch her, to imitate her graceful gestures: moving my hands gently when I walked, bending my elbows just so, making sure that my fingers did not brush my hips. At synagogue, I blinked up at her, smiling openly, watching her long eyelashes flutter as she tried to resist a yawn, pressing her hand to her lips.

All of Bethany had exploded in celebration this past spring when she'd wed the handsome Gad.

Our mother let us bring flowers to Ester in her home as her relatives dressed her in deep green cloth and placed cold metal necklaces over her bosom. We offered baskets heavy with fresh violets, lilies, and irises bruised by the weight of their own lips.

"Here, girls," she had said, kneeling and pressing a feathery kiss to our cheeks, showing us her hands that were hennaed with curling vines. I inhaled deeply. She smelled like cinnamon and musk. "One day you will have wedding flowers, too."

"She is lucky to have a young and handsome husband," Marta had confided in me when our mother pulled us from the room. We went to wait on the path that led to Gad's home. "A girl as beautiful as Ester would have been prized by a wealthy man, an old man."

I nodded, agreeing. How lucky Ester was! How beautiful they both were when they kissed under the chuppah. It felt like starlight to watch them. I wished I could drink their love. Save it and taste it when the cold winds of winter arrived. God must be happy to see such young people come together.

Ester's own father had clapped Marta and me on the shoulders, bending down with a wry smile, his breath already laced with drink. "I've spent enough on this wedding to shame your father into spending even more when your time comes! Five lambs slaughtered, and I bought out the market's entire supply of wine! What lovely brides you both will be!"

We had blushed, lowering our eyes like our mother had taught us.

Ester was a queen out of scripture when she came to meet Gad. Dark kohl made her almond-shaped eyes even bigger, and gold bracelets blazed at her fragile wrists. The midday sun glinted on her lips, which were wet and red as if she had just licked them with her own tongue.

"She is so lovely," my friend Yohanna gasped, clutching my hand tight.

"One day we will look just as beautiful," I declared, echoing the words of Ester's father.

But Ester did not look beautiful now.

"Oh, no! No!" she screamed. Her eyes were glassy and unfocused.

"Shame on you, whore!" snarled Caleb. I flinched, remembering his fatherly touch. "You have brought disgrace to your father, your mother, your husband!"

I could see red welts rising where her nails had broken the skin of her throat.

I glanced over my shoulder. Marta clutched Lazaros to her side as she scanned the shrubs near the path, looking for me. I hid in the wet shade of the fig tree, watching the scene unfold.

"This is the way of an adulteress!" shouted Gad. The word hung in the air—an open wound.

Adulteress. What did it mean? I clutched my chest again. I would be sick. I would explode. Something was wrong with these men.

Gad's face was contorted with rage. His fists shook at his sides. "She eats and wipes her mouth and says, 'I have done no wrong!'"

"We can show no mercy! Her impurity will corrupt our daughters and our wives!" Efraim pointed a short, swollen finger at Ester. He no longer looked like the father who gave Yohanna and me a coin to spend at the market. He was a bloated monstrosity, his face spidered with red capillaries.

Ester's scream pierced the dull, hot air.

"And where is your lover?" Gad howled at her. "Shall I kill him in front of you? I can't! He doesn't care enough to save you!"

I did not understand. What lover? Didn't Gad and Ester love each other? Hadn't their wedding been beautiful?

A dusty streak of cloud fissured the blue of the sky in half. The heavens would fall in on us. I held onto the fig tree.

Ester's father joined Gad. "Shame! To think I reared a whore like this!"

"Father!" she wailed. "Father!"

"You are no daughter of mine!" he declared.

Her screaming opened up like a flower then—blooming bigger, louder, higher—until I thought my ears might bleed.

Where was *my* father? I scanned the mob but could not see his face.

My body was shaking, my heart beating in my eyes. There was blood at the edge of my vision. Ester's moans were shaking something loose inside of me. An animal curled into position under my skin. Behind my knuckles, claws clicked invisibly. I would hunt these men down and rip the skin from their backs with my teeth. I would eat them and spit out their bones. I would turn them back into dirt.

"Whore!" Gad kicked a cloud of dirt down onto Ester's face and she lost her balance, falling backward.

"The Law of Moshe says we must stone her!" the old rabbi proclaimed, holding his hands upward toward heaven. A cheer resounded through the group.

How many times had I walked past this ledge with our servant woman Kemat, accompanying her into the fields to bring her husband, Meshkenet, his lunch? As Gad flung a first rock at Ester, I trembled, past words, past thinking. It hit her in the shoulder and tore her dress, but she hardly noticed. Blood dripped down her arm. Now I saw the piles of stones next to the men. They were stones like the ones I'd often gather in my skirts, collecting them for their pretty colors; stones Lazaros dipped in water to make bright and shiny.

What a strange child I was, often filled with an overwhelming emotion for the trees, the beetles and the flies, the mangy camels tied up outside of town, flicking their long tongues in my direction. I was suddenly filled with rage that these stones should be so misused! Baked with sunshine, dusty with the summer wind. They were not meant for cruelty!

But I was wrong.

These stones had been wielded before. Women had died here. There, just beyond Ester, I saw a vision of the piled, limp bodies of women who had been stoned here. Skipping past them down the path to play in the fields, I had not known this.

Even as a little girl, I had heard from my father about men with the ability to see angels or fiery chariots. These were men who could look across the desert and see the rain coming before it ever crested above the horizon. I wanted to be like these men.

But no one had prepared me for the visions of women in which we see each other. We see what has been done to us. We see our dead.

In every town, in every land I have ever traveled to, the women have been waiting for me, clustered in front of the city gates, always the color of winter—even in lands where winter never comes.

They are the dead women. The women who have been murdered by their fathers, by their brothers, by their husbands. The harlots trying to staunch their slit necks. They are the girls with black eyes, blood dried down their legs, their hands outstretched and pleading. They ask to be seen.

"No!" I struggled to speak. My voice was too thick with disbelief to leave my throat.

There was more ceremony in the slaughter of animals. At least their blood was spilled with sacred purpose. Ester's blood would seep deep into sand where nothing would grow.

Did my God want this? I could not imagine that he did. But what did I know? I was but a child. And a girl.

All I knew then was that my sight was splintering. I could see the wildflowers, the soft, almost liquid beauty of spring rolling forward, carrying pink almond blossoms over Bethany toward Yerusalem. And I could also see the spectral heap of dead women, their heads caved in by jagged rocks. I could see the kind-faced men that I knew fondly as my elders, my protectors, my father's friends. And I could also see a crowd of monsters, capable of incomprehensible things.

"Miriam!" hissed Marta. She had spotted me hiding near the fig tree. But she was too late.

I had already leapt from the bushes, throwing up clouds of red dust as my feet pounded the dirt. I was a tiny girl, blurred by speed, and howling with a fury that rose from my lungs. Down the embankment I slid, skinning my knees as I hurled myself before Ester. I felt her arms grasp me close, her hair hanging over my back. "No!" she cried. "No, Miriam!"

"What is this?" There was a moment of confusion. Then Gad kicked the ledge, sending a rain of gravel down upon us. "Kill them both!" he bellowed.

But it was not to be. "Stop!" shouted a voice. It was Gilead, the rabbi. "That is Nicodemus's daughter, Miriam!"

"This is no girl!" Ester's father hissed. "Nicodemus has raised a wild animal!"

I pulled myself to my knees, gazing up at them through the glare. The sun behind the men made them appear as shadows silhouetted by an unearthly glow.

How do I explain what happened next? Later no one could be sure. Someone came into me. Except that someone was *me*. And I was no longer a girl. I was dark. Old. I was terror. I was horror. I was the face of the deep. The blackness that came before God shaped the world.

"Shame upon you! Shame!" My body vibrated with something beyond anger. It was the rage of trees. Of roots. Of dirt. Radiating up from the ground, it filled me with a woody strength that forced words from my mouth. "Who gives you the right?"

"Miriam . . ." Ester begged. "You must go home."

From the edge of the path, Marta pleaded. "Miriam! What are you doing?" She was holding Lazaros in her arms. But I was beyond their concern. The anger thrummed through me and back into the ground. A second passed and the earth responded with its own pulse.

The rage that grew before me was like a bruise, a great shadow that spread across the ground. Then something darker and stranger than the opacity of shadow eclipsed the void above us, filling the air. And there was a noise, too. Like clouds scraping over a mountaintop, or a thousand blades being sharpened against a stone.

Vultures swooped down on the men, so many of them that they blocked out the sun. They beat huge wings against the men's faces, knifing sharp beaks into their heads.

"Demons!" screeched Ester's father, raising his hands to defend himself. "She has summoned demons!"

"Someone stop her!" Ephraim yelled, blood filling his eyes as the birds scratched at him with their talons.

Stop me? Not yet. This was the earth's answer to their violence.

Ten vultures. Twenty. And still more fell out of the sky, rasping and hissing. A great shadow covered the rabbi, then it lifted the hat from his head.

"Shame!" I screamed at them. "Shame!"

"Get out of here!" Gad yelled to the other men.

"Leave her!" Achan screeched, "Let the birds pick her bones clean!"

"They will eat you all! All of you!" I yelled at the men as they fled. But the hoarse cries of the vultures drowned out my words. My voice was small again; the voice of a girl.

In the midst of the chaos Marta had run through the great flapping bodies of the birds, impervious to their wings. She scrambled down to us now, pulling Ester to her feet, and whispered something into her ear.

The last men fled, the birds chasing them back to the village and their homes. There would be no stoning.

Ester would live.

"You foolish, foolish girl!" Marta slapped me hard across the cheek. "What will I tell father! What? What . . .?" she trailed off helplessly, gazing about her in awe as the birds settled blackly along the ledge, fixing us with their inky eyes. They shifted their feathers impatiently. One of them made a groaning sound like that of a wheel spinning against rock.

I gasped, tears springing out of my eyes as I touched my face.

Marta swung her arms. "Get! *Get*, you foul creatures!"

One of the birds beat his wings heavily as if to say, *Who are you to command us?*

Marta pulled Lazaros away, back up the stone steps toward Bethany. I followed behind her, but not before looking back.

"Thank you!" I whispered, my hands still vibrating with dangerous heat.

Ester was gone.

The vultures bowed their naked heads, touching their beaks to the ground. They blinked at me with their dark eyes before lifting like smoke from a fire, into the high, thin blue of the summer sky.

Two

My father was waiting for us outside our home, framed by the trellis of roses that arched over the front gate. My mother stood behind him. They already knew.

"Achan and Caleb have just been here! Yelling like madmen! Telling me my daughters are demons!" he thundered, his face the color of a pomegranate under his black beard.

"Nicodemus..." murmured my mother. Her face was painted and composed. She looked more like a Roman statue than a real woman. But her voice was clipped. I could tell she was angry. "What have you done, Miriam?"

Our servant Kemat hovered in the doorway, her hands set firmly on her hips. Was she angry, too? I could take my mother's icy rage. But Kemat! I couldn't bear it if Kemat was ashamed of me.

At last I began to cry.

"Oh, stop it!" Marta pushed past me. "Miriam is playacting. She doesn't want to get in trouble."

"Marta!" my father stormed. "You are as much at fault as your sister!"

Now Lazaros was weeping, too, choking back sobs that left him breathless and gasping.

Kemat scooped him up, cooing into his ear. "Hush now. Do you want to hear a story?"

My mother looked down at me coldly, but she spoke with practiced tenderness. "Don't be frightened, Miriam. Nothing bad will happen. Just tell us what happened."

"Nothing bad will happen... we will see about that," my father grumbled, narrowing his eyes at us. He was easily angered, but bad at punishment.

He had slapped Lazaros once when he tripped and broke an expensive jar of wine. And he had whipped Marta when she snuck into the dining room to dance for one of his youngest students.

But he had never hit me. Not yet at least.

It was my mother who'd pinched and slapped me. She hardly even needed an excuse.

"Miriam," my father said sternly, his voice steadier now. "I heard everything from Achan. Now tell me yourself."

Drying my eyes on the hem of my dusty cloak, I took a breath and drew my small body straight, looking up at my father.

He was not so old then, and handsome in the way that birds are handsome, with sharp, narrow shoulders and a pointed chin like Lazaros. He clipped his beard short; in those days it was still black with only a sprinkling of gray.

He had a short temper and snapped at us constantly. But I lived for the moments when he engaged with me fully. He would erupt in laughter when I said something impertinent or asked a question about scripture. Or he would bang the table when I crossed him, frightening everybody, telling me to hold my tongue.

He glared at me now. His eyes had grown dense, small, and black.

Still I held my ground.

"I am ready for my punishment," I said bravely, trying to keep my voice even. "If you must disown me, I understand."

His eyes widened unexpectedly. Then he laughed, shaking his head in disbelief.

Was he mocking me?

Tears were falling from my eyes again. My throat was thick with phlegm and an emotion so clotted it was beginning to choke me. But I did not stop speaking. "I would protect Ester again. I would! I do not believe that God who would kill a woman like her! It is terrible! A *sin*!"

"Miriam!" my mother gasped. "Hold your tongue!"

But my father was laughing in earnest now, one hand stroking his beard. His anger seemed to have vanished.

"Stone me!" I shouted, grabbing the front of my dirty shift as if I would rip the cloth. "Stone me! But do not mock me!"

"Miriam!" My father's bushy eyebrows wiggled as he tried to get his laughter under control, putting a bony finger to his lips to hold back his mirth. He knelt so that our faces were level. "I am not mocking you."

I stared at my father, examining the pleasing hue of his high brown cheeks, the gleam of the straight teeth that, remarkably, he would keep his whole life.

"Miriam," he said, reaching out and cupping my chin with his hand. "I will never disown you. And I will never harm you. There is nothing that would make me do such a thing."

"Nothing?" I gulped, trying hard to believe him.

My mother stepped forward and squeezed my shoulder.

"Nothing," he promised.

"Father!" Marta interjected. "Punish her for being so foolish! We all could have been killed!"

"I will do no such thing!" My father's voice was immediately sharp. "She has been punished enough."

And he was right. I wept for the rest of the day, blubbering into my bowl of stewed onions and lentils that Kemat served to us out in the courtyard under the whir of insects. I blinked up at the purple-veined sky, feeling pitiful and small, watching as the blue gave way to a deeper magisterial sunset. At last Kemat scooped me up with her thin arms and carried me to the room that Marta and I shared. She settled me into bed and drew the heavy wool blanket up to my chin.

Oh, Kemat. My true mother. My sister. My great love.

To feel her arms around me again just once would be enough! I grow old. But one day I will slip off this wrinkled skin and become young again. Then I will run to her and bury my face in her dark, coarse robes and hear her telling me that she will never leave me.

Miriam. Your soul is as light as a feather. You are perfect. You are beloved of God.

She smelled of honey and almonds.

Kemat's face comes back to me like the sun every morning. Even as old as I am now, in a country far from my home, I still open my eyes to the dawn and expect her to be sitting on the bed beside me.

"There is much to do today, Miriam. Do you want to pick herbs with me in the forest?" she would say. She couldn't have been more than twenty, a thin Egyptian woman with a narrow face and straight

black hair cut at her shoulders. Every one of her gestures gave my
world meaning. Her stories stirred my heart. She taught me the secrets
of the flowers, the right herbs for bellyaches, the rhythm of the warp
and weave in the loom, the intense effort it took to move the stone
that milled the corn.

"Kemat!" I whispered to her that night as she convinced me to sip
some honeyed milk, hoping to settle me down enough to sleep. "You are
like a flame!"

"A flame?" She sighed, patting my chest through the blanket. "Shall
I take that as a compliment, Miriam?"

"No . . . I mean you glow like you are made of fire."

"Miriam. *You* are the flame," she whispered, pressing her thin lips
to my forehead. She extinguished the lamp. "Remember that, my little
one. You can give the gift of light. Or choose to burn everything down."

· · ·

A full day passed before Ester's father and husband showed up at our
house.

It had been too hot to play outside, and my mother took pity on
Marta and me, letting us watch as she washed herself and applied her
makeup using a smoky circle of mirror hung on the wall. My father had
bought it as a gift for her at the market a long time ago.

My mother's beauty intimidated me. Maybe it is for that reason that
I cannot truly summon her for you. Her beauty resists my memory.

I have spent many hours staring at my own reflection in the hope
that she will surface. Sometimes, for a moment, she does, but only as a
faint outline of individual attributes. The small, narrow nose. The full
lips. The jutting collarbones and supple, womanly figure. I remember
that she was stately, always well perfumed, her eyes ringed with kohl.
For some reason I never discovered, she only ever wore green or red,
her clothing fashioned from cloth she had woven on her own loom and
which she barely decorated. Occasionally she allowed for embroidery at
the cuff of her sleeve.

That day she was sitting at a low stool, brushing out her long hair.

"Mother! You look pretty without paint on your face," I told her,
eyeing the assortment of oils and powders scattered across the cedar
table below the mirror.

"Thank you, Miriam." She smiled at her own reflection, letting her free hand flit to her cheeks, fingertips brushing against a faint spidery vein that curved away from her nose. "But I am getting older."

"May I have jewelry, too, Mother?" Marta asked. She was rummaging through the box of my mother's treasures, adding bangle after bangle to her bare arms.

"A woman should shine brighter than any finery," my mother advised. She beckoned Marta over to her, slowly removing the bracelets, leaving only one on Marta's wrist. "You would do better with fresh flowers in your hair than gold and silver at your neck. You have no need to distract the eye from wrinkles. Your face is still lovely and smooth."

I watched transfixed as my mother rose and went to her trunk, selecting a pale green linen tunic. She lifted her arms and it floated over her, curving to her contours like water over a shelf of rock, sliding down around her long thin legs. She belted a red slip of silk at her narrow waist, turning this way and that to observe her figure in the mirror.

My mother. *My mother,* I thought with awe, having to repeat the words in order to truly believe them. How could I have come from such beauty? I saw my own anger and frustration in my father, my quick wit mirrored in his intelligence. But my mother was always foreign to me. I had none of her grace.

I frayed the edge of my tunic as I studied her. She ran a well-organized household, overseeing the grinding of the grain and the pressing of the olives. She often went down to our fields outside of Bethany to check on our crops, raising her slender hand up to shield her eyes from the sun. She would ask Kemat's husband, Meshkenet, questions about yield and irrigation.

As far as I knew, my father never set foot in the fields. It was enough that they had belonged to his father before him. It was enough for him that they fed us.

My mother, despite all her fine attributes, was far from perfect. She was a slave to that blurred version of herself in the mirror. She never let my father see her without her eyes and lips painted. And she did not speak up when he criticized her cooking or complained that she was looking haggard.

"You should rest more, Hadassah," he would say, pinching her waist.

"You are getting too thin." And she would laugh, a cascade of nervous bells, neglecting to remind him that she had been up all night the past week with Lazaros, who had been sick with a cough.

"Aren't we rich enough to have jewelry?" Marta complained as she plopped down on the bed. She already looked like my mother. Her skin glowed golden and her fingers were long and tapered. She could pout and complain all day and still look pretty.

Whenever I chanced to look in my mother's mirror, I saw a skinny child with big eyes and wild hair. And yet sometimes I also saw a face that did not belong to me. Someone older, with black bangs and a neck circled by a heavy golden necklace. Someone wiser. At other times it was a face so black it was almost blue looking back at me.

But I never told anyone about these visions. They were my secret.

"All of my friends have pretty things," Marta continued when my mother didn't immediately respond. "Elisabet has a ring with an emerald from her father! I look like a peasant girl. No one will ever want to marry me..."

My mother stopped brushing her hair and gave Marta an appraising look: half-annoyed, half-entertained. I suddenly felt certain that she was seeing herself in my older sister. Had she asked for finery when she was younger? She hardly ever spoke of her childhood. Her only sister had died in childbirth and her father and mother had died of the fever before I was born.

"I need pretty things to attract a man!" Marta huffed.

"Keep your lives free from the love of money and be content with what you have..." I announced primly, parroting the scripture I remembered overhearing from the dinners my father had with his colleagues.

"What?" Marta wrinkled her nose, confused.

"It's scripture," my mother explained, but she was eyeing me suspiciously. She flicked her tongue over her unpainted lips as if she was tasting the air for some misdeed. "Where did you hear that, Miriam?"

"From Father," I said stiffly, crossing my hands in my lap and looking up at her defiantly. "Scripture is his work. I listen to him when he speaks of his work."

I said this but the truth was that I barely understood what it was my father did. I knew he sat on the council of Jewish elders: the Sanhedrin. He worked in Yerusalem during the day. Sometimes I climbed up on the roof in the morning and watched as he made his way down the winding path out of Bethany. He would grow smaller and smaller until he disappeared over the Mount of Olives, heading into that great pulsing city with its dense smoke, its pilgrims, its bleating animals. It was close to nightfall when he returned with all its smells trapped in his beard, bringing other dignified older men or boisterous young students home to dine with him.

When the men came, we surrendered the largest room in the house so that they could relax on the scrolled couches. Their voices carried all the way into the courtyard where Kemat fed us in the mellowing twilight, her inky black hair turning blue as the shadows crept up the walls behind her.

I would always find a reason to slip inside and hover in the shadows near the doorway, trying to listen to the men.

"Worshipping trees as they do, do they think they are really Jews? Working on the Sabbath? And they never come into the city to sacrifice at the temple. They have no right!" I heard one man say.

My father would wait a beat, nodding I'm sure—although I couldn't see him—before responding in amicable tones. "Levi, be careful not to fall into hypocrisy. Our forefathers were also far from the temple when they lived in exile. If their prayers could travel from Babylon, then surely Galilee is not so far!"

"But the pagan whores with their Asherahs and their shrines to idols! It's practically Roman!"

Inevitably someone would knock over a glass. There would be a rumble of laughter. An exclamation. A servant would come running and I would flee back to the courtyard, blushing, even though no one had noticed I had left.

My mother broke through my reverie. "Miriam, I wish you paid as much attention to your spinning lessons as you do to conversations not intended for your ears." There was such flatness to her expression as she said it. Even without her makeup, it was hard to read anything but placid disinterest in her beautiful features.

I think now that she had not always been so practiced at tranquility. My mother learned out of necessity to keep her feelings below the surface. The turbulence, if she had let it reach her face, might have destroyed the beauty men so prized.

A loud banging resonated through the house. Someone was at our door.

"Nicodemus! I know you're in there! Come out and explain your-self! You owe it to us!"

The blood drained from my mother's face.

"Children, stay here," she said. I could tell it took effort for her to keep her voice steady.

Home for once, perhaps because he had been expecting this visit, my father had no doubt answered the door and let the men inside, because suddenly the voices were louder, echoing down the hallway.

". . . all through Yerushalem. We've scoured Bethlehem and the nearby villages, and she's nowhere to be found!"

"The adulteress. The deceitful woman. She could be with any man."

I shuddered at the words. I did not need to see the faces of these men to know who they were.

"I assure you she is not here," came my father's equanimous reply. "I haven't seen Ester since her wedding day. You have relatives up north. In Yericho? Have you sent word there?"

No! I thought, scrambling to my feet, my heart beating so fast that the world shimmered, and my fingers vibrated with the music of my blood. *Don't let them find her.*

"Stay, Miriam!" my mother commanded before stepping into the corridor. "Do not leave this room!"

"Miriam, why did you have to do that?" Marta suddenly seemed to be younger than her twelve years. Her lower lip was trembling.

"What?" I asked fiercely. "Do *what*? I didn't do *anything*!"

"You called on those vultures," Marta said thickly. I realized she was beginning to cry. "You attacked those men and now *we* will be beaten because of it!"

"Father would never beat us," I said with confidence. "He may slap us. But you watch. He will send Gad and Ester's father away."

But Marta only sobbed, burying her face in the blankets. "You don't know anything . . ."

"I know more than you!" I snapped. "I know scripture and you don't!"

It makes me blush to tell you such things. Marta was old enough to understand the danger all around us. She was already wiser than me.

"It was your daughter Miriam's doing!" Gad was speaking now.

"She summoned devils to attack us. Then Marta gave Ester spells to take her away from this place."

My father was silent.

"You must answer for this, Nicodemus! The town's justice has been thwarted by your children!"

I flinched, remembering when Ester's father had touched my shoulder at the wedding.

"The town's *justice!*" It was my father's turn to roar. "Do not speak to me about the town's justice! Had I been asked, I would *never* have allowed a stoning! Such things are not done near Yerusalem. They pollute the holy city!"

I leapt to my feet at this, edging into the hallway, pressing my back against the wall. Father would put them in their place! The men of Bethany all looked up to him.

"Look, Nicodemus." Ester's father sounded calmer. He was trying to be reasonable. "You will understand when your daughters are grown. They are too young to cause you trouble now. Have sympathy for a father like me, with sons to provide for and a reputation to protect. No one will do business with me if they think I cannot get my women to behave."

My father did not answer. I edged down the dark hallway.

"My wife is gone," Gad insisted, his voice a weapon now. I could feel it shaving close to my skin as I flattened my shoulder blades into the stone, keeping my breath low and quiet, stepping sideways to get closer. "I will never get the justice I deserve. And your daughters are to blame. The least you can do is serve justice to them. *You!* You who claim to know the Law better than anyone! Use that Law on your own family. Otherwise, I will have it known that you are a hypocrite and a eunuch."

A eunuch!

Lazaros and his friends sometimes used this terrible insult on each other. Once, Enosh had hit Lazaros hard in the crotch, and my brother had been slow to react, his rosy mouth forming an *O* as a glazed look came over his eyes. Enosh had hooted with laughter. "If you don't cry, you're a eunuch!" he'd taunted my brother who, as he did when almost anything bad happened, at last began to weep.

A eunuch was a man without a sex. How could my father allow it?

But he did.

He addressed both men. "I feel your pain. You have lost a wife, and you a daughter. The circumstances are questionable. I am aware that my daughters interrupted the proceeding. But they certainly did not summon the vultures or perform magic. However, I will honor your request."

"Marta!" my father cried.

I didn't understand what was about to happen. But my body did. My stomach was roiling and a bitter taste was bubbling at the back of my throat.

"Marta!"

Surely Marta saw me hiding in the shadows of the hallway. But she stared straight ahead as she brushed past, any trace of her childish tears now gone. Her lips were frozen into a small smile. She was still wearing the single gold bangle my mother had let her keep. And she was wearing my mother's face.

The rest happened outside. I imagine Marta kept her eyes lowered as my father led her out the front door and into the road where all could see. I could hear the men mumbling, but Marta remained quiet.

Did Gad hand my father the switch, already cut and ready? Or did my father walk into the nearby trees, his hand testing the resiliency of the branches, his finger squeezing the tender shoots until he found his weapon?

I crawled to the nearest window. But I was a coward. I could not bear to watch. I shut my eyes as Marta's cries, whimpers at first, finally turned into a rising and falling wave of moans.

"Miriam!" My mother lifted me up by the back of my shift, choking me.

She slapped me. Hard. Her ring cut my cheek. But I was relieved to feel the pain.

"I should be punished! It should be *me!*" I wept, looking up at my mother through my tears.

She hesitated. She was looking at the hand she had used to slap me. Slowly she flexed her fingers, turning the ring's black stone face up again. "Forgive me, Miriam," she said softly. I think it hurt her every time she hit me. And yet she slapped me again and again, year after year.

My mother went to witness Marta's pain. She could not stop it.

But she could stand there, across from the men, and fix them with her gaze, saying silently, powerfully, with her whole presence: *Shame! Shame! Shame!*

I know now why my father punished Marta instead of me. Marta had been in charge when she lost control of me outside of Bethany. She had let me interfere with the stoning.

But I am no fool. I have since witnessed men scorning women, hitting women, punishing women. And I have come to understand what satisfies their hunger for violence.

My punishment would not have given Gad and Ester's father any pleasure. A child could not possibly stand in for Ester. For her sensuality. Her disobedience. Her desire. But Marta's womanhood was dawning. Her breasts had begun to swell. Her hips were already widening. The men could look at Marta's body and imagine she was Ester. But not at me. I was still too young.

My father refused to meet my eye for the rest of the day. His face was ashen and there were lines on his forehead I had never seen before. He disappeared into his study, and when I walked past I heard the rustle of unfurling scrolls. He was looking for some passage from the scriptures to give him solace—some ritual to cleanse him of his violence. The next day he would bring one of our youngest sheep into the city to sacrifice at the temple. He would offer blood in atonement.

Even then—young and unlearned—I knew that something was wrong. Why did he need forgiveness from God when he should have knelt before Marta to beg for *her* forgiveness. It was a forgiveness she had already granted him, I noted with disgust, when at dinner she served him wine with a smile.

And yet at least my father knew that he'd done wrong. From that day on, whenever I saw Gad or Ester's father, I would shiver, trying to summon the deep inhuman power of the vultures.

Let them die. Let them all die.

Later that night, after Kemat had applied a cooling salve to Marta's welts, my sister eased into bed beside me with care, exhaling loudly as she pulled the blanket up over her legs.

It was dark, but I could feel my shame like a blistering burn covering my whole body.

It took a moment to summon the courage to speak. "Marta. It should have been me."

She did not respond.

"Marta," I tried again, rolling over onto my side so that our faces were very close. How was it that her breath tasted as sweet as meadow grass? Shouldn't she exude the bitterness and pain of this afternoon?

"Yes?" Marta whispered. "What is it, Miriam?"

"What did you tell Ester?"

She was quiet for a long time. Then, just when I had given up, she answered. "I told her to run. To get as far away from this place as she could. That she should go to Yericho. Or further. Past Galilee."

Starlight spilled from the open window, sparkling in her dark pupils.

I nodded, staring at my sister, "Do you think she will be safe?"

"No, Miriam. She will never be safe again."

We breathed steadily, the silence darkening between us, our inhales aligned. I thought Marta had probably descended into dreams. But I spoke again anyway. "Marta. Marta, I think I hate all men."

From outside the window, the hum of insects was like the sound of a stream. "It is all right to hate them, Miriam," Marta said softly. "But someday you will also love them."

She grasped my hand, pulling it to the warmth of her chest so I could feel her heartbeat. Soothed by the song of my sister's blood, I was soon asleep.

Three

What is it about happiness that discourages memory?

I ate fresh dates, ripe pomegranates, sweet citrons. Every morning I forgot the day before.

Those days are a blur of color, laughter, smells. The laughter of my friends as we played together among the gnarled olive trees. The joyful songs of pilgrims twining with birdsong, becoming something inhuman as they rose with the heat. The golden cloud of spices that Kemat would cook with when a holiday approached.

Our home was always full of guests—old men and my father's young students. Ours was a sprawling one-story house made of stone. We had a dining area, a storeroom with a wine cellar tucked underneath, and a small corner room where my father kept his scrolls and my mother her loom. All these rooms were built around a small courtyard, which held a modest kitchen garden, a cooking fire, and three fig trees. Our furniture was plain but made from expensive wood that included cedar from Lebanon, spiced cypress, and bone-white Aleppo pine. I can't imagine our home without a chorus of voices, arguing, telling stories, exchanging gossip. My father made sure we were never without company.

I think this was because he was a generous man. I also think it was because he did not want to be alone with my mother. Better to distract himself with the company of other men.

On those rare nights when my father would preside over our Sabbath meals, I would delight in his long rambling stories about our ancestors and their trials. I wanted most to hear about the prophets. The men who had received visions from God. What did it feel like to be chosen?

I knew to wait until he was deep into his wine cup. Only then, when his cheeks were flushed above his dark beard and he patted his midsection with contentment and belched, remarking on the good food, did I dare begin my questioning. And there was not a question that he did not answer at length. His eyes would brighten, and he would sit straighter, preparing for a solid hour of explanation.

Of course, this meant that I was always looking for a question he could *not* answer. I was always looking for the limit of his knowledge. "Father, why must we wash our hands before we eat?"

"Because the Lord said unto Moshe, 'They shall wash their hands and their feet, so that they may not die: it shall be a perpetual ordinance for them, for him, and for his descendants throughout their generations.'"

He would pat me on the head, pulling at the short curls behind my ears, and glare at Lazaros if he was nearby, adding, "My son, it would be good for you to remember these things."

"Why would the Lord make us dirty?" I would persist. "Didn't he create man in his own image? Does that mean *God* is dirty, too?"

"Leave your father be, Miriam!" my mother would scold. "He is a busy man."

She would hold my gaze until I nodded. But later she would find a way to draw me into her arms, pressing me into the cinnamon perfume that hid in the pleats of her dress, whispering, "You are too curious, Miriam! It will do you no good!"

I wish that I could open my eyes inside that memory and summon her face instead of her smell. How often I dream of her as a gray presence! Featureless and smooth as the hills covered in morning mist.

I have failed my mother. I cannot bring her back to me. I cannot properly give her to you.

Let me instead summon Lazaros as a little boy! He had round cheeks but was so skinny that his bones often looked like they might poke out of his skin. I can describe him to you but I cannot really *see* him!

What had Lazaros looked like when he ran into our house covered in mud from head to toe? His eyes were the only clean part of him. He claimed that it had been Achim and Enosh who had tricked him into rolling around in the puddles!

"I swear. They always trick me!" Lazaros was lying. He had rolled in the mud unprovoked in order to make his friends laugh. Always the joker.

It's all ashes now. I couldn't even return to the house where we grew up. It has been burned to the ground.

And my memories are the same: fine ash, sifted through my fingers, that shows me I once kindled a brilliant fire.

For a little while, as a child, I lived a perfect, ordinary happiness.

• • •

"Give it back!" Yohanna shouted.

"No!" I clutched the leather ball Kemat's husband had made for us. I ran down the narrow street, darting back and forth so that Yohanna couldn't catch me.

"No fair!" whined Lazaros, lagging behind us both. His long hair was slick with sweat and he was hardly running. He puffed and wheezed. Sometimes when he got overexcited, Lazaros would stop breathing. He would turn blue, his eyes growing larger and larger. Kemat took to hitting him on the head with the heel of her palm and he would snap out of it, gulping down air greedily.

"Miriam! It's my ball! No fair!" he gasped.

"Here! Catch!" I swirled around, lobbing the ball over Yohanna's head toward Lazaros.

"Agh!" It hit him right in his sweaty face. He stood there dumbly for a second, then toppled over.

He moaned, turning his face into the dust, his fingers twitching toward the ball.

"You're fine!" I yelled. But I stopped, leaned over, and grabbed my knees, breathing hard. Yohanna caught up to me and we both watched to see if he was really all right.

"I win! I win!" He rolled over, grasping the ball triumphantly.

"Those are *not* the rules of the game," Yohanna laughed. She loved to laugh with her whole mouth open. I'll never forget how she would make a whistling noise, grabbing my hand and pulling me close to her when she thought something was strange. Her fine hair could have been silky, but she was like me: preferring to get dirty and stay dirty. Her mother dealt with this by plaiting the strands into a long braid that thumped between her narrow shoulder blades when we ran through town.

She was making the whistling noise now, narrowing her eyes at Lazaros. "You know the rules, Lazaros. Whoever runs past Enosh's house while holding the ball wins, but only . . ."

The midday sun was shining brightly, but everything around me was growing darker as if a cloud were passing overhead. The stone walls that bordered the road appeared black and seemed to narrow. I could feel the very earth beneath me rolling. I stumbled forward. Was this one of those earthquakes spoken of in scripture? I could hardly stand.

My heart hammered in my ears. I looked down at my hands, but they were glowing so white I could hardly see them.

"Yohanna!" I called, but the words died in my throat.

After that I saw nothing. My body disappeared. Or perhaps it would be better to say that my body scattered: each particle of me riding a different strand of wind away from what was once my flesh and blood.

I heard a loud noise. It was rushing water moving at a great speed all around me. A river.

Oh! was the last thing I thought. This is *God*.

• • •

I woke in my own bed, with my mother hovering over me, weeping.

"Miriam, Miriam," she whispered. It was more a prayer than a name.

"Mother!" I cried. I inhaled deeply, feeling my own skin like tight, uncomfortable clothing. I wiggled my fingers.

"Nicodemus, come quick!" my mother cried. "She's awake!"

I gazed up at her tear streaked face. Why was she so sad?

My father, his eyes like fiery wheels, burst into the room. He looked at me as if he might kill me.

Now he will beat me. Now he will show no mercy, I thought dispassionately.

I felt huge . . . inhuman.

"Nicodemus, don't!" My mother stretched her arms across my body.

But my father only took a long slow breath that flared his nostrils.

He sank heavily to his knees. "God is merciful!" he cried out in the same voice he reserved for the reciting of the Torah. "God has heard my petition!"

"What happened, Father? I was outside with Yohanna when the sky went dark . . ."

My mother covered her mouth with her hand, but my father shot her a look that said *Do not scare the child*. And then he went on to scare me himself. "Miriam," he said solemnly, taking my hands in his. "You were seized by a demon."

I nodded, not truly understanding.

I remembered a little boy named Yamin shaking wildly, his eyes rolled back in his head. He'd fallen down in the sandy square one Sabbath as we were filing out of the synagogue. His older sister had shrieked and, kneeling down beside him, had struggled to control his wild movements.

"Someone help me!" she'd pleaded. A group of men had rushed forward, but her friends had scattered, making signs against the evil eye.

"Do not get near!" my mother had warned me, clutching my hand. "There is an evil spirit in him!"

But I had peered through the mayhem with curiosity, craning my neck even as my mother led me away. I had never forgotten the absent look on Yamin's face, his arms bent up rigidly like the frozen wings of a dead bat I had once come upon at the edge of the old vineyard beyond our garden. The bat had been dry and brittle. Yamin looked like that, except that he moved, shuddering against the restraining hands, spittle foaming out of the corner of his mouth.

"Did I . . . was it like Yamin?" I asked. I noticed that my head hurt above my left temple.

They did not answer, but stared at me silently, the tears still brimming at their eyes.

"Will I die?" I asked.

I saw my mother's hands twitch. Did she want to ward off the evil eye?

"You will not die," my father answered finally. But he had waited too long to answer.

I looked to my mother beseechingly, but she refused to meet my eye, staring instead at my father, her lips trembling. Was she praying under her breath?

"What does it mean, Father? How did the demon get into me?"

"It means nothing," my father said brusquely, squeezing my hand so tightly it hurt. "And it will likely never happen again. Don't speak of it to anyone."

I nodded, choosing to believe him.

But of course, it did happen again. And the next time I did not dissolve or disappear.

I remembered everything.

Four

On the hushed nights before the rainy season, my mother would let Marta and me sleep on the roof.

Kemat would bring a clay brazier up the ladder and we would huddle around its orange glow. By the time Kemat had gotten our beds made there was an edge to the air and we were thankful to crawl below the heavy wool blankets. Those late days leading up to the Feast of Tabernacles, the winds churned in the west, blowing the charred breath of the temple's fires all the way up to Bethany.

"Watch carefully. If you see a star fall, remember where it fell so we can go and find it tomorrow!" Kemat instructed us. She was most comfortable in the darkness. Her inky black hair melted into the shadows and her onyx eyes dilated, fed by the moon and the wet smell of dirt digesting a day of sunlight.

I laughed. I wanted to find a silver shard of starlight lodged in a bush. Kemat's mischievous smile made all manner of things feel possible: people becoming trees, stars with human faces, golden scales weighing human hearts.

Marta sniffed. She already felt much too old for these sorts of games.

"I'd rather you tell us a story," she suggested, lying back and pulling the blanket up to her chin. "One about love. And a king."

"You're so boring, Marta," I complained as I dove under the blanket, wrapping my arms around my sister's waist, nuzzling my head into her soft belly. She smelled like rosemary and yeasty bread. "All you ever want to talk about is love!"

Marta reached over and tweaked my ear affectionately. "Hush, Miriam. You'll be lovesick soon enough. And then I'll get to make fun of you, too."

I peeked over the blanket and watched Kemat's face turn red as she blew into the mouth of the brazier. The embers glowed and smoked. She stared wistfully into the night for a long time. A few thin strands of hair blew up and across her face, reaching toward the field. Her lips parted, letting that darkness enter into her.

Was she thinking about her home? Egypt? I could see something moving in her eyes. Golden hills. A river. Wide-winged graceful birds fanning hot air. Trees with long leaves like fingers.

I could taste her melancholy. It was not unpleasant—the taste of water seeking an ocean.

Oh, I thought, nuzzling Marta's stomach, still watching Kemat. *I know that feeling! An ache for the distant past. A yearning for what is lost!*

But what *had* I lost? I was hardly eight years old. I hadn't lived long enough to lose anything.

"Have I told you the one about Isis?" Kemat whispered, interrupting my reverie. The night pulsed! A radiant blue glow emerged, revealing the line of the horizon. The stars winked above us, their light showing the curves of a few gray clouds usually hidden at this hour. The chorus of frogs and insects paused their music making, and when they resumed, their singing was an octave higher, almost celebratory.

"Isis," I whispered, feeling the name imprint permanently on my tongue.

A thirst. A hunger. A power.

"Who?" Marta wondered.

Kemat turned back to us, half her face eaten by the dark, the other cast red from the fire. "Isis! She is the mistress of all the stars! The lady of magic."

"Tell us! Tell us!" I squealed. I loved nothing better than Kemat's strange stories. They were about men who became birds. Women with the faces of lions. Queens with skirts as wide and purple as the night sky. Men who lifted the sun from below the horizon every day. Most of all—and I could not have put it this simply back then—Kemat told us stories of gods and goddesses that were not so different from the stories of men and women. They quarreled. Made mistakes. Got lost. Fell in love.

"Isis was a beautiful queen. She was the queen of Egypt. The country where I come from."

"*Was* she beautiful?" Marta asked skeptically. I knew she did not think much of our slender Egyptian maid. How could the queen of such a land rival the beauty of a Judean woman?

"As beautiful as your mother." Kemat's face nearly split in half, she grinned so widely. She was deft at unseating my sister's petulance. "In fact, they looked very similar indeed."

"Go on," Marta prompted her, happy with this answer.

"Isis knew all about the river, the Nile, that ran through Egypt. She knew about how it flooded once a year and nourished the land. She knew about the power of the moon and the stars. She could harness starlight to make the wheat and barley grow. But she wanted more. She wanted to be as powerful a goddess as the sun god Ra."

"She sounds greedy," Marta noted. But she was transfixed, biting her lip in anticipation. "Go on, Kemat."

"She wasn't greedy. She was cunning and she was desirous." Kemat's eye flared with the reflection of the flame. Her iris thinned into a vertical line and for a moment she resembled an amber-eyed cat. "It is not a bad thing to want something, Marta."

"She wanted power?" I asked.

"Isis wanted the night to be equal to the day," Kemat answered, sharing the firelight of her eyes with me. "She wanted to claim a royal throne for the moon." I felt the burning travel through me, tingling in my core.

"What did she do?" Marta prodded impatiently.

"She made herself a snake. She took clay and sand and river water and fashioned a long, lethal serpent." Kemat stretched out her arm, letting a wave of movement travel from her shoulder down to her fingertips. I could imagine the shadow of a forked tongue extending beyond her gesture, the glittering star of a reptilian eye blinking on the golden skin of her hand.

"Ugh," Marta shuddered under me, her stomach tightening. She hated snakes and screamed whenever they knifed across our path. Once I'd picked up a harmless black serpent and chased her around the garden, threatening to throw it at her face.

My mother had slapped me so hard that it left a fingered bruise on my cheek. But it had been worth it.

"What did she do with the snake?" I asked.

The crescent moon of Kemat's smile returned.

"Isis knew the path Ra took across the land each day. And so she set the snake in his path. Ra was self-important. A proud man. When he walked, he didn't watch his feet. He barely respected the ground he walked upon. So when he came upon the snake, he stepped on it. It bit him and he immediately fell. The venom was fast-acting, and he started to grow pale with death."

Marta gasped and then pretended to cough. She wasn't as immune to Kemat's storytelling as she would like to admit. "Did he die?" she murmured.

"God can't die!" I interrupted. "God came before the earth."

"How very wrong you are," Kemat said, silencing us both, placing her hands flat on the grass mats, looking deep into the brazier. "A god can certainly die. They can make mistakes. They can suffer."

"Father would be angry if he heard you say that," Marta warned, and I could hear in her voice that she was genuinely afraid for her.

Kemat's expression was bemused. "It's a story, Marta. What harm is a story?"

I sighed impatiently. "Keep going, Kemat!"

"All right, little one," she glanced down at her hands, which were covered in cooking burns. Divets and cuts. Dried skin across her knuckles. I knew the texture of her touch well; the gentle pressure of her fingers at my temple when she was trying to soothe me into sleep. She squinted, raising her hands, letting the orange glow of the brazier play across them. Was Kemat reading her story in the lines etched across her palms?

Perhaps. When she looked up at us her eyes were distant. But she began to speak again. "Ra moaned and screamed. He called to all the gods and goddesses of the land. He called to his children for help. But no one had the antidote. No one could save him from the spreading poison."

My stomach lurched. I felt sick, but I took a deep breath, focusing my eyes on the pulsing flames in the brazier, listening intently to the story.

"Isis came to him then. She told Ra she was the only one who could save him. But she would only do so on one condition: he must reveal to her his true name. The name that held his power."

"His name?" Marta scoffed. "What good is that?"

"A name is everything," Kemat answered gravely. "It is the music we respond to when we are lost. Someone goes down to the river and calls out our name and, somehow, we hear it and return."

I could smell her words. Fresh split cedar. The sourness of wet clay. The unmistakable sharpness of running water. There was a rushing sound in my ears. I tried to ignore it.

"Ra was in agony. He knew he had been tricked. But he wanted to live. So he told Isis everything. He told her his secret name. It was then that Isis assumed her role as queen of the heavens and the earth. The stars shone brighter! The river gushed forth with life and nourished the land. She was all-powerful. And a powerful queen needed a powerful king. A lord that would match her wisdom, her grace, her beauty . . . "

The rushing was so loud in my ears that I could hardly hear Kemat. But it didn't matter. I watched her lips moving. I had an uncanny sense that I already knew the ending to the story—a terrible, terrible ending.

"Oh, God!"

Did the voice belong to me? It seemed a long way off.

"Miriam."

I heard my own name spoken in a man's voice. It was a voice distorted by a rush of running water. I couldn't see anything.

But this time I did not dissolve.

My vision sharpened. I swallowed, tasting the sweet warmth of decomposing plant matter. The moon was no longer a crescent as it had been seconds before. No! It pulsed, engorged and full. There was enough silver light that when I waved my hands in front of me, I could see their shadows below me.

I was standing in water up to my waist. And I was naked.

Oh. My body was different. Longer and wider. I saw pearlescent drops of sweat collecting around the large dark nipples of my heavy breasts. My hand pressed the softness of my belly through the water.

There was another gust of air as warm as breath. A briny, intimate smell.

A marsh! I realized. *And I am a grown woman! What is this? Where am I?*

"Miriam!" The man's voice called again. I could feel it move the hair on my neck, curving to the delicate skin below my chin.

But I did not turn around. Something had caught my eye—something ahead of me, sparkling underneath the water and the dancing reeds. I pushed forward, squelching through the mud and grasses, trying to move aside the reeds.

"Ah . . ." The voice was so close to me it could have been my own. I felt it move through my body and into the water.

The surface rippled. And when it settled, I could see what lay below.

It was a face. A human face. Pale and still. Shining up out of the inky depths.

Oh, no. Oh, no!

I splashed forward frantically. My fingers connected with something straight and hard. I pressed my hand against it, realizing I had found a large, submerged box, large enough to hold a man.

The man's face hovered just below the surface.

You!

I had never seen this man before in my life or in my dreams. But the overwhelming feeling I had was one of recognition. And relief.

He was handsome, with a strong jaw and a cleft chin, as well as a long narrow nose, almost Roman, that had been broken before and had healed with a slightly flattened ridge. It was a lion's nose. Black curls streamed out above his tall forehead and he had full, almost feminine lips. He reminded me of the beautiful god flanked by satyrs and women that I had seen a painting of in the Yerusalem market. "Dionysus," my father had explained, noting my curiosity. "The Romans' lord of wine and . . ." he paused, a wry smile curling his lips. "Lord of trouble."

You! I thought once more. *Where have you been? It has been such a long, long time!*

The man was certainly dead. His cheeks were slack.

I had to get him out of the box. I had to breathe life back into him. I had to touch him.

But as I reached in, stretching my fingers toward him, a high-pitched keening broke the spell. The darkness of the marsh faded and shimmered, then began to shift into leaves, interlocking roots, glistening webs of starlight. A meshwork of hush. A blinding dust.

I could see nothing. I was held inside of a scream that was growing louder and louder.

No! I must stay with him! I cannot let him go again!

The strange thought filled me with terror. I clenched my stomach and gritted my teeth, trying desperately to stay in the marsh. But the water began to recede. And I could feel the grass mats of the roof below my shoulders again. I was back in Bethany.

I opened my eyes. Kemat, Marta, my mother, my father, and Lazaros were all kneeling around me.

Only then did I realize that the screaming belonged to me.

• • •

Marta and my mother were weeping.

I sat up, nauseated but well enough. The night smelled fresh and dry. Gone was the brine and heat of the marsh.

Where had the full moon gone? Had it been real?

It felt *more* real than anything I'd ever experienced.

My father was kneeling at my feet, gripping my ankles, staring at me solemnly. A lamp flickered beside him, its flame pushed almost horizontal by the night wind.

"What happened?" I asked him.

His hands twitched on my ankles. He said nothing. My mother's weeping swelled into a low sob. But I refused to look at her, staring intently at my father, waiting for his eyes to answer me if his lips would not.

Finally, he swallowed, wet his lips, and answered. "You had another spell, Miriam. Do you remember nothing?"

Lazaros peeked from under Kemat's arm. I saw by the wetness of his eyes that he, too, had been crying. "Father says you have a demon in you!" he told me. "But I will help you get it out!"

I ignored him. I was desperate to talk with Kemat.

"Kemat! Kemat!" I whispered. "I saw him! Someone . . . a man! He said my name. He called me Miriam."

Kemat's eyes widened but she said nothing.

"Who?" my mother cut in sharply. "What are you talking about, Miriam?"

"I saw a face, Kemat. The face of a dead god. He was in the marshes."

Seeing that Kemat would not respond, I turned to my father. "He was like the lord of trouble. The lord of leopards! The one in the painting with a beautiful face and sparkling eyes!"

My father stiffened and pulled his hand from my grasp. "What are you speaking of, Miriam? God has no face."

"You are wrong, Father." I was still too stunned by the experience to hold anything back. "God *does* have a face! And he is beautiful! But it was terrible. He was dead . . ."

"What is she saying?" My father turned to Kemat, his eyes narrowing dangerously. I was suddenly worried for the Egyptian maid. "What nonsense have you been telling my children?"

"Nothing, master," Kemat said demurely, her eyes lowered, her hands tightly knotted in her lap. "Miriam speaks of dreams. She is unwell. Have pity on the girl."

My father looked back to me. He rapped my shin with his knuckles as if to test the solidity of my body. I winced. It hurt.

"Never speak to me of such things again, Miriam. It is madness. It comes from the devil that has possessed you."

Never speak of the man again? His beauty? The terrible sorrow in my breast for him?

Impossible.

But I nodded, too dazed to argue.

Later, my mother insisted I sleep in Kemat's bed with her, sending her husband, Meshkenet, to sleep on a blanket in the storeroom.

"Why can't I sleep with you, Mother?" I asked, frowning as she carried me to the servants' quarters at the far end of the house.

She did not answer me. But when I looked up into her eyes, I saw fear. My own mother was afraid of me.

"Am I unclean, Mother?"

"Be quiet, Miriam. Be quiet!" she begged before depositing me onto Kemat's mattress. "Look after her."

She left us.

"Come here, dear one." Kemat pulled me to her thin body, running her fingers through my hair and massaging my tender scalp until I finally relaxed.

I wrapped my arms around her chest, thankful for her embrace. I felt that without someone to hold onto I might dissolve. There was a sadness in me with no root, no explanation. I felt I had lost my entire world.

"Kemat?" I whispered through the darkness, my lips moving against the skin of her arm.

"Miriam."

"Who is the god in the box? Is it Ra? The sun god?'

Kemat was quiet for a long time. Then she answered. "No, Miriam. He is not the sun god. He prefers the darkness. The underworld."

"Who is he?" I pressed on. "Is he the one my father spoke of? The Roman god of leopards and goat men?"

But she would say no more.

For a while the spells came so infrequently that we could pretend they did not exist. No one in Bethany knew. I was not yet an embarrassment to my family.

Five

"Lemuel is here!" Lazaros cried excitedly. He burst into the room that Marta and I shared. I was sitting on the bed sorting colored beads. Some I had found among the rubble in the street. Others were gifts from my mother and Kemat. I liked lining them up, as if each one symbolized a prayer or a word. *Carnelian. Green glass. Onyx. Wood. Bone.*

Was that what writing was like? I mused, recalling the long powdery scrolls my father pored over for so many hours.

"You're not listening!" Lazaros stomped his foot impatiently. "Lemuel has presents for us!"

"Lemuel!" The name finally broke through my daydreaming. I did not like many of my father's friends. But I loved Lemuel! Lemuel was not a rabbi or a doctor of the Law. He was a merchant, a man made of pure energy weathered into thick, bark-like leather, his muscles almost comically overdeveloped, but with a substantial gut. He was as clean-shaven as a Roman, with eyes as gray as thunder. Expensive perfume wafted from his wide sleeves. He always wore jewelry, and a chunk of ruby hung from a hole in his left earlobe.

"He makes his wealth selling oils and perfumes," Marta had told me the last time he'd visited. "Myrrh and aloe. Cedar oil from the north." She was concerned with understanding other people's status in our community. "He is the wealthiest man in Bethany! And he dresses like a madman!"

Lemuel had a large home but spent most of his time on the road, carting his products to and from foreign lands. When he was back in town, he would always come to dine with us, sporting outrageously colorful jackets, his hands glittering with rings, relaying stories of run-ins with leopards and lions.

"I don't care about cats!" Lazaros would cry when Lemuel began one of his stories. "Tell me about the *lestai!* About the bandits!"

"Ah, yes," Lemuel would chuckle, smacking his big trunk-like thighs. "The time I outsmarted those brigands outside of Yericho. That's the story you want to hear, son?"

The best was when Lemuel brought along gifts: thin purple slips of silk for Marta, a bundle of peacock feathers for Lazaros, exquisitely embroidered belts for my mother, and little wooden boxes for me, engraved with running lions and deer.

For my father, he brought tightly coiled scrolls. And he brought news: "The Galileans are stirring up trouble again. I wouldn't travel north if I were you. It's only a matter of time before the Romans make another example of those brigands."

My mother would cough loudly and suggest that Marta sing a song to entertain Lemuel. But my father, eager for information, would wave his hand at her, clicking his tongue dismissively. "Has there been outright violence?"

"Violence!" Lemuel would chuckle, clasping his hands around his ample midsection. "Well, of course. The Romans make a point of scaring a village every month or so. Go in and rough up the brutes who are too poor to pay taxes. Drag a whore out into the fields and give her a go . . . But nothing more than that recently."

"Such behavior will only incite them to rebel." My father would sigh. "It would be wiser to treat such simple folk with gentleness."

"They are not gentlefolk!" Lemuel would raise a bushy gray brow, grabbing his glass and gulping down the last of the wine he had brought as a gift. "The Romans know that to discourage another fellow like Yudas they must regularly remind the Galileans of their power."

"Two thousand crucified for that man's idiocy! The damn zealots!" My father, ruddy with wine and outrage, raised his fist into the air and shook it futilely. "To think that anyone would need a reminder! I heard that the smell of rotting bodies clung to the road out of Sepphoris for weeks . . ."

"Nicodemus!" My mother stood up, nearly upsetting the low wooden table we were gathered around. "Enough! There are children present!"

Tonight, however, there would be none of this talk; only good cheer. Even before I reached the courtyard, I heard the swell of Lemuel's laughter. And there he was! Cross-legged on the ground, chuckling at something my father had just said.

"Miriam! You are taller every time I see you!" Lemuel exclaimed, his gray eyes wrinkling with merriment. "Come. Sit! Eat! Your mother has outdone herself again."

Of course it was Kemat who had done the cooking. But I held my tongue. I would tell Kemat of Lemuel's praise later. She would shake her head, her silky hair swinging across her face to hide her blush.

"I was out with my sister Marah and her husband, Ohad, in Arimathea for a week," Lemuel explained, his big hands dismantling a whole loaf of bread and dipping pieces into the fatty juice of goat stew. "But I'm worried about my brother-in-law. He hasn't been to the temple in ten years, and he is ill with dropsy. I told him he must travel to Yerusalem to give sacrifice if he wishes to get well. I told him to bring his son, my nephew Yosseph, and I will host them."

Lazaros was imitating Lemuel's sloppy manners, grabbing a piece of bread and dipping it into a bowl of lentils. My mother shot him a dangerous look and he froze, the bread halfway to his mouth.

When the last of the wine had been drunk, Lemuel motioned to me that I should come over to him. He looked slightly embarrassed. Or drunk. Or both. But his eyes twinkled as he held out his calloused hands, cupping a shiny white treasure of some sort.

"What is it?" I breathed, hardly able to contain my excitement. A part of me wished the gift would turn out to be alive, an exotic animal I could train to sing or talk and sit on my shoulder.

"A very expensive gift for a very beautiful girl," he chortled, opening his hands further so I could better see what he was holding.

My mother peeked over my shoulder and asked, "What on earth, Lemuel?"

Marta who had, moments before, been gleeful with her gift of ribbons for her long dark hair, looked confused. "What is it, Miriam? Show it to all of us!"

Lemuel transferred the object to my hands, and I was surprised by how cold and heavy it was for something so small.

It was a moderately sized jar, shaped like a teardrop and bleached bone-white, with triangular grooves around the top that narrowed to a small opening, stoppered with a small black stone.

"It is a fine jar, made of alabaster," Lemuel explained. "But that's not the gift, my dear."

He reached over, gently taking the jar from me and popping off the top.

Perfume! I gasped with joy.

Lemuel had only ever given perfume to my mother, and I had always been jealous of her sweet smells: the honey and cinnamon that lingered beneath her gestures, jasmine heating up on the veins of her wrist, and the delicate aloe she applied after a bath.

But I was still young. Perhaps too young for perfume. My own body still so fresh that it did not even produce its own musk.

Even now, even here so far from home, I can smell the perfume that rose from the alabaster jar. Can you smell it in this small hut? A blue flower close to the dirt. The armpit of a lover. The smell of doorways guiding us into and out of life.

This was not one of my mother's sweet scents. This odor was discordant, thick, and herbal, piercing me low in the belly.

"Nard! Spikenard!" My mother exclaimed faintly, wafting the smell up to her narrow nose, making a show of inhaling deeply. She reached out and rapped Lemuel's shoulder. "What a ridiculous thing to give a young girl, Lemuel! What will she possibly do with it?"

"How could you, Lemuel? Three hundred denarii, at least!" My father was surprised, too, chewing his lower lip, leaning forward so that he could smell the expensive oil.

"Ah, it is nothing to a man like me!" Lemuel scoffed. But he was bright red with embarrassment.

It was a more expensive gift than anything he had ever given Marta or Lazaros or my mother. It was more expensive than all the scrolls and wine he had ever delivered to my father.

"Why me?" I asked, clutching the jar to my chest, feeling dizzy with its dense smell.

Lemuel looked at my father instead of me. He flung out his big arms and laughed nervously. "Forgive me, Nicodemus! I can only answer that I had the strangest dream. In it Miriam was holding this very jar of spikenard. And I knew that she must have it."

A dream?

"You have dreamed of my daughter?" My father's eyes were sparking like struck flint. "Is this what you are telling me, Lemuel?"

"Yes! The silliest dream. She was wearing stars on her head, clothed in light, riding in on the moon. Trust me that I know I sound like a madman. But I felt it would be worse to ignore such a dream. I had already acquired the jar!"

Slowly my father nodded, relaxing.

He had studied scripture enough to understand the power of dreams. He knew of Yosseph in Egypt, interpreting dreams sent from God. He knew of Daniel's nightly visions. "Miriam. Do you understand how precious this gift is?" he said sternly. "Lemuel has given you an anointing oil. It is holy. For ceremony. It is not to be worn like a perfume."

"It is only fit for a king or a queen!" I replied grandly. "I shall wait for a king before I use it!"

All the adults burst out laughing, breaking the tension. I blushed hotly. Even Marta snickered.

"You *are* a queen, Miriam," Lemuel assured me. "Never forget it."

My father's eyes flashed and my mother rested her fingertips on my shoulder protectively. But Lemuel was no lecher. He was embarrassed but too superstitious to keep his dream a secret.

Marta scowled again, sticking out her tongue at me over Lemuel's shoulder. But she could not upset me then. The jar steadied me. The smell was making my blood thicker, sturdier, darker.

Later that night I left Marta snoring in our bed and snuck out into the courtyard. A nightingale roosting invisibly in one of the trees broke the silence, sending a complicated entreaty of whirs and whistles up to the stars. I settled myself deep in the shadows of the fig leaves and opened the jar again. I inhaled and was immediately dizzy. I shut the jar suddenly, wrinkling my nose.

It wasn't that I disliked the smell of the perfume. But it made me feel very strange—as if I was about to remember a sorrow so vast, so deep, it might break me apart forever.

Six

"What an oaf!" Lazaros whispered in my ear. "He's making Yosiah nervous!"

A Roman solider with legs as thick as olive tree trunks was standing behind the tax collector Yosiah in the marketplace outside the gates of Bethany. Yosiah was a pitiful man: one of his legs was shorter than the other, giving him a dragging limp. His features drooped to one side. He resented any help, cursing if anyone offered to carry his bags for him. He was not loved.

I stared at the Roman solider. His breastplate gleamed almost white in the noon sunlight. He scowled as he oversaw the poor man's duties. I thought of my father and Lemuel discussing the mass executions outside Sepphoris. The soldiers pillaging villages and raping women. The Roman presence was so entangled with ours that it was hard to see where their power ended and our submission began. I sometimes forgot they were behind every event, deciding whether we could live or die in our own city, our own land.

An old woman with a shiny bald patch on the back of her silver head was pleading with Yosiah, obviously unable to pay her yearly due again. She wrung her bony hands, rocking back and forth, her voice rising with agitation.

Yosiah glanced up at the soldier, closing his lazy eyelid against the sun, grimacing.

The solider didn't say anything. He reached out and slapped the woman hard. She was so little, almost made of parchment, that she hardly even fell. Instead she appeared to *flutter* to the ground, her thin hands spread out in surprise. She yelped feebly like a wounded animal.

"Stop it!" I yelled, before anyone could tell me to keep quiet.

Yohanna pulled at my braid. "Remember what my mother told us about the soldiers, Miriam. They will ruin us if we challenge them. They will cut our hearts out or worse! They will defile us!"

"What do you mean?" Lazaros asked. "Yohanna, I am confused! Will they defile *me?*"

"No, of course not. Don't be silly." Yohanna rolled her eyes. "But Miriam and I are daughters of Yerusalem! They will take their weapons and stick them up . . ."

"Stop!" I reached behind me blindly, pinching whatever bare piece of flesh I could reach first.

"Ah!" It turned out to be Yohanna's nose. Her eyes watered. "You're awful, Miriam!"

I glanced back. No one in the marketplace had gone to help the old woman. The soldier was grinding his foot into her skirt. As I watched, he swelled his cheeks before spitting forcefully into her face.

The woman moaned and turned her other cheek. He spit on her again.

Oh. I understood, my blood boiling as I watched Yosiah look away, his hands shaking. The young men who walked past kept up their playful banter so as to pass by the soldier unnoticed.

I understand now. Every time we look away from this violence, we all betray each other! And yet, when we openly oppose it, we risk doing nothing and losing our own lives.

The world fell away. Suddenly all sensation was gone. My body was as numb as stone. I could still see the soldier laughing, his lips drawn back to reveal his rotten teeth. His face faded. But not my anger. It swelled larger and larger until it was no longer inside my body. I felt porous; washed clean.

I was no longer in the marketplace. I was alone, drifting on my back in water. I felt that I might be the water itself, my body the smooth muscles of the current sliding over stones and sand.

Somewhere, someone was crying.

What is your name?

"Miriam." He knew mine. His voice called to me from across the marshes, across a distance of dreams.

But he did not appear. I continued to float in the water, listening to a woman weeping.

After a long time, years perhaps, I woke to the sound of my mother's voice. "There's no use, Nicodemus. Everyone saw it. And everyone will know by tomorrow. You have to *do* something."

"Do you dare tell me what to do, Hadassah?" He was more petulant than he let himself be when he knew I was listening. "How about *you* attend the assembly tomorrow? Instruct my students? You seem to think you know perfectly well how to dispense justice."

My mother was quiet. I inhaled slowly so that my parents would not sense I was awake.

Kemat, with honeyed goat milk, came in soon after they left. She played with my hair, tucking it behind my ears, tickling the soft flesh under my chin. "Oh, Miriam. You are too fierce for this land!" she whispered.

"It is not right to hurt an old woman," I said, sitting up.

"It is a terrible thing to do," Kemat agreed. "But," she continued, "it is done all the time. And not just to old women. Young women, too. And babies. Killed for sport. It is the Romans' way."

She stared at me, her black eyes as impenetrable as the sky on a night when the moon does not rise. "Are you ready for the world, Miriam?"

No one had ever asked me such a strange question. It sent shoots of lightning down to the very soles of my feet.

"Men like that should suffer," I insisted.

Kemat burst out laughing. "Oh, they will Miriam! Perhaps not in this life. But surely they will suffer in their lives to come."

• • •

Within hours everyone knew that Nicodemus's daughter had thrown a fit in the market in front of a Roman solider. She'd endangered the whole town with her public display.

My family filed into the synagogue the next day, and my father headed, as always, to his place of authority at the front of the room. My mother led us to the gallery, and I felt all eyes upon me. My mother's friends smiled at Marta and Lazaros, but when I passed, they visibly shuddered. One or two women made the sign of the evil eye, then spit on the ground.

Yohanna's eyes were fearful. She moved closer to her mother, clutching her skirts. Serah hissed and reached up to clasp a small blue talisman on a rope around her neck. This was the same woman who just the week before had let me stay the night with Yohanna. She'd made a bed for us out in their garden so that our chattering wouldn't keep up the whole house.

We found our spot against the wall, and I stood with my back uncomfortably straight, facing the reader and the hazzan supporting the scrolls.

Usually I listened intently, trying to memorize all the words I could. This was a window into the world of the scholar, which I was denied. But if I tried hard enough, I could walk away with *something*.

The best Sabbaths were the ones when my father would step up in front of the community and offer a long commentary on one of the teachings. But my father was not reading that day and he had not spoken to me since my spell. I had waited for him at the door as we'd left earlier in the morning, but he had grunted without saying anything, pushing past me. He walked ahead of us all the way to the synagogue. My mother held my hand but she, too, would not meet my eye. I felt her fingers trembling on mine. Was she frightened to touch me?

Oh. I am a burden to them, I thought, a sour taste in my mouth. My father was pensive, sitting next to Lemuel, with his hands folded in his lap over unsaid words. I watched my father rather than meet the suspicious gaze of the children and women.

A part of me, a small wicked part, wanted to fake madness. I saw it clearly. I would writhe and moan on the floor. Perhaps a snake would slide into the synagogue and wrap around my body. Or a great wind would push through the windows, blowing off the women's scarves. I'd stand, drape the snake around my shoulders, and feel that dark reptilian power pulsing through my veins. I would go in front of the rabbi and rave about the end of the world—when mad women like *me* would drive the Romans from our holy city.

Ester would come back to avenge herself. The old bald woman from the marketplace would drive a sword into the soldier's breast.

And I would lead them.

Toward the end of the service, my mother pinched my arm, disturbing my dark fantasies.

"Try to act normal. Blink!" she whispered angrily.

As we left the synagogue, Lazaros's friend Achim yelled after me.

"Miriam! Miriam! Show me your devils! Lazaros says you are filled with unholy terrors!"

His mother put her hand over Achim's mouth, and he wriggled frantically, trying to get free. His mother was a broad, strong woman, and she had an easy time restraining him.

My mother grabbed Lazaros by the ear and dragged him, crying, all the way home. He was barely breathing by the time we were inside. But my mother wasn't fooled. She slapped him soundly and ordered him to his room without bread or milk or water.

"I thought Achim could help!" Lazaros protested. "I want to *help* Miriam! He said you can beat wickedness out of a woman! He said if you beat them hard enough, the demons will come out!"

"Pray that I don't beat the wickedness out of *you!*" my mother stormed. "Now go! Before I think of some worse punishment."

At the Sabbath dinner, after the prayers had been said, my father finally broke his silence. "We must go make an offering at the temple, Miriam. We must help you become clean again." The expression on his face was neither angry nor stern. Strangely, it seemed quizzical, as if he were waiting for me to offer a better option.

I tried. The thought of losing my visions, losing the chance of seeing the strange man's face again, did not feel right. "Why can't I just go to the mikvah with mother and wash myself? Why do I have to go to the temple?"

My father's brows shot up in surprise. He was so young then! Now I know with certainty that he already had growing qualms with the temple practices—serious questions about issues of impurity, ambivalence toward his fellow doctors of the Law. But he took his role seriously, performing it for our family even more frequently than he did for his peers or students. No one had yet come to show him another way, although sometimes I felt him looking at me with a hunger for an answer. *Why me?* I would think naively. *You are the one who can read! Teach me, Father. Only then will I teach you in return!*

"Is Miriam going away forever?" Lazaros asked, having recovered from his temper tantrum. He reached out a small hand to clutch at my arm, his eyes as soft and brown as a doe's. I forgave him immediately.

"No, my son. She will be back tomorrow night and she will be better," my mother explained.

Lazaros didn't believe her. I wondered what else Achim had told him about "curing" women. I had a suspicion it might involve stones.

Lazaros followed me around for the rest of the night, right into bed where he promptly began to weep. He was like a difficult vine twining around my body. I had to unwrap him from me and carry him to his own bed.

"Tell me a story, Miriam?" His voice was already thick with sleep.

But I began anyway. "There was once a woman and she was very sick. Sick like me. But sick with sadness. She was sad because she had lost her husband, the king. So she decided to go out and find him . . ."

• • •

The next morning, I woke early with my father. After we had shared bread with honey, he blinked sleepily, spit out a seed, and suggested that I join him in his morning prayers on the roof. It was the first time he had allowed such a thing. I nodded stiffly, holding my breath, trying to hide my excitement. I followed him up the ladder, looking at his long striped shawl dangling above me, smelling the fresh, wet dew on his feet.

We stood facing the west, toward Yerusalem, and I watched, imitating him, as he raised his hands up toward the sky. He recited the Shema and I did too, bowing my head, putting all my energy into the words.

"How do you know your prayers so well?" he asked later when we were headed to Yerusalem.

"I listen when you pray, Father. And I remember everything," I confessed. I didn't confess that I also listened in on Lazaros's lessons.

"It is good to remember these things. They may be saved on scrolls. But writing is dangerous! It can so easily be changed or destroyed. Your mind, though, will never lose track of the right words." He smiled as if surprised that he endorsed what he'd just said.

"How did you learn the Law?" I skipped to catch up.

"I learned it all by listening. I listened to my teachers. And I haven't forgotten a single word they told me." His voice sounded like a closed door.

I didn't like limits. Whenever Marta was irritated with me, I would continue to tease her past the point of return. She would retaliate by pinching me or telling my mother. Then my mother would hand me over to Kemat, who would once again say, "Miriam. I am beginning to think you *like* making people angry!"

So I asked my father another question. "Father, when will *I* learn to read? When will *I* learn the Law?"

We had reached the market, where vendors were already beginning to set up their stalls. Women unfurled leather satchels of dried herbs, and men stood behind their earthenware, which was piled up on flimsy wooden tables.

Father did not answer my question. We walked on, our sandals making a powdery music of slaps and thumps against the dust of the road.

It was not until we had ascended the Mount of Olives and the city had become visible again, blazing in the pinkness of early morning, that he stopped. Yerusalem looked like a dangerous bug with a hard shell and sharp pincers: the walls beyond the ravine of Kidron rose up two hundred feet and were topped by several pointed towers. The temple's gilded spires stung the sky.

The city was beautiful and impressive. Even my father, when approaching Yerusalem, would rest his hand on his heart and breathe deeply, as if savoring the view of a beautiful sunset or a lover. It did not move me in the same way that it did others.

Now I know that the more important view was the one that lay behind me, looking back over the olive trees, the hills furred with wildflowers and grass, the fields dancing with heavy-headed grain, all the way to my home in Bethany. What I would give now to spend just one hour looking at my home from a distance! And maybe if I watched long enough there would be one window illuminated, letting me know that my mother had begun to light the lamps.

But no, the best I have is what I can tell you: that the land outside of Yerusalem, its tides of barrenness and fertility, its fevered wind and gnarled trees, was holier than whatever lay inside the city. The smallest, most insignificant stone from the hill outside my home was more sacred to me than whatever it was the priests guarded.

"You will not go to school like Lazaros," my father said quietly. I turned away from the view to look up at his face. But I could not interpret his expression. His lips were set in a thin line, disappearing into the darkness of his beard. His gaze went past me, unfocused. "You will marry like your mother and keep a good house."

I would not learn to read. I would not learn the scripture. I would marry. Like Ester had married Gad.

I would not make a good wife. I didn't care about household chores. If I was forced to marry, forced to be a simple woman, I would surely die! Would I end up on the hills outside of Bethany? Would men stare down at me with contempt?

But I didn't say anything. We walked on. To argue with him would be to admit defeat. At that time in my life I had never seen my father lose an argument. It didn't seem wise to begin it until I knew full well that I *could* win. *How can I continue my studies? How can I convince him to teach me?* I schemed as my thoughts raced. I had to understand how God could allow the Romans to rule over us. I had to understand how God could allow men to throw stones at Ester.

By the time we neared the city the day had begun in earnest. Large crowds of pilgrims clogged the roads, singing songs of praise, some dragging sheep and goats alongside them. Animals bleated and screamed, pulling against their tethers so violently that the ropes cut into their sinewy necks. I shuddered, trying not to make eye contact with these animals. To witness them would be to disappear into their terror. I knew that I couldn't hold it all. We entered alongside these crowds, through the Fountain Gate.

The crush of people pricked a strange feeling of anticipation. I glanced from side to side, peering down alleyways as my father hurried me along. I scoured the passing faces. Old men. Young girls. Handsome youths with their hair recently cut and oiled back. I was looking for someone. Someone I had never seen before but who I was sure I would recognize.

There were centurions on every corner once we'd entered the city. Big men who hummed with violence. Their eyes were cold and gray as metal.

I made a point of staring up at each of these soldiers, enjoying the moment that they realized a girl was trying to catch their attention. They would startle, stepping backward, even though I was tiny. A little girl. The force of my gaze was enough to make them physically retreat. One spit after me, mumbling something about Jewish whores, grinding his heel into the dirt.

I smiled secretly, hurrying to catch up with my father's brisk pace.

My father refused to acknowledge the soldiers, but he nodded and talked with a great many other men as we made our way through the Wool Weavers Square, the Fullers Square, and finally entered the Upper Market.

Here the smells were packed so densely into the stagnant air that it was a wonder we could even breathe. The noise was overwhelming. The pilgrim's songs were more desperate. I could hear the ragged edge of unhealed wounds in their keening. "I call on the Lord in my distress, and he answers me! Save me, Lord! Save me, Lord!"

These desperate chants were matched by the haggling of the merchants. "A Tyre coin for a dove! But a coin for this bird!"

The chaos did not distract me from the rising feeling of reunion. Someone was about to arrive! If I kept looking through the crowds of people, I was sure to meet his eyes. I craned my head around, staring intently at a passing man whose silver curls brushed his deep red cloak. I stared at an older woman behind him, her clouded eyes blinking blindly. Older men with their heads in dun-colored turbans turned away from my searching eyes. However, a few children were intrigued, returning my gaze eagerly and smiling before they were dragged onward by a parent and my own father ushered me in the opposite direction.

Where are you? Who are you?

"Move along, Miriam," my father said, walking in front of me as we left the market and the street narrowed. "We must get to the temple before the second sacrifice."

The closer we got to the temple, the more frantic the screaming of the animals became. Perhaps they did not yet know their fate. But I think the sheep and goats and birds smelled it on the air. The blood of their brothers and sisters was already rising on the smoke that belched from the temple rising before us. The animals yapped and chirped and bayed unhappily.

The expensive clouds of perfume no longer disguised the stink. It was a mixture of animal fat, incense, and blood. I put my hand over my mouth to keep from retching.

"How can such a holy place smell like death?" I questioned, tugging at the fringed edge of my father's shawl. "How is this *clean?*"

My father squinted down at me. "How can such a young child possibly know what death smells like?"

Death smells like spikenard.

That's what I wanted to say, although I had no idea what it meant. I pushed this strange thought away.

I had seen animals die. I had watched Meskhenet butcher a lamb for a Pesach meal. I had seen dead jackals outside our town. But my father was right; I had never been close enough to death to really note its smell. Still, I knew for certain that the heaviness in the air was the heaviness of final breaths. It made me dizzy.

In the outer court people idled in groups, gossiping. In the shade of the porticoes, vendors had set up their shops. They offered every animal for sacrifice: Goats. Lambs. Sheep. Doves. Dusky-colored pigeons with shiny wet eyes. Some vendors sold fatty little cakes of incense. The moneychangers targeted the pilgrims in their weather-stained garments. But I hardly paid any attention to this. I was more interested in the men who were dressed like my father. One, usually older, would stand gesticulating, surrounded by a group of seated men, younger with their beards clipped short.

I imagined the glow of knowledge hovering above these men's heads. They were filled with an internal fire that fueled their energetic voices. *Have they understood God?*

I tried to imagine myself sitting alongside these young men. I desperately wanted to feel the same fire kindled within me.

One day. A certainty like sunshine flooded my body.

As we made our way through the chaos, one of these young men, clothed in freshly dyed blue robes, came through the crowd. "Nicodemus! I was wondering if we could continue our conversation. I have a question about the doctrine that holds we have a duty toward our own body as it is in God's likeness . . ."

"Hold your thoughts, Avram. This is perhaps a question better suited to the school of Rabbi Keziah. He knows Hillel's stand on this. I am about to offer a sacrifice with my daughter." He spoke with warmth and ease. "However, I *will* be holding a conversation later tomorrow with the others if you would like to discuss it then."

Avram noticed me, his big mouth curling into a grin. "Of course, Rabbi! I will see you tomorrow." He bowed to my father and gave me my own exaggerated bow, practically touching his forehead to the ground. "Good day, my lady!"

"Avram. Always the joker . . . " my father said, pulling at his whiskers, his eyes wrinkling with affection.

Oh, I realized, staring after the handsome young man. *My father's students are his real children. He reserves his real wisdom for them!*

My father led me straight across the outer court to a vendor who was practically obscured by his wares: unstable stacks of wicker boxes filled with puffs of feather and flashing eyes.

I couldn't help but draw closer, extending my hands toward the birds. Who would stop their flight intentionally? I stuck my fingers into the cages, gently brushing the glossy beak of a sparrow while my father negotiated with the small, one-eyed man who was selling them.

The cages were caked in shit, and some of the doves and sparrows were sitting in it, gawping at me, too exhausted to beat their wings. One dove, so gray that it was almost blue, opened and closed its beak silently. It stared at me with intensity. There was not a word in the dove's gaze. It was the bird's entire *soul* that it communicated: every glen it had found safety in, every nest it had built, the whole sky it had swept clean day after day. Every song it *could* sing but now would not. My stomach tightened.

"This bird will stand in for your troubles, Miriam," my father said to me, coming over, clutching a small white dove.

In the past I had given bloodless sacrifices, small cakes of the best flour mixed with galbanum, storax, and incense that my mother helped me prepare.

"What do you mean it will *stand* for me?" I asked, surprised to hear anger in my voice. How was the dove going to the same fate as the shewbread? Still holding the struggling bird, my father led me up the steps to the Court of Women.

A enormous bronze gate guarded the next level of the temple. It glinted like a knife blade in the midday sun.

"Wait here. You can go no further." My father stopped me at the foot of the curved steps leading up to this door. A priest with a short flat nose stood at the top of the steps, his thin hands hooked into a wide belt. I knew he was a priest by his white tunic and coned hat.

"Give me back my bird!" I cried out desperately. I knew I must seem like a spoiled child. But I didn't care. I tried not to cry.

But my father did not turn back. I stood there, alone, amidst the chatter of women and the recitations of the pilgrims, as he disappeared through the gate with the dove. A lone white feather hung suspended in the air for an instant before coming to rest on the dirty stones.

It looks like a bone, I thought. I began to shake.

I shook as if all the caged birds were inside of me, beating their wings to get out. I could feel the wicker cages constricting my heart and my lungs. A cold sweat broke across my forehead.

"Is she all right, Papa?" A little boy was pointing at me as I shook, half bent over, in front of the gate.

"Leave her alone. She's possessed," hissed the boy's mother, pulling him away.

Let him bring back the dove. Let him bring back the dove, I willed.

But when my father returned, he was empty-handed. I could barely stand, I felt so ill. He took my hands and bent down to look at me closely, "It is done, Miriam. You have been purified."

"Where is the bird, Father?" But I knew I would never see it again.

"Its blood has been offered so as to clean you of this ailment." He was terse as he led me back through the gate into the outer court.

"No!" I screamed, wrenching my hand out of his. "I want it back! Go get the bird, Father!"

"Miriam! Be quiet! You are making a scene!" He grabbed my arm, pulling me close to him. Passing women stared at us.

I trembled. I could feel something rising in me, as if I was about to vomit or explode. My vision blurred.

"No! Stay! Stay! Stop them!" Someone was yelling and birds were squawking. The sound of their beating wings was like thunder. Something was happening.

One by one the cages fell over and shattered open. The birds burst into freedom, flying upward in a blur of white and gray and brown. They were like tiny stars, spinning light and fire and feather, yearning to return to the heavens.

When I turned to my father, my mouth open in awe, he was watching me in shock. There was fear in his eyes. Fear of *me.*

He grabbed my hand and pulled me away, leaving the chaos behind us. No one acted as though we were to blame. No one stopped us. He dragged me forward, refusing to slow down or look at me.

On our walk back to Bethany, in the grass-sweetened air, I recovered. The smell of the temple, its reek of blood, still clung to my clothing and my hair, but the fig and vine trees bordering the roadside offered up their healing perfumes, swayed overhead, and cleansed me with their bending shadows.

"You are clean now, Miriam," my father said, breaking the silence.

"What does that mean?" I asked, kicking up dirt with the toe of my sandal.

"You will no longer fall into trances. The devils that were within you have gone."

I nodded, slowing my pace so that he soon outpaced me. I stepped from one shadow to the next. A vulture, high above the trees, cut the same circle again and again in the gray dusk.

I stopped for a moment and looked up, wishing stupidly: *I wish I could fly. I wish I could escape with the doves.*

My mother welcomed us home with fresh bread, lentils, and salted fish.

Later that same night, I collapsed with another spell.

Seven

Just when I should have been allowed more independence, I was put under the constant supervision of Kemat.

"She must be watched," my mother told her. I sat at their feet in front of my mother's looms. They had paused in their weaving to speak. My mother's fingers played with my hair so rhythmically that I was almost lulled to sleep. I had a wad of wool in my hands that I had been stretching apart, but I let it drop into my lap, thinking it looked like a little rain cloud settling into the dark valley of my skirts.

"I am often called from the house," Kemat began, her eyes cast down respectfully, her voice low and controlled. "Shall I spread the news that I can no longer attend to births?"

"Oh. Yes, yes . . ." My mother's hand rested heavily on my head. "I mean no! You are the only proper midwife in Bethany. It would be shameful to keep you from your duties."

Midwife. I had heard this word before; it was used to describe Kemat. I knew it had something to do with how children came into the world, but such things were never discussed in our home.

"What does a midwife do?" I asked.

Kemat's forehead was furrowed with lines that I didn't often see. I knew she was trying her hardest to be respectful.

I was sympathetic. We both had to protect my mother. Her feelings were so easily hurt. The one time she had heard me call Kemat "Mother" she had flown into a rage, grabbing me by my braid and yelling at me. *You think this girl is your mother? This unclean woman who does not even go to the mikvah for cleaning? Who doesn't even bathe?*

I had wept and wept. Not because of my pulled hair. I had cried to know that Kemat stood by impassively, hearing my mother's ugly insults. Words like that stung for long after they had been said.

The truth was, Kemat *was* my mother in most ways. She bathed me. She put me to bed. She fed me. She taught me how to spin, how to cook, how to tell stories.

"They pay you, don't they?" my mother said absentmindedly to Kemat, her hand beginning to play with my hair again.

Kemat answered me first, sweetly. "Miriam. A midwife helps mothers give birth to their babies. It is a dangerous business."

"It is a dirty business!" my mother added. "Blood everywhere!"

Kemat's left eye twitched but she kept her face composed. "It is a sacred event, Miriam. Life enters into the world. It enters so forcefully, so intensely, that it often brings death along with it!"

"Oh," I nodded, although I did not really understand.

Kemat was still smiling; a smile so threadbare I was surprised it fooled my mother.

"Hadassah, what shall I do with Miriam when I am called to a birth?"

"Well . . ." my mother faltered. "Take her if you must. It won't hurt her to know what is coming for her. She is close enough to her child-bearing years."

Kemat nodded. "I think it will be good for Miriam to see such things."

• • •

Before heading out to a birth, Kemat would take a strip of muddy red cloth and slip it down the front of her shift.

"What's that, Kemat?" I asked.

"It's blood from my own birth. At least that's what my mother told me," she said softly, looking at the cloth, pinching the stained part, the dark pupils of her eyes swelling, holding back sorrow.

I had never before entertained the idea that Kemat came from her own family. "Where is your mother, Kemat?"

She paused. "She is dead. I saw it in a dream. She came to me and told me I would see her in the next life."

"The next life?" Now I was truly confused.

"Yes," Kemat began her work again, picking up a long leather strip and folding it over a bundle of herbs. "When I am born again."

"Is that what Egyptians believe?"

"Some," Kemat nodded. "Some don't. But I know we are born again and again. We come to fix old mistakes. We come to heal old wounds."

"How do you know this?" I leaned closer to her, feeling a power in her words that was similar to the yellow energy that hovered between the horizon and the gathering storm clouds.

"I have looked into so many newborns' eyes," she whispered. "And they are not new. They are very old. I am always certain they know more than I do. They are closer to the doors of life and death."

Doors opening and closing. A rushing sound. Water moving impossibly fast, driving over cliffs, boring through stone and mud and wood, making its way to the ocean. A feeling of leaving my body. Slipping through warm caresses. Grasses. Waves. A blast of saltwater.

I nodded and didn't press her further.

• • •

Kemat did not let me actually witness a birth at first. I think my mother asked her not to. I have a vague memory of her hovering in the doorway before we left one night, her nostrils flaring with each deep inhale she took, trying to summon the nerve to speak.

"Keep her away from the worst of it, Kemat. I saw my sister's birth . . ."

Hadn't my mother's sister died? In childbirth? I had heard such things mentioned in whispers. Is that why my mother always looked pained when Kemat left with her satchel of herbs?

Kemat showed me how to mix honey, carob water, *kheper-wer* plants, and goat milk to create a salve. "If we massage this into the woman's secret place, it will bring on cramping and she will begin to deliver the child," she explained as we stored it in a wide stone jar. Rosemary-infused oil was for after the birth when the woman's womb was dangerously open. "This herb will prevent a fever or an ill spirit from entering inside of her," I was told as I snapped a twig and inhaled. The herb smelled clean and blue. Healing. Kemat taught me how to lay the birthing bricks.

Sometimes while a woman moaned, Kemat let me dab her forehead with a wet rag. But always, at a certain point, she would send me out to stoke the fire in the courtyard and keep hot water available for washing.

Certainly I heard the moment when the screams of the mother were joined by the squalls of the babe. I saw those little pink faces, mouths like berries, ears flat against their heads, soft skulls coned from their tight exit, eyes closed against the brightness of the world. But I did not get to see the actual births.

I loved attending those births because of the women. There was much seriousness. All the women past a certain age had seen a mother die in labor. But there was always a feeling of festivity, of something wondrous about to occur. The grandmothers of Bethany would crowd into the house, their long skirts making a comforting whistling noise as they pushed through the hallways. They had accepted Kemat unofficially, forgiving her foreignness when her herbs proved more effective than those of other midwives. But the most important role still belonged to the grandmothers.

Calling back to our ancestors, they would raise their voices and summon the old songs.

"Come here, little one," a crone would beckon to me as the women filled the birthing room. "Sing along so that you will know the words when it is your time."

And when the baby was born and the mother safe, the real celebration would begin. Seedy cakes with flaked almonds on top! Honeyed nuts! It was better than any holiday we celebrated at home. I began to look forward to the nights when Kemat took me along with her.

That all changed a week before the Feast of Tabernacles.

It was late at night and Marta had already gone to sleep. But I had refused to go to bed. The moon was a week from full and already I could feel its waxing light energizing my blood. I bounced around the house—somersaulting on the soft rugs in the hallway, peeking in on the long room where my father was entertaining his students— until my mother screeched that I must go sit with Kemat and *not move.*

Kemat was with Meshkenet in their room, repairing his cloak. When I tiptoed in, he had his strong jaw against her shoulder, nuzzling her neck. He was a handsome man with sharp features that seemed to have been cut with a knife. He had long ropey muscles from his work in the fields.

Kemat blushed when I cleared my throat.

"Oh! Miriam. What is it? I thought you would be in bed?"

"I'm not tired." I said plainly. "And mother says I must stay here and calm down."

"Would warm milk soothe you?" Kemat started to rise and I noticed—although it happened in the fraction of a second—the hungry look she shot back at her husband and the way his lips curled upward. But then it was gone and she was standing up, smiling down at me. She tightened her red-and-green embroidered belt, one of my mother's own cast-offs.

"No."

"Are you always this hard to please?" Meshkenet joked.

"Yes," I answered bravely. I liked Meshkenet. His voice was soft, almost feminine, and he would sometimes sing in his native tongue. However, he only did this when my mother and father were far away, letting the words drop from his tongue as sweetly as if they were drops of nectar. "My mother says I am a fright."

"Come now," Kemat knelt down and shook her head. "Who says being a fright is a bad thing?"

"I would rather be a lion than the quivering lamb," Meshkenet offered. "I would rather own my own life and be able to defend it."

I didn't think of it then, but as slaves they would have understood the difference between those with power and themselves. Those who were tied to duty. To pain. To other people's lives. I wonder now if they had served someone else before my father? Someone less amenable perhaps.

"Kemat!" A plump servant girl appeared. She was distraught. "My mistress has sent for you," she said. "It is an emergency. There is no time!"

"And your mistress is . . . ?" Kemat was all business, standing somehow a foot taller, her face composed, almost regal.

"The wife of Othniel. Rebekah. The baby is coming very quick!"

Kemat wasted no time. Meshkenet got her herb satchel from the chest at the end of their bed and handed it to her wordlessly. I stood to the side, feeling the shadows around me like a physical weight, not sure if I wanted to disappear or step into the light.

But Kemat looked back at me as she slung Meshkenet's cloak, which she had just finished mending, around her slim shoulders.

"Are you coming?"

"Yes," I said, joyfully. "Yes. I am coming."

• • •

There was a very different tenor in the air when we reached Othniel's house. It vibrated with emergency. The grandmothers were not singing, preferring to stand solemnly in the hallway, their faces drawn and worried.

I could tell that the woman's labor was going badly, not just by her pale face but by Kemat's expression as she bent down to examine her.

Serah, Yohanna's mother, was there and she shot Kemat a meaningful look. "I am glad you are here. No one else has been able to turn the babe . . ."

Two older women who I recognized as Othniel's sisters were in the room. The younger of the two was kneeling next to Rebekah, speaking soothing words, gently brushing the struggling woman's sweaty hair away from her face.

But Rebekah was past words, moaning and writhing in her bed.

"Can I pull back the cloth from the windows?" I asked Serah.

Serah looked down at me distractedly. "Yes. That might help."

It smelled stale in the room. Was it Rebekah? Or was the smell lingering from some previous unpleasantness? The plump servant girl hovered in the doorway, steadied by two old grandmothers: small wide women with shiny black eyes. I had come to recognize them as the town elders, Ophri and Marah. Their faces were resigned.

"Get us hot water," Kemat commanded the servant girl. I was surprised that she didn't send me. Instead she beckoned that I should kneel beside her.

"Look. This is the doorway between worlds," she murmured so softly that only I could hear.

Rebekah's sex looked like a purpled flower that was past its peak, the petals bursting away from the controlling energy of its center and stem.

"The child is breech," Kemat whispered to me, her fingers still inside the woman. "And it's a large child for such a small woman."

She was right. Rebekah was young and her body was poorly formed for bearing children. I looked up past her bent knees at her drawn face. Her eyes met mine unseeingly.

"No! No! No!" she screamed.

"I can do it," Kemat said, talking to herself, but I nodded anyway. She got up on the bed with Rebekah and began to murmur to her.

Just then three other young women pushed their way into the room. They were singing, their clear, resonant voices immediately cutting through the fetid stink of the air. I was glad for the shift in energy.

"Go away!" Rebekah screamed.

"My dear, it's me, Elisabet! Your dearest friend!" the oldest girl cooed. "We have come to sing the birth songs."

"I have to turn the child," Kemat tried to explain over the confusion.

"Rebekah!" Kemat got close to the pale woman. "You must imagine the baby turning over. We are going to hold your feet up. There will be great pressure. But perhaps we can shift his position."

The authority in her voice rippled through me. I almost never heard a woman speak with such confidence and knowledge.

"Yes. I have seen it done! We will help." Ophri scrambled up on the bed with as much vigor as a child. She grasped one of Rebekah's swollen ankles as Kemat reached for the other.

"Someone get a stool or a pillow to support her hips. We must tilt them upward!" instructed Kemat. "And do not stand silent! Sing! The baby will hear and dance. We need the child to move."

The younger women exchanged worried looks, but after a moment's pause they began their songs again. Tentatively I added my own voice to the music, comforted by how it was immediately embraced, swallowed, and eclipsed by the others women's singing.

We would sing the baby out of her. All would be well. Kemat was powerful and experienced.

For the next hour and a half Kemat and Ophri tilted Rebekah upward even as she struggled and moaned and called out for her own mother, long dead. We worked against the narrowness of Rebekah's body and her own unwillingness to bring the baby into the world.

Finally Rebekah was lowered down and Kemat guided her onto her hands and knees, into a crawling position. She placed her hands on Rebekah's hips and rocked her back and forth rhythmically.

It was the hardest I had ever seen Kemat work, and she was *always* working: weaving, mending clothing, cooking, grinding grain, carrying water. But this was the work of the spirit. Her body and her being were perfectly aligned as she finally brought Rebekah into a squat.

"It is time. The babe is turned. You must push. You must push to get through to the other side."

And somehow Rebekah, although her jaw was rigid and her eyes squeezed shut, her face as red and shiny as a pomegranate, somehow she began to push. I could tell by the way her whole body seemed to contract and pulse around her belly. Her knuckles whitened as her hands curled inward.

The older women joined the girls' singing. Their rasping, yearning voices quickly overpowered the sweetness of the original melody as they began a new song. It was slower, with huge pulses that I now know imitated the squeezing of Rebekah's womb. Rebekah's screaming surfaced in the moments of silence and then Ophri's rough voice would surge forth.

I could almost see the silvery tendrils of music rooting themselves below Rebekah's open sex, opening up a space for the babe to drop into.

And then it happened. Another voice was added to the music.

The babe came out wailing, as red and pulpy as some squashed berry.

"Thanks be! Thanks be to my mother and her mother!" wept Ophri.

Marah took the babe into her big, soft arms, using her own shawl to wipe his face clean. Kemat leaned in, blowing in the child's face and smoothing back his slick black hair.

"You must make sure his nostrils are clear," she said, showing me how to do this. "You must make sure the child can breathe."

"She has delivered a healthy boy!" Serah called out into the hallway. "All is well!"

Everyone crowded into the room. Young and old women reached out to touch life as it began—wet and loud.

I could feel the immediacy of twined pulses—mother and child—snaking around us all, weaving us in a circle that would not soon be broken. All our exhales—mothers, grandmothers, sisters, daughters—braided together to flood into the lungs of this new child! Every hair on my body shivered with a low, thrumming music. I wanted to move, to exclaim and sing! Surely *this* was more holy than the temple. We didn't need goats or doves for sacrifice in the birthing room. We had the spilled blood! The cries of the newborn child made scripture seem complicated and abstract.

"Here, let me clean him." Kemat took the babe over to a stone bowl of water that the servant girl had brought in. With a delicacy I had never seen her perform, Kemat began to bathe the baby boy.

I looked back at the bed at the mother. Worn. Spent. Smiling. Pale. Pale as death.

"Kemat. What is wrong with Rebekah?" I asked worriedly. But she did not hear me.

Rebekah was smiling wanly, nodding at the other women even as her lips grew blue. "I feel cold," she murmured. "Will someone close the windows?"

"The windows *are* closed, dear," Serah reassured her, sitting down on the bed. "Would you like to hold him?"

"She is bleeding!" Kemat had come to give the child to his mother. But she immediately passed him to Serah instead.

"What . . ." Rebekah's voice was faint, slurred. She could hardly focus her eyes on Kemat.

"I see no blood!" Serah countered vehemently. "Except for the blood that has already passed! She is not bleeding."

"No. The bleeding is inside of her." Kemat had her ear to Rebekah's wrist. She was listening to her pulse. "It is secret bleeding. Would that we could see it. But there is no way to staunch it."

I was colder than I had ever been. I could taste bile on my tongue. I knew my face must be screwed up with the effort it was taking me not to be sick, not to cry out.

No. This was not how it was supposed to happen. The celebration in the room was dimming. Everyone was beginning to panic. Rebekah moaned, "Oh, God . . . Oh, God. Give me my baby. Give me my baby."

"Give her the child," Kemat said gravely to Serah. "Let her hold him once."

She glanced back at me with a resolved expression that seemed to squeeze her narrow features closer together, giving her a hawklike appearance.

Kemat told me quietly, drawing me close to Rebekah, "Come here, Miriam. It is important you understand this. It is important that you look this death in the face and honor it."

"No! No! Get me Othniel!" gasped Rebekah. "Get me my husband . . ."

"Somebody get her husband," Kemat's voice rang out, clearly, so that everyone could hear. "Rebekah is dying. She will be gone soon. Someone fetch a rabbi."

Serah backed out of the room, her face nearly as gray as Rebekah's. Ophri was moaning, holding onto one of the younger women whose face was rigid with shock.

"Is there *nothing* you can do?" the servant girl pleaded. She was trembling, her hands hovering over the crumpled blankets, the pink stains. Rebekah's left leg had begun to jerk spasmodically. Kemat took back the baby that was crying and squirming in Rebekah's slack arms.

"There is nothing when the bleeding is inside," old Marah said bitterly. "I have seen it too many times."

Kemat touched my shoulder lightly. "Watch, Miriam. Death is much like birth. It is just as hard."

But I pulled away from Kemat. Something was tightening in my chest. It was the uncomfortable sensation of repressed motion—like I must cough or be sick or run.

I crawled onto the bed next to Rebekah. Her eyelashes were fluttering, and her body was unnaturally cold. I placed my cheek to her cheek, breathing softly into the corner of her mouth.

Please. Return. If you can heal, heal. But if you are claimed by death, go.

The voice was low. Supple. It flowed through me with the certainty of a river flowing toward an ocean: ivy growing precisely through the cracks in a wall.

"Miriam . . . Miriam," Kemat scolded gently. "Get up before her husband comes. They need to do the proper things. I know it is hard."

But I ignored her, pressing my hands to Rebekah's breast, feeling her heartbeat flickering, fading.

"Oh!" I gasped, shocked when an almost uncomfortable heat pulsed in my palms, corresponding to the pumping muscle below them. Slowly my own hot pulse seemed to regulate Rebekah's blood. Her heart beat more surely under the fire in my hands.

"What is she doing?" Ophri asked with concern. "What is the child doing?"

"Let her stay," Kemat said hesitantly. "Watch."

Watch? I didn't care what Kemat said—only that I stay connected to Rebekah. Her blood leapt up under my hands, its current pushing life and heat back through Rebekah's veins. Her skin softened, grew flexible again under my touch. Her pulse was stronger, steadier.

And still the energy surged through me, aching in my palms, burning the tips of my fingers. I wasn't sure how I knew this, but I felt certain that if this transfer was stopped abruptly, before I was completely finished, it might kill us both.

"Ah!" Rebekah jerked under my hands, her back arching. Her eyes flashed open, unusually alert. "Oh, Mother!"

"Rebekah!" Marah cried. "Live! Tell me you will live!" Her young friends were crying with disbelief, with fear, with joy.

The woman's whole body twisted. She embraced me. "Where is my baby? Where is my *baby*? Someone bring me my child!" The wire of need in her scream relieved me. She would live to see another day.

"What is it?" Her husband, Othniel, burst in through the doorway, immediately putting his hand up to his mouth in revulsion when he cast his gaze over the room. He took in the bloodied sheets, and his half-naked wife with a haggard face, sitting up, weeping, her hands outstretched—not for him, but for her child.

"A miracle!" some were calling.

Another turned to Kemat: "Thank you. You have done a good thing."

"I did not do it," Kemat said flatly. "Thank the child."

But the woman laughed, patting me on the head, sure that Kemat was joking.

We left soon after, Kemat with a bolt of fine blue linen as her payment. The moonlight was almost a heaviness, something I had to shrug off my shoulders as we made our way through the narrow streets back to our home.

At the door, in the dense blue darkness cast by the house, Kemat turned to me.

"What did you do to Rebekah, Miriam? How did you heal her?"

"I put my hands on her," I said quietly. "I don't know."

"Don't tell anyone about this," she whispered, laying a soft finger against my lips before ushering me inside.

But she didn't have to tell me. I stared down at my trembling hands.

If they could give life and heal, could they also cause pain? Could they draw life *out* of a body?

It was the first time I felt terrified of myself.

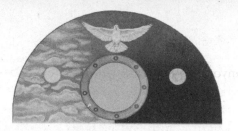

Eight

I had passed over to the other side of childhood. Something dark had bloomed inside my heart. It was powerful. But it was also frightening. I avoided Yohanna and the rest of my playmates after that night.

Lazaros complained that their games were boring without me. "When we play Wedding, Yohanna always makes *me* be the bride. And I said that's not fair! Because I'm a boy!"

"Why do you play with her then?" I asked disinterestedly. "She's not even *your* friend."

"Because . . . because . . . " His lower lip wobbled. "Don't be mean, Miriam. I like it best when you play with us!"

But I could still feel Rebekah's spirit shivering under my palms. What did it mean to be so close to death? And then to ask it directly: *Do you want to take this life? Or will you leave her alive?*

There were many nights I lay awake beside Marta, my mind filled with these questions. Kemat still took me to births, three in the following month, but they were all without incident. Mostly I ran errands.

"Kemat?" I tried to ask her once more when we were walking back from the fields in the late afternoon, "What happened with Rebekah?"

"A spirit moved through you," she said plainly.

"Was it God? Will it happen again?" I asked, squinting through the slanted golden rays that obscured my view of her as she strode ahead of me. She didn't look back.

"We will have to wait and see."

"Wait for what?"

But she didn't answer.

Finally, one night I felt my bones might burst through my skin and run out of the house. I had to get outside. I was filled with a wild energy that needed release.

I waited until my father stopped pacing back and forth through the hallways. Some distant cousins of my mother's had visited. They were hard, scrawny people who she didn't seem to enjoy, but much had been drunk through the meal. I felt certain that once asleep, my family and our guests would sink deep into wine-laced dreams that were not likely to be disturbed by my leaving the house.

Slowly I eased out from under the blankets and went to the chest for my cloak. I lifted it over my head and backed up to the doorway, holding my breath as I tiptoed to the front door.

Once out of the house, my whole body prickled pleasantly, and my toes sank into the grass as I ran to the very edge of our gardens. I felt as if I could shoot down roots and leave behind me an irregular line of child-size trees.

At the very edge of our land, I paused before the family tombs. The wind blew the scent of woodsmoke all the way from the house. I could smell freshly turned soil from the fields, and something thin and piquant that might have been the scent of a star. A shiver traveled up my spine. My father had built these tombs some years ago—in preparation, I suppose, for his own death.

I felt at once the fragility of my body and, at the same time, the certainty that I was something *more* than my body: indestructible, huge, and ceaseless. I had sensed this before, of course, when I was almost asleep or emerging from one of my spells. But never had I felt it so directly.

I felt myself swell to the size of the sky and then shrink smaller than a crystal of sand as I stared at the dark blue mouths of the twin tombs. They stayed still, stayed empty. And I knew somehow, no matter how far I wandered that night, I would be safe.

An old stone wall bounded our property and I hopped over to the other side of it. I knew the land outside of Bethany well. I knew the gnarled olive groves that bordered the terraced fields, and the old vineyard just beyond, but I had never been there alone and at night. My eyes adjusted to the dark.

An ancient field tower stood out darkly against the sky. Long ago it had been erected for shepherds to watch their sheep when this was still grazing land. The tower drew me with such intensity that I felt there must be a strong wind behind me, driving me forward.

But the night was still.

Stones were strewn on the ground and old wooden planks leaned against the rotted door.

With a gentle push it swung open soundlessly.

Inside was completely black. I stuck out a foot and felt a stone step. With care I made my way upward until I emerged into the tower's top room. The ribs of the roof were all that was left, making the window that looked out over the vineyard unnecessary: starlight and fresh air came in from above and beyond. The floor at my feet was a mess of rubble and debris.

I peered up at the stars. A thin sliver of moon turned the fields silver. In the distance was the feeble light of a lamp in Bethany. A strange, huge version of myself stood just behind me.

At the eastern edge of the vineyard, dark shapes drifted in and out of the shadows. I squinted, watching them move long and low and serpentine amid the ordered vines.

Leopards. The same cats I remembered flanking that wild god in the painting my father had called Dionysus. Liquid flame. I could make out the wave of their tails, the yellow glitter of their eyes. They circled closer and closer.

But I was not afraid. I descended and emerged from the tower to meet them.

They flanked me from a distance as I headed home, twisting in and out of the trees, moving with the same fluid turns as a meandering river. I heard the wet sound of their breath.

Should I have run? No. Strangely, their presence made me feel safe.

After I scaled the wall, I sat atop it, looking back toward the tower. The leopards, three of them, stood in the middle of the field. They blinked up at me before disappearing back into the trees.

"Who are you?" I called out. I could have been talking to the night itself.

• • •

I began visiting the tower whenever I could slip out unnoticed. And the leopards always came, following me, their long tongues flicking in and out of their furred jaws.

I collected stones and flowers and brought them to the upper room. Sometimes, standing there, looking out at the night, the wind would rise and swirl through the broken rafters, blowing my blessing into the darkness.

Yes, I thought. *I must feed the night. And it feeds me, too.* Every morning after I visited the tower, I felt stronger.

I was so preoccupied with my growing sense of a power that had no name and no explanation that I did not immediately notice when my mother became ill. It was a slow diminishing that took months. At first she was just too tired to fetch the water from the village well.

"Are you not sleeping well?" I asked her when she sat down heavily with her face hidden in her hands. Her once lustrous hair was tangled and dull.

"All I do is sleep!" she snapped. But I could tell that she regretted her tone. She tried to smile.

Soon she was too tired to grind the grain for our bread, and so Marta and I took over the work. My arms thickened with new muscles as my mother's own body wasted away.

"Can I massage your shoulders, Mother? Or braid your hair?" I asked one afternoon when I saw her warming herself in a ray of sunshine behind our home, her face turned up to the light, her cheekbones jutting out like wings from beneath her dark-circled eyes.

She startled, crying out like a bird, her eyes flashing with fear when she realized I was beside her. "No! Don't touch me!"

Her words brought tears to my eyes. I felt rejected. I was too young to understand that she spoke from pain and not fear.

"No, Miriam! That's not what I meant! You surprised me!"

She no longer came into our bedroom at night. She began missing meals so that she could rest.

But I was resentful that she seemed incapable of enduring my presence. She let Marta play with her jewelry and dresses. Me? She could not look me in the eye. When I brought her teas that Kemat had brewed to give her strength, she would shrink from me, having me place the cup on the chest near her bed so she wouldn't risk touching my hand.

Today, when I remember her fear of me, I try to let my anger immediately sink in my body, like dirt in water, settling slowly in my feet, and sinking lower still, safely back into the earth.

Sometimes she would tell me to come sit beside her while she worked at her loom. But she did not want to dialogue. Instead, she wanted to tell me the stories of the mothers and daughters that had come before us, when we were exiles. I would yawn and grow bored. These were the same stories I had heard countless times. About women who let their husbands rule; who let their husbands take their babies up to be slaughtered! Women who felt unreal. Meatless. Without the details and fire and flaws that would properly bring them to life. Now I know I was longing for my mother's own story, in all its heartbreak and complexity.

"Tell Kemat to come tell us a story!" I complained one day, flicking at a stone that held her standing warp in place. "I already know all about Ruth."

To her credit, my mother did not scold me. Instead her hand trembled as she plucked the taut wool. "All right, Miriam. Go to Kemat."

She no longer did any housework. She barely ate.

Marta wasn't sleeping or eating, either. She was consumed with worry, picking at scabs on her arm until she drew blood and my mother snapped at her. She said that Marta was lazy and neglecting her duties.

Later that night, I could feel Marta shaking beside me in bed. Was she crying? I curled into her body, nuzzling my chin into her shoulder.

"What's wrong with Mother?" I whispered.

"Go to sleep, Miriam. Leave me alone."

But she let me hold her as we both fell asleep.

In the early evening when the sky was growing purple, my mother would sit out alone behind the house. Her lush beauty was gone. Her shoulders slumped inward around her pain. Sometimes she would rock back and forth, her eyes closed, cradling her stomach, which had grown swollen the more emaciated the rest of her had become.

Kemat cared for her.

"Anise, fennel, clove, cinnamon . . ." Kemat instructed me as she made thick syrups for my mother. "Next we will steep myrtle leaves in water for her pains."

She paused, clearly worried.

"What's wrong, Kemat?" I asked.

"Miriam, can you not see that your mother is suffering? We must try to make her life easier and help her."

"Should I touch her?" I asked, remembering what I had done with Rebekah. I had never done it again, but wondered if I *could*.

"Do what you will, Miriam. She is your mother and deserves your love and help."

"But what . . ." I couldn't bring myself to say it. I could taste fear under my tongue.

But Kemat was gone, rushing into the courtyard to help my mother as she struggled to stand. My father noticed but said nothing.

Now that I am old, I feel an ache of tenderness for my mother. Did he turn from her bed? Was he repelled by her illness? Her unclean pain? I'm sure he offered doves and lambs for her healing. But he did not offer what was needed. Affection. Support. His arms around her. His voice uniting us as a family, letting me and my siblings know that our mother was surrounded by love.

How could he go about his daily business when she lay in bed in pain? How could he continue to have students to our home, laughing and drinking wine while he knew that she was curled on a couch in the next room?

I don't blame him now. Men are trained to ignore women's suffering. My father had been told since he was a young boy to look away when a woman wept or screamed or complained.

How else could men inflict suffering with such callous ease?

The men always refuse to bear witness to the horrors of the world! But no matter. I will not call upon my anger just yet. Otherwise I would never be able to tell my story to you.

My father avoided us all. He was always in the city for meetings with the Sanhedrin.

Every morning Kemat would take out her store of dried spices and herbs and begin to work. We cooked golden thistle leaves in hot water with honey, hoping the concoction would ease the agony in my mother's stomach.

While Kemat grew most of the plants she needed in our kitchen garden, there were some herbs that, she explained, could not be cultivated. We went out to pick the pink mallow flowers growing wild.

Their juice must be squeezed and served fresh. There were many plants that had to be sought out in the wilderness and often were only useful during specific days or stages of the moon.

"The moon draws the water up from the roots and fills the plants with power," Kemat explained, kneeling down next to a wizened scrub. Her hands handled the base of its woody stem with the same tenderness that she used to touch her husband.

The tea Kemat made for my mother required that we pick out the seeds and the slender leaves of wild coriander plants. A domesticated version of the plant could be found in our back garden, but Kemat was insistent that the plants for food and for medicine were different: "The medicinal herbs have a more important job. They must be sturdier and wilder in order to bring your mother a similar strength."

It was on a day that my mother could not rise and lay reclining on a couch in her room that Kemat and I realized there was no more wild coriander to be found on our land. We left Lazaros with instructions to bring my mother diluted wine if she should ask for something, and headed out beyond Bethany.

Kemat's blue cloak stood in sharp contrast to the reddening landscape. We walked through spare fields harvested of their barley and millet. Crows wheeled above us, insistently sounding the same impatient word. I paused, shielding my eyes from the midday sun, and looked up at them, aware that I was receiving a warning I did not yet understand.

I followed Kemat into abandoned groves grown wild with brushwood and grasses. We stopped under the shade of a fig tree and Kemat pulled the last of the autumn fruit off the lowest branches and passed them to me. The flesh inside was sweet and resistant.

We walked deeper into the trees, through clouds of myrtle and swaying towers of acanthus, searching for the bright leaves of the wild coriander.

Unexpectedly, Kemat discovered another plant she needed and squatted down to harvest its roots. I wandered off through the trees, putting my hand to each olive trunk. It was as if each tree had its own individual pulse, a vibration of internal strings. Each time I touched another tree, its chord was added to a growing choir of voices: olive, terebinth, pistachio, carob, almond.

I didn't notice how far I had wandered until I looked around me and was startled that Kemat had disappeared from view. I searched for her blue cloak between the meshed shadows of branches. My breath caught in my throat as I recognized the glint of golden eyes in the undergrowth.

The three of them were watching me from a few paces away, closer than they had ever approached me in my nighttime adventures.

The leopards stepped into view. They were muscled stars, eyes and sharp teeth gleaming, golden pelts shooting out strong, insistent rays of light. Their fur rippled over sinewy shoulders and haunches like the sky molded to the landscape. Their spots were the darkness of clouds moving between moonlight and starshine.

The biggest cat stepped closer. He opened his mouth and flicked his tongue over his black lips. He drew an audible breath.

As children we were warned about dangerous animals. There were jackals that stole our sheep and goats. Wolves loomed at the edge of the gardens. I had even heard tell of a lion, a large yellow cat that stalked through the pages of scripture, his face circled by a tawny beard.

But these leopards were my nighttime partners in adventure. I was overjoyed to meet them at last in the light.

"Thank you . . ." I said hesitantly, feeling embarrassed by my clumsy human speech. The biggest leopard cocked his head.

I tried again, silently, concentrating. *Thank you for protecting me.*

"Miriam!"

Kemat had found me, her fists full of dangling roots; her eyes wide with alarm. "Miriam. Step away slowly."

But I ignored her and reached out my hand toward the leopard's wet black nose. The cat blinked and for a moment, he had human eyes. Big, brown eyes with flecks of gold around a black iris. Eyes I recognized but could not place.

Is it you? Are you the one I am looking for?

The leopard nudged his huge head into the curve of my hand.

Oh . . .

He nudged closer to me. His breath smelled like soil softened by rain. I swear I could hear the ripe fruit of his mind whirring and humming with a music too fast, too powerful for humans to understand.

He licked my forehead, slowly, intentionally, with his rough, muscular tongue.

"Miriam!" Kemat was almost screaming.

The leopards' fur bristled. Their lips twitched over glistening teeth.

The two smaller cats lurched forward, growling like thunderclouds over the hills, settling at my feet. They touched their noses to the forest floor in front of me.

I'm not sure what compelled me, but I raised my hands over their forms as if in blessing. It was the same stance my father adopted each morning when he prayed on our roof.

The leopards melted back into the trees, their tails becoming vines, their eyes turning into golden spots of sunlight falling through the foliage.

I stayed still for a moment, hugging myself tightly, remembering those human eyes looking out of the leopard's face.

I expected Kemat to scold me, to drag me back home, and tell my father. But, like the leopards, she was kneeling.

"What are you doing?" I asked, bewildered. "Get up!"

She didn't answer. She shook her head, wiped her wet eyes, and rose.

I ran to her, hugging her slender waist, looking up and trying to read her golden face. She peered back at me, her eyes guarded.

"Tell me this, Miriam. Did you know those leopards?" she asked me when were close to the village.

It was my turn not to answer.

• • •

Kemat's tinctures kept my mother's pain manageable for the duration of the rainy season. My mother slept almost constantly. After Kemat suggested it, I took to sitting beside her for hours, stroking the bird-like bones of her hands.

She had to stop her beloved weaving altogether. This happened without mention. But the night she told Kemat she would no longer help with the cooking, she wept.

"The smells make me ill! I can no longer sit next to the heat of the fire. What is this poison in me that turns me into the worst type of woman? Lazy! Useless! I cannot even draw water!"

I paused in the hallway outside her door when I heard her complaining to Kemat. "He should put me out on the streets. I cannot feed my own family!"

"You are lady of this house," came Kemat's tempered reply. "There is much dignity in that."

"*You* are the lady of this house! You have drained me of my life! You have stolen my children's love!" My mother wailed, collapsing into breathless coughing.

"What's wrong with her?" Marta whispered to me late one night. She reached across the blankets and squeezed my hand. "Do you think she'll get better?"

Her hand trembled when she said it. She knew the answer to her own question. But to speak the question into the soft gray night between us was to honor the possibility that she *might* be healed.

Marta pulled me closer to her, burning her face in my shoulder, both of us crying so insistently that soon our braids were matted together with our tears.

After Marta finally fell asleep, I stared up at the flat black of the unlit ceiling. I knew my mother would die. I could see the event ahead like a star. A star I did not want to follow or look at.

Heal my mother please. Give me the power to heal my mother.

I went to her while she slept sometimes and rested my hands on her body, surprised by how she felt more alive the closer to death she came. It was as if her spirit was closer and closer to the surface of her skin. I could feel it moving under my palms.

But I could not feel any power in me. No visions arrived. My hands did not buzz or warm up. I worried that, somehow, I was making her sicker.

"Kemat, am I making my mother ill?" I asked quietly, early one evening as we made flatbread over a metal dome we had placed on the cooking fire.

She looked at me sharply. "No, Miriam. But could you make her better?"

I lifted the irregular round of bread off the heated dome and placed it on a wooden platter beside us. I didn't want to tell her that I had failed.

"I don't know how to make medicines like you, Kemat," I finally answered. "I'm just beginning to learn . . ."

"You know that's not what I'm speaking of," Kemat said, her voice very quiet. She took the pitcher full of flour and water and poured the mixture over the dome.

I watched as the paste bubbled, turning a pleasing gold at the edges.

I was a failure. Why could I heal Rebekah but not my own mother?

Later that night I snuck out to the tower. The night was still, and no eyes looked back at me from the darkness.

Once I was in the upper room I concentrated, trying to feel that huge part of myself that was more likely to emerge at night. Nothing happened. I was skinny and insubstantial: exactly the height and strength of my childish body.

My father taught that God was all-powerful, all-seeing. This nameless, faceless entity came to our forefathers to grant them miracles. He could raise light from nothingness and control the waters of the seas.

I bowed my head and raised my arms, reciting the Shema. I concentrated so hard that I could feel my heartbeat throbbing between my eyes.

Lord! Lord! Help me! Please heal my mother! Elaha! Lord, come! Please make her well.

I recited the words, the prayers, the pleas I had learned from my father again and again. But they did not kindle any power. They did not comfort me.

I pity myself now. I pity that young girl asking for the help of a faceless god.

Oh, Miriam, I want to say to myself. *Pray to the leopards. Pray to the night. Pray to death itself.*

I squeezed my fists so hard that my fingernails dug into my palms and drew blood.

Help me. Help me!

Somewhere a lovesick animal cried for its mate.

I stayed in the tower much longer than I had in the past. The night's blackness drained away, leaving behind a pale, indifferent gray. The vine tree's leaves were little bone-colored fishes in a sea of shadow.

I dragged my feet on the return. God had not come to my aid. I shivered and paused at the wall. I remembered my father telling the story of the cursed man Iyyob at the dinner table.

Iyyob had been good to God and lived an honorable life. And he had endured the worst punishments. For no reason. His family and loved ones had been killed. His wealth depleted.

Everything I fear and dread comes true. I have no peace, no rest, and my troubles never end.

I hopped over the wall and raced through the fields, running from my own mind. I stopped to catch my breath at the edge of our gardens—and there before the tombs, like a white flame that would be extinguished by the rising sun, was my mother. Her shift wafted in the wind.

I tried to will myself into invisibility, but she had already noticed me. It was the first time she had returned my gaze in months, and I was surprised by the vitality that gleamed in her eyes.

It would take me many years of tending to the sick and the dying to recognize that power. It is a life force that has nothing to do with the body and everything to do with the spirit. It is the heat of the blood preparing to release the breath that lives, briefly, within the bounds of bone and skin. My mother was burning up.

"Oh, Miriam. Come here, will you?"

I approached nervously, studying her face.

She looked haggard and spent. It is strange to think that I am now years older than she ever lived to be.

My mother, in my memory, is never younger or older than she was that night. Sometimes I imagine myself in a reversal of roles, holding her body to my breast, my long, white hair mixing with her black curls.

My mother. Years after your death, I am still trying to heal you.

Her face was pinched. "You are a good girl, Miriam, already such a beauty. You will attract a fine husband, I'm sure. And have many, many children."

Cold air bloomed around us, promising winter. I shivered, still staring up at her. Willing her to weep. To smile. To frown. To become human!

"Mother. I cannot have you go! You must not go!" I reached out my hands to her beseechingly.

Now I know that she had received that deep knowledge that lets us move onward, out of one life and into the next. When she spoke, it was with the authority of death itself. The death that had already claimed her.

"Peace, Miriam. Calm yourself. I will go. All happens in its right time."

I could hardly look at her, I was trembling so hard. My eyes fell to her hands, and I realized she was holding something small and hard.

"What is that, Mother?"

Without saying anything, she unclenched her fist to show me a dark little statue.

I had seen them peddled in Yerusalem by Roman vendors. I knew it was forbidden to make images of human beings. And as she held the statue out to me, I gasped, realizing that it was a small woman.

"Take her." My mother folded my hands around the image.

Made of onyx, the statue was small but heavy. The figure's breasts nestled into the curve of my fingers. Her tiny, carved face rested against my thumb. I imagined wee stone lips kissing me.

"Mother . . ." I whispered. "It is forbidden."

She smiled. "I want you to have this, Miriam. It was my mother's before me. And her mother's, too. It goes all the way back to Canaan before Abraham. But you must promise not to show it to your father or your brother," she added gently.

"Who is she?" I asked. She was naked except for a skirt around her wide hips.

"I don't know," my mother admitted lightly. She laughed then. "Maybe she is Abraham's wife!"

"Was Serah so black as this?" I asked her.

"Hush," my mother said, placing her hand over my own, feeling the statue through my grasp. "She is just a mother. She is just a stone."

I was perplexed. "But you are my mother!"

She was silent for a moment. Her hand on mine was cold. "Let us go back before your father rises to say his prayers."

She did not ask why I was out at night, and she did not explain further about the statue. I knew instinctively to keep it secret, wrapping the anonymous woman up in my finest silk scarf, a present from Lemuel.

Now I recognize her curling hair. Her curving figure. Her pointed breasts. I have seen statues of her spread to distant lands.

My mother was right. She was a stone. And she was also a mother.

What she didn't tell me was that back in the days of Canaan she had been called Asherah. Wife of God.

But I did not know that then. I knew only that the statue pulsed below my pillow. The little black woman sent me dreams about trees that became men and walked beside me in the night. Hawks with human bodies perched high in the branches. Women with snakes twisting around their elegant arms.

A week later, in the dawn hours while all those in the house slept, my mother died.

Nine

Shortly after my mother's death, my father did two things. He put my brother in school at the synagogue, and he freed Kemat and Meshkenet from their service to us.

It wasn't a customary erasing of debts—not a Sabbath or Jubilee year. Instead, as the spring anemones reddened the hills, flaunting their colorful celebration in the face of our sorrow, my father decided to honor Kemat's service to my mother by letting her go.

Oh! It was terrible! Worse in some ways than my mother's death. That year I lost them both.

I knew I should celebrate such a thing. I loved Kemat dearly and wanted nothing more than for her to be happy. She deserved to have her own home. But couldn't she stay here? She could live and be free with us.

Poor Kemat. I'm sure she felt terrible guilt. How hard it must have been to hide her happiness from me. She would finally be allowed to return home!

And my poor father. I can pity him from the vantage point of my own age.

There had been no passion between him and my mother. But he had loved her. And although he did not cry at her burial or in the days following, neither did he smile or laugh.

The image of Kemat was irrevocably twined with the image of my mother. In the last month, Kemat had lifted my mother up from the couch every day and walked her in the sunlight. Kemat had sat with my mother when the pain was at its worst, massaging her hands.

I'm sure that every time my father looked at the Egyptian maid he thought of his loss. And what better way to deal with his sorrow than to do a little good? He could make a gift of his pain and release the woman and her husband! He had lost a life. But he could also return one!

The day arrived when Kemat would leave and I woke, already weeping.

What a fool I was! My anger and sorrow had kept me sulking in the shadows. I had wasted my last days with her! The realization propelled me out of bed to run to her.

Kemat knelt on her mattress, carefully packing up their belongings.

I was weeping like a baby! I sank onto the mattress next to her, grabbing onto her arm. "Kemat, can I go with you? Please?" My voice quavered.

Kemat shook her head, clicking with her tongue disapprovingly. "Hush, girl. Crying like that won't help you," she scolded me softly, continuing to fold a blanket up neatly.

"Where will you live in Bethany?" I continued, wringing my hands uselessly, my eyes bleared with tears. "Will you live on the other side of town?"

Gravely, she looked at me, her hands planted on the blanket in her lap. "I am planning to return home, Miriam. It is a long way from here."

"Where?" I demanded.

"A place called Alexandria in Egypt, where your ancestors once served our people as I have served yours," she explained, folding up a muted brown tunic and stowing it in a leather satchel.

I nodded, struggling to think of a reason for her to stay. "But what will I do without you? What will I do when I have one of my spells?"

Kemat stopped what she was doing. "Miriam. Do not let anyone tell you your spells are evil. Do not be afraid of them."

Not understanding, I knelt beside her. She took my small hands in her own. "You have been given a gift, Miriam. A powerful gift."

I was eleven years old. Four years had passed and I had spoken to almost no one about what actually happened when I fell into a spell. I kept these visions locked inside, where they vibrated like a seed that knows it is being held above wet soil. The secret longed to be planted. To be told. To burst through and to grow.

"Kemat," I asked quietly, rushing, knowing there was no more time. "Was it God who helped me heal Rebekah? Why is he helping *me*? I don't understand. Is it Serah or Leah or Rachel or one of the other grandmothers?"

I thought of the statue wrapped up in silk, hidden under my pillow. Was it that dark woman who worked through me?

Meskhenet entered the room then, smiling benignly down at me. He had the strong body of someone who worked in the fields, and his high cheekbones never burned but seemed to glow like burnished metal the more he was under the sun. I wonder now how they had not yet born a child? Kemat must have used some herb to keep the children at bay, knowing it would not do them well to raise them in a life of servitude.

"Miriam, I don't know what works through you," she said under her breath, shooting Meskhenet a sidelong glance. "But I know one thing. You will come to Egypt someday. Come and find me."

"I promise," I said, squeezing her hand tightly, tears dripping from my chin onto our fingers. I had no idea what she meant.

Early the next morning, Meskhenet and Kemat left on an ass my father had gifted them. We stood on the roof and waved goodbye. Wrapped in her blue cloak, Kemat sat on the animal, while Meskhenet led it slowly through the crooked streets of Bethany. The stars were still visible in the sky; one, crowning all the others, flickered directly above the receding figure of Kemat. I thought that the star had appeared to guide her home, away from me.

Or maybe the star would stay in the sky for years to come, and one day I would look up at it and say, "Please show me how to get there. Show me how to get home."

Home—a place where I still had a mother.

Ten

My father immediately hired two new women to help with the household chores. Apphia was broad-shouldered and tall but with the clouded wits of an old woman. She was overseen by Beltis, who tutted and murmured in a fricative language I couldn't understand.

They listened vaguely to my father's instructions that first morning. Apphia stared blankly past his shoulder, picking a piece of her nail loose with vigor until blood beaded from her finger. Beltis nodded but her eyes were hooded. I was almost certain they didn't understand my father when he pointed to me and warned them that I must be watched carefully.

My intuition proved correct. The new women stayed busy with the chores. They had no interest in caring for me or asking me where I spent my days.

"You must keep an eye on your sister," my father said to Marta over our Sabbath dinner. "You must see she that grows up into a marriageable woman."

Marta stifled a laugh, taking a big bite of bread and chewing with puffed out cheeks until she could get control of her mirth. "Of course, Father."

But the conspiratorial glance she shot me said the opposite. Marta cared little for my education. The wilder I looked, the more beautiful and refined she appeared by comparison.

Marta let me do what I wanted, when I wanted. She wanted to spend time with her friends, gossiping about the young men, practicing with makeup, perfume, and ribbons. These young women laughed cruelly when I tried to tag along.

Once when I tried to follow them on their weekly trip to the market, Rebekah's cousin Tali made a retching noise. "Get away, Miriam! The men will never speak to us if you're along. They'll think we consort with animals!"

Even Yohanna no longer wanted to run and get dirty. She spent hours gazing into a mirror her mother, Serah, had given her. She was becoming more and more like Marta: concerned with her ornaments and ribbons, batting her eyes at the village boys.

"My mother says I shouldn't play with you," she said spitefully one day when we were picking wildflowers on the hill just outside Bethany. I had run into her walking to the market and convinced her to come with me. But she stepped daintily around the thornbushes, wrinkling her nose when I ran through a muddy puddle and the brown water splashed up onto my bare calves.

I had tied my skirt up so that I could move more freely. But Yohanna's red dress was spotless and modest, falling almost to her feet. Her lips were pink, and her olive complexion was blanched by some sort of paint.

"Why does your mother say that?" I asked, pausing, the red of the poppy in my hand suddenly reminding me of blood. I twisted it, and the broken stem leaked silvery water onto my arm.

"Because you are untamed!"

I looked down at my ripped dress. I hadn't changed out of it in days. My feet were caked in layers of dirt. I reached up, patting a rat's nest that was forming in my hair at my neck. Perhaps Yohanna was right.

"Fine! Go then!" I yelled.

Yohanna ran from me. From then on, she no longer met my eye. And sometimes, as we left synagogue, she would laugh when I passed, whispering something to another girl named Lilah.

At night in our bed, Marta no longer snuggled up close, groaning that she was too old to share a bed with her little sister. How lonely I was. The women in my life had abandoned me. My mother was dust. Kemat was gone. Marta despised me.

I wondered if perhaps it was time to try to become like the men. I watched jealously as Lazaros returned from his lessons at the synagogue with his friends Achim and Enosh.

"Let me test you," I would say to Lazaros. "You must practice to make Father proud!"

And so my brother fed me the lessons and the Torah that no one else would give me. Lazaros, my dear brother. Always giving me gifts without a thought for it. His entire life was a gift to me; his whole being sacrificed to my whims, my loves, my sorrow. I wonder sometimes where he would be without me.

Perhaps he would still be alive.

I grieve for him when I remember him as a small boy, perpetually hungry, eating whatever was within reach but burning it up immediately, his cheeks ruddy with feeling and his hands flowing through the air as he tried desperately to explain how deeply he felt everything!

"Look! The clouds are so beautiful today! I saw a dead bird by the road and my heart broke!"

I made fun of him for his easy tears. But they taught me to appreciate the wilting wildflower, to tip upward its papyrus-thin petals, and to smell the last of its perfume.

How foolish I was to think it was his scriptural knowledge that was the blessing.

"Tell me about cleanliness, Lazaros?" I prodded one day as we walked home from the market.

"Father says there is much debate over the difference between living water and the mikvaoth we use," Lazaros answered, his words halting. "I think . . . See, there are wild men and women in the north who are never properly pure and only bathe in rivers and streams! They don't have the right water."

We were eating dates, chewing the sugared meat carefully so that the treat would last longer. I flicked the leftover skin from my finger.

"Why would water caught in a container by men impart more purity than water that comes directly from the heavens?" I asked, bemused.

Lazaros was stumped. "Don't ask me questions like that Miriam," he replied. "It's no fun."

He kicked up a plume of dust that caused our feet to disappear momentarily.

I felt bad and offered him my last date. He took it from me, ravenously splitting it open.

"What does the scripture say happens to our *rouach,* our spirit, after we die, Lazaros?" If he couldn't answer my questions, I would ask different ones. Just as he was greedy for sweets, I was greedy for knowledge.

"The Berakoth says, 'We bless Thee, oh Eternal God, who restoreth the soul to the bodies of the dead,'" parroted Lazaros. After a moment of picking his teeth, he added, "We go back to our fathers in the Sheol."

"And our mothers," I snapped angrily as we approached the little gate leading off from the street to our home. "We go back to our mothers!"

Lazaros looked up at me. His cheeks turned red and tears leaked from his eyes. "Oh, Miriam. Will we see Mother again?"

I couldn't answer him, for the more I learned, the less I was certain about anything.

Even my own body felt uncertain. Unlike Marta, who was already entering womanhood, I was skinny, steadily growing taller without full breasts and hips to show for it. My hair, once sleek and dark, had reddened slightly, and the only way I could tame it was to plait it tightly every morning. I had never given much thought to beauty when I was younger but, as my sister started to darken her brows and rouge her lips with my mother's old paints, I became painfully aware that I still looked like a child.

I told myself that I would rather run freely, think freely, and speak freely to the brooks and puddles and wind than start to mold myself into a wife.

I felt at home outside of my home in the company of trees, darkness, animals.

And in front of the tombs.

Large stones had been built up in front of the square door to block me from my mother's body. Spring came and went, leaving behind a fine net of vines over the stones. By summer's end the tomb was circled by tall grasses.

I left pebbles and rocks, polishing them in my mouth before planting them in the grass at the tomb's door. Animal bones. Dried roses. I opened my jar of spikenard and left some of the sticky oil on the stone, pressing my forehead into the slick spot, wishing I could feel her bones on the other side—some reassurance that she had existed.

I barely slept. Hardly ever washed. And rarely remembered to eat.

"Miriam refuses to help me with any of the household work, and she's always covered in dirt," Marta complained at dinner one night.

This was not untrue. I picked at my stewed onions.

Lazaros giggled from the end of the table.

My father frowned. "Marta is right, Miriam. You will never be married at this rate."

"I don't want to be married! I'm too smart for marriage! I want to go to lessons with Lazaros. You know I'm right, Father."

My father slammed his fist onto the table. "That is enough, Miriam! You are impossible!"

I stayed cool, unsurprised by his rage. I expected it. He had been even quicker to anger since my mother's death.

Often when I returned from a long, roaming night there were still students sitting up, debating issues of purity with my father. I would stand at the door, listening, holding my breath. I longed to be truly heard. And to be seen.

"Miriam doesn't need to study," Lazaro said, his face reddening with emotion. I could see the vein in his neck, which resembled a blue snake. "Miriam already knows more than I do!"

"Miriam knows nothing, and her husband will like her the better for it!" my father said with finality, his eyes black and dangerous.

Later that night, as I watched Marta brushing her hair at the foot of our bed, I announced dramatically: "I don't want to marry! I don't want to belong to a man! I'd marry a leopard or a lion! But not a man!"

For once, Marta laughed. Heartily. All of her carefully practiced poise dropped away. She threw her head back, clasped her breasts, and hooted with laughter. Finally, when she caught her breath, she looked at me with a kindness in her eyes I hadn't seen in a long time. "All right, Miriam. Marry a leopard. And please remember to invite me to the wedding. I wouldn't want to miss such a spectacle."

• • •

My father invited his students back to our home almost every night. Beltis complained about having to make so much food all the time. And it was true. Although the students were thin, studious men who talked about controlling their appetites and getting closer to God, they demolished whatever was put in front of them.

They threw crusts and nutshells and scraps onto the floor. They spilled wine. Cleaning up after them was always a chore. But I tolerated their presence because their conversations with my father gave me a rare window into the Targums I did not yet know. Here were the stories and theories of scripture that Lazaros was too young for! I only needed to stay out of the way in the corner, pretending to sweep the floor or polish our metal pots.

The men hardly noticed me. I was invisible. I could listen.

The same could not be said for Marta. She would primp before they arrived, applying jasmine oil to her wrists, pulling her hair up into a complicated hairstyle I had seen on Roman women in Yerusalem.

When my father turned his head, these men looked for Marta, grinning like hungry jackals when she swept into the room with a jug, leaning across them to pour more wine. She would smolder under their gaze.

"You look like a fool," I said one night as she passed by me on her way to the storeroom. Her cheeks were rouged and her eyes were heavily ringed with kohl. She had clearly disregarded my mother's rule about jewelry: four different bangles clanked at each wrist.

"Oh, cheer up, Sister!" she said lightly. I was surprised she was not angrier. She squeezed my chin. "You will be pretty one day and the men will all look at you, too."

Oh, the terror! I did not want to be looked at! I wanted to speak! I wanted to debate!

Did she like one of these young men? Did her eyes seek a particular student, her cheeks warming when he smiled at her? I never asked and so I do not know.

• • •

The second spring after my mother's death arrived like a revelation following a longer, wetter winter than usual. The women dawdled at the well in the middle of Bethany, pulling back their scarves, letting the sun wake up the color in their cheeks and hair. The men headed back into the field and returned at sunset with black mud staining their knees and hands.

On the first warm, dry night my father joined us at dinner. Apphia served us lamb to celebrate the occasion. At the end of the meal, when Lazaros was sopping the juice out of his bowl with the last piece of bread, my father cleared his throat. We all paused, turning to him. He tucked his chin into his neck before looking at each of us intently, one by one. "There is something I must tell you. A wonderful thing."

Marta squirmed beside me. She was beaming.

Strange, I realized. *Not a fleck of paint on her face!* But she had never been more beautiful. Her cheeks were brown with sun, and her freshly hennaed hair flowed down to her waist in chestnut curls. She looked as dark and ripened as the figs that would soon weigh down the branches over our heads.

"Marta is betrothed to Amos," my father explained. "They will wed soon. Your sister has made a good match."

I was confused. Yes, Amos was a wealthy merchant. But he was also an old man. Now, I know he couldn't have been more than forty years, some would say at his peak, but Amos had already had a wife. A wife who had died childless. He was ancient! And Marta was *perfect*. I remember watching the dimples in her plump cheeks, the sparkle in her eyes.

My sister deserved a beautiful king with a slender waist and oiled curls. A man with a strong jaw and fiery eyes! She deserved a Solomon out of scripture who would write her songs and kiss her sweetly.

A good match indeed, I snorted to myself. *A waste is what I call it!*

That night I inched close to Marta in bed and reached for her hand. She didn't resist, letting me squeeze her fingers. "I am so sorry, Sister," I murmured.

"Why are you sorry?" she asked scornfully, wrenching her hand away. "Sorry that I will be wealthy? That I will live in a beautiful home?"

"I am sorry to lose you," I admitted, stunned by my own words. Yes. That was the worst part of it. Not that Marta would wed, but that I would lose my sister.

I hiccupped as I tried to quiet my sobs.

"Oh, come now," Marta hushed me, curling closer and wrapping her arms around my shoulders. "I will be just on the other side of the town, Miriam. We will see each other all the time."

This didn't comfort me. And my own grief made me feel ashamed. It was so selfish! I should be rejoicing for my sister, not grieving for her like she was dead.

The betrothal period was short. Amos, due to his work, was often on the road and wished to be married before he and his caravans set off on another venture.

On the day of the wedding Amos's relatives and friends began to stream into the house along with the first lemony rays of sunshine. They were as unattractive as he was. A woman I took to be his sister pinched my cheek and slapped my bottom, saying in a gravelly voice: "This one will be pretty soon, Amos. You sure you can't wait until she starts her blood? Or are you happy to take the sister?"

But thankfully Amos was too busy overseeing the delivery of the wine to respond.

Yohanna and her mother, Serah, arrived. Serah showered me with sugary exclamations for which I was totally unprepared. She hadn't looked my way in years.

"What a special occasion!" she said, embracing me and pressing her bony cheek to mine. "I'm sure your mother would have been very proud of your sister."

Yohanna fiddled with a delicate gold necklace at her throat. She wouldn't meet my eye.

"Let's go help Marta get ready," she suggested, pulling her mother away. "We must give her the perfume and the ribbons for her hair."

Rebekah arrived with her cousins Tamar and Vashti. She hardly glanced at me—the girl who I had given back her life!

And still more people arrived. Lazaros and his friends hovered at the gate, watching as the young women passed by. Enosh, the shortest of the boys, and the most confident, greeted each one.

"Hello, Lilah! You are as pretty as a lily!" he called out in his squeaky voice. But his compliment made Lilah, a rather unremarkable girl my age, blush and laugh nervously. She looked at Enosh as if he was a full-grown man.

Old friends of my mother's delivered delicacies of roasted nuts and honey. Then they went to find Marta, who was being kept apart from Amos.

When I peeked into her room, it was a storm of rippling fabric and musky perfume. Her friend Serayah was winding a golden belt around her waist.

"Here, Miriam," Marta said, batting Serayah away and leaning over her open trunk. She handed me a dress as yellow as the spring flowers blooming on the hillsides. "You can have this. Amos has promised me a new wardrobe."

The whole room tittered with excitement.

"Clothes for his queen!" Serah exclaimed, shooting Yohanna a glance as if to say that she should remember the material benefits of marriage.

"Yes." Marta preened in front of my mother's old mirror that she had brought into our room for this occasion. "He will get me embroidered coats! Egyptian silk! Roman styles!"

I shrugged out of my dirty dress. It had been pale blue once, but was now the color of ash. I turned away from the women, hiding my skinny chest. My nipples had puckered and grown larger in the past month, but I was still flat-chested.

The dress was much too big for me. The sleeves hung past my hands.

But Marta was wearing my mother's old dress. Green as moss, it hugged her shape perfectly. And there it was, hidden deep in her big eyes: the glint of my mother's own dissatisfaction. Her worry. Her fear.

"Why don't you girls go gather flowers for the bride?" Tali suggested, eyeing Marta's naked head. I could see her small eyes narrowing with jealousy. She was older than Marta by three years and had not received a single inquiry from a suitor. She was not an ugly girl. She was wide hipped, with a softness to her face that made her look a little childish. But, I thought spitefully, she has an ugly mind. I remembered her making fun of me.

"How about that, Marta? You'd like flowers?" Tali put her plump arm around Marta's shoulder. "Send the girls out for the lilies in your garden."

"Yes, yes!" Marta's eyes flicked from the mirror to me and Yohanna. "You two go and fetch me some."

"Do I *have* to?" Yohanna complained, but her mother Serah frowned and shook her head as if to say, *Behave!*

I slipped out of the room, not looking behind me to see if Yohanna was following. It was a relief to leave behind the closed room full of perfume and sweat. Outside, the wet dirt enhanced the high-pitched sweetness of the almond blossoms.

"Slow down!" Yohanna complained.

"I'm moving slowly enough," I responded.

Yohanna sighed as she struggled to keep up. I glanced behind once and saw that her cheeks were flushed with anger.

"There! See!" I pointed out some red lilies in the dark grass near an olive tree. I slid to my knees, knowing that the grass would leave a green stain on my yellow dress. I curled my hand around the tender stems of the lilies, peering into their dark center where the golden stamens appeared star-like. "I will pick only three and leave the other two," I explained, remembering Kemat's lessons. "I have to respect the flowers so I can pick more later."

But Yohanna had vanished.

The sunlight blinded me momentarily. I shaded my eyes with my hand, getting to my feet slowly, twigs stuck through the thin fabric of my skirt.

Yohanna was speaking to someone on the other side of the trees. "Who are you related to?" I heard her ask.

It was a man. A breeze pushed the dark hair away from his face. His embroidered cloak opened up behind him like wings, his blue tunic showed off a slender waist, and gems glittered on his fingers. Yet the sun's glare obscured his features, making his face a golden blur.

"I'm Lemuel's nephew Yosseph. He says these gardens are the finest in Bethany."

"My father's gardens are better!" Yohanna asserted. "There are too many thornbushes here."

"Really?" he responded lightly. "I rather like how wild it is." A cloud obscured the sun and at last I could see his face.

He is handsome, I realized.

His eyes were almond-shaped and light brown. His mouth wide and expressive, with thin lips. A fine stubble of hair covered his jaw. His dark curls gleamed with oil. If he had not been tall and broad-shouldered, with a confident swagger to his step, I would have said he was pretty. But his whole being radiated such self-assurance that he was, in fact, truly beautiful.

I guessed he was twenty-five years or so.

Suddenly I burst out from the shadows, stumbling. The lilies fell out of my hands.

"What are you doing?" Yohanna yelped.

But the young man came to my aid and offered me a smooth hand. I took it and felt a shiver pass from my fingers down to my stomach. "And who are you?" he wanted to know. "Are you one of the thornbushes I have been warned about?"

I struggled to my feet, still holding his hand, transfixed.

"She is Miriam," Yohanna said. "And I am Yohanna. My father is Efraim. He imports cloth from the east . . ."

"Miriam!" he cut her off, squeezing my hand, his eyes crinkling at the corners. "I have heard much about you from my uncle! You have a quick wit I hear."

"I . . ." Whatever wit I possessed had fled.

I could feel the small hairs all over my skin, a warmth in the bowl of my hips, sweat beading in my armpits.

"Miriam runs around barefoot," announced Yohanna.

"You have pollen in your hair," he said, releasing my hand. "It suits you."

He waited for me to respond. But my mouth felt like it had been sewn shut.

Instead, hardly knowing what I was doing, I crouched down and picked up the lilies intended for Marta's hair and handed the bouquet to Yosseph. "Our garden may be wild. But its lilies are most fragrant," I said softly.

He breathed in deeply. "My business is perfumes. And I agree. Will you show me back to the house, Miriam?"

"Are you visiting? What are you doing in Bethany?" asked Yohanna.

He addressed his answer to me. "My uncle is getting too old for the travel that his business in oil and perfume requires. I have helped him for some time. And now I will take it over."

"So you will stay in Bethany?" Yohanna's eyes sparkled as she stopped to catch her breath when we reached the top of the hill.

"When I'm not on the road," he answered placidly. "It is nice to be near to the city. And to men of learning. I have a great desire to study with your father, Miriam."

"I do, too," I answered honestly.

He laughed with surprise.

We had reached the house, entering through the back hall, and I was suddenly flooded with embarrassment. Stopping at Marta's door, I turned to him, wishing I had remembered to brush my hair, to keep my dress clean. "I apologize for my impertinence. I meant to say that I like being close to the city as well . . ."

Yosseph nodded, looking at me with his hand hooked in a leather belt covered in a lightning-like design. "Yes. I think it will be good to be close to the city."

He left with that, his words traveling straight to the bottom of my spine, pooling there like dark, undiluted wine in my womb.

"Who was that?" Marta asked as we entered back into the suffocating room. Someone had hung a shawl over the window so that no curious men could peak inside at the women changing clothes inside.

Marta's friend Dina wove long red ribbons into her hair even though it would soon be covered by a scarf. This sight was for her husband alone. Tali was slipping my mother's old rings onto Marta's right hand. But all the women were looking at us.

"It sounded like a man," Tali noted.

"It was Lemuel's nephew Yosseph," Yohanna announced proudly. "We ran into him in the garden."

"Yosseph, Lemuel's nephew from Arimathea, come to help with the business!" Serah beamed at her daughter, coming and taking her hands. "He's almost as handsome as he is rich! Did you behave well?"

The women all exchanged knowing glances, tutting and chuckling.

"He would make a fine match. Someone should catch him fast!" Rebekah chimed from her seat in the corner. She was holding the long, gauzy cloth that Marta would wear over her head when she went to meet Amos.

"I *did* behave well, Mother," Yohanna answered primly. "I think I made a favorable impression."

No one asked if I had caught the young man's attention. *But I had!* The knowledge bloomed inside of me. It summoned the words of Solomon's lover to my breast. "Let him kiss me with the kisses of his mouth—for your love is more delightful than wine. Pleasing is the fragrance of your perfumes; your name is like perfume poured out!"

The ceremony itself was a blur of relatives kissing my face and rubbing my cheeks. My father grew redder and redder the more wine he drank, standing up and raising his cup, making wild pronouncements about the joining of families, although I knew he thought Amos churlish and uneducated. I had heard him say as much behind closed doors.

Candles were lit leading down to the garden. The youngest children carried baskets of flowers up to the house, where Marta went to meet Amos. The petals hung weightless in the air as Marta leaned in to receive the ceremonial bracelet from Amos's hand. He pressed his thin lips to her smooth cheek, and I tried not to wince.

After the meal, when the moon had risen, Amos and Marta would go to sleep in a chuppah under the trees.

"That is where the *real* wedding takes place," Rebekah laughed, nudging Tali.

Taking advantage of the disorder, at the feast I managed to drink more wine than I ever had before. I snuck sidelong glances down the table to where the handsome Yosseph sat on Lemuel's right hand. Lemuel had his arm slung around the young man's shoulders, gesturing to Rabbi Achan. Yosseph shook his head, laughing.

Was I imagining it, or did he often look in my direction? When our eyes met, the wine throbbed behind my eyes. I swallowed nervously, looking away immediately.

By the end of the night I was drunk. It manifested mostly as fatigue. I rested my head on the table. Eventually Beltis took pity and shepherded me, like a drowsy child, off to bed.

I dreamt of darkness. A darkness so dense and green that I knew it must belong to a forest. But then, just swiftly as it had begun, the dream shifted under my feet and I found that I was walking along a road.

The dust of the road was red. It stretched ahead of me to the holy city and beyond that, to another city. But something was wrong. Corruption filled my nostrils: blood and vomit and the sour sweat of human pain. It was worse than anything I had ever smelled.

The horror registered physically. My lower belly clenched and cramped. I could feel something squeezing my intestines. A pain knifed up through the hinges of my jaw.

Lining the road as far as I could see were those stark crucifixes we had sometimes passed on our way into Yerusalem. I had only ever seen one or two, far enough away that they barely suggested their grim purpose, but here were hundreds close enough to touch. The bodies on them were alive and in agony.

This is what the Romans do to us, I thought with revulsion. *They kill our trees and then they nail us up on them and kill us, too.*

Men and women stared down at me. Some cried out for water. Some moaned. Names. Not of God. But the names of lovers and parents.

I started to run, but realized that unless I headed out into the blank expanse of the desert, I would never escape their suffering. The crosses were planted at every step of the road. It was then that my own voice rose to meet those dying screams.

Of course, now I know it was not a dream.

This horror had really happened. I was much older when I finally heard the full story of Yudas's rebellion twenty years before I was born. The brash Galilean had gained popularity in the years just before my birth. But the Romans had come down hard. They set an example. Two thousand men, women, and children were crucified on the road leading out of Sepphoris.

I have heard that the cries reached the very heart of the city. Whole families were wiped out.

But that night I had no context for my dream, nothing to anchor me in the midst of these people's torment.

I woke in my bed alone, shivering in the thin water of my own sweat. It wasn't until I rose and the morning light crept through the window that I realized I had left behind a crimson stain on the bed linens almost the exact color and shape of the lilies in our garden.

I was no longer a child, no longer clean. I had begun to bleed.

Eleven

If I had worried that I might not see Lemuel's handsome nephew Yosseph again, that fear was soon put to rest. On the Sabbath following Marta's wedding, he began attending the dinners my father gave for his students.

I was suddenly Eve in the garden, embarrassed by the dirt caked deep into my skin, my hair so knotted I worried I might have to cut it all off. For the first time I wanted to look like a woman. So against all better judgment, I sought Marta's advice. Already, too, in the week since she'd been gone from home, I had begun to miss her.

Her new house was on the far side of town: huge, with two stories and several additions tacked onto the main building as an afterthought. Her young serving woman Atalyah let me in, shooting me a frightened expression, hiding her face behind a curtain of oily hair.

I see! I realized. *She is expecting mistreatment.*

"Is Amos a good master?" I asked. "Have you been in this household long?"

She made a strangled noise, refusing to answer.

Atalyah led me through a main room that was decorated with colorful tiles depicting small glittering fishes and foxes, then through a dim hallway lined with ornate carpets, into one of the side buildings. These were Marta's rooms. I peeked into one that had a huge window. An Egyptian loom hung down from the ceiling, the warp already threaded with white wool.

Marta didn't share a room with her little sister anymore. She had multiple rooms. And servants. And beautiful scents blowing through the open windows from a garden that a gardener tended.

Well, if she didn't get a handsome husband, she did get a handsome household, I thought as I paused to run my fingers along a wooden border that ran the length of the hallway, covered in a red swirling motif that reminded me of the wildflowers outside.

"Here," Atalyah bowed her head, gesturing to a door to my left. "She is in here."

I looked inside, narrowing my eyes against the dense, stale air that greeted me. I could smell burning galbanum. Someone had drawn a cloth over the window so that the smoke had no way to escape.

Through the shimmering dust particles and curls of smoke, I saw Marta reclining on a couch.

Atalyah bowed her head, bending her knees. I thought she might curl up and roll over like a frightened insect. But instead she spoke in a strained voice. "Is there anything I can get for you, mistress?"

Marta didn't say a word. She merely flicked her wrist and the girl backed out of the room, leaving us alone.

Although only a week had passed, Marta was pale. Her face looked larger, flatter, robbed of its curves and vitality, as if someone had taken her and pressed her between two stones. And although her face was beautifully painted, it showed signs of use: the kohl around her eyes was thick enough to hide a lack of sleep, her red mouth was slightly chapped.

Was she sick? What was wrong? Just days ago, decked out in silks and flowers, she had looked like the Queen of Sheba, practically jumping into her older husband's arms, her skin like smooth, golden honey.

"Come, Sister," Marta commanded. "Sit next to me."

As I joined her on the couch, I was worried to find that she *smelled* different. Powdery. Like dry skin and musty blankets that had been folded and stored in a chest for many seasons. And worse, under that, was the sour bodily smell for which I now have a name: sorrow. It comes out in the sweat. It seeps into our pillows when we sleep.

But Marta was also examining *me*. She lifted a tremulous hand and tucked a stray curl behind my ear, letting her palm rest against my cheek. Her eyes traveled down to the dirt under my fingers and the patched hole in my tunic.

I finally spoke. "What is wrong, Marta?"

She blinked several times, the whites of her eyes appearing almost blue. She pursed her lips, turning from me. "It is a strange thing, Miriam. There are a great many things I can't possibly tell you."

"Then who *will* tell me?" I argued, reaching out for her arm. But she winced. I pulled up the sleeve of her tunic to see a dusky bruise traveling up from her wrist.

Her eyes widened. As if she, too, was surprised by the bruise.

"Marta! Shall I walk blindly into the world! Mother is not here to warn me. Tell me what it is like!"

I should have been sweeter. I should have embraced my sister and taken her out of that home. But I was young and angry. And her secrecy felt like an insult.

"Miriam," she said slowly, trying to unstick the words from the wound of her mouth. "I am alone, too. Mother told me nothing. She did not tell me what to expect . . ."

Outside, muffled by the curtain, a warbler whistled. The noise was so tempered, so pure, that it deflated our words. We were silent for a long time, my hand still clutching her bruised arm.

Finally I spoke again. "I became a *niddah* for the first time. I used the cloth to clean up the blood just like you and Kemat showed me."

It was the right thing to say. Marta knew all about monthly bleeding. She had been bleeding for years. I was relieved that I had given her a foothold. To see my sister powerless was to feel powerless myself. But now a haughty expression transformed the flat planes of her face.

"And you waited the seven days before bathing? You used the bedikah cloth to see when it was finished?" she asked sternly.

I nodded, relaxing into her authority.

"Yes. I did it all," I assured her.

But what I wanted to say was, "I'll do more if you tell me more! Tell me, Marta! How does one become a woman? Does it hurt? Do you regret it?"

It would have been easy to abandon these procedures and remain unclean. No one would have known. There was no longer any governing female presence in my life to supervise my initiation into womanhood. Telling Marta made it feel real—as if I had the cloth in my hands and was showing her the flower-like stain of blood that my body had produced.

"Oh, Miriam," Marta drew me close to her. "You are a woman."

It was as if she was saying, "You are unclean! You are doomed!"

"Yes . . ." I said, then hesitated for a moment before deciding to go ahead and ask her. "Could you could teach me how to do my face and hair? Like the women in Yerusalem?" I cringed inwardly at my stupidity. Did other girls like Yohanna learn grace innately? Did they wake up one day and know how to appear beautiful?

"I am surprised, Miriam," Marta clapped with delight, looking more and more like her old self.

She showed me to a room with a bed and a small pinewood table covered in her pots of scent, oil, paint, and jewelry. There were new gems in the midst of my mother's old gold bangles and emerald rings: carnelian beaded like blood in the center of a silver cuff, and long earrings made of colorful glass.

I sat on the edge of the bed and allowed her to brush the knots out of my hair. It hurt but in a way that made me want to cry with happiness. Kemat had brushed my hair. And even my mother, on occasion, had untangled my curls.

How good it was to be cared for. To be touched. I hadn't even realized how much my body ached for intimacy until I felt Marta's fingers deftly pulling apart the rat's nest that had formed at the base of my neck.

Her hands worked magic. Soon my hair was smooth and silky, my whole body relaxing as if I had drunk wine.

"If you wear it pinned up like this, you will look positively Roman," she explained, twisting and turning my curls.

"I should *want* to look Roman?" I asked with slight revulsion.

"They are the most stylish. It's what all the Hellenized women in Yerusalem are doing. I saw Herod's wife, Phaesalis, there last time when she was visiting for Yom Teru'ah. She had her hair done just like this. Not that I'd be seen showing my hair . . . but still a fine look." Marta's fingers deftly pulled a few stray curls out of place and let them fall against my cheek. I knew I would never have the patience to complete such a style by myself.

When she was done, she brought me a mirror with which to see her handiwork. I tilted the reflective metal up toward the window, catching the light. My face seemed to belong to someone else. Someone older with high cheekbones, full lips, and wet, dark eyes.

But the completion of her task left her with nothing to distract from her distress. As she watched me watching myself, her face a dusky orb reflected behind me in the mirror, Marta's upper lip began to tremble.

In moments she was sobbing. It was the kind of crying that produces almost no sound, but just shakes the body. She sank back down onto the bed.

"Forgive me," she choked out. "I don't know what's come over me." The kohl, carried by tears, branched out along the pinched skin near the corners of her eyes.

I wrapped my arm around her slumped shoulders. "What is it, Marta? What is making you so sick?"

"No. It's not like that. It's just that marriage is so different from what I thought it would be. Amos can be . . . he can be rough," she tried to explain.

"Rough?"

"He is not gentle with me," she shuddered, her eyes drifting to the left above my head, as if she could not meet my eye while she revealed her pain. "Mother told me that knowing your husband could be better than the sweetest wine, but I do not find my relations with Amos to be sweet. They are . . . " she searched for the word " . . . painful."

I have never been good at listening when women give their confessions. I am immediately spurred to action, infused by an anger larger than any human can possibly hold.

"I will kill him, Marta. I swear it. I will kill him."

"Don't, Miriam," she said. "I know you can. But don't do it."

It was the first time she had ever admitted that there was something strange about me.

My face must have shown my disbelief because she continued brusquely, glancing over her shoulder as if someone might be listening.

"To take a life is to offer your own. If you hurt Amos, then someone you love will hurt, too."

"But *you* are hurting," I pleaded.

The room darkened. Perhaps a wind outside blew the leaves of the nearby fig tree over the view of the sun. Perhaps the weather was honoring what happens when one woman realizes that another woman is in danger and there is nothing she can do to help.

"I feel his dead wife around me in this house. Her *repha* stands right behind me as I blow out the lamps each night," Marta confided, shivering. "Last night I felt a weight in the bed beside me. But when I put my hand out . . . no one was there."

The shadows in the room intensified, grew bluer, and for the blink of a moment I saw something the color of rain clouds shimmering just beyond Marta in a corner of the room.

"Don't worry, Marta," I said without thinking. "If anything, his wife will protect you. She wishes you no ill, only safety."

"What?" She pulled away from me. "Are you mad, Miriam?"

"I don't believe I am," I responded, but I wasn't completely sure that I was telling the truth.

"Well, Amos will be leaving on a trading trip soon. I will have time to rest." Marta was retreating into a performance of dominance. She stood up.

I stayed seated, saying nothing.

"Here, take these ribbons." She pushed a couple of slips of green and red silk into my lap. "Tell Father we would love to host the family for a feast during Tabernacles."

There was nothing to be done. Her moment of vulnerability had passed, and I had failed to reassure her or offer any advice. She had the servants bring us an early dinner of salted fish before sending me on my way.

The night hovered like a storm above the town. The whole land grew red briefly as if, unclothed of its bounty, its blood could finally show.

My hands, holding the ribbons, were clenched into fists.

What could I do to protect Marta? Who could I tell?

I could go out to the tower and talk to the owls. I could summon that huge, dark part of myself and strike a bargain. But Marta's words were heavy in my heart: "To take a life is to offer your own."

I remembered the figurine stuffed below the pillow. *Sara,* I said, trying to summon her power by gifting her with the right name. But it slid away. I called on the matriarchs of my mother's stories: Moshe's sister Miriam, Zipporah, Salah, Leah, Dinah. But they felt unreal. I could imagine the course fabric of their clothes, the silhouettes of their bodies. But their faces blurred like the bottom of a bowl filled with water.

I tried to imagine the nameless women who had come before. Whose names had flattened under the heavy weight of their husbands. But I couldn't find them.

Do stories preserve us? Outlive us? Or do they erase everything that came before? I wondered.

I gave up on the women. I focused instead on trees: the gnarled olives outside of Bethany, tufted cypresses like towers of black smoke, thick-bodied terebinths I had wrapped my arms around, the fig trees in our courtyard that fed us every year. As I made my way through the crooked streets, I knotted their roots and branches into an impenetrable forest around Marta. I wanted to put her into a garden and then I wanted to close the door and shut out the world.

"An enclosed garden is my sister, my bride, a hidden well, a sealed spring."

I unlatched the front door. Always these beautiful fragments of scripture! And then what? How I longed to access the entire song! All of the knowledge that my father *could* give but chose to withhold.

"It's a matter of protocol. We do what our fathers did!"

Men were arguing with my father. Curious, I slipped into the storeroom and retrieved a jug of watered-down wine with honey as an excuse to go and see who was present. The jar was heavy, and I steadied it at my hip, walking slowly.

At the door, I paused in the shadows.

My father, looking more cheerful than he ever did in *my* company, was seated in the middle of the table, gesticulating with one hand and gripping a metal cup in the other. His newest students were seated around him: Hanan, argumentative, with an aquiline face and grating voice; Issachar, who shared the same narrow features and sharp tongue; and a boyish student with pale eyes called Amram who smiled at me when I served him wine. They had eaten well. The remains of the feast lay scattered across the table: fish bones, stewed vegetables, nut shells, a bowl of olive pits.

There, on the right side of my father, was Yosseph. His sleeves were rolled up over his long, sinewy arms. I could see the wine in his eyes. He was laughing. Laughter that was almost feminine. Musical. A cascade of birdsong.

Hanan was speaking loudly. "Still! I am positive that any type of healing constitutes work! I don't see how you can allow for it on a day of rest. Rest is rest. Healing requires great work."

My father shook his head, smiling, "It is more complicated than that, Hanan. Would you not take up a sword to defend another if he were attacked on the Sabbath? Generosity of spirit cannot be called work."

Yosseph asked, "Are there different types of healing that are allowed for? What of exorcism?"

"Better not to risk becoming unclean by having contact with a demon on a holy day or a day of rest," my father said decisively before taking a deep draught from his cup.

Issachar cut in, his nose red with excitement and drink: "But you hold that it would not be improper to put your hands on someone in a fever in order to heal them?"

I remembered Kemat mixing up herbs for my brother's cough secretly in her room during the Sabbath. I entered the dining room with my head lowered, interrupting the conversation on purpose.

"Oh, Miriam. Good, you've come to top us off!" my father said, his eyes going straight to the wine. Yosseph smiled at me with a kind of openness that felt inappropriate. I blushed. But as I lowered the jar to pour wine into my father's cup, all the anger of the day washed back over me.

How could you give Marta such a terrible man to wed? How can you dine with your friends and talk of these things when your wife is dead?

"What is it, Miriam?" My father tilted his head, as if sensing my thoughts.

I took a breath and poured the wine. "Nothing, Father. I am tired, that is all."

I nodded at the men and, for once, did not look for a reason to stay. What violence were they capable of within the secrecy of their own homes?

Twelve

Marta became pregnant almost immediately. Amos may have been violent, but the promise of a son stayed his hand.

I have enough distance now to understand that man better. His violence was a desperate effort at ritual. When he hit Marta, he was doing the same thing that his father and grandfathers had done. He was communing with his ancestors. Oftentimes violence comes down to us through our blood. We must understand that in order to halt its progress.

Perhaps that is why Amos was afraid of me. He could sense that I was there to protect my sister from passing on that poison to her own children.

"I am his queen," Marta confided in me. "He no longer even expects me to share his bed! I am allowed to stay in my own quarters."

"What a wonderful husband!" I joked sourly. "You don't even have to see him." But I was glad he was no longer hurting her.

• • •

The months passed. Summer fell softly to the earth. Marta blossomed. She grew more and more beautiful, the happiness she had lost after the wedding slowly returning to her cheeks, her smile, her eyes.

A child must be a powerful sort of medicine, I concluded, *if it can heal such a wound.*

"I will be an uncle!" Lazaros declared one morning, accompanying me on a walk. I needed herbs for the coming rainy season when we would be more susceptible to chills and fevers.

"Are you ready to take on such a big responsibility?" I asked, half joking.

Lazaros stroked his chin. His eyelashes fluttered with the force of the emotions running through him. "Oh, Miriam. What if I'm not a good uncle?" he asked, panicked.

I laughed and he looked even more distressed.

He continued, blushing, squinting up at me. "I'm not even very good at study or the Law! I'm not good at much of anything!"

"Hush. Hush!" I pulled him to me, comforting him as much as I was comforting myself.

"Father thinks I'm an embarrassment . . . " he mumbled into my chest, the basket of herbs squashed between us exhaling the peppery smell of earthy roots and freshly cut stalks.

Oh, my poor little brother. Perhaps he would have been better born to a farmer. Some man who could have taught him to use his hands.

"Lazaros," I said gently. "It does not matter if you are good at school. You know more than me already. You delight in every day as it comes. Your heart is always open to beauty. Even after mother died, you did not weep for long."

He pulled away, looking up at me. His nose was dripping tears. His lips were dark with blood. Sometimes I worried that the force of his emotions would cause him to explode.

"I love you, Miriam. Never leave me? Don't go away like Marta? I don't think I could bear it."

"I promise," I said, knowing that he was wrong. I was the one who needed *him*—for so many reasons, one of which was to help me manage Marta's pregnancy. She was so pregnant that she had difficulty walking. Her ankles swelled up, and when they did I visited her with the salves Kemat used to make and rubbed them into the veins of her legs.

"Ah. . ." Marta would sigh, tilting her head back onto her pillow when I pressed the tender spot on her feet just below the big toe; the little valley where her heel met the ankle. "Your hands are so strong! When did you get to be such a healer?"

The new midwife in town was supposed to be a fool. She had lost three women in the past year and Amos refused to let her near Marta. I jumped at the opportunity to use some of the skills Kemat had passed down to me.

I moved the energy down her legs, unclogging her muddy veins with my fingers. I gave her cooled cucumbers to nibble and had her drink ginger tea to help with her nausea. Sometimes I would make a plaster of wheat and spices and rub it over her stomach to ensure the healthy growth of the baby.

But there was a difference between the tenderness that made me want to massage her legs, to bring her rich, nourishing broths, and the power that had heated my hands in the past. I didn't think that power would ever come to fill me again. I had not healed my mother.

The rainy season blew in early, coming a few days before Sukkoth. Marta was due any day. I told Atalyah to send for me as soon as her labor began. I wanted to be there to witness that electric moment when one life splits in two, when two hearts stop sharing the same pulse and blood.

It was too cold to go on the roof and, as was the custom, watch for the temple smoke carried by the wind. The air had already shifted into blades, knifing a chill into our skin at night. For the first time in my memory, we held our Tabernacle feasts inside our home; my father had rejected Amos's invitation. He hardly even bothered to send a messenger to Marta telling her we would not be attending, until I reminded him.

Why didn't he care about Marta? Was she no longer a part of our family? I asked as much over dinner. "Why do you refuse to go see Marta? Her husband is unkind to her. Shouldn't you intervene?"

He turned ruddy. With embarrassment or anger, I couldn't tell. His hand twitched. "Marta is with child. Her husband sees to her care. She is safer kept apart from us."

"Safe from us? Or do you mean we are safer kept from her?"

He roared, throwing his cup to the floor. "Enough! Go to bed! You are worse with every passing day!"

I backed out of the room slowly, refusing to lower my eyes, ignoring the hiccups of Lazaros beginning to cry beside my father.

It's as if he believes pregnancy is a disease, I thought when I was in the darkness of my own room. *As if he believes that her husband's anger is* her *fault!*

The winds made their way inside of our house. I set up a brazier in my room at night and brought in an extra woolen blanket.

When I finally woke, it was well past sunrise. Clean, hard sunlight pierced my eyelids and I sat bolt up, knowing something had happened.

After I had dressed hastily, I ran into Lazaros, who had been coming to get me.

"Miriam! It's wonderful!"

"What is?" I blinked sleepily, pulling my cloak closer to my chest.

"It's Marta!" he cried. "I've just received the messenger. She gave birth last night! She has a baby son! I'm an uncle!"

• • •

It had happened too fast to call for me. At least that's what Marta told me when I went to see her the next day. But I suspected that Amos had threatened her.

"You are too quiet—like a thief!" he said, when I arrived at the house.

"Just like a thief, and here to steal your wife," I replied happily before rushing away, knowing I was only safe if I moved fast enough.

But Marta seemed fine despite my absence. Her friends had attended the birth. Serayah had cleaned and braided her hair. Tali had caught the baby. "I'm unclean," she explained cheerfully. "So Amos may not come see me for another week. I can rest and just enjoy being with *him*."

He was a small boy with tufts of dark hair on his head, and he appeared as insubstantial as a cloud. When he buried his head in Marta's bosom, I was surprised it kept its shape. I expected him to dissolve and shift form in response to her firm physicality.

The air of the room smelled like soft goat cheese; the same intimate, briny smell that sometimes emerged from between my own legs. I wasn't sure if I liked it or not.

"Come and hold him," Marta instructed me. He was heavier than I expected and as warm as a sunbaked stone.

As I held the child, something intense stirred in me, a nameless memory summoned by the smell of the baby's head that disappeared almost immediately. It did not attach to an actual word.

"How pretty you look holding a child!" Marta exclaimed. She was unkempt and relaxed.

"I'll never have children," I said.

But I was smiling, and Marta smiled back at me. She knew I was lying.

• • •

The servant Beltis hummed and shook her head when she saw me. She was wringing her hands, clearly distraught.

"What is it?" I asked.

She shook her head again, mumbling incoherently, before hurrying away.

Two different messengers arrived and spoke to my father. And it was from my father, his face ashen and his lips withered as if with poison, that I finally heard that Marta had fallen unexpectedly ill.

"We must go to her!" I insisted, my whole body vibrating with fear.

"We cannot risk contamination," he said stoically. "She is still unclean."

"She will not make us dirty. Are you afraid?"

"Miriam," he gazed at me intensely. "She thrashes with fever. The child will live. Amos has already found a wet nurse. But there is not much to be done for your sister."

I realized again that he blamed Marta. Somehow my sister had created her own misfortune.

"So you care for the child? But not for your *own* child?"

"There is *nothing* to be done, Miriam," he said, getting up from his seat across the table. "You must pray. And I will pray, too. But God willed that women feel sharp pains when they bear children."

"Did he will that she die? Is *that* God's will?" I exclaimed. "I wish you could feel her sharp pains! I wish you knew what it was like!"

"Silence!" he yelled.

My father stopped me before I left the house. "I forbid you from going to her," he said.

"You forbid me?" I echoed his words back, so consumed by panic and fear for my sister that I couldn't immediately understand that he would truly keep me from her. "I saw her just days ago! Why can't I go now?"

"Damn you, Miriam! Must you make me say it? Amos, Marta's husband, will not have you near her. He is afraid of you and claims that it's because of you his wife is so ill. I cannot defy Amos."

"You have lost your wife. And you will lose Marta now. Is that what you want?"

But he only disappeared back down the dark hallway without another word.

For, you see, he *did* lose everything. Marta. Lazaros. Me. Within ten years he would lose us all.

• • •

I did not care if my father punished me. I would rather be with Marta than suffer the rest of my life imagining that I might have been able to save her.

Although it was very late, there were still lamps burning in every window of Amos's large home. I banged on the door.

Atalyah opened it, her eyes wild with fear. "Miriam, you should not be here!"

"Who is it?" a voice thundered from inside. But something had come over me. I could feel the earth surging up through my feet.

"It is me, Miriam! I have come for my sister!" I boomed, sweeping into the house.

Amos swelled with anger when he saw me. He was surrounded by friends, rich men in embroidered vests with jewels on their fingers. There was wine on the nearby table and a bowl of honeyed nuts. Had they all gathered to say the right prayers when she passed? Or was he preparing to celebrate? He had his son, didn't he? Now he could get rid of his wife.

"Who is this girl?" one of the men laughed, gesturing at me.

"Let me see her!" I demanded.

"GET HER OUT!" bellowed Amos.

"Master, forgive me," Atalyah apologized.

I ran to Marta's room. Women were praying at the foot of her bed and Rebekah sat next to her, her hands hovering uselessly over the rumpled blankets. Tali was weeping. In the corner. I could smell urine, blood, putrefaction. Marta's face was gray and slick with sweat.

"Marta!" I whispered.

"Someone get her off the bed!" Tali shrieked, pointing at me. "Amos said she must not come in here!" But I ignored her.

"Marta!" I shook her shoulders, shocked when I found her skin burning hot. She *looked* cold but this disguised the fire that was burning her up from within.

"No. Let her work!" ordered Rebekah. She fixed me with an intense gaze. "Go ahead! Do what you did before! Do what you did for *me!*"

She had never before acknowledged that I had healed her. But her desperation, her love of her friend, brought forth the knowledge from within her.

Raw power surged through me. I could feel buds and flowers and leaves in my fingers.

Come, come, come! I thought desperately, rubbing my palms together. *I bid you work through me!*

Marta moaned.

I began to cry, and with the tears came the heat in my hands. *I'll meet fire with fire,* I thought deliriously. *My fever will burn out hers.*

I thrust my hands under Marta's dirty shift and pressed them to her chest.

There was a pressure at my temples. A whirring noise in my ears, growing louder. Water running off a ledge, plummeting into an abyss.

Perhaps I would die, too. The fire was too much to bear. I felt it rising up my arms. The pain would swallow me whole.

Just at the moment when I thought I could bear no more, Marta sat up with enough force to throw me backward. Her eyes flashed open, blood flooding back into her cheeks and lips.

"Oh!" she gasped. "Oh! Oh!"

"Yes! She did it!" Rebekah yelled jubilantly.

"A miracle!" wept Atalyah, prostrate on the ground, her palms open.

"Thank you!" I cried lifting my own hands up through the incense smoke toward the ceiling.

Thank you. I said it with every part of my being, every inch of my shaking body.

I wasn't thanking God. I was thanking my own hands. I was thanking every woman in that room.

Perhaps I could only heal when they were around me. Crying, singing, demanding that we save each other.

• • •

When I was sure Marta would live, I slipped away, going home and climbing up on the roof where I thought I might be able to return to myself. I needed the cold clarity of the starlight.

A light wind came from the west carrying the fragrance of a garden that did not exist: the perfume of mandrakes, cane and cassia, the high pure odor of flowering henna.

There was a rattle from the ladder that led up the side of the house to the roof. Through the dark I recognized my father. Without a word he came to sit beside me.

We were quiet for a long time, watching how the purple sky broke into the yellow streaks of dawn like a wild iris. I think I knew then, in that silence, that my father *had* loved my mother. I felt him carrying her memory, her linen shroud, her final days of pain. She was there with us on the roof, telling us that we were still together, still family.

Finally he turned to me. He looked suddenly older, his beard grayer than it was black.

"Miriam, what did you do . . ."

I shook my head and the words died in my mouth. I did not know who had told my father. It could have been the women. Or even Amos.

The heat still vibrated in the center of my palms as if I were holding two burning stars and waiting until the right moment to return them back to the sky.

Speak. This is the moment.

"Father, will you promise me two things?"

His eyes were tight but he smiled. "Yes, of course. At this moment, I would promise you anything."

"You must promise to teach me. Really teach me . . ." I was thinking out loud. "Teach me like you have your other students. But most importantly, you must not make me marry."

"Why are you so hungry for knowledge, Miriam? Does it look like it has made *me* happy?" He pulled at his mustache, frowning heavily.

"Father, it is all I want," I insisted.

After a moment or two he took my hands in his and nodded. "If that is what you truly want, Miriam, it will be so. I will teach you."

The sun was rising, orange with fire. I pressed my palms to my chest, feeling for the hole left behind by Kemat and by my mother, wishing that I had the power to heal myself.

Thirteen

I was obsessed with understanding purity. I bled quietly every month, making sure to keep myself separate from any men. But a secret was growing in me.

I never felt cleaner than when the blood pulsed between my legs. It was as if my womb was giving a gift to the dirt. I shared the darkest, sweetest parts of myself with the hungry roots fingering through the soil. I would take my dirty rags and bury them by the tower, knowing that my blood was powerful. It would draw the moonlight down into the owl's nest. It would tell the stars where to shine.

At my father's table I was finally able to speak. And not only to speak but to argue and debate! I could question the laws. I could interpret scripture. But could I tell these men anything of what I really knew? Of course not.

Now I know that it is not wise to sit at a table with men when there are no other women present. They will tell long stories about other men. They will tell stories that mock the women who support them, bear their children, nurse their wounds. They will talk of nothing. A perfect, strange nothing. A nothing that is God.

My father was ambivalent about our lessons, and I had to remind him daily to sit with me, transmit Targums, explain the current debates of the Law, and critique my ability to apply scripture to practical matters.

At first he insisted that Lazaros join in on these lessons, but soon he saw that I was fast outrunning my brother in my ability to memorize and understand his teachings.

Lazaros had finally begun to grow, shooting up above my father in what seemed to be the space of a day. He could not keep still and was always drumming his fingers on tables and the walls themselves, bouncing through the house with such force that I was surprised when he *didn't* break something. He did not want to sit still for hours with me and my father. He wanted to run about with the other boys of the village and exercise his newfound strength. And so when my father started to devote more time to my studies, Lazaros was not jealous.

It was my memory that most impressed my father. One night, having finished our lesson after he'd returned from Yerusalem, we sat in the courtyard sharing pomegranate wine and he turned to me, quoting a saying I had heard many times before: "Miriam, the man that does not recite is impious. And I must say you are well practiced in the art of remembering my lessons."

Instead of dropping my head in deference to his authority, I kept my eyes raised, fixed on him, and said nothing.

"Your brother is a good boy, but he has trouble learning by heart," my father continued, pulling at the wiry ends of his long beard, curling them around his forefinger. "He would have it that everything was written down for him. But you cannot count on papyrus. The heart and mind are more reliable."

"But have I not heard your fellow students say, 'It would be better to see the Torah burnt than to hear it on the lips of women'?" I shot back, raising my eyebrows. This was the kind of banter I regularly heard at my father's dinners, and there had been many times when he had agreed with such pronouncements.

Much to my confusion, he replied: "You are not a woman; you are my child, and our Lord commanded us, 'Thou shalt teach my children my commandments.'"

I didn't contradict him, but I couldn't help but laugh. Seeing that I was not serious about the issue, my father began to laugh as well.

So I was no longer a woman in his eyes. Was that a victory? I wasn't sure.

"You are a good student, Miriam, so let us leave it at that," he finally said.

"Am I a good daughter?" I countered. I could tell he was increasingly uncomfortable.

"No, Miriam. But you never wanted to be a daughter, did you?"

I nodded. But I felt a widening gulf between me and my father just at the moment when he was choosing to draw me closer as a student of the Law.

Still, within several months of study he relieved me of my serving duties at dinner and allowed me to sit at the table and join in the discussion.

My father's disciples did not like the idea of a girl sharing the same status as them. True, there were those men who realized I could keep pace and welcomed my participation. Amram commented on my wit. He had a soul like water, gently steering the conversation toward issues concerning love and duty. But the kind men who called me by name and nodded respectfully when they left were outnumbered by the students who deeply resented my contributions.

Issachar would not meet my eye. He pretended I did not exist. Alvah and Dan, two pretty brothers from Yerusalem, stared me down with such hungry intensity that I couldn't help but blush. When I lowered my eyes, they would exchange congratulatory laughter, kicking each other below the table.

But no one was more enraged by my presence than my father's favorite student, Hanan.

He was a tall and narrow man who, as hard as he tried, could grow no more than a few bristles on his pointed chin.

The first several times my father allowed me to join the table I remained silent and listened intently. Once or twice I asked a question about the butchering of sacrificial animals, but then I would recede into quiet attentiveness. My father's students obviously thought my inclusion in their meals was an eccentric gesture on my father's part and that I was mainly present to support him.

What a good daughter I was. Sitting at his side. Cutting the tough meat for him! Making sure his wine glass was filled!

After one of these meals, I heard Yehiel say to Hanan as they prepared to leave, "What can he think she will learn?"

Hanan gave a sly smile. "I say that she is learning to be the wife of a scholar."

They both chuckled, fastening their thick cloaks with studded brooches before heading out into the night.

In bed that night bitterness filled my mouth. A wife. Never a wife! How could they look at me and not fear me?

The next time my father invited his students to dinner I did not hold back.

It had reached a late hour and much wine had been drunk. Hanan, relishing his status as favorite, had gotten progressively louder and more contrary. He was the only one who openly disagreed with my father and sometimes even tried to goad him to anger. My father liked this about him and told me that Hanan's badgering kept him sharp.

Hanan, dipping a crust of bread into a dish of honey, questioned my father: "Tell me, Nicodemus, is not the nature of a woman that of a thief if she steals a rib from the sleeping Adam?"

My father chuckled, leaning back on his stool. He twisted his beard thoughtfully.

"Have you ever been robbed?" I asked, the sound of my voice surprising everyone at the table. I had directed the question at Hanan.

"God's will has protected me from such misfortune," he replied, still grinning at his own wit.

"Misfortune?" Now I was the one laughing, sitting up straighter and gesturing with curt broad strokes, as was the men's style. "My friend was recently robbed," I said. "Thieves got into his house in the night while he slept. They stole from him a silver ewer. It was a disgrace!"

Hanan, annoyed, interrupted: "What can your story possibly have to do with this discussion?"

Ignoring him, I continued, "They stole the silver ewer and, in its place, they left a golden pitcher. The man, robbed, woke up richer."

Then I went silent, watching the men around me.

My father, quicker than his students, broke into laughter. "You have been bested, Hanan!"

Hanan looked befuddled so I added, "God takes a mere rib from man and in return gives him something much more useful: a wife."

Yehiel slapped Hanan on the back. "Let me be robbed every night then! It seems as if *you* have been robbed, too, my friend. You have been robbed of your argument!"

After that night, I became more vocal with my thoughts. Perhaps it didn't help that as I began to assert myself in these discussions, I was visibly becoming a woman. It has been my experience that men are distrustful when beauty and intelligence meet in the same form. An old woman is allowed to be wise—at least in relationship to womanly concerns. But a young woman must be lovely—lovely and, most importantly, *silent*.

I did not inherit my mother's full breasts or her elegantly curved body. But my hips had widened and my belly turned soft. There was a new sheen to my skin, and my hair had darkened, turning so black it was almost blue except when the sun hit it. Then it would shimmer with red as if dyed by henna.

On those occasions that I went to visit Marta, she would coo with delight over my changes. "You would look wonderful in this green tunic Amos bought for me. Here, have it! If only you spent less time in the sun, you wouldn't be so brown! Then it would be even lovelier against your skin. But you must promise not to run around like a child with it unbelted. Cinch it just below your breasts to show off your figure."

Marta was moving slowly since her illness. Most days she did not get dressed. And Amos had strictly forbidden me from visiting the house again. I had done the worst possible thing apparently. I had healed his wife.

Thankfully he was away on business for long stretches of time and I took advantage of his absence.

I brought my sister flowers. Fresh herbs I gathered in the fields and woods outside Bethany. I brought her gossip.

But she mainly wanted to sit quietly in the sunlight, letting Atalyah bring her tea that she did not drink. While I started to glow and grow, she was withering, and she barely wanted to talk. Occasionally she would brighten when I asked her about the latest fashions. But it was rare that she roused from her melancholy. She hardly even spent time with her son, Kernan.

"Do you remember what happened?" I asked one day.

"No," she said softly. "But perhaps you should not have brought me back, Sister."

After that I no longer went out of my way to visit her. The thought of her ingratitude made the bile rise in my throat. She had her life! Her son! Why could she not fight for her joy?

How young I was not to see how desperately she *was* trying to surface.

I had brought her back to life. But she was still underwater. The fear of Amos's violence kept her small and afraid. She must become pregnant again to escape his wrath or find a way to escape his attention.

When I held Kernan, letting him play with my hair, she watched me knowingly.

"You are nearing the age of fifteen, Miriam. You are ready for marriage." There was the slightest glint of the old Marta in her eyes.

I shifted the babe in my arms. "I would rather not marry."

"Come now!" Marta chided me, biting her lip and smiling. "Your little friend Yohanna seems to have done quite well for herself. I heard that she is betrothed to a man by the name of Chuza, steward to Herod. And she isn't half as pretty as you."

Yohanna?

I was caught off guard. I'd been so immersed in my studies that I hadn't thought of Yohanna once. I realized that I hadn't seen my friend in a long time.

Had it truly been at Marta's wedding that I had seen her last? A year before?

She had looked lovely with the golden chain around her neck and her dark ringlets! But she still seemed like a girl! Like a girl my own age! Why did I feel so sad? Was I sad for Yohanna's fate? Or was I sad to have lost my friend?

"I heard he spotted her when she was at the temple for Sukkoth and sent an intermediary to her father," Marta continued, loving the authority that good gossip gave her.

"I've no interest," I asserted again.

Marta was finally angry, "It doesn't matter if you don't want to be married; you *will* be married. And it will be a patient man who agrees to put up with your nonsense!"

She was right. The more I attended my father's dinners and spoke my mind, the more I made an enemy of his students.

"Nicodemus, you have trained your monkey well!" I heard Hanan say to my father one night when several smaller discussions had fragmented the table.

"She is no monkey, Hanan. The girl surprises me every time she opens her mouth. I can take no credit for her wit." He was smiling good-naturedly at Hanan but his words were a warning to the men.

I pretended not to hear, keeping my eyes locked on the moving hands of Yehiel as he explained to Issachar the issues involved with the purity of vessels for the scrolls. It was the first time I had ever heard my father publicly give me praise.

But as the weeks followed, he ended the dinners with a comment about my progress. "Miriam is advancing faster than all of you! How can this be?"

Each time he said such a thing I felt the pulse of Yehiel's distaste. Issachar's resentment. And Hanan's anger.

Some nights Hanan waited at the door to leave, waiting for me to pass on my way to my room, the blade of his nose turning his profile into a weapon.

At what point do you truly feel yourself to be a woman? At first blood? Betrothal? Marriage? The birth of a child?

I say it is when you notice that men will no longer meet your eye, but you feel their gaze on you when you look away. Their eyes on the rest of your body as you walk by, cataloguing its faults. Its beauty. Its purity. It reminded me of the way men examined the doves and lambs outside the temple. Was this dove pure? Did it have a bent wing? Was the color of this lamb too muddy for sacrifice? How much does it cost? Would the spilling of this bird's blood bring you closer to God?

As a child I had exchanged cheerful greetings with most of the men in Bethany. They were friends of my father's and knew me as his daughter. But at some indefinable moment during the summer of my fifteenth year, it became inappropriate for them to speak to me. I could no longer be treated like a child out on an errand. I was old enough for marriage.

It was at the market that I became aware of the change. I exchanged a few coins for a bundle of spices from a man so weather-beaten that with every movement of his thin body, I half expected him to crack open and blow away like sand in the wind. I smiled when I spotted Lazaros's friends Achim and Enosh talking near the wine merchant's table.

They were growing into themselves. Enosh had sprouted up several inches in the past year. Achim was sturdier, but still had the round face of a child. He glanced away from my smile.

Only a month or so before they would have come over and teased me or asked where my brother could be found. But this day they looked away nervously, ignoring me. When I took a step to go and say hello, Achim tugged at Enosh's sleeve, whispering something into his ear.

The two boys took off back into town, obviously avoiding me.

Was something wrong with me? Agitated, I put a hand to the wild strands of my hair.

"Shelama, Miriam!"

The sound of my name on a man's tongue was a relief.

I turned to see Hanan walking up the hill toward Bethany, crossing through the market to join me.

Hanan hates me, my mind whispered. But it had been a long quiet day of study. I had talked to no one. I was bored and Hanan did not look unhappy to see me.

"I was coming for dinner but have just seen Yehiel," he explained, scratching the course black hair on his long neck, peering down at me. "He says the Sanhedrin will be convening late into the night."

I nodded, my eyes flashing to the table behind him where a little, yellow-toothed woman sold fresh muskmelons. I would not have to buy as much food as I had expected. A simple meal of stewed lentils and old bread would feed me and Lazaros. I was thinking this over as I turned back toward the village gate.

"For once that tongue of yours is still. Are you disappointed that you won't have a chance to perform for us tonight?" Hanan asked, walking alongside me as I began to make my way home.

I wasn't yet offended. It was nice to have a companion. I was alone so often in those days. Lazaros was busy with his lessons, trips into Yerusalem, and his friends. I often went for whole days without hearing my name said once. Without opening my mouth.

So I did not think too hard about how we must have looked walking together.

I was a young girl, coming to fruit. My hair was still unbound and free. My feet were muddy and bare. I walked side by side with a man who was neither a family member nor my husband.

And we were walking toward my home.

Without a mother's instruction I was blind to certain conventions. But Hanan knew better. He should have, like Lazaros's friends, kept his distance.

"Disappointed? I'm pleased I don't have to watch you chew with your mouth open," I replied playfully. "And you must be pleased to escape my questions."

True, I disliked Hanan and found him bullheaded in conversation. He was close-minded and rarely ceded a point. But there has always been something attractive to me about adversarial interactions. I liked that he challenged me. It made me work harder to construct strong arguments. And when my father saw me going head-to-head with his brightest student, he always beamed, pleased to see that I could keep up.

Hanan frowned. He was allowed to tease me. But my own quick tongue was not so welcome.

"Come now," I said lightly. "What is that you're carrying?"

A leather pouch was slung across his back. "These? Scrolls! For your father. He requested them. I'll leave them at your house for him."

I quickened my pace to get ahead of him. The road was narrow and uneven with stones. I could almost feel the pebbles pressing into my soles, sending a quiet, wordless message up into my legs. *Escape him. Walk faster.*

"Oh, Nicodemus!" Hanan exclaimed in that grating, pompous voice that annoyed me. He lengthened his stride to keep up with me. "He is so lenient with his princess! She can have everything she wants. Everything but letters."

"What do you mean?" I asked, feeling a blush creep up my neck. Was it anger? Was it shame? I didn't own the emotion yet. It was wordless, from below my brain, from deep in my belly.

Hanan squinted one eye at me, the corner of his mouth twitching with mirth. "Don't tell me you haven't noticed? Your father taught your brother, Lazaros, how to read. But he continues to deny *you* such a gift."

My jaw snapped shut. An inhale caught in my throat.

I felt like I might faint with anger.

It had *not* escaped my notice. When my father called Lazaros into his study, I hovered in the hallway, breathing hard, wishing I could access that last mystery.

If I couldn't read, I couldn't be sure if I was getting the whole truth. Perhaps my father was withholding the most important laws, the holiest secrets.

Some nights I stole into his study and carefully picked up the heavy scrolls, never daring to unfurl them. They felt like bodies wrapped in shrouds. They concealed something within that had once been living but was now just a shadow, a symbol, of the original life.

Now I would laugh at Hanan. I would laugh at his thin, useless book learning!

Oh, my father. There are many things I resent him for. But it was a strange gift he gave me when he did *not* teach me to read or write.

You are stunned, Leukas. I see your mouth hanging open! You, who call yourself a bard, collecting stories so that you can write them down. Forgive me for insulting your trade. But I believe strongly that stories live longer and stay closer to the truth when they are only stored in human hearts and heads. How many times did my father tell me that it was foolish to depend on the written Law when it could be corrupted or miswritten?

Already I have seen my life written down wrong. My love and my heartbreak have been turned into words as dead as those scrolls. Dry, bleached, white bodies that cannot possibly summon the vitality, the juice, the sorrow, and the abundance of my life.

But being only fifteen years old, walking beside Hanan, glancing at the scrolls on his back, I felt the sting of my father's refusal.

I can read the right herbs for healing, the sky for weather, the air for rain, the trees for seasons! I wanted to declare but found that I could only redden silently with anger. When I asked my father why he wouldn't teach me, he would laugh and say, "Do you need to read something to remember it, Miriam? I don't believe you've ever forgotten a thing I've said."

When we reached the house, Hanan entered before me, undoing the latch as if it were his own home. As I followed him into the crisp darkness of our dining room, I was struck by the fact that the house was truly empty. The servants had brought their husbands lunch in the fields and Lazaros was at the synagogue studying. I pushed passed Hanan out through the opposite door into the courtyard, needing the reassurance of the sun on my face.

He was close behind me and I could smell the stink of his body, the oil in his hair. I was thankful we were outside and not indoors. "You who bathe every day and speak endlessly of purity! You are soiled! You are corrupted by pride and anger."

I avoided his eyes and clutched at my pouch of spices. "Please leave the scrolls in my father's room. I must go tell the servants what to prepare for my dinner."

"Tell the servants, ey?" Hanan mocked me. He stepped closer. His breath was heavy and audible. "So you act the part of the little house-wife? Do you grind the grain, too? Do you step on the grapes in the spring and squeeze out the wine?"

Something told me not to answer. The tensed nerves in my jaw sent a pain down the side of my neck, into my breastbone.

"What other tricks are you hiding from us when you meddle in men's business?" Hanan's tongue flashed behind small brown teeth. A pale tongue. Coated in something the color of dust.

Never before had I felt truly frightened for myself. I had felt sorrow and worry. But even when the leopard had touched his mouth to my head all those years before I had, somehow, known I was safe.

It is the unknown that inspires fear, I think. And I did not know what would come next.

He touched me. He put his uncalloused hands to my face.

Something shifted in me. I felt as if I was filled with water so cold it was almost frozen—but still, slowly, pulling the current forward.

"A pity you are so bent on learning the Law or you might make a pretty bride. I hear your mother was beautiful. Perhaps one day, if you learn to hold your tongue . . ."

I could bear it no longer. A buzzing had begun in my feet and my hands. Hanan kept his palm on my face, savoring my paralyzed docility.

Darkness bloomed above us and suddenly the air was bruised with black feathers, beating the dust from the ground, the dried leaves from the trees. They arrived so suddenly, descended on us so completely, that it appeared as if the vultures had come from inside the air itself.

One of the great birds landed on my shoulder, gripping me with its powerful talons.

"What magic is this?" Hanan gasped with horror.

Another bird dropped like a black cloud from the sky, and another, and another.

The huge birds swarmed. One vulture balanced on the fig tree's long, jointed branch that passed just over my head.

They opened and closed their beaks, making a din of rasps and clicks, and the bird on my shoulder released all his breath in one grav-elly groan.

I had never felt cleaner, stronger, purer than I did surrounded by these birds. I felt protected by the great shadows of their wings, their knowing eyes. These beings understood death. And yet, they did not die! There could be nothing more powerful than that. To stick your head into death. To *eat* death! And to transform it into flight and feather and force.

Hanan had backed into the doorway, his legs wobbling, his face blanched.

"It is true! You are filled with demons!" he exclaimed, his voice strangled and high. "You have bewitched your poor father to do his bidding! I see it all now! He has fallen under your power!"

"Go from this house!" I commanded, feeling a new strength fill me now that the vulture was steady at my shoulder. "And never come here again."

Without another word, his terrified eyes fixed on the birds, he withdrew into the shadows of the house and was gone.

I stood there a long time, feeling the power running through me, into the bird on my shoulder, up into the sky itself. Finally I began to shake. But no tears came. And although my mouth was open, I made no noise. Quietly I sank down under the vulture's weight. He hopped off to join the rest of his kin on the ground around me.

They were making soft sounds now. Almost cooing. One bird cocked his head with something like worry.

"I'm all right," I whispered.

The birds blinked at me knowingly.

"Thank you," I murmured. "Thank you."

I stood slowly, bouncing my knees to make sure they would hold me. I waved my arms over the vultures' heads in the semblance of a blessing.

Slowly, as the sun tilted toward the long yellow of late afternoon, the birds began to hop away and take flight.

Each one made sure to meet my eye before leaving. I nodded in thanks.

I stood there and watched them circle higher and higher until all of them, all seven, disappeared into specks in the skies beyond Bethany.

Strange, the things we are known for, the names that stick after the years have passed.

Hanan never returned to the house, and my father, although

confused, did not seem to mind his disappearance. There were always new students to fill an empty space at the table.

But it wasn't long after that the rumors started. They still follow me to this day. I heard them on the tongues of merchants and men when we traveled into Yerusalem for holidays. *There goes Nicodemus's daughter Miriam. Miriam of the seven devils.*

Fourteen

I was surprised one evening to see Yosseph again sitting out in the courtyard with the rest of my father's students, picking at a bowl of figs and grapes. He had been gone for a long time on a trip up north on business. In the months of his absence, I had thought of him frequently.

Yosseph was nut-brown from the sun and a drop of gold dangled from his left earlobe. His wide expressive mouth was open with laughter, his sun-bleached eyebrows rising with delight. I didn't need to be told of his worldliness. It hung on him. A red stone flickered on his fingers.

"Tabariyyah is like Yerusalem," he was telling everyone. "But without us Jews, it is without a moral center. There is pomp everywhere and not a single sanctuary to utter a prayer or make sacrifice. No true synagogues! Can you believe that?" He looked around at all those seated, nodding as they opened their mouths in shock. I could tell that he liked to share gossip. It made him feel important. He continued, "And yet! I've never met such people as I've met there. Philosophers! Plenty of them. Women with hair the color of blood, who paid their own way and come from some northern island. I bought dinner for a small, dark man called Sanyat from the Far East. He told me that his people worship a human man; a man who walked on earth and spent all of his days sitting underneath a tree!"

"So they worship a fool?" My father was delighted with this information.

"A divine fool," Yosseph explained lightheartedly. "For while he is a man, they also believe that some time before that, he was a god." He picked up a fig, splitting it with his teeth, taking a bite of the fleshy center.

I was aware of his body's lean muscles and strength, its warmth and shape and otherness, and hair where I had none.

Slowly I exhaled, feeling itchy and hot. Worst of all, being near him made me feel dull-witted.

Lazaros was seated next to my father, listening for once. He turned and spotted me hiding in the doorway. "Come and sit, Miriam! Yosseph is telling us about Herod's city Tabariyyah!"

Yosseph's eyes flickered to meet mine as I came into the courtyard and settled down on my father's right side.

"Yes, tell me about Tabariyyah," I asked, arranging the folds of my green tunic carefully over my knees. Hours spent with Marta, looking into a mirror, had given me a different understanding of my body.

Recently I had received an interesting gift—a beauty that could attract male attention while also deflecting any notice of my hunger for information, my intelligence, my strange intensity. Miriam, who suffered from spells and ran wild in the woods, disappeared when I smiled just so. I could become pleasant Miriam! Lovely Miriam! Desirable Miriam.

I liked how Yosseph leaned forward when he spoke, directing his whole physicality toward whomever he was addressing. "Tabariyyah is Herod's new city. He called it after the Roman emperor Tiberius. To get in good favor with him. But the scandal is that the city is built on old burial grounds. It's unclean. No one will go near it."

"*You* went near it, obviously. Are you so very brave?" I asked, blushing as I heard the flirtation in my voice without having intended it.

Yosseph didn't respond like my father's other students might have. Instead he reflected for a moment, picking up a piece of bread with his elegant hands. "I'm no braver than the next man. But I am a merchant by trade and must go where others will not in order to bring back goods and information such as this."

"You are a trader of stories then," I concluded. "Just as much as perfume."

He smiled, pleased. "I'd never heard it put that way. But yes. I love a good story. Almost as much as I love to tell one."

"And what of the mood in Galilee?" my father interjected.

"It is a land of lestai. Rough brigands and the storytelling *Chasids*. You would think that after the massacre of Yudas and his followers, the Galileans would be more cautious about aligning themselves with someone in opposition to the Romans. But there are many preaching an end of days and many more following these men. Herod seems to execute a new messiah every day." Yosseph was not smiling and I could see that he had chosen to conceal something.

"Have you seen violence?" I asked.

"Miriam!" my father exclaimed.

"What do the Romans *do?*" I asked. I wanted to know what I had long suspected: that we were protected because of our proximity to Yerusalem. Protected because my father was part of a council put in place by the Romans themselves. But the pilgrims coming into Yerusalem brought the stink of suffering with them.

Yosseph denied me the truth. "Enough of my travels!" He clapped my father on the back, grinning again. "Tell me news of our new high priest? Is Caiaphas a Roman puppet or a man of God?"

I was shocked to hear someone talk so brazenly about the state of the world. My father and his students would debate a piece of scripture for hours, but the minute the Romans were mentioned they would speak in subtleties and riddles.

I know now that the Sanhedrin of my father's time was not the institution it had been in the past. It was a new court that had been installed after the massacre of the elders by Herod the Great. While my father and his colleagues despised the presence of the Roman soldiers and our occupation, they could not openly criticize the emperor. It was Rome who had given them their power.

Yosseph was tied to no one. His wealth was his own. He was free to say many things that my father would not.

My father smiled conspiratorially. "If you know anything of our last high priest, Annas, then you know a little of Caiaphas. It is Annas who orchestrated the appointment of his son-in-law as high priest."

High priest. I remembered seeing the man in his sky-blue ceremonial garb standing on top of the steps leading up to the inner courts of the temple. A man who was close to God.

"Then he is a Roman tool," Yosseph said coolly, folding his slender hands in his lap. "Annas has handed down his legacy of submission. He will do whatever Herod and Tiberius want."

It was strange to think of a man of God being the same as a Roman tool. It was the first time I had heard it put so baldly.

"We all submit to the Romans, Yosseph," Issachar argued. "You cannot blame one man more than the rest."

"If the high priest does not represent us, then who *should* I blame?" Yosseph countered. His tone was light but cutting. I could see the merchant in him: able to gossip and tell stories for leisurely hours, but equally capable of striking a hard deal and inspiring respect in his adversaries.

Lazaros chimed in, "Father, don't you despise Caiaphas? Is he not the man who has spoken of exiling the Sanhedrin council to the Mount of Olives?"

I met Yosseph's eye for a second as my father reddened. Yosseph did not look away. Instead he tilted his head down, deepening his smile. Oh, he was not leering. But to be looked at like that—frankly, admiringly— was terrifying!

He made me anxious. I broke our gaze, tearing loose a yellow thread from my dress and winding it so tightly around my finger that the tip turned blue.

"Now Lazaros," my father said, trying to regain his composure, "it is not as simple as dislike. I can dislike the man Caiaphas. But as high priest, Caiaphas is the human manifestation of God's Law. We must not forget that. It is true, though, that he has suggested some rather unorthodox procedures. He would have all the rest of the vendors from Chanuth come into the main court to sell their animals."

"Then he seeks to undermine the power of the Sanhedrin?" Yosseph asked flatly. "He will make you obsolete."

Issachar looked at my father in shock. Yehiel and Amram exchanged uncomfortable glances. Alvah spluttered into his wine cup. Dan seemed utterly confused. To say such a thing outright was almost treason!

Yet my father was thoughtful. He must have been thinking about these issues daily but keeping his opinions to himself. *This* was the conversation he was longing to have. My father finally spoke, agreeing with Yosseph: "Yes, I believe that is his aim. Caiaphas would have the temple free of our presence. Sometimes I think he would rather be the *only* priest, in charge of a few Roman soldiers to control the chaos."

Yosseph nodded, satisfied with this answer, and shocked everyone with his next question. "Nicodemus, do you believe in the Messiah? Is it possible we will be saved?"

My father laughed with amusement as if that were answer enough.

"Yosseph is wise," my father said later that evening, weighing a few olive pits in his hand as I cleared the table.

"Yes, Father," I agreed.

"He questions everything. He will not accept falsehoods."

"And *I* will?" I poked my father, a little peeved that my spot as favorite student had been usurped.

"You are not wise, Miriam. You are unwieldy."

I could not argue with that.

But I know that if I had not been so intrigued by the handsome man and his stories, I would have become jealous. But it was no longer my father's attention I was striving to hold. Now it was Yosseph's gaze that I sought.

One night he arrived early, before my father had returned from the city. Spring was thickening the air, erasing the hard edges of the hills, the rooftops, and turning the flat blue of shadows into something vibratory, filled with hidden life, purpled. Pollen coated the stones, the roadside. The sky seemed deeper, as if it was an ocean that had suddenly received an influx of water.

After washing up, Lazaros said the prayer over our wine and we were quiet, enjoying our simple meal of stewed meat and spiced vegetables. By the time Beltis came in to announce that Yosseph had arrived, we were nearly finished with the meal.

"You receive him?" Beltis asked in her halting Aramaic.

I drew myself up to my full height, remembering my mother welcoming guests into our home. I straightened the dark blue linen of my skirt. Tonight I was to play the lady of the house. "Yes. Tell him to come and sit with us. Father will be home soon."

Yosseph hovered in the darkness of the threshold. He was freshly shaven and his hair fell in burnished waves to his shoulders.

"Shelamah, Miriam." His voice was courteous. "Shelamah, Lazaros. I did not mean to disturb your meal. I wanted to drop by. I've a gift for your father. I will have my servant leave the wine by the door. Will you let Nicodemus know that I stopped in?"

The earliness of the season made the whole earth hum; everything was days away from blooming. White roots threaded through the dust, searching for water. Green lips spoke their first words through the black soil. I felt similarly, as if my skin was the thinnest veil between my blood and the world. The wind was expectant; it filled the courtyard, blowing the shadows of the fig tree's new leaves across the doorway and Yosseph's shadowed figure.

"No, please. Come sit and eat." I held my arm out in welcome, gesturing to the pillows and the remains of the meal. "My father should be back any minute and I'm sure he would be pleased to see you."

Yosseph spoke softly to someone I could not see. I heard a rough dragging noise, a scuttle of feet.

Yosseph explained: "Then I will have my servant bring one of the jars of wine. I would be honored to share it with you and your brother."

"Oh! I can't take any more wine," Lazaros said, patting his thin stomach and belching dramatically before leaping to his feet. "I've eaten my fill and I promised I'd go on a walk with Achim and talk with him. He wants to go over our lessons."

"He wants help from you?" I asked rudely. Then I blushed, worried Yosseph would think me cruel.

But Lazaros chuckled as he picked up his cloak and draped it around his narrow shoulders. "Trust me. I'm even more confused by it than you, Sister. But Achim seems to think I can help him."

His ears, slightly too large for his bony face, had turned a bright red. I had the feeling I had nearly caught him in a lie. What mischief was Lazaros really up to with his friends?

I resisted teasing him, though. "Take care and be back soon. The last time you were out past dark Father got worried!"

"Yes, Sister," he answered, but he was already distracted, picking up a last piece of bread and nodding goodbye to Yosseph before slipping out the opposite door to the courtyard.

Somewhere a bird made a long, open noise. The music seemed to register in the clouds above us, darkening their bellies.

Yosseph came into the courtyard, purposefully, pulling straight his embroidered vest, before sitting down in Lazaros's empty space.

Oh! I could smell him! Balsam. I imagined sap in his veins; his whole body filled with a tree's blood, pulsing with liquid shadow.

What did his neck smell like? The secret parts of him? What would it feel like to trace the sharpness of his profile with my finger? To let my palm hover over the honey-colored skin of his chest, the dark hair just sprouting from under his tunic.

I couldn't stop these thoughts. And they arrived so loudly, I felt sure he could hear my desire. My hands shook slightly as I passed him a metal bowl filled with clean water.

"Thank you, Miriam," he said, his voice slightly uneven. Did he feel my intensity? Was the night making him dizzy, too?

He removed his rings before carefully washing his hands, making sure to clean under each fingernail.

"You can bring it in now." He flicked his hand toward the doorway and a swarthy man with a shiny bald head and a long scar across his left eye waddled into the courtyard carrying a heavy stone jar. He was wearing a vest similar to Yosseph's, but on the stout man it looked ridiculous.

He puffed up his cheeks as he strained to open the crate for us, and then with a curt nod to his master, he vanished back into the house.

The servants had withdrawn. My father would not be home for some time.

The silence made me tingle. I would do something rash.

I would say the wrong thing. Or more frighteningly, I would say the *right* thing.

Yosseph saved me by speaking. "This is the finest wine. Cypriot. It should be drunk unmixed with water—and in moderation so that its taste rather than its effect will be savored."

"And you will waste it on me?" I whispered.

He poured a bit into the metal chalice in front of me and then into his own cup, before quietly reciting a prayer. I held his gaze and brought the cup to my mouth, tasting the metal rim and slowly drawing in a mouthful of the wine.

Blood rose to my cheeks as I held the taste under my tongue: surprisingly a touch of something keen and wooden, maybe pine, followed by a sweetness unlike fruit or honey. It was more like the breath a hot field exhales midsummer.

Yosseph took a sip and, after swallowing, he looked up at the sky. "Nothing quite like it," he said. "It is a cleaner wine; not so cloying as the ones produced here in Yudea. Perhaps it should not be used for meals or pleasure but, rather, saved for ceremony and ritual."

"Don't be foolish. Sharing wine with a friend is ceremony enough. It is just as holy, if not holier, than anything that happens in the temple," I replied, surprised that I had spoken my mind.

The gold in his eyes twinkled. He leaned forward, closer to me, laughing, "You are probably right, Miriam. Who am I to call for formalities? I spend enough time among rough traders and the road's dust to worry that I might become as godless as one of those barbarians to the north."

I longed to know of the lands and the people beyond Bethany and Yerusalem.

"Yosseph . . ." I liked the sound of his name on my lips. The first syllable was a swell, followed by a glide forward. His name sounded like running water. "Yosseph, tell me more about the heathens you've met? You speak of strange gods. Gods that are men?"

"Strange gods . . . and goddesses," Yosseph added, pouring more wine into his own cup. "There are a great many Phyrgians and Egyptians around the remains of Sepphoris. And in Tabariyyah there are many who worship Isis. They have had great statues of her erected, and some keep images of her in their houses."

Isis.

Isis was the goddess of Kemat. The Egyptian goddess who tricked the sun god with a snake . . . Why did her name echo through my body?

"Who is Isis?" I asked.

"Some call her Aset," Yosseph began to explain, looking above me into the sky that was contracting darkly around its first stars. "I don't quite remember the legend they believe, but it has something to do with her husband. He was the king of the land. But his brother tricked him into lying in a box and cut him to pieces. They say Isis went out searching for his body. I've heard she brought him back to life . . ."

The birds wheeling above us paused mid-flight. Their straight black wings were like the inked symbols on my father's scrolls.

I remembered Kemat's voice many years ago describing the Egyptian queen Isis and her husband. I had not known the story had such a gruesome ending. I felt something twist in my chest as if the queen's loss was my own, reminding me of the rootless grief that haunted me ever since the beginning of my spells.

Men fell over and died sometimes. Perhaps I would die now. I thought my heart might explode.

"Are you all right, Miriam?"

I kept my eyes closed. There was a warm pressure on my shoulder, sending life and goodness back into my body. I blinked to see that Yosseph had his hand on me.

"Are you all right?" he asked again. "Your father mentioned that you occasionally fall ill."

"No," I insisted. "He is wrong. I *used* to as a child, but it has not happened for many years."

"I am happy to hear it, Miriam. I would have you always be well."

Soon after, my father arrived home. I could tell he was surprised to see Yosseph and me alone in the courtyard. But he said nothing of it and only smiled. He sampled the Cypriot wine and, as we debated what mischief Lazaros must be up to with Achim and Enosh, my father kept looking between me and Yosseph with a peculiar expression on his face. It seemed, partly, to be a look of great sadness but also one of joy. By the end of the night he had smiled more than he had in weeks. "What good conversation the two of you make. Both wise. Both inquisitive! What a pair . . ."

Lying in bed much later, my body felt heavy. I imagined that having been immaterial as a cloud for years, I had finally been transformed into water—enough water to fall as rain and fill an ocean.

Fifteen

I did not know that these days, so warm and thoughtless, were numbered. I did not notice how they repeated as, every morning before my father woke, I would climb up onto the roof and watch as the day drained out the darkness of the night's rich wine.

Standing there, my shawl wrapped tightly around my shoulders, I would murmur to myself: "And the earth was without form, and void: and darkness was upon the face of the deep. And the spirit of God moved upon the face of waters."

I would try to concentrate on the landscape, the trees inside our garden wall, and the light cutting between the ordered lines of the vineyards beyond Bethany. Just as I could not picture the face of the deep or the face of the water, I could no longer picture the face of the man who had for years appeared in my dreams.

The world was beautiful, but it was ordinary. The birds made noise as the day began, but the noise was no longer song.

I make it sound unpleasant when the routine of that time seems, in retrospect, a kind of blessing. The flaxen grasses of the fields waxed and waned. The moon did the same and my body placidly complied. I grew used to the monthly confinement my blood necessitated, even taking the time to dust off my mother's old looms and beginning to weave long blank sheets of linen. Without design. Without color.

I have seen men escape their fate. There are those who go silent and choose to fade, faceless, into those shadows that lie outside of legend. I think this was such a time for me. The ground was soft enough to absorb the sound of my footfalls. The stars no longer noticed me at night. God's hand relaxed its hold.

As I walked unnoticed, someone matched my stride.

I was fascinated by the stories Yosseph brought back from his trips. Fiends to the north who wore animal clothes. Women who led armies and rode into battle on the backs of wolves. Listening to him I realized how sheltered my life in Bethany was, and how small.

He would arrive, sometimes after dinner, and my father would nod before calling my name.

"Miriam! Yosseph would walk with you? Will you come?"

I was already perfumed and dressed.

As we strolled around Bethany, I would sometimes lean closer to him, feeling how the neck of my tunic slipped to reveal my collarbone. I would implore him, "Tell me more about this miracle worker you saw?"

And Yosseph, always leaning away from my intensity for the sake of modesty, would answer honestly. "There was a woman whose legs had ceased to work. She had to be carried around on a pallet by her children. And the man made her pay handsomely. But afterward he spat in her eyes repeatedly and drew a circle in the sand around her body. And she did get up and walk. If only for a few steps before falling."

"So did he really cure her?" I wanted to know. "Or did he convince her to stand up and try to walk? Did he put his hands on her? Did he say what it felt like to do such a thing?"

Sometimes he would come to a stop, reaching up to pull at his earring reflexively.

"You are very curious, Miriam!"

I knew Lemuel no longer traveled. He had almost completely transferred his business to his nephew. But I was surprised that he did not come around to our house anymore. My father had mentioned that he had been ill this past winter.

"He is old, Miriam. He has swelling of the arms and legs. It makes movement difficult."

"Yosseph, what is it like to sleep out under the stars on the road? Do you wake feeling more alive?"

"Ah!" His golden eyelashes would flicker, his hands coming together in a joyous clap. "There is nothing like it! To wake and feel the dew on your tongue. To know that you will be moving your body all day."

Our sandals slapped against the gravel in the road. The children, playing in the square outside the synagogue, cried and cheered. I waited for him to ask me about myself. *So, Miriam. What is it that makes your heart sing? What troubles you? Tell me about your dreams . . .*

But he never asked. He would smile placidly, occasionally stealing a glance at me. Happy to be seen walking at my side. Happy to have me as his companion.

One evening—it was one of those attenuated dusks that come just at the close of summer—an especially large crowd arrived for dinner, which made it impossible for me to hear Yosseph over the chaos of arguments and voices. After we had eaten, Yosseph and I slipped into the garden. Gnarled olive trees pointed with their long, black arms to the whitewashed tombs at the farthest edge of our property.

Although it was my land and I knew the way through the mesh of roots and leaves better than anyone, Yosseph led the way. "Miriam, have you heard of our new prefect?" he asked me solemnly as we came to a clearing.

"Yes," I replied. "Father told me he arrived in Yerusalem with great display. He had his soldiers flanking him and holding up standards that depicted the face of the emperor."

"Indeed." Yosseph looked from the sky back down to me. "Pilate does not disguise his hatred for us. It is a scandal to let the picture of a man enter into the city."

"Is it true that Pilate keeps the high priest's garments hostage between festivals?" I asked curiously. However, I was also curious to see how close I could draw to Yosseph without alarming him. The last of the daylight, filtered through trees and the humid air, struck like flint against the dark gold waves of his hair.

"This is true. I believe it is an attempt to control any rebellion that could emerge during those times when there are many outsiders in the city. The prefect will not release the proper garments to the priest until he has proven that he can keep control of his people," he said, stepping away from me, back into the trees.

It often struck me as strange that the men around me—men as rich and learned as Hanan and Issachar, Lemuel, Yosseph, or even my father—could withstand our oppression. Could they not, with all their power, both financial and spiritual, find an intelligent way to relieve us from our Roman oppressors?

I now know they felt the weight of their grandfathers' defeat, their ancestors' sorrow in exile. They were not timid. These men were trying their best to protect their families.

"Who will do something?" I asked. "Who will rid us of the soldiers in the Antonia Fortress?"

"What you speak is treason," Yosseph asserted, but not unkindly. His eyes tightened with something like amusement. "It may be fine to say such things in the safety of Bethany, but I bid you hold your tongue in Yerusalem. Pilate has soldiers stationed at every street corner."

I bit my lower lip, clenching my right hand until my fingernails bit into the flesh of my palm. How could I express the growing anger in me when I saw soldiers laughing at us? Pointing at my father's hanging tefillin, his ceremonial cap. Every time I went into the city with him, I loathed the way the centurions watched me.

These men have made a sport of killing my people. Bleeding our coffers dry. Burning down our temples and our homes, I mused to myself.

"Are you not outraged enough to take action?" I finally asked, my voice thick with emotion. "I am always surprised that you men can complain all night and then bow your heads like slaves to the tax collectors! We should refuse to pay! We should refuse to hand over our ceremonial garb!"

Yosseph responded physically, his hand breaking the distance between us, gripping my slender wrist. At first I thought he was angry with me. But his grip relaxed and his fingers lightly circled the bones of my hand.

"Miriam . . ." he said gently, shaking his head, his swaying hair sending out the scent of lily oil and balsam. "Miriam, you are a good girl! And you are smart. You have certainly heard what happened before?"

Slowly I nodded, breathing heavily. He was right. By then I had learned about the rebel massacres. My father had described the horror of two thousand crucifixes lining the road leading out of Sepphoris.

Yosseph continued, peering deeply into my eyes, "Are you not happy with your home? Your life? I would not have you meddling in matters that could get you killed. Perhaps our messiah will come someday. Perhaps he will not. It is not for us to say. It is God's will."

I ignored the real question; the one Yosseph thought was rhetorical. Was this placid life for me? Was I happy with my home? My walks with Yosseph? My long, meandering conversations with my father's students?

Yosseph took my silence as an opening to step closer to me and to brush my cheek with his hand. The breath caught in my throat. Our faces were very close. I could take one step closer and press my breasts against his chest. Close to Yosseph, my worries faded below the strong pulse of my desire.

But later, alone, the question of my satisfaction resurfaced.

Once the questions had been asked, I could not return to the former sleepiness of my life. I found that I had no more patience for weaving or embroidery. Late at night, I was still wide awake; caught between my desire for simple happiness, for Yosseph's approval, and for something entirely different and wordless.

This *something* was growing. I could sense it looming like a thundercloud in the distance. Yes, right now the air was still calm and sweet. The sky above my head was still blue. But the clouds were gathering. Yellow energy was coiling in their heavy bellies. Soon it would pour down on the land. There was a hunger in me to go out and meet the storm.

Hurry on! Move me past these simple days! Deliver me into my destiny! It was a prayer I willed myself *not* to utter. And still it flowed through me.

What *was* the storm? Was it my visions? My sense of God working through me?

I tried hard to subdue myself. But the harder I tried, the more it seemed that the chaos rippled from inside of me out into the world of Bethany.

In no time, the rumors had begun again. The longer I remained unmarried and under my father's instruction, the more I aroused concern in the men of Bethany. Nicodemus's daughter did not have a husband.

"He is making himself look like a fool," I overhead my father's friend Caleb saying to Rabbi Achan. I was standing outside the synagogue, waiting for Lazaros to catch up with me. But he was taking his time, laughing with Enosh.

I looked over my shoulder, wondering about whom the older men were speaking. Caleb met my eyes, answering my question.

"Nicodemus should betroth Miriam to some man from the north who does not know about her troubles. That way her father can clean his name of her. And the poor man will be chained to her before he finds out the mistake he has made."

Achan, his silver beard stained yellow with food, eyes rheumy and small, gave a nervous laugh, seeing that I was now fully aware of their conversation.

"Come now, Caleb. Don't speak so harshly of the girl."

"She is no longer a girl. She is a woman." Caleb's eyes flickered upward reverently as he drew on scripture: "'Charm is deceitful, beauty is vain.' She must practice being a woman who fears the Lord—a woman who fears her husband and keeps a tidy house."

Something was wrong with me. And it wasn't just the older men who thought so.

The disdain of the women stung the most. At the Simcha Torah feast held at Lemuel's grand house the day after Sukkoth, I overheard Serah, Yohanna's mother, Tali, and Rebekah all talking about me.

I had told my father and Lazaros that I would meet them at Lemuel's home. But I realized my tardiness as I made my way through the front door without being stopped by a servant. There were people all about. Lemuel never passed up an occasion to share his wealth with friends and family. And now, having handed over his business to Yosseph, he could relax and fully delight in the riches that his long years of travel had earned him.

Once inside, the confusion of smells and voices overwhelmed me: two servants were hauling a slaughtered lamb out to the courtyard to be cooked over the fire. My eyes widened as I looked at its marbled flesh. The creamy blues and whites of the animal's muscles peeled apart.

What an intimate thing! To see flesh opened up. To imagine our own hearts and wombs with their secret colors inside our own bodies. I wasn't sure if I was revolted or awed by the sight.

Spiced smoke blew in from outside. Coriander. Saffron. Rosemary. I almost sneezed, the aroma was so dense.

I spotted Marta's friend Tali. She was heavily made up, her small eyes swallowed by rings of kohl, big green-jeweled earrings making her face look unbalanced. She grabbed my shoulder in greeting, yelling over the noise, "Go to the side courtyard! Help the women with the vegetables!"

I nodded and hurried back outside. As I was about to step into the courtyard, I heard my name spoken from beyond the door.

"Miriam has grown into quite the beauty," said Yohanna's mother, Serah.

I smiled with pleasure, patting my delicately arranged hair, feeling the complex texture of braids Marta had woven into my scalp.

"It's a pity she's such a nuisance," said Rebekah. "If her mother were around, she would put a stop to Nicodemus's lunacy."

"And her sister did so well for herself," came Lilah's voice. "I can't bear to imagine what Hadassah would think if she knew Miriam was eighteen and still unmarried."

Lilah was a short, unassuming girl with pretty, olive skin. I bore her no ill will. Why was she speaking of my mother as if she knew her? She had never spoken to her!

"At this point, she is spoiled for marriage," Serah confided.

There was a peal of laughter. More smoke reached my nose and the bite of burnt coriander made me want to cough. But I swallowed it back, staying hidden in the shadows.

"She's obviously trying to seduce Yosseph," Serah said, something in her mouth. There was a pause. A smacking of lips. They were trying some of the food. Testing the herbs. Adding more rosemary. I imagined their heads crowded together over a steaming pot of lentils and onions.

"I know!" Rebekah finally agreed. "She follows him around like a little lamb with a shepherd. And Yosseph has no idea what danger he is in. It would be an ill-advised match."

The women were right. It would be a terrible match. I would be bored of Yosseph in minutes. I would go mad being a good housewife. I desired him. I liked to look upon him. But the idea of *marrying* him made me hot and nauseated.

Serah spoke decisively: "If she really cares for him, she'll remove her attention from him. Her mother was a great woman, keeping the burden of her illness from everyone until the last days. She cared more for her husband than for herself. It is a pity Miriam has not inherited her sense of duty."

"I wouldn't worry," Rebekah assured the other women. "Even if she persists, I can't see a well-traveled a man like Yosseph falling for the cunning of such a girl. Other than her beauty, she has no virtues. Without a mother's guidance, she has become unmanageable."

Slipping into the shadows of vine and almond trees, I tried to steady my breath. The tears dried into tight lines of salt on my face in the cold night air.

"Mother," I said, not truly speaking to my mother so much as the night itself and the comforting, weightless embrace of the darkness. "Help me. Deliver me to my destiny. Whatever that is."

I gripped so hard at the sleeves of my dress that the fabric ripped in my hands.

By the time I returned to the house, the lamps were lit and the feast was well underway. I washed up and joined one of the tables, glad that the many guests covered my late arrival. Seated among the other women, I kept my eyes down.

I could see Yosseph, seated at the men's table. He laughed heartily, using his slender hands to eat. Occasionally his face would appear serious, his wide lips pressing into a line as he listened to someone. He looked like a king, dressed in his fine clothes. Solomon from the stories my father had told me when I was younger! A sparkling brooch was pinned to his purple cloak.

Later, when the lamps had been relit and cast their pure white tongues upon the stone walls, I got up to go. Many would stay at the tables until the last of the wine had been drunk. The women were already drifting away to reconvene at the cooking fires in the courtyard. Stories and gossip would be exchanged. Mothers would play with their children's hair.

I resolved to slip away. But I was surprised when Yosseph appeared in the door to the courtyard. His cloak was askew over his shoulder and his hair, usually oiled into place, was rumpled as if he had run his hands through it several times. He leaned against the doorframe, crossing his arms across his chest, smiling too easily.

"Behold!" Yosseph whispered huskily. "You are beautiful! Your eyes are doves!"

"Yosseph! You are drunk!" I cried, jumping back as he reached out for me.

"True. Aren't you?" His eyes glittered with confidence and entitlement. "You are Solomon's beloved tonight, Miriam. A rose of Sharon. A lily of the valley!" Throwing out his arm like he was about to perform a song, he recited perfectly:

"Awake, north wind; and come, you south!
Blow on my garden, that its spices may flow out.
Let my beloved come into his garden,
and taste his precious fruits!"

It was my favorite scripture: the Song of Solomon, and it dripped with pollen and pomegranate wine and frankincense. Deer jumping through the syllables. Trees furred with needles and moss sprouting through the lines. Words fashioned from fragrance and bodily desire.

Yes! I thought, feeling drunk myself. *Love is holy. I had almost forgotten. God inspired this poetry. Maybe there are secret things I can only understand with my body. With my love for a man.*

"Miriam . . ." Yosseph was just tall enough that he could have rested his sharp, freshly shaved chin on my head. But he was staring down at me, staring at my lips, daring me to come closer. I tilted my face up. Our chests brushed and one of his hands grabbed mine, squeezing my fingers tightly. The low light had the effect of flattening his angular, well-formed face into a sort of drawing. He looked like an idea—like a king of old stories, preserved only as a few lines of pretty poetry, a gestured painting fading on an old stone wall. His breath smelled like bread and heat.

"Miriam. I would make you my wife."

"Then make me your wife," I said, hating myself. Loving myself. Knowing that by saying yes to Yosseph I was saying no to something else.

I was saying no to the storm.

• • •

Yosseph came the next day to speak with my father. I heard their voices in the courtyard.

"Go away!" Beltis scolded, her watery eyes narrowing as she saw me edging toward the window. "You must not look! It is not proper."

She would not leave me alone until I promised her that I would stay away from the men. She pushed a piece of bread into my hand and I took it out of the house, back into the garden, where I crumbled it in my hands, scattering seeds for the birds.

By the time I returned home, Yosseph was gone. And my father made no mention of his visit. In fact, he hardly even looked at me over dinner.

It was only much later, a long time after Lazaros had gone to bed—as Apphia and Beltis blew out the lamps—that he knocked at the door to my room.

"Come and sit with me in the courtyard, Miriam," he commanded. "We must talk."

Filled with nervous energy I practically jumped out of bed, throwing my heaviest cloak over my shoulders.

But the night was warm, and once in the courtyard I found that I could remove it. I folded it up on the dry dust at the edge of the cooking pit and sat down, my knees underneath me. My father sat down across from me, placing a lit lamp between us.

The flame danced between our exhaled breaths.

"Look at the lamp, Miriam," my father said.

But what about Yosseph? What passed between you?

Still, I fixed my eyes on the flame. "What am I supposed to see?"

"Just continue to observe it. Look at the place where the flame meets the night." My father's own eyes held twin reflections of the lamp. These little white stars blinked at me and then I returned my eyes to the real flame.

"There is more to the Torah than talk, Miriam," he finally said, after I had been watching the lamp for a while. "Sometimes understanding does not come from another man. It comes from God's world. But we must quiet ourselves in order to receive these messages."

I didn't respond. I was locked into the lamp. It was as if my vision had shrunk to the exact thickness of the flame; nothing else was visible. There was a slight pressure at my temple and a tingling sensation at the spot between my eyes. Breathing deeply, I watched as the whiteness of the fire darkened, revealing a gradient of color: red, black, and, surprisingly, a blue as pure and strong as a summer sky. Then, strangely, these colors, without disappearing, became secondary to the experience. Darkness unlike anything I had ever seen in a shadow or night sky began to emanate from the lamp's wick. The only comparison I could make was to that dim memory of the man's face from my dreams; this was the blackness of his eyes, the hypnotic center of his dead irises.

"The lamp has turned into blackness," I said, and although I was perplexed, I did not break my gaze.

"There is the lamp we see and then there is the lamp of darkness," my father said quietly. "This lamp can only be seen through deep contemplation. In such an image we can begin to understand those things that the prophets said, which seem impossible to comprehend."

But there was a feeling building in me, halfway between ecstasy and panic. The blackness was not static; it seemed to be drawing in the air around it. The pressure in my head grew. I was alarmed to recognize that the strange state that accompanied my spells was beginning to overtake me.

I trembled, willing my whole body to reject the spell. After a tense moment, the pressure released at my temples. My breath came easily and I felt normal again.

My father looked intrigued: his brows were knotted together and his mouth curved up to the side.

"What did you see, Miriam?"

"Nothing. I don't like this practice. Do you teach it to your other students?" I asked. The wind had died down and the lamp's white flame grew tall and straight.

"No. It is not a practice I teach to all my students. It has been known to provoke madness." He put his hands together as if about to say a prayer but then thought better, folding them in his lap. "I thought, perhaps, it might suit your gifts."

"What gifts?" This was a totally different conversation than I had been expecting. "No one else seems to think I have gifts. Apparently, I am full of devils. Everyone in Bethany says so."

My father did not deny this. Slowly, thoughtfully, he nodded his head in agreement.

"Yes, there are those who believe you are possessed. But I think you know that there is more to it. You are very quick to learn, Miriam. And God has worked through you to heal."

He had never said it so plainly. I hadn't realized my shoulders and jaw had been tense until he spoke. I had been holding my worry in my muscles for years, clenching myself tight against his indifference. Or worse, his scorn. Even when he let me sit at the table, I felt there might have been a mistake.

"Miriam. Have you changed your mind about marriage?"

The question caught me off guard. I had left any thought of Yosseph far behind.

I sat up straighter. "I fear it," I answered truthfully.

My father frowned, tucking his chin into his chest, looking at me hard. "What if you loved the man that would be your husband?"

I squeezed my eyes shut. The black flame of the candle appeared in my mind. "Father, I love my God with all my heart, my soul, and might."

It wasn't a lie. But it wasn't the whole truth.

When I said "my God" I meant the power that had flowed through me when I'd put my hands on Rebekah and Marta. I meant the owl in the tower. I meant the leopard's wet nose against my face. I meant the pale face of the man in the box.

"Repeating scripture will only get you so far." He put a hand out to the lamp's flame, cupping its slender heat. "Love of God is also love of his men and his creations."

Above us a bat swung across the stars, his dark wings writing something invisible in the sky. I imagined his little body serving some larger purpose, his dusky fur and tiny, thorn-like teeth all in service to his energetic message.

He dances for God. He lives for God. Eats God's bugs. His whole body is love!

"Father, did you love Mother? Did she give you joy?"

My father coughed nervously, shifting his whole body away from me, glancing back into the dark house.

"What does it feel like to love?" I didn't mean to push. But I was desperate. "Is it better than meditation? Than studying?"

He opened his mouth, only to close it. He bent his head, rubbing his eyes hard, pinching the bridge of his bony nose. Finally he spoke. "Yosseph has asked if I would give you to him in marriage."

"Yes, I know," I answered briskly. "I know already."

"Well. What then? Will you refuse him?" My father asked wryly, finally looking up at me, the whites of his eyes glowing blue in contrast to the darkness pushing in on us, eating up the lamp's feeble light.

"No."

He laughed.

"Miriam. You love him. I have seen it in your eyes."

I wanted to argue. I wanted to say that I *desired* Yosseph. I wanted to touch him, smell his hair, taste his wide lips.

But I wasn't certain that I loved him.

"Yes," I said because I couldn't say this to my father. I couldn't speak of my desire. Or my intuition that something stranger and bigger lay ahead for me—something far beyond Bethany.

"You will make a fine wife, Miriam. I know it."

"When will it come to pass?" I asked, unsure what I had just done.

"He has left for a journey up north to procure aloe and myrrh. But he will be home in the spring. You will be properly betrothed then."

That was the last of it. He was quiet but emanated cheerfulness, humming a praise song, getting up and going back into the house without another word to me.

Later, in bed and unable to sleep, I turned over on my belly, bunching the linens around my feet so that the backs of my calves were exposed to the slight chill in my room. I could feel the flower of desire pulsing in my belly. I pushed my fingers underneath my body, pressing the tender mound of my sex, feeling the concentrated heat, the soft, silky folds. I breathed hard, thinking about the vines heavy with grapes, the pomegranates stretching their leathery skin, the mighty sinews of summer sun streaming through any leaf, any opening, to reach bare skin and turn it to gold.

Miriam.

The man's voice did not belong to anyone in the room.

I shivered. My hand pulled away from my sex.

It was not a memory. Not a dream. The voice did not belong to Yosseph.

I rolled over, back onto my back, my eyes shut, seeing the image of the lamp's flame burned into my eyelids. As my body grew heavy and my mind opened blankly into those underground vaults that are only accessible during sleep, the image of the lamp's flame transformed. It lengthened and grew blacker, black as ink, until it seemed a morphing line detached from the lamp.

Slowly the line fragmented into those curious shapes I knew were the letters I could not read. A word hovered, black against something white, perhaps the illuminated skin of my eyelids, perhaps the lack of anything at all.

Much later I would learn this was an experience that highly practiced Chasids and rabbis achieved during their deepest contemplation. After pondering and praying over the name of God, it would reveal itself like black fire on white fire. In fact, my father told me once, it was said that this was how the Torah was originally composed.

Each holy word had burned into the eyes of the prophets.

Ignorant of any letters, I had no idea what I was looking at. I felt that it must be a name. But I knew it was not the name of God.

It would be years before I would recognize the letters, scribbled onto a page of a long story—my own story. I would cry out, pointing to the symbols, and ask the author what they meant.

And he would squint at me as he explained, surprised that I did not already know.

Yes, they were a sort of name.

Son of God. Son of Man.

Sixteen

Almost the entire winter passed before Yosseph returned. I kept my ears alert for news of him at my father's table, but it was not until the ground began to soften that word came that Yosseph was in Bethany. On the day that I knew he would come to our house to dine with my father's students, the clouds merged, forming a dense cover, and the air was brisk and wet. The season seemed to be waiting for my own heart to open to warmth and light.

In the early morning I went into town to bathe at the mikvah, and afterward rubbed oil deep into the chapped parts of my skin, willing my body to shine like polished metal. Those first moments of cleanliness after walking through the bath were like being born.

Cleanliness is a physical state, I mused. *Not something abstract involving rules!* It was simple! It involved water and being properly in my body. Feeling the skin of my cheeks prickling with cold. The flutter of my spirit in my chest, straining toward its destiny.

On my way back home, wrapped in a woolen cloak, I felt as if my eyes had been clarified, and that I could see colors for the first time in their true vibrancy. Some early *achna'i* blossoms appeared unnaturally blue at the roadside. I picked a few, storing them under my tunic above my belt, feeling the soft petals tickle my nipples, waking up the spring in me. I knew that within an hour or so of being plucked, they would turn—like the sky during sunset—from blue to a deep pink.

Later on, as the light purpled and people began to arrive and settle on cushions in the courtyard, I carefully applied a mixture of jasmine and olive oil to the place on my wrists where my veins were closest to the air. Marta had shown me that the blood would heat the scent until it flowered outward. Initially I took out my favorite tunic: a striking red of pomegranate seeds with embroidered sleeves, but then thought better of it. There was something pure about Yosseph, something that deserved to be free of the flesh and its colors. I settled on a plain linen dress that I had made for myself on my mother's looms. It was a bloodless white, like goat milk mixed with water.

I hovered invisibly at the door to the courtyard, watching as the men gesticulated and ate. My father was still in his city garb, the tefillin dangling at his forehead, his prayer shawl about his shoulders. And there, just at the edge of my sight, was Yosseph. He was thinner and browner, which had the effect of making him appear burnished rather than worn down. A new green gem dangled from his earlobe. His hair was shorter and oiled away from his face.

I stood for a moment, drinking in the thin odor of the pomegranate wine in the jar that I held to my chest. My eyes had unfocused as I mused, and suddenly I was surprised to see the shadow cast behind Yosseph shiver, dilate, and grow dark. It was as if there was someone else, huge and invisible sitting just outside the circle of men and listening in on their debates.

Oh. The storm.

The shape disappeared and my gaze refocused. The image of Yosseph grew sharp and strong against the courtyard's backdrop of trees and the kitchen garden. I realized that at this hour of dusk no shadows could be cast.

It had been an illusion.

"Miriam!" Yosseph cried out, spotting me in the doorway. "Come and join us!"

And I did, letting Yosseph rise and kiss me on both cheeks in greeting, signaling to all the men present that it was done.

I had been claimed. I would soon belong to him.

• • •

I was ready to be married that night.

Or at least I was ready to be touched. I thought I might go mad with anticipation.

But Yosseph was formal. After a discussion with my father, he decided to delay our betrothal until after Pesach.

My father explained this to me one evening as we shared a simple meal of flatbread and stewed onions. "He plans to send messengers to his mother and brothers to see if they approve of the match. I believe he also has a wish to honor you with a proper betrothal banquet. He feels this will be appropriate only when we have fully entered into the harvest."

"But the betrothal period is already long enough," I complained.

My father laughed. "For someone so sure she would never marry, you are eager to be a wife now! Yosseph comes from a large family with many responsibilities. We must honor his wish to include them in this transaction. We will write up the ketubah soon enough and settle on the mohar that Yosseph will offer for your hand."

But the weather filled me with urgency. As Pesach approached, the trees blossomed with such intensity that one flower seemed to push the previous one off the branch. The ground was soft and pink with rotting petals. The hills reddened with anemones. And the wind woke me early every morning, hotter each day, telling me that I must rise and say my prayers on the roof.

From that vantage point, I could see all the way to Yerusalem, which was surrounded by tiny dots that were buzzing in and out of the great gates. Hordes of pilgrims poured into the city from every road, dawn till dusk.

Even Bethany was beginning to fill up with family and guests. There were new vendors at the marketplace, men with faces so scarred and sunburned they looked like they had been whittled from wood. Men who had lugged their precious goods with them from far away. Salted fish from the north. Metalware and trinkets from Egypt. Earthy-smelling perfumes in glass bottles sold by a man with no nose.

Little children ran through the streets, discarding their traveling hats and cloaks, dropping crumbs of bread, delighted to be reunited with their cousins and friends for the holiday. Feast days rejuvenated Bethany. Suddenly I could taste the lives that existed beyond my small realm. Life always felt more possible during these moments.

With my impending betrothal and the pleasant weather, my father's mood had lightened. I even heard him laughing at something Beltis had been grumbling about. "Good woman, you worry too much!" he reassured her, handing her a pouch of coins to take to the market. "We will get more wine. We will not run out."

Over dinner that night, he suggested that Lazaros and I bring an offering to the temple in honor of the approaching feast.

"Invite Yosseph," he told Lazaros, knowing I would need an intermediary to make the interaction appropriate. "It would not be unwise to offer a sacrifice and receive a blessing before the betrothal."

We set out early the next morning, the sky above us veined with watery pinks and blues. There were no clouds yet, but a white haze obscured the horizon. After we had passed the Mount of Olives, the natural smells gave way to the dense odor of foreign spices, hot oil, and the sour, fertile smell of animals.

I had to close my eyes and breathe deeply through my nose to focus on the pure green scent of the almond blossoms and the vine trees underneath the stink.

How was it that this city was holy? Why did we have to enter it to become clean? One should get as far away from the chaos as possible. Cleanliness was back in the country, standing knee-deep in living water, away from the crush of desperate humans.

Lazaros, taking his role as chaperone seriously, walked between Yosseph and me as we prepared to join in with the crowds of pilgrims.

"It's madness!" he exclaimed, clapping his long hands together. "Look at those Cypriots in those colors."

In the past year Lazaros had sprouted up taller than most of the men we passed. But if it was possible, he was even skinnier. His body was so awkward and sharp I often thought it must be hard for him to get comfortable. How did he sleep at night? Did his bony knees bruise when they knocked together? Yet he was filled with spirit. His big eyes grew wider still as he craned his head to watch the passing strangers. Quickly he forgot his role as chaperone and picked up his pace, eyeing a pretty girl with a bright red scarf around her hair, walking next to a man on a donkey.

Yosseph kept his distance but I felt his gaze like a hand at my back: warm and steady. "Would you want to live in the city, Miriam? It would still be very close to your family." His voice was low and respectful.

"I don't like the city," I responded without thinking, wrinkling my nose at the stench of refuse that filled the air the closer we got to the gates.

He nodded thoughtfully, straightening the front of his tunic. It was a rich, dark blue, the plainest piece of clothing I had ever seen him wear.

His beard was so freshly shaved that the olive skin of his face looked as smooth as a woman's. His features were relaxed, handsome, and controlled. Men wearing the tefillin and hats that identified them as scholars nodded at him deferentially. Rich men, walking beside their wives, called out his name, raising their hands in greeting. Even the centurions eyed him respectfully. Yosseph was a merchant. A city man. He radiated wealth and sophistication, commanding attention from the Romans and the Pharisees.

A woman shrieked, dashing across our path and off the road. I stopped, peering behind us to see that people were falling back like water from oil, clearing the way for someone.

"What is it?" I asked, confused.

Yosseph grabbed my hand, pulling me near him.

A beleaguered man came closer, his stride uncertain. He held his arms out in front of him as if feeling for support. His whole body was swathed in muddied bandages, and strips of cloth dragged in the dust behind him.

"*Ame! Ame!*" he cried, to warn everyone of his impurities. But it was unnecessary. The leper's illness was visible; at the ends of his arms were short, fingerless stumps.

Yosseph made a hissing noise. For the first time I saw his composure break. His eyes narrowed with revulsion. He stepped in front of me, raising his cloak to protect me. "Stay back, Miriam."

I pushed down the cloak, watching the leper as he passed us.

The man sensed my gaze, pausing, leaning forward, his knees bending inward as if he might crumble into himself. Visible through a slit in the bandages wrapped around his face, his eyes were disconcertingly wide and vital, fringed with thick lashes.

My hand twitched. Something cramped in the arch of my foot. I started to step forward.

"*Ame! Ame!*" the man warned. "Do not come close, mistress!"

"Miriam!" Now it was Lazaros who intervened, his skinny arms surprisingly strong as he pulled me out of the leper's way.

"Stop!" I squirmed, trying to loosen myself.

The leper had passed on. I watched as he hobbled into the city.

"What can a man do to deserve such pain?" I murmured quietly, my hand at my heart. It was pounding. I felt intensely alive. Intensely uncomfortable. My own hands felt numb, as if they, too, were rotted away.

Yosseph blinked down at me. "What do you mean, Miriam?"

"Does he really deserve such an affliction?" It was a question that had troubled me since my mother's death. I remembered her huddled in the back of our house, her body twisted by suffering.

"He suffers for his sins," Yosseph said solemnly, ushering me onward now that the man was a safe distance away.

Lazaros laughed, breaking the buzz of intensity. "Miriam has great pity for the lepers, Yosseph. You should be careful with her. She was always trying to give them food at the market when we were younger. And she brought bread to Mahli the Cripple every Sabbath, even when he cursed her. My mother had to forbid her from doing so."

I felt a growing anxiety. I couldn't seem to draw a full breath. I was relieved when we arrived at the Zion immersion pools and I took my leave of the men before going to bathe with the other women. Taking off my cloak, shawl, and outer tunic, I was shivering in my white shift.

An ancient woman was supported as she walked through the water. Each step registered in the widening of her yellowed eyes.

I waded in slowly, feeling the coldness enter me from the tough soles of my feet and travel upward. Dipping my hands into the water, I imagined the invisible impurities of the past week being pulled away. Was my skin lighter now? How come the water, burdened by so much sin, was yet still clear and blue, reflecting the sky above me?

A young woman with thick hair as pale as wheat was beside me in the pool. She coughed so hard that I was worried she would die. I put a hand on her back, feeling her ribs, the gray energy of her illness rising up to meet my palm. She stopped and twisted to look up at me, exclaiming in a foreign tongue.

She gripped my hand, tears rimming her brown eyes.

Thank you. I didn't understand her language, but I knew what she was trying to say.

But for what?

As I stepped out of the bath, I looked back to hear the woman chattering excitedly, arm in arm with a blonde woman who was pointing at me.

I rejoined Yosseph and Lazaros by the Sheep Gate. Yosseph's hair was wet and black. He had put his head under one of the fountains attached to the pools.

The city made me feel edgy. But today the feeling was intensified. I noticed that where there had only been vendors of the most necessary sacrificial animals, now there were many stone tables set up within the colonnades of the court. Sheep and cows set their eyes into me, bleating hopelessly.

Yosseph, although he was committed to playing the part of a wealthy, well-behaved man, eyed the moneychangers who sat closest to the gates. He couldn't help but thrust a hand into the purse attached to his belt as if to check that he had enough coins to avoid interacting with such men.

Pilate had recently ordered the merchants from the Mount of Olives into the sacred space of the temple. There had been uproar at the time, and much talk around my father's table. But seeing it up close I was no more outraged than I had been my first time here. There was still the smell of death, still the same sense of chaos and destruction. I preferred to say my prayers in the clean wind at the top of my roof in Bethany. There I could offer myself without the sense that I might, at any moment, fall into the shape of a dove or a sheep being pulled under the sacrificial blade.

I drew my arms around myself protectively, and Yosseph, assuming I was being demure, stepped closer as if I needed the defense of his body against the push and shove of singing pilgrims and squabbling men.

Lazaros was in love with the confusion. His cheeks were red with excitement, and he kept pushing back his unruly curls, peering over my head. He dwarfed most of the men around us. I wondered where his height had come from? My father was not very tall. Perhaps his height derived from my mother's mysterious relatives to the north. The ones who were mostly dead. Mostly nameless. Even as Lazaros left us to go and speak with a vendor of brightly colored birds, I could still see his dark head over everyone else.

Yosseph went to bargain a lamb for our offering while I looked about.

A woman had fixed her eyes on me. As old and stooped as the olive trees outside the city, her eyes gleamed like milky pearls against the tight black skin of her face: so tight, in fact, that it gave her the appearance of a skull, and yet she was not hideous. She reminded me of the silvery ash at the bottom of the cooking fire. Used up but finally light enough to be carried on the wind.

She was seated amid a pile of rags near the steps that led up to the Court of Women. People shuffled around her without looking down, and yet I wondered how they could ignore her. She was the oldest woman I had ever seen.

Her eyes tightened, almost disappearing into the darkness of her winkled brow. She lifted a hand and beckoned me.

It was as if God had struck me temporarily deaf. The cacophony of songs, prayers, and bleating animals receded. A woolen silence took its place; people's mouths still moved and the sheep still kicked at the dust, but no sound reached my ears.

Without thinking, I approached her. She stared up at me, her hand still curled in the same gesture she had used to summon me. Her fingernails were long and brittle, yellow as piss. One was long enough that it curled in on itself.

"Behold!" She reached out, grabbed me by my shawl, and pulled me roughly down to her.

Overwhelmed, I had no choice but to sink to my knees.

"Behold!" She placed her palm against my chest, the long nail pressing into my sternum. "Daughter of Yerusalem, who is that rising from the desert?" she asked. Her eyes held mine, but they did not see *me*. They penetrated me, straight through stone walls of the temple and the city to the empty, wind-drawn center of the wilderness beyond.

When had my voice deserted me so completely? I tried to swallow and could not. My blood was thick and cold. It clogged in my chest, freezing up the muscles of my heart.

She rapped her hand against me with such force that it seemed she might actually harm me. I gasped and my pulse skipped.

"Behold, he is here. He is here in this city. He who shall cause the fall and rise of many men!" she boomed. Thunder flew through her. How was she so loud? "The man who is not a man! The man who is the Son of man!"

People were stopping to look now, holding their children back protectively even as they craned their necks forward. The vendors had stopped their transactions, pointing at us instead, exchanging curious looks.

One squat money changer went so far as to make a show of getting up, slamming shut his box. He puffed up his square chest, stomping over to us as if he would stop this nonsense.

The woman did not care. She gripped me harder. I could smell her breath, thin and sour as old milk.

"And you! Oh, woman in the garden, a sword shall pierce your heart!"

"Oh!" I spasmed, feeling her nail in the center of my chest. The pain flooded into me. Had she killed me? Had she thrust a hidden blade into my breast?

I moaned, looking down at her, trying to keep the tears from spilling from my eyes, choking back bile.

"You are the first and the last! The whore and the holy one! Wife and virgin!"

Her words released, my stuck voice. "What do you mean?" I asked angrily, trying to shake off her grasp. "What are you doing to me? Stop!"

"Light and glory! There comes salvation. There comes desolation! There comes the end! The beginning! He is here, now, in this city of . . . the storm!"

The energy was too much. Her eyes grew milky with cataracts that had not been there seconds before. She had been a flute blown through with wind. Her voice lost its vigor and died in her throat.

Suddenly Yosseph was there, shoving the woman off me. "Unhand her, crone!" he yelled.

I saw her fall back hard, her fragile shoulders making a painful, crunching noise as they slammed into the flagstones.

Others rushed around us and Yosseph pulled me away, holding me closer to him than ever before. I could feel the hard jut of his hip against my waist, the blood pumping in his chest.

And my own body felt more alive than it ever had, as if the woman's long-nailed finger had reached into my chest and kindled the flame in my heart. I could hear every sound around me again, painfully. I swallowed, tasting each particular smell. Human piss. Dirty wool. The sweat of a person about to die. Gummy and blue, like rainwater caught in a stone's cleft. Bird droppings. Balsam perfume. Galbanum incense. The dense, moist center of yeasty bread.

I stood, frozen, watching as a young man kicked at the old woman half-heartedly. The temple guards advanced to take control of the situation, carrying the scent of blood and smoke with them, the secrets of the inner temple.

Would they drag her inside and slit her throat like they did to the little lambs? Would they offer her ancient blood up to our invisible god?

No. A crazed laughter bubbled up from somewhere deep inside me. I started to tremble. *The only blood these men did not want was a woman's. Any other blood would do. But not the blood that women gave freely, without sacrifice, without death, each month! No! A woman's blood they despised. And squandered.*

"Miriam! Are you all right?" Yosseph grasped my waist. I could feel his fingers pinching the softness there, taking advantage of the situation to feel me, to relish our closeness.

"Who was that?" I asked weakly.

Lazaros pushed through the crowd to us, putting his arm around my shoulders, usurping Yosseph's position.

"How dreadful, Miriam! What was she saying to you?" he exclaimed. But his eyes were bright and he couldn't hide the smile that danced on his full lips. He loved the madness. The activity! This would all make a wonderful story.

"Yes, yes. I'm fine," I assured them, nodding, "But who *was* she?"

"That's Anna, she's a madwoman," Yosseph answered, letting go of me and resuming the distance that was appropriate to stand from a woman who was not yet his betrothed, not yet his wife.

"She's not mad," Lazaros argued. "She's just mad with grief." Her husband died years ago and she's come here to pray every day since."

She was gone now, swallowed by the crowds.

I let them lead me out of the temple. I let them go into the courts without me and offer our sacrifices. I stood in the shadows of the temple walls watching as people hurried by.

My tunic felt itchy and heavy. It rubbed uncomfortably against my nipples. My sandals were rigid against the arch of my feet. I wanted to run my hands through my hair. Remove my clothing. Sit under a steady stream of water. I tasted the salt of my own sweat, longing to suck the salt off someone else's skin. To press my face into the ground and breathe in the fertile black loam. The old woman's words rang through my mind. *Behold, he is here. He is here in this city. He who shall cause the fall and rise of many men! The man who is not a man! The man who is the Son of man!*

Had I imagined it?

I thought not. She had said *the storm*. I was sure of it. She had looked into my heart and understood me. She had sensed the clouds crowding closer.

She had said they were here.

He was here. But what did that even mean?

I turned my head this way and that, searching every passing person's eyes.

When Yosseph finally returned and we made our way back to Bethany, he had to pull me along. I kept pausing, as if stunned, to peer behind me. I was filled with the sense that someone huge, blue, and practically inhuman was following behind me. It was an energy that pressed against my spine, and the delicate dimples placed low on my back. The presence seemed to say quietly, in a low, resonant voice, *Miriam.*

The sun slid down our bodies like liquid butter as we left the city, melting Yerusalem, causing the temple's roof to glitter, and the metal coins in people's hands to flicker like flames. I stared deeply into the eyes of every passing man. They coughed uncomfortably and looked away. A few smiled lasciviously. I could tell this behavior was unnerving to both my brother and Yosseph, but I ignored their disapproval.

The woman's words echoed in my head. *He is coming. He is here. He is in the city.*

Seventeen

When I woke the next morning, it was with a sense of urgency. The air felt electric. The hair on my arms stood up. I was dizzy and nauseated, but it was hard to call it illness. It was like the apprehension that floods the body before jumping into cold water.

Still, there was food to be arranged for the Pesach festival. I oversaw the making of the nutty pastries, instructing Beltis on how much coriander to add. But I could not sit still long enough to eat anything myself or wait to see if the pastries turned out all right. Instead I climbed up on the roof and scanned the distant hills, sure that I was waiting for something to bloom out from beyond the heat-hazed horizon.

A storm. I swear I could feel it. The sky was blue, but one long sheer cloud divided the heavens like a thread that had escaped from my spindle.

That year we planned on attending the celebration at the grand home of Amos and Marta. Amos enjoyed throwing huge parties in honor of even the smallest holiday. However, I observed that, unlike the selfless generosity of Lemuel's feasts, this was out of a desire to display his wealth and provoke envy.

I set out early and the springtime swallowed me. Early violets crushed underfoot reminded me that the earth could sweat sweetness. I knelt beside the path and plucked one, gazing into its tight purple eye.

A passing serving girl sneered at me. *Miriam. The mad daughter of Nicodemus.* I could practically hear her thoughts. But I did not care. The words of the woman in the temple had set something afire in me. What, I did not know. But the colors were so bright I could almost hear them. The new tufts of green grass lining the path chimed, bell-like.

The pale red roses climbing the gate to Amos's home were as breathy and low as a lover's moan.

Tendrils of wind, scented greenly with almond blossoms, tangled me in their embrace. I avoided the house and slipped into the back garden, escaping the bustle of people arriving. Leaning against a steady olive trunk I looked up through the latticework of foliage. "What is this? What am I feeling?" I whispered, the words seeming less like a question and more like a prayer.

When I finally climbed up the hill and joined the women at their table to eat, Marta was furious.

"Flowers in your hair! Eyes like a rutting donkey! Don't tell me you've been embracing your betrothed."

"He's not yet my betrothed," I countered gaily, surprised that I felt the need to assert this. "And look. He's seated over there with Lazaros. I've just been sitting out in the garden."

Tali was boasting about her betrothal to Eran, a member of the Sanhedrin like my father. Rebekah poked fun at her friend. "He is practically a Greek with those pillars he's put up in his home. But I heard they're just painted plaster . . ."

I poured myself some wine, taking no care to dilute it. What was wrong with a little drunkenness? It amplified the sense that everything was chattering with aliveness. Even the cups seemed to vibrate. I studied the way mine reflected the dim glow of the full moon just rising above the trees. I watched the candlelight play off my sister's hennaed hair, which was sneaking out from beneath her scarf. Her tresses transformed into snakes dancing from her head down into the mouths of our hungry cups.

Could I feel it then? Was it then that God's eye noticed me? Or earlier in the city, when Anna had put her finger to my chest?

I think that when we grow very close to our fate, the world tightens around us like a skin. There will be no deviation. No escape. The shape of our lives finds us, fresh and unformed. When our fate arrives, we find that we are only able to walk in one direction.

Directly into the storm.

I stood up from the table, almost upsetting the cups. Yosseph caught my eye over the sea of heads and mouthed my name, "Miriam."

Did he think he owned it; owned me already? I found that I did not want to hear or feel my name on his long, thin lips.

"Miriam! Go lie down in my rooms! You're drunk!" Marta commanded, gazing up at me with disgust. She slapped me on the hip. "You are making a fool of yourself."

But once inside the house I felt like a dove in the marketplace, wings beating against a wicker cage. I paced the halls and escaped out a side door into a night that was so dense with pollen, with perfume, with moonlight, that it was less a color and more a material. It was a skin I walked into and felt smoothly adhere to the curves of my body.

The garden was a vibrating purple mass against the sky. The moon was so low and so swollen I felt I could reach out, dip my fingers into its bowl, and remove a droplet of golden honey. Glinting from between the trees was a star I did not recognize. It hung alone, bright and almost red: a pinprick of blood under the moon.

I let the star pull me. I needed to get up higher in order to see it clearly. Unsteadily, I felt my way around the side of the house until my hand connected with that object of my quest: a ladder I pulled out and away from the wall.

It was some mercy I managed to get up to the roof without falling to my death. But once on top of the house I could see the whole violet ocean of the sky awash with stars. I looked down upon the bustling feast below. The candlelight merged seamlessly with the stars and the silver olive leaves. I could not tell where the heavens met the land.

And there below the moon was the strange star. I gasped to see it so clearly. Where had it come from? I swore I'd never seen it before.

"So you've noticed it, too." The voice was low, yet bright.

Someone else had made it up onto the roof before me. I could tell by his size that the man, although seated, was tall.

"Yes. I've never seen it before."

"Really?"

I thought of my nights in the tower, praying to the sky, to the leopards and the darkness. "I am no stranger to the night sky. I would like to think I know its face as well as my mother's."

"It's been in the sky for some weeks," the man offered. He spoke with a slight lilt. An accent I thought might be northern.

"That's impossible."

"Perhaps. But I followed it here."

"You're jesting." I knelt down, my body closer to his, my eyes still on the star.

"I dreamed I must go on a journey. And I didn't want to. But then the star arrived. And you see . . ."

I could smell him. Musky sweat and split cedarwood. Rainwater on hot stones.

"You see I'm here tonight, and I haven't the faintest clue why."

I turned then to look at him, and he must have felt the same urge, too. His face, half-shadowed, appeared blue. His eyes were wide with curiosity, owl-like, a little too big for his face. And yet despite this, he was handsome in an odd sort of way, with a strong, cleft chin covered by dark stubble. His nose would have been the only refined part of him, long and narrow, had it not been broken and healed slightly crooked.

"Maybe you can tell me," he said. "Why am I here? Why did I have to come all the way to Yersulaem? God knows, I do not love cities."

I was filled with the impossible urge to reach out and touch him.

"Miriam!" The voice came from below.

"Miriam, where are you? Miriam, come now! Let me see your beautiful face!" called out Yosseph, obviously drunk. How did he know I was outside? I could hear his soft footfalls tracing the house's periphery.

The man's expression was suddenly serious. "Who are you?" he asked. "I swear I know you."

"*Miriam!*" Yosseph's bellow was so loud it made me jerk upward to my feet. I backed away slowly toward the ladder.

Although he was almost swallowed in darkness, I could still see the glint of his eyes watching me.

"I know why you're here," I offered, as I lowered myself down on the rung.

"Why? Why am I here?" the man called after me.

Sometimes we speak with our future tongues. We give breath to the spell of our own fate.

"Don't you see?" I called out to him. "You came here tonight to find me. I am the star."

• • •

"Where have you been?" Yosseph asked, having spotted me leaning against the wall. He was smiling with relief. "I've been looking for you for ages."

"I don't know." My voice sounded funny and high. "Yosseph, do you know a tall man with wild hair?" I asked, "He was here tonight. I think he had a northern accent—maybe Galilean?"

"Galilean?" Yosseph was taken aback. I lurched forward drunkenly into his embrace, gazing up at the clean, sharp line of his jaw.

"What is it?" Marta joined us, holding a lamp ahead of her. "What is wrong with my sister?"

Her face was a blur of yellow lamplight. The corners of her eyes sparkled until I couldn't focus on anything else. The dizziness had returned. I leaned into Yosseph's chest, hoping the steadiness of his very real body might root me in the real world.

But neither Marta nor Yosseph could keep me from overflowing my edges.

The world dissolved. Miriam dissolved.

• • •

I awoke hours later in my own bed. My father was at my side.

Slightly sore and heavy limbed, I sat up and rubbed my head. But I did not feel alarmed or sick. Instead my body thrummed with blood. Blood moving with the same vital current as river water. Although the spell had passed, my vision sparkled like ice. The edges of objects pulsed with an inner life. The candle was alive. The walls were alive. The rocks and sand and dirt below this home were the body of the entire world.

"Father," I exclaimed, watching his eyes widen with alarm as I clutched his hand fiercely, digging my fingernails into his knuckles. "I am clean! I am whole!"

Eighteen

It was as if the dream world I entered during my spells and the real waking world had exchanged places.

In the days following Pesach, I fell into a trance again and again. Seated in bed or out under the blinding sun in the kitchen garden, my hands that had been weeding or picking herbs would fall open aimlessly, more interested in the sensations of wet dirt between my fingers. More than once, I was so overwhelmed with the beauty of a stammered dove song that I burst into tears, and Lazaros—his narrow cheeks flushed with worry—would try to console me, hugging me to his body.

"Miriam! You are acting mad! Did that woman in Yerusalem do something to you?"

"I'm not sick Lazaros, I'm well," I insisted, even as my tears wet his shoulder.

The third morning after Pesach, Yosseph came to the house to visit me. My father ordered that I stay in bed and, dazed beyond resistance, I complied, staring up at the ceiling and imagining stars, clouds, faces. One face in particular.

As if my altered state had somehow amplified all my senses, I could easily hear my father speaking outside my room; his voice was low and worried but came to me as clearly as if it had been breathed into my ear.

"She's had them her whole life, but not for many years," he was telling Yosseph. "I thought they were resolved, but I am worried that this time she may be beyond help."

When Yosseph finally entered my room, it was as if his face was obscured by a screen of smoke. I could still distinguish his features, regular and well groomed, but the spark that had illuminated them before seemed obscured. I could no longer see him clearly.

My hair was unbound. I hadn't bathed in days, and I wore only a white shift that, as I struggled to sit up, sank below one shoulder, exposing my naked skin. But I was alert to every mote of dust in the room, every shifting breath exhaled by me, by Yosseph, by the insects hovering in the ceiling's corner. I couldn't have cared less how I appeared.

"How do you feel, Miriam? Your father tells me you don't remember fainting at the feast." His voice seemed like a thin stream next to the deep ocean of the man on the roof.

Oh no. I couldn't marry him. I couldn't give myself to Yosseph. Not after seeing such a man. Not when I was so intensely alive. It would kill me. There was nothing left of my desire for him. He was lovely as a flower in a garden. But I would not pick it. I would not bring that fragile bloom into my house only to watch it wilt and fade.

No. I wanted a tree. A storm. A disaster. Someone huge and strong and rooted. Someone who was of the ground and the water and the sky.

I so seldom held my tongue that my silence must have been worrisome to him.

"It is no secret that I have come to care for you deeply. I would have you better soon so we can be betrothed and wed. There are healers in Yerusalem to whom we could bring you . . ."

Betrothed and wed. It was all I could do not to cry and rip out my hair. Yosseph's presence in my room was unbearable. He had to get out. Couldn't he see that I didn't want him?

But I nodded carefully, my eyes lowered demurely.

Yosseph noted my disapproval and sighed. "Miriam, do you want good health? Do you want to be wed? Or are you too filled with demons to know what is good for you?"

When Yosseph realized he would get no response from me, he left, promising to visit again soon.

I was glad when he was gone from me.

That night, when everyone had gone to sleep, I got up quietly and made my way out the back of the house.

I headed straight to the tower. The black shape against the purple night made my heart race. It reminded me of the man on the roof: dark against dark. A new moon night when absence was really presence and I could feel a pulsing void where the moon had hung just days before.

Entering the tower was entering into mystery. I could feel the cold, wet air. I paused on each rounded stone step, feeling the grit and brittle leaves between my bare toes. It had been a long time since I had visited.

Standing once again at the open window I felt returned to myself as, after a spell, I came back into my body. It was as if the tower's rubble and vine-covered sides were an extension of my own skin. I could feel the foundations firmly in the hillside in the same way that I could feel the steady anchor of my own hips. I opened my mouth, feeling it as vast as the sky above me.

Huge. I was huge. I was stone and dirt. Protector of the vineyard. The fields. Watchtower and lighthouse. Beacon. My spine straightened, simultaneously driving upward into the sky and downward into the roots and rubble below me.

The words of Micah came to me now. "And you, O tower of the flock, the stronghold of the daughter of Zion, to you shall it come, even the former dominion shall come, the kingdom of the daughter of Jerusalem."

There was purpose in me. A driving energy as insistent as water pushing toward the ocean; rain plummeting from the heavy-bellied clouds.

Yes, something was coming for me. But I could no longer wait patiently.

It was time for me to seek the answer to the mysteries of my life.

For a long time I stood still, thrumming with the night and the tower. When I tired of looking out at the stars, I settled on the floor, slipping my fingers through the moonlight, turning the air into dense white lines streaming through the holes in the roof.

Come! Show me where to go! What to do!

How can I put words to it? I am not sure if it is possible. That is the problem with dreams and visions. They are hard to describe or explain, even to oneself. Often we are left with only a taste in the mouth and the barest shape of a feeling.

I was aware that I was no longer in the tower. The familiar darkness of my earlier visions opened before me and, sitting up on my knees, I felt the tickle of weeds, and water surrounding me.

Except as soon as the darkness appeared, it began to lighten as the night does in the hour before dawn. The water did not stay around my

knees but began to rise and pull with a strong current. I was forced to
stand as it reached my breasts and pushed my shift against my body.

Looking through the dim light, I could see for the first time that
there were shores on either side of me, and that they were bordered with
trees. I was standing in a river. And as I felt my way with my feet across
its pebbled bottom, I saw a man on the shore. He was tall and still. I
walked against the current, my hand out to steady myself, struggling
to get close enough to see him. But as I fought against the river, I was
wrenched from the dream. I woke up back in the tower, gasping, lying
flat on my back.

I knew then what I must do, where I must go.

In the morning I tried to make myself presentable and went to
join Lazaros in the courtyard to share a meal. As I joined him, serving myself a piece of bread that Beltis had just baked, he gave me a
wary look.

His worry made him look younger: a curly-haired little boy with
eyes and ears too big for his pointed, narrow face. "Can I trust you not
to fall into the cooking fire? You've got everyone worried, Miriam."

Casting a sidelong glance at the small fire, I smiled as the flames
seemed to flicker brighter and longer than I'd ever noticed. I shook my
head, trying to clear it so as to appear normal. "Forgive me, Brother.
I cannot help myself. I feel terrible that I have caused you and Father
such worry." I bowed my head and tried to arrange my face into a somber expression.

Lazaros laughed, his mouth full of food, his eyes twinkling.
"You're a terrible liar. What is it that you want? I know you don't
think you are ill."

I smiled, hardly surprised that he had seen through the ruse. He was
younger than me. But he was attentive; too keyed to the minute shifts in
other people's emotional states. It was always hard to lie to him.

"I heard father telling Yosseph that I may need to seek a cure. I was
wondering if you have heard of any healers?"

"Why do you want to see a healer?" A tiny indent appeared between
his bushy brows. He cocked his head curiously.

"Everyone seems to think I need to be healed." I looked away from
his ink-black eyes that were so like my own.

"I don't care about everyone. Be truthful with me, Sister."

"All right, fine," I huffed, finally glancing back at him to see that he was grinning expectantly.

Did he know what I would say?

"Do you ever get tired of our life here, Lazaros? Do you ever wish you were like Yosseph and could travel to distant lands and see strange things?"

His eyes widened with understanding and he nodded slowly. "So you would leave and go on an adventure?"

"Yes. I would leave," I said, knowing that telling Lazaros was irrevocable. He would either be sympathetic or destroy any chance of my leaving Bethany. He could go directly to Father and explain my deceitful behavior.

Lazaros looked up through the fig leaves for a long time before answering. "There is Dov, who styles himself after Honi the Circle-Drawer. He comes to Jerusalem. But I think he is false and mostly likes to draw the crowds. I've never actually heard of him healing anyone . . ."

The image of the river flowed in my mind.

"Let's travel outside Yerusalem, Lazaros." My voice was husky with intensity. "Let's go somewhere far away. I want to see the world before I am a married woman. I want to live."

"Yes. Yes!" The blood rushed to his cheeks. His hand curled around the knife he had been using to cut the bread. I could almost hear his heart picking up pace. "A real adventure! Well . . . Honi's grandsons, Abba Hilqiah and Hanan the Hidden, are also said to practice magic and healing up in Galilee."

"Galilee . . ." I echoed, thinking of the man's rough accent. He had sounded Galilean.

Lazaros continued to rattle off names.

"There is a rabbi by the name of Eleazar, who is said to cast out demons. He is with the Essenes at Qumran. And Shamgar has told me of a wild man up on the Yarden River. He is called Yochanan the Immerser and claims to remove people's impurities by bathing them in the living water."

Blue flooded my vision, as if someone had taken crushed cobalt and blown it into my face. It was a blue of river water that reflected a great, pure expanse of sky . . . the blue of a man's skin absorbing garden shadows.

"Tell me more of this man Yochanan."

Lazaros picked up a stray pebble from the ground, turning it over in his fingers. "Well. I've heard he lives on locusts and wears the skin of wild animals. But that is not why I mention him. He is said to have attracted exorcists who can perform miraculous deeds. I think we could convince Father to let us go. I've heard him mention the man before."

The world constricted. The roots below us seemed to surface, nudging our tailbones. The sky was closer. Heavier. The insects wheeled in ever-closer circles around our heads. My own skin felt tight and hot.

Yes. This was the sign. The world was pushing me out of Bethany. Into my destiny.

"Let us go to the river," I resolved.

"Yes!" Lazaros beamed, his hand reaching out and grasping mine with surprising strength. "Let's see the country! It will be good to leave Bethany for a while . . ."

I'd been so caught up with my own desires and troubles that I hadn't paid attention to my brother. His excitement bubbled up so easily. Had he been suffering, too? Was he stifled by the routine and safety of our lives? Did he listen to Yosseph's stories with growing envy?

Later that night, after my father had returned from the city, Lazaros made our case over dinner. "We must purify Miriam, Father," he hedged as we neared the end of our meal. "We must find her a healer. Do you agree?"

It was fascinating to watch him play at this. Lazaros was so red that I felt sure my father would see through our deceptions immediately.

But he listened carefully as my brother explained his reasoning. Everyone spoke highly of Yochanan. Achim's uncle had gone to him for a persistent affliction of the skin, and he had been healed! He also cleaned women who were troubled by demons.

My father shelled a walnut and popped it into his mouth. He chewed thoughtfully before swallowing, raising his eyebrows and letting out a long, defeated breath. "I had thought you healed of these spells, Miriam." It almost felt like an accusation, except that his eyes were soft and sad.

"I did, too," I answered, perhaps too quickly. "But they seem worse this time. I cannot be married until they are gone. Yosseph will not take me in such a state."

His head sunk into his hands. There was a small bald spot forming that I had not noticed before, brown and shiny from the sun. "This is true."

"Yochanan has exorcised many other women," Lazaros continued. "You have heard of his wonders yourself!"

I tried to hide my smile by raising my cup. Apphia had overwatered the wine. It barely tasted like anything.

My father snapped. "I have heard he preaches that the kingdom of God is near. That is all I have heard."

"Yes. But I have also heard his followers are capable of miraculous deeds. They can heal the sick." Lazaros grew stronger in his resolve as he went on. "Miriam is in need of cleansing *and* healing. Where else would we be better going?"

"The temple," my father murmured almost to himself. "The temple is the only place where she can be cleansed."

"You know that is not true," I retorted, unable to keep quiet any longer. "What about the baths? The rivers? The living water Ezekiel speaks of?"

"She has been to the temple," Lazaros said, coming to my aid. "She has made offerings there many times. And yet, still, she suffers possession."

My father knotted his fingers together in deliberation. "You must know that I have little faith in these men of deeds. But we have tried all other methods."

Both Lazaros and I nodded fervently.

He looked to me. "Miriam, will you go to this man with an open heart?"

"I will, Father. All I wish is to be well."

It was done. Lazaros pinched my arm as we went back into the house, his smile comically large. "Do you think we will run into brigands?" he whispered with excitement.

"I hope so," I joked, laughing softly so that my father wouldn't hear.

• • •

The next day, as Lazaros made preparations for our trip, my father summoned Yosseph to the house.

I had gone into town to the mikvah to be cleaned earlier and had done my hair modestly under a dark linen shawl. When Yosseph arrived, the two men secluded themselves to talk. I sat in the courtyard, baking bread over the dome I'd placed on the fire, happy the eight days of Pesach were over and I could go back to making ordinary flatbread. I had it down to an art. I could pour the mixture and peel it away so that the bread was just browned on the surface. My hands flew back and forth, settling into the rhythm, piling the finished rounds up in a basket to my left. Finally my father appeared in the doorway, his expression somber.

He must have watched me for a moment before speaking. Did he see my mother in the sureness of my hands? With my hair as a screen between my face and his, could he pretend that it was her touch that would shape his bread?

My bread, my body . . . the thought arrived unbidden in a voice not my own.

"Come, Miriam," my father said, interrupting my reverie. "Yosseph would speak to you."

Yosseph stepped into the hard sunlight. My father looked between us and smiled before retreating into the house, leaving us alone with the fig trees.

I stood up from the cooking fire. Crumbs of bread fell to the ground at my feet. Yosseph came to me, closer than I'd expected, immediately clasping my hands in his.

"Miriam . . . Miriam!" His voice was hoarse with feeling and his eyes were blurred with tears. "You are not to be controlled, are you?"

"I cannot stop these things, Yosseph." I tried to soften my voice. "I would give anything to be healed and betrothed to you already."

I tried hard to let his angular beauty, the goodness of his wide thin-lipped mouth, erase the burning eyes of the man I had encountered on the roof. *Here* was a real man! A man who would easily and quickly be mine to touch and taste. But the warmth of Yosseph's body and the fruity odor of his breath did nothing to stir my heart. I was water rushing forward to whatever lay ahead.

Still I leaned into him, putting my head to his chest. I could feel the light dance of his heart against my cheek, his desirous inhale as he clutched me. He smelled too clean, as if he did not sweat like other men.

"I will be back in a month's time and we will be betrothed in the height of summer," I said reassuringly. "Pray for me, Yosseph. It is not a long journey."

He touched the soft palm of his hand to my cheek and slowly, keeping his eyes fixed on mine, he leaned in and kissed the side of my mouth.

I pressed my lips tightly together, refusing to taste the heat of his desire.

"I will wait for you, Miriam. I will wait for as long as it takes."

What a fool I was. Now that I am old and slow, I know that the moments we hurry through the fastest are the ones most worthy of our attention.

Inside this memory, I now want to ignore my youthful impatience and linger on his brown eyes and the yellow flecks radiating from his irises . . . the sun glinting like flecked gold on his oiled curls . . . the emerald hanging from his ear bringing out the green thread in his embroidered vest. His skin—smooth and brown and unwrinkled.

It is funny that I think of him as being so much older than me! Remembering him, as he was that day, he seems a boy.

Yosseph, who is dead now. Yosseph, who I will never lay eyes on ever again.

And if I step outside of my younger self, I can see through the square window to my father standing in the darkness of the hall, worrying the fringe of his prayer shawl, a furrow burrowed deep as a wound between his eyes. Somewhere nearby my brother is negotiating with a merchant to get supplies for our journey. The long hair at the back of his neck sticks straight out and, as he speaks, he reaches up and pulls at it distractedly. Farther still, if I follow the wind through the tree trunks behind our home, I'll reach the calm, chill air that pools around the base of my mother's tomb. I will see Marta and her son in Amos's house just a few streets away.

If I pull back more, all of Bethany will be visible. The workers have paused in the fields for a drink of water. The sheep on the hills cleave so close that they appear as if clouds have come down to graze on the new grasses.

Now I see us—my brother and I—as small as insects, crossing the sand and slipping between the tall shadows of the palm trees, and I wonder how we did not notice those cold patches of air that often accompany a memory so terrible it has imprinted itself into the very land.

We were walking over the dried blood empires had left behind. The many massacres my people had endured. The road had not forgotten a pain so thick that it was an actual color. Yellow. Hanging in the air like poisonous dust. Anguish so heavy it had not dissipated many years later.

But I see it now, the overlap of time only possible in recollection: the ass walking us away from the only place we had ever known, the heaviness of the sky, the same inevitable pull of a story that is moving faster than its characters. From where I sit now, I finally understand.

We thought we were riding away from Yerusalem.

But we were really riding toward it.

PART TWO

The River

Nineteen

"We are free!" Lazaros declared, not once but four times that first day. We walked against a heavy flow of pilgrims on the route that led from Galilee into Yerusalem. Their faces were sun-darkened and the sour smell of exhaustion drifted up from their dusty clothes. They were desiccated by travel—and by the pain that had, perhaps, sent them on pilgrimage in the first place.

Some eyed us disdainfully. Our hands were soft! Our sandals were crisp and stiff and new. It was obvious that we had not traveled for days as they had. Why were we headed *away* from the temple?

But by late afternoon, as the sun stained the edges of the clouds a fleshy pink, the road narrowed and the pilgrims' songs of praise and piety died away behind us. In some places the road faded into the red dust of the landscape, washed out from the winter rains. We were headed into the wild.

"It's different from home," Lazaros noted, his hand running across the ass's coarse fur. The animal made a grunting noise to signal that she enjoyed his touch.

"Yes," I agreed happily. "It is very different."

There were no more vineyards or farmland or gardens. This was a barren, rocky land, enlivened only by short green shrubs and broom trees whose black trunks looked like old hands holding up the smoke of their leaves.

That night we slept on our cloaks under the open sky, curled close to each other, as we had when we were children.

"Tell me a story," Lazaros whispered as the stars pulsed above us.

"I don't remember any stories," I lied, watching the starlight twinkle in his black irises.

190

"You're lying!"

"No, I'm not," I insisted. "I'm too tired."

"Tell me about Orpheus. The musician prince. The one who followed his dead lover into the underworld."

I acquiesced, repeating the story that Yosseph had first recounted to me.

"Orpheus was huge. He had to have an enormous lyre fashioned for his big hands. But the music he played on that lyre was as beautiful and delicate as spiderwebs strung with morning dew. His music was like the dawn. But he was dark with tangled hair as black as night . . ." Before the story's tragic ending, Lazaros fell asleep, his faint snoring making me feel at home even in such a strange place.

The next night we stayed in a pilgrims inn. Our sandals were caked with limestone. With the hems of our tunics ragged and dusty and our cheeks brown with sun, we were beginning to fit in.

"Where should we find our accommodations?" Lazaros asked the fat man posted at the door who had cheerfully pocketed our money. He had a strangely childish face submerged in such girth. His rolling chins were hairless and his cheeks glowed rosy. His fat red fingers had squeezed each coin as if trying to extract juice from the metal.

"Accommodations!" he laughed, slapping his stomach with amusement. "Do you think yourself a king? You'll have the same accommodations as everyone else. The floor."

Lazaros blushed, his hands gripping his cloth pack so hard that his knuckles whitened. "Oh, I see . . ."

Inside, burping drunkards and heavily painted women passed around jars of wine and beer. Couples were dancing in the courtyard without any concern for decency. Musicians drummed and piped. I felt my face warming as I watched a handsome man with ebony skin pressing his lips against a woman's throat. She arched her back, pressing her ample breasts into his chest, throwing her arms around his neck. They flowed and danced, becoming one body, finally slipping out of view into the shadows.

Surely they would make love. They would sleep entwined, heads pressed so close that they dreamt one dream. Oh! I could feel their movements echoing in my own flesh.

"Come now, Miriam," urged Lazaros. "We must get some sleep before tomorrow."

We laid out our cloaks on the second floor of the building.

As we drifted off, Lazaros murmured, his voice slurred with fatigue, "I would love to dance . . . Maybe at the next inn."

"I would, too . . ." I agreed.

"Will there be dancing at your wedding?" He turned onto his side, gripping the skirt of my tunic as if to keep himself awake.

"If Yosseph allows it," I answered stiffly.

Lazaros mumbled something indecipherable before passing over into sleep, but I was restless and awake. At some point the fat innkeeper waddled up the stairs and meandered down the hallway, humming an oddly mournful song as he blew out the lamps.

"Don't vomit on my floor . . ." he whispered to a drunk man curled up near us, who was moaning about his stomach.

Then he was gone down the stairs, leaving us in darkness.

• • •

As we followed the road to Yericho the next day, the air became muggy: threads of humidity and heat blurred the horizon. We removed our shawls, tying them around our heads to soak up our sweat.

We stopped for bread and water at midday and I massaged Lazaros's feet and legs. He hadn't complained, but I noticed his ankles were red and swollen. But he rallied quickly enough. "We must keep going," he insisted. "We can get to Yericho by nightfall. I am sure of it."

I didn't protest, for we couldn't rest under the glare of the sun. And it would be cold out here at night. We had to find somewhere better to bed down. We would take the road into the valley I had heard called the Wadi Qelt, or "Valley of Darkness."

It ran along a rift in a series of hills that swelled up out of the desert. As we descended, I thought that the rock of those hills seemed almost alive. They were fleshy heaps of matter that sucked up all sunlight so that, unless we looked directly up at the circle of the sun above us, it was dark as night. Did I imagine the squeeze and release of those hills we walked between?

"I think the land is breathing," Lazaros said, apparently noticing as well. It was hot in the valley, and I had tied up my skirt so that fresh air could reach the skin of my legs. It felt good to walk.

We emerged back into sunlight as the final rays of the day turned the oasis of Yericho into a flame. From the rooftops of a hundred houses came blue lines of smoke rising straight up to the heavens like fine silk on a freshly threaded loom.

Huge, baked, sandy voids surrounded the city. Did God love deserts? What purpose did they serve? Why did he clear the trees and flowers and greenery away? Was it good, sometimes, to leave space for something? A whole landscape of space? Or did that emptiness leave room for something else to take root? Something not necessarily holy. Not necessarily good.

"So this is the center of debauchery!" Lazaros exclaimed as we made our way down into Yericho. "I think it's very impressive. And look, there's Herod's palace!"

I remembered Yosseph describing it to me. "A city of sweetness!" he'd called it. "The date palms make for the best cakes I have ever tasted. You should learn to make them, Miriam . . ."

"It's an abomination," I shot back at Lazaros. "It is Herod's city, and Herod is for the Romans. Do you sympathize with Rome, Brother?"

Lazaros reached down and slapped me lightly on the shoulder. "Calm yourself, Miriam. You must admit it is beautiful to behold."

Merchants pushed past us, leading camels heavy with chests, jars, satchels, and rolled up rugs. A few soldiers sauntered by on horses, eyeing us suspiciously.

What I knew of Herod I had gleaned from Yosseph's stories. He had fallen in love with his own brother's wife and stolen Herodias away from him! When I had heard the story I had smiled inwardly, thinking that Yosseph was naïve and that all the men listening around me were naive. Perhaps Herodias had wanted to be stolen. Perhaps she had escaped.

The palace was out of place in this land. It seemed to me that it sprawled uneasily on top of the natural swells of the desert. Pillars sprouted up like dead trees, stripped naked of bark, holding up roofs so high that six or seven men could stand on each other's shoulders without reaching the ceiling. Cities. I wanted nothing to do with them. With their filth . . . their crowds, like flies on a dead carcass, feeding on death, exchanging sorrow and excrement and stagnant breath.

But the aqueducts fascinated Lazaros and, as I negotiated replenishing our food supplies in the huge marketplace, he insisted on having a long conversation with the vendor about the mechanics of the system.

"Come on," I nagged, feeling like the younger sibling. "I am tired, Lazaros."

He looked genuinely angry when I forced him to keep moving.

"Why are you in such a rush? Isn't this why you wanted to travel? To see the sights? To come back with stories?"

No, I wanted to say. *I came to put my feet in the river. But I do not know why.*

By the time we reached the next inn, I felt exhausted by the barrage of colors and peoples, sounds, and smells. We put the ass in the stable and paid for the night, and Lazaros suggested we cook our vegetables for supper.

To my relief, the inner courtyard of this inn was different from the last. There was no music. No one danced. I was happy to see several quiet groups sharing food and wine around their own fires. I let Lazaros lead the way as I looked through the dusk light at the people's faces.

My feet tingled. Some wind was blowing through me that would not stop until I had *arrived.* We were close.

A group of young women barely older than the babes in their arms stared at me. I knew that when they looked at me—nineteen years old, uncovered hair, unwed, and slender-hipped as a youth—they were confused. How could someone so old still be without a child?

"Here?" Lazaros asked, pointing at a circle made up entirely of men at the farthest corner of the courtyard.

"Yes. There. That's fine." I breathed a sigh of relief.

Why am I afraid of other women? I wondered. *Why do I always go to sit with the men who I know will not respect me?*

They were having an animated discussion. Lazaros held up our last skin of wine and asked confidently, "Might I offer you men some wine in exchange for a share of your fire and company?"

They were welcoming, and when I stepped up beside Lazaros and sat down beside him, their smiles widened even more.

"And who are you, lovely lady? Is this your wife?" The question was addressed to Lazaros by a thin man with a square jaw. He was bald but with an impressively full beard.

Lazaros chuckled, blushing slightly as he opened up the wineskin and passed it to the man on his other side. "No. This is not my wife. This is my sister, Miriam."

"Ah! So such loveliness is yet unclaimed," the bald man continued, arching an eyebrow and pulling on his beard.

"I have no need of claiming," I declared boldly. "I claim myself."

"She is to be betrothed to a wealthy merchant from Yerusalem," Lazaros added quickly, putting a hand on my shoulder to calm me.

"But she is not *yet* betrothed," suggested the bald man with a knowing leer.

"That is enough, Chislon!" came a reprimand from behind Lazaros. "Have you no respect for a woman?"

This man was small and compact, the hair of his beard and head dense with curls. He had a heavy brow that was ill matched with his small, weak chin. But his dark eyes were kind. He took a swig of the wine and addressed my brother and me in a loud voice. "Pay no mind to Chislon. He is always rude when he is drunk. Perhaps we will not allow him to sample your wine. What brings you to Yericho?"

Lazaros hesitated, looking to me for an answer. I shrugged. I didn't care what he said. These men were strangers.

"My sister is ill," he began, the lie constricting his throat. "We are seeking purification and a cure from a man by the name of Yochanan. Have you heard of him?"

The squat man's face broke into a large smile. "Of course I have heard of him! I am a *talmid* of Yochanan. Call me Andreas. I am just returning to his camp after celebrating Pesach with my family in K'far Nahum."

An older man joined in. "You say you are student of Yochanan's? I would not voice that widely. Last I heard, he had greatly displeased Herod."

"Why is that?" I asked, turning to Andreas.

Andreas shook his head and frowned deeply, his chin practically disappearing underneath his big, expressive lips. "The Herods of this world will always be afraid of men like Yochanan."

"He has publicly condemned Herod for marrying his brother's wife," the man across the fire explained. "And as I've heard it, Herod already thought him a troublemaker before Yochanan personally insulted him."

"Does it not say in Malachi that God would send us the prophet Elishah again before the coming of the great and terrible day of the Lord?" announced a clean-shaven man.

"He does not say he is Elishah," Andreas answered, but he was smiling as if he disbelieved himself. "He is humble."

Lazaros was intrigued. "So there is more to him than his immersions? I had thought him simply a man of deeds."

"There is *much* more. If you are a pilgrim seeking purification, he will offer his teachings of repentance. But if you choose to stay and keep learning, as I did, then he will teach you the contemplation of the *Merkabah*." Andreas gestured as if pulling apart the very air to set stage for some revelation.

"And as I looked, a stormy wind came out of the north: a great cloud with brightness around it and fire flashing forth continually, and in the middle of the fire, something like gleaming amber," I said, quoting Ezekiel. The words were like a fire that burned my lips. "And in the middle of it was something like four living creatures. This was their appearance: they were of human form. Each had four faces, and each of them had four wings. Their legs were straight, and the soles of their feet were like the sole of a calf's foot; and they sparkled like burnished bronze."

The room became silent. Andreas was stunned. "It is surprising to hear scripture from the lips of a woman. Not even I know Ezekiel's visions by heart. Where did you come by such knowledge?"

"But is it not dangerous to contemplate the chariot?" I answered his question with one of my own. "I have heard that only the most skilled rabbis are capable of teaching and practicing the Merkabah."

"Yochanan is as skilled as any rabbi I have ever met, if not more so," Andreas said defensively, crossing his arms across his chest.

"Forgive my sister," Lazaros interjected, fishing some date pastries from our satchel. "Share our food with us and tell me how we may find Yochanan? We have heard that he has several camps along the Yarden River."

Something sparked in Andreas's eyes. His spirit radiated wonder and openness. Someone at the river had set him on fire.

I want that! I thought jealously.

"I, too, was doubtful of Yochanan," he replied, addressing me now instead of Lazaros. "But now I am all faith. All wonder. You will see soon enough. If you wake early with me tomorrow, I can take you to his camp. I am headed there myself. It is only a day's walk from here."

"Is it worth seeing him?" Lazaros asked in a manner that was perhaps a little too inquisitive.

Andreas's eyes flashed dangerously. "Would you have gone to Moshe had you lived in his time? Would you have sought healing from Elishah? Would you answer God's call?"

Lazaros was speechless. But I knew my answer. Yes. I would answer this call. Whether from God or not, I did not know, but I would follow it to the river.

Twenty

I slept heavily that night and awoke feeling there was something I was just on the edge of remembering. But by the time the sun had risen and we had made our way out of the city, the feeling had subsided.

Andreas was friendly, patting the donkey on the rump and joking that we would dine well that night. "We'll eat the ass! The wild men of the river love roasted donkey."

Lazaros laughed louder than was necessary, his eyes sparkling with a sense of adventure.

As we walked, Andreas told stories of his large family back in K'far Nahum. "If you think me a loud man, imagine a family of thirty or so sharing a meal together. It has been said that when we gather, we can be heard on the far shores of the Gennesaret Sea. The worst is when my brother Shimon and I are out fishing in our boat. I think sometimes our laughter frightens the fish away!"

"You are a fisherman?" Lazaros asked, enthralled by this turn in the conversation. "What is it like to go to sea? Do you ever get ill from the waves?"

"Ill from the waves?" Andreas roared, slapping his thick thigh. "I am happier on water than I am on land. You see how flat-footed I am?"

As we entered the wooded valley near the river, a cool wind breathed through the trees. Vines twined around tree trunks and delicate flowers nodded their heads as we passed. Pink petals. White petals. Golden pollen. Our path was decorated with riches that would rot by tomorrow morning, turning into something richer than an ephemeral bloom: dark, black, fertile. River dirt.

Andreas pulled purple fruit out of a bramble bush. "We are all wealthy in the forest. We never need worry about buying food. Food is everywhere!"

I took a bite of the fruit, which was surprisingly tart.

"She likes it!" Andreas winked at me and I couldn't help but give him a slow smile.

"I do. What else can I eat?"

"The entire forest," he joked. But as he pointed out various flowers, crisp leaves, and berries, I saw that it was true. I remembered Kemat stepping carefully through the olive groves near Bethany, teaching me which plants provided nourishment and which were medicine.

We drew closer to the river, and the balsam, oak, and pistachio trees gave way to tamarisk, date trees, and willows.

Clean me of the city, I prayed, not just to God but to the land itself.

Lazaros whispered once, "Where are we?" But Andreas never seemed lost, even though there was no path for us to follow. From time to time he would put a hand to a tree and lift his nose as if he were scenting our way. Another time he pinched a branch and licked his finger.

We pushed through greenery so dense and undisturbed that I wondered if it had ever been entered. We were in a womb of green. The sky, barely visible through breaks in the branches and foliage, took on a deep, mossy shade. And the world *smelled* green, too. Even the flowers carried a muscular, earthy smell inside of their perfumes. I was dizzied by the scent, the pressure of so many beings, so many flowers and trees and birds, the radiance of the yellow *karkoms* dotting the ground. The red date trees held out their tight little fruits on thin arms.

I could feel the donkey stepping more carefully now. She was smart enough to know what this land required. Each press of her hoof was a form of bodily reverence, an acknowledgement of the tender soil below her.

The river announced itself first as a sound. Indecipherable. Inhuman. The voice of water white with turmoil.

At last we came to the rocky shore. The donkey trembled slightly, flicking her tail as she navigated the irregular stones. As we walked, the river widened. Its waters grew heavy and calm, turning from white to a deep, ponderous blue. Up ahead rose plumes of gray smoke.

Rounding the river's meander, the camp became visible: the shore was wide and sandy and dotted with people. Small makeshift huts dotted the forest's edge. A large crowd was amassed on the banks while many more people were standing in the water. Some were finely dressed. Others wore threadbare shifts and seemed at home in the encampment.

"You are in luck!" said Andreas. "He is giving immersions today."

Some of the men and women were completely naked.

"Oh!" I exclaimed, as blood flooded my cheeks.

Full-grown men stood in the shallows, their strong, muscled backs visible, hair snaking up their lean legs. Women splashed about in water-soaked shifts, their dark nipples showing through the sheer fabric. Fat men with pregnant bellies sat cross-legged on the shore.

There was something at once lovely and foolish about their nudity. I had only ever seen small children naked. I was struck by the long, taut muscles of these people's thighs and the dark tangle of hair at their groins from which their male members emerged. I was shocked. Delighted. Embarrassed.

Andreas was scratching the tight curls on his head. "You are scandalized."

Was he sympathetic, or did my embarrassment give him pleasure? I couldn't tell from his expression. I slipped off the donkey, immediately bending down to pull off my sandals. I stepped into the water-softened soil. "I am ready," I responded confidently, squaring my shoulders. "Lead me."

We set off toward the large group waiting at the river's edge while Lazaros tended to the donkey.

Some men eyed me intensely although their scrutiny didn't feel like lust. They were wondering what sin or sickness made me step into the river. Why had I come to Yochanan for immersion?

An old woman with painfully swollen joints caught me staring and smiled widely. What a beautiful thing it was to wear down your teeth with good bread and good love. What soft, breakable, difficult creatures we all were! And without our clothes on it became clear we were all the same. Naked as babes in the river. I returned her smile.

In my mind's eye I saw Moshe in the rushes of the river. Egyptian prince or Jew? Nobody knew. In the river, did it matter?

A voice boomed from the middle of the water. "Come! Repent! Let the water cleanse you!"

The huge voice was emanating from a small man. The water was almost up to his chest. He could have been forty or four hundred years old, so dark was he with the sun and weather that he appeared shrunken like a dried fig. I watched, fascinated, as he dipped his hands into the water and brought them back up, cupping water over a man's head. "Repent! Immerse for the release of your sins and be purified!"

"Do you see him?" Andreas asked, pointing. "That is Yochanan."

There were other men practicing the same ritual. They were dressed like Yochanan, in simple flaxen tunics.

An uncomfortable buzzing rose in my breast, as if my heart were vibrating, and I felt a painful pressure between my eyes. Once I stepped into the river, I would never be the same again. I felt sure of it.

I hadn't come for a cure. I didn't need healing. Still, I knew I would be transformed.

"You came all this way to be cleansed by the living water," said Andreas kindly. "Why wait to immerse? Go now and change your life."

Change my life.

I unwound the shawl from around my shoulders and, pulling off my outer tunic, I stepped into the river.

"Ah!" The cry turned into a sigh. The water was much colder than I had expected. But after a long, hot day of travel, the temperature was a relief, and I eased in more quickly, relaxing as the chill traveled up my spine.

"Come!" A young man with girlish curls beckoned. "Receive the immersion."

He reached out his hand and I took it, surprised. There was no modesty here. No decorum. I could take a man's hand. No one would think less of me.

He smiled, leading me into the deeper water.

Watching a pair of older women washing their hands, I followed suit. I scrubbed the dried sand from the cracks in my palms and scraped the dirt from under my nails. The sun was invisible behind the trees now, but I could still feel its warmth on my face. The current pressed against my spine, massaging the sore muscles of my calves.

As I waded further into the river to take my turn, Yochanan fixed me with eyes so light they appeared almost yellow in the midst of his leathery face.

"Are you ready?" he asked. "Do you want to be clean?"

"Go on!" The woman behind me pushed my shoulders lightly. "Have no fear!".

I bent my head, struggling to speak, feeling like I might faint.

Yochanan's voice thundered in my ears as he opened his hands over my head. "Repent!"

Tears of river water ran down my face. I spluttered, stepping aside as another person took my place. I was in the river. And I was still Miriam.

A peal of laughter sounded from the shore. I startled, splashing water. Andreas was embracing another man in greeting: a big man with long athletic legs. The hands that thumped Andreas's back were covered in black hair. His flaxen tunic was rolled down to his waist, exposing the bare sunburned skin of his back. His tangled black hair obscured his face.

He threw back his head to laugh again, pulling away from Andreas—and he saw me. He grinned, and it transformed a face made for brooding into something beautiful.

It was the man from the rooftop.

I could not breathe. There was a rushing noise in my ears that was more powerful than the river's voice. It thrummed inside my head. Perhaps it was the sound of my own blood.

It was certainly him. He had the same crooked nose. The same square, cleft chin. The smile did not leave his face. Instead, it deepened, revealing a dimple in his left cheek.

What will I say to him? What shall I do?

The water moved around me, through me, and at last I found myself able to lift my feet from the pebbled bottom to step back to the shore. But as I neared the sand, the man broke my gaze, squeezed Andreas's arm, and strode off into the trees.

"Miriam!" Lazaros was sopping wet, his black curls plastered to his forehead. "Miriam! I was immersed!"

He threw his arms around me, guiding me back to Andreas.

"So! How do you feel?" Andreas drew both of us into an embrace, the bristles of his curly beard cutting through my wet shift.

"Andreas. Who was that? The man you were just speaking with?"

Andreas glanced behind him. "That's Yeshua. We must join his followers for a meal later tonight. He's the camp's best storyteller."

• • •

Andreas introduced us to his friend Thoma, a sallow-faced youth with the receding hairline of a much older man. Thoma smiled easily, though, and was as excited as Lazaros. The two were immediately like brothers.

"Any friend of Andreas is a friend of mine! And I'd love friends in Yerusalem. Can I stay with you when I come for Pesach next year?" Thoma wanted to know.

"Of course!" Lazaros was blushing. "And you will come to our meals. Miriam is a wonderful cook."

We sat on the shore, letting the last rays of sun dry our shifts clear of the river water. Andreas kept waving people over to introduce us.

"Andreas, I tell you, things are changing," said a short bald man sitting down with us. "Increasingly, people arrive with news of Herod's wrath. The mood has changed in your absence. I'm feeling that we may need to move soon." He spoke loudly, insistently, in a voice raspy with woodsmoke. He ignored my presence.

"Calm now, Yoses. Will you let a man relax and eat before you launch into your worry? Always you are worrying!"

"Ignore my brother," said the handsome man who was with him. "He is hungry. And his hunger makes him worry. We must get some wine in him!"

"Yeshua said we must stay to listen to Yochanan tonight," Yoses said, his voice quieter, almost conspiratorial. "He says we must not disrespect Yochanan by avoiding his teaching altogether."

I wanted to learn more about the man called Yeshua, but I was overwhelmed as more and more people were joining us.

A foreign woman with blue eyes and yellow hair knelt down beside me. She took my hands in hers and I was surprised that there was no heat in them. They could have been the wind-chilled leaves of a tree. She introduced herself as Salome. "It is a pleasure," she said, smiling. "I spent some time in Bethany a long time ago. I much prefer the town to the city nearby. I like the trees. The gardens . . ."

Andreas chuckled, and Salome's eyes flashed with anger, her bloodless lips flattening into a line. There was some undertone to the interaction that I did not yet understand. I wanted to know all of the relationships threading these people together at the river.

"You will join our meal?" Salome asked us as she straightened up to her full height. She was impressively tall.

"Yes, yes . . ." Andreas promised her.

Slowly people dispersed. We watched as two young girls played in the shallows, darting their hands in and out the water, trying to catch fish. A plump woman walked to the shore, calling out for them. Her voice mixed with the river's babble, the evening birdsong, and the children's laughter.

"To think that people live like this!" Lazaros whispered to me.

"Yes," I replied, laughing. "And we didn't know. We thought you must grind the grain and go to synagogue always. And clean the house."

"We didn't even need a house," Lazaros exclaimed. "Or any money. We could have just gone into the forest and lived on berries and leaves."

"The Romans have no dominion over the wild . . ." I whispered to myself, not totally sure what I was saying.

An unfamiliar bird made a whooping cry somewhere in the forest to signal the end of day. Dusk descended, rendering the divide between sky and trees, river and shore, ambiguous. Eventually everyone, in and out of the water, moved through a blue landscape. The children who remained in the shallows appeared to float in a realm without edges or texture, made invisible up to their waists by the water. As I watched, another mother came to collect them.

"You could watch forever," Thoma said, leaning back on his elbows beside us and looking down into the river. "New people come every day. Some are very rich and come from far away. A man from the east came last week with a pouch full of the most beautiful salt I have ever seen. Pink as a babe. And you know what he did? He threw it in the river! Disgraceful . . ."

When the first stars appeared, Yochanan finally finished his immersions and came back into the encampment.

"It is time," Yoses announced, rubbing the top of his bald head nervously. "You must come and sit with Yochanan, Andreas. You must show your respect."

"All right! All right!" Andreas grumbled, getting up and brushing the dirt from his bowed legs. "Come all. It is time to *receive*."

I looked at the men's faces, which expressed more than their words. Yoses's eyes narrowed perceptibly as Andreas joined him, as if to say,

"Let us keep this quiet and not make a show." Was I imagining an almost dangerous undertone to the conversation? Why was Andreas so ambivalent about the teacher he had been so excited about just the night before? What was I missing?

Andreas and Thoma led us to a huge willow where Yochanan was settling himself on a blanket next to a small fire. I saw that no women were present in the group. They had gone to the far edge of the camp, and I could hear their laughter as they cooked and prepared food for everyone. It didn't take long for me to realize that no matter how free with each other everyone had been at the river, the men and women had now fallen back into their usual roles.

"Should I be here?" I asked nervously. Andreas shrugged noncommittally.

Lazaros pulled me down next to him, letting me know that I could not abandon him.

Yochanan fixed his eyes on me. His voice, when he spoke, was no longer loud. It whistled like a reed riddled with holes. "I will speak of things unfit for a woman. I will speak of mysteries. I will speak to the men who will continue my teachings."

Even here I was not allowed at the table. "Worry not," I said, rising abruptly. "I will not pollute your group with the impurities of my sex."

As I walked away, Yochanan began to speak again. Lower, secretly. His Mishnah: the teachings that neither I nor any woman would ever receive.

I wandered down to the river, thankful for the darkness.

"What are you doing, love?" The voice was both delicate and sharp and belonged to a pretty girl, almost the same age as me. Her mouth was heart-shaped and a babe at her breast was fussing with her tunic, trying to find a way to her nipple.

"Come. Do you want food? You must be hungry."

She headed toward the women and I followed after. What else was there to do? I did not want to sit among dirty bowls and crying children. She placed her babe on the ground, putting a hand on his back to see that he was balanced and could walk. "Go, Gera, and find your sister," she commanded, pointing at some children playing at the forest's edge. She picked up a basket of freshly baked bread and I breathed in the hearty smell of the browned crust.

"Follow me," she said, slipping her free arm through mine. "You looked lost. Yochanan does that to women. He would rather they disappear at night."

"Why is that?" I asked, already knowing the answer. It was that way for all men. Women were for the cooking of meals and the bearing of children. And they should disappear when they were not useful.

But the girl's response surprised me. "Well, I think it is because he will not lie with a woman. God knows why. I think he was married many years ago but his wife died of a flux . . . Perhaps he resents that the other men will go and lie with their women tonight."

I blushed. I had rarely heard a woman speak so candidly!

"What is your name?" I asked, enchanted.

"Adah." She squeezed my elbow as if to press the name into my skin. "My husband, Philip, brought us to follow Yochanan two years ago."

"And you are a follower of Yochanan, too?" I asked as she led me into an impenetrable night of twisted trunks and branches. She seemed to know the way.

"Well . . ." she bit her lip, clearly reluctant to explain herself. "Philip would be angry to hear me say it. But I prefer the stories of Yeshua to the teachings of Yochanan."

"Yeshua?" I couldn't help myself. His name buzzed like the tang of citrus on my tongue.

"Yes. That's where we're going now."

The ground was so densely covered with moss that it silenced the sound of our footsteps. But I could hear *something*. Somewhere in the darkness, people were singing.

Led by the red glow of a fire, we pushed through the tamarisks into a clearing. *Here* were all the women! And the old men. Children flashed by with honey-slick faces. I could smell burning sugar. I watched as a woman flicked a sweet date pit into the flames.

Women were dancing around the fire. Young boys were singing, their voices unbroken and gentle. People lay with their heads in each other's laps. A couple on the far end of the clearing were embracing; their faces blurred together as they kissed. Men and women sat side by side. Salome, the woman I had met earlier, was listening to a skinny man who ate while he talked.

Was it a dream? Had I fallen asleep down by the river?

Adah pulled me into the warmth of the fires. "Let's sit and eat. And you can tell me a little about yourself. Andreas said you come all the way from Bethany . . ."

A man reached up to pinch Adah's rump. "Oh, good. You brought more bread."

"You'll only have it if you behave," she scolded, ruffling his wiry hair. "Miriam. This is my husband, Philip."

"Oh! Yes!' he exclaimed. He pulled Adah down into his lap now, reaching into her basket. "I've heard of you! Andreas brought you and your brother. And you are seeking an exorcism or some kind of healing?"

"Yes. We are from Bethany and have traveled from there," I replied, blushing. I settled down with my legs underneath me, straightening my tunic. Such questions made me nervous.

But at that moment Lazaros appeared. "Miriam! I've brought wine!" He winked at me. "I couldn't stand such boring blather. That is why I left Bethany. Andreas is coming, too. And Thoma."

"Wine?" I asked in confusion, remembering something Andreas had told us on our earlier journey. "I thought Yochanan's talmids followed his ascetic strictures. Doesn't he teach that one should abstain?"

"Well, you're a nosy one, aren't you?" Philip exclaimed, peering at me around Adah's shoulder. "What do you know about Yochanan?"

"I know that he barely eats," I responded eagerly. "And that he does not drink. But you do?"

"I don't deny myself pleasure." Philip pinched his wife's wide hips and she giggled. "Not wine, not food, not women . . ."

"And yet you are his student," I observed. "How will you learn with your mind clouded by such things?"

"I'd be careful, Philip," Andreas interjected. "This woman is a better scholar than any Pharisee I've ever met. She was speaking of the chariot last night with ease . . ."

Philip had a tuft of gray beard at his chin and I wondered how much older he was than his radiant wife. He stroked his whiskers, smiling good-naturedly. "It is true that Yochanan follows strictures that make the Essenes look flexible. But he does not require that his talmids abide by these rules as obediently as he does." He shot a look at Andreas. "And anyway, I'm not sure I would call myself a student of Yochanan's these days . . ."

Andreas shook his head in reprimand. "*He* would not like to hear you say such things. There is peace between them now." Andreas turned to me, clearly changing the subject. "I was raised in Bethsaida. But my brother and I moved to K'far Nahum to take over my mother's family's residence. My father died young and did not leave us any land."

Salome had tucked her pale hair behind her ears. She was leaning in to speak to a young couple, both dressed in fine blue silk with large rings flashing on their fingers. Wealthy Yerusalem Jews like my brother and me, they stood out among the sun-darkened Galileans. Most of my company seemed to come from around the Genasseret Sea. Across from us sat a woman as black as the new moon sky. She was laughing so heartily that her breasts shook visibly under the thin cloth of her shift.

I would like to be her, I thought. *So at ease! So at home in her body!*

Startled, I realized that some of the women might be prostitutes, particularly those who sat without a brother or husband or chaperone and carried their own money pouch. And something in them seemed hardened against the world. The paint on their faces did little to disguise the pain in their eyes. Yet when they looked at me it was with such a direct, unflinching gaze that it left me breathless. Hardship had honed them, making them strong.

The children were playing a game in the dusk that involved running around in circles and hopping over each other. One was riding on the shoulders of a man who was imitating a beast of burden, his knuckles pressed into the dirt like hooves. The child held fast to the man's black hair, directing him through the throng of small boys and girls. Another child, a little girl, climbed onto this man's back as well. He pretended to buck her off and then laughed—a joyful, almost deranged sound. In seconds, the other children had all swarmed around him and the man sank to the ground, pretending to be besieged. He rolled onto his back and put up his hands playfully, crying out, "I yield! I yield! I beseech you to have mercy on me!"

His face became visible as he shook out his long hair. This madman, his tunic covered in dirt, playing like an animal with the children, was Yeshua.

Oh, Leukas! You don't believe me? You would have him arrive, solemn in clean white robes, sitting at the fire and explaining matters of the spirit? Is it hard for you to hear your savior called a madman? Let me assure you. He *was* mad. Irresistibly mad.

How can I describe for you the man who everyone believes they already know? You are no better, Leukas. You who have said his name with the intimacy of a lover! And yet you never met him. Never touched his clumsy, calloused hands. Never heard his laughter. That was no holy music, I can assure you. It was thunder echoing off slabs of rock.

Over the years so many have tried to describe him. Even to me they would tell of his magnificence! What can I tell you that you do not think you already know? You would rather see him as you do in your mind—thin, sad, and already cleansed of the dirt of this world.

Yeshua had the muscular body of a big Galilean farmer—a man who had worked in the fields with his brothers and helped his father carry heavy beams on his shoulders across town. He had a badly healed broken nose, flattened at the ridge, which gave him the appearance of a lion. His eyes were too big for his face.

His body commanded attention, even when it was relaxed or asleep. And yet there was something comical about him as well. Was it the ears that stuck out a little? His huge, hairy hands? He was too big, too loud, too much. It was what the children loved about him.

Yeshua threw back his head and roared. He bounced into a crouch, planting his hands on his thighs, grinning down at a young girl who had come to join the game. "You have won me as your steed, mistress!" he declared, and bowed his head to her. He let the child tug on his hair and lead him forward again, back into his role as their lion.

I swallowed, raising my hand to the pulse in my neck. My blood was giddy.

Were some of these his children? He was still young. But not so young that he would be unmarried. I looked around, a sour taste flooding my mouth. There were plenty of women with golden skin and plump arms cradling babies in their laps. Adah's words returned to me: "The men will go and lie with the women tonight . . ."

I blushed, turning my attention back to the group around me. Andreas and Philip were shaking their heads.

"He's drunk," Andreas observed.

Philip shook his head, smiling. "No. I assure you he is not. Ever since he got back from Yerusalem, he's been denying himself. He's back to his old ways, abstaining from all good things. He wouldn't even touch the lamb some women brought with them last night!"

"No longer a glutton? I don't believe it." Andreas's eyes crinkled with affection. I could see from the way he watched Yeshua that he loved the man. "Have you tried tempting him?"

Salome spoke seriously, changing the mood. "No. Philip tells the truth. Yeshua himself said that he received a dream while he was in Yerusalem for Pesach. That he should live simply again."

So he *had* been in Bethany.

"And how does your sister come by her formidable knowledge of scripture?" Andreas asked Lazaros. "How does she know about the chariot?"

"My father is a member of the Sanhedrin . . ." Lazaros declared proudly. His hair had dried in disordered curls that framed his angular face, his pointy chin. It suited him.

I shuddered. Pharisees were not looked upon kindly outside of Yerusalem. They were seen as squabbling pointlessly over rules and scriptural debates and despised as puppets of the Romans. Yosseph had told me as much: "The Northerners believe we concern ourselves with petty things while outside the city people are starving." The complaint did not seem completely unfounded. And yet I saw the effort with which my father tried desperately to keep our faith alive under the weight of Roman violence and surveillance.

Philip and Andreas exchanged knowing looks as Lazaros continued. "And once Father believed Miriam to be unmarriageable, he decided to give her a proper education."

"Unmarriageable?" Adah was perplexed. She eased off Philip's lap, turning to me.

"I have suffered spells," I said dryly, trying to suppress a smile. It felt silly to say it, especially when I no longer believed it myself. Better that I should say that I was *blessed* with spells! Blessed with a mysterious power that had saved my own sister's life!

"And she seeks a cure," Andreas explained to the group.

I nodded. "Although I was cured of my spells for several years, they have recently returned."

"She is to be betrothed when we return," Lazaros added, his cheeks flushed with what he knew to be a lie. "But first she must be made whole!"

"Yeshua is a skilled healer . . ." Philip said thoughtfully, reaching over to help himself to a sweet. "Yeshua has performed exorcisms successfully in the past. But I think he prefers not to make a show of it . . . ."

"Ask Yeshua at the end of the night," Thoma advised, "when there are fewer people around. He might do it then."

I felt a precipitous feeling, as if I stood at the edge of a cliff.

The man himself, covered in dirt and grass, emerged from the forest and sat down between Andreas and Thoma. He reached up and pulled a twig out of his hair. His mouth twitched, a dimple appearing in his cheek. "My friend! Have you received wine and food?" he said to Lazaros.

"Yeshua is trying to play the caring host!" joked Philip, reaching across Thoma's lap and squeezing his knee.

Yeshua's eyes twinkled merrily. "I guess I should trust you two to get a man drunk."

Lazaros lifted our wineskin, which had finally come back round to him. "I have brought wine all the way from Yericho."

"A good man!" Yeshua's voice thundered once again. How could he be so loud? But I liked his loudness. It was so very different from the mannered, self-aware voices of my father's students.

"And yet you will take none of it!" teased Andreas, poking his friend's arm. "You've become dull in my absence. No wine for Yeshua! I can't keep up with your constant changes."

"Yes, I am refusing wine," Yeshua admitted with good humor. "But only so there is more for you and for our guests. I could drink three whole jars and just be getting started. I'm really doing you all a favor."

"Ah!" Thoma laughed boyishly, his cheeks already flushed. He reminded me of Lazaros more and more. "I remember the time at the last harvest . . ."

But Yeshua playfully put his finger up to Thomas's pale lips. "Don't embarrass me in front of strangers. I'd like that honor myself!"

"I'll happily drink your share." Philip took a deep swig before passing the wineskin behind him. "But Yeshua, how will you be merry enough to tell us a story?"

"He is a foolish drunk," Adah confided in a whisper. "God help us. I will not let him bed with me tonight."

I almost cried out at the audacity. But I giggled instead. And

Yeshua, hearing the noise, looked over to me. "And you. Will you have some wine?" he asked, noting that I had not taken any.

"I've had wine enough," I responded playfully. "I think I'd prefer river water. If it makes you all act as wild as you do, then I think it must be stronger than the grape."

"Ah! A wit *and* a scholar!" Andreas guffawed, thumping his leg. "Yeshua! She is a sharp one!"

Yeshua smiled, gently, mischievously. A stray curl had fallen into his face and he would have looked like a boy had it not been for his beard.

Salome was sitting very straight, her thin hands folded in her lap. "Yeshua. Will you tell us a story tonight? Will you teach us?"

"He's sober!" Thoma slurred. "How will he tell a story?" He'd thrown an arm around my brother's shoulders. Lazaros grinned at the intimacy and pulled his new friend closer.

Yeshua laughed heartily, "I'm offended, Thoma! Must I be drunk to tell a story?" He stretched his long arms above his head then, as if preparing for a physical task rather than the telling of a tale. He squared his broad shoulders, straightened out his spine. I could almost see a cord of energy running up through him, coiling in his throat.

A hush fell over the group. Adah pinched Philip as he went to drink from the wineskin again. He groaned as she shook her head, but complied, setting it down.

Above us silver specks of insects slowed their flight, hovering in the air like suspended starlight. The blue shimmer of a fly floated effortlessly above Yeshua's head, crowning him.

"Listen closely, then," he announced in a mock whisper. Everyone inclined their heads toward him. "Listen closely, as little children would listen . . ." He was making fun of us. I could tell.

The handsome Yohan Ben-Zebedee had joined us, leaning at such an odd angle that his whole face screwed up in concentration, and all it would take to topple him over would be a *whack* on the head from Yeshua.

"You fools!" Yeshua scoffed. "Do you think I'm going to speak to you secretly? That wouldn't be fair!"

Lazaros laughed with surprise, looking over to me and saying with his wide bright eyes, *What a strange man! Isn't he wonderful?*

Yeshua shouted over our heads, "Everyone! Everyone! Do you want to hear a story?"

"Tell us the one about the farmer?" pleaded a young girl with freckles across her wide face.

"I just told that one, Mari," he said more quietly. "But I'll tell it again to you tomorrow."

Some men who had been dancing paused to listen. Yoses, Yohan's bald, outspoken brother, turned away from the dark-skinned beauty I had been admiring earlier, drawing closer to Yeshua. The mothers gathered their children onto their laps, offering them leftover sweets to keep them quiet. From the distant edge of the camp someone yelled, "Tell us a story, Yeshua!"

"I will, but stop me if it's bad!" he called back over the sea of heads that were all turning to face him. "Have you heard the story of the man with two sons?"

Some shook their heads, but no one spoke. A wind rose, twisting the branches above our heads, releasing the sharp, peppery smell of the woods. The waxing moon stood paused above us, as if deciding whether to expand into her fullness. The starlight seemed to draw closer as the night contracted around us, darkness pressing against our skin.

An owl floated down noiselessly onto a low branch. I wondered if anyone else had seen the great bird. I doubted it, for everyone's eyes were on Yeshua. A hush fell as the invisible breath of those beings we forgot to acknowledge stilled: the snails, the frogs, the snakes, the vines, the green buds, and the river itself were all listening.

He began to speak slowly: "There was once a father who had two sons . . ."

His eyes caught mine for a moment. His voice was smooth. Practiced.

Oh! He's showing off! I thought and shivered. Was he showing off for *me?*

His Galilean accent was not as strong as Andreas's or Philip's, but it still made certain words seem heavier. He spoke as if he were relaying the latest gossip told to him by a neighbor the day before.

He is handsome, I thought nervously. He was not well-groomed. He was coarse and big, but also more striking than Yosseph.

And he was very tall. Yeshua always seemed a little uncomfortable in his height. It was as if he never had enough room to fully stretch his legs. He inhabited closed spaces—rooms, houses, courtyards—with the same explosive energy as a caged animal. *It looks like he might jump up at any moment,* I thought, amused, watching his fingers tapping against his thigh as he spoke.

"The older son was a good boy, a dull boy," he said, "and he loved his father dearly. The younger son was a rascal who caused no end of grief to his mother, constantly flirting with girls and shirking his chores."

Here Andreas interrupted, his face wrinkling with mirth. "Let's call the younger son Yeshua!"

"Or we could call him Andreas?" Yeshua shot back. But the interruption didn't faze him. "All right. We can call him Yeshua. Can you see him in your mind? A big, ugly brute. Ears sticking out like a goat."

There was a round of laughter. Mari, the little girl, clapped her hands with delight. "Yeshua! Yeshua!" she cried.

"The younger son was ready to live like a king. He went to his father and said, 'Father, give me my share of your wealth,' and so the father divided his wealth evenly between the two sons."

"What a silly father," the dark-skinned woman noted.

"What a silly son!" Yeshua countered. "Don't judge the father too harshly. We all make bad decisions for love's sake, do we not?"

People nodded in assent. Some women glanced sidelong at men I took to be their husbands.

Lazaros was listening with his mouth open. This was not the same brother who fell asleep during my father's lessons.

"Soon after, the younger son went off to the city where he squandered his wealth on wild living. He bought women. And wine. And food. Within two years he had spent his inheritance. Then came famine, and the younger son found that he could not feed himself. In order to eat, he even hired himself out to a citizen of that city who sent him into the fields to feed his pigs . . ."

"Serves him right!" a young boy called out. "Thou shalt respect thy mother and father!"

Yeshua grinned, tipping his head to acknowledge the boy, but did not stop his story.

"The son was so hungry that he even ate the pods the pigs were eating. And that is when he remembered his father was a more gener-

ous man than his master and would feed his workers better. The son was starving and so, despite his shame, he decided to return home and become a servant to his father . . ."

At that moment, something hit Yeshua from behind with unbelievable force. A little boy rolled over his shoulders and Yeshua gripped the culprit by the feet. The young boy's dirty shift fell over his head, exposing his nakedness. He screeched and wriggled, trying to get free.

But Yeshua was not angry. He laughed so hard I was afraid he might drop the boy on his head. "You little scoundrel! You have not caught the lion! The lion has caught *you!*" Slowly, gently, he flipped the boy right side up, and put him on the ground.

When Yeshua sat back down, the boy did not leave. He toddled in front of him, chortling and bouncing and waving his tiny hands in the air. It was almost a dance.

Yeshua nodded in time with the boy's rhythmic movements while continuing his story. "As the young man approached his old home from a distance, his father saw him and was filled with love. Such was his gladness that he ran to his son and kissed him."

Yeshua paused then for effect and looked around, his face suddenly intense and serious. "And the son said, 'Father, I have sinned against heaven and against you. I am no longer worthy to be called your son.'"

I'd been holding my breath. I gulped the night air greedily, realizing I had dug my fingernails into the dark soil beneath me. Everyone else was similarly transfixed.

"But the father was overjoyed and ordered his servants to set up a feast in his son's honor."

"That is outrageous!" exclaimed an older man sitting behind me. "No father I know . . ."

"I do not speak of the father you know; I speak of the father you *should* know," Yeshua replied sternly, no longer playful. "Open your ears and let me finish."

The man grumbled but soon went silent, listening. The young boy danced beside Yeshua, sticking out his little stomach and putting his hands at his hips.

"Meanwhile, the older son, who had been in the fields, came back to see what the uproar was about. When he saw that the celebration was for his brother, he said, 'Look! All these years I've slaved for you and

never disobeyed your commands. Yet you never threw me such a feast or killed a young goat on my benefit. Yet for this son who has squandered your wealth, you have killed the fatted calf!'"

The man who had interrupted now nodded his head, pounding his fist on the ground in agreement.

But Yeshua was not finished.

I could tell by the glint in his eye, his practiced fluctuations in volume and tone, that he was used to telling stories to large crowds. He knew how to build suspense. Pausing once more, he took a sip of water from a small earthenware cup, and then made a snarling lion face at the child who was standing guard beside him. The boy giggled delightedly and crept behind Yeshua, pulling at his hair as if to resume their earlier game.

Ignoring his tormenter, Yeshua brought the story to a close. "And the father replied, 'My son, you are always with me, and everything I have is yours. But we must celebrate and be merry because this brother of yours was dead and is alive again; he was lost and now he is found.'"

And with that, finally, his body relaxed. He was done.

"But what does it mean?" the old man asked.

"Are you troubled?" asked Yeshua, instead of answering the question.

"I'm not troubled," he said. "I'm offended by such injustice. The younger son did not deserve to be rewarded above the elder."

Yeshua sighed. "Keep seeking, good man. When you find the answer, you will be troubled. When you are troubled, you will finally be able to marvel at the world around you."

There was finality to Yeshua's words—words spoken with such confidence they had the ring of scripture. But I had been raised to question scripture.

"The Father you speak of is no human father. Am I right?" I asked, and the crowd that had begun to make noise again fell silent.

A small furrow appeared between Yeshua's brows. His eyes threw the question back at me. *And who are you?* they said.

"God welcomes back those who have been lost to him," he said enigmatically. Then, much to my surprise, his demeanor shifted. He laughed lightly, adding, "This woman is sharp! Sharper than all of you! She knows where the wind comes from that fills her with spirit."

"You did not answer my question," I said under my breath, not thinking he would hear.

But he scowled, clenching his square jaw. He *had* heard.

Lazaros yanked at my ear. "Be quiet, Miriam! Don't you know when to hold your tongue? That man speaks with authority."

"What authority?" I said softly. "Tell me, Lazaros."

"Well, I don't know!" Lazaros admitted with a chuckle. "But he's very convincing! What a story!"

"There is much to think on," pondered Philip, looking up at the sky as if he would find the answer to his confusion in the stars.

"What a patient father," Andreas noted wistfully. "I'll take him over my own blood."

I settled back, watching as Yeshua rose and found the little boy. He lifted him onto his shoulders and ran a circle around the fire as the boy screamed with delight.

"He will spoil the child," grumbled a mother. "Life is not all games!"

As the fires burned down to embers, Adah joined Salome to round up the children. "I have three," she told me as she put the leftover crusts of bread into her basket. "Gera is the youngest. And two older girls: Adina and Hodiah."

"Can I help?" I offered, chastising myself internally. I wanted little to do with childcare. I wanted to speak with Yeshua.

But Salome shook her head, giving me a small embrace, her cool hands at my neck.

"It is good living among so many mothers," Adah explained. "There are plenty of women here to help. There is always someone to help. Women like Salome."

I watched as they walked off toward the group of playing children.

It had been so long since I had spent time with women my age. Women other than Marta. Women who knew themselves and spoke with humor and lightness and honesty. In truth, I had only ever known one woman like them. They reminded me of Kemat.

All around me women departed with their children. And with their men. Tonight they would lie with them. Practicing sweetness. Making love.

I shivered, looking around me carefully. Would one of the women claim Yeshua? Had his wife remained hidden until now?

"How long do you two intend to say?" Andreas asked Lazaros.

Lazaros glanced at me sheepishly. "I don't speak for Miriam . . . but

I find this place invigorating. I wouldn't mind staying to hear this man's teachings."

"Yes!" I agreed, my heart fluttering again. "Why leave when we have just arrived?"

Bethany felt further away than four days of travel. It felt like it belonged to a different lifetime. Shuddering to think of returning to Yosseph, I chastised myself. Hadn't Yosseph's love been my greatest wish? I must try harder to imagine myself his wife!

"My lady," Andreas interrupted, and for a second I was worried he had read my face. But then he spoke again, "Aren't you in need of a cure? This is the best time to approach him."

Lazaros laughed. I resisted pinching him, speaking loudly to cover his obvious amusement.

"Yes. I do need a cure. A cure from possession."

Yeshua was now speaking with a young man at the edge of the forest. Only their faces and gestures flashed in the firelight, creating the illusion of trees having grown heads and hands in order to have a conversation.

"Then go to him."

"Yes. Go, Miriam, and be healed," Lazaros added, grinning so widely I thought his face might crack. He was entertained at the thought of Miriam, his proud sister, having to play the invalid. Play the fool.

Yeshua must have heard me coming, but he did not turn, preferring to gaze into the undergrowth. What did he see there?

"What is it?"

I dug my toes into the damp soil beneath my feet, hoping for some inspiration. "I have come to be healed," I said at last.

He turned to look directly at me then. His gaze had the same force as weather. Like hard rain on dry soil. I felt my body shifting its landscape under his eyes.

But he only smiled. "You have no need of healing."

"What do you mean?"

He seemed to be thinking very hard. He inhaled slowly, his nostrils flaring. I was so close I could smell him. Earthy and sharp. The scent of split cedar wood. "Answer me this. What are you *really* doing here?" he asked softly.

"I came to find you," I answered honestly, and immediately regretted it.

He did not smile, but his eyes widened. He tilted his head, appraising me, then turned to disappear into the forest.

Later that night, sleeping in a hut between Salome and an old woman, I peered up through the slats in the grass roof. My eyes followed thin strands of moonlight spilling down on Salome, turning her pale hair an iridescent white. I breathed slowly, trying to calm my speeding heart. But as hard as I tried, I could not relax, knowing that close by, somewhere in this camp, Yeshua lay in his own bed.

And perhaps he lay awake, thinking of me.

Twenty-One

"Come. We must get started with the cooking." Salome woke with the dawn, rousing me gently. I startled out of a dream, a chaos of indescribable color and sensation.

The sun had not yet risen but the world was already pale and soft, as if cleansed by the passing of night. It was strange to see the encampment full of women moving silently to ensure that grain was baked into the morning's bread, and the children's dirty clothes washed in the shallows of the river.

"We must prepare food for tomorrow's Sabbath," explained the older woman who had slept beside me the previous night. She introduced herself as Michal as she led me to a cooking fire just under the shadows of the jujube trees at the edge of the encampment. We quickly got to work cutting up vegetables, throwing them haphazardly into a large basket. Each day, I realized, new pilgrims and visitors must add to the pile of food, and this woman's job was to find some way to blend every odd offering into one meal.

"The little ones kept me up all night," said Adah as she arrived, her face swollen with lack of sleep. "I slept for but an hour."

"Give them to me next time," Salome offered, scooting over as Adah settled down, opening up a bundle of cucumbers. "I don't mind spending time with babies."

There was something wistful about the way she said it. I felt heartache hovering in every one of her careful gestures—as if it were her slow, purposeful movements that kept her from falling apart.

"Gera wants to suckle at all hours," Adah explained as she began to expertly cut up the cucumbers. "But he is nearly two, and Philip thinks I should wean him."

I remembered Marta back in Bethany, handing Kernan off to her maid Atalyah, and my own mother who had allowed Kemat to raise me.

"Why have you left your families?" I asked bluntly, then blushed, worried I had been too forward.

"This place has *become* family," Adah said simply. "I have more help from other women here than I ever did back home. Most of my kinswomen are dead and Philip's family disapproves of me. They knew I was poor and had no dowry . . ."

"You married for love," I said, hardly able to contain my smile. "Was that your crime?"

"Yes," she replied, laughing, as she smoothed a stray curl away from her face. The day was already hot, and perspiration was beading along her hairline.

Slowly, as the morning gained body and color, the men began to emerge from their huts or from the depths of the forest, barefoot women holding their hands. I watched, spellbound, as they leaned close and kissed. There was no shame. They had lain naked together under the branches and the stars and the moonlight.

The men went to wash in the river and then came to us for food, each one giving thanks and bowing his head.

"Shelama, Miriam." Thoma's already pale face was accentuated by dark circles below his eyes. "Give a man a scrap of bread. I don't think I could eat much more."

"Serves you right," Salome chastised him, even as she ripped him off a hunk. "You drank like a pig last night."

"But what fun it was!" he laughed, winking at her despite her humorless expression.

Lazaros overflowed with a vitality I had never seen before. His face looked fuller; his height suddenly impressive rather than awkward. "It is good to sleep outside," he confessed as I served him some stewed vegetables. "I feel like my dreams have room enough to bloom."

"What poetry is this?" I laughed.

"No! Truly!" he insisted, although he smiled bashfully. Then a shadow seemed to pass over his face. "I dreamt I was in a boat on a misty lake. Green hills surrounded me. And I was hurt. Wounded badly I think."

"And *I* am the one who everyone thinks is mad . . ." I joked.

Finally, after the men were served and the children had scampered over to sit around us and eat, Adah instructed us to serve ourselves. The bread was coarser than I was accustomed to but full of taste.

"Miriam, how is it that your husband allowed such a journey?" Adah lifted her eyebrows in curiosity. I could tell that she had been dying to ask this question since the previous night. Adah was only two or three years my senior. And yet she already had three babes of her own.

"I am not yet married," I answered defiantly, preparing to defend myself, but Adah's face remained calm and curious. There was no hint of judgment there.

"Is it because of your illness?" She welcomed Gera into her lap and opened her tunic to offer the child her breast. "Gera, Gera," she muttered as his lips sought her nipple. "What are we going to do with you? You are even hungrier than your father."

"Yes," I answered, "but I am to be betrothed . . . if I return home cured."

The boy at Adah's bosom let out a satisfied burp and she patted his back affectionately. "So there *is* someone who waits for you. It does not surprise me. You are a beautiful girl!"

"Don't presume, Adah," Salome said softly. "Marriage is not always as pleasurable as it has been for you."

"Oh, it has not been *all* pleasure," Adah huffed. "The things I could tell you . . ."

I felt blood rush to my cheeks but found myself confiding in her. "I'm not sure how I feel about marriage. Nervous and excited. Perhaps it could be a good thing."

"An appropriate response to such a commitment!" Adah exclaimed, laughing and tucking her breast back into her tunic. She patted Gera on the head before pushing him off her lap. "At first it seems too sweet to be true and then, very quickly, it becomes ordinary. But I tell you, there are still moments when I see Philip as if for the first time. I hope that you know such joy soon enough!"

The rest of the day was occupied by a series of chores, a fact I would have resented had I been back at Bethany, but I was no longer alone in a house. With Adah and Salome's company, the time passed quickly. What a joy it was to laugh with them! To play games with the children and keep them from wandering too far afoot. To giggle while we collected food offerings from that day's new arrivals. And there was still plenty of time to walk down to the water and cool our feet.

At midday, a group of Egyptian men arrived: all brothers I decided, by their similar, lithe builds and heavily-lashed eyes. Adah shook her head, complaining that we would have to prepare more food for dinner than she had previously reckoned.

As the day deepened into its final golden hour, Lazaros chatted amiably with Thoma and the Ben-Zebedee brothers, receiving some sort of initiation into the teachings of Yochanan. But Yeshua remained noticeably absent. And he did not appear next to Yochanan in the river, either. I resisted asking Adah as to his whereabouts, but it took all my effort to silence my questions.

His words resonated in my head. *What are you really doing here?*

To distract myself, I helped the old woman Michal clean some rags in the river shallows as the final crowd lined up to step under Yochanan's handfuls of water.

Michal's cracked lips flapped over a toothless mouth that always appeared to be scowling. Her eyes were flinty and she narrowed them whenever I tried to smile and hold her gaze. But as we worked side by side, I sensed that her defenses came from a lifetime of hardship. Silence was the best way to earn her trust.

Our hands brushed each other's as she handed me a faded red scarf and her lips twitched with affinity. "You are a good worker," she allowed, beating a white shift against a rock. "Although you look like a fine lady."

I wrung out the red scarf. The sunlight was tinged pink as it sifted through the threadbare fabric. The light was the color of intimacy. The color of lips. Women's secret lips. Roses.

The river carried laughter and voices downstream. Men and women were playing in the water, splashing each other while they waited for Yochanan's blessing.

"Michal, why do men and women choose to be immersed again?" I asked, twisting the water out of a dirty shift.

Suddenly she was animated, her eyes bright as shiny hard-shelled beetles. "Why do you think?" she cackled.

Trying not to take insult, I thought for a second but could not come up with my own answer. "I have no idea. Tell me?"

"They have made themselves unclean with loving during the night and need to be purified by the living waters once again," she explained. "Although Yeshua does not believe you need to repeat immersions."

"What *does* he believe then?" I tried to keep my voice even. I could feel the cold tongue of the river lapping at my ankles as I stepped further into the water; a shiver of pleasure traveled up my calves to my thighs. I stood still for a second, savoring the feeling.

"I think . . ." Michal squinted, her voice slow as she thought through her answer. "I'm not sure, but I'd say that Yeshua believes you must immerse and *then* change your life. The water only cleanses you enough to begin—to begin to live outside of sin."

It was the most she had spoken to me. I wanted to push, but I resisted. I did not want to risk offending my new friend.

I watched transfixed as men and women whose bodies must have mingled the night before now stood a proper distance from each other, receiving the Yarden's purifying water.

I was sure that Yeshua would appear at dinner, served early to accommodate the coming Sabbath. But after the meal, when I had finally joined Lazaros and his new friends, I was agitated to discover that he was nowhere to be found.

Instead I tried to listen to Yochanan's teaching from a distance. But it was hard to hear from my shadowy spot under a squat terebinth. And the teachings were inscrutable.

"The key is to repent. Do not flee harm. Do not count yourselves as lucky or blessed. Do good deeds in keeping with repentance."

And of what do I need to repent? I thought sourly. *Tell me something more interesting!*

Later in the day I reunited with my brother.

Unlike me, Lazaros was enflamed by the day spent with Yochanan; his brows wiggled as his animated face passed through a wild series of emotions. Joy. Wonder. Confusion. A dent appeared in his forehead that was entirely new. He was thinking hard. Trying to make sense of something.

He is so ready to feel included among the elect that virtually anything could heal him, I thought bitterly, as with a few clarifications from Thoma and Andreas, Lazaros repeated what he had learned: "We must think of repentance as a return to our God! When we sin, we miss the mark. And we stray farther from God *each* time we sin."

"But as far from God as we are, we must not despair," Andreas added gruffly. A day immersing in the full sun had left the stout man as red as a turnip. "We can always begin. We can always step into the river to be cleansed!"

I nodded tolerantly, pretending I had not studied the question of sin intensely with our father for years.

But I resented being tutored by Lazaros. The brother who had squandered the knowledge my father offered him freely! The brother who had been taught to read, though he didn't really care to know!

"You see, Miriam, it is a question of *wanting* to change," Lazaros continued. "When you receive immersion, you must truly want to receive purification."

"Yes," I interrupted with annoyance. "'Purge me with hyssop, and I shall be clean; wash me and I shall be whiter than snow.' We must beg for God's forgiveness and purification. Purification must be active rather than passive."

"Well said!" exclaimed Philip, coming to sit beside us with a piece of bread piled high with onions and dried fish. "But you are only speaking of the body and its impurities. What of the spirit and the heart?"

I was taken aback. Every time these men complimented my knowledge, I felt a surge of pride mixed with confusion. Yochanan would not teach a woman. But his followers were remarkably open about spiritual matters.

"Body and spirit . . ." I murmured.

I had never before heard anyone divide the two. It was a new idea that purity could represent two separate matters. Avoiding a direct response, I replied with a psalm: "Create in me a clean heart, Oh God; and renew a right spirit within me."

Yoses Ben-Zebedee brayed with laughter. "She is a quick study! You must work harder to unseat her!"

But I did not feel that I had bested Philip. Instead I was curious and, relinquishing any attempt at superiority, asked, "But what do you mean when you speak of cleansing the heart? Is it not accomplished through immersion in the living waters as well? How is it different from the impurities of the body?"

Andreas chimed in: "Philip is only repeating Yeshua's words. You would do better to ask *him* to clarify the matter."

Philip, who had been ready to speak as an authority, sighed and nodded his head. "This is true. I can tell you what I think it means, or you can go directly to the source. These are Yeshua's teachings, not Yochanan's."

But I could not question Yeshua because he did not appear. And the next day he remained absent as well. The longer he was gone, the more a jittery nervousness built inside of me. My legs felt twitchy. I kept glancing over my shoulder. A starling's surprising swoop overhead could set my heart aflutter.

"Walk with me, Brother?" I asked Lazaros as the day wore on, but he declined.

"I do not want to miss Yochanan's teachings! Oh Miriam, you would love to hear him speak. He knows his scripture well!"

"Yochanan will not tolerate me," I complained.

"Oh come now!" Lazaros shook his head, but he was already distracted. Thoma was waving him over.

I let him go.

I was thankful when I spotted Adah, Michal, and Salome sitting farther down the shore, watching as a group of children splashed in the shallows. Gera was squatting in the wet sand, afraid of going in further, screaming at his older sisters and throwing fistfuls of sand into the water.

"Have you received immersion?" Adah called out, and I appreciated her mocking tone of voice. "Do you feel like a new woman?"

"I am healed. It's a miracle!" I swept my arms out as if to display my new wholeness.

Salome gave us a disapproving look. I was coming to expect her dour nature. But it did not make me dislike her. "I, too, came here for healing. And I *was* healed." Her voice was as weightless as the sound wind makes as it passes over a leaf.

"You were ill?" I asked with surprise.

Salome shot a glance at Adah. Her mouth pressed into a bloodless line that I recognized; she was preparing for my judgment. "I do not believe I was ill in the way you have been. I was afflicted with sinful living. But I have changed my life."

I struggled to keep my face composed.

Salome chuckled, the first time I had heard her do so. "You don't believe me."

Her face was not painted. But this woman who looked as pure as a spring flower could only be referring to a life of prostitution. "So if I understand correctly, you are referring to Yeshua's Mishnah and not Yochanan's?"

"My husband was right, you are quite the scholar," Adah noted, reaching beside her in order to catch Gera running by. She lugged him onto her lap, where he resisted for a second before wilting into sleepiness and comfort, his hand grasping at her shawl.

I could sense Salome's relief in the way she smoothed out her skirt, pulling hard on a stray thread until it ripped free. She was glad I had not asked for her story.

She answered in a measured voice. "Their Mishnahs are one and the same. But you are correct: Yeshua has a different understanding of purity and redemption. He is more accepting of women such as me and believes that as soon as we change our ways, we are freed of our impurities."

Adah turned to me and said seriously, her brown eyes wide and sincere, "Yeshua is very learned."

"Learned?" I asked imperiously, remembering those many dinners exchanging scripture and arguments with my father's students. "Has he studied the Law?"

"Not formally," Adah conceded. "But he has a better knowledge of it than any man I've met. And that is only a small part of his knowledge. He has studied with many teachers."

"What do you mean?" My curiosity could no longer be contained. "Who is Yeshua exactly? I've barely seen him since I arrived. But I have heard so much talk."

Adah nodded at this, stroking her boy's curly hair absentmindedly, "Yes. You're right. I suppose he has gone into the forest. He does that sometimes."

"For what purpose?" I looked behind her into the vibrant shade that pulsed between the jujube trees.

"Sometimes he goes away for weeks at time," Salome explained. "He deprives himself of food and drink in order to reach higher states of contemplation. I hear he once went into the desert and . . ."

Adah broke into laughter, interrupting Salome. Gera startled awake in her lap, his face turning red. He began to struggle, but Adah kept him prisoner, locking her arm around his waist.

"He sounds like an Essene," I noted, thinking of the ascetics who lived outside of Yerushalem, wearing only white, observing rules even more intense than those of the Pharisees. "Why are Yeshua's teaching's more lenient than Yochanan's, if he is so strict with himself?"

"Don't let him fool you!" Adah said. "Yeshua can't keep up the ascetic routine for long. He never does. Mark my words, he'll be drinking and feasting by the end of the week. And if you think he is such a devout man, you should have seen him several years ago . . ."

Now Salome looked as confused as I felt. "What do you mean, Adah?"

Adah's wide grin accentuated her pretty, plump cheeks. She lowered her voice and said knowingly, "It's widely known, really. Perhaps not among the most recent members of Yochanan's students . . ."

"Yes?" I prodded.

Adah continued gleefully. "I have it on good authority that Yeshua used to be a very different sort of man. Apparently, when he was much younger, he left his family in Nazareth and went off to Tabariyyah in search of adventure. It is said that he ran with a very wild crowd and was the wildest of them all, drinking, feasting, and keeping the worst sort of company . . ."

At this Salome's whole body tensed. But Adah continued without notice, rocking her disgruntled son in her lap as she spoke. "Philip tells me he was particularly fond of women and lived in a brothel in Tabariyyah for a time . . ."

"He was just like the younger son from his story . . ." I concluded with disbelief, trying to merge the image of the tall, powerful man with that of those pleasure-loving fools I had often seen keep Lazaros's company back home, men with loose tongues and nothing to say, always in search of a better party, a more perfect wine.

"Exactly," Adah nodded and Salome's eyes widened. "Except that when he grew tired of his wild ways and returned home, there was no father to welcome him back."

"What do you mean?" I asked.

Adah lowered her voice. "Philip tells me that when Yeshua returned home to Nazareth it was to find that his father had died."

"How terrible!" Salome cried.

Oh, Salome. You who felt things so intensely. Every sorrow—whether it was yours or belonged to someone else—was a thorn in your skin, a sword at your throat. Sometimes, still, I pray for your purity of feeling.

"But when did he become as he is *now*?" I pressed on, still unsatisfied. "Why is he so highly respected here?"

"Have you not heard his stories? Have you not spoken with him?" The look of adoration on Salome's face irked me. "He explains things as they are!"

Adah was less reverential. "Many years have passed since he returned home. It is said that he has studied with all of the great rabbis and maggids, even spending some time at Qumran with the Essene scholars there. For the past five years he has been with Yochanan and is now his favored student."

"And yet it seems he offers Yochanan competition," I countered, remembering the exchange between the men at the fire that first night.

Adah's expression became serious. "I would not say that. Yeshua loves Yochanan dearly, and it would cause him grief if he thought there was animosity between them."

I was smart enough to know that a comment like this only affirmed that a conflict existed between the two men. But I let the matter drop and soon the women were laughing again and telling other stories.

As night fell, there remained no sign of Yeshua. The humidity made me restless and I couldn't sit still. Eventually I made an excuse to go check on our donkey. I led him on a walk about the whole encampment, but Yeshua was nowhere to be found. I pictured him deep in the woods, sitting so still that even the passing beasts might mistake him for a tree. Or maybe I was wrong. Maybe he was on all fours, living as an animal, lapping water from a puddle like a thirsty lion.

At the dinner that night I found that I could not stand any more of Lazaros's enthusiastic recitations of Yochanan's teachings. I loved my brother, and loved to see him genuinely enlivened, but I was impatient.

Why was I here? Surely I had not traveled so far for Yochanan's useless immersions . . . Was it true what I told Yeshua, that it was for him I had come to the river?

I managed to keep still just long enough to eat the lentils we had prepared the day before. I stood abruptly. The men looked up, surprised. Not wanting to offend my brother or his company, I smiled and explained that I must go check on the children.

Michal and Femi, the dark-skinned beauty, were serving them supper. They sat around the cold firepit, nibbling the fish that a group of pilgrims had brought with them earlier in the day. Thankful that the Sabbath provided a cover of darkness, I sank into the shadows next to Adah's little daughter Hodiah.

Hodiah, no more than three, skinny and brown like her father, recognized me as one of her mother's new friends. She crawled to my side. Sitting on her bony knees, her hands placed on her thighs, she looked up at me expectantly, blinking. *Yes,* I thought. *She takes after Philip, but those are Adah's eyelashes.*

"What is it, Hodiah?" I asked. Why did she look at me with such anticipation?

I was reminded of the leopard's yellow eyes watching me as I walked to the tower at night . . . and the black irises of the vultures as they descended to my aid. The girl radiated the same powerful attention; the same silent insistence that we were intimately connected and that I must provide something.

But what did *I* have to offer?

More children emerged out of the blue dusk behind Hodiah. They formed a circle around me. Two fat little boys who must surely be twins . . . Adah's little one Gera, dragged along by his other sister Adina. Several girls toddled over, all holding hands, smiling with front teeth missing, sunburned noses like rubies pressed into their faces.

An older boy plopped down close to me, sitting on a flat stone that bordered the firepit. "We want a story!" he demanded.

"Yeshua tells us stories," said Hodiah.

"Then go to Yeshua," I said trying to keep my voice kind.

"*You* have stories." Adina gazed up at me with her head propped in her hands. "You tell us a story."

I reached out to touch Adina's head, an almost maternal feeling coming over me that passed as quickly as it had arrived. She did not seem surprised by my touch and nestled under my arm.

"All right, then," I paused to think. "I'll tell you a story you've never heard before . . ."

Looking at my captive audience, I suddenly felt the shadow of Kemat at my shoulder. I did not want to instruct these children. I wanted to give them a gift. I would tell them a story Yosseph had brought back with him from one of his journeys to a far-off land.

"There was once a prince, a very beautiful prince, who had the gift of music . . ." I began tentatively. With the eyes of the children on me, I grew more confident. "He played such beautiful music on his lyre, and sang so sweetly, that wherever he went animals would follow. And one day it was not just the animals he charmed, but a girl. She was the love-liest maiden in the land, and they were soon married."

Adina twisted her head around, rapt, her mouth slightly open. The older boy was rocking back and forth, anxiously absorbed.

"They had everything they needed there in the forest, and they were very happy for a while. But one day the girl was walking in a field when a viper bit her. She died immediately and went down into the . . ." Here, I struggled to find the word that Yosseph had used to describe this place. "The place under the ground, where the rephaim . . . where the spirits live."

The little boy sitting on the stone screwed up his face. His lower lip wobbled and the corners of his eyes glistened. In a comical imitation of an adult's worry, he put his hands up to his cheeks.

"No! Don't worry!" I smiled reassuringly. "The prince was too sad to let his wife disappear into death. So he went down to find her."

The boy's face relaxed. Transfixed, the children had drawn close enough to hear me now. Even little Gera, too young to really under-stand, was watching intently.

"So he traveled deep into the earth, under the roots and the rocks and the soil, playing music the whole time, and his song was so enchanting that when he finally reached the place where the girl was kept, the rephas and demons could not help but be charmed. They were so pleased with his music that they granted him back his wife. But on one condition."

"What?" breathed Adina. *"What?"*

It was then I realized my mistake. The story was romantic, but also tragic. The ending would devastate the children.

Children are wiser than adults, you see. They take grief seriously. They mourn for the dead characters in a story as if they had really lived. They beat their breasts for a tragic poem. Forgive me, Leukas, for speaking like an Egyptian about such things. But I truly believe children's wisdom comes from how close they are to their last lives. Recently born, they are closer to death. Closer to heartache and separation. They understand that the stories we tell are not make-believe tales. They are memories.

How different would my life have been had I known that then. But I did not.

That night in the forest I cocked my head with detachment, considering my young audience. I took a breath as I composed a new ending for the children.

"The prince was told that he must not look back at his wife as he led her back above ground, back to the land of the living. But thankfully the prince was determined to bring his love back to life, so he kept his eyes fixed ahead of him for the entire journey. Before long they broke into sunlight and were returned to each other's arms."

The children were smiling. Hodiah squealed with delight, crawling close enough to bang on my knee emphatically.

"And they lived to be very old and had many children and many animals. And all of their children were strong and good and could play the most beautiful music, just like their father . . ." I said, finishing.

Satisfied with the story, the children began to disperse. Gera shrieked at Hodiah and she ushered him away. Adina stayed at my side, sinking her head into my lap sleepily. Soft and golden skinned, she was like a little Adah. She smelled sweetly of meadow grass heating up under the sun. The warm weight of her was comforting and I stroked her cheek, feeling her velvety skin and the softness of her curls falling onto her face.

Fireflies flitted about us and I smiled, feeling sleepy myself. It was easy enough to imagine that we were suspended in the sky itself, hovering amidst stars. Stars seeking each other. Flying toward the dark unknown. Returning, always returning.

"That is not how I've heard the story told." At the dark edge of the forest, Yeshua was leaning against a tree. He had been there the whole time, listening, disguised by the shadows.

His voice startled me and woke Adina, who rolled out of my lap, frowning as she stood unsteadily.

"You tell them of the Romans' Orpheus?" he asked. The darkness hid his expression.

I nodded, remembering Yosseph telling me about the Roman rites to honor their lovesick musician.

"But they both die in the end," Yeshua continued. "He does not trust the miracle. He looks back and damns his beloved. She stays in the land of the dead, and he is pulled apart by wild women."

I shivered, overcome by the irrational desire to touch him.

"Yes." I remembered what Adah had told me earlier about Yeshua. "If I am not mistaken, you too enjoy changing the endings to stories?"

I was used to my father's students; men who were easily angered.

But Yeshua was not like other men. Slowly a catlike smile spread across his face. He began to chuckle, a deep rumble as if the earth below were rearranging its stones. "Perhaps you are right." His voice was low and intimate. It took me off guard. "But I happen to believe there is no such thing as an ending."

It was the wisest thing he ever said to me.

Before I could respond, he was striding over to the big group, calling out jovially, "Please tell me there is some leftover food! I'm starving!"

Twenty-Two

"Do not say I am against the Law!" Yeshua's voice was emphatic. I tried to keep my attention on Gera, who was dipping his fingers into a bowl of water. I whispered a prayer, helping him to wash his hands.

Lazaros spoke in response, but I could not hear clearly what he was saying from where I was eavesdropping.

Yeshua's voice, however, was loud enough that his words could be heard from every spot in the clearing. "We are here to make the Law alive again, to truly observe the commandments, unlike those men who seem to cherish it so highly but practice no devotion behind closed doors." This was how he taught, informally, as people ate and drank around him, as if it were a conversation among friends.

"Are you well, Miriam?" asked Adah with concern.

"I am fine," I said. But I wasn't. My hands were sweaty. A tight knot had lodged behind my breastbone. Was it terror? That didn't seem the right name for it.

I left the meal early, heading to the river. I was so dazed that I didn't even startle when a snake as thin as a black thread slipped over my feet. I stopped dumbly, watching him. He coiled, the tip of his tail flicking alongside his slender neck, hissing lightly so that his pink throat was visible. A young viper! But my body still didn't register the danger.

Slowly he slid toward me again, curling around one ankle and then the other.

He felt like water against my skin. And then he was gone, swallowed by the dark undergrowth.

"Thank you," I whispered, unsure if I was thanking the viper for sparing me his venomous bite or for blessing me with his magical embrace.

The snake. The fireflies. The soft mossy ground absorbing the sound of my steps. The high, frantic music of the tree frogs. All of it gave me the sense that I had entered into another realm as I reached the river's edge. Starlight streamed down from the sky and etched white lines of movement on the river's surface. I imagined these as threads, weaving in and out of a long cloth and leading toward a finished whole: a tapestry of the forest within which I was only a tiny speck, no bigger than an embroidered flower.

As always, the vision of myself as insignificant, swallowed within an all-encompassing world, was comforting rather than frightening. It was like those nights spent in the tower, feeling myself rocked by a pulse more powerful than my own. I picked up a stone, small and flat, flicking it over the water. Circles opened like tiny mouths as it skipped several times before sinking.

Later, crawling under my cloak next to Salome, I imagined the stone in my mind, still turned by currents deep underwater. I felt like the stone when it had been poised just above the water, a moment away from being consumed by the river.

I see myself from far away now, lying straight on the ground, hands folded above my breasts, fingernails dirty with silt, eyes peering up through dust and pollen to the slats in the hut's grass roof. My face was smooth except for a tiny indent between my brows. Now, old as I am, that furrow has deepened until it can no longer be erased by sleep or meditation. Then it was only visible when I was deep in thought.

How beautiful to see oneself before our story shows up on the body. My flesh is a jumble of words now, each wrinkle and knotted joint the tale of how my sorrow happened and how I continue to carry it to this day. Do I even need to tell you my story, Leukas? Perhaps. Or perhaps you only need examine me closely, look deep into the lines at the corners of my eyes to know the truth of it.

But peering through memory, looking down on myself that night, nothing can be read on me as yet; no sign of suffering in my face. I am still untouched as I lie there—still safe. The water has not yet swallowed me and drawn me into its currents.

I bid you let me pause the story and stay here a moment. If you are impatient with my silence then I bid you look at these hands and their crooked bones. It is easy to see that they have touched and been touched. Read between my fingers the love I have held and the love I have let go.

• • •

The following morning I woke while the world was still dark. Everyone was asleep, even the most industrious of the women. Salome's breath whistled gently through her lips. I left the hut slowly so as not to disturb anyone. The leaves on the trees were silver and motionless.

The air still held the warmth of yesterday's sun and, inconceivably, another heat had been added to this one: a dense warmth that rose from the ground itself. I folded my heavy cloak, throwing it back into the hut behind me. Even my shift felt too heavy; I could feel drops of sweat beading in my underarms, beneath my breasts, and at the crest of my upper lip.

I wandered down to the riverbank to see if there was a relief from the heat nearer to the water but, if anything, the air was even more stagnant there. Was it unsafe to wander off? I had never been afraid to escape into the wild back home. And as I listened for my own fear, I heard nothing. My heart beat steadily against the hand I pressed against my chest.

Wearing a skin of dark, waxy leaves and muscular vines, the forest was a living body. Dense. Opaque. As I hesitated, watching the trees, I thought I could see it breathing, exhaling out a humid, glistening mist.

Go on. This is the real temple, a small voice—mine and *not* mine— sounded in my head.

I stepped into a grove of tamarisks. My bare feet pressed into moss and dirt that exhaled a smell as pungent and intimate as the odors of my own body. The serrated leaves of an ash tree grazed my arm. A line of ants emerged from the flesh of pink oleander flowers. Here I could forget my worries. I was part of a larger, stronger body than my own. A body that cared little for men and women, little even for time.

I made my way unevenly. Sometimes the trees thinned and I could see through the gaps in the leaves and branches to the silver sheen of the water.

How long did I walk for? Quite a while, I suppose. The longer I was awake, immersed in the forest, the more I found myself slipping back into a dreamlike state. Small eyes glinted like embers in the undergrowth and yet, unafraid, I brushed past them and watched as they closed and reopened deeper into the darkness.

I followed a direction that sprang up from the ground and not from any personal sense of destination. Perhaps I was heading toward the center of the forest—that place, like the city's temple, where the trees all prayed toward when the wind blew through them.

At last I broke through to the sandy banks of the shore. The other side of the river was closer here.

The water looked almost still: one uniform, silvery thread that slid off into the mist.

I'm not sure what made me stop, but something gave me pause. I turned back to look across to the other shore. There, dark as ink against the white mist that wove in and out of the tree trunks, was a woman.

She was holding out one arm as if in greeting. Uncertainly I lifted my own, returning the gesture.

We stood there for several breaths, facing each other across the water. Finally, as the morning light pierced through the clouds, her face became visible.

It was my mother.

I knew it was impossible. But she was there. On her face was that familiar expression of gentle reservation.

"Oh!"

Without thinking, I stumbled into the river. It was bracingly cold as I staggered across the rocks, shivering already.

The current was strong and I struggled to keep my footing.

The woman lowered her hand and stepped away. The mist obscured her features once again.

"Mother!" I cried desperately, stepping deeper into the river, oblivious to the dangers of the current. She waved at me again, no longer in greeting, and seemed to be saying something. But her words were swallowed by the roar of the water.

Oh! I realized too late. *She was warning me, telling me to turn back!*

I sank underwater, my vision blurred and shimmered. As I burst up into the air one last time, I finally saw her clearly: her face younger than I'd ever remembered it. She was smiling.

The water consumed me. And then I saw nothing at all. I struggled blindly, unable to surface. How stupid! I would drown. Alone. Unremarkably.

But then I was held. Strong hands hoisted me from the water, dragging me roughly up onto the pebbles.

I could not see or breathe. But I could feel the hands on my chest, pressing the air back into my lungs. There were lips on my lips, blowing deep into my mouth.

"Breathe!"

And I did, coughing water onto my chest.

That first breath came like fire through my throat. My whole body was shaking uncontrollably. Before me was a deeper blue than I had ever seen. This was the blue of angels! The blue that cannot be seen from below, but only from *inside* the sky.

I had to close my eyes again.

This was the true immersion. Now I was born again. I breathed, greedy for air.

"Why did you go into the water?" Crouching at my feet, Yeshua braced himself against my knees, sending a surge of heat up into my body. I could feel it pooling deep in my belly. Aware of my sheer shift sticking to my chest, instinctively I covered my breasts.

"How?" I asked thickly. "How did you save me? Where *were* you?"

He sat back on the stones, simultaneously bashful and self-possessed. "I . . ." He shrugged. "I followed you."

"You followed me?"

"Yes." He said it plainly, unapologetically.

I pulled my knees up to my chest, hugging them, feeling that I must hold my body together or I might fly apart.

Yeshua was wearing nothing but a loincloth. It was a feeble attempt at modesty, barely covering the hair on his upper thighs where it became dark and curly. A violet vein in his thigh pulsed under my gaze.

"Did you see that woman?" I asked. "On the opposite shore?"

"No. I saw you go into the water."

"Why did you follow me?"

He planted his arms and hands behind him so that he could stretch out his long torso. It was all I could do to keep my eyes on his face. His nakedness intrigued me: the lean muscles of his crossed legs, the curious path of black hair trailing down from his chest to his stomach.

"I often sleep in the forest," he explained. "I come out here every morning to sit quietly and to bathe. When I saw you walking along the banks, I decided to see where you were headed. The better question is, what were *you* doing outside the encampment at such an early hour?"

"Looking for you," I answered, surprising even myself. I hadn't realized it was the urge to find him that had propelled me into the forest. But it was true.

He laughed, the force of the noise surprising. It would be a long time before I would grow used to his habit of swinging from one mood to the next in a matter of seconds, a look of reproach melting into a huge smile, or that always unexpected laugh that seemed to belong either to madness or drunkenness.

"Thank you for saving me . . ." I said.

"You'll save me someday, I expect," he replied, looking away from me, hiding an expression I had just seen surfacing. Clouds in his eyes. Storm clouds. "The scales will balance."

He leaned back, the shoulders of his muscles bulging as he shifted weight from one arm to the other, stretching his fingers deep into the sand. He gazed up through the foliage above us. Morning birds were beginning to flit in and out of view. A white-throated kingfisher dipped across the river, dropping down to puncture the current with the needle of his beak. The blue bird rose victorious with a twisting fish, flying back up into the trees on the opposite bank.

I glanced at Yeshua, wishing I could remember how to breathe normally. But every inhale brought me a taste of his sweat, his warmth, his nearness.

He eyed the spot in the river the kingfisher had entered.

His body was dappled in the shadowed shapes of leaves. It gave the illusion that he was wearing the spotted pelt of a leopard. *A fitting description,* I thought. He had the easy grace of a cat: its lithe body slipping unseen through the forest. Until the moment it was startled by a butterfly and fell over itself, tail up in the air. I remembered watching some kittens that had snuck into the grain store at Yohanna's home. They would sit regally on the stone jars, pointing their whiskers at us as if they were sure of their royalty, and then immediately leap into the air, pawing at a fly or a moth.

"How do you heal people?" I asked.

If he was surprised by the question, he didn't show it. "I give exorcisms," he answered. "It is a good trick. I give people the healing they already have inside of them. They believe they are well, and it becomes so."

But I could feel him withholding something from me.

"No. That's not what I mean." I stretched out my legs, relaxing.

"No?" He brought his hands together, eyeing me curiously, unaware that a white moth had just landed in his hair, opening and closing its wings.

I would regret not asking. Why else had I come here? I had never before met someone who might understand what I had done for Rebekah and my sister, Marta.

"No," I said confidently. "I'm talking about the heat. That thing that comes up from the ground through your feet. I feel it in my hands. Buzzing. It's almost painful. And then . . ." I struggled. To say it aloud was prideful. Maybe I would be struck down. Maybe he would laugh at me.

But he reached out then and touched my hand. Tentatively. A finger pressed into my open palm, urging me to speak.

"And then if I put my hands on someone, I can heal them," I concluded.

"Yes," he nodded. He shook his head and the white moth flew off. "That's what it's like. Like fire in my hands. And I feel a pressure between my eyes, too."

A heron flew overhead, embracing us with its shadow. The great bird seemed to hover for a moment as it reached the river's edge, confounding time itself. Yeshua and I both turned to watch as, with a piercing motion, it dipped into the shallow water and settled upright, balanced on its leg. As it steadied itself, it swiveled its head and fixed us both in its vision. A strange sense passed over me that perhaps we were only real when looked at by birds; by animals who could see the whole story from above as they flew over the deserts, the forests, the oceans. Perhaps Yeshua and I would be intractably merged if we were both held, our materials mixed and concentrated, in the gaze of a single eye.

"Do not let anyone tell you that you need healing, Miriam." It was the first time he had said my name.

His dark skin was burnished by the rising sunlight. The world was remembering its color now: the blue leaves faded into various greens. The river reeds were no longer like shards of gray metal standing upright in the water, losing their fearsomeness as they finally leaned into their natural yellows.

"Will you teach me?" I asked breathlessly.

He frowned. "No."

It was the right answer. Had he known I'd been testing him? Testing his pride? But there were still things I longed to know. To understand. "Andreas tells me you believe the purity of the spirit is different from the cleanliness of the body?"

He reached up absentmindedly to brush away a fly. "I do."

"Then the living waters only wash my skin, my body. And my spirit is left unclean . . ." My voice was light, but I was not being playful. This question had been bothering me since Lazaros and I arrived at the river.

"Just the opposite." Yeshua spoke with great seriousness. "For someone like you, the world of men is unclean and can touch your skin. But your spirit is inviolable. Your spirit makes you clean, not any waters."

"Can you see into me?" I asked plainly, feeling naked despite the thin shift that separated my body from the air. "Am I pure?"

He studied me then for a long time, examining the curve of my belly, my legs, my calloused feet, and dirty toenails.

"You are not pure. But what a good thing it is not to be pure! Do the birds worry if they are pure? Does the river try to wash itself? If we scrubbed away all the dirt, we would have no earth in which to place our seeds."

My stomach tightened. I leaned forward as if drawing physically nearer might bring me closer to understanding him. I could smell him. The irrational desire to touch him throbbed painfully in my fingers.

"Careful," he whispered, the trace of a smile on his lips.

"What were you doing in Bethany?" I asked.

Something flashed in his eyes, and he looked down at his hands in his lap, breaking the intensity between us. "I was visiting friends in Yerushalem for Pesach. They invited me to the Seder."

Why did my whole life change after I saw you? I yearned to ask. *Who are you? Who are you to me?*

"It was an outrageous spectacle," he continued. "Out here you forget how foul the cities are. How full of unhappiness. All those people can think of is money. Coins won't sprout if you plant them in the ground. They won't grow anything." His voice became passionate and he sat up straightly. "To think how many believe they are only clean when they can make it to Yerusalem, the dirtiest city of them all. My friends told me that we would be dining among Yersusalem's finest minds: Pharisees with a complete knowledge of the Law. But isn't it funny how those who teach the Law with such zeal are the most likely to disobey it?"

"My brother-in-law is the host you speak of, and my father is one of the men you condemn," I replied crisply. Silently, I added, *And the man who would be my husband is the richest of them all.*

But Yeshua did not seem surprised by this information. Did he already know I came from wealth and privilege? He must have laughed at highborn women pretending to be Roman, spending all their time on paints and jewelry and gossip.

"If I believed such men were irredeemably sinful, I would never speak a word. I'd go off into the wilderness by myself. But I believe it *is* possible for them to recover their goodness. If they give up their wicked ways, they can be born again," he said firmly.

I picked up a small, rose-colored stone, feeling a pit in its surface. "And I suppose *you* must be completely sinless in order to say such things?" I countered.

He looked me straight in the eye. "I have never claimed to be without sin. In fact, it is only because I have known great sin that I can recognize its presence and prescribe its cure."

"Oh I've heard you were very sinful indeed," I said before I could stop myself.

He laughed again. "I was. I still am." He rose easily, as if he had been ready to spring onto his feet the entire time he'd been sitting there. He had that same energy that pushes the mushrooms up from under the ground in the course of a single night. "Shall we go back, sinner? Saving you from drowning has made me hungry."

Grinning dangerously, eyes sparkling, he offered his hand.

I grasped it, but misjudged my own strength, standing up too quickly and too close.

It would have been easy. Coming together. His lips had already touched mine when he had given me back my breath.

I could return his breath, I thought, opening my mouth slightly.

We stood there, my hand in his, both of us sensing the storm-like energy created by the nearness of our bodies.

My head came up just to his chest and I tipped it back to look into his eyes. They were slightly hooded, his own mouth open. He was not as calm as he appeared. His heart was racing, too.

He dropped my hand, shaking his head and laughing lightly. "You are dangerous," he added, heading off into the forest. Yeshua padded silently along a path he knew by heart. I made a point of hanging back so that I could watch the muscles ripple in his shoulders, the stretch of his long legs moving confidently across the uneven ground.

After a moment I dropped in behind him and in minutes we burst back out into the encampment. The day had already begun. People were breaking their fast. I saw the old woman Michal tending to the arrival of new pilgrims, showing them where to tie up their animals. Adah and Salome were making a stew in a large pot. As I went to join them, Yeshua's hand came down on my shoulder.

"They were able to cook and care for everyone perfectly well before you came. You need not join them."

I looked up at him, narrowing my eyes. "You would have me shirk my duties? For what?"

Removing his hand from my shoulder, he answered in a low voice, meant only for me. "Do you really think those are your duties? You have already chosen other responsibilities, even if you do not know it. Come, let us eat with Yochanan and see what he thinks today."

"I don't care what he thinks," I snapped. "I would keep talking to *you.*"

"Then come," Yeshua rolled his eyes impatiently. "Come and keep talking to me."

Was he tricking me? I glanced back at Adah. She waved at me, not necessarily gesturing for me to join her, but I was sure she expected me to.

Yochanan was speaking near the water. There were the Ben-Zebedee brothers next to my brother, Lazaros, sharing a bowl of walnuts. Andreas was cross-legged, sitting so straight that a small curve in his lower back became visible. He was as still as a little forest creature— the human embodiment of a stump softened by time, already wearing ivy and yellow fungus.

When I nodded quietly and sat down beside Andreas at Yochanan's feet, it was not because I felt I might receive some wisdom from

Yochanan. I was already sure he had nothing for me to learn. What I really wanted was to sit next to Yeshua, to feel our hands brush as he passed me the bread.

What was this feeling? Desire? Love? Fear?

Whatever it was, it was very different from the sunshine of my feelings for Yosseph.

Yeshua made me frantic. And yet it was not upsetting to be with him. What I felt was almost hunger, but as I put a piece of bread to my mouth, I found that I had no appetite.

The question perplexed me enough to put all thought of my mother's apparition out of my mind. She faded into the morning shadows, eclipsed by the blood and flesh of Yeshua; the closeness of his body. It was only years later, stepping into a very different river far from my home, far from the Yarden, that I realized that the woman I had seen waving at me had not been my mother after all.

Having stepped into so many different currents in my life, I now know an important secret: rivers disrupt time. Rounding a bend, the turbulence of the water confuses the solidity of the landscape and causes events to occur differently on opposite banks.

Years later, drawing close to another river at daybreak, I was startled to see a young woman looking at me from the opposite shore. I raised my hand. She raised hers, stepping toward me into the swiftly moving water. And I realized that it had not been my mother waving to me that morning. It had been myself.

What would have happened had I made it across the water? Away from my brother. Away from Yeshua. Away from this story you have traveled so far to hear, across the water, through time and into the safety of my own arms?

Twenty-Three

My blood came later that day. Caught up in the enchantment of the jungle, I had forgotten the reality of my womanhood. I stood there bathing in the river with the other women and groaned with disbelief as I wrung out the cloth, letting the river eat away the color until only a smudge of pink, the clouds of a feeble sunset, remained visible in the weave.

Unfair!

I'd wanted to spend time with Yeshua, and now it was all ruined. For how long would I remain unclean? It could be a day or two; or it could stretch out longer than a week. The uncertainty of my own body frustrated me. I splashed water up onto my face, imagining it washing away my features, leaving behind a pale moon whose thoughts and passions were unreadable.

"The hut farthest from the encampment is used for women during our blood," Adah explained simply, holding a sleepy Gera up against her bare breasts as she used a cup to pour water over his head. He spluttered, reaching a fat hand up as if he could stop the flow.

"Mama! No water!"

"Then you'll have to stop getting so dirty," she chastised her son while running her fingers through his wet locks. She wrinkled her nose, looking at his scalp. "I'll never understand how you get food in your hair."

"I'm a terror," Gera said to me, proudly echoing the words of his mother and father.

"Yes, you are," I giggled, bending down to look him in the eye. "Your mother is a good woman to tolerate your mischief."

Adah walked to the shore, setting her son down in the sand and removing her clothes to bathe in the shallows.

When she turned back to me, I was struck by her beauty. Pale seams traced the curve of her soft belly, showing where it had swelled with pregnancy. From prominent collarbones, her breasts hung down, heavy and full with big, dark nipples. She stood straight and strong without any shame, fully inhabiting her beauty, her short legs slightly apart, water dripping from the dark coil of her pubic hair.

Let me feel so powerful! So inside of myself! I mused.

"We will bring food so that you do not have to wander far in your condition," Adah promised me. "Here, let me show you where to go."

I knew that my brother, Lazaros, and Yeshua were sitting together and sharing stories in the camp just across the river. But more than trees separated us, I thought bleakly as I let myself sink into the cold water. It cupped my breasts under my shift, and I felt the current slide along the sensitive ridge of my neck. I stayed there, looking at the pale blue sky banded by thin clouds that seemed, with every movement of wind, to strip the sky's color even closer to a bare white.

Femi, the Nubian woman, was also in the hut. We shared a simple dinner of lentils and bread. She was not interested in talking, spending all her time beading a little necklace of stones and nutshells.

"Who's that for?" I asked, trying to ignite a conversation.

She gave me a hard, appraising look and did not answer.

We fell asleep early.

Once, through the din of the night wind and the river's roar, I was sure I heard his laugh. Or it could have been the yell of a wild animal, deeper in the forest, signaling that it had caught the scent of its prey.

Femi left the next day. The old woman Michal delivered food, unwilling to share any gossip when I pressed her. "Life is the same every day. Calm yourself," she chastised me before leaving. "You are missing nothing."

But how wrong she was! I wandered down to the river, skipping stones for hours. Each one the river swallowed reminded me of a wasted minute; a minute I could spend back in the camp with Yeshua. With everyone! Why must my body betray me now?

Kemat's voice came to me, softened by years. *It is not bad blood,* she had said once when I caught her cleaning her *nidah* cloth. *It is good blood. It is the blood of possibility.*

It was a restless night, and I couldn't be sure if I was dreaming or awake for most of it. An owl's sonorous cry stretched out endlessly and the sound of wind was like a foreign human tongue. When I finally roused to the white light of early morning streaming in through the hut's open door, I crawled out feeling more tired than rested, and was surprised to see that something had been placed deliberately in the way of the entrance.

A small stone. A bundle of black irises.

I picked one of the flowers up and twisted it by its severed stem, examining its details: delicate veins and faint purple skin just thin enough to let through light from the other side. The smell of the flower was light and sweet in contrast to the heartier aroma of the nearby cedars.

I handled the stone, pink with one small pit. The breath caught in my throat. It was the same one I had picked up the other day. Had Yeshua kept it? I turned the stone over and over in my hand as if it would eventually reveal the answer. But it remained a stone and, no matter how I peered through the trees, I could see nobody.

As I paced around the hut that day, willing my blood to stop, I tossed the stone from one hand to the other. Finally I knew what to do with it and stuck the small weight in my mouth.

I could taste the salt of someone else's sweat, the waxy residue of a warm hand closed over its small body. My tongue's tip fit perfectly into the pit. When I spit it out again, into my hand, it was glistening: pink and wet as something that had just been born.

Late the next day my bleeding stopped.

You are made clean, I thought bitterly. But I was also relieved.

Clambering up onto a rocky outcrop that jutted over the river in this hidden spot, I shook out my hair, freckling the stone at my feet with dark spots. The water glinted where I had just left it, as if my body was still there, disturbing the current.

Spreading out my arms, certain for a moment that no one but the sky and the river were witness to my nakedness, I was sure that there was no such thing as purity. Sometimes my blood was inside my body. Sometimes it wept from my body into the water. My body was the same as the river, the willows, the vines, the doves, the herons. Its scripture had no language. It was never finished. It was always being written and washed away. Surely it had no rules, no laws.

I stepped back onto the soft sand of the shore, making sure to return the black iris to my hair.

"Miriam!" Salome startled me. She had run to fetch me, crossing the shallow portion of the river without changing out of her skirts, which hung damp and heavy in the wildflowers. "You must come!"

"Now?" I asked in confusion, resisting the urge to cover my nakedness.

"Yes! Now! We are leaving!"

• • •

The camp was in chaos. People ran back and forth with bundles of vegetables. The cooking cauldrons exhaled the smell of steaming food. But alongside the expected commotion, men were loading up the donkeys with supplies. Yohan Ben-Zebedee and Thoma were at work pulling apart one of the men's huts.

Salome led me around an outcrop of willows to a small stretch of pebbled beach; the willows' drooping branches offered privacy there.

Adah stood alongside Philip, talking animatedly with Yoses Ben-Zebedee and my brother. Yoses's head was badly sunburned and his face was even redder with emotion. "We should have known it would happen," he growled. "It's been building for months."

"You say it like it's a bad thing," Adah responded, her voice controlled. "I no longer need to be part of Yochanan's community. Are you so attached to him?"

"What has happened?" I asked, turning to my brother. Lazaros was two shades darker than when I had seen him last, his hair tangled with twigs. But he had never before looked so vital, so joyous.

"You should have been there!" Lazaros answered, unable to contain his excitement. "It was as if Moshe and Elishah were allowed to spar!"

"What do you mean?" I looked to Adah and Salome. Salome pursed her lips solemnly. She had refused to explain why the camp was disbanding when she'd come to fetch me. I could see that she was holding her elbows very closely to her sides, tensing her jaw. She was worried.

Philip butted in. "Miriam, Yeshua and Yochanan have had a falling out."

"It was years in the making," muttered Yoses, flaring his nostrils and shaking his head. "Yochanan said he was attracting the wrong people. Too many whores."

"Yoses!" Adah snapped, eyeing Salome. But our friend did not appear wounded.

"I thought Yeshua did not wish to offend his teacher," I offered.

"Don't play dumb, girl," said Andreas, a heavy cloth satchel slung over his bulky shoulders. "You see the difference. Yeshua will teach you. He will teach Adah and Salome. He likes having the children around. And Yochnan would prefer to go out into the wilderness and fast with his closest students."

"There is no reconciling them," Philip added, frowning at his own pronouncement. "Yeshua called Yochanan a snake. They threw many insults."

"A father and son's spat," Yoses disagreed. "Perhaps if we give it time, things will mend."

I was still confused.

Lazaros sought to clarify the issue for me. "You know that Herod has been displeased with Yochanan? Some men arrived a day ago with news that he has sent out *conternubias* of his men whose aim is to find and capture Yochanan."

"Yochanan does not approve of Herod's sinful marriage," Andreas added. "And he continues to preach against him."

I nodded in understanding. "But what does this have to do with Yeshua?"

"It all started around that," Adah explained. "Yeshua believes that Yochanan is in danger and should disband for a while and retreat into the forest. But Yochanan would stand his ground here at the river. Eventually a compromise was made to move to one of our remoter locations."

Andreas clicked his tongue with frustration. "It is madness! And Yeshua knows it. Herod has eyes everywhere. He knows where Yochanan is in every season."

"He will be fine," Yoses argued. "I believe that was only the excuse for the argument. Yochanan seems certain that the Lord wills him to stay."

Andreas was more and more exasperated, his rough cheeks growing beet red. "Are you all so naive? Herod will kill Yochanan."

"So the split is about Herod . . ." I suggested.

They all looked at me. But Salome shook her head. "It is what they tell themselves. But they have been threatening to part ways for some time."

"Is it wrong that Yochanan is unafraid?" Lazaros asked the group.

"Of course he's unafraid," Philip declared confidently. "He has God on his side!"

"And how has that helped all the other prophets?" Yoses thundered, so loudly that I almost jumped. "Habakkuk stoned in Yerusalem. Yeremiah son of Hilkia stoned in Egypt. Ezekiel, Ahijah, Zechariah. All slain. And God was surely with them."

"Is it certain then that Yochanan is a prophet?" I interrupted.

Everyone fell silent. Andreas opened his mouth as if to speak, but decided against it. Adah looked up at Philip as if searching for her opinion in his face.

"What does it matter?" I continued. "I don't see what the quarrel could be if they have agreed to move downriver."

"Yeshua calls Yochanan eccentric and forbidding. It has all finally been brought into the daylight," Philip explained. "And Yochanan called Yeshua's stories childish."

"Do you think they will truly part ways now?" Yoses said; he did not seem convinced of it himself. He spat on the sand then rubbed the spot with his bare toe. "They have had arguments in the past. We must give it time . . ."

Andreas lowered his voice. "Yeshua has long tolerated Yochanan's inconsistent favor. Remember last spring when he would not speak to Yeshua for a month? Yeshua goes to great lengths to prove his asceticism, refusing to drink or lie with women . . . and yet Yochanan has said that in order to be his true successor Yeshua must mortify himself further."

I laughed, startling everyone. "I am sorry. I just don't see how a man can become more holy by leaving behind his duties."

"His duties?" Yoses asked, his eyes blank.

"To love his children and his wife! To make children! To care for the land. To drink and eat good food in celebration of our Lord. How can you uphold the Law when you are suffering from privation in the wilderness?"

Adah nodded in agreement. "Yes. Listen to Miriam. She speaks for us women."

Lazaros shook his head in warning. But I continued. "We must weather the hardships of winter, but we must also accept and celebrate the bounty of spring. If we refuse the bounty, we refuse God."

"Do you accuse me of refusing God?"

Turning, I realized that Lazaros had been alerting me to the presence of Yeshua, who had arrived just in time for my speech. His eyes were black fire and his curly hair was wild with leaves and burs. Had he just woken up from a nap beneath a tree? Still, his expression was unreadable. Something about him appeared to have been locked away. He addressed the group. "You were speaking of me?"

"Yeshua, we were wondering if we will follow Yochanan downriver when he leaves tonight or perhaps go . . ." Yoses offered feebly, finding it impossible to vocalize the possibility of a split.

"You mean to ask if I am parting ways with my teacher? You ask if I call myself rabbi? Master?"

Yoses looked away, embarrassed, and Andreas grimaced.

It seemed as if Yeshua might shout at all of us. But then like a cloud breaking up over the sun, his face relaxed and he smiled lightly. "I tell you that the *least* man is better than Yochanan. And the least man is better than I. Be careful when you speak of prophets. You have only one teacher, one master. And he is your Lord in heaven."

"Forgive me, Yeshua," Yoses bowed his head in shame. "It is hard to think of leaving Yochanan."

Yeshua laughed and stepped over to him, wrapping his arms around Yoses's shoulders, shaking him playfully. "You don't need my forgiveness, friend. Forgive yourself!"

"What Lord do you speak of who is so lenient?" I asked.

But Yeshua directed his gaze to Lazaros instead. "For now we will stay with Yochanan and travel with him to the next camp. We must leave tonight so that tomorrow we are not found by more pilgrims."

Lazaros nodded. "Then we shall leave today as well," he said, speaking to me now. "I am sad that our time here is done, but we were to return soon anyway . . ."

"*Leave?* What do you mean, Brother?" I asked him. "Should we not go with Yeshua's group?"

I could feel my brother wavering beside me. He looked so happy in the wilderness.

But it was Yeshua who spoke next. Coldly. "I forgot to congratulate you on your marriage, Miriam."

"Yes," Lazaros said. "I told everyone about your impending betrothal. It would be wrong to stay away too long. Yosseph and father might worry . . ."

I stared at Yeshua, and he gazed back at me.

"You are right, Lazaros. I am healed and can return home." My mouth was filled with the bitterness of metal.

"Blessings to you and your betrothed," said Yeshua formally, dispassionately. "I hope he is prepared for your sharp tongue."

Everyone laughed and the matter was over.

But I could feel the blood rising in my cheeks and pounding in my ears. The ground felt like rolling water beneath my feet.

The women led me to prepare food for travel.

"What will *you* do?" I asked Adah as I stirred the pan of vegetables over a small fire.

Adah sighed. "God knows. I will go where Philip goes. Perhaps it is time to return home to K'far Nahum."

Salome seemed to be in turmoil. She packed away flatbread between pieces of cloth with such tenderness I thought she must have pain in her hands. "How nice to have a family to return to . . ." she said softly. "I think I will follow Yeshua if I must make a choice. Where else would I go?"

Adah touched her friend's arm gently. "All shall be well, Salome. I know it."

"Did you see it in a dream? All has not been well many, many times . . ." Salome replied. Her face had aged years. I could see a network of lines around her pinched mouth that had previously been invisible.

Adah honored her friend's pain stoically. There was nothing comforting to say. Instead she turned to me. "We must celebrate Miriam's triumph! She is returning healthy and ready to wed a wealthy husband!"

Yosseph. I wanted to tell them that it was no triumph.

I forced a smile. "Yes, I am very lucky."

The truth was, I could hardly remember Yosseph's face. And even worse, whenever I tried to bring him to mind, something else arrived in its place: Yeshua's strong, muscled body at the river, his mischievous smile. The burn of his lips on mine, bringing me back to life. Why had my visions led me here? Life at the river had brought me nothing but dissatisfaction.

I saw to it that Lazaros and I had enough food to get home without need of more supplies. And as I was securing a last bundle, Adah found me again amidst the chaos and pushed a full wineskin into my arms. "For you, my friend. We have too much to carry already." But as her soft face crinkled with emotion, I knew what she was trying to say with the gift of wine was that she was sad we had to part.

I would lose my first real friend in years and it was too much to bear. Impulsively I grabbed her hand. "Adah, you have been a true sister. I hope we see each other again."

Tears beaded at the corner of her delicate lashes. "And you will be fat with a child by then! I wish you many blessings, Miriam. You deserve them."

We embraced then, and I tried to imprint the feeling of her safe, confident body into mine.

Let me absorb her sureness! Her goodness! Her love!

I loaded the ass heavy with our bags and the wine. I rubbed her damp nose and patted her side as she made whistling noises through her big teeth. In truth, I was not comforting the donkey. She was comforting me. The feeling of the animal breathing at my side kept me from the overwhelming feeling that I had lost something I would never find again.

Lazaros approached, the rich color of his cloak throwing into relief the red in his cheeks. "We should leave soon to get to Yericho before it is truly dark."

"Don't you want to say goodbye to your friends? To Thoma?" I asked, hoping to prolong our departure.

"I've said goodbye," he said simply.

"Lazaros, we could go with them . . . we could refuse to return . . ." I tried.

He laughed nervously. "Would you really do such a thing to Father, Miriam?"

He was right. It was a selfish thought. A cruel thought.

"Lazaros!" It was Andreas, helping two other men haul a heavy bag of provisions across the camp. "Don't leave just yet! Lend a hand."

And Lazaros was off for a last melancholy farewell.

I looked around once more. In an hour all traces of the camp would be erased. There would be scuffed footprints and hoofprints in the wet sand, and dirt thrown over the last embers of the cooking fires, the ashes of which would blow away by the following day. Even if I wanted to come back, there would be nothing to which I could return.

I still had the pink river stone knotted into the sleeve of my tunic. Now, as sunlight streamed down illuminating the world with the brightness of ordinary life, I pulled the stone out, fingering its small pit, balancing its negligible weight on the skin of my open palm.

How could I return to Bethany? It would be like commanding the river to turn back on itself, travelling against its current, away from the ocean.

"Miriam."

Somehow Yeshua had approached without my noticing. He stood so close to me that I could feel his breath against my neck.

Turning quickly, I caught a fleeting look in his eyes—almost desperation. Then it was gone, replaced by a blank expression.

"Yes?" I said, wishing I could say the word a thousand times more.

Yes, Yeshua. Yes! Show me where to go. Yes, touch me. Say my name one more time and save it from being said by other lips. Save me from my life!

He stood next to me, his hand also on the ass, gently stroking her flanks. She flicked her ears, blinking slowly with pleasure.

I imagined our shared touch running through the animal, finding union in her heavy, thick blood.

The river. The sleepy-eyed donkey. Golden mice streaking through the thornbushes, their mouths full of grass, leaves, berries. The dew-encrusted morning. Dragonflies piercing the damp air with their glittering wings. Stones glistening pink and smooth. Things that we had briefly shared that would disappear from our lives in a moment.

The sun was behind him. It lit up his silhouette, turning white the edges of his wild black curls while darkening his features. I noticed a scar at the corner of his upper lip, only noticeable in this half light. Sweat beaded at the point where his neck disappeared into his tunic, pulsing along the ropes of his veins. I fixed the image of him deep in my memory so that I could summon it later.

I will remember you when I am very old, and it will be like opening a bottle of perfume that has not aged, I thought. *I will inhale deeply.*

I was not wrong. I am doing it now, summoning him from my deepest memory. And he is as flawed, as frustrating, as irresistible as he was on that day. Even now, years later, having heard the rumors and the stories, I mourn the fact that he resists representation. No portrait can summon the strange union of childlike wonder and keen intelligence that danced across the features of his face.

Perhaps I am telling you this story because I think it will help. At the end he will stand as he was in life: stark and uncreated as a stone that stands in the middle of a flat land, like those stones that stand in circles in the Tin Islands. Stones that confound even those who live among them. How did they arrive? How do they persist through weather and time to stand so tall?

I hope I can give you something that lasts as long. Something that can be touched and tasted. Then maybe he will return to me . . . stand before me . . . say my name as he did that day.

"Miriam," he said again, and his voice was the voice of the river. "I have come to bid you farewell."

I hesitated, wetting my lips. What was there to say? I could not even tell myself what I felt. "So it is goodbye." My words felt flat, meaningless.

His black eyes narrowed and he stepped closer. I longed to reach out and take his hand, press my fingers to the callouses on his palms instead of speaking. My touch would say more than my tongue. And what if he would let me kiss him, just once? Put my lips into the corner where the black stubble met his full lips. Kiss that small white scar. Surely, then he would understand everything.

But I chose to speak instead. "I feel you should know that I am not *yet* betrothed, not *yet* a married woman. I have made no vows. I belong to no one."

He folded his arms across his broad chest. "You belong to yourself," he said simply.

And he left without looking back. Without touching me.

I leaned against the donkey for support. Lazaros returned with another wineskin, a present from Andreas, and he helped me up onto the ass. As I felt the warm body of the beast begin to move under me, I looked back at the river.

Take me to the ocean, I pleaded with the water.

But we set off for home. Backward to Bethany.

Twenty-Four

I watched the slender sliver of blue sky above us, peeking through the willow fronds. Birds darted from branch to branch. Sometimes one of them let loose a cascade of frantic music.

"Love songs," Lazaros laughed. "They are all courting each other."

No, I thought bitterly. *They are songs of longing.*

As night tipped over us like a black bowl placed over a pair of insects, I noticed how the clouds did not disappear but faded into black, just as dreams disappear back into the grain of our wordless thoughts in our first waking moments. *The sky's dream,* I thought wistfully. *Let me relax and fade. Let me forget myself as well.*

Each flower and tree we passed was another painful farewell, another bright exuberance that could not be preserved accurately in memory. In a perfect world I would commission a scent to be made for each of these flowers. I would squeeze the mild, clean odor that the stones had given off near the river when the noon sun hit them. It was as if the forest had become another skin. Another kind of body. I would leave its protection raw and unclothed.

"I can't wait to tell everyone of our travels, Miriam. We have truly adventured!" Lazaros shook his head in disbelief. "And Thoma will come for next Pesach, and Andreas has also promised to visit. I never thought I would make such good friends."

"Why did you feel we must leave?"

He looked up at me, his eyes tightening with distress. "I didn't want to go, Miriam. But it is our duty to return. To Father and to our lives. We must take care of our home. And I must go back to my studies . . . so that I may be a scholar."

He was as upset as I was. Poor Lazaros. We were both bound by roles we found little pleasure in performing.

Night had fallen completely as we approached Yericho's gate. I watched the balsam trees suspiciously. Such cultivated greenery felt artificial compared to the lush forest of the Yarden. *Why make a forest by hand when one has already been given to us?* I wondered.

The city was noisy and dirty. Women squawked, bargaining over food and spices. Men appeared to argue in a foreign tongue that was so slow and rounded I wondered how anyone could ever launch a debate with its honeyed words. Little children caked in filth wove through the crowds. I saw one try to grab a man's money pouch hanging from his belt. But the man was quicker than the boy and grabbed him by his collar, hitting the child, who began to scream indignantly.

At the market I realized I had become accustomed to the silence that surrounded Yochanan's camp. True, people were always talking, teaching, and listening, but there was a sense that as soon as someone closed their mouth, the soft, insistent drone of the river would reassert itself. In Yericho, one voice falling quiet only made room for another. Someone shouted out a good price on Cypriot wine.

Lazaros led us back to the inn where we had made Andreas's acquaintance. But a squat woman informed us that they were at full capacity and could offer us no board. She sent us on to another lodging.

Even from the door I could hear the clamor from inside. Once we'd stabled the donkey, Lazaros grinned to see that in the main courtyard a group of fools were giving some sort of performance by the light of a huge fire.

There were women, too, more draped in cloth than legitimately clothed, their bare arms and legs flashing in the firelight, dancing, beckoning us, leaning up against the porticoes. They smiled at Lazaros, reaching out to us so that the hot blood in their wrists unfurled waves of perfume. Cassia. Lily oil. Juniper. Cypress. Powdery flowers: their tight, sweet fruits, their shade, their clear, nourishing sap.

I couldn't blame Lazaros when he ogled the women. One, older than the rest, her thin lips extended by bloodred paint, reached out and pinched the skin of my waist through my tunic.

"Ow!" I jerked away from her, looking to Lazaros for help.

But the old woman was already propositioning him. "Young man, sell me your whore? I could do good business with such a face."

"I am not his whore," I replied indignantly.

Lazaros blushed all the way down his neck, his eyes wide with discomfort. "It is true, my lady. This is my sister." Lazaros pulled me away quickly.

The old whore cackled, nodding at me as if to say, *it's your choice, not his.*

"I don't think you look like a whore . . ." Lazaros whispered in my ear.

"I'm touched," I snapped.

He looked longingly from me to the bawdy crowd gathered around the fire. "I'm going to make use of our last night of freedom . . ." he said, already approaching a woman perhaps twice his age but with the small, clear features of a girl. Heavy silver earrings stretched out her delicate earlobes. As I watched, Lazaros knelt beside her and said something soft. She laughed, brazenly bringing her hand up and touching his face.

I sighed. My brother could have his pleasure.

Above me the sky withheld its stars, pulsing clear and black as the center of an eye. Each one of my thoughts, no sooner than it had arrived, led back to the river to Yeshua's impassivity, his back turned to me as he left without a proper farewell.

You belong to yourself.

"You look sad. Do you need a kiss?" A girl with dark straight bangs approached me, curling her fingers around my arm and smiling enticingly. Her thick hair and almond-shaped eyes reminded me of Kemat.

"I'm not sad. Leave me be."

She shrugged and turned to a passing man, leaving me with the fragile smell of rose water.

I drifted away from the crowd, kneading my chest with my fingers as if I could loosen the pain there.

Perhaps the loss I felt that night was a premonition. It rattled with each breath I sucked in, tinged with the fire's smoke and the sweat of the men around me. My hands trembled and shook, and every time I swallowed, a burning sensation spread from my mouth to my belly as if I had taken poison. I could taste salt on my bottom lip, could feel my tears sticking my eyelashes together.

Wine will numb my body, I decided, returning to Lazaros for the wineskin. He hardly acknowledged me, much too engaged with the pretty woman who was now sitting in his lap.

I was thankful when the warmth of the wine overwhelmed my senses. My drunkenness lent everything the quality of a dream. It seemed that the people around me were wearing faces I recognized.

An old man with a gnarled cane inset with milky crystals wore the same eyes as Yosseph. The same golden yellow petals spread out from dark irises. Another tall, bald man with a small bone hanging from his ragged ear was certainly Meshkenet, Kemat's husband, until he turned and revealed a stranger's face. The harlot who sat in Lazaros's lap looked at me through the flames of the fire and, for a second, I was sure she was Yohanna, my childhood friend. Yohanna with her rosy cheeks and dark curls. Her habit of pursing her lips while smiling to show she could disapprove of something and enjoy it all the same. Where was she now? Married to a steward in some distant land? Would I ever see her again?

I was overcome with a sadness bigger than my own life. A sadness that everyone I knew would die. Had, perhaps, already died.

At that thought I realized suddenly that I was about to be sick. I lurched out of the courtyard, swallowing back bile.

The hour was late and the lamps that lit the upper level of the inn had been extinguished. The feeble light of the stars came through the windows and revealed dark puddles of blue. Dozens of sleepy exhales rose up from the floor, pushing me forward.

Something sharp sat in the center of me, agonizing even with the wine. I was a lamp's light, weightless with heat and fire except for the darkened wick insisting on its presence in the flame's center, insisting that there was still something being destroyed, still something that could feel pain as it burned down.

I returned to the ground floor, leaning against the arch of the first portico that looked into the courtyard, trying to catch my breath. My stomach roiled and I squeezed my eyes shut, trying to regain a sense of balance.

"What is your name?" The old whore's voice was resonant with a graveled edge. Her painted lips appeared black in the darkness.

"Miriam," I answered.

The harlot barked with laughter, spittle landing on my face. "No. Not that name. What is your *real* name?"

> *I revealed myself to those who did not ask for me;*
> *I was found by those who did not seek me.*
> *To a nation that did not call on my name, I said,*
> *"Here am I, here am I."*

"Here I am," I whispered, echoing Isaiah's words, confused by both the woman's question and my own answer. Still, my drunkenness tipped me forward. I leaned into her body.

"Yes, you are," she agreed quietly, pressing my face to her breasts.

Up close, beneath her kohl and the tightened lines drawn in her skin by years of hardship, she was a handsome woman. She had wide, flat cheeks and a short, well-formed nose ending with delicately flared nostrils that seemed ready to scent danger. The lamplight's pulse made her seem as if she was caught between youth and old age, glow and shadow.

She studied me for such a long time that it felt like years, and I had difficulty drawing a full breath. Finally, she licked her lips and squinted as if she had identified the one wrong loop in a weave. Reaching out, she tucked a loose strand of hair behind my ear. Her hand next to my cheek was warm. She cupped the back of my head. It felt good to have that heavy weight supported by someone else, as if I could release at last the burden of my thoughts.

"You must forgive me for calling you a harlot earlier . . ." she murmured, her mouth so close to me that I could smell mint and cassia on her breath.

"But *you* are a harlot . . ." I responded without thinking.

"And you are *not*, and I am apologizing for my mistake." She did not seem offended and continued to examine my face.

"But you will be mistaken for a harlot again and again . . ." her voice was much softer now. "You should get used to it."

"What do you mean?" Suddenly I was filled with the sense that, perhaps, *this* was the moment I had gone all the way to the river to find.

Not Yeshua. Not the river. But this old whore breathing into me. Telling me my true name. This was the moment the fragments of my visions and dreams would begin to form a full picture.

"In the future," she continued. "In the future, you will wear a whore's face. And we will call to you. We will ask for your help. And you will come to our aid."

"Why?" I didn't feel the need to ask her how she had this information. I felt certain that anything she might tell me would be true. There was a building sense of unease in my stomach, the product of too little food and too much wine. But it was also the strange sense that one gets when they realize they have unwittingly strayed into danger. It was as if I had looked to my side to see a cliff edge and, far below, the unforgiving stones of a gorge.

She shut her eyes and pressed her bright lips into a line. Slowly she nodded. "You are the name of the sound and the sound of the name." Her eyes opened, brighter than before, polished by a few surprising tears.

"What lies ahead? Is it danger? What are you talking about?" I was desperate now and grasped at her shawl. "Should I refuse to return home?" I asked after she did not respond. Only once it was said did I realize it had been my unspoken wish ever since Lazaros and I had left the jungle.

She smiled tenderly, her hand moving from my head to my neck, pressing her thumb to my pulse there. "Even if you do not return to Bethany, you will still arrive in Yerusalem . . ." she said, her voice almost inaudible.

"Miriam! What are you doing?" It was Lazaros, his eyes wide with alarm. In a second, he had the woman by the neck of her tunic. "Take your hands from my sister!" he roared.

"No! Lazaros! Stop! She has done nothing wrong."

But the woman retreated back into herself. Lazaros released her, shaking his hands uncomprehendingly at what they had just done.

She bowed her head and said to my brother, "I have told your sister everything she needs to know."

Lazaros's brow knotted with confusion. But I had no time for him. I turned to the old woman and pleaded, "What do you mean I will end in Yerusalem? How do you know about my life?"

But she melted into the shadows without another word.

"Miriam!" Lazaros was grasping me by my shoulders now, and before I knew what was happening, my body convulsed with a violent wave of sickness, and I vomited down the front of his tunic. "There, there, Sister! Get it out. You will feel better."

When I was done, Lazaros led me upstairs and made us a makeshift bed. He pulled his cloak up over himself and promptly fell asleep. But that whole night I did not sleep. Slowly I shook off the last of the wine and felt my mind become sharp and painful again.

The next morning, as Lazaros packed up our supplies in preparation for our journey home, I searched through the inn for the old whore but I could not find her.

I even went to the innkeeper. "Have you seen a woman . . . a loose woman? She is older, with darkly painted eyes?"

"Older?" The woman chuckled, patting her belly. "There are no old women here but me. No one like that works here."

As we rode away on our beleaguered ass, I couldn't help but wonder if the old harlot had been a dream.

Only now, telling you this story, can I say with certainty that she was real.

And I expect, in the stories written by men like you, I will wear her face.

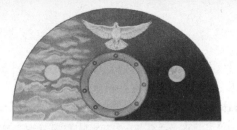

Twenty-Five

The house was empty when we arrived home. The table had not been set. The fire was smoldering into embers.

"Where is everyone?" I called out.

There was no one around. Not even next door. Lazaros was as concerned as I was. I was struck by the strange feeling that more time had elapsed since our departure than we knew. Lazaros called out loudly, surprising me: "Enosh!"

Hurrying up the road was Lazaros's gangly friend, tilting forward as he walked, like a huge crane about to lift off. "Lazaros! Come quick, friend. There's a healer in town!"

A young servant girl appeared a second later, holding a fistful of leeks in one hand and a long, wooden ladle in the other. She had rushed out in the middle of cooking.

"Come on, silly!" Enosh yelled behind him as he raced onward.

But we were both so weary from days of travel that we did not immediately follow.

"Shall we wait? Or go?" Lazaros asked, rapping his knuckles against the stonework of our gate indecisively.

"Maybe we will find Father."

"We've just seen great healers!" Lazaros patted his hollow stomach. "We could stop and have a piece of bread . . ."

But I could feel it: a buzz in my palms, a pooling heat low in my belly. Something important was happening. "No!" I decided. "Let's go!"

I set off, glad when I heard the sure slap of Lazaros's sandals behind me.

Our journey had not come to a close quite yet. We were still moving forward toward some inscrutable destination. Something could still be attained.

In our absence the fig trees had spread out into the fullness of their foliage and the town was dappled with shadows once again. It quickly became clear that everyone was walking toward the center of Bethany. The deeper into our village we moved, the more shadows we crossed: those of leafy branches, short square buildings, the spiny trunk of a dead pine. I measured my breaths in these blue spaces, inhaling during stretches of shade and exhaling in the slanted rays of the sun.

I looked over my shoulder at the purpled hills just visible above Bethany's rooftops. They were quickly taking on the same color as the sky, the whole world one uniform shade and texture so it felt as if, the closer we got to the center of Bethany, the deeper we were inside the body of a huge stone.

My reverie was immediately broken by the chaos of voices rising from the street in front of the synagogue.

The crush of people was so thick—perhaps all of Bethany condensed into one space—that I had trouble seeing what they had gathered to watch. Even Lazaros with his formidable height was forced to rise on his toes, his hand up over his eyes to shield them from the last arrows of sunlight.

Young children were running free, weaving between our legs and pulling at the tassels to our cloaks, their parents too distracted to control their antics. I spotted Yohanna's mother, Serah, talking with her older sister Yahel. At their feet were jars of water and portions of grain; apparently, they had put their daily chores on hold in order to witness the spectacle. As we pushed through the bustle, I saw that my father, in his full ceremonial attire, was standing with the other village rabbis on the steps. He was wearing his best prayer shawl, crisp and bleached bright by the sun.

"What is this?" I asked Lazaros, clutching at his arm so that we would not be separated amid the chaos.

"Be gone, sorcerer!" someone bellowed right behind my shoulder. Nearby, an old man hunched so terribly that his bald head appeared to sprout from the center of his chest. He shook his fists in the air, and I couldn't tell if he was outraged or overjoyed.

"He is a sorcerer, for sure!" Lilah, Yohanna's friend, exclaimed vehemently. "Bethany will not soon cleanse itself of this stain."

"Isn't your mother ill, Lilah?" Serah responded. "Would you deny her such a miracle?"

"Keep moving so we can see," Lazaros suggested.

He ducked under Serah's raised arm, and she squeaked with surprise. "How rude!"

I had left Bethany a dull place. And now that I had returned it was transformed.

Yosseph saw me before I saw him. He stood on the distant edge of the crowd where I could just spot him through the gap between two old serving women. He raised a hand to greet me.

The surprise was just arriving on his face; happiness as light and brittle as a crust of ice on a field. It had not yet penetrated his being. I could still see some last thought hovering in his features, tightening his pupils. Something smoky and heavy and complicated. Something having to do with money.

Yosseph. Slender and as handsome as something made by man. A glass flute designed to hold wine. That was it—he looked as if he had been designed. Each dark wave of hair was oiled perfectly in place. His sandals were polished and new. His whole *presence* was polished and new.

I could not marry him, I realized.

Forgive me that my eyes are wet as I tell you this, Leukas. To think I was so very afraid of happiness and its promise of obscurity. Forgive me if I sigh at my younger self. It is a terrible thing to relive one's foolishness.

I honor that small life now. The one we never had. The long, golden days of peace. Yosseph's uncle Lemuel having come to dinner. My father sitting under a fig tree planted to celebrate the birth of our first child. The house we never shared. The garden. The rock-hewn tombs cradling our bones.

As if he could hear my heart closing to him, feel my feet rocking backward, about to carry me away from Bethany, Yosseph started pushing through the crowd. "Miriam!" he cried. "Miriam!"

I knew then that he trusted me completely. While I'd washed him away with the cold water of the Yarden River, he had let Bethany's sun bake me deeper into his heart.

"Miriam," his voice was quiet honey meant only for my ears. It was the voice of a bridegroom stealing a moment with his bride before the wedding festivities pulled them apart once again. A voice anticipating a soft mattress stuffed with sweet grasses, the gentle sigh of surrender and release. Union. I could taste the perfumes that he traded on his skin, deep in the thick fabric of his scarlet cloak.

"Miriam," he said again, and this time he nearly pressed his lips into my cheek

That is not my name. The thought arrived in my own voice but I couldn't tell where it had come from.

"What is happening, Yosseph?" Lazaros peered over our heads as he spoke, looking toward the synagogue steps.

"Praise be! Praise be!" called out the voices of women and men. They were braided together in wonder.

"The most extraordinary thing has happened!" Yosseph explained. "A man has come and healed Mahli the Cripple. I saw it happen with my own eyes. He bent over and talked to Mahli, and then Mahli rose on his two legs and walked as well as I."

"Mahli?" Lazaros asked. I was surprised to see skepticism in his narrowed eyes. "But Mahli has *never* walked."

An old woman interrupted. "Lazaros, he tells the truth! Mahli can stand and walk."

Lazaros shot me a look as if to say, *These silly people of our hometown. Now that we have traveled, we know better. We are of the world.*

The energy in my palms flamed painfully. "Oh!" I exclaimed, doubling over. There was the buzz of bees in my ears, growing so dense that it was hard to hear anything else. A phantom flavor flooded my mouth. Nectar. Mead.

But a voice rose above it all. Forceful as thunder cracking apart an olive tree, yellow energy splitting into the wood's soft, vertical heart. "Ask and it will be given you," the voice boomed. "I cannot promise that I will be able to heal anyone! But put your faith in God. Everyone who searches finds. Perhaps you will find the healing inside of yourself!"

Lazaros, tall enough to see past the crowd, laughed, clapping me on the shoulder. "What is *he* doing here?"

I could feel energy leaving me, sinking down the veins of my legs, penetrating through the thick callouses of my feet. If I had looked down to see purple blood seeping from me, I don't think I would have been surprised. Some muscular root of the underworld was sucking me into the soil. Someone was using me. Summoning my energy. Calling for it through the ground itself.

"Off of me!" I gasped as Yosseph leaned close. "Don't touch me!"

The sky was the color of stone, and Yosseph's face peering down at me was bloodless.

"Yeshua!" Lazaros called out happily, oblivious to my distress.

But I already knew that Yeshua was there. I'd felt him seeking me, drawing me to him like water into the cracks of a thirsty field.

I elbowed past Yosseph and a woman with a crooked spine. I ducked under Lazaros's arm, until, with a deep breath, I broke out into empty space.

It was like being born.

I breathed and the inhale was laced with the sweat, the pain, the black splinters of desire hidden in everyone gathered around me. It was agonizing. And it was delicious. Each exaggerated feeling woke up a new part of me . . . the pale skin between my toes, the veins tucked behind my ears, the inner corners of my eyes. Whatever energy was being called from my core was not leaving me empty. It was leaving me more alive than I had ever felt. I was finally inside the real world.

Yeshua was standing with his back to me, but I knew it was him. Made more respectable by his flaxen tunic and with his long hair tamed, he raised his arms as if he was about to part the seas.

Tali's blind mother was kneeling in front of him, her narrow eyes opaque and unseeing.

"Please . . ." she begged, twisting her fingers together. "I have never seen my daughter's face."

It was true. She had never seen the plump Tali with her hundred different expressions of dissatisfaction.

"Do not treat this man like a miracle worker! We do not yet know by whose authority he does these acts!" The voice belonged to Rabbi Achan, who stood grasping at a staff next to my father.

"Only a demon can command other demons!" a man called out.

Achan blew air through the gap in his front teeth in agreement, pounding the butt of his staff into the dust.

"I make no claims for myself!" Yeshua responded. Was there anxiety in his voice? Or was it the nervous animation of the crowd I heard instead, making its way into every spoken word?

Mahli was standing to the side, his legs two thin stalks. But he *was* standing, his face slick with tears. He was too overcome to speak as he clutched at his withered torso, shaking his head.

I stepped into the empty circle. The sun behind me pushed my shadow onto Yeshua's back. Into him. Could he know me by my shadow alone?

It seemed so. He dropped his arms and straightened his back without turning.

"Shame on you for doubting a man who does God's will!" The voice was fierce and loud. It resounded off the face of the synagogue, pulsing through the crowd so that everyone jumped with surprise. It was my own voice.

Rabbi Achan wheezed with horror, pointing his staff at my father. Serah turned to Tali and her sister Yahel. "Look! It is Miriam! Miriam of the seven devils. She is possessed!"

But for the first time I truly did not care.

"This man does God's work," I repeated and came to stand beside him, not yet letting my eyes turn to see his expression. "All of you know that I have suffered strange spells my whole life. I have returned to Bethany to tell you that I am healed. And this is the man who healed me."

If I was worried Lazaros would argue against this, I was immediately reassured. Pushing out into the circle, he addressed the crowd. "It is true! My sister who was sick is well. This man called Yeshua is a man of deeds."

Lazaros gave me the most fleeting look. We were agreed. This was the way forward. Although I didn't understand it yet, his eyes said to me, *Yes. This is it! This is how we escape.*

Why did I do it? Without meeting Yeshua's gaze, I saw his hand twitch and open at his side in surprise; I could feel the air contract around us as he inhaled quickly. Why did I need to give him this authority?

"Blessed be his name!" someone called out.

My father broke from the rabbis and came to me, taking me in his arms. I breathed in the familiar scent of temple smoke and oil that was always caught in his clothing. His arms were thin, more like those belonging to a man older than I remembered, but his embrace was strong.

It was over my father's shoulder that I finally met Yeshua's gaze. There was a look on his face I did not recognize, halfway between surprise and intense concentration. It was the look of a young boy seeing how long he could stare at the sun before going blind. And I realized it *had* been nervousness I'd heard in his voice. His whole body was a question quivering at the end of a half-said word.

Why are you here?

And, in answer to my soundless query, he nodded his head and smiled an uncertain smile, just curling the edges of his full lips. But as soon as my father released me and turned to Yeshua, the smile was gone, replaced by a stoic expression. It had been meant only for me.

The crowd grew noisy again, tightening their circle around us. Enosh was animated, waving his big, skeletal hands and crying out that he had never seen such a wonder. Tali was crying so hard the kohl streaked down her cheeks, calling out to her healed mother.

The mood was no longer one of condemnation. No. This was a celebration. A wonder. A miracle.

My hands knew it. My womb knew it. Even my feet knew it.

"My daughter was lost and has been returned to me," my father said gravely, grabbing one of Yeshua's hands in both of his. "You have given me back my daughter!" Yeshua shook off the polite gesture and drew my father into a tight embrace, kissing his cheek.

"When I saw you heal Mahli, I knew you were in possession of extraordinary power. I was not sure from whence it came. But having healed Miriam, I know your authority must come from God."

Yosseph was there, too, his rings glittering as he moved to touch me again.

But I stepped out of his grasp, closer to Yeshua, who did not move away from me. He leaned into the air separating us. Behind us, our shadows merged into one flat blue body.

"Father," Lazaros spoke. "This man was Yochanan the Immerser's favorite student. But he is a teacher in his own right now. Truth be told, I only knew of his parables and exorcisms. I did not know he could heal the crippled."

"So you, like Yochanan, are of the belief that the river's living water washes away sin?" my father asked Yeshua. I could see the spark of flint in his eyes, the click of his jaw. *Oh no.*

Yeshua deliberated for a second. I wondered if he was going to defend his teacher and humble himself.

But he did no such thing.

"I am of a different belief." He rolled on his feet, shifting his weight back and forth from his heels to his toes. It was that energy of a leopard poised to pounce that made people listen. Later, having known him for a long time, I noticed that he grew restless when he was about to say something new—something that surprised him as much as it surprised his audience.

"Heal me! Heal me!"

I glanced around as the men continued to talk leisurely, as if they were totally alone. Meanwhile the crowd was growing larger. We needed to leave.

"Yes, son. Please share your belief with us. I'm always eager to hear about teachings that don't find their origin in the temple." Was my father encouraging him or baiting him? His knuckles were white as he clamped his belt, tapping his foot on the ground.

If Yeshua could pounce, then again, so could my father. Debate was his purpose in life—the thing he practiced most passionately.

"Are we not filled with *ruach*—with spirit?" Yeshua asked in response. But he directed his question to the whole crowd instead of just my father.

"Are we?" A little boy hiding behind Yahel's skirt cried, "What *are* we?"

But my father agreed loudly. "God breathed life into Adam's nose. It is so."

"And yet how did your life begin?" Yeshua prompted.

"Do not play a silly game with this man . . ." Rabbi Achan wheezed, trying to edge in front of my father with his staff. "He will corrupt your ears, Nicodemus!"

But my father easily pushed the old rabbi aside. His eyes were wide and his face was transformed: the dent between his eyes that I had thought permanent was gone. His curiosity had smoothed out his face, making him appear a much younger man. "That's a complex question . . . Yes, God made me, but . . ."

The crowd was holding its breath. And suddenly my father was laughing, clutching his stomach with uncharacteristic mirth. I was so surprised that I reached out to steady him, feeling the boniness of his arm.

Finally he replied. "I would say that my life began after my mother birthed me."

"Exactly!" And now Yeshua was laughing, too.

He made sure to turn his eyes to the crowd, taking care to smile widely at a little girl gaping up at him, her ragged doll forgotten in the dust at her feet. "You are born of flesh! Your mother's flesh! That much we all know. But you cannot enter the kingdom of God unless you have been born of flesh *and* been born of spirit. You must also be born, like Adam, of God's breath."

My heart was melting. Or expanding. I could feel something like lamp oil, golden-green, burning, spreading out into my arms, my legs, and rising upward into my throat.

Yeshua's cheeks were ruddy with passion. His hairy hands were declaratively open at his side, as if this was a teaching he had offered many times, but I noticed an uncertainty quivering behind his eyes. It was clear to me that he had never uttered the words before, not even to himself.

"You hear the wind and don't know where it comes from and how it fills you. Yet it does! So are all who are born of the spirit."

"This is a very interesting idea . . ." mused my father nodding, even as Rabbi Achan spluttered with disbelief behind him. Then he peered around, his black eyes widening as he remembered how many people were gathered around us. The crowd was tightening its circle and growing louder.

"Let us depart," Lazaros suggested quietly.

"Yes, yes . . ." My father nodded slowly, rubbing his hands together. "Will you celebrate my children's return with us? We will have more privacy around our own table."

"We would be honored to have your company and conversation," Yosseph added, his expression one of polite interest. He had heard wild things from many *Chassids*, many storytellers, during his travels. But he would do anything to make my father happy.

He wanted to make *me* happy.

Lazaros embraced Yeshua, clapping the back of his broad shoulders. "Of course he'll come! He hosted us at the river. It's the least we can do to return the favor."

"I fear we will never be able to properly repay you for the healing of Miriam . . ." I heard my father say quietly to Yeshua as we pushed through the crowd. Women reached out, tugging at Yeshua's tunic as we passed. He gently shrugged free, continuing forward.

"I hope you never repay me for something I did not do," Yeshua said wryly, catching my eye. "Your daughter was well when I first met her."

"Don't listen to him, Father," I joked lightly. "He is full of compliments because he knows you promise him a good meal." All the while my pulse was hammering in my throat. He was here. He was in Bethany.

As usual there were many dinner guests. Marta arrived, looking slightly more brittle than she had only a month earlier.

"The child," she said, then sighed, gesturing to the purple circles below her eyes, gripping my shoulder in greeting. "He keeps me up. Keeps me moving. He wants to suckle. And worse, he wants to babble. Constantly. I would have you come and distract him."

Lazaros invited Achim and Enosh, and my father's students began to arrive as night finally settled into the land. It pressed in through the windows of the house so that it seemed we were on an island in the middle of an ever-growing expanse of black water.

I took too long washing my hands at the door, carefully removing the grains of river sand still imbedded under my fingernails until the water in the bowl turned brown and opaque. I could see the murky reflection of my own face, my eyes two black holes, my mouth a wavering smudge that disappeared when I let my fingers brush the water's scummed surface. Did I look the same? It was impossible. My face must reflect how much had changed in me.

"Are you coming?" Lazaros asked

I waved my hand over the bowl of water to erase my face before following after him.

Everyone was seated and my father and Yeshua were already deep in conversation. The only place left to me was next to Yosseph on a scrolled couch covered in a dark green cloth. I crossed my legs under my dress, noticing how Yosseph's breathing quickened in my presence.

I resisted the impulse to shake him roughly. *Wake up!*

"Are you in pain?" he whispered intimately. "Was the journey hard on your body?"

"I am not so fragile as that," I grumbled. "Do I look ragged?"

"No!" he exclaimed, blushing. "I didn't mean to insult you. You are more beautiful to me with every passing day . . ."

Why couldn't he do something to deserve my revulsion?

I am wasting love, I thought with a flutter of fear. *I am wasting a good man for one I may never have.*

But then the sound of Yeshua's easy laughter and the deep rumble of his voice made me forget my fear. What mattered was Yeshua.

"You were gone so long . . ." Yosseph murmured and under the cover of the table he grasped my hand tightly, crushing my fingers. I could feel one of his rings grinding into my palm, leaving a mark.

Yeshua saw us, noting our closeness. I raised an eyebrow as if to say, *What of it?* His smile disappeared. He turned back to my father, pulling a piece of bread through a dish of honey and almonds, a few stray drops catching on the sleeve of his tunic as he lifted it to his mouth.

But Yosseph hadn't noticed any of this. "Are you tired, Miriam? Shall we go somewhere more private to speak?"

"No!" I said unthinkingly, "I would prefer to sit and rest my legs."

Yosseph nodded and turned to study Yeshua. "And you encountered this man at the river? I've never met anyone like him . . . There is something akin to madness in his eyes."

"You think him mad?" I asked sharply, setting my wine cup down with a clink.

Yosseph's face rearranged itself to please me. "No! Not at all." He smiled gently. "In fact, I think the opposite—although I am not trained in Targums and scripture like your father. I can still tell that Yeshua has a keen grasp of the Law . . ."

Yeshua, who had been listening, broke in on cue, his voice rich with wine and mischief. "And yet I've no formal training! Unless you have a question about the making of tables or the setting of beams . . ."

"I find that hard to believe!" Yosseph countered politely. "You speak with great ease about difficult matters."

"Believe it!" countered Yeshua, turning to serve himself more of the lamb that had been replenished by one of the servants. "If you wish to speak to someone well versed in the Law, I expect all you would need to do is turn to your side."

It took me a moment to realize he was talking about me rather than my father or one of his students.

"Oh yes. I know," answered Yosseph mildly. "Miriam never forgets anything. She can recite any song she has ever heard . . ."

Miriam. The good girl. The girl who could recite rules and recipes and songs. Was that all I was to Yosseph?

I stood abruptly, nearly upsetting the dishes. The wine in my cup jumped and wept one red tear down its side, onto the table.

Yosseph flinched, twitching his heavily embroidered sleeve away from the spill.

Suddenly I was struck by how much the wine looked like blood.

Why is blood so frightening to men? I wondered.

"I am tired after many days on the road," I announced to the whole table. "Forgive me. I must retire for the night."

"Of course," my father said, standing up hastily. His eyes went small and wrinkled at the corners with emotion. "Rest, my daughter. I am blessed beyond measure that you have been returned to me healed."

I turned back and Yeshua's eyes searched mine. He seemed to speak without opening his mouth.

Miriam . . .

I broke away, breathless. But I did not go to bed. Instead I slipped out of the house and clambered up the ladder that led to the roof. The air up there was fresh, and insistent spring smells rose from the flowers and fruits below.

The night shivered. Folded. Something darker was blotting out the stars. Wings swept over me, rearranging the heavens. The owl's feathers brushed the top of my head, anointing me with the hunter's flinty determination and clarifying the thoughts that had been circling smaller and smaller inside my head.

Why is Yeshua here? What will I say to Yosseph? Why do I feel so torn?

The great bird carried away these concerns. It swooped down into the garden toward some unsuspecting heart, hidden like a gem in a handful of silken fur, tucked in the shadowy grasses.

My mother's bones lay in the dark garden. The footprints of my childhood, long overgrown with thornbushes, still existed in memory. I could place my feet on them, walk my old path to the tower. I could stand in the fields where I had watched Kemat bring Meshkenet his lunch.

I sighed, bent over, and pressed my hands into my stomach, breathing in deeply through my nose. Then slowly I sat down on the grass mats, remembering that night many years prior when, on this very spot, Kemat had told me the story of the Egyptian queen.

The same stars above me had illuminated that long-ago night.

As I watched, they blinked in and out of focus, like sleepy, dispassionate eyes. They were eyes from above that belonged to beings much too huge for me to see . . . faces too dark, too vast for the size of a human mind.

All was sky, and as I quieted myself, my heartbeat imitating the rhythmic sparkle of the heavens, I could pretend that I did not exist at all. My eyes were just another part of the firmament: two stars blinking back at those other beads of light.

Stars. No stars. Stars. No stars.

Perhaps someone else in some other world was staring up at the night sky, at the stars, and looking into my own eyes.

"Miriam."

It was not a question.

Yeshua had come to join me on the roof. His shape was somehow darker than the darkness that had swallowed all else. I could see him like the owl, a vibrating shadow approaching and obscuring the stars, carefully lying down beside me.

He stank. Perfectly, his sweat so pungent it made my skin prickle and set a thirst in my throat that I knew water couldn't quench.

"What are you doing here?" I asked him.

He said nothing, but I could hear the air moving into his huge chest as he took a long, deliberate breath. "I was invited by your father." There was a smile in his voice.

"I thought you were going to follow Yochanan downriver. Why are you in Bethany?"

The owl answered for him, hooting from the garden with such exultation that I knew he had caught his prey.

"I thought you hated Bethany and all the Pharisees here . . ." I said when he offered no answer.

A wind rose from the west, dry and smooth, drifting over the roof and sending my hair wild. It drifted over my lips. I knew that it had tickled his face when he chuckled quietly.

How very close we were! His features appeared blue and strange, only faintly illuminated by the scythe of a moon just cutting through the sky's hard shell. He was inhuman: a strange mixture of weather and animal, thunderclouds growing thin and tall as pillars as they rose above the mountains. Movement itself. Snaking ivy, leaves flickering with sun. Plural.

I drank in his heat and it only made me thirstier.

"What are you doing to me?" he asked huskily.

I was surprised enough by the question that I cried out lightly. Almost a laugh. "I am doing nothing," I said. "I am asking you very simple questions that you have refused to answer. Why did you come here?"

When he spoke it was not an answer. His voice was softer than I'd ever heard it, almost musical.

"When I was a young boy, I had very strange dreams . . . Dreams that did not happen when I was asleep. Yes, they did come late at night. But I was always awake. I would sneak out of my parents' home and walk up into the fields. I would run to a nearby hill where I knew there was a view of the valley. But all would be black. I would stand there watching that blank expanse and then my vision would begin to shiver.

"I would see shapes in the blackness, Miriam. People walking, holding torches and great stone bowls of ochre and blood. They were heading into the hills. Into the rock. And then I would be inside of the earth itself with these people. I could feel the warmth of their strong bodies beside me. But all I could see were tongues of flame licking the walls, veining the darkness.

"Slowly in this dream world, the light would reveal animals. Not real, but painted. On sloping walls of stones, long muscular legs appeared that seemed to run across the rock as the torches flickered. Women dipped their hands in the bowls of ocher and then pressed their palms next to pictures of men with the heads of beasts. I knew that these were my people. A people who had lived inside of the mountains and had been able to slip into the minds of animals . . ."

I could see his visions clearly because they were my own. The same huge, inhuman power that had flooded through me in my youth when I had looked in the leopard's eyes, when I had raced through the trees at night.

I startled at the lightest pressure of a touch tracing the long bones of my hand. His finger moved down to the place where my veins surfaced in my wrist.

How wrong to think that this man's touch could heal. It did much more than that. Let me tell you that his touch could set you afire.

"Your hands are hot," he whispered.

"Yours are, too," I answered.

We were quiet. Then he continued, letting his hand slide to my upper arm.

"As I grew up, the dreams stopped. I traveled far and sought wise men who could tell me what these visions had been teaching me—or teach me how to coax them back into my life. But I became convinced that they would never return. Then miraculously they began again: more vibrant and more intense than they had ever been before."

"Why are you telling me this?" I asked finally. "Are you trying to teach me something?"

"Do you want me to teach you something?"

"No," I said decisively.

I felt exposed, as if the whole of my body was in my words: my sinews and muscle and reserves of milky tears bursting into my voice.

"Maybe I'm asking you to teach *me?*" His breath was sun-warmed grass. "I only want to tell you that I studied and meditated and could never again reach that bliss. I could only remember the magic of my childhood from a great distance."

He came closer still and his curly beard brushed against the softness of my cheek.

"But the dreams *did* return. Incredible dreams . . ."

His voice disappeared under emotion I could almost taste. Thick. Melancholic.

I let the silence swell, bloom. Whatever came next would change our lives. "Do you know when the dreams returned?"

I shook my head. My whole body was aching.

"They returned the night after I first saw you. Here in Bethany."

I felt that I would fall into a spell and never return. But it was not frightening. Finally I felt alive.

"How did you do it?" he asked.

"Do what?" My voice was rough with hunger. I could not disguise my desire for him any longer.

"I could feel you," he replied. "I feel you through my feet when you're near. Sending me energy. Today at the synagogue. Like lightning traveling through the soil itself and into me. I've never healed a man before."

"You're speaking of Mahli the Cripple?" I reached out to touch his shoulder, shocked by how real he felt, how sturdy, taking pleasure in the swell of his arm through the rough flax of his tunic.

"Yes. The cripple." When he spoke it was slow, almost halting. "I bent down to give him a blessing . . . and then suddenly he was rising to his feet, proclaiming the miracle. I swear I did nothing. It was you. Nearby. I knew it. You were helping me. We did it together."

"You are not an ordinary man." I said plainly, claiming no responsibility.

"You are no ordinary woman."

We were silent for a long time. He leaned into my touch. I felt the night between our bodies grow frantic and hot as a flame does around the lamp's last inch of wick.

"I came to Bethany to find you," he murmured.

I drew my hand back and it burned with absence as I laid it on my own chest. "You have found me. What will you do now?"

I already knew the answer. I was singing it with every inch of my skin. But he spoke my own mind for me, from the root of my own desire.

"Miriam. Now that I have found you, I will *have* you. I will never be parted from you again."

• • •

I can smell Bethany now better than I can picture it: wind threading through the fig trees, picking up the sticky pollen hidden on the leaves, the wetness of olive leaves making the air something thick, sweet, and drinkable. I would wake with it in my mouth, making me thirsty, not for water, but for colors and sensations.

The next morning I emerged from sleep with that smell coating the back of my throat, tickling a sigh that had been held there, curled into a ball, since I had first seen Yeshua in front of the synagogue. It was a sigh that was caught halfway between relief and sorrow.

It was barely dawn, the light wavering through my window so that the shifting shadows of olive leaves—interstices of circles and curves that danced and swam like fish—were thrown up against the far wall.

An ocean. In my future. The cold sweep of waves bringing these fish to the shore.

Was I dreaming?

I sat up, clutching at my body to prove that I was real and awake. My breasts were still high and small, the nipples hard little berries. My palms drifted downward to the soft curve of my belly, my finger pointing toward the hair that curled protectively over my sex: dark, tangled, and fragrant.

Time was happening differently to me, stretching forward slowly as within a dream. Maybe it was still Pesach.

The house was asleep, the lamps unlit, the corners filled with puddled darkness and the morning mist.

I went back up to the roof where the sky was still stained with night. It was a violet color that looked as if it could so easily break, falling as shards of dawn around me until I stood somewhere else entirely . . . somewhere without roofs and towns, without people, without a sky.

The kingdom of God is like this . . .

Even on the roof the words managed to reach me, a black pulse of them against the back of my eyes. They signaled his voice without its actual sound.

I clutched my arms around my elbows, pressing my palms into the sharpness of my joints, feeling as if I might become the wind itself if I squeezed myself tightly enough.

"Shall we say the Shema together?"

My father surprised me. I swung around just in time to see him pull himself up from the ladder, crawling onto the roof on his knees and hands before stiffly rising.

Surely he was not so old as this. How had he aged so while we were at the river?

Without a word exchanged, he joined me and we fell into the rhythm of praise we had shared for so many years. Praising the land.

The dawn. The sun. The city. We raised our hands and recited the words that summoned my childhood.

We will always stand here together, I thought. *Our praise has been stamped onto this roof, into this morning, so completely that it will never truly fade or pass away.*

Perhaps that is true. Yerusalem has been sacked. Bethany is burned and gone. But I would like to believe that some spectral presence of love and devotion—a father and daughter standing side by side—still shimmers in the sunlight over that desolate land.

While the sun rose and signaled the beginning of a new day, a new life, I could feel our words hovering at the end of a story, putting its characters and poetry to bed.

The last of the wine, I thought as the fields reddened under the new light.

When it was done we stood shoulder to shoulder, watching as these brilliant reds grew keen and fresh before, in a matter of seconds, they faded into the pale blues and browns of ordinary life.

Daybreak.

I turned to my father, knowing that the words I spoke would change my life. They could exact a punishment so complete I would no longer be his daughter, no longer be Miriam. I remembered the crumpled face of the adulteress Ester all those years before. A woman who had followed her desire rather than the will of men.

"Father, I cannot marry Yosseph. It is not possible."

He looked at me, his face unreadable, eyes impassive, hardly seeing me. He laced his fingers together over his stomach and lowered his chin as if in grief.

I could hardly breathe.

Then to my surprise, his black eyes flashed with good humor. The furrow in his brow disappeared again and he smiled with more ease than he had in years.

"Of course, Miriam. I know. You belong to another."

In the distance a dove began to cry, something halfway between a song and a warning.

Twenty-Six

It has taken me my whole life, a life of impatience and hot blood, to realize that the greatest sin of all is the sin of speed. To move quickly is to go against the natural sway of seasons, the river's meander, the slow pulses of dawn and dusk stretching out the day's colors.

But to be young is to be quick and to desire swiftness from those moments that should be savored.

We were betrothed by the end of the week: a simple ceremony held in the garden with my father, Marta, Lazaros, and Lazaros's friends Achim and Enosh in attendance. The fig tree's fallen fruit sent up the resplendent smell that comes just before rot, and the delicate mustard blossoms crushed underfoot seemed a better seal of our promise than any spoken words.

I can still see Yeshua, all outline and gesture, wearing a cloak with blue-threaded borders I had sewn the previous year on one of my mother's grandest looms. Earlier in the day, Lazaros had taken him into the city to a barber so that now the strong line of his jaw was visible under his clipped beard.

Yet there was no taming him. He had laughed as Marta struggled to comb down his wild curls.

"It's no use!" she exclaimed when one of the comb's teeth broke off in his tangles.

"My mother used to complain about our hair, mine and my brothers' too," he explained genially, fishing out the broken tooth and examining it. "She called it a weed that was worse than anything that grew in her garden!"

I thought he looked perfect. He was too big, too wild for Bethany. And I loved that his very body reminded me of the forests and rivers.

Messengers were sent to his hometown of Nazareth to make preparations for the wedding and to ask for his mother's blessing. We were allowed no time alone.

I felt myself turning into steam at the edges whenever we were close, my blood moving so quickly that it couldn't help but slip out of myself and into the wind.

On the second morning after our betrothal, he left for Nazareth. He would gather his relatives for the wedding and then send for my family and me.

My father, upset that Yeshua had refused a pouch of coins, had pressed a wineskin into his chest. "I would not have you travel such a distance without some sustenance. And what would you give a lestai if they tried to rob you?"

"I would give him the cloak from my back," Yeshua replied, laughing and grasping my father's shoulder firmly. "I would give him everything I own."

My father laughed and laughed at this. His time with Yeshua had made him lighter. Even his eyes appeared more brown than black.

Finally, alone in the morning light, thin and clear as water, we stood close to the front gate. With nothing but a simple pack swung over his shoulder for the journey, he no longer tried to hide his desire.

His eyes, which had been so guarded when we'd first met, were as open as the late spring flowers bursting into full bloom around us. His mouth parted around the shape of my name. "Miriam," he breathed, as if to ask me a question.

"What is it?" I wanted to touch his chest but knew that we were not yet allowed such intimacies.

He squeezed my hand, sending a shiver up my arm and down into my belly.

I felt *planted*, like roots sinking into the soil between my toes. His touch was the touch of a gardener placing my seed in the flaky soil as slowly and intimately as a lover. This, so that I would burst and begin to grow. A hundred years later you could return to this place and find me a head taller than the house, my leaves providing ample shade, my trunk thick and twisted in a slow, weathered dance.

Yeshua brought my hand to his lips and, lowering his chin, looked down his long nose at me, the scar at his lip just catching the light. To my surprise, he tasted the tips of my fingers.

"Miriam." This time he smiled. "Soon you will be mine."

Each time he said my name it felt more like my own. Each time he looked at me, it was as if I was finally becoming myself.

Without another word, he turned and departed through the early morning shadows.

Afterward I floated through my chores, hardly feeling my feet on the limestone floor. I tripped and laughed, bumped into Beltis carrying a jar of water, and hugged her when she began to curse at me. I surprised her when I asked to take back charge of the oil press.

"It will be good to keep busy while I am waiting!" I explained. "I don't think I could bear to sit still."

But it didn't matter. Time sped by. Sunsets lasted as long as a quick inhale. It was as if the days themselves were conspiring toward my happiness.

I would be married to Yeshua. We would be together.

But Yosseph did not yet know that I belonged to another. He had stopped by the day after we arrived in Bethany and my brother turned him away with the excuse that I was still sleeping, recovering from our month of travel.

As the days following my return turned into weeks, Yosseph was not so easily dismissed.

"She cannot *still* be tired," he'd complained when my brother made my excuses yet again. "If she is ill, should we not send for a physician?"

Lazaros, who had been strangely unsurprised by my betrothal to Yeshua, confronted me over our morning meal. "You can't let this go on any longer, Miriam. The man deserves to be free to find another wife."

I nodded stiffly.

Yosseph. What could I possibly owe him? He hardly seemed real to me anymore.

But Lazaros had splayed his hands on the table like spiders and would not look away from me.

"Are you saddened that Yosseph will not be your brother?" I asked, returning the challenge.

"Are *you* saddened that he will not be your husband?"

I closed my eyes and took a deep swath of the scents around me: dust riding the air, temple smoke thinned by the distance between Bethany and the city, and the unmistakable tang of my sweat rising from the secrecy of my own body.

"I'm happy that Yeshua will be my husband," I finally said.

"Then I, too, am happy." Lazaros's sharp cheeks reddened with an excitement that I realized he had been holding at bay. I had given him room to reveal his true feelings. "I already feel that Yeshua is a brother."

It was later that same day that Yosseph came to call again. I knew that I must face him. But I underestimated him. My desire for Yeshua had simplified Yosseph into a pretty sketch: all surface, with no depth of intelligence or intuition.

But when I greeted him, I saw that he already knew. The vigor had gone from him. His lips were pressed into so flat and wide a line it looked as if his face had been split in half.

He had cut his hair short, above his ears. I had never seen him look so austere. Even his earring was gone, leaving behind a tiny pinprick in the lobe that seemed to me like the absence of a star in the night sky.

There would be no beauty between us. No softness.

"I don't know why I even came," he said.

"Yosseph . . ." I didn't know what to say. I felt like a fool standing before this man I had been supposed to love.

And did I still care for him? There was a part of me that was pained by his coldness. I longed for him to smile and sweep his hands out magnanimously, saying, "We shall be good friends forever. Nothing has really changed between us."

A group of children cried out cheerfully from the next street. The thin, gray shadow of a lark sliced across the mellow, cloudless sky.

I felt silly, almost greedy, at my wish for a reconciliation between us. Why couldn't I let him go more easily?

The trellis that curved in front of the path sighed briefly in the afternoon wind, its sinewy vines relaxing enough to let fleshy, pink rose petals flutter down upon our heads. Yosseph didn't even reach up to brush them away.

Crowned with roses, I noted that the familiar gold flecks ringing his irises appeared less like flower petals and more like tiny golden blades circling dangerously in his eyes. Something had shifted in him permanently.

Yosseph. Forgive me! I think now. I didn't understand our story—a story that was already longer than one life. It stretches in many directions: snaking river-like into the distant past and more uncertainly, a silver thread of stream water licking through the hills of the future.

We had been wed before. We had been husband and wife before. I am sure of it now. And he expected that it would happen again. Even if he did not know, his soul thrummed with this ancient certainty.

But I already belonged to another; someone whose hold on me was thousands of lifetimes older than his.

It was agonizing. I rocked backward on my feet. My hand rose to my neck, trying to relax my throat enough to speak the words that would send him away. "Yosseph, I am betrothed to someone else."

"Do not patronize me, Miriam. It is the talk of the town." His voice was acerbic, and his elegant narrow nostrils flared with anger.

But I saw that his anger was a mask for the deeper, more hopeless sorrow that lived just below the surface. My eyes were suddenly unveiled and I saw him as he would look many years later: beard long and dove white, age-frosted eyes sunk deep in his delicate skull, resigning himself to another fate he had not expected.

In that moment I saw Yosseph as he looked when he left me here. Here. Sitting where you sit now, Leukas, on the day he left this hut for the last time.

The words I spoke next were true but empty. "I made no promise to you, Yosseph. And so I can break no promise."

"No promise . . ." he echoed, turning from me and shaking his head. He chuckled dryly. "No broken promises. Yes, Miriam. Don't worry. You are absolved of all guilt."

Yosseph bowed his head and backed away, and a space opened inside of me, hollow and ragged-edged as a death wound.

I brushed the roses off my shoulders, watching as they fell, bruised and folded, onto the dirt.

Oh, do not mourn him! I long to tell my younger self. The sorrow was not in his departure, but in the fact that it was impossible for him to break free of me.

Yosseph walked away that day, and he is gone now, certainly dead. But I have never lost him. I can feel him yet; I can still bring every age of his face to mind.

No matter how hard he tried, or how far he walked, Yosseph never left me.

Twenty-Seven

Marta came to help me pack my belongings, bringing to me a satchel of my mother's old dresses. We sat in the bedroom we had shared years before, laughing and sifting through dusty silks and creased tunics.

Yeshua filled every inch of my being. His smell. Sweat and sour, split wood. Something nutty and freshly alive, just having sprouted up through the ground. The memory of the dimple pressed into his cheek. I longed to kiss the corner of his full lips, taste the smoke caught in his beard, run my fingers down his long spine to the taut, tight muscles of his lower back.

"You are distracted!" Marta complained, smiling good-naturedly. She put down the wooden bangles she had been holding. "You seem drunk."

"I feel drunk," I admitted, blushing. "I feel almost mad."

"It is really love, then." She pinched my cheeks as if to examine how their color might enhance this fact. Her breath was wildflower-laced honey. Her eyes were wide and dewy—fringed with sparse lashes that clumped together. The same shape and color as my own.

"It *is* love," I assured her. "Is that such a bad thing?"

"No." She pursed her rouged lips, placing her hands in her ample lap. "But it is a dangerous thing."

"Love is dangerous?" I asked with a laugh.

She did not laugh in response. Her face was suddenly serious. "Yes, Miriam. Men are dangerous. Never forget that we make them even more dangerous when we give them our love."

I smiled haughtily, brushing off my sister's words. But now I remember them like bright flags flapping in the wind, a red warning against the flat expanse of the desert.

My sister warned me. And I failed to listen.

• • •

Our wedding was scheduled for late summer.

"Why wait a whole year when the harvest will soon arrive? You are already past your best childbearing years . . ." Marta reasoned one night when she joined us for dinner. Amos was away on business and she had left her son Kernan under the care of Atalyah.

"Is that all you care about?" I joked, arching my eyebrows at my sister. "My breeding?"

My father reddened with embarrassment to hear it spoken of so plainly and tilted his head back toward the pale blue sky. Some sparks from the cooking fire floated up above us like the afterimage of a star. Late afternoon winds had lifted the heat and it was cool enough to eat in the courtyard.

"It is time you started your own family," Marta kept on. "What would Mother say if she knew you had stayed unmarried for so long?" Marta rose to clear our dishes, but I beat her to it, stacking my father's cup neatly into mine. Robbed of her role as housewife, my sister patted her hands aimlessly on the fine weave of her skirts.

Misinterpreting our play as an actual argument, my father broke in gruffly. "Miriam, calm yourself. Are you not happy?"

"Yes," I said simply, "And let me be happy for a while before I become a mother."

"It is not for you to decide," my father replied, but not unkindly. "God will give you a son when the time is right."

A son.

I tried to imagine a younger version of Yeshua: his face smooth, eyes unnaturally large without a beard or a man's strong jaw to balance them out, his legs having just grown long, carrying his new height awkwardly. My imagination would prove very far from the real thing. We can make our children from our flesh and blood. But we cannot simply make them up in our minds.

Marta seized on my silence. "Will we shoulder the whole cost of the wedding? I understand this man comes from a poor family. We can't let circumstances steal Miriam's occasion."

My father grunted, spitting off the side of the table, "Silence, Marta! It is unseemly to speak of money for such occasions. Of course we will supplement his family's offerings."

"He has a wealthy relative in Kanna, and the wedding will be held there," I interjected, having placed the dishes to the side. "They will provide their own food and wine, and we have every cause to believe that it will be a splendid affair without our meddling."

I shook my head in disbelief. To think the girl who had bargained with her father for freedom would so willingly give herself over to a man.

I didn't dare say what I actually felt: that I cared little for the finery and ritual. That all I wanted was to touch him.

Twenty-Eight

A retinue of my family and friends approached Kanna, our sandals worn down by three days on the road. The salty air from the Gennaseret Sea blew across the fields. The hills were so green that they appeared almost blue, as if the sky had become heavy enough that some of its substance had slipped down to cover the dirt and the grasses.

Explosions of white-flower squills, standing as tall and alert as candles, blurred the road's edge, along with purple henbane and red poppies bleached pink and papery by the summer sun. Mice danced through the bushes, more a movement than a visible presence. Paths snaking through the fields showed where the foxes had run the past night.

Finally we arrived at a small village of rough-hewn homes. There was a well, animals, children. Sheep wandered through the grasses without a shepherd in sight.

The town was lifted above the rest of the landscape by a series of swelling hills that had been terraced into farmland. I could smell citrus groves on the wind. Orchards, too, seemed to spill out of themselves, sending out low, heavy branches that blurred their borders. Almond and pomegranate trees wove their fragrances through the air, and the red-grape trellises of the passing vineyards showed their empty vines in prelude to the fresh harvest wine I knew we would soon be served.

A tall woman was waiting for us on the muddy road. At her feet was a water jar she must have been carrying when she saw our retinue.

As we approached, her features sharpened. Big, deep-set eyes were shielded by a heavy, masculine brow, and her lips were full even in her advanced years. She was not beautiful—not compared to the pale sketch I still held in my mind of my mother's graceful figure. But she was a handsome woman with her straight back, wide hips, and skin that, although wrinkled, looked like it would be warm to the touch: an even shade of dark gold.

This was a woman who had stood under the sun her whole life—washing babies, stomping grapes into wine in the green air of the orchards, tending to animals, reaping her reward from the fertile land.

"Shelama!" Lazaros cried up to her. I pushed between him and Enosh, wanting to be the first to officially arrive. Everyone had come along; my sister had even insisted on bringing Atalya. Kernan babbled, "Sheep! Sheep! More Sheep!"

"Hush . . ." Atalyah sighed, barely able to make the words out.

"Greetings!" I called out to the tall woman. "We have come to Kanna for a wedding. Do you know where the house of Shimon lies?"

The woman laughed a big belly laugh. She clutched her stomach, her eyes twinkling.

Her mirth seemed to make her actually expand. Then her lower half swelled and another form detached from her, its small hand tightly clasped in her own: a girl no older than nine or ten.

At this she pushed back the rough, undyed shawl so that several silver strands escaped. "You speak of my own brother! Are you *her?*"

My father had come up behind me without my noticing. "Do we have the honor of speaking to Yeshua's mother?"

"Yeshua! Yeshua!" The young girl interrupted, tugging at the rough edge of the woman's sleeve. The child was covered in dust from head to foot, her long, messy braid almost white with caked mud.

"Quiet, Yael!" the woman scolded. "Show some respect for your brother's betrothed."

I blushed. Should I kneel? Lower my eyes? How was I supposed to greet my new mother?

She answered the question by coming to me and embracing me with such vigor I was worried I might snap. A big, warm heat emanated from her sturdy body, like the comfortable even pulse of a cooking fire. "So! You are the one who has made my son act like a proper man!" she thundered in my ear. "I must thank you! Shelama, Miriam. I, too, am called Miriam. As we share a name, we shall soon share my son."

"May I call you Imah?" I asked quietly, and something stuck in my throat. *Imah.* Mother.

"Of course! You could call me 'old hog' if you want. I'm nothing!

Just a poor old woman worried sick about her sons." Miriam waved her hands back at the village as if to implicate the entire population.

Yael piped up, "Call me sister! For I am his *best* sister. Yeshua says I am his favorite!"

Imah yanked on Yael's braid, chuckling. "This dusty beast is the last gift I have from Yeshua's own father. This next Sukkoth will mark ten years since his passing."

A rasp as my father cleared his throat alerted me to his discomfort. His hand went to my elbow, pinching my arm as if to assure himself that his daughter was still real.

He is reminded of his loss. My mother gone. Marta married off. And now I am to leave him too . . .

"My sympathies . . ." my father offered in a dry, mannered voice.

"Sympathy! Keep it for yourself, old man!" she squawked, holding her belly again. "Let us get moving! Follow me!" And she took off, a steady stream coming from her mouth all the while.

"There is much to do before the wedding. I will need all the hands you can spare. And as usual, my son will not bother himself with any of the details. Even though it is his responsibility. Even though he has left everything to me his whole life. Do not mistake my impatience with his behavior for ingratitude. But shouldn't a mother expect that her own son will lighten her load or provide? Nothing. I have received nothing these past five years. I still believed he was with the madmen up at Qumran. I had no idea he was with the river prophet . . . no message. Imagine how my heart jumped when he walked into our town this summer. I had long ago decided he was dead. You see, I am a woman who expects death . . . Thank the Lord for my son Yakov, or I would surely have been crushed by this world."

Even with Yeshua's sister dragging her feet, Imah set a fast pace. We made our way through the crooked streets until it seemed we had walked around the whole town several times over. I was sure we had passed the same squat, one-story building almost consumed by vines at least three times when we finally rounded a corner and came out on a ledge.

Imah slipped easily down the uneven steps of a stone stairway cut into the hill. We made our way down one person at a time, the donkeys resisting the sudden descent. I hung back and laid a hand on each of their heaving sides as they passed.

"My cousin is wealthy enough. Not that he is very generous . . ." Imah informed us as we reached our destination. My father had to stifle his laughter with a hand, pretending that he was coughing. Imah didn't notice, waving up at a house sprawling just on the edge of the last hill before the land of Kanna sank back into flat, sprawling greenery. "Do you see this monstrosity? Who needs two stories? Who needs servants? He has a room just for bathing! I raised seven children in two rooms."

"Seven children!" I exclaimed. I had not known Yeshua had so many siblings.

"Seven that lived . . ." Imah said flatly, but I could see a sinew tighten in her thick neck, the muscles of her body twitching around old wounds.

The path leading up the hill was almost entirely overrun with late summer lilies. The smell was dizzying as I bent down to pick one, pinching a bit of pollen and rubbing it between my fingers. It was as orange as the pure flame produced by old pinewood.

"Pretty!" Yael hopped over to me and I smiled, tucking the lily behind her dirty ear. She looked up at me with those preternaturally big eyes. Yeshua's eyes.

He was all around me. In the lilies and the sprawling rosebushes shifting with the wind like big, sleeping cats on the hillside.

And then I heard his laugh, rumbling from inside the house and making it seem as if the stones themselves were amused with our arrival.

"Drunk! Of course!" Imah screeched, surprising Lazaros so much that he almost tripped. He reached out and grabbed my shoulder to steady himself.

Imah muttered something unintelligible under her breath, her tongue half out of her mouth. "All of them. Drunk! Drinking up the wine meant for the wedding. When I left them, I was assured that they would not touch the good wine. I should have known . . ."

"Do not worry, Imah," I tried to calm her. She seemed so agitated. But she surprised me with a burst of sarcastic laughter.

"Worry! Don't worry? What do you think it is that mothers do? You will know soon enough! We love! We love—and then we worry."

Imah led us through a house that was spacious, cool, and dark. Musty, embroidered hangings depicted serpents, fishes with long forked tails, and people, too. One jar, the size of a man, was covered in Grecian illustrations. A naked man was chasing a woman, her hand drifting out behind her like a wing tasting the air, preparing to take flight.

Miriam hurried us along and back out into the light, where grasses grew up around an orchard in a trough of land just below the house. "I'll not direct you men. Go and be fools with my sons. Drink!" Miriam declared loudly. "The women should come with me."

I looked back at Lazaros and he grinned, the tip of his nose peeling with sunburn, communicating wordlessly. *Go be a woman! Me? I'm going to have some fun.*

Marta pushed ahead of me, peering around curiously, her rouged mouth quivering with a repressed smile. I knew what she was thinking: what a relief that this house was not as nice as her own! Marta wanted me to be happy. And she wanted me married. But not into a richer family than her own. She could enjoy herself now that she knew this "wealthy" relative of Yeshua's represented no real competition.

"Filthy!" she mouthed to me, pointing a limp finger back at the house. "Dust everywhere!"

"This is where you will stay until the wedding," Imah informed us, showing us into a squat addition at the side of the house. Fragrant herbs were tied up in the corners. Rosemary exuded its clean blue scent. Sage. Lemon balm.

Marta and Atalyah took little Kernan off for a nap, and I was shown to a longer room I would share with Imah and Yael. Standing at the long window overlooking the flowering citrus trees, I breathed in deeply, enjoying how the air felt as nourishing as food . . . as cleansing as water.

"Leave her trunk here," Yeshua's mother instructed a serving girl with a dark, almost handsome mustache. The girl huffed as she deposited the heavy load at the foot of the bed, dusting her large hands off on her tunic. "Heavy! Do you have gold in there?" she asked in a resonant, almost masculine voice. "Your dowry?"

"Hold your tongue, Metis!" snapped Imah, whacking the girl on the side of the head.

"Aye!" Metis cried out, dancing away from Imah's hand, still hanging sharp and ready in the air.

"What *is* this?" Imah flipped open the trunk, gazing inside, and repeated the girl's question. "What need do you have of so many dresses?"

On the opposite bed a meager pile of folded blankets and cloaks belonged to Imah and Yael. What would Yeshua think of me dressed in the finery and pomp it seemed he despised so much?

"These are my mother's things," I tried to explain, embarrassed by how weak my voice sounded. "My sister bid me bring them." I wanted so badly to impress this woman. But I knew it would not come easily. I would have to sit in the dirt with her and weed her kitchen garden for days, if not years. I would have to give her grandchildren.

It had been a month since I had seen him last. For all I knew, he was another sort of man entirely in his native village, born and bred of a wild land with no hint of tenderness.

These thoughts plagued me as a group of women I did not know gathered to begin fitting me with wedding adornments.

Their hands smelled of cinnamon and cardamom. Were we being made into sweets? A woman with Imah's strong jaw gently touched my elbow, offering me some honeyed nuts in a little blue bowl. An older woman with Yeshua's big eyes lit a powdery lump of incense on the windowsill and soon the room was so smoky with gray perfume that I felt perhaps we were inside of a cloud, lifting off from the ground itself.

"What a flower of a lady! A delicate rose!" cooed a young girl, holding hands with Yael. "Are you a princess?"

"Foolish girl!" exclaimed Beulah, Shimon's wife, reaching out to tussle the girl's short, silky curls. "Do you think a princess would marry our Yeshua? This girl must be very brave indeed."

Beulah was closer to the kind of woman I'd grown up with in Bethany. Her eyes were lightly ringed with kohl and her hair, which should have been gray, was pink with henna. "Here, I have set aside some of my jewelry," she explained, unwrapping a small satchel. "Pretty? It belonged to my mother. And her mother wore it before that . . ." she explained. "It has been worn by many brides on their wedding days."

Beulah was both a comfort and a disturbance in that she reminded me of my own mother. Her beauty was a strange combination of feminine care and familiar discomfort.

Imah, on the other hand, smelled of sesame oil and her own sweat. She had me try on an old tunic that she had worn at *her* wedding to Yeshua's father. She pressed her calloused hands to my bare back as if she might coax my slender frame into something more womanly, someone who would fill the old clothing with her original flesh.

"How funny," she noted, pulling a belt tightly around the heavy green cloth so that I had a shape. "While I was but a babe of fourteen at my own wedding, you, the elder, are the one with the body of a child."

Only the top of her head was visible as she said this, and I stared down at the sunburned skin revealed by her parted hair, showing that while she had made herself seemly with a head scarf for our arrival, she usually worked with her hair free and her head uncovered. Beulah had left us to oversee the making of the household supper and I felt suddenly more relaxed.

"Imah . . ." my voice was hesitant at first.

"Yes, child?" She sat back on her feet, her knees dusty from the ground. "What is it?"

"Were you very frightened before your wedding?"

Instead of answering, Miriam closed her eyes, the wrinkles in her face relaxing into depthless lines. Her mouth went slack. Had I said something wrong?

But then she smiled wistfully, nodding her head, and I realized she was consumed by memory. "Yes. I *was* frightened. But my mother and her sisters had told me what to expect and I knew it was my time," she finally said.

I remembered Marta's discomfort and fear following her own marriage bed and felt my heartbeat begin to speed. "What *should* I expect?"

Miriam's big eyes grew wider still. She barked with laughter, so like the laughter that belonged to my betrothed. "Has no one told you about the making of a child? The love that is as sweet as wine?"

I remembered the couples at the riverbank. The dancing couple at the inn. Kisses that looked as if they must burn. I remembered the feeling I'd had at the pit of my stomach when Yeshua had touched me on the roof. "I think I know . . ." I stuttered.

"Child!" Imah exclaimed. "Do not be afraid. It is only unpleasant with a man one does not love."

I was quiet.

She narrowed her eyes and rose to her feet so that our faces were nearly at the same level. "Do you love my son?"

Love. It felt like a paltry word, something thin and sheer floating through the air after a storm: a moth's wing. What I felt for Yeshua was something without a word. It was blue and heavy. It lived between joy and despair, refusing to identify itself completely with either extreme.

But even without answering, Miriam seemed to understand. She pressed her forehead to my own. "It is a powerful thing to love. It is a great joy. But it can also give you great sorrow."

"Why is that, Imah?" I asked, feeling the warmth of her skin and the shape of her skull beneath it. It felt as if our thoughts might merge and leave us as one being.

"My daughter, death may take the one you love and leave you alone. As soon as you love, death steps to the door." Her voice wavered as if coming to me from across water or down through a distance of years. Within seconds, however, she composed herself, tidying her steely hair and drawing her scarf back over her head. "That is enough for now. Let us get you fed so that you do not swoon from exhaustion."

The meal was served in the courtyard. I had thought the men might join us but, while I heard their loud voices echoing through the late summer air, they were obviously being kept separate from us. Our wine was watered down so that it barely warmed my throat as I sipped it from a small cup.

Marta and Beulah had quickly realized their shared affinity for weaving. They talked at length about the difficulty in procuring certain herbs for dye. Meanwhile, Atalyah struggled with a grumpy Kernan who kept reaching out for his disinterested mother. Marta barely turned when he moaned out her name. Atalyah kept him tightly secured with her left arm while she used her right to eat lentils and onions with a portion of bread.

Yeshua's mother, in her rough cloak, her cheeks ruddy, did not even try to contribute. She was busy taking care of the girls, of whom there seemed to be many. Yeshua's relatives far outnumbered my own and they all seemed to have children. Yael was the oldest of them and fancied herself the leader, dragging two small girls no older than three by their hands. None of the children would sit still; they raced about us, weaving in and out of the circle, running into each other until someone fell noisily to the ground. Finally, unable to stop them with words alone, Imah removed their agitator by pulling at the oldest girl's long plait and sitting the girl in her lap. The game quickly dissolved, and the tired children found their way to their own mothers—some young enough that they pulled at the women's dresses, demanding milk from their bosoms.

Although we had traveled for several days and I had walked much of the way, I did not have an appetite. After nibbling at the coarse bread soaked in wine, I rose to my feet and headed back inside.

The bed was a stone outcropping from the wall covered in wooden slats, with a lumpy mattress stuffed full of grasses that was uneven to lie upon. I pulled my heaviest cloak over me, although the weather was mild, and tried to straighten my back against the rutted surface. *At least I am by the window and can pretend my home to be the orchard itself,* I thought as the night wind crept into the room, tickling my nose and lips with my hair.

At some point Imah tiptoed into the room with Yael sleeping in her arms. I watched them from behind the arm I'd thrown up partly over my face so that she thought me asleep. There was a mattress on the floor for both of them to share and, with great care, she changed the girl's loose slip and tucked her underneath a blanket. When she was done, she leaned down and pressed a kiss to Yael's forehead. I was surprised when she then came over to me and, with just a brush of her lips, pressed a kiss onto the top of my head. Then she, too, went to bed, her quiet breathing quickly becoming a steady rhythm of rasp and snore.

The sound soothed me, and I let my senses open up to the frog song coming from the window. I could hear the men as well, their voices louder now that their meal was finished and the wine drunk. The higher, reedy tones of young boys wove themselves through the low thunder of the older men's guffaws. Was that my own father, laughing as loudly as a peasant? Someone was hooting like an owl, and I was sure an actual owl was hooting back. There was a pause between the cascades of calls that suggested a question and a reply.

The scent of someone's jasmine perfume still hung in the room. The sweetness of late apricots, citrons, and pomegranate fruit wafted in with each breeze. The grass itself had a warm, peppery aroma that reminded me of watching clouds with Lazaros when we were young, our cloaks pushed into the fields below us so that when we came back home my mother despaired at the green stains that couldn't be removed from our clothing.

It was not like a vision or a dream; instead, at some indefinable moment, the world softened. Dust in the air of the room remained suspended and began to glitter. Each breath made me lighter so that I felt almost as if I was floating above the straw mattress.

Interspersed between the men's voices were the caws and yowls of real beasts. I heard twigs breaking. Branches twanged. Something was nosing through the bushes. Someone was singing—a hectic, high-pitched song that was not in our language. *Greek?* I wondered, perplexed when the glossy sibilants withheld their meaning from me. Were there going to be foreigners at my wedding? I wondered if Yeshua, with all his traveling, had friends outside of Yudah.

At the thought of foreigners, Kemat appeared in my mind, her straight black bangs blown sideways by an invisible wind. Her palms were open at her side, dyed yellow with saffron and the green juice of freshly cut herbs. A honeybee climbed up the neck of her blue cloak, its small wings glistening like flecks of rainwater.

It was as if I had spoken her name aloud and the world was responding: the smell of embalming herbs peddled by Egyptian vendors in Yerusalem seeped into the room from the dirt floor itself. Almond oil. Rose. Aloe. Myrrh.

And there! I could hear a new sound. Something fast and high-pitched. It was the clicking speed of Kemat's own language, just outside the window. I recognized it from those times I had surprised her in conversation with her husband, Meskhenet. Yet it was neither of their voices. Instead it was a low voice: a voice I could only imagine belonging to an ancient tree, saying something in a tongue I couldn't understand but whose message felt intended especially for me. A voice that had been calling to me since I was a child . . . calling to me since before I was born. It arrived to me from another life. Another love.

Miriam.

I was nine years old again, wandering through a strange, shadowy forest of trees. I could see their slender forms rising through the darkness and feel their surfaces with my fingertips: sometimes the cold of smooth stone, sometimes the rough, braided exterior of bark and branch.

He was here somewhere on this land. He was close.

The thought of him made me sit up suddenly, unsure if I had ever truly been asleep or awake, sweat sticking the front of my shift to my breasts.

"Miriam." The voice was real; a husky whisper coming from the window. "Miriam. Are you awake?"

I reached my hands out into the darkness.

"Oh!"

Hands grasped mine, pulled me forward. I nearly tumbled out the window into the night. I braced my knees against the stone ledge, fully awake now, and peered out at the darkness.

He was there, looking up at me with his owl-like eyes. The brown skin of his face was turned blue in the late summer darkness, the whites of his eyes almost blindingly bright. His wide smile had hunger in it. If I had not found him the most handsome man in the land, I would have been terrified. His hair was wild with flowers woven through his curls. Smudged mud ran down the center of his forehead.

"What are you doing here?" I whispered, injecting as much stern-ness into my lowered voice as possible. "Do you want your own mother to wake? Your sister? They will surely think me a harlot."

He laughed with such low, soft force that it disturbed the air. His hands tightened around mine, sending a slow yellow energy into my body. Honey. Sunlight stretched out and slowed down and made into something thick and edible. "Miriam, we are already betrothed. Do you really think it so unseemly for a bridegroom to see his bride?"

The smell of him erased all trepidation: musky and human yet with the tang of living water—the kind of water that is never still but always in motion, like streams and rivers flowing between oceans.

I slid my hands up his muscular arms and gripped his shoulders so that I could climb down from the window. He shook his hair like a beast, and wound his hands around my slender ankles, steadying me.

"My queen! You are beautiful to behold!"

He let go suddenly, and I leapt into him, crushing against his huge, solid chest.

"Come," he breathed into my ear, causing a shiver to run from my tongue deep down into my belly. "Let us go into the orchards."

I tried to calm my heartbeat but found it impossible. I wound my arm around his waist, feeling the heat of his bare skin. Was he naked? No. My fingers brushed something as silky as water. But no. Not fabric. *Fur.*

"What are you wearing, bridegroom?"

"I'm not wearing anything," he answered.

But I had touched something that was not skin. I pulled back, squinting. He was wearing an animal pelt, thrown loosely over one shoulder like a toga. But it barely covered him.

"How fearsome you seem!" I whispered, finding that I could hardly speak. "Will you eat me?"

"When I was much younger my brother Yakov and I found a dead leopard on the edge of our village and took the hide for ourselves. He has brought it to me as a wedding gift and the fool in me thought it would delight the children to pretend to be a beast. But I have scared them . . ."

I let my hand grasp at his hip bone, sharp through his skin. His breathing quickened.

"You don't scare *me*," I said.

"What a shame . . ." he said gruffly, pressing his hand into my lower back and pulling me close.

I gasped at the intensity of our chests touching, the softness of my thighs against the hard muscles of his long legs.

"Miriam . . . Miriam," he murmured into my hair. "I was no longer sure if you were real."

"I feel as if you, too, may be a dream . . ." I answered.

It was true. He was like some creature of legend: a mixture of the old stories my father had told me and those foreign tales Yosseph had brought back from his travels.

The god who goes underground. The lord of trouble. Of wine and leopards and satyrs. The youth, wreathed in flowers, who sings for his lost lover. The king who raises the grain from the soil, I mused.

"I am the giver of unmixed wine," he said as if he had heard my thoughts. But he was simply handing me a wineskin.

Moving quietly away from the house, we sank to our knees in the soft grass below an old fig tree that was heavy with fruit, determined that its second flowering of the season would outdo the first.

"You are a flower of the plain . . . the valley's lily," he said softly into my cheek, reciting the words of Solomon. "Let me support your head and hold you."

It was easy to sink into him, to close my eyes and surrender to his heaviness on me and the burning of his lips at my neck. "Am I a fool to be seduced by poetry?" I inquired.

"Miriam. I *am* the fool. Never think me more or less than one."

His hands buzzed as if filled with storm light, making my skin prickle. He let them drift from my shoulders down to my waist.

We would become one. I felt fate drawing us together as surely as water falls from the heavens. We would fall into each other, never to be individual bodies ever again. I would disappear. He would disappear. And I felt sure that whatever came after would be bigger, stronger. And dangerous.

"Forgive me. To touch you is to feel as if I might do anything." His fingers drifted to the dimples in the small of my back, pressing into them as he spoke. "I am suddenly filled with the sense that mountains can be moved."

I raised my head so that I could see the moon's orb made miniature in his eyes.

He was right. That familiar energy was in my hands. My feet. The same inhuman power had flowed through me when I had healed Rebekah and Marta. I could see and feel with every part of my body—as if my senses were not confined to my flesh. Even as his eyes moved from the moon back down to meet my gaze I was also seeing us as if from above, from the eyes of the leaves themselves. We were intertwined, our skin glowing indigo in the moonlight as if we were joined petals, freshly colored and released from the center of the same flower.

Kanna itself shrunk to a flickering speck on the landscape as I rose higher into the heavens. I could see it as a single star in the constellation of Galilee's villages.

With you the whole world becomes the night sky.

"Or an ocean," he suggested aloud, answering my silent thought. "And we are but light caught on its surface."

It did not surprise me. My thoughts were his thoughts. My hand on his breast felt his heartbeat because it was *my* heartbeat, shared blood pumping through both of us.

It happened then. His features appeared to ripple as if they were made of water. His nose shortened, the bridge pinching inward. His hair was gone. His eyes were narrower, a light green. Then just as suddenly, another transformation began. He had long, fair hair, a reddish beard, pale, freckled skin. A thinner face. A small, pointed chin. And again his face changed, and again he was younger, tanner, older—and once I could have sworn he wore the face of an ancient woman.

Yet somehow his eyes were always the same. And they were looking at me with the same wonder that I felt.

"When I look at you, I see many faces and I recognize them all. Sometimes you have a high forehead and pale skin. Or you are as beautiful and dark as ebony, with curling lips. What dream is this?" he asked.

I thought of Kemat many years before. "It is not a dream. It is other lives. From before. I am sure of it."

"Yes. I have loved you before." He nestled his face into my neck. "I feel it is true." He squeezed me to him then, opening his mouth against my flesh and biting softly: not hard enough to leave a mark but with enough pressure that it was as if a fire had shot through me.

Then to my surprise, he sprang up, pulling me with him. "You are right, Miriam. It is too dangerous to lie with you. I do not know if I could resist taking dishonorably tonight what I can have honorably tomorrow."

"I will stop you if you ask me for sweeter wine than I should give," I promised, feeling the mischief in my words.

"I can assure you that you will not, and even if you did, I might not listen." His eyes flashed like struck flint. He was right. He would take me. I knew it. I wanted it.

Yet I also felt naive. Yeshua had shown himself to be changeable above all else. He could transform from a wild man in animal skins to a forbidding temple scholar in an instant. Who was I to think I knew anything about this man?

But the knowledge that I didn't truly know him only made me hungrier. I longed to learn his mind, his spirit, and every inch of his muscled, mysterious body.

"Shame on you to think you could tame me!" I announced. "You will have me not when *you* will it, but when *I* will that you are my lover."

He laughed and reached for me, but I twisted away, half hiding behind the tree I'd been leaning on.

"Our union must not be spoiled," I warned, even as my body contradicted the words my mouth spoke. I leaned forward so my face was near to his. And he leaned into me.

What happens when two storms arrive in the same bowl of the mountains?

Fire. Cracks of yellow energy splitting tree trunks, exploding the grain stores in a dance of sparks . . . a drumbeat too big for the sky. It ruptures the long purple veins of the clouds and releases rivers. No downpour of raindrops, but sheets and sheets of solid water, waving and folding over the mountains like curtains fluttering in the wind.

That is what it was like to kiss him.

The whole night celebrated with us. The frog song went up by a pitch and somewhere a wild dog screamed.

His hands were in my hair. But I no longer had edges. I was the grass underfoot. The heavy branches of the citron trees. The soft, silken head of the bat parting the olive tree leaves, seeking a white ray of starlight.

And then, although it was almost a bodily pain, I wrenched myself away.

"*Oh.*"

It was done. There would be a marriage. There would be songs and prayers. But whatever difficult destiny I'd been seeking had arrived.

The voices of men interrupted us.

"Go!" Yeshua urged me, and I stumbled away, back up the hill.

The shadows swallowed him, but I could hear him chuckle.

"You play a dangerous game, bride! But I plan on winning you by tomorrow at nightfall . . ."

I ripped my shift climbing back through the window. The exposed skin of my belly tingled under the night breeze for a long while.

Sleep never came, and yet I dreamed. I dreamed that I was with Yeshua but he was smaller, lithe and lean, with a smoothly shaved head and a long, aquiline nose. We were standing knee-deep in moving water and he was saying something to me. The leaves of palm trees waved sword-like overhead. A heron flew above us with wings as extended and relaxed as my father's unfurling scrolls. It had the feeling of a farewell.

Then the world shifted and Yeshua was present again, but old and battle-scarred, hair flaxen like a foreigner's and with a metal-gray beard. He was standing at the edge of a lake, reeds swallowing his lower half, making him appear spirit-like, floating, holding the hilt of a sword.

A dark-skinned man, taller than anyone I had ever seen, stood in a white room with columns of marble holding up an impossibly high ceiling. He was arguing with an old woman, her gray hair like woven snakes down her back.

A boy. A baby. A girl. An eagle. A lion. We were two snakes, our hearts like flattened blades inside our simple bodies, twisting about each other, threading our love into thick fragrant vines girdling a pomegranate tree.

Yet no matter how many different faces we wore, I always recognized him.

Each time our eyes met, our hands touched.

You. Thank God! It has been such a long time . . . I have so much to tell you about, I intoned silently to him.

That night I lived a thousand lives.

Twenty-Nine

They came for me just after sunrise: the women, young and old, my own kin and strangers, all loaded with armfuls of flowers so varied and lush that their combined perfume made me dizzy: crimson *susons* with their long tongues and tart smell, some late-season karkoms giving up puffs of petals the color of sunlight, sprays cut from blooming tamarisks, and deep-throated hyacinths. Beulah herself had worn orange lilies pinned to her bosom and had applied a pale powder to her cheeks so that when she first approached me, I did not recognize her and thought her youthful.

Marta was lovely. She appeared a softer, happier version of my mother in a red-and-yellow-striped tunic she had cinched tightly with a dark leather belt. And I realized I had never seen Atalyah without a dull, colorless scarf around her hair. She now wore a scarf of bright, banded colors and had applied some rouge on her cheeks, calling attention to how all her small features seemed to gather in the middle of her wide face, too frightened to fully inhabit the space provided.

Yael and a dozen other girls were laden with straw baskets of Galilean roses. Two very young girls, hardly able to speak, reached out their hands to pull at my curls and draw me from my bed. The older women lifted my shift from me so that, without properly waking up, I was already naked among the many different female generations, their hands, gnarled and smooth, working my skin with perfume and my hair with brushes.

"Ah! What lovely nipples," Beulah noted as she massaged oil into the thin skin covering my rib cage. "Like rosebuds." I relaxed under her sure touch. Marta was behind me, combing jasmine and myrrh into my hair, the slick perfume escaping her fingers and dripping down my spine.

Someone was burning hyssop. The dense, purple smell coiled into our lungs, turning our exhales into something rich, fragrant, and almost colorful. I imagined I could see the essence of each woman lifting from her lips. The yellow light of the children. The radiant blue of Beulah and the older woman. Marta's fiery orange. Flower petals crumpled underfoot, adding their own bruised nectar to the air.

Yael pressed a thick unguent of lily oil into my feet. She used both of her hands to circle my ankle, massaging the blue veins that surfaced along my shin.

As the women busied themselves making me beautiful, I couldn't help but notice their own finery: the simple, rust-colored tunics of the young girls, and the golden earrings that dangled from my sister's ears. Beulah took an intricately embroidered leather belt and wound it around the shift I was wearing.

Imah was the only one who seemed careless of her own appearance. Her gray-streaked hair was swept back into an orderly plait that she had secured by coiling it into a bun. She wore an undyed shift that swallowed her sturdy form. Yet to me she was the most beautiful of them all because, in her face, I could see Yeshua.

When I had been fully dressed, Marta and Atalyah stepped forward to adorn me with flowers and set my hair in a series of ornate curls and braids. Beulah appeared with a polished silver mirror, which she held up so that I could see myself.

There were three chunks of turquoise pressed into the mirror's handle. The metal was blackened by age. It looked like a mirror fished from the ocean, having only reflected the sleek, glassy faces of fish for hundreds of years. My reflection was waved and distorted.

"You are a true daughter of Yerusalem," Beulah said, sighing with satisfaction. "And to think you are wedding such a beast of a man!"

Imah, overhearing this comment, stopped her stitching of the veil I would wear for the ceremony. "It is not your place to speak ill of my son, Beulah," she said firmly, the gossamer fabric drifting weightlessly from her hands.

Beulah narrowed her eyes, her elegant face twitching with the energy it took to control unseemly emotions.

But Imah roared with laughter. "It is not your place because it is *my* place to speak ill of him! Even now, in the early morning, I predict that he has found a way to get all the men drunk."

We did not break our fast except for some stale bread soaked in water that was brought to us as we continued our preparations. Once again I was too nervous to eat. Something tightened expectantly deep in my belly. Every clear thought melted into a bodily sensation. I was thinking more with my flesh than I was with my mind.

Here is the corner of my mouth that he tasted. Here is the small of my back, still tattooed by the pressure of his fingers . . . the surface of my thighs enflamed with the strong feel of his muscular legs against mine. When would he come and unite all these sensations? One kiss would not satisfy me. I wanted all of him.

Hours passed. Time had paused. The scents and fabrics that wound around me wove a gossamer spell. Would we forever float between birth and death in this series of warm rooms, women touching each other, long skirts brushing along the floors, voices blooming soft and warm? Maybe the lamps would sputter and fade. But they would revive to grow straight flames again. Everything was tidal . . . the arms that floated up and then down around me, all of our interconnected heartbeats. The oil would never run out. The older women, laughing and telling stories, would grow younger.

Songs from the bridegroom's retinue floated in through the windows. The day's last light slanted in on us: a pure streak of apricot puddling on the ground and turning everyone who walked through it into a living flame.

Marta was at my side, draping her soft arm around my shoulders. She whispered, tickling my ear. "You are the loveliest bride I have ever seen." Her eyes sparkled with tears as she slipped a gold ring affixed with a translucent beryl stone onto my smallest finger. "It was our mother's and then, at my wedding, it was mine. Now that you are to be a wife it will be yours. And you will to give it to your daughter someday, too . . ."

Interrupting her, a young woman by the name of Mibtachiah called from the window at the far side of the room. "Who is that man walking through the field to meet us?"

The room grew silent. The air flickered with golden dust. Dense purple smoke hung above our heads like mist.

Mibtachiah, unmarried and bare-headed, her long, straight hair plaited with tiny, white flowers, turned back from the window to face me. She smiled gently, her round cheeks dimpling, and then repeated the phrase that signaled the beginning of the ceremony. "Who is that man walking through the field to meet us?"

"He is my master," I said softly, surprised by my quavering voice. I thought of Rebekah saying the same words, watching as Isaac approached through tall grasses and wind.

Daughter of Yerusalem, who is that rising from the desert? Were those the words of the crazed old woman from the temple? Or an echo of Solomon's Song that was, at that minute, coming in through the window on the wings of an early autumn wind?

"He is my master!" I cried out and flung my arms open.

And the wedding began.

The young girls were each given a small torch that Beulah lit using a red clay lamp decorated with an ornate etching of roses. The flames, as they caught the dry grass at the torch's end, drew in the sunset's colors and gleamed like the stones set into the necklaces that weighed heavily around my neck. The girls' faces were light itself. Outside the singing grew louder, one bright clear voice overwhelming all the others: "I came to thy house for thee to give me thy daughter to wife; she is my wife, and I am her husband this day and forever."

I was at the door now, the girls floating about my skirts, and I could see the men.

He was carried up on a palanquin, and at first I barely recognized his bare face and short hair. With his beard shaved cleanly away and long hair cut, his beauty was now human. Before he had seemed the product of curling ivy and tree roots. Now, with his cheeks bright and sun-kissed and his forehead clear of stray curls, he looked almost vulnerable, years younger. Here was the man I could imagine as the prodigal son of that story he had told by the river. A stone, blue as the sky that framed his head, gleamed on his fingers as we waved to me.

My father was overcome with emotion. I could tell by the defensive scowl that weighted down his jowls. He stepped from the throng of men and boys to join me. Putting an arm around my shoulders, the hard bone of his forearm reminded me of his age and my softness. At last he spoke: "My daughter, will you go with this man?"

"My father, I will," I answered. The doves echoed my coo of "I do, I do, I do." The youngest boys quieted, closing ranks around Yeshua's palanquin, and a great hush came between the two groups: women and men, the hearth behind us and the orchard behind them. Lazaros, flushed with joy, helped Yeshua down to the ground.

We stood face to face. The air between us shivered with our matched desire. And for the first time, instead of feeling agitated by this tension, I reveled in it, knowing that everyone here was gathered for one purpose—*to honor our desire*. Perfume was visible, beading into sweet honey above the sweat on the women's upper lips and the oiled curls of the men's hair.

"We rejoice and delight in you!" Yeshua's brother thundered. "We praise your love above wine!"

Now it was the women's turn and I could sense Marta's warmth behind me, her weaver's hands touching my back as she would a bolt of fine silk. She spoke, "Hark! Behold! He comes, leaping upon the mountains, skipping upon the hills."

But it no longer mattered what words were spoken or which people were present because his eyes had met mine and the part of me that had coiled tight and tense the previous night grew tighter still. Suddenly I wished I were clothed in water alone, standing waist-deep in the Yarden River once more. The weight of the necklaces at my throat were the weight of the words I wanted to speak without ceremony, without an audience: "I am yours. I am yours. I am yours. And you are mine."

"Let us go to the chuppah, my friends," Imah's cousin Shimon invited us.

And the children began to herd us like shepherds with their flock of sheep. Their baskets of flowers and dancing flames narrowed our party from either side until everyone was walking two by two, Yeshua and I at the head of the long procession.

I dared not meet his eye but stared at his hand, open and relaxed. I hardly recognized the man in finery, but I knew the rough callouses of his palm, the strong fingers. *Those hands have touched me and will soon touch me again.*

His fingers curled inward as if around mine. "Miriam. . ." He said my name softly so that no one could hear. Now the children were singing again, the music seemingly a continuation of my own name spoken from his lips.

> *You shall eat the fruit of the toil of your hands;*
> *it shall go well with you, and your wife within your*
>   *house*
> *shall be like fruitful vine; your children round your*
>   *table*
> *like fresh olive branches. Thus shall the one be blest*
> *who fears the Lord.*

The chuppah had been erected at the distant edge of the orchard. The canopy billowed upward as a wind scented by the nearby almond trees pushed its way through the four posts. At the foot of each of these posts a tall tallow candle had been lit, sending up elongated tongues of flame that appeared to bow to us as they bent under the wind's force.

"Miriam."

I could smell the earthy, pungent odor of his own sweat mixing with the spiced oil someone had applied to his skin. His face gleamed clean and darkly tanned.

He was real. *I* was real.

The murmur of wind mixed with the chatter of voices to weave a spell of quiet around us. "Miriam. Do you take me? Are you sure that this is what you want?"

The whole world spoke for me. A nightingale whistled. The frogs croaked with joy. And somewhere an owl opened up the night with a cry that radiated outward, rippling through the orchards, the leaves, the grasses, like the force of a stone penetrating water.

He gripped my hand, raising it up in celebration.

"It is I—the bridegroom! He who has the bride is the bridegroom!"

Without waiting for me to speak, he leaned in, his huge hand supporting the base of my spine, and he kissed me.

The crowd cheered. The trees swayed, shuffling their clustered leaves, twisting branches with approval. I tasted honey . . . sunlight as dense as actual gold, heavy enough that it sinks in the water, collecting in the bottom of cups, riverbeds, oceans. Captured inside of him.

Released by me. A golden wine aging and deepening its flavor until I arrived to taste it.

"I want you," I said again, quietly, into the corner of his mouth.

"And I you. As I have before."

He kissed me again.

The flowers fell from my hair. My body softened against his body.

We were wed.

Thirty

The feast was sumptuous: Marta's husband, Amos, brought an offering of exquisite spices that were used to flavor the food that appeared on tray after tray. There were fig and date pastries flecked with slices of almond. Three lambs had been slaughtered and cooked slowly so that the meat tenderly fell apart over stewed vegetables. The first wine was as thin and yellow as moonlight, and after I had downed it, I was not sure I would be able to stay seated. My skin vibrated and my feet flexed as if I were already dancing. The cup was copper with a braided design around the lip so that when I raised it to my lips, I first tasted the texture of the cup, its uneven mouth, the cold darkness of the earth's metals, and then finally the warmth of the wine.

Remembering it now, I want to tell myself to slow down—to taste each dish with relish and sample the many varieties of wine that the guests had brought as gifts.

But with Yeshua at my side, I found I had lost my appetite once again. His feet, bare of sandals for the ceremony, tickled my ankles. As I cast him a sidelong glance, he smiled secretly, all the while holding a calm, courteous exchange with a distant cousin who had come to offer his congratulations.

"Good Sister, as I am now able to call you!" said Yeshua's brother Yakov. "I must thank you heartily for bringing my brother back into the fold."

He was sturdier and shorter than Yeshua, with a barrel chest and coarse hair. It was only in comparison to his brother that I could look at Yeshua and see the elegance of his form and not the brutality. With his hair oiled and his face shaved clean, Yeshua was as handsome as any man I'd ever seen. He caught my gaze and gave me a pinch on my thigh through my skirts. My breath caught in my throat, but I ignored him and smiled kindly up at Yakov. "Truly? I fear you'll find I've led him farther astray."

Lazaros chuckled knowingly, his eyes sparkling with wine-fueled mirth. "Miriam is a terrible influence. When we met Yeshua, he was the ascetic, and now look at him! He eats and drinks like a common glutton."

Yakov threw his head back in raucous laughter, his big hand flying up to his chest. "You think *this* is his most immoderate behavior?"

"Don't reveal all my secrets, Brother!" jested Yeshua, half standing to clap Yakov on the shoulder. "What will my new bride and I talk about if you expend all the best stories now?"

"I don't think your profligate youth is any secret to me," I quickly countered. "It seemed to be common knowledge in Yochanan's camp."

Yeshua's eyes flashed darkly. But after a breath, his face was joyous and composed again. Yochanan's name had stirred some anger in him I had not known existed.

But I barely gave any thought to this at the time. I was preoccupied by how quickly the sunlight was seeping into the ground, its glow giving way to the soft lilac clouds of night over the treetops. Soon the only illumination came from the cooking fires and assorted candles; people became blurred assortments of garment and face. In the half light, the gilded embroidery on their cloaks, flashing rings, and the glowing whites of their eyes became the only proof that they existed.

Seated on her son's right side, Imah kept up a steady stream of chatter. "And you will have to give thanks to Samuel and his wife. Lord knows why they came at all! They remember you from when you were a boy and set loose their sheep. So it is time to correct their unfavorable impression . . ."

Yeshua nodded without responding, watching me all the while. His lips were wet with wine. He tilted his head as if to say, *And when shall the games begin?*

I could still feel where his hands had burned into me the night before.

In the shadows someone began to beat a drum, slowly, then with more force. Yeshua's youngest brother, Yudah, a slip of a youth with an oversize mop of curls, sang with a high, girlish voice. As if summoned by the sound, some hired girls that Amos had sent for filled the empty circle that the feast tables surrounded and began to dance, rotating their hips purposefully as if stirring something in a large pot. Lifting up their feet, they pointed their toes with such exquisite purpose that I felt their movements must be working magic. They were summoning seeds from the ground! They were sending the air in different directions so that their potent odor reached every one of us: sweat and musk and the smell a cooking fire sends up when you pour water over the coals.

All this distraction was supposed to allow the wedded couple to slip off unnoticed.

I could feel the strong muscles of Yeshua's thigh close to mine. Now that the night had truly fallen, he let the cover of darkness cloak how his hand traced circles on my lower back through the fabric of my dress. His touch was steady and rhythmic, like the beating of the drum. He nudged his knee against mine, and I took a deep breath. It was as if I had drunk wine instead of air. I was drunk and couldn't help but lean into him, resting my head heavily against his shoulder.

It must have looked a pretty scene: the bride, grown sleepy with wine and food, relaxing against her new husband. But the force between us was far from peaceful . . . It was a ravening forest fire bursting dry seedpods . . . oceans flooding the lowlands and never melting back, transforming grain fields into complicated jungles of seaweed . . . wind so insistent it blew the moss and dirt from the tops of mountains, changing a terrain of peaks into softened hillside. Our bodies could not meet and stay the same. There would be a fundamental shifting of our shapes, our elements.

The words had been spoken. But our union had yet to be consummated.

Then there bellowed the sober voice of Yeshua's mother, "My son, you are a fool!"

Yeshua's hand froze on my back. He narrowed his eyes. Imah looked extremely annoyed. A knotted hand was raised as if to slap a small boy but, confronted by the large man who was her grown son Yeshua, her palm hovered without a purpose.

"I warned you, Yeshua, and I warned Yakov, and still you did not listen . . . you think we live in a land of milk and honey where all things are provided without any effort on our part?"

Yeshua gestured as if to sweep crumbs from the table and, as agitated as she was, Imah immediately fell silent. "What seems to be the problem, Mother? What responsibility does the bridegroom have that I have not already fulfilled?"

She barked with brittle laughter. "The wine! You and your friends have drunk it all up before the festivities and now there is none left. What will these wealthy guests think of us? That we are extravagant peasants?" She lowered her voice, hissing. "I cannot go before her father and tell him there is no wine when the wedding celebrations have hardly even begun."

"Be quiet, woman!" Yeshua's voice was harsher than I'd ever heard it. "What does this have to do with me? I am drunk already and have no need for more wine."

She opened her mouth, about to argue, when I interrupted. "And you are the only one allowed to drink to excess? We should provide for all our guests. My sister's husband has offered us a sum of money as our wedding gift. Can this be used to purchase . . ."

But he cut me off, squeezing me lightly at my side. He raised his hand to his forehead as if he had just remembered a dream. "Wait! Imah, have you checked the stone jars by the distant kitchen garden?"

She snapped, "Don't toy with me, Yeshua. You and I both know those are water jars."

There was a sparkle in his eyes, the same gleam that had appeared when I'd seen him romping with the children by the river. "I think you are wrong, Mother. I would check again."

She was exasperated and threw up her hands as if to shake him. "You disgrace your father's memory! He would never let such a thing happen. At our wedding there was no shortage of wine . . ."

At the mention of his father, Yeshua's spine grew rigid, but his voice remained carefree.

"Boy!" Yeshua called, and a young servant came over.

"May I be of service?" he asked.

"Your name is Obadiah?"

The boy turned red and nodded.

"I seem to remember that I helped make a table for your father,

Kenaniah. You must have been a babe back then . . ." Yeshua scratched at his cleanly shaven chin. "I was never a skilled carpenter like my father, but I remember thinking that table was some of my best work."

The boy couldn't contain himself. "Yes! We still have it and use it for feast days. I remember you well. You told us stories when you dined with our family after the workday. I've never forgotten what you said about a lion eating a human and becoming human . . . it still puzzles me to this day."

Yeshua nodded slowly. "Yes. I was rather foolish back then. I am glad my stories entertained someone. My mother can tell you she found them tiresome."

Imah shook her head. "And now you have a wife to bore with your antics. I'm well rid of them."

Yeshua kept his eyes on the boy. "Obadiah, you can refill everyone's glasses with wine from the jars near the kitchen garden."

The boy opened his mouth to object but then remembered that he was speaking to the bridegroom, "I . . . well . . . I may be mistaken, but I believe those jars only hold water . . . "

But Yeshua was already pulling at me as he turned away from the festivities and his indignant mother. "Check again, boy! Pour yourself a glass and drink deeply! If you still find it to be water, then perhaps it is true that I am a drunk bridegroom and do not know of what I speak . . ."

Imah was red with vexation. She pounded the table with her fist. "You will celebrate, and I will despair! The trouble will always fall to your poor mother!"

"Come, my love," Yeshua breathed into my ear, and a shiver went down my neck so that I couldn't help but leave the feast behind us.

"Yeshua! You are a disgrace to me and a dishonor to the memory . . ." Imah's voice faded behind us as we set a quick pace through the forest.

The trees here were thick and twisted as if they were the muscled arms and legs of giant men. At any minute it seemed they could break through their sinewy stillness and begin to march onward toward the ocean. But Yeshua was at home among them, letting his free hand drift over their bodies and outstretched leaves as if greeting old friends. Once he stopped and let me go for a minute as he pressed both his palms into a gnarled almond tree. Then he pulled me to him once more and led me farther into the dark.

Light from the moon came down as a thin, singular shaft ahead of us and, as we drew nearer, I could see that a tent had been erected. Its mouth was a bower of twisted branches and its sides were protected by a linen cloth. The entrance was alive, exhaling the perfume of henna blossoms and jasmine oil.

"The lush foliage is our canopied bed; the beams of our house are cedar; our bedroom's rafters are pine."

The song, surely sung by him, emanated from the trees instead. The earth, moist and resilient below our bare feet, pulsed with its sound.

My hands touched his forearms. He pressed his palms into the curve where my waist broadened into my hips. I let my fingers slip under his tunic so I could feel the heat of his chest and the coarse hair that grew there. "I could hardly sit next to you the desire was so great . . ." I whispered.

His mouth was at the corner of my eye and he licked the crease there. "It seemed a sin *not* to touch you. And it would be a sin now not to drink of your wine."

As much as I wanted to relax into his body and let him do what he wanted, I could not control the part of me that was always on fire to argue. "All this talk of sin bores me. Must your desire for me have to be coupled with an idea that belongs within the bounds of the temple?"

He bit me in response. Hard. At the spot where my ear met the skin of my neck.

I gasped and my hand tightened at his shoulder. And he bit me again, only much more softly now at my collarbone as he drew his other hand down my thigh, pushing through the folds of my skirts until he reached bare skin.

He knelt as if to grasp me at my waist but then made to climb into the tent. Looking up, he flashed me the same look from the night before: hunger and madness merged into one. "Can you forgive me?"

I knelt in the soft moss at the bower's edge and let him pull me inside.

• • •

What happens when the river meets the ocean? Does its fresh water feel the sharp tang of otherness as it enters the salted waves? Is there pain? Or is it thoughtless pleasure?

And what of the rain? It sinks into the soil to nourish the crops, but is there not a moment of impact where its softness breaks against the land?

We strive for union our whole lives: with God, with our purpose, with each other. But union is not a sport for children. It is not a game. It is the loss of a self. The rain does not just break against the ground— it *becomes* the ground. The river consumed by the ocean *is* the ocean.

What can I tell you of that night? That it was easy and ordinary? That I was the same Miriam afterward, only wiser and more complete as a woman?

The truth is that the kisses that came before had been sweet, but the lovemaking was past song or perfume.

It was what a mirror must see when the only thing that it faces is another mirror.

He was not rough. But neither was he gentle. My finery did not live to see another day, shredded to pieces by his eager hands: the studded belt his mother had carefully cinched around my green overdress came apart immediately, spitting beads across the blankets below us so that, as we rolled deeper into the tent's darkness, the places where they pressed into our flesh left behind indented constellations. Without the clear lines of our separate bodies, we slid into the same skin. I pressed my hand into the spot between his shoulder blades and could feel us breathing through a set of shared lungs.

There was pain but it was passing. There was pleasure, but it seemed like a single star in a night sky scattered with countless lights. I felt as if I might disappear below his weight. And then I was on top of him, my skin prickling like sunlight on moving water. His arms were knotted with scars that, as soon as they rose under my fingers, faded back into dream.

Then he was over me again, his knees locking in my thighs, pinning my arms up above my head so that I had to arch my back into order to touch him, my breasts pushing up into the hard, wide planes of his chest. And he was transformed again: his shoulders narrowed, and the bulky muscles of his body were made sleek and long under skin that began to ripple under my hands as softly as water. Again and again, he changed. He was a tangle of vines. A plant. A shadow. Various as stars in the sky, he was older, younger, a man, a woman.

To say more is to betray the magnitude of such a thing. Lovemaking is no secret, and it would have done me better if my own sister or mother had prepared me when I was still a girl. But union—the meeting of two equals in love and celebration—is one of the great mysteries.

I keep it secret because the words for the telling do not yet exist.

When it was done, I was no longer Miriam. Or perhaps better said, I was no longer *just* Miriam. I felt myself poured into him, inhabiting his breath. I touched my mouth and it was his full lips, the first prickle of whiskers growing back just at the corners.

I need only blink and I was seeing myself: blurred and soft, cheeks rosy and chin rubbed red by the scratch of his stubble.

But the change I'd undergone paled beside the transformation that had happened to my new husband.

It was not physical. He looked the same, his big body wrapped around mine so that the sweat beaded in the curled hair of his chest mixed with my own perspiration. There was a smell in the tent that was rich and dark like spices, and under that a sharp, tart note—as if fresh figs had grown overripe and burst as they'd fallen from the branch. His hands knotted deeply into my hair and the hinge of his hip bone pushed into my upper thigh. I was not sure if we could part even if we tried with all our might. Our limbs belonged to the same center, like petals circling a flower's bud.

"And to think that when I first saw you, I thought you unreal. A dream . . ." His voice was a low rumble in my neck.

I pushed up on my elbows and he sat back so we could see each other in the dim light of the tent. The moonlight shimmered.

"On the rooftop?" I asked.

"Yes. I was terrified. As if I had seen a terrible angel. As if the world would end."

I remembered him from the previous night, robed in animal pelts, his eyes lit by some internal fire. I did not believe that he could be frightened. But I stayed quiet, savoring the heat emanating from his bare skin, pressing my palm into it—and then to his arm threaded with veins. I could feel his life beating just below my fingers, insistent as the drums I heard still coming from the festivities beyond the grove.

"You make me feel as if I might go mad." His voice was less a sound than a vibration. He blinked and his eyes gleamed with surprising tears.

I thought of my own visions and the way the world would shiver and shift into a different land, a different time. And yet I was always confident of my sanity even when others mocked and ridiculed me.

"When I saw you at the river, it started again. I sat in the darkness of the forest that night and suddenly a brightness circled my vision as if dawn was arriving only for my eyes. Then clouds, fire, and a feeling of pressure at the center of my brow. It was mostly a feeling—as if I had been drawn through the center of a lamp into the flame's mind."

He was lying back now, looking up at the striped cloth of the tent's arched roof. He pointed his finger, tracing circles in nothingness as if he could draw his dreams for me. My eyes followed his touch, pretending that it stained the air with a warm glow. Circle connected with circle until I could almost hold it in my imagination: a sky filled with moons and suns, a world where light arrived in the morning and then never set. "It was as if torches were going back and forth between living beings. Everything was light and everything was in movement. And yet there were others present."

I opened my mouth to speak, then decided against it. I felt justified. It was just as I had expected. In this we were the same.

"These visions continue to come and go without my bidding. I cannot explain it, but somehow I feel as if they bring me closer to you. That they are about you. About us."

I thought of him as I had first seen him on the roof: his hands and profile glowing against the darkness so that he appeared more plant than human being.

"I went mad *after* I saw you . . ." I admitted, then bit at my lower lip, hesitant to explain how desperately I had yearned to find him.

He laughed, his whole body trembling. "It soothes me to hear that. So afraid was I of losing all touch with reality that I retreated into the strictest asceticism. I refused drink and rich food like the Essenes I'd first studied under. Even Yochanan believed I was living too narrowly."

"I like the glutton and drunkard better, I think," I responded, rolling over so that once again I was on top of him. I wrapped my hands around his wrists, pressing my breasts into his chest, and pulled our arms out straight, our wings matched and outstretched.

"Let us not live in fear," I murmured. "I think the fear was less that we would go mad and more that, having found each other, we would not be allowed to come together."

"Is that so?" His breath was shallow and even. He was holding something back. "Sometimes I worry that our coming together will be our undoing. That we will run into the hills to make music and drink wine forever. That we'll grow our hair so long and tangled that others will mistake us for animals."

"And that is a bad thing?" I chuckled. "Don't the animals seem happier than we do under the thumb of the Romans? The birds don't sow or reap or store their harvest in barns, and yet they are fed and live full lives. They have no one to answer to, and yet they are well cared for."

He gave a bark of laughter and his eyes sparkled through the darkness. "What wit you have, my fine wife! I've more wealth in your mind than your dowry it seems."

"Be careful not to spend it all at once," I warned, giving his shoulder a gentle pinch.

"I won't spend it at all." He lifted his mouth to mine and licked the salt from my lips before stealing the breath from my throat, pulling me fiercely into a kiss. "In fact, I'll order us both deaf and dumb so that we may be happy brutes. Let us go back to the river and live among the fowls there. We can catch fish and drink the nectar straight from the flowers."

I sat up to look at him, the shocking nakedness of my beautiful, wild husband with sunburnt cheeks and a bump in his nose from some far-off brawl. He was both fresh to me and also familiar. There was a jagged white seam that ran along the top of his right thigh from an incident I would only learn about later, from his mother, where as a babe he had fallen off a ladder into a sharp piece of wood. I felt I knew every freckle and hair, but my eyes were greedy to mark and memorize each one.

It was as if I already knew the more important scripture to commit to memory was not the Targums and psalms I had learned growing up, but the living, breathing being in front of me.

And yet how often have I have heard even his body misquoted. In the stories I catch from travelers at the marketplace, he is as whittled down as a dead twig. His flesh grows paler and paler until he is less man than moonlight, unencumbered by the blood and bone that once made up my husband.

You have made him shorter. Paler. Practically sexless. You have erased his scars. His wily humor that expressed itself as much through his body as it did his voice. His twitchy legs, ready to leap into a dance, a run at any moment. Where is his dimple? His stink?

My husband . . . I thought again and again that night, running my hands along the length of him, the coarse fur of his arms and calloused hands. Then I would relax under his reciprocations, his intelligent hands exploring the parts of me I had often pretended did not exist. Now that I'm older, I know his intelligence came from his history with other women. He had not always been an ascetic. Perhaps he had been unsure and gawky at first. I'll never know. There were many women who came before me.

That night he was clever and confident. And whenever I responded in pleasure or surprise, his eyes would widen and he would laugh with delight as if I were his first—as if he had never suspected what joy lay inside of the bridal chamber.

But just as I was not his first, so was it not *our* first time together. I could feel the pith of our spirits echoing in other beds, beds of pine needles and damp soil. As we moved our bodies, it felt that we had fallen into a dance. And when he grasped my upper arms and stared into my eyes, I knew he felt it, too.

As the night grew sheer and let through the pink and gray of dawn, I was certain we had known each other before. But where? Something was coming into view at the edge of my mind. It tickled my consciousness as I drifted in and out of sleep, nestled under his arm.

"I wasn't jesting . . ." he said quietly into the crown of my head; I could feel his voice like a wind through my hair. "Let us go back to the river and make our home. I would bathe in its fresh waters every morning with you."

I turned my eyes upward. "Yes. Let's do that. Would you rejoin with Yochanan?"

He was quiet with thought for a moment but shook his head. "No. I am grateful for his instruction, but I find that our views are too divergent. I will offer my services to those who want them . . . I think Andreas and Philip would join us as well as a few others . . . "

"Then it will be like a small river village . . . and we shall soon add our own family to their numbers," I whispered, thinking of Adah and Salome, their arms laden with babes. Suddenly a new image rose to meet these: me with the heaviness of my own child in my arms, wading slowly into the shallow chill of the river, ready to receive immersion not from Yochanan but from the strong hands of my own husband.

He was excited at this thought and he squeezed me to him, exclaiming, "Let us have a brood to rival Yakov's sons and daughters, so pure of the world that they can move through the jungle like birds and survive on herbs and seeds."

"Then we must get to work . . . " I teased and climbed back on top of him.

At some point in the early morning I fell deeply asleep. And yet the sleep came on in such a way that I still felt awake as I watched the tent and trees dissolve around me, until I was lying naked in an immaterial world of sparkling dust.

Drifting downward, my edges relaxed, hardened, and relaxed again as if I were slowly falling through my own body. Except I was no longer in the orchard. I was running, my breathing labored and quick. Every part of my body told me one thing: *Escape, escape!*

Buildings and walls shot up like gray columns of smoke beside me. Their windows glowed, not with lamps but fire. Rocks and dust plummeted from high above me and crashed at my feet so that I had to cover my mouth as I coughed through explosions of ash. The stones of the street were slick with blood. All around was the smell of filth. This was not just the stench of animals burning . . . People were burning as well, rancid fat sizzling, popping, hair melting into oil and cinders in the wind that whipped back and forth through the city.

It was Yerusalem. But it was Yerusalem in ruins.

Where was my father? My brother? My sister?

I pushed through the throng of people running, scrambling in the opposite direction. Was I imagining it, or did I recognize these faces? Was that the sturdy back of my brother's friend Achim? But it couldn't be! His hair was white. The hands at his side were dappled with age spots.

When I finally reached it—and I had not known that was where my feet were leading me—the temple was a ruin standing on colonnaded coils of charred smoke. With a strange sense of release, I realized that amidst this disaster no one would forbid me going further than the Court of Gentiles. The fire had destroyed all intimations that this was a forbidden place. Was there a small sense of victory, a kernel as compressed and lustrous as a pearl, that formed in the moment?

I entered the temple's inner court and altar. And no one rose to stop me.

Sacrifices were piled high. Yet these were not oxen and lambs! They were the members of the Sanhedrin. Men with their bellies slit open, spilling their innards, useless hands trying to stopper rivers of blood. Mothers whose deaths had suffocated the children grasped in their arms. Young men gurgling as they convulsed, their throats weeping blood noiselessly onto the tiles.

How do I explain what I saw? I still have no idea what it meant and have seen nothing like it in my life since. At first it was the Romans destroying the city. And then they faded. Time swelled and passed and overlapped.

Men wearing metal streamed through the city now.

I was choking, holding my own throat as if I had to stop my own lifeblood from leaving me. Still, I couldn't look away and found myself stumbling backward down the steps until I finally made contact with something hard and alive. A man put his hand on me and spun me around.

The metal he wore made him appear as a serpent with scaled skin about his arms and legs. And he wore a starched tunic over this strange dress. In one hand he had a lethal sword that was caked in blood up to the hilt. And in his other hand he raised a strange flag: forked like a serpent's tongue, white with a cross painted on it, as red as the blood on his sword. His face was pale, with ruddy cheeks, and he had a shock of ginger hair on his head. His eyes were a most unusual color: flat and dense as steel.

"Stand down, woman! I come to claim Jerusalem in the name of Jesus."

He flipped his sword up and its blade pierced my heart.

There was no pain. But my breath left me, and I found myself weightless. I sank to my knees, drawing my hands around the blade as if I might pull it out or force it deeper into my breast.

That was it. A whole life. It came down to one surprising moment. A sword penetrating me as easily as light enters river water.

As the front of my dress grew warm with my own blood, my eyes flickered up to the white line of the man's flag. I remembered the madwoman's strange ramblings at the temple all those many months before. "Behold, he is here. He is here in this city. He who shall cause the fall and rise of many men. And you, oh woman in the garden, a sword shall pierce your heart!"

I awoke back in the tent in the orchard, drenched not in blood but in sweat. The space where Yeshua had lain beside me was empty.

It was then, confronted by his absence, by the very shape of it left behind in the blankets, that I realized what had been threatening all night. In fact, it had been there since the first time I'd seen him on the rooftop.

Yeshua's face, tanned and alive, flickered behind a mask I knew even better: the white face of the man from my vision, stony with death and blurred by a screen of water. The man in the box. Yet, as I saw the two faces in the same place, I realized that although one was living and the other entombed, they were the same.

They are the same man. And one is dead. One of them is already lost to me . . .

My heart racing, I sat up in a panic, pulling what remained of my green tunic over my nakedness and running my hands through my snarls. I couldn't explain the fear that had enfolded me, but it forced any other thought from my mind.

There wasn't time to try to make myself presentable, so I grabbed the rough woven blanket that we had slept upon and drew it around my shoulders.

Why had it taken me so long to recognize him? It was *his* voice that I had heard calling me from inside my visions. It was *his* voice that echoed from the underworld, trapped beyond the land of the living.

I tripped through the grass, glossed with morning dew. There were empty cups thrown to the side and the smoking remains of fires. One or two guests lay on blankets, still curled together in sleep. In the light of my dream, they all seemed corpses, fallen where they'd been slain. The scarlet scarf around a sleeping woman's neck was a mortal wound. The whistle of a snore coming from the man's mouth beside her was a death rattle.

With relief so great that I almost sank to my knees, I found him on the edge of the orchard closest to town. He was no longer dressed in finery, but in the rough, flaxen tunic he most often wore. And his back was to me.

I raised my hand to touch him, to prove he was real. At that moment he turned, sensing my presence.

It was then that I saw the shadow of Andreas behind him. As the stocky man came closer, the early light showed that his face was grave and his gnarled hands were knotted over his stomach.

And here was the confirmation I did not need: Yeshua's face drawn thin and pale, his lips blue as stone and his eyes filled with tears. He was the very image of mourning. Already half past the world of the living, he wore the face of the man in the box.

"Miriam . . ." Yesuah's voice was hollow as he reached for me, pulling me to him with shaking hands. "Miriam. It has happened. It has happened because I was foolish enough to leave him. I have forsaken my greatest friend . . . my father."

"What is it? Who do you speak of?" I gripped his shoulder, turning his body to face me so that I could look him in the eye for the answer to my question. But he twisted away, turning his head into my shoulder. Yeshua was reduced to a child wracked with sobs, grasping my upper arms tightly in order to stay upright.

"What is it?" I looked to Andreas now and knew my voice had the flavor of accusation to it. He grimaced and opened his mouth.

"What have you told Yeshua to trouble him so?" I hotly inquired of Andreas, who lowered his head, his chin disappearing into his stubbly neck. He swallowed carefully before speaking. "Miriam, my lady. Herod captured Yochanan. He captured him a fortnight ago. Then, yesterday, he killed him."

In a flash I saw the small, wizened man from the river. But he was no longer clothed and standing waist-deep in the currents of the Yarden. Instead he was flung back in a scarlet puddle, his head a great distance from the rest of his body.

We stood there for a long while. Yeshua wept. By the time the sun had risen high enough into the sky to signal the start of a new day, and the wedding guests had woken and begun another day of festivities, my husband was a different man. His eyes were dry and his mouth was as straight and thin as a knife's blade.

Without a word, he loosed me from his grip, turned from us, and walked into the woods. Not daring to follow him, Andreas and I shared bread in the shade of an almond tree. When Yeshua's mother came over in confusion, it was up to me to explain what had happened.

Just as the sun began to sink again, he emerged from the forest. He poured himself a glass of wine and, after a sip that he held in his mouth and tasted before swallowing, he turned to me and Andreas and nodded as if we were at the end of a long conversation. "It is decided then. We must go to K'far Nahum."

PART THREE

The Sea

Thirty-One

My most important possession has no weight. It cannot be picked up. It cannot be unfolded like a tapestry before you. My memories of those two short years together are my only true treasure.

We barely ever slept indoors.

We set up camp on the Genasseret seashore. Our driftwood fires sparked green and blue against the greens and blues of the water. We made our bed from spongy moss beneath the big sycamores, sleeping curled together, our hands pressed to each other's faces, always checking to see if the other was real. We would awaken in the middle of the night to a full moon turning the world silver and strange, as if time itself had gone slow, thick, and visible, coating every leaf and branch and hill with its luminous expanse.

"How do you do it?" he would ask, kissing me. He explored my whole body with his lips. He tasted my navel and my sex, his strong hands cradling my hips. "This magic?"

Our lovemaking didn't just summon our souls into our mouths, didn't just set our nerves on fire. It summoned *animals*. Foxes came to watch us. Sand cats curled around tree trunks, their honey-colored fur releasing puffs of musk and dust as they rubbed against the bark and kneaded their claws into the dirt. A murmuration of starlings appeared, so large it seemed like a huge, shadowy being dancing above the landscape. And once near K'far Nahum, standing waist-deep in the sea late at night, locked in each other's arms, I felt a silken nudge against my leg. And then another. And another.

"Fish!" Yeshua exclaimed, leaning down to brush his hands through their smooth, twisting bodies. Hundreds of them, come to celebrate with us.

Even when the friends and followers around us began to swell, we managed to sneak away and perform the most sacred rite of all.

"We are always laying our hands on others in healing," he murmured one night, his scratchy beard against my breast, his hand gently circling the flesh around my nipple. "But you are the only one who can heal *me*."

"It's not just you," I confessed, looking down into his dark eyes, taking my own fingers and tracing the faint white scar on his lip. "It feels as if, when you touch me, we are healing the world."

A dragonfly landed on Yeshua's long spine. I told him not to move, before leaning close to look at its iridescent wings catching the dawn light. Later, owls hooted as I cried out, amplifying the music of my pleasure, and hummingbirds churned the air over our union. The crickets vibrated deep in the grass, and a hawk made a high, clean noise in the sky.

Often during our travels, we would return to a former encampment to find the place where we had slept overtaken by irises, wood violets, and roses.

"Yes," the bees said, their wings laden with pollen, ensuring that these blossoms would seed and erupt. "This is where they slept. This is the shape of their love."

You don't believe me, Leukas? You think these memories fanciful? Every lover invents magic when they remember the first sweetness, you will say—the wonder of their first nights together.

Then answer me this.

You believe he rose from the dead. That he turned water into wine and summoned fish and bread from thin air.

Why not believe this, too?

Thirty-Two

Why K'far Nahum? I asked him many times.

The sea, he would say. The water. The confluence of many rivers.

I understood.

Just as I understood that the river of many lifetimes was arriving, at last, in the ocean of my present. My present with Yeshua.

As we neared the town, Andreas suggested we stay with him and his brother Shimon's family.

Shimon, who had the same corkscrew curls and barrel chest of his brother, was initially distrustful of our arrival. "I don't need a common magician stirring up trouble in my household—or an amulet for a hurt tooth," he had rumbled. "What I need is good weather and a net full of fish." He was sitting at a low table with his wife. Ivah was still young, but her features were pinched and her hair was already flat and thinning. She had a babe in each arm.

"All boys . . ." Ivah muttered, almost under her breath. "Is it wrong of me to wish for a daughter?"

"But your boys are good, solid boys," Yeshua joked warmly. He took the babes from her, bouncing them on his knees.

Ivah sat back in relief, watching as her youngest boy, who had been crying since our arrival, became quiet.

Yeshua loved children. It was something I had noticed at the river, but only fully understood later. Given a choice between the company of toddlers and adults, he would always pick the dirt-caked boys, the sleepy-eyed girls handing him flowers.

His dark eyes dilated and he opened his mouth as if in awe as he gazed at Ivah and Shimon's little boy. He made a grotesque face, baring his teeth like a wolf and flaring his nostrils. The child gurgled and gave a peal of laughter, hitting at Yeshua's chin.

"Why feed *him*?" Shimon complained to Andreas. "I've been feeding *your* wife and children for months now while you run after these magicians! And you expect me to provide for them, too!"

Shimon was incredibly loud. I wondered if shouting was his normal voice. But Ivah and the children were used to it. The babes blinked up at Yeshua, unperturbed. This was the ordinary volume of life in this household.

Ivah rolled up the sleeves of her tunic and rested her elbows on the table. I saw that, while her hands were red and calloused from housework and handling the salting of the fish her husband caught, the skin on the inside of her forearms was still golden and smooth. She had the veiled beauty of a bird that from afar seems brown and unremarkable, but when it finally sits still on a nearby branch, reveals the gem of its bright eyes and the sheen of its plumage. "Forgive my husband," she apologized. "He works too hard, and he has cared for Andreas's family in his absence. It has not been easy . . ."

"And you have worked hard as well," replied Yeshua. "And I am thankful that you did not let Andreas's children and wife go hungry while we had the pleasure of his company."

"Enough!" Andreas boomed, proving that he could be just as loud as his brother. "It will be only for three nights. And they will help us with the chores."

"Put me to work!" Yeshua called out merrily. "I'll gladly do anything!"

"Build me a boat," roared Shimon. "Can you do that, fool?"

But it was settled. We would stay with them.

The brothers had two houses with a courtyard in common. Their widowed mother, Orpah, lived under Andreas's roof. She was a woman stooped by age, but under her decrepitude I spotted the origins of the brothers' square build; she was all one width from her shoulders to her waist.

That first day she came to serve us a lunch of dried fish and fruit. "Aren't you a handsome brute?" she noted, cocking her head at Yeshua.

Orpah took a shine to my husband, immediately giving him a big, toothless smile, but one look at the rich red dye of my shawl and she sniffed, smelling the lily oil I had applied to my wrists. "Is she . . . *Roman*?" she asked Andreas, as if I could not hear. "Why have you brought a Roman whore into our home?"

Yeshua's face hardened, and he put his arm around my shoulder, pulling me protectively to his side.

My mouth had been half-open, ready to let loose my sharp tongue, but he spoke before I could embarrass us both. "Mother, I am profoundly grateful for your hospitality and the company of your sons. But I will not have my wife spoken to like a common harlot." His anger vanished almost at once and he startled everyone by giving one of his wild barks of laughter. "Now that I think of it, I won't have a *harlot* spoken to like a common harlot! Let us all break bread together and treat each other as family."

Orpah laughed and soon she was asking Yeshua bawdy questions. "How is it that you make men clean when you are still wearing the threads made dirty by your work? Wouldn't you have to go into the water as bare as a babe?"

He chuckled, and to my surprise, blushed under her hungry eyes. "Mother. You are right that we must shed all our belongings in order to enter into the kingdom. But at the river I saw fit to keep on my tunic."

Still, she would not serve me food or look me in the eye. Instead she handed the bowl of stewed vegetables meant for me to my husband. He patted me on the leg under the table and as he handed over my food, he whispered in my ear, "She treats you as she herself has been treated."

He was right. Orpah was distrustful of other women: curt with Andreas's wife, Yiska, and outright combative with Ivah. Yet her sons could do no wrong, especially Shimon, who seemed to have inherited a good portion of her foul temper.

I smiled at Shimon sweetly that first night and asked probing questions about his work. *He will soften,* I thought smugly. "Andreas tells me your father was not a fisherman. That he farmed outside of Bethsaida. What draws you to the water?"

"My uncle, who made enough money to feed his children, unlike my father," Shimon said curtly, eyeing me suspiciously as if my curiosity was something to be distrusted. "Why do you want to know?"

"Do not speak ill of your father!" Orpah spat at her son, making the sign of the evil eye. "He was a good man."

"He was a stupid man who could not maintain a field of grain. He was a debtor," Shimon snapped back at his mother. "I feed you with the money I make from fish. Be grateful, woman."

Yeshua was eyeing Shimon with interest. "I abandoned my father's trade, too. As he had abandoned his own when my grandfather lost his land to a bad loan. My father was a carpenter. And I am a vagabond storyteller. Must we all abandon the Father? Is it fated that we must do so?"

I knew he was thinking about Yochanan.

But Shimon was not paying attention. He was still glaring at me.

I tried to infuse my voice with sweetness. "Have you ever been caught out in a storm and been thrown overboard? Do you swim?"

"Do you always ask so many questions?" he shot back.

"She does!" Yeshua laughed. "Almost as many as I do. Although I think the most important question right now is if there is more wine."

Shimon smiled begrudgingly at that and went to retrieve another jar.

The next morning Yeshua woke me early to say that Shimon had agreed to take him out on his boat.

By the time they arrived back, late in the evening, they were holding each other, laughing. Andreas walked behind them, a perplexed expression drawing his eyebrows together. I cocked my head at him, gesturing to the two men who seemed to be unexpected friends. Andreas shrugged as if to say, *He loves my brother more than me! What can I do?*

Shimon had caught not one or two nets full of fish, but four—so many that the other fishermen could not believe his fortune. "This man is a lucky charm!" he joked, slapping Yeshua on the back. "I'll have to take him out with us more often."

"Good," Ivah whispered at my side, shifting the babe at her breast with such carelessness that I was afraid she might drop him. "Get him back in his boat and out of the house."

Does your husband beat you? I wanted to ask the pale woman. But it was not the moment.

Later that night as we settled down on the makeshift bed that Ivah set up for us in the storeroom, Yeshua pulled away from my embrace and folded his hands over his chest. "He doesn't believe a thing I say, but I like him better for it!"

"Who?" I asked drowsily, nestling my head under his arm, drawing comfort from the perfume of his sweat mixed with the salt of the nearby shore.

"Shimon. Can you believe he advised me to give up my vagrant ways and join his netting team? He said I seemed better suited to fish than to men."

"Yes?" The rumble of his voice in his chest was soothing.

"And do you know what I said to him?"

"You know I do not . . ."

"I said I had no need of switching professions. That I'm already a fisherman. A fisher of men!"

"How very clever of you," I replied, reaching around his chest and pulling him into the curve of my body. "And here I was, mistaken, thinking that *I* had caught *you* . . ."

And, of course, I *had* caught him. But only for two years.

When did it happen that he was no longer mine? When did he start belonging to the entire world?

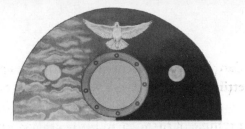

Thirty-Three

"They say he took a boat to the far shore," I overheard a woman at the market gossiping.

"You are mistaken," answered another. "Just this morning I spoke with a man who knows one of his brothers. He told me, with a promise of secrecy, that they have set up camp in the hills where their cooking fires cannot be spotted."

These women seemed an extension of the Genassaret Sea itself, their gray shawls curving to their heads like a wave does to the shore's sand and stone. Other vendors arrived tugging donkeys laden with jars of wine, rolled up rugs, oil, bags of grain, and cheap trinkets.

I was looking for salted fish and a few hard loaves that would soften in water or wine.

I bent over a display of crude leatherwork set out on the bottom of an overturned jar. An older man smiled at me up from where he sat cross-legged on the ground. He exuded a funk that was more energy than it was smell. "A belt for your husband? A small satchel to put herbs in to ward off the evil eye?"

I shook my head, unwilling to speak and reveal my refined accent, so noticeably different from the rough Galilean voices around me.

"He's an accomplished exorcist is what I hear," came the high voice of a woman who sold spices and herbs. I liked the precise way she swept her herbs into little conical piles and pinched up a bit of powder for someone to smell. "Apparently a man, deranged by a demon, burst into the synagogue in Nazareth, and the Rabbi Yeshua told the man to be opened and he was immediately made clean."

"It's all hearsay," scoffed a young man with his hair clipped straight across his forehead in the Roman fashion. "I've heard it all: he healed a cripple near Nain and turned water into wine in Kanna. But as far as I see, all he's actually good at is telling stories."

"I wonder what you'll do if you ever fall into misfortune," an older man interjected. "If you were made mute or deaf or crippled, would you not put your doubts aside and seek his healing?"

The young man snorted with derision. "I gather you're the sort to pay a year's salary to any wandering Chassid who draws a circle in the sand around you and spits in your ear. The only power they have is to empty pouches."

The young woman was shaking her head fervently. "You are wrong. He asks for nothing. He is a true man of deeds. Every miracle he performs he does free of charge."

"My husband's brother was a leper and now his skin is as clean as a babe's," remarked a gray-haired old woman. "I saw him before and after with my own eyes. Puss and sores and all manner of filth—completely gone! And it disappeared as soon as this man Yeshua laid his hands on him."

I clutched one of the vendor's belts so tightly it bit into the palm of my hand.

"Are you going to buy or break?" the leather vendor demanded.

"Forgive me." I bowed my head to him and moved closer to the conversation. Here was a table full of trinkets and cheap jewelry. I ran my hand over the clumsily hammered necklaces, pinching at their chains as I listened.

"A man who sits down to dine with harlots and Pharisees is no friend of mine. He is as good as Hellenized. I wouldn't be surprised if he counted Antipas among his followers soon enough," the cynical youth complained.

"You are a fool!" The young woman was so exasperated that she had spilled ochre- colored powder onto the table. "Yeshua is as far from a Roman as you or I . . . if not farther. It is said he was a talmid of Yochanan's down by the Yarden. Antipas slaughtered his teacher and is his sworn enemy."

The young man was sobered. "And my father's father and brother were also killed. Dead among Yudah's followers less than thirty years ago. Strung up on crucifixes and bled like animals for sacrifice."

"If you have reason to hate the Romans, then you have reason to love this man . . . or at least listen to him," the young woman continued.

"He speaks of all our debts forgiven. He speaks of a kingdom . . . and a time when his sword will be raised and see the Romans gone from this land."

I dropped a thin, silver bracelet I had been handling and turned away. There was always a point when the gossip veered so far from the truth that I found it useless to listen any longer.

The fishwives were quiet, their lips slim and dry as the fish they wrapped carefully in linen for me. I handed over some coins and tied the bundle into my skirts so that my tunic rode up like a farmer's trousers. My calves were sun-browned and muscled from walking and I relished that this was not Yerusalem: a lady could bare her ankles and let her hair fly freely unbound without worrying that some young Pharisee would chastise her.

K'far Nahum was no Bethany. It was closer to the bustle of a city, and with the Hellenized metropolis of Tabariyyah nearby, there was a constant influx of foreigners and gentiles.

As I walked through the pebbled streets, I passed more Romans than I did fellow Jews: some centurions who were unafraid to meet my eye and leer, and groups of women in richly dyed dresses who were obviously the wives of those soldiers. They laughed, throwing their necks back to expose the white skin of their collarbones and the tops of their breasts.

I took the long route through the town, following the street that led me right to the harbor. The boats were coming into dock already with their early morning catches. I kept my distance, watching as the gulls darted down and the men, their bare backs glistening dark and wet under the noon sun, struggled to empty their heavy nets. The sky behind them was so cleanly blue that it looked like a bolt of dyed cloth stretched as a tent above us.

I had spent enough time in K'far Nahum to know that the weather could change almost instantaneously, clouds blooming from the horizon until the water churned black as old lamp oil. Sometimes the fishermen did not return. Daily the sea gave up its plenty of fish. But sometimes, on a stormy day, it claimed its due.

Yeshua would have reproached me. "The earth is not as cruel as you believe, Miriam," he would explain. "We must not pay for our every joy. Sometimes the joy itself, felt fully in the moment, is payment enough."

Looking out at the jewel of the sea, feeling my bare legs beneath me and the wind braiding its salt into my scalp, I thought that perhaps he was right. I reached up to pull the shawl away from my head and ran my fingers through my hair. It was two and a half years since Yeshua and I had been wed and, although the circumstances of our life together were unusual, I had never been happier.

No storm had come to swallow up the boats of my contentment.

One of the jetties was crumbling into the sea, the fishermen having left it long ago to be claimed by the waters. I had taken to walking along its stones on my trips into town. I had to step carefully. When I reached its end, I sometimes felt that, if I were to take but one more step, I would remain aloft, walking weightlessly over the water.

My hair blew out toward the horizon, and the hills of the distant shore blurred under the screen of dark curls. I brought a hand up to my brow to block the sun and saw Shimon, stripped to the waist, paused next to his nets, watching me. Seeing me turn toward him, he quickly busied himself with the cleaning of his nets, gesturing to another man to come and help him.

In the time since we had met, I had managed to understand some things about this stormy man. He disliked scholars. He disliked "fools" and "madmen" and "whores" and "tax men." He disliked Romans. He disliked his wife. But mostly he disliked me. Although he did like my cooking. I had been able to summon a small smile from his stony face with my spiced lentils.

"Lady lighthouse! Are you standing there to guide the boats safely to shore or direct them into the rocks?" called out a familiar voice from the pier.

"Yudas. I didn't think we'd see you again so soon!"

The slender man offered me a hand as I stepped down from the jetty. He was hardly thirty yet had the face of an old man, his well-trimmed beard already streaked with gray. Wrinkles spread out from the corners of his eyes.

He had been blessed with a wife and a daughter, both of whom had died several years earlier when an ill vapor passed through his town. He never spoke of his loss and seemed to have no inclination to start another family. *How do you do it?* I longed to ask him. *How do you live on?* But it felt like bad luck. To acknowledge that one could lose such happiness was to invite that possibility into my life.

May it never happen. Let us linger in this perfection forever. Never aging. Never parting. Never to die.

It was a prayer and a promise to myself. Most of all, it was a way of ignoring the memory, buried deep within me, that we had been separated before. We had died before. In those many lives, had we ever grown old together? Leukas, I tell you now, I still do not know.

Yudas dropped my hand and walked up to the edge of the pier. He looked for a while out at the water. "Are you surprised that I am returning? I only left in order to settle my debts and transfer my home to my brother and his wife."

"So you have erased your past . . ." I noted. Yeshua would say that Yudas was coming home, remembering himself.

And I would argue: *Look at the man! His pain has delivered him past all desire. He has no appetites. And I don't think it is a good thing! Desires and appetites keep us alive. They keep us grateful for the present. The food in front of us. The lovers that we might someday meet.*

How right I was! To be so hollow is to be vulnerable to fate! Our love, our pining and striving, our very desire keeps us filled with our own stories, our own needs. When we empty ourselves too thoroughly, the winds come to fill the void.

"You think me rash?" Yudas questioned.

I tasted the sea salt on my lips before speaking, twisting the edge of my shawl as if I could squeeze out the right response. "If you are rash, then I too have lost my mind. I gave to him my whole life when I agreed to wed him."

Yudas stopped at a stall and handed over a few coins for fresh fish. When we had passed under a stone arch into the shade of the almond trees at the edge of town, he spoke pointedly. "They do not come just for him, Miriam. Surely you must know."

"I heal," I admitted after a long moment. "But it is not the same. He teaches, and tends the hearts of the men and women who come to hear him speak."

Yudas nodded at that, adding with a flash of amused disapproval, "Maybe you, too, will teach someday. Life surprises us. And you are still young."

We slowed our pace as we entered a clearing circled by pines, tall and straight as sentinels. Out from under their protective shade, the ground was a baked red powder.

"No one listens to women when they teach," I complained, knowing that Yudas would agree with me, or worse, chastise me for being so brazen.

We came into sunshine and his face expanded into an expression of rare joy. "Wildflowers! So early!" he exclaimed, bending down by the side of the path.

It was not yet spring, but already an assortment of colors dotted the grasses. Yudas stopped, tucking the bundle of fish under his arm, and pulled a sprig of early flowering bindweed. He held the delicate pink blossoms up, examining the darker red veins that divided the flower into discrete petals. He took a fingertip and traced the color lightly, completely absorbed. But then, with his face half-obstructed by the blooms, he started to muse.

"Of course, I should not be surprised that the bindweed comes early when Yeshua and his retinue approach. The whole world wants to celebrate, even if it means disregarding the natural order. Soon all the seasons will be untimely: every blossom blooming prematurely when it feels your footsteps. Will that be how we know the kingdom has arrived? When the summer comes in the winter? Or when there is no more winter at all?"

I plucked one of the flowers out of his hand and twisted it between my fingers. "Don't ask me about the kingdom. Today, K'far Nahum is the kingdom."

"You speak in the same riddles as he does." But Yudas was not upset and began to walk again briskly. "But tell me the news of our friends. I have been a long time gone . . ."

Happy that he had changed the subject, I gossiped cheerfully as we walked the last winding mile through brush and wildflowers until we came to the encampment. So many had joined us. We had picked up a whole family, including an old grandmother named Atarah. On first glance she was frail and small, bent over a walking stick as crooked as her own spine. Yet the minute she opened her mouth she transformed: her voice was ageless and clear as the shofar's call. And she always had something to contribute, insisting on clarification every night when Yeshua told his stories, and often rejecting outright what he had said.

"What is this narrow door? What if a woman is good and fat from giving you children and she cannot pass through? Will she not be able to enter?"

She never failed to make Yeshua laugh. "Atarah, are you worried that you will not be able to follow the way? Trust me when I say that you will have no trouble passing through the gate. You are a thin blade of grass."

But she always had the last word. "Rabboni, I am not worried for my own sake, but . . ." and here she reached out to pinch a large woman sitting beside her with a small babe nursing at her breast, "I am worried for my daughter-in-law. She is not made for narrow gates!"

I relayed all this to Yudas and more. And he brought his own news. Some men in Upper Galilee had found a strong youth they insisted was to be the new king: "He is a shepherd, and handsome, too. But the trouble is, no one has forgotten the fate of those who followed my namesake, the rebel Yudas. Strange that I should share my name with so many infamous men . . . I say that it will do us no good to be brave if we are dead. The Romans won't let anyone proclaiming himself the Messiah live for very long."

"Yochanan made no claims," I noted. "And still he was struck down."

"Yochanan should have stayed at the river," Yudas replied. "When he insulted Herod and his wife, he entered into a game he had no right to play. His place was the wilderness."

I thought of that small brown man, more wooden than he was flesh, standing in the Yarden, making proclamations. It was hard to believe him dead. It was as if he had only been washed away downstream and into the ocean.

We reached the camp and children ran headlong into us. Women were making bread over the fires.

"And where is your brother, Lazaros?" Yudas asked me. "He was with you last I remember . . ."

"Lazaros is back in Bethany. But I expect we will see him again soon. It does not seem that he ever wants to be long away from his beloved . . ." I joked.

But it was true. Yeshua and Lazaros were as close as blood. The last time they'd been together, Yeshua had taken my brother out on the sea with Yohan and Yoses Ben-Zebedee. They had come back exultant and empty-handed.

"I think my shadow scares away the fish," Lazaros had confessed. "And I kept going to the side to look out into the water!"

Lazaros and Yeshua would stay up half the night talking together. "Tell me how to build a table! How do you pick out the correct wood?" my brother asked once.

And Yeshua grumbled. "I'm sitting barefoot in a forest, a disgrace to my family, in order to *never* speak of such dull things again."

"I don't think they are dull," Lazaros responded lightly. "The world must be made, isn't that right? Someone must make us houses and chairs and beds."

And Yeshua would answer in detail. "My father preferred oak for tables. Or occasionally a holm tree. But I was partial to cedar."

I wondered how long it would be before we were all together again.

"They are truly brothers," Yudas agreed. "I will have you know that when I first joined your fellowship, I was sure Lazaros was Yeshua's blood and not your own."

"My blood is my husband's blood," I said, smiling.

I spotted Salome seated under the shade of an olive tree. A blanket spread out in front of her was covered with an assortment of bundles. Every new member of our group brought some gift: sesame oil, wine, kerchiefs filled with seeds, grain, dried fruit. It was Salome's job to see what we could use immediately and what we could store for our inevitable return to the road.

"I don't mean to make your task more difficult, but I have more to add to your troubles," I told her as I untied my skirts, handing over the loaves and fishes.

"No. This is good." She nodded slowly, biting her pale lower lip thoughtfully as she unwrapped the fish. "Something that I don't have to cook tonight. A group from Tabariyyah brought these vegetables and they are almost rotten. We'll have enough to feed an army tonight and nothing next week . . ."

"Forgive me then . . ." Yudas said, presenting her with his fresh package of small barbels. "These too will need cooking."

Her face fell, but she took the fish, muttering something under her tongue. A complaint. A recipe. I wasn't sure. Whenever I felt bad about how much the slender foreign woman was responsible for, I remembered the brief week where I had insisted she do nothing. She had shadowed me, utterly forlorn, her hands twitching whenever I set about a task.

"Please!" she had enjoined me. "I need to keep busy. It quiets my mind. Give me something to do!"

Later, when we were seated around the fire for our evening meal, Salome brought the barbels out on a wooden board. She had dusted the fish with spices and cooked them so that they fell apart as she served them, their pale flesh gleaming in the firelight.

I served myself eagerly, but unexpectedly the fish revolted me. They tasted too much of the sea, and I struggled to swallow. It was strange. One of my favorite parts of our stays in K'far Nahum had been the daily catch. Our last visit Yeshua had joked that he would have to become a fisherman in order to keep me in fish.

I smiled at Salome in admiration for her cooking while concealing the uneaten barbels under some bread.

Yeshua sat at my side, picking the fish bones with his fingers while talking with Yudas about a centurion who had donated the funds for a synagogue to be erected in Bethsaida.

"Is it compensation for the horrors inflicted on us by his brothers?" asked Philip from across the fire. Adah was at his side, an arm slung over his shoulders. "Does he think he can buy our forgiveness?"

"He should not have to buy it," scolded Yeshua. "Haven't you already freely given it?"

Philip went to speak again but his wife cut him off. "You forgive too easily, Yeshua, as someone who does not have children," scolded Adah. "What if that same soldier had hurt your daughter? Or slain your son?"

"Yes! This is true. Ease of forgiveness is a privilege. I'm sure it gets harder when one has more to lose . . ." I could see the sparkle in his eye as he changed his mind, his heart. I loved such moments. Shift. Adapt. It was the same intelligence he brought to me at night when he touched my body. When he asked me, "What do you want? Where is your pleasure today? How have you changed?"

But Yudas was shaking his head vigorously. "You all misunderstand me. The man truly believes in our God. But he still prays to the idols of his homeland. He worships some crazed man who, as far as he could explain to me, is divine only in that he inspires drunkenness and lust in his followers."

"How can this be?" I butted in, stealing some bread from Yeshua's hand. But when I took a bite, I found that its taste was dull and chalky.

Yudas pressed his lips together and peered upward, as if the stars would help him to explain. He nodded as if he had received his answer, but made no move to speak. It was the pale-haired Salome who broke the silence, with the certainty of someone who had been raised in the world of centurions but had not been born a Jew.

"It has to do with the land itself. Men like that believe they cannot carry their gods and goddesses from the groves and waters where they were born. They cherish the memory and long to return to their holy ones. But I expect that now that the centurion is in our land, he feels he must honor your God born of these oceans and mountains and deserts."

"So he believes in many gods at once," I concluded.

"I do not see how it is profitable for a man to serve two masters," Yeshua said, cocking his head to the side and wiping his oily hands on my leg. I squirmed away but he laughed, giving me a wink. "He will only love one and hate the other."

"This man's faith is a performance then. He dishonors his false god *and* our true one," Philip said, quick to agree. He stood and came to sit closer with us.

"The man's faith is different from yours. That is all," Salome said sharply. "Is that so wrong?"

I watched Yudas, who was tapping his fingers on his knee with some agitation. It was not in his nature to immediately disagree with Yeshua. He rarely asserted his opinion. He was the one talmid of Yeshua's who I associated with silence. And yet his silence in no way rendered him invisible; he was always noticeably present, nodding his head and keeping his eyes fixed intently on whomever was talking, giving them his full attention until the end of a long conversation. Only then, after deliberation that wrote itself clearly on his face as a tightening of the muscles in his hollow cheeks and a furrowing of his brows, would he ask some probing question. And as soon as it was asked, he would retreat once more into the role of observer as the others jumped in to voice their answers.

The olive trees held us that evening. The soil below us was bound together with their roots, the air above us veined with their leafy branches. No conversation was too unwieldy for their shade. All was softened, colored by their invisible, woody exhalations. The firelight cast shadows and tongues of light upon their trunks. The flame pretended to eat them, but kept its distance.

"Worshiping the land does not require the dividing of your faith," I suggested. "But the land, although whole, does not always appear the same. Our Lord tells us that there are barren deserts like Egypt cut through with mud and water, and then there is the milk and honey of our homeland. There was the garden that man was born into. And the small, sparse kitchen gardens we plant now, here by the sea. Perhaps this man's god is just a different version of our own god; he just looks different clothed in the vines and flowers of a distant land."

Yudas smiled again, as he had earlier at the flowers, unexpectedly pleased.

Salome reached out and pinched my hand with thanks. "Yes, Sister," she whispered just for me. "That is the truth."

"Perk up you fools!" Shimon boomed, emerging from the trees with his brother Andreas, his voice thundering through the clearing.

"Friend! You have joined us!" Yeshua cried out, rising to embrace him. "I thought you were too busy!"

Andreas shrugged. "Do I count for nothing, Yeshua?"

"Don't be silly, Andreas. You always dine with us. I am only surprised by Shimon also joining us tonight."

"Did you think we were Romans?" Shimon laughed as he pushed his way into the circle. "Here to interrupt your rabble-rousing? Has it been so long since I saw you last that you have started to teach fear instead of kindness, Yeshua?"

"Guess what we brought," joked Andreas, his customary good humor restored. He deposited a smelly bundle in front of Adah and Philip.

"No more fish!" Adah groaned, pretending to kick the bundle into the fire. "We have more fish than hungry mouths!"

"Don't listen to my wife," countered Philip as he shifted over to give his friends room to sit. "We've never once gone hungry, and yet we never seem to have any extra. One loaf of bread feeds twenty!"

"Are you all right, Miriam?" asked Yohan Ben-Zebedee with concern. "You have eaten no fish and barely any bread."

I didn't respond immediately. I was watching as my husband wandered off with Shimon and Philip. A young widow named Marah who had come to us only a month earlier, plagued by a paralysis of her hands, sought to join their conversation. I watched as Shimon pointedly turned his back to her, shutting her out of the discussion. Yeshua was too excited by the arrival of his friends to witness her exclusion.

I sighed and slowly turned back to Yohan. "I see how it is! You are not so much worried about me as you are about my dinner going to waste! Do you want my fish?"

He laughed. "I wouldn't say no if you offered but—truly—I wondered if you were ill?"

"She is not sick, Yohan," Yudas said. "Leave her be."

I looked back at Yudas, but he offered nothing more before giving me another rare smile and joining the other men.

I gave Yohan the rest of my fish and then went to help the women with the cleaning. There was a small stream nearby and we brought the dishes down there to rinse.

When we were done, I lingered, my feet in the stream, enjoying how the water cooled my blood.

Water. The stream circled my calves and then passed on. Washing me. Tasting me. Water from the sky. Rain, heavy with pollen and red dust and starlight. Water from the earth's thinnest, most superficial veins. Brooks. Creeks. Overflowing springs and wells. Opalescent droplets beaded on the morning grass. Milky white water running from the fig tree's broken branch. Deeper water. Water of the sea, as flavorful and salty as sweat. My husband's sweat.

For in his innermost being will flow rivers of living water . . .

Finally I could understand scripture. Because I could feel it. The words lived in me. Outside of me. I had never felt fresher or more alive than I was when inside the current, the liquid dance of the earth itself—cleansed by living water every day.

I stepped deeper into the stream. The silvery bark of each tree was visible and each blade of grass sparkled with its own light.

How could I have forgotten? I wondered, throwing my head back to look at the star-speckled sky. The moon, having just risen, was so full it looked ready to overflow. I could feel the pulse of its glow like the beat of my own blood.

The full moon comes again, I thought, putting a hand to my belly.

"Miriam!" Adah called to me. She had turned silver and blue by the moonlight. "Are you coming? Are you all right?"

I stood with my feet in a vast landscape, stretching from seaside to mountaintop. I felt sure, all of a sudden, that my intelligence was not isolated to this body. It flowed out of my feet into the stream, over rocks and sand, through the cracks in the earth that led deep underground.

He had opened me to this. It had always been there, but his body and his touch had shown me that I was not limited by skin, by bones, by lifetimes. Each time he looked into my eyes and put his hand at my breast, pressing into my heartbeat with his fingers, I remembered everything. I remembered what it was to be a river stone. A hummingbird. A storm cloud. A leopard. A drop of rainwater.

"Yes!" I exclaimed finally, jumping out of the water and sending droplets flying. My skirts dragged in the dirt as I scrambled up the rocky hill and grasped the softness of my friend's arms. She smelled sweet and damp. Like milk and children.

"Have you gone mad, Miriam?" She swayed backward under my weight and we almost toppled over.

"I've always been mad!" I laughed, hugging her to me tightly until she surrendered, returning my embrace. "It's just that I've never been so happy!"

The joy was too much for me. It overflowed into that ecstatic realm that tears belong to. They streamed down my face and dampened Adah's cloak.

She pulled back, looking at my face closely. "Oh, Miriam! Me too. Me too."

The sky stretched purple and dense over the blue-black of the forest. "What a beautiful night! What a paradise we live in . . ."

It was true. I never could have imagined such happiness, trapped in the small world of my father's dinners. His dry debates. The world of men and their rules.

Here we lived to breathe and eat and love. To sleep and awaken was a miracle. Each dawn revealed a new array of colors. Purple as a secret vein one morning and the ashen pink of a frost-covered pomegranate the next. Each day was a universe of delight. Adah taught me and the little children to squeeze nectar from the honeysuckle. We ate wild berries and picked fruit from the trees. We pinched spices from wild gardens and used them to flavor the pigeons that the local shepherds offered to us, strung up on long sticks by their limp feet. We ate fish from the streams, with sea salt. We slept with the starlight and the silken shadows as our blankets. New friends arrived every night with gifts, wonders, stories. The young massaged the gnarled hands of the old. And the elders taught us how to become slow and quiet, and to receive the tender, pink prophecies of flowers in our dreams.

Sometimes I dreamed of the rose—her lazy, flesh-colored petals waving in the breeze, barely protecting her pollen-powdered heart. And sometimes I dreamed of her stem, all thorns and no blossoms, each thorn exuding a tiny, perfect bead of crimson blood.

Adah clutched me to her soft breasts. We stood there watching the moon as it slowly lifted upward.

And inside of me I felt something else tighten and swell.

There was a moon in me, and like the moon in the sky, it was rising.

Yeshua liked to stay up late talking. I was happy to see it was Marah, the young widow, who held his attention. She was waving her hands now, made whole by his healing, her eyes glued to them as she pinched the air, flicked her wrists, and then squeezed them into tight fists. She wasn't smiling. The miracle was bigger than joy for her. It inspired scrutiny and attention.

How? I knew that was what she was asking. *How did you heal me?*

Faith, he would answer. But I knew the real answer. The answer he whispered to me late at night when everyone else was asleep. *I don't know how it happens. Tell me, Miriam. How do we heal?*

After helping put the children to bed with Adah and Marah, I sought out the small glen just inside the forest where Yeshua and I had made our bed. I stretched out the cloaks and blankets and lay down, clasping my hands protectively over my stomach.

In. Out. In again. A dry inhale. A long, whistling exhale. I listened to my breath.

"Hail my love! My favored one!"

I rolled onto my side as Yeshua sank to his knees on the blankets and stripped off his tunic. He smelled of wine and woodsmoke and fish as he lay down next to me and pulled me into his arms. I nuzzled into his collarbone, enjoying the softness of his chest hair against my cheek.

After two years, his body was an extension of my own. I felt I knew every part of him. And yet there was something so miraculously *different* about his physicality. His hard muscles against my softer limbs produced a kind of tension. Perhaps it was the same joy that water feels when it meets stone. The river carving through a mountain. The sloping rock face directing the rain into the valley. A wedding of elements.

"Where have you been all night?" he wanted to know. "You disappeared after Shimon and Andreas arrived."

"You are wrong. I was by the fire a while longer. And I helped Adah with the cleaning."

"Ah! Forgive me. I had not seen Shimon in a long time."

"I saw him earlier," I admitted.

"Oh? He didn't mention it." Then he chuckled dryly, squeezing me slightly. "You still haven't cracked him! You will have to cook something particularly delicious to get into Shimon's heart."

I ignored this. Given that it had been two years, I had concluded some time ago that Shimon would never treat me as a friend. "Does he still complain about the Romans? And the bad weather? And his dull wife?" I asked. "If I remember correctly, the last time we saw him, the two of you were arguing about kings and you came away angry . . ."

"Ah! That . . ." Yeshua relaxed his grip on me and through the shadows I could see the telltale twitch of his lips. That tick always let me know that he was thinking of something unpleasant. "Time takes away the sting. It seems like a trifle now."

"He said you were a charlatan who worked for the Pharisees to keep us under the Romans' thumb. He said you taught passivity and meekness. He said you would fall under the sword of a new David, come to claim Yudea and free our people."

"The one who is much keener to argue is Yudas," said Yeshua, redirecting the conversation. "Yudas, who will not stand behind his own arguments and prefers to place them between us and then look in the opposite direction like an innocent child."

"Come now," I said, pushing myself up on my elbow so I could look down at him. My long hair pooled on his chest. I placed my hand to the side of his face. "You love Yudas. He has given up his entire life to be with us."

"Yes, he has," Yeshua admitted. "But I didn't ask him to do such a thing."

"Hush . . ." I leaned in, kissing the side of his mouth, letting my tongue flick out and taste the day's sweat and dust caked into his skin.

Since our wedding, he had kept himself clean-shaven and his hair clipped short. But that night there was a fine stubble at his chin and I let my fingers brush against it. At first he turned his head, still troubled by my words, but as I breathed softly against his cheek he relented, running his warm hands up my back and turning his mouth toward mine.

"What Yudas and Salome said was true and you know it. There are as many gods and goddesses as there are trees," I implored.

"There is one goddess. One queen. And she is you."

"I don't respond to flattery," I said, even as I pressed my cheek to Yeshua's and took his hand in mine, twining our fingers together.

"I am happy we are close to the water again," Yeshua whispered into my ear, his breath sending a shiver down my spine. "It reminds me of the time we walked into the ocean and the fish came to meet us. And then later, lying in the sand, testing the limits of . . ."

"We are even happier now," I interrupted. "Now we have grown ourselves a family and are not thrown out of every village we enter."

I could feel the dimple in his cheek as he smiled.

"Don't pretend you didn't find it exciting," he reminded me. "In fact, it could be argued *you* were the one who had us chased from Shunem. You insisted on staying with that pregnant girl who was besieged by demons."

"She had no demons in her. You know that!" I poked his chest with my finger. "She was feverish, and if I had left her, both she and the child would have died."

Yeshua pulled away slightly so that he could gaze down into my face. "How wild you looked with your hair down, crawling on top of her, her gray skin turning ruddy under your hands. It was like watching spring descend on the mud of the fields, waking the flowers from their sleeping seeds."

"Yes. I'm sure that's why we were thrown out. It would have *nothing* to do with your argument at the synagogue."

"Fair enough," Yeshua admitted. But he gave me a half smile that let me know he was not conceding. "Perhaps the blame belongs to both of us. At least K'far Nahum tolerates us for now."

I let my hand trail back down to the warmth in my stomach, my finger pressing against the soft curve of skin between my hips.

"We must leave K'far Nahum soon though. We must go and see your mother. I have a gift for her . . ." I let my words trail.

"What gift? We have only just returned to our friends here. Must we leave so soon?"

"Not so soon." I could no longer contain my delight. "We have a long seven moons before we should return to your family."

"Seven moons?" He sat up, his arm around my shoulders, not yet understanding—although it seemed his body did, as one of his hands traveled to my belly and the other cupped my hip.

"It cannot be so . . ." He did not finish his sentence, but tightened his hold on me, his eyes wary. "These two years there has been nothing . . ."

"I, too, was worried," I responded lightly, knowing what he and all our other friends and family members had long suspected—that I was barren. "But it has been two moons since my last blood, and I am sure that I am carrying your child."

Before I knew what he was doing, I was lifted up in the air, supported by his strong arms. His hands curled around my legs and my shoulders as he planted a series of kisses on my face. As he tasted me, he started to walk briskly, deeper into the forest.

"Put me down! I thought you would be overjoyed!" I complained, twisting and beating a hand uselessly against his breast.

He responded by laughing darkly, throwing me up and then catching me again. I grasped at the short hair at the back of his neck and bit his ear. Hard. The wet dirt taste of blood filled my mouth.

But he did not cry out.

"Careful now, wildcat. I too can bite!" he warned.

It was only then that I saw he had carried me through the forest to the top of a hill that looked out to the sea beyond.

Yeshua gripped me by my waist and easily lifted me up as if offering a sacrifice to the night's splendor. "Here my love! Let us receive the *real* immersion."

I struggled free.

Right behind his head, as if it were a crown, I saw the moon, full and risen to the sky's center. Just to look at it was to be made clean and new under its white fire. The stars, too, bathed us in their radiance. Slowly, so that I almost thought he was melting into the earth, he sank to his knees, bringing his head and hands to my belly, his lips moving against the curve of my hip.

"Can you feel it? It has happened."

I took his head in my hands and nodded, although I could not give the feeling words.

"My love. It is as I always wanted." He looked back over his shoulder at the moon. "We were parted. We were two. But now—now the two have become one."

Thirty-Four

Salome and I were replenishing our supply of herbs for medicine and cooking in the woods. We paused at a creek to wet our scarves and tie them across our sweaty foreheads.

I watched how carefully Salome moved, her elbows always bent, pinned into her narrow waist. We had spent years together talking of everything. Roman brutality. The way the moon seemed to communicate with women's wombs. Cooking. Herbs.

The most useful information was about lovemaking.

The first time I asked her for such guidance I was worried she would be offended. But she smiled and squeezed my arm. "I thought you might ask soon."

She offered her love lessons easily, in the same flat, matter-of-fact tone she used to speak about the weather. How to make a man moan. How to increase a woman's pleasure. How to hold off the moment of release so that when it finally came it was more powerful. Pleasure was something Salome had much experience in.

Once or twice, I made the mistake of pushing her for the story of how she had ended up a prostitute. She would immediately freeze, her pale eyes going milky as if she were temporarily blind. "It matters not," she said curtly the first time, and left abruptly. It was the same afterward: at a stream washing clothes. Baking flatbread over a metal dome. Lazing in the sunshine. Up. Gone. She would avoid me for the rest of the day.

Yet it was in my nature to try again. I wanted to understand why she moved like she was made of open wounds. I wanted the *story*.

"Look at that!" Salome noted, streaks of red appearing on her pronounced cheekbones. "The khatamit zifanit blooms!"

355

We had come out into a field covered in tall stalks of blooming flowers. Two years in Galilee had acquainted me with them. Now they were still the intense dark magenta that later in the spring would only remain as a thin corona around their pistils. The process of blossoming would dilute the color, drawing it out into frothy pink petals.

Fingering the buds that were as hard and promising as a nipple ready for suckle, I was suddenly moved to tell Salome about my pregnancy. It was new yet, and it would be a month or so before I even started to show, but I felt that the more people I told the news to, the more real it would feel.

Make me feel heavy, I thought as I plucked a flower and handed it to my friend. *Let me feel your eyes on me, seeing something more than me* inside *me.*

"My blood is two months late . . ." I began.

Salome's reaction surprised me. She instantly sank to her knees, bringing her hands to my stomach, lightly cupping the curve that was barely even noticeable under the folds of my tunic.

"Shifra and Puah watch over her," she murmured. Rather than comfort me, the invocation of the ancient midwives Shifra and Puah, charged with killing all the Jewish infant boys in Egypt, made my skin prickle with gooseflesh. I thought of Miriam, my namesake, saving her brother Moshe, watching him float away from her on the river. I resisted recoiling from Salome's touch.

"Salome, stand . . ." I said, trying to get her to rise. I had never before seen her so overcome.

"And you are named for Moshe Rabbenu's blessed sister, Miriam," she murmured so that I could barely hear, her thin lower lip trembling. "Miriam, who guides all babes safely down the river. It is right that you should carry your own child through waters, close to the sea."

"Rise, Salome! You are soiling your cloak!" I exclaimed, squeezing her shoulders. But she only pressed her cheek into my stomach more fiercely.

"Grant me a second, Miriam." Her voice, which had been controlled and ceremonial a second before as she spoke of my ancestors, had gone unexpectedly hushed. "Let me feel this new life as if it were my own."

It was only then that I realized my friend was crying. The dark, charcoal dye of my skirt absorbed the stream of her tears, but as she turned her head, giving her other cheek a turn pressing against my belly, I saw that her eyes were swollen and red.

"Salome . . ." I lowered myself to the ground and embraced her, feeling the wide, delicate wings of her shoulder blades heaving with silent sobs. She sank into my softness. "Many women in our encampment have come to us heavy with child. Adah herself is just recently delivered. What is it about my child that troubles you so?"

The number of births we experienced in the wilderness would have been a problem had Kemat's training not prepared me so well. I had been ready to sit at the feet of many birthing women in the past two years, and had massaged their swollen bellies. I had even used the heat in my hands to stop bleeding and slow the frantic dance of a fever.

And now it would be me. Who would sit at *my* feet? Who would guide *my* womb? An image of Kemat flashed in my mind, more a portrait of textures and smells than anything visual. My pregnancy made the loss of her fresh again. I wanted her beside me, showing me how to make life inside my own body.

Salome was busy murmuring in a tongue I knew to be Greek, her hands clutching at different parts of me as if I were clay she was molding into shape.

Finally she calmed and drew away from me so that we were face-to-face, our knees kissing.

"I know what it feels like."

"What?"

"I said I know what it feels like," she repeated.

A fan of shade unfolded, folded, was gone. By the time we looked up, the bird's shadow had disappeared. Suddenly the gnats were gone. The low whir of the crickets flattened back into the grass.

I stared into the blue of her eyes.

"I know how it feels. Like being a tree. Growing roots. Getting heavier with sunlight and water. I, too, once carried a child." She said it slowly. The word *child* had been spoken with such intensity that I was almost ready for something of substance to issue forth: tiny black pearls scattering from her mouth into my hand or the yellow kernels of grain shaken free of their sheaf.

Again the bird was overhead. We glanced up. It was a kestrel. I could tell by the way it hovered in the air, searching for the twitch of prey below.

Something was happening to my friend. Her hair, always pale and flaxen, seemed made of the finest gold. Her watery eyes glowed like the first blue of a bruise—that place where the blood has come close to tasting air.

She was all her selves at once. The old woman she would become, as flat and white and thin as a shaft of morning sunlight. A young girl infused with color and verve, whose breasts were still high and whose lips were wet and rosy, hands resting lightly over the swell of motherhood. I could feel the phantom of her pregnancy between us: a real physical weight, the push of her belly against mine.

"I was lax in my devotion. I thought the mother had abandoned me, so I did not ask for her assistance . . ." Salome's word blended together, almost inaudible curls of breath and emotion.

A quiver in my throat . . . tickling my voice. As if I had inhaled pollen. I thought I might accidentally say her name . . . disrupt the flow of words.

But her words became louder, embodied. Each one coursed through her hands on my belly, vibrating into my pelvis. "I cursed my mother for my misfortune when my lover Tarquinas died of the flux before we could be wed and have my virtue protected by the Law. My father threw me into the streets when he found that I was pregnant by a man not yet my husband; the proprietor of the pleasure-house I sought refuge in sold my body although I was with child, and I lost the child so close to birth that the bleeding almost killed me . . ."

I was perplexed by her words. "Salome, what mother would curse you to a life of harlotry? I don't understand."

Her eyes flashed. "*My* mother?"

Then she shook her head. "No. Not *my* mother. *Our* mother. The mother of Horus. Our blessed lady Isis. I thought she had forsaken me. But she had not. She was testing me as she, too, was tested when Seth murdered her love and sealed him up in a box. As when Seth again betrayed her trust and took Osiris's body and cut him to pieces, scattering him about the land."

A wind blew up from the sea. It teased tendrils of our hair out from under our shawls and snaked through the low branches of a nearby sycamore. I looked closely at the tree and, as it trembled with the wind, I felt that it was more alive than any man or woman I'd ever seen. Wider than it was tall, the thin shoots of the topmost branches seemed almost animated, bowing and twining each other in a complex dance. But the tree was bottom heavy and the lower branches, longer, stretched too far unsupported to remain aloft. They sagged to the ground—one so twisted that it seemed as if it were a surfacing root, poking its leaves and silvery bark through the sparse grasses and moss that grew in the tree's shade.

"Isis." It was not a question. I knew the name as well as I knew my own. *She who goes into the river to find her husband. The husband who has been killed and whose parts are scattered. She who searches through sea and marsh, gathering his pieces, in order to once again make him whole.*

Kemat was there beside me. No longer just a smell. A wash of golden skin. Here were her almond-shaped eyes, her sinewy arms around me, her voice in my ear whispering. "Isis assumed her role as queen of the heavens and the land. The stars shone brighter! The river gushed forth with life and nourished the land. She was all-powerful. And a powerful queen needed a powerful king. A lord that would match her wisdom, her grace, her beauty . . ."

Could Salome feel Kemat, too? Here beside us?

"I thought, if you followed Yeshua, that you must be a Jew . . ." I said to Salome. "But you follow Isis?" As soon as I spoke these words, I was embarrassed by my naïveté. Salome with her unusual, flat accent and pale skin was obviously a gentile. The only gentile in our group.

But she was not offended. "It is a compliment that you do not immediately connect me with those violent curs that call themselves the Roman Army. But those brutal men and silly women *are* my blood. I was born in Miletus, city of Apollo. I am lucky that my mother taught me the secret ways . . ."

"I thought you had already taught *me* the secret ways," I joked.

"No," Salome said, pressing her hands to my stomach again. "Not *those* ways. Yes, pleasure is a part of the secret rites. But there is much more."

This is what I had sensed all these years. This was why I had pushed her to confide in me again and again, even when I saw that it made her uncomfortable.

"When I was fourteen years my mother took me to participate in the Great Mysteries. The worship of Osir-apis and his queen, Isis. I always thought there would be a temple up in the woods—one to rival Apollo's grand house. But the older priestesses showed us that the temple was our own minds. Under moonlight, I drank a strong brew of wine and herbs with the other young girls. We were made to remove our robes, and after long hours of retching, during which my vision narrowed into blackness, a sense of calm filled my body like warm honey. And when we stood up again, we were as goddesses."

Something inside of my belly twitched. I knew it was too early for my child to move in my womb, but I was sure that a new heartbeat had started its rhythm. I could feel the tide of a secret blood begin the complicated work of tying together a body and a soul.

"Do you still pray to Isis?" I asked quietly. "Do you still pray to the Goddess?"

"Miriam," she said with a laugh like frantic frogs signaling the first frost. The cold rains. "What do you think?"

"I don't know . . ." I admitted. "Who do you pray to, Salome?"

She was a young woman. And then an old woman. Her skin darkened and her hair curled. And then, for just a moment, she looked like me. How could she be so many different things at once? Was it a dream?

She answered finally. "Miriam, I am old enough now to know there is no one god or goddess. I pray to every blade of grass. Every flower. Every person I meet. Every person I hate. But most of all I pray to the women. All of us. For it is we who give birth to the world."

We sat in the woods for a long time, holding each other, completely silent, praying to those tiny insects churning the air, splitting through the sunshine with their bladed wings.

Later that night I chose to announce my pregnancy to my friends. Marah's newly healed fingers shook as she touched me. Adah's smile was knowing, her dark eyes dancing as if with candlelight. She giggled. "You think I didn't know already?"

"But temper your hopes," advised old Atarah pointing at my belly with her crooked walking stick. "You could miscarry. I lost my first three pregnancies."

"Now that my wife is with child, I see that she no longer belongs to me!" joked Yeshua as he came to join us after the meal.

Atarah scoffed, rolling her rheumy eyes. "This woman has never been yours! A mother knows to say it: she belonged to her child before he was ever conceived."

"So it's a boy?" Yeshua played with her. "Can you tell?"

"It is too early to tell." Atarah lifted her wizened chin defiantly and I held back a chuckle. The proud old woman wished she could give my husband an easy answer. She loved to feel like the authority on anything from local history to the proper cooking of freshly caught musht fish.

"Are you asking because you want a boy?" I asked Yeshua. "Perhaps you are trying to coax my womb into carrying one?"

"Of course. Eventually. Even if we are first blessed with a girl. I've always dreamed of myself no longer a son but the *father* to a son."

"A son?" I laughed. He had never shared this dream.

But he ignored me. "Have you heard the story the Tarsian travelers told last night? About the ass that fell in love with the maid? You ask me how the men knew it was love and not merely friendship. Well, let me tell you that it was quite obvious . . ."

He launched into a story so bawdy even I couldn't help but blush.

Funny that those stories are already gone. The pointless ones. The gossip. The travelers' tales. The stories he told to make old women squeal with glee.

Even Atarah forgot herself and opened her toothless mouth in a wide guffaw.

Thoma came to join us, eager to know what was making us all so merry, and I sat back, imagining a new presence between me and Yeshua; the warm and earthy smell of this child. No doubt it would have Yeshua's curls but my small, sharp nose, Yeshua's wide shoulders and long spine, the same hidden dimple in his left cheek.

This is my son, I thought. *Whom I love and who brings me great joy.*

Yeshua shifted as if he sensed the weight of the child I imagined at his side. He glanced at me, and for some reason I could not fathom, his eyes were filled with tears.

Thirty-Five

"They say you are a harlot with hennaed hair and a face made up like a Roman woman," Shimon explained to me. We were walking through the market together, eating dates. "And they also say that before his touch you were filled by demons that inspired you to offer your flesh indiscriminately."

I snorted with amusement, although Shimon's expression suggested he was anything but playful.

"What's worse, some of the young boys at the wharf asked me if it is true that you service all his followers. That you call us all brother and we call you sister."

"Service?" I asked, feigning ignorance. "What can you possibly mean? You forget I had a protected upbringing and do not know much about *indecent* behavior. I could use an explanation."

"Miriam. I tell this to you for your own good." His voice was concerned. "So that you may put a stop to this poisonous gossip."

"How may I put a stop to something I did not start?" I asked mildly. The sun was high and hot, and for once I did not feel like quarreling.

I stared into the straight, white light of midday. My head felt heavy. Was it the pregnancy making me feel so queer? Only a few days prior I had looked into the stream near our encampment and found my own face a stranger's: that of a much older woman with long, white hair. And I kept seeing different faces behind the familiar features of my friends.

Adah's soft beauty darkened. She seemed to transform into a small hairless boy the color of onyx, flashing pearly teeth, a tight necklace of red coral around his slender neck. Philip's hunched back straightened out. He grew longer, sturdier, until I saw he was an old, regal woman.

The elegance of the woman's posture contrasted with a jaundiced complexion, her two front teeth chipped and decayed down into needles. Yudas wore broader features: a great hawkish nose with a black mustache and a gray beard, with eyes as blue and chilly as a pond reflecting the sky.

I glanced back at Shimon and did not see the sunburned, curly-haired fisherman. I saw a tall, handsome man with a shiny bald head and a narrow, almost feminine chin.

You are not dreaming, I told myself, knowing that what I had seen was in the past or yet to come.

I inhaled, tilted my head back. Cooking spices. Cassia. Cumin. Animal dander. Dried sardines warming up under the sun.

Above us a few sheer clouds moved lazily through a sky so blue it appeared unreal: the intense indikon dye that the Greeks brought from the east poured across a white cloth. I lifted the heavy skin of water I'd been carrying to my lips and drank deeply.

"Are you listening, Miriam? I'm speaking of your reputation." Shimon's voice was loud and grating. "You must cover your hair and wear shoes like a wellborn lady."

Shimon turned to Yudas, who had just rejoined us with a fresh pouch of cooking herbs. "You see how she lives to vex me? She plays the adoring student whenever her husband speaks, but when *I* speak her eyes go blank."

"If Yeshua heard you speak so, he'd knock you to the ground," Yudas warned, getting in line at a table where a young girl was scooping portions of grain out of a sack.

"Knock *me* to the ground?" Shimon scoffed and pushed out his barrel chest. "His student and friend?"

"You think he is so peaceful?" I raised my eyebrow at Shimon and slipped the waterskin back into my satchel. The strap tugged heavily at my shoulder. I'd bought some plums and peaches I knew were close to being overripe and they were weighing down my load. They wouldn't survive the heat of the following day, but their fresh tang and sweetness was the only thing I could think of eating. I brushed the fuzzy skin of the peach, thinking how it reminded me of the softness of a baby's head.

I used any excuse to care for the encampment's young children these days. I had recently helped Yohan Ben-Zebedee's wife, Tirtza, give birth to twins. The delivery had taken all of three hours—the tiny, soft-spoken woman displaying a surprising physical vitality.

"I thought you might die," I had confessed as I rubbed a salve of coriander and honey between her legs to prevent festering and fever. "How could you push two babes through your slim hips? And so quickly!"

Tired as she was, she had given a hearty laugh. "My mother was smaller than me and she had seven babes. Each within an hour. They slipped right out."

"May it be as easy for me," I said, half to myself.

Every day I let Tirtza rest while I took care of the twins. I loved their deer-like eyes that widened in surprise whenever I spoke, that crinkled in joy whenever I smiled.

"Yeshua's Mishnah is peaceful . . . problematically peaceful," grumbled Shimon. "I've asked him if he will hold a sword against the Romans when we finally rise, and he laughs at me."

"I think he would protect himself if the time came," I said, not totally sure I believed it myself.

"Hush," Yudas said, reaching over and boxing Shimon's ear. Shimon spat with disbelief, then massaged the side of his face. He was too astonished to react.

Yudas drew closer, whispering. "We are among centurions and gentiles. Galilee is *not* the place to be speaking of rebellion. Do you not remember what happened to our brothers and fathers just thirty years past?"

"So you are a lamb? Ready for the slaughter?" Shimon shook his head. "Say it. Admit that you are dying to fight!"

"Shimon," I interrupted, trying to diffuse the tension. "How is Ivah?"

His brown forehead folded into a stratum of wrinkles. I could tell he hadn't thought of his wife in days. I had grown closer to Ivah since our return to K'far Nahum, stopping by with sweets for the children when I came to market. She sold salted fish to provide for her growing brood of children while Shimon stayed with us and made no profit from his fishing. I knew that she suffered from Shimon's absence.

"I haven't been back to Ivah in days," Shimon admitted, his voice rough with regret.

"Go to her," I encouraged him, both for Ivah's sake and my own.

He looked at me and for once his face was open, his big, chapped lips purpled by sunburn and weather. "I shall. I shall go to her."

"Bring her some sweets," I suggested. "Something for the children."

"Miriam. Do you know that woman?" asked Yudas, motioning with his head toward a crone who was staring at me from across the market. I looked to see if her eyes might be seeking out someone else behind me. But she shook her head to say, *No—it is you.*

My first thought was to protect the child. I clasped my belly.

She took a few halting steps toward us. On her feet were fine woven sandals that contrasted with her appearance of decrepitude.

"Is she one of us?" Yudas asked as he drew close. "She seems to know you."

"No. I've never seen her before."

"Damned hag!" Shimon spat in the dirt.

"Imah, what is it you want?" I asked, approaching her.

"You are Miriam?" Her voice was an insubstantial whistle.

"Leave her alone!" scolded Shimon.

But the older woman was unruffled by his anger. "You must help," she said softly. "You must come with me."

"Why?" I asked. "How do you know my name?"

"Leave us be," Yudas petitioned her gently.

But she stamped her foot in the dust. "I must bring Miriam to my mistress!"

The young girls selling salted fish were staring. A stocky man with a silver beard pointed toward us.

"Come," she beckoned again. "Away from these eyes. I will explain on the way."

I could feel the old woman's demand tugging at something in the center of me. My lungs tightened around my heart and I swallowed nervously, trying to relieve the constriction.

"I can't allow it," Shimon said loudly.

An old fisherman who had been watching us asked, "Is there trouble, Shimon? Who are your companions? Do you need help? Shall we force her out?"

"Come with me," the old woman repeated, her eyes drilling into me. "It is *now* that we must go."

Seeing that no one was going to make a decision either way, I held out my hands. For someone with small, fragile bones, her grip was surprisingly strong.

Her smile became conspiratorial. "You will come." It was no longer a question.

Shimon's mouth opened to argue, but I shot him my iciest look and spoke under my breath. "If you do not approve, then leave us. And I swear I will tell my husband you called me a harlot. Let us test his peaceful nature."

"This way," said Yudas, leading us out of the market into a nearby alley.

"My lady extends many thanks," she said proudly. "She has asked me to keep watch for the rabboni's followers."

"You are a spy? Who is your master?" questioned Shimon suspiciously.

"What is it you want?" I asked now. "How do you know my husband is a man of deeds?"

She laughed again. "You come into town and buy enough food to feed a Roman army! You hide under an expensive shawl. I am old, but I am no fool."

She was right. It was no miracle. She was just observant. Would the crowds descend on our encampment soon? The sick women with their sick babes? The palsied? The crippled?

It was not a bad thing. But each time we arrived somewhere there were more people to heal. I had been enjoying our brief moment of anonymity camping out in the hills.

"Are you bargaining for money to keep our secret?" Yudas asked evenly. Was there anger behind his voice? Derision? I kept searching for a potent emotion in my friend. But his eyes were hooded and blank.

The woman was finally taken off guard. She shuddered at Yudas's suggestion. "I would think of no such thing! I am not so dishonorable. I mean only to ask for your help with my lady. She is not well, and I am worried she will not last the night. You must come now."

"The night? Is she ill?" I was incredulous now.

The space between homes widened. Gardens offered shady clusters of palms and trellises covered in sea roses. One house at the very edge of K'far Nahum was more impressive than the rest. Made of sturdy basalt painted white, it had two stories. A stone wall enclosed a private garden. Above the doorway was a mosaic of tiles. A rich Hellenized Jew's home, I decided. The lack of a washing bowl at the doorway further confirmed my suspicion. The woman led us into a courtyard, and then into the house through a series of low-ceilinged rooms.

"Do you know this place?" Yudas asked Shimon under his breath.

"Who do you think I am?" Shimon answered. "A fisher of gold? A tax collector who empties others coffers to live in David's palace?"

"My lady's husband left this home to her," the crone explained, overhearing Shimon. "Her husband was a good man—my master for many years before my lady."

I marveled at the exotic tapestries hanging on the walls. Yet dust hung heavily in the air. There was but one sputtering lamp in the niche of the wall, the burning sesame oil's nutty scent discordant alongside the damp mildew of the hallway, the aching blue smell of stones that had not seen sunlight in years. On the walls I noted shadowy depictions of fish, men, women, and some being that seemed a boy but had the lower half of a goat. All were dancing, intertwined.

A girl appeared. "Good, Zillah. She has been asking for you." This girl, though, did not fit into this poor imitation of a Roman's home. Her skin was the same honey as mine and a shawl respectfully covered her hair. In her hands she held a bundle of wet rags that was letting a slow drip of water onto the ground. But she paid the mess no notice. "Is this the man they speak of? Ben-Avram told me he heard a rumor that the rabboni was near."

"This is not the rabboni," I explained.

"You see before you a fisherman from this very town," added Shimon. "Now answer me this: who calls this their home?"

Zillah and the young girl exchanged a worried glance.

Finally the old woman, spoke: "This is my lady's house. Rebekah, take them to where she is resting."

"Resting? She no more rests than a sick babe sleeps!" the girl complained. "She tears at the skin of her face and weeps when you are gone. I shouldn't be responsible for a demoniac. Perhaps her demon will come into me!"

Yudas seemed concerned at this revelation, but Shimon was as curious as I was now. He strode alongside Zillah and Rebekah as they led us through a small arched door to a room richly tiled with azure and alabaster.

A large window cut high into the opposite wall let in a little light. I saw a figure on a couch, curled in on herself so that she appeared to be more of a lump than a human form. She was moaning. I thought it must come from the very bottom of her bowels—a low, foul noise full of distress and desperation.

"Is she a lunatic?" Shimon's voice was sour with distaste. He stepped back, reaching for the front of his tunic so as to draw it over his mouth protectively. "Woman, answer me!"

"Zillah . . . Zillah . . ." the woman on the couch slurred.

"Have care, Miriam," Yudas warned. "I would never forgive myself if I let you put yourself in danger in your condition. She could be a leper for all we know . . ."

"She is *no* leper," Zillah said indignantly. "My lady is the most beautiful lady."

I knelt beside the couch and peered into the mistress's face.

I knew her at once. The snub nose. The delicate eyelashes. The faint, dark fuzz above lips that she had inherited from her mother, Serah. "Yohanna!"

All of her cruelty and coldness was forgotten. It had been years since I had seen my childhood friend from Bethany so long ago married and moved away. "Yohanna! It is me, Miriam! Miriam!"

I was a little girl again and filled with the same vibrant energy that had propelled me through the dusty streets. Across the fields. Up trees. Into dark, damp caves in the hillsides. All alongside my pretty, mirthful little friend.

"Yohanna, please . . ." My voice was desperate.

"You know this woman?" Yudas asked. He knelt at my side.

"Yes. Yes."

Her complexion was the yellow of piss-colored smoke hanging above the city—the yellow of death.

Yohanna began to moan again. Down her neck were scores of angry red sores. I'd seen them before. On cripples and invalids carried to us on stretchers by their family members, those too ill to rise from bed and clean themselves.

"We were friends as children in Bethany. She is called Yohanna." The name hung in my mouth, as sweet as the caramelized pistachios and almonds Kemat had fried in oil and served to us when we were young—her name was a small jumble of syllables as unblemished as she had been the last time I had seen her.

Yohanna had grown into a beautiful woman with long, dark, lustrous waves down her narrow back. Staring at me from across the synagogue, her arm linked with Lilah's . . . whispering something to her new friend . . . calling after me as I passed her in the market: "Miriam! Filled with devils! No one will marry her . . ."

Yohanna who had hurt me. Who had left me behind. Yohanna who I still, somehow, dearly loved.

"It's no use," the girl muttered as she came over with her wet rags. "She's filled with a devil and will surely be dead in a day. I have never seen anyone go without food and water for so long and live."

"Can you take her to the rabboni?" the old woman Zillah pleaded. "She would accept healing, I know. She is in desperate need."

"Take her to Yeshua?" Shimon asked in disbelief. "How do you suggest we transport your lady?"

Though the words were callous, Shimon was right. I let my fingers press at the feeble pulse of Yohanna's neck. I was quite sure she wouldn't survive any journey—even a short one into the nearby hills where we were camped.

"What happened to you?" I did not expect a response as I rocked her head back and forth between my palms.

"She began to refuse food after the passing of her husband," Zillah explained quietly.

"And for the past two moons she has refused everything but water, sops of bread, and a little wine."

"And now, going on a week, she has accepted no water," added the servant girl. "She would follow her husband into the underworld, where he deservedly belongs. He who worshipped mammon, and only returned to love his wife when he was tired and in need of a good meal."

"Hush, Rebekah! You speak wickedness," scolded Zillah. "She loved her husband as the Shulamite loved Solomon. There is no sin in loving."

Yudas was thoughtful. He squinted as if trying to see something dim, something very far off.

"What is it?" I asked.

"I have seen this ailment before," he confided quietly. "It has nothing to do with death, and more to do with God. My wife's sister died from it. I don't think she wished to die. She believed that all food was poison. She said her mind was clear when she could feel hunger but otherwise it was clouded."

It would be the only time I ever heard him mention his wife.

As if summoned, she appeared in my mind. His wife. Wide-faced, wide-hipped, and impossibly young, an expression of mischief turning her plain features into something enchanting. And then she faded. Although she never really left. From then on, if I looked out of the corner of my eye, there was a gray shape behind Yudas, dense as a raincloud, which sometimes sharpened into the shape of the woman. Often, she was holding the hand of a child.

Blessed are those who mourn, for they will be comforted.

"It is so with my esteemed lady!" Zillah said. "She swore that it was her impurity that led to her husband's death, although it was the fever that took him. She broke the laws of kashruth and handled his food improperly during her monthly blood, although she did not know it had come on. She did not tell him and so he did not bathe in the mikvah. It is a great chova—a great debt—she feels she owes him. She atones by denying herself food . . ."

"Force some milk and bread down her throat and leave us be," Shimon interjected.

I rose to my full height. "Hold your tongue. You know nothing of healing. If she eats something rich now, she will surely die."

As if to reinforce my point, Yohanna's eyes rolled back into her head. She was in the grips of some terrible pain. Or terror.

Zillah despaired. "Please. Anything you can do."

I knew what I must do.

During our travels in Galilee I had healed countless people. And although I was now comfortable putting my hands on someone's fevered forehead, I was still freshly amazed when the power *did* come into my hands. What a miracle that I could perform miracles! The gratitude never faded.

I worked my hands under Yohanna's dress, pressing against the cold, bare skin of her rib cage. I shut my eyes and prayed. *Please. Come. Come through me. Heal my friend.*

"Ahh . . ." I felt my womb tighten. But it was not painful. In fact, the feeling was almost pleasurable—similar to that thrill I had when my husband first came into me, our bodies merging as one. My fingers prickled with fire and I could feel the familiar pressure building between my eyes.

"Oh!" Yohanna gave a sharp cry and her hands relaxed. Gently her eyes closed.

Please. Please. The words pulsed in my hands. They beat into Yohanna's heart.

I remembered something my father had said many years prior when he had first instructed me in Torah. "Faith cannot be blind. We must always doubt that we are clean enough—that we are good enough—to receive the bounty of our Lord. We must be always striving."

I bowed my head, continuing to send up my silent prayer.

I felt the fire in my hands grow to an almost unbearable burn before it began to ebb out of my palms into my friend's body. The release was intense, numbing my legs, my face, my arms. But I had done it often enough not to be afraid.

Unbidden, the pale body of the sycamore Salome and I had sat beneath many days earlier came to mind. I felt as if my arms were its white branches sending messages of leaf and seed into the winds.

"*Ephatha!*" I said loudly. "Be opened!"

Zillah shuddered in surprise. Rebekah shrieked.

Yudas and Shimon exchanged knowing glances. They had seen many such healings. They were no longer surprised.

I moved my hands up to Yohanna's neck, pressing on the sores and feeling the lines of her veins. I was trying to draw her blood to the surface, and she stiffened again. Then her legs shot out straight, her knees locked.

"Have mercy! She is taken by a demon again!" Rebekah moaned. "My poor, poor lady. How she suffers."

I held up a finger. "Hush. Let me finish."

Yohanna's pulse was still feeble under my fingertips. But I envisioned dark sap, reawakening the dry deadwood of her heart.

"Ephatha!" I repeated and from the window a great wind rushed into the room, whipping the servant girl's scarf from her head. She screamed. A jar on a table was knocked to the floor, shattering and spilling wine across the tiles.

"Mother!" cried out Yohanna. "Mother!" She sat straight up, as if shot through with lightning. Her hands were knotted into her matted hair. "Mother . . ." She drew me to her.

"Do you know me?" I whispered as the wind subsided.

She whispered something I could not understand.

"Yohanna . . ." My lips brushed her ear. I leaned in closer, listening. "Who am I?"

"You are the first and last," she murmured faintly.

"What?" I said sharply.

"You are the honored one, the scorned one, the whore, and wife, and the virgin . . ."

I see myself now, as if outside of my body. See my heaving chest, my hands gripping my knees, eyes like smoldering embers. The pregnancy making my hair appear longer, more lustrous.

Make them swear to remember, I want to say to my younger self. *Make them swear that they will tell this story, Tell Yohanna. Shimon. Tell Zillah. Tell them all!*

Yohanna collapsed again, back onto the couch. But something had changed. The sunlight streaming into the room seemed to find her all at once, illuminating her skeletal frame. True, she was not strong yet. But a thread of energy hummed through her now. I could see it. Her breath no longer smelled stale and putrid.

Zillah threw herself on Yohanna, embracing her tightly. "Speak to me, lady. Speak to me!" she begged.

'Hmmm . . ." mumbled Yohanna. "Water, please . . . Maybe bread."

I stood up and straightened my skirt, feeling unsteady.

Yudas took my hand, as if he too had been healed for a moment and was able to speak from his heart. "You have done it. Thank you, my lady."

I squeezed his hand back and looked up at the window. The sky was clear and the few clouds I could see moved hardly at all. The air was still.

There was a hiss from behind me. Shimon's hands were raised as to ward off the evil eye. He spat on the ground at my feet.

• • •

"She is your friend?" Yeshua asked as he helped me wash the wooden trays we had used to serve our dinner. We were kneeling by the stream as the light grew pale, working against the Sabbath that approached with each dimming minute.

"We grew up side by side," I explained. "But I think she has been abused by the years and a strange marriage. I knew she had wed Herod's steward. But it came about during the years of my education. I was not much interested in those things at that time . . ."

Yeshua sat back on the muddy bank, the cleaned wares piled in the grass behind him. Inky shadows flitted across the pale, twilight sky—birds searching out the last lazy insects and bats unfolding their warm wings.

"Yudas tells me you healed her with your own hands." There was a quizzical look on his face, something between amusement and displeasure. "That you summoned the wind, and Shimon was so frightened he nearly fled the room."

"I did nothing," I said, resting my head against his strong shoulder, running my fingers against the grain of the dark hair of his forearms.

"Never deny your own deeds, Miriam. You need not preach them from the mountaintop. But do not call them nothing. It is an affront to God, he that grants you such a gift."

"Fine," I sighed. "Then I did it. I performed a great miracle. But I think you healed her more completely tonight by offering her a place with us."

"That is the gentle magic that any man or woman can do," Yeshua corrected me. "She is a lonely woman, imprisoned by wealth. I merely gave her a way to live lightly in the light of love."

Having regained her senses, Yohanna was overjoyed to recognize me as her old friend. None of her disdain or judgment from our adolescence remained. She clutched my hands and asked after Lazaros. She remembered the games we three used to play together.

"She's used to finery and being the lady of her own house," I said, worried.

"She is used to being in a great deal of sorrow and pain," Yeshua countered. He reached out, tapping me lightly under the chin. "She will do fine. You watch."

"It *is* a paradise here," I reasoned. "And anyone who stays long with us sees it, too. But sometimes I do miss the river. Remember the plan we made to return on our wedding night?"

I regretted the mention of our wedding night immediately. He shivered under my touch.

"Yes. The river was shelter from the storm. A fool's paradise. A kingdom already past."

I knew he was not speaking of a place, but of a man: Yochanan.

"You say she was a member of Herod's court?" he asked, and the pivot confused me.

"Yohanna? Well, yes, I guess she must have been," I realized.

"That fox . . ." There was a venom in his voice. "If I were a man who acted only through his own authority, I would go and slaughter him."

"And on whose authority do you remain peaceful?" I inquired.

I could feel turbulence in his body. Clouds passing up his muscular arms, causing his shoulders to hunch. Lightning in his tongue, stinging his words, turning them yellow with fire. He brought his hand up to his forehead, letting his forefinger tap the soft skin between his eyes.

"Miriam. I would say it is our Lord of Hosts who comes to me. But I am not certain. Sometimes it is a human voice prompting me. But mostly it feels stranger and bigger than any man. Could it be a demon? Or some malevolent force come to tempt me with power? Sometimes I feel that I should go back into the forest for a long time to make clear who it is I am speaking to . . . and speaking for. It must be God. Otherwise, how can I heal those who are in pain . . ."

I remembered that moment of doubt earlier, my hands on Yohanna's cold flesh. Who worked through *me?*

Was it all good, this power? Or could it be misused?

Oh, Miriam, I long to tell myself. *Confess your worries! Share your questions with him!*

But I hid my fear that night. I wanted to comfort him. What good could come from giving voice to the uncertainty, allowing it to open up between us?

I did not honor it back then. Now I know that uncertainty is the greatest miracle of all. When we hold ourselves open to the possibility of error, a blessing can arrive that we never imagined possible. The oceans can part and offer a way forward. A question blooms season after season, yielding new flowers, new ideas. But an answer is solid. It bears only one fruit. And very often, it is the wrong fruit.

"How can you doubt that you do good?" I asked. "There are a great many who now owe their lives, their sight, and even their sanity to your words and to your touch."

"And I resent them all for it," he confessed. He was red with embarrassment. He cast his eyes down as if waiting for me to scold him.

"It relieves me to hear you say so," I said. I took his calloused hands in mine and squeezed them tightly. "I feel it, too. I love that we are both needed. That we can relieve pain. But often I wish a life for the two of us alone."

"I wish it, too." His voice had turned husky.

But I kept speaking. "And the fishermen! Those stupid men! You spend so much time teaching your fishermen, and they are the most stupid of the lot. Each day they understand you less and less. Why waste time on them?"

He chuckled. "The ones who understand do not need to be taught! You will never see me among those who are most ready for the kingdom. They are fine left on their own."

"Then I guess I must be in sore need. For you seem to be in my company a good deal."

"Don't twist my words, Miriam." He pulled his hands from my grasp and placed them on my shoulders. "You hold the greatest paradise of all: the world that will arrive alongside our child. I can feel it closer and closer: the time when the scales will balance and our people will know justice. The time when the Romans will leave our lands. It is near."

"And so our child is the Messiah then," I joked. "Shall we call him Iman'uel?" This was my growing confusion—that he could seem profoundly doubtful one second and then so certain the next that the very light seemed to bend toward him, affirming his position in the center of events.

"Perhaps the name will come when he is born," he said, and his eyes drifted to the stream's opposite shore and the purple puddles of shadow beneath the trees.

"And if *he* is a girl?" I prompted.

The dimple appeared in his cheek as he smiled. "We will call her for you and my mother: Miriam."

"That's dull." I snuggled back into his warmth and drew his arm around my shoulders.

"We should go back," he said finally. "I promised Philip and Yoses Ben-Zebedee I would speak to them after our meal."

I stood up and mud fell away from my skirt. My feet were black with it.

"I forgot to ask. Why did Shimon not come for dinner with you?" Yeshua questioned as he picked up the cleaned trays and bowls. "It is unlike him."

Shimon. For the first time, his name made me shiver.

"Yeshua, I must confess. Shimon makes me hesitate."

I saw my husband's eyes widen, but I continued. "I am afraid of him. I fear that he hates women."

Yeshua nodded gravely.

It was a long time after that I realized he had not really heard me.

Thirty-Six

By the time we moved onto Nain it was midsummer and I was heavy with child. The trip took two days of walking, during which I realized how much our numbers had swelled.

Every day they came. Yochanan's old students found us. The invalids joined us as soon as they heard word of the healings. Old ragged men and women covered in pustules or with milky, unseeing eyes. There were wild girls with bound hands, restrained by their relatives, spitting and biting, eyes rolling back into their heads. A boy possessed by demons thrashed and snarled. Family members dragged their loved ones who could no longer walk to us on pallets.

Everyone came. Pharisees like my father showed up, looking for a good debate. The bored and wealthy came bearing gifts and coins that we used to feed our ever-growing numbers.

I loved the old women. The widows and old aunts. The ex-harlots who clucked over my pregnant belly, massaging my travel-sore feet.

We left K'far Nahum as the summer reached its height. The purple globes of kipodan flowers dotted the fields like fine beads of perspiration on a lover's skin.

"All flesh is grass, and all its beauty is like the flower of the field," I whispered as I walked between Atarah and Yohanna.

"She is going mad," Atarah said across me to Yohanna. "The heat and the child are making her mad."

"Then being mad seems quite pleasant," Yohanna shot back, reaching out and squeezing my hand. I shared a secret smile with my friend. It had been surprising how quickly we had slipped back into our old intimacy. We had no need of words sometimes. A look or a gesture were enough. A shared childhood is something that connects people. The same sunshine, the smells of our home moved through both of us, connecting our minds and hearts.

"She must rest!" Atarah muttered, hitting her walking stick into the dust emphatically.

"I'm fine," I reassured the old woman. But she was right. My feet were so swollen from the pregnancy that I had forgone my sandals. Each stone that pressed into my bare soles sent a dark secret up into that part of me that was busy growing.

I struggled to keep up. But by the time we reached Nain I was drenched with sweat.

"You really must rest now!" Atarah commanded. "Tell your husband to get you to an inn where we can wash your feet and make supper."

Tired as I was, I could still laugh, patting the warm, rippling side of one of our donkeys.

Atarah's watery eyes grew smaller: "What? You think carrying a child is funny?"

"It's a funny business getting with child," I replied, grinning as I unpacked a skin of wine and handed it to the old woman. "Surely you must agree with that, or have you forgotten?"

She uncorked it and took a sniff before sipping. "Your ankles are swollen and your color is bad." She was in no mood for play.

"It's true I'm tired," I acquiesced.

"Tired?" As we all gathered under the shade of a black mulberry tree, Yeshua came to check on me, plucking one of the drooping blossoms as he drew near. I knew in a month's time these delicate white blooms would wither and give way to tart purple berry clusters. He rubbed the blossoms between his fingers and a fine white dust caught on the wind.

I let him put his arm around me. His touch was like medicine. I could feel my weary joints loosening and my breath returning to me. Nearby, Philip was tying an ass to a pine. Adah fed nuts to the horde of children that was always following her these days. Yeshua's beard was growing in. He reached up to scratch the hair self-consciously, tugging at his chin. His black eyelashes had sweat beaded into them and I could smell the intimate perspiration of his underarms.

If only we could leave our friends and go into the woods. I would have my fill of him again and again. I would demand the healing that is only possible between a husband and wife.

"She needs to rest!" Atarah tapped Yeshua aggressively on his other arm. "She needs food, water, and sleep."

"We will go into town for provisions and see if anyone is kind enough to offer us shelter," Yeshua offered lightly.

Grumbling, Atarah went off to help Adah with the care of the children.

"Rabboni? What comes from the gate?" Thoma asked, paler than usual.

We were far enough away that we could see the whole village. A disorganized group of small houses, unprotected by a wall, bled into gardens and fields across the landscape, all nestled between verdant hills that unrolled into the distance to the foot of Mount Tavor.

I noticed a skirmish of red dust at the entrance to the town where the road narrowed between two squat homes.

"Listen," I said. I could hear keening.

"Master, we have interrupted a funeral," Thoma realized. "They are bringing a body out of the town."

Squinting, I could just make out a white litter held on either side by large men. They must have been headed toward the rock tombs in the hills. A woman wailed.

"An ill omen," noted Yohanna. Despite the heat and days of travel, Yohanna looked immaculate, her hair healthy and shiny now that she was eating and drinking again. She had plaited it in a long braid that hung down her back.

Yeshua, too, was frowning. He narrowed his eyes against the glare of the sun.

"Shall we make camp here and wait till they are done with their grieving?" Yudas asked, coming to join us. "We have enough supplies to last the night and the weather is fair. We can sleep comfortably under the stars."

The entire village was pouring forth with loud lamentations. A few young boys held torches aloft. The day was so still that the thick gray smoke rose in direct lines up toward the heavens. The woman raised her hands into the air, sobbing.

"We must go to them," Yeshua said decisively. "That woman is in need of comfort."

Those around me nodded firmly. But I could tell, although he spoke confidently, that Yeshua did not speak with an otherworldly authority. It was Yeshua the man wanting to quiet the woman's cries.

"Let us leave them to honor their dead," I suggested, putting my palm on Yeshua's lower back, feeling a knot of tensed muscle. "We will only confuse their ceremony. We can comfort the woman tomorrow."

"Are you so weary of service? Would you deny your husband's gifts to those in need?" Shimon reprimanded me. A wet cloth was slung behind his neck, sending a steady drip of water down the front of his tunic.

"She means no ill, Shimon," Yeshua countered evenly. He then turned to me. "Miriam. We *must* go. Can you hear how she wails?"

"I am not your master," I said. "Go forth."

He smiled with relief. It was the answer he wanted.

I remained under the shade of the mulberry tree. A white butterfly circled around its trunk, skimming flower petals with the ragged edge of its wings. Suddenly I could feel the wear of travel on my body: An ache in my lower back. A needle of pain in my sex. The uncomfortable twang of overworked muscles behind my knees.

I tasted the shade—blue and tranquil—disinterested in the sorrows of men. I tapped one of the tree's low, strong branches, sensed its deep, slow intelligence, and was comforted. But I needed to be with my husband and join the fray.

The men bearing the dead body tensed their shoulders, squaring their feet as if there was still a life to protect on that slat of wood.

But the elderly woman was unafraid. "Have mercy on me! Leave us be!"

An old man hobbled forward, leaning heavily on a polished stick. He pushed in front of the woman protectively. "If you seek food, we can offer it to you when we have buried our dead!" he declared loudly. "My name is Obed. I am Nain's rabbi and I must insist that we honor the widow Shifra. She, who buried her husband and two children last year, buries her last son today."

Hearing the story of her own suffering was too much for the woman.

"Hush, Shifra," Obed said. But she was inconsolable, beginning to weep again.

Yeshua stepped forward and put his arms around her. The rabbi was shocked. His eyes grew wide as the woman trembled violently and then stilled, slumping against Yeshua's solid embrace.

"Have no fear and do not weep," he said tenderly.

My upbringing had been one of formalities and rules. True, I was good at finding ways to break them. But I was always astonished when Yeshua touched a woman. A woman who might be bleeding!

Not that I believed in the importance of cleanliness anymore. At least not in the traditional sense that my father had taught me. But I knew that most men did. Most men looked at women and wondered what impurity, what filth, was hidden in their bodies.

"Disgraceful!" The rabbi screeched. "Who are you to lay hands on this woman?"

A young girl startled the crowd. "Hold your tongue, Father. Are you blind? *This* is the man we have heard of!"

"Who have I heard of, Sera?" Obed asked, squinting at Yeshua.

"It is the magician Medad spoke of!" said his daughter. "He said he was a big Nazarene brute who traveled with harlots and tax men."

The others had pushed to the front of the crowd—Shimon, Andreas, Philip, and Yudas.

The air was still and the day was oppressively hot. But I could feel the invisible pressure of a storm. Something dark and muscular was closing its fist just below the horizon.

"A magician?" the widow Shifra's voice was a dry whistle, barely able to carry her words. "You can perform deeds?"

"Let me see your son, lady," Yeshua said softly. "Let us see if we can ease the cause of your sorrow."

Your son is safe. Although I feel your pain. He is safe in the belly of the world. He will be born again. Plant him in the stone tomb and he will grow again. In a different life. Where did these strange, certain words come from? They flooded through me and it was all I could do to keep my mouth closed.

"Yeshua . . ." I said. "Yeshua, leave the boy be . . ."

I am certain that no one else saw it, but doubt spread across my husband's face. His eyes narrowed and the right corner of his mouth turned down. But then it was gone and he ignored me.

"Bring him!" he ordered confidently.

No one moved. The men bearing the body looked to Rabbi Obed for a sign.

Yeshua waved a hand in exasperation. "Would you let her suffer longer? Bring him!"

"Bring my son to me!" Shifra screeched. "Bring Levi to me!"

I could feel her sorrow in me like it was my own. Desperation is an animal that makes us bite and scream.

Where does this sorrow come from? I wondered, pressing my swollen belly, feeling almost paralyzed by dread and anguish. Yeshua must not touch the boy. But oh! To let the mother suffer was unbearable.

Haltingly, the men bearing the body carried him to us, laying the wooden slat gently on the ground next to Yeshua and Shifra.

"This is not right! It is not done!" Obed despaired, but he was ignored. The townspeople were too interested in the spectacle to protest.

"What can he do?" Salome whispered in my ear. "The boy is dead."

"I am wondering the same . . ." I admitted, watching as Yeshua began slowly to unwrap the body.

"Have mercy!" a squat woman cried out.

I was struck at once by the boy's face when it emerged through the swaths of cloth: it was still, as if in sleep. His lips were pale, but not the grayish purple I expected of those who had been dead some time.

"Let me see him!" I declared, pushing between Andreas and Philip who were blocking me. I sunk to my knees next to the corpse.

"Miriam! The child!" Adah cried from behind me, reaching out to grasp the back of my dress. "Do not risk impurity!"

But I didn't listen. The boy's flesh had not yet grown cold.

"What do you think?" Yeshua asked under his breath.

"My son! My son!" Shifra wailed.

"I'm not sure," I finally managed to whisper. I leaned close to the boy, smelling shit and bile even though I knew he had been cleaned. I could tell he had been pale and sickly before his final illness.

But there it was—my suspicion confirmed—a pulse so dull at his throat that I could have mistaken it for the movement of my own blood in my fingers.

Could I have hidden it from Yeshua? I think not, for he was watching me.

Yeshua's eyes sparkled. "He lives."

"Yes." There was too much clamor for us to be immediately over-heard. The disciples were talking among themselves and the townspeople were arguing as they tried to push closer. Rabbi Obed kept up a stream of complaints so steady and well-spoken they almost seemed a recitation of scripture.

"He lives," Yeshua said. He seemed to want to share the good news with me privately for a moment. "I knew it."

How could I tell him? And by what authority? It had been tugging at my womb from the second I put my hand to the boy's forehead and, as if I needed more confirmation, I looked into the clear sky to see the black shadow of a lone vulture drawing a circle around the sun. With each rotation the circle tightened until it seemed that the bird was totally consumed by the light.

The boy was alive, but he was receding from his blood with each soundless, motionless breath. It was no surprise his mother and the townspeople had mistaken him for dead. He would be soon enough.

Perhaps his spirit is already departed . . . nearby, but not truly in his body, I mused, staring out at the distant hills, the mountain, the green smoke of trees hazed by heat and sunlight. The vulture swung back into view, cutting a straight line across the sun.

It is not sorrowful, I tried to remind myself. *Life comes and goes and comes again. Where will his spirit go? To a stone? A tree? Another man?*

I thought of my own child, only recently planted within my body. Where had that life come from?

The boy was not dead, but he had been claimed by death itself. To take him back would be like trying to return water to a broken bowl. He was moving on from this body.

"Yeshua . . ." My voice was husky and low. Certain. "Yeshua. He should not be healed. He is already gone."

"What?" He was confused. "Why?"

"Get on with it!" a bearded youth cried. "You desecrate our dead without introductions. You let a whore touch the beloved son of Shifra."

"Be quiet!" Yeshua roared and sprang to his feet. "While you were bickering, my wife has determined that this boy still lives and can be saved."

I groaned. It was too late now. How easily provoked he was!

"Alive! You must heal him, Rabboni!" It was Shimon, pushing alongside me. "Show them that you are no Chassid come to tell stories and milk them for money. Show them *who* you are."

I didn't have time to wonder what Shimon was referencing. Who was Yeshua but *himself*? A healer. A teller of stories. My husband.

"Yeshua," I raised my voice. "It would be unwise to heal this boy. He is passing onward."

"What does she speak of?" It was Rabbi Obed. "Is the boy alive? What does she mean, *onward*?"

Onward. Into the next life! Just as Elishah was reborn. Just as every piece of the earth circled in and out of being. The water, the very breath in our lungs. I knew that death was the fertile black soil that all fallen branches and faded blooms fall back into; and death had already claimed this boy for itself. The boy would nourish and grow and change in the earth's soft embrace. It would be no mercy to wrench him back into this sick body, away from the fertile darkness that lives between death and rebirth. His life had already closed.

"Yeshua. Hear me please. He must not be made to rise. Let him be at peace." A river surged through my voice. I could feel many women speaking through me—the grandmothers of my bloodline. The women who had lived on this land for many years. The women who *were* the land.

A shadow drifted across my husband's face. He shaded his eyes with a hand. He had seen the vulture flying back and forth.

"Please!" begged Shifra. "Please do something!"

I think maybe it was then that Yeshua began to ignore his instincts. *Our* instincts.

Because I must believe that our instincts were aligned before that moment. They had curled into the perfect kernel of the child I held within me. We were one. We thought and felt and breathed the same desires. I slept beside him every night, shared my body and my secrets with him, and believed he shared the same with me. There were times during the first two years of our marriage when I would see through his very eyes. And he confessed that he had often experienced the same, feeling his own body with my hands, inhabiting my skin.

His lips twisted with indecision.

For a second I was sure he could sense the heaviness of the bird's flight, the open bloom of the boy's spirit already curling brown at the petal's edges, turning toward rot. I was convinced we were of the same mind.

But then the widow Shifra spoke again. "Prove it! Are you truly a man of God?" she wailed. "Show me your power."

"Do not weep! I will do what can be done."

Yeshua straddled the body, breathing lightly on the boy's eyes, nose, and mouth.

"What is he doing?" Obed asked, flustered.

"Stop!" I said. But the word made no sound. I spoke from an older version of Miriam; a Miriam who wore a different face. A version of myself that had lived before and was called to service that day by the sight of the vulture.

The flight of the bird wove in and out of the sky like a thread through cloth. Needling through to another sky, the vulture drew together the fabrics of different lives like a long, black stitch.

Yeshua leaned over the boy, spitting lightly on his dry lips, and rubbing the wetness into the boy's slack mouth.

For a moment I thought we were saved. My husband's power had wisely deserted him.

But then the boy sneezed.

Then he sneezed again. And again. His cheeks grew pinker with each convulsion, and his body jolted violently: his knees bent and his hands jerked up to clutch his face.

"Praise be!" exclaimed Rabbi Obed.

"Agghhhhh . . ." the boy moaned, spitting up gray liquid and wracked by a spasm of coughing so hard that it pulled him upright.

"A miracle!" Adah exclaimed. "A miracle!"

"Is this what you did to me?" a shocked Yohanna murmured from somewhere behind me.

"Levi! Levi!" Shifra ran to her son.

"Mother," he said softly. His voice raised the hairs on my arms.

"He lives!" Shifra cried. She proclaimed it to the gathered crowd. "My son was dead, but he has been returned to me! Surely this is a man of God."

Still crouching on the ground, his palms in the sand as if to steady himself, Yeshua appeared dazed.

"She speaks of you," I whispered.

"You are right!" Shimon announced. "This is a man of God. He has come to fulfill the scripture. A great prophet is among us. Let it be known far and wide."

"Hold your tongue," I exclaimed. "You don't know what you are saying."

"Rise, Miriam. You will be trampled," urged Yudas. I grabbed his hand and struggled to my feet, feeling my new heaviness as a burden for the first time.

"What has he done?" I murmured, looking up. The bird was gone, leaving no sign of its flight in the cloudless blue of the sky.

"He has vanquished death," Yudas answered quietly. Simply. "He has shown us that it has no power in his kingdom. He is the Lord of Life."

"He cannot vanquish death," I said to Yudas. "It is from death that he draws his power."

I knew Yudas well enough to tell that he was alarmed by my words. But typically he said nothing as he led me away to find us rest and food.

Rabbi Obed sheltered us in his own home that night and I was thankful to lie back on a mattress in a small room and straighten my back. I rubbed the skin that stretched over my widening hips and groaned. Every one of my muscles ached. There was a dull throb behind my eyes that only went away when I pushed hard against them with my thumbs. Was the child sore, too?

"There you are." He stood, filling the entire doorframe, a candle in the hallway illuminating his curls and turning them to fire. His tunic was dusty, but his face was scrubbed clean. He tilted his head, watching me. His expression was tender, his eyes soft with feeling.

"Are you pleased to see me so beleaguered?" I joked.

"No. But I am pleased to see you bearing my child." He knelt beside me and took my hands in his, carefully squeezing them, pulling at my fingers in the particular way he knew relaxed me. I could not help but close my eyes.

After a while he climbed into the bed with me, curving his body to mine. He drew a finger down my bare neck and his hot breath on my skin sent a ripple of pleasure through me.

"You told me not to heal the boy . . ." he said, letting his voice trail off like a question.

"Was it right to steal what already belonged to death?"

"But he was fine," Yeshua insisted. "He eats and drinks with his mother this very night. I sat and ate with them. And nothing bad has come of it. I wasn't sure I could do it, but I did."

"Perhaps you are right," I conceded, wanting to put to rest the sense of foreboding that had been building in me from the moment I'd first seen the funeral retinue. What was done was done.

There was such celebration after the first day's commotion that we stayed on in Nain for three days. Everyone wanted to host the famous healer and his students. And I relished the opportunity to rest.

On our final day, as we were packing up our beasts with gifts of food and wine, a young boy ran into the village, screaming. The rabbi's daughter Sera had been climbing a tree and had fallen to the ground.

Everyone ran up into the hills.

The girl had fallen headfirst. She must have died the second she hit the ground. Bone had ruptured the delicate skin of her throat.

There was no talk of bringing her back.

Thirty-Seven

"He drags you from village to village? He forces his pregnant wife to lodge with strangers?" Yeshua's mother shook her head in disbelief.

I was helping her knead the bread dough. A small hut, open to the elements with a grass roof, protected us from the sun, but we were sweating. We smelled of salt, yeast, and the nutty aroma of the good wheat corn Yeshua had brought as an offering to his mother. And Imah had her own scent—something at once peppery and rich that I recognized as a variation of Yeshua's own odor. I could smell it sometimes when the sleeves of her dress opened as she wiped the sweat from her forehead.

"Wheat?" His mother had said, almost in disgust, accepting the heavy sack of grain when we'd arrived. It had been a gift to us from a woman Yeshua had cured of a skin affliction on the road to Nazareth. "What? You are too important now for barley? Is your stomach grown as soft as your head?" she inquired of her son.

Yeshua hugged his mother, ignoring her protests. "Give us this day whatever bread you please. We are not picky after a day's travel. Consider it payment for our troubles while we stay with you."

"I will ask Yakov to kill one of his goats. We must celebrate." Imah dusted her hands off on her apron before ordering her many children and grandchildren about, organizing the bed and board of our entire company.

It was a large group. More than forty women, men, and children had followed us to Nazareth. Some were hardy enough to camp out under the trees, but others, those with the very old and very young to care for, were thankful that my mother-in-law, Miriam, held an esteemed position in the little village. She found a home for everyone who needed a bed.

I was allowed to help Imah with her tasks, but not to attempt any chore or errand that took me out of her company.

"A child! To think that my dolt of a son has done something worthwhile. He has given me a daughter and a child. God is generous!"

I sipped from a stone cup that Yael had delivered to us earlier. The water cooled my throat and belly.

"Here, rest." Imah put a hand between my shoulder blades and began to work the muscles. "Your worries all live here."

"Ah . . ." I sighed and closed my eyes. Her hands—accustomed to kneading bread, grinding grain, and braiding unruly curls—were strong and dexterous. I felt my body unraveling. It was at once pleasurable and alarming, as if I could slip out of myself like a river exceeding its banks in the rainy season. I stopped her hands.

"What?" she asked, perturbed. "You don't like it?"

"No . . . It's not that." My hand dropped. "But I am under your enchantment. I could fall asleep now and perhaps sleep for days. Don't you want me alert so that I can help you prepare supper?"

"I would be happy if you slept for days. A woman carrying a child must respect her burden." Imah's voice was low, resonant, commanding. Yeshua had so much of his mother in him: his tall, muscular stature, his broad, high cheeks. His explosive laughter. I wondered for a moment what of Yeshua's belonged to his father. Yeshua seldom mentioned the man. The few times I pried for more information he had turned surly and defensive. "What do you want to know?" he would say to me. "He taught me to talk to wood, to mend roofs and beams. He loved my mother well. He's dead now. I am not here for the dead. I'm here to speak of the living."

But sometimes I woke to feel someone sitting beside us: the shape of a large man who took his body from the night. I was sure it was his father. And I knew we must speak of him someday.

"You have a lovely, straight back," Imah remarked as, ignoring my protests, the warmth of her palms moved down to the painful knots near my tailbone. "At first I thought my son had only fallen in love with your beauty. He was always following the prettiest girl when he was a child."

I was too relaxed to argue with her compliments. Instead I inched backward into her embrace so that she could reach around my hips. Only as my muscles smoothed and my breathing slowed did I realize how long I had felt like a stranger in my own skin. Her strong, guiding hands taught me how to come back to myself.

"There was Michal, until she left to marry a farmer in Bethsaida. The slim-hipped Simera, daughter of a trader who stayed here for a season. Who knows where she is now . . . But Elisheba was the one he loved best. I thought surely he would ask for her bride-price. But he was a scoundrel and left us about that time . . . still practically a boy. The disappointment of his father, although he was best loved, above Yoses and Yakov. I can only imagine the women he tumbled with in Tabariyyah. Harlots, I'm sure of it. Yakov and Yoses heard talk. But I'd bet those harlots were the most beautiful ones. He always had an eye for beauty; bringing me armfuls of the most colorful violets and lilies, insisting on putting a silky finish on a table, taking the basket of grapes and picking out only the smallest, duskiest ones."

My breath caught in my throat. I was always hungry for details about Yeshua's past, his habits, his childhood. I wanted to remain silent and let her wax on. I knew, propelled by the sound of her own voice, Imah would let one story branch off into another.

Simera. Elisheba. I had always known my husband had been with others. His body had been loved before. He came to me with the confidence and warmth of someone who knew what it is to love. But I was sure, each time I brought him into me, that I loved and touched him better than anyone who'd come before. I looked into his eyes and was certain I had erased my predecessors.

Imah felt my unease through her hands. My shoulders tightened again and a muscle in my lower back twitched.

"You did not know?" she asked. She was not being cruel. The softness of her hands on my body communicated her love.

"No. I did," I assured her. "I am no fool."

"You are no fool?" Her eyebrows rose, folding her forehead into lines, and she grasped my upper arm to make her point. "Then get my son off the road! Have him settle down and care for you. Start a household. How will he provide for a child living like a wandering madman? Who will perform the berith if you give birth on the road?"

Yeshua had warned me about her anger. "She will call me an idiot," he'd said. "She will harangue me our entire stay. Then—watch—she will make us all a feast fit for a king. When we leave, our animals will be heavily loaded with gifts and provisions. Her mouth is sour, but her hands do the work of sweetness."

Imah grunted. "It is a pity you are as stubborn as he is. But it seems your father raised you as a man and saddled you with a man's pride. I thought you might talk sense into my son."

"You have heard of his cures? How he brings peace and healing to those in need?" I pulled my shawl back around my arms. I said nothing of my own healings. It was not the time. "You should be proud of him, Mother. He does good wherever he goes."

She cupped my chin in her hand, tilting my face toward her. We were eye to eye. Her face was tight with sunburn, but she was a handsome woman and still had most of her teeth. "Let me ask you this: does he bring *you* peace? Does he bring *you* healing? Or does he hurt your heart? Do you sit up at night worrying that he may come to harm or, worse, bring harm to others? His old teacher is dead. Why should he think that he will pass unnoticed by Herod?"

"You speak of your own pain, Imah, not mine," I corrected her sternly. "We are not the same."

She didn't answer. She only looked at me sadly, her calloused hands folded in her lap, before returning to the bread. We set it in the shadows to rise.

His mother was right. This I now know. There was no difference between us. Not even in name. Her sorrowful heart was a shadow. Her pain upset me then because I knew it was the prophecy of my own.

• • •

Yeshua rose early the next morning. "Shall we walk?" he whispered in my ear. I nuzzled back against him, trying to draw some warmth from his body. The storeroom had no windows and it cooled off in the morning; I could feel the chill in my bones.

"Come back to bed and finish my dream for me," I murmured. "It was a good one."

"Here, sit up!" he commanded gently. I saw that he had opened the door to the courtyard and the glow of the approaching dawn. His face, bathed in pale light, was one color, hewn from stone. He knelt before me, holding out yesterday's bread and a flask of water.

I shook my head at the food and arched my back, enjoying the stretch.

Six moons, I thought with a mix of pleasure and frustration. *Three more to go.* How much bigger would I get?

Yeshua was impatient. He tried to haul me up with him. I groaned, "Why must we walk now?"

"Now is the kingdom!" he whispered.

I couldn't tell if he was joking or not.

"Now is the time of birdsong!" He tugged at me again and reluctantly I rose. "The kernel before the wheat springs forth! The mustard seed before its weed takes over the field! The calm before the heat of the day! The festivity!"

"It's too early for this nonsense," I complained. "The kingdom is letting your pregnant wife rest and making sure your mother doesn't overwork me today."

"The kingdom is my wife!" he said, laughing and giving me a squeeze before leading me out into the fresh morning air.

Nazareth was built into a rocky hillside. Pastures sloped up to a rocky ridge. Yeshua led me alongside the fields that were twining through the blue shadows of palm and olive trees. We were both barefoot, and mud squelched between our toes. Somewhere in the foliage above us a dove emitted a cascade of coos. The sound amplified the muffled quality of the diffuse light, the lack of wind, the blurred shadows. The dove's call originated in sleep. It reminded me of a dreamer struggling to wake but finding he has gone in the opposite direction: dreaming himself into an even deeper sleep.

We broke through the trees just as the sun rose above the horizon. The clouds appeared as flowers, rosy and voluminous. Their white bodies stretched away from the sun as petals do from a blossom's seed-studded center.

I let out a cry of wonder, gripping my lower back and leaning backward to take it all in. Yeshua stepped up to the edge of the hill's craggy ledge. The wild groves of olive and vine trees beyond the rocks glowed silver under the sunrise, the leaves flipping up in the wind like metal fishes swimming in a sea of shade.

"I would come up here when I was young," he said softly. "Always in the hour between darkness and dawn. I would sit and stare at the hills for so long that it seemed they changed shape. Some strange thing would happen. The mountains would move; the sky would switch places with the land. The very fabric of the world would ripple. It was dizzying."

I could almost see that boy, hardly grown into his full height, beardless, with fresh, young skin.

How the land must have loved to look on him, too! I thought to myself. *How the sun must have risen in order to bring light to those eyes.*

We stood side by side, watching as the hills slowly woke into daylight.

"You are happy here?" he asked me, touching my shoulder hesitantly as if we were strangers and he was asking me something in passing.

I did not answer immediately. His manner was disarming. I turned to him and grabbed his forearms, squeezing tightly. "Yeshua. I am happy *with* you," I insisted. "Wherever that might be. Here or elsewhere." I was still young enough to think that exaggeration was more important than truth in such moments of intimacy. The truth was, I had been happy by the river. I had been happy in those first days of K'far Nahum before needy fisherman besieged him. I even enjoyed the traveling, as long as it allowed us darkness and time alone together. I enjoyed sitting with him and the children and the other women. I was truly happy when he came to help the women with the day's cooking, wherever we were camped. But I could feel how fragile that happiness was.

What if I had been honest in that moment? If I had disregarded the romance of the dawn, the beauty of my husband's face, the mistaken sense that I must calm him and help him at the cost of our shared happiness and understanding? If I had forced him to sit beside me on the ground and talk for hours about the child I was carrying. What if we had discussed a shared happiness we could seek out and secure for ourselves—not as teachers or healers or wandering magicians—but as a family?

Would it have saved him?

I tell this story knowing that I am no storyteller as Yeshua was. I cannot draw out a lesson from the sequence of events or deliver you to the final wedding, the joyous song, the parable's neat conclusion. I can only tell you what happened. I can only tell you that he said, "I am happy with you, too. I am happy here in Nazareth." And the moment for truth had passed.

He gripped my hips. The child in my stomach stirred between us. We were almost a family. He knotted his hand in my hair and pulled my head backward to kiss me.

Yeshua took me there, on the hilltop, the rocky ground digging into my back so that I had a tattoo of stones and grass pressed into my skin for the rest of the day.

I tell you this not to change what happened. Not to atone for the mistakes I've made. Don't mistake me for a penitent.

I want only to reach back and touch those moments when I remembered to keep my eyes open. When I bit his shoulder and crawled on top of him, gripping his waist with my thighs, riding the tide of the ocean that existed between him and me and breathing into his ear, "Husband, what is the kingdom like?"

"This! This. This is the kingdom!" And he came into me with the force of the strong waves arriving ahead of a storm, clawing at my buttocks and legs.

Our cries were swallowed by the birdsong in the valley below.

They echo there still, somewhere just beyond Nazareth. And they tell a story that has no end and no beginning.

Thirty-Eight

"How much longer must we remain in this little town?" Thoma had cornered me on the outskirts of town. We had been in Nazareth for a week. "It's hot and there's nothing to do."

"We are not helping anyone here," Shimon complained. "There are others to be healed elsewhere."

I shrugged and told them to speak to my husband. The festival preparations for Tu B'av were well underway and Imah had promised to make her famous almond sweets.

"They are his very favorite," she confided. "I will teach you how to prepare them so that you can always satisfy your husband."

Cooking had never been my strength. But I was learning from the other women. Old Atarah taught me how to dry and preserve the cumin. Adah showed me how to forage for the wild jeezer, a powerful herb that would enliven my lentils. Even Yohanna, privileged as she had been in Chuza's household, had extensive knowledge of savory spices. She shared a recipe for an excellent honey sauce that sweetened tough goat meat. I had my own spice pouch now, and sometimes I would hold the bundle of treasures up to my chest and recall gathering plants with Kemat in the forest outside Bethany all those many years before. Sometimes I could feel her hands working through mine.

Where was she now? I wondered. Had she made it back to Egypt with Meskhenet? Did she now have a child? The memory of Kemat inspired me to wander out into the fields in search of wild herbs. "I'll bring you back armfuls of fragrant greenery," I promised Imah.

"As long as you bring them back soon," she snapped. "We have so much to do before tomorrow!"

Adah flashed me an understanding smile. "Go, Miriam. We have enough working hands here."

I wandered for a long time and laughed to myself with surprise when, from a distance, I recognized my husband. He was sitting in the dirt in a nearby almond grove playing with Yael. He drew something in the sand with a long stick and Yael peeked over his shoulder, yelping with laughter. Smoke curled up from the courtyard, reminding me of my abandoned chores. It rode the wind blowing up the hill, against me, threading the smell of baking bread and spices into the wild grasses.

It was a relief to feel invisible and aimless for once. I sat with my back against the rubble of an old pasture wall and watched as a bumblebee attempted to enter a blossom nearby. He clung to the stem as I imagined a fisherman might cling to his sail in a storm. Beyond the pasture, a few lazy sheep massed at the crest of a distant hill.

I must have fallen asleep for many hours. When I awoke the sky was lavender and the air had cooled. Someone was touching my shoulder.

"Come now, Miriam. How long have you been up here?" asked Yeshua's brother Yakov.

"I . . ."

Yakov had a dirty rag tied around his head, soaked by a sweaty day spent in the confines of his workshop. He was clean-shaven for the approaching holiday.

I liked the man well enough. He was Yeshua's blood. He had the same physical power. The same intense gaze. But without my beloved's humor or lightness of spirit, the effect was one of stagnation. The skin of his forehead stretched red and tight across a mind that never allowed itself enough space to think.

"Dinner is about to be served, and Mother is flustered because Shimon, Thoma, Yudas, and the Ben-Zebedee brothers have appeared and demand to be fed as well."

He offered me his calloused hand and I rose, looking back for a moment at the circle of flattened grasses. *My nest,* I thought sleepily.

"She knows they are here to convince Yeshua to leave," he continued as we walked down the hill side by side. The wind threaded through the grasses. "They tried to bribe her with walnuts and a jar of wine. But she was not so easily fooled."

"Do you enjoy your work?" I asked. I was curious about his life as a journeyman. I knew he had to travel once or twice a week to a well-paying job in the nearby villages, or in Herod's city of Tabariyyah.

"Oh yes. It is better work now than it was during my father's life. The building of Tabariyyah has brought me many new clients."

"And Yeshua learned the trade from your father, too?" I prodded.

Yakov paused, rocking backward on his heels before turning to look at me. "Yes. We studied under our father together." His voice was measured but I could hear a warning under his calm demeanor.

Something made me push. "Tell me something of your father. Yeshua and your mother speak so little of him."

Yakov stopped. "You think you know your husband?"

The question caught me off guard. I didn't know what to say.

"You think it is all fun and sport? The feasting and friends?" He flung the dirty rag from his head down into the grass.

I said nothing.

He shook his head. "Do you know what he did when he came home and found that our father had died while he rutted in Tabariyyah? He yelled like a madman. He went into the synagogue screaming like one of those demons he claims to now have power over. The rabbi threw Yeshua out and told him to leave town. So he did: sleeping naked with sheep and goats and pigs until he wore a thick crust of mud and shit. And when my mother wept and asked him to come home, he tore at his own skin, weeping at her feet. I slapped him then, for he deserved it. And he turned the other cheek. So I slapped him again. And again, he offered his cheek until I could no longer raise a hand. He slept in the dirt in front of our home that night, and when we woke, he was gone. Gone for eight years. For eight long years we thought he was dead."

Somewhere in the trees the bewildered call of a hawk sounded. Was it looking for something? Its prey? A child?

The noise brought Yakov back to himself. "We all love him. But we have grown used to his disrespect. Forgive me for upsetting you."

"I am not upset," I insisted, although we both knew it was a lie. "These are things I should know."

Yakov said not another word and soon we were at his mother's house, where the dinner was already underway.

"You can't leave before Tu B'av. It's improper to travel on a holy day.

Where will you make your wood offering?" Imah complained as Yakov sat down next to his brother Yoses. "You come and eat up my stores and then depart before the holiday."

Imah was ladling out a vegetable stew as the disciples devoured a basketful of fresh wheat loaves. I found my place on a blanket next to Yeshua.

"It is decided: we are leaving in the morning," Yeshua countered, dipping a chunk of bread into a dish of olive oil.

Shimon and Andreas exchanged knowing looks. The brothers had been trying to convince Yeshua to move on for days.

"The provisions have been made," Yeshua told his mother. "We will head back toward K'far Nahum."

"This is the plan?" I, too, was surprised. Only a night before I had asked my husband when he wanted to go, and he had said sweetly, "Go? We are fed well and cared for here. You make my mother happy. We could stay until the child comes. My mother has been at many births. She could help you."

Yael spoke up now. "Is it true, Brother? You are really going?"

I realized she had only ever seen her older brother for two or three days at a time, and when she was younger the family had believed him dead.

"We'll be back," Andreas butted in. "Don't let your worry ruin your pretty face."

Yeshua turned to his little sister. "Yael. It is not just me I must consider. There is much work to be done elsewhere."

"Work?" Her lower lip quivered. "Aren't you happy here?"

Yeshua's smile disappeared. His lips tightened into a line.

"Yes, son. What work?" His mother crossed her arms across her chest.

"It is hard to explain, Yael," he struggled. "My happiness is not of much importance. It will not do much good."

She frowned in confusion, setting down her half-eaten apricot.

"And I *can* do good," he began slowly. "I can do good for many people. But I must keep moving. I must heal in every town. I must find those who have been passed over and neglected. We must keep spreading the teachings."

Yael nodded slowly, sucking on her lower lip.

His mother snorted with disapproval. "The good you speak of is imaginary. *Yes.* You are special. Special to me! To your wife! Pride goes before destruction, my son. You can do good for us and for your wife. But don't try to convince others of your greatness. It will bring *no* good."

Such words from anyone else would have provoked Yeshua into a defensive fury. He might not have spoken or come to blows, but he certainly would have stormed off into the forest for hours of angry reflection.

His face was red with embarrassment rather than anger. He bowed his head without responding. Yakov took a bite of bread. His younger brother Yoses shook his head. The brothers were used to this dynamic.

"Here is how it will be . . ." His mother placed her roughened, red hands on the table. Her back was straight and her face glowed with motherly authority. "You will stay on in Nazareth for Tu B'av. Then you may go."

Here, she turned to Yudas, Shimon, Andreas, and the Ben-Zebedee brothers. "And *no.* I am not speaking of you. Leave whenever you like. Go impose on your own families. Eat someone else out of hearth and home."

Yudas grimaced. I could tell he resented being lumped in with the other men. "Imah, I am sorry we have taken advantage of your kindness. Let us help you with any chores or needs you have in preparation for the holiday."

But before his mother had a chance to respond, Yeshua spoke. "Yes. You are right, Yudas. We must stay on for the holiday and help my mother." He seemed almost under a trance. I put my hand to his forearm and squeezed to show him my support, asking silently, *Is this really what you want?*

He pulled Yael onto his lap. "Wouldn't that make you happy? Shall we send you into the vineyard this year to find a husband or are you still too young?" he asked the girl.

Yael squealed, pretending that she wanted to escape his grasp.

"Good!" Imah stood suddenly, towering over us all. "We can start our celebration early then. I will fetch the pastries."

The men were soon placated by the delicate, flaky sweets. Imah brought out more wine, and everyone feasted and told stories and drank until late in the night. By then the disciples had all decided there was no point in hurrying to leave in the morning.

Adah took me aside and whispered, "Have care, Miriam. He grows childish in his mother's home."

"Yes," I said, nodding, watching Yeshua laugh with his mouth wide open, full of food, his arm around his brother's broad shoulders. His face was somehow smoother, younger. "I have noticed."

● ● ●

Holidays in Galilee were wilder than in Bethany. There was less scripture and more storytelling. Less finery and more wine. Men and women sat at the same table—that is, if there was a table at all.

Tu B'av in Nazareth reminded me of a wedding—but not between two people. Instead, the village was offering its bride-price to the vineyards: bundled wood tied with colorful string, cut flowers, loaves of bread in strange shapes, songs sung by young boys in the forest, so sweet and piercing I wouldn't have been surprised if a bird had fallen out of a tree, stunned by the beauty of their voices.

Tradition had it that the young, unmarried girls brought blankets and baskets into the vineyard to collect the ripe grapes. But the real reason they went there was to offer themselves as potential wives for the unmarried men of Nazareth.

"We never did such a thing in Bethany," I announced.

Yohanna slipped her slender hand through my elbow. "Of course not! So close to the temple? It was only after I came into Galilee with Chuza that I began to realize how different the customs are up north." She giggled, raising her thin, black brows. "You know why the loaves are shaped so queerly?"

I shook my head. "I don't."

"They're modeled after a man's . . . his secret parts." She blushed, but continued to speak, her voice lowered. "It's supposed to ensure that the young women in the vineyards get with child. They offer the sacrifice to the fire in hopes that the women's wombs will take up their new husband's seed."

I chuckled, thoroughly surprised.

"But don't ask Imah." She pointed at Yeshua's mother, passing out pasties to Adah and the widow Marah's children. "These country women have grown used to protecting their traditions. She'll lie and say the loaves have no particular shape."

Everyone was dressed in their finest—whether that was a scrap of brightly colored cloth pinned to the front of a rough tunic, or a crown of flowers woven by the nimble hands of Nazareth's littlest girls and scattered about for the taking. The finest of all were the young maidens, holding their jars of wine and empty baskets, blushing and whispering intimacies to each other. I smelled sweet water when they passed, wafting from the skirts of their best clothes, handed down from their own mothers' weddings. Yael was the most striking of them all, with her wide hips and her height. She had grown up since the last time I'd seen her. Her beauty was masculine, like her mother's. She often made a cutting motion with her hand, just like Yeshua did, when she spoke.

Where are you now, Yael? Your name is sand. Your body dust. You must have died before anyone asked for your story. But that night you were the loveliest girl I had ever seen.

"She's too young for marriage," Yeshua grumbled. We had lugged an old wooden bench out to sit beneath the trees as night fell and the girls headed off into the vineyards. Fireflies flitted in and out of the darkness like misguided stars.

"You say that only because you married me when I was well past the age for marrying," I countered.

"Nineteen years?" he scoffed. "That's not so strange."

"I was married at thirteen," Yohanna responded. She feigned relaxation, playing with the end of her long dark plait, pulling at the split ends of her glossy hair. But I could see her swallow slowly, as if trying to keep down sickness. What did it mean to speak of her husband? She always avoided my questions about him. "And most of our other friends found husbands soon after."

Yeshua scratched his head and smiled like a sleepy child. He had been out under the sun all day, helping to erect bowers in the vineyard. "I wonder where I would be now if *I* had married at thirteen," he mused.

"Yes?" I questioned sharply. "And who would have been your wife?"

"Ah!" His face split into a toothy grin and he grabbed me, pulling me over onto his lap. "You can't trick me, wife. It's a holiday. Let's speak of nothing unpleasant."

"You have always been such a nuisance, Miriam," Yohanna said. And something about her tone reminded me of the prissy little girl she had once been, flirting with Yosseph at my sister's wedding.

"Tell me, husband, did you ever follow the young maids into the vineyard on Tu B'av? Did you ever taste the sweetness that only a virgin can offer?" I had sipped some of the strong wine and was feeling impish.

"Virgins!" he joked. "What good are those? My lovers were well past their vineyard days. I wanted a teacher not a student . . . so that I would be ready for you."

"Enough!" Yohanna's limit had been reached. She was scarlet with embarrassment.

"Enough of what?" Shimon and Andreas came to join us, sitting in the grass and setting a bowl of honeyed nuts and dried figs between them to share.

"We were speaking of marriage," Yohanna replied sharply, glancing at me and Yeshua.

"Marriage," Andreas intoned, nodding his curly head thoughtfully. He elbowed Shimon, winking. "What would you give to be one of those young men tonight? To have your pick of the fruit? Aye?"

"I'd ply you all with drink so that when you finally entered the grove, you'd be too drunk to do anything but fall asleep underneath a tree," I offered dryly.

Shimon grunted derisively. "You sound like a grandmother."

"Respect your grandmother then," I shot back.

I am surprised to remember how easygoing I was back then. Men no longer dare say such things in front of me. They know that just as I heal, I also protect. And protection for young girls often looks like punishment for men. What of it? It has taken me my whole life to understand that I was not born to serve everyone. It was one of my misconceptions then, back in Galilee: that I could love everyone, help everyone.

It is not so. I am here for the trees. The women. The children. The birds. I am not here for the men who would hurt them all.

A strange expression had come over Yohanna's face. "I was very frightened of my husband after we married. But he did not even take me to bed until three months had passed. He had other lovers to keep him satisfied. And for them I was always grateful." The words poured forth almost beyond her control, as if she were releasing some poison that had long been stuck inside of her. "I think long betrothals are best. So a man and a girl may truly get to know each other."

"Your husband was Herod's steward, was he not?" Andreas asked, his mouth full of nuts.

I resisted pinching him. Yes, Yohanna was healed. But there was still harm in her. Harm that might take lifetimes to heal. The one time I had pressed for details about her marriage, her eyes had welled up and she had begun to shake. At the time, I was unsure whether this reaction was due to her love for him or the harm she'd endured as his wife.

Yohanna nodded her head vigorously, coming back to herself a little. "Yes, he was Herod's steward. We lived as part of Herod's court. It was such a change from my life in Bethany. I arrived the same week that Herod insisted on marrying his brother's wife. It was chaos."

I could feel Yeshua's legs beneath me tensing. "You saw that fox? You knew him?" he asked.

"Not often," she answered. "Chuza only allowed me to attend the most important events. Herod was practically a Roman. He had small teeth and would order the prettiest wives paraded before him so that he might have his pick of them. His favorite, though, was the beautiful daughter of his own wife. Behind closed doors Chuza would call Herod a violent dog, ready to bite at anyone who challenged his authority."

"His *daughter?*" Shimon's nostrils flared as if he had picked up on the smell of something delicious. "I have heard she is a devil beyond imagining. Was she not the instigator of our late master's execution?"

"I never heard any such rumor," Yeshua said quietly. "Is it true?"

"Salome?" Yohanna shook her head. "The poor girl is not to blame. Herodias, her mother, made a jest that if Herod wanted to see the girl dance anymore, he would have to bring her a worthy gift. It was all in play."

"Yes?" Shimon inquired. "What gift?"

"Herodias did not say. It was only a jest. I'm sure she meant finery or jewels. But Herod has a dark sense of humor. He delights in torturing women with horrors and obscenities." Unlike the men, Yohanna was aware of my husband's growing discomfort. She grimaced slightly, her hands twisting in her lap. I could tell she didn't want to continue.

"What gift?" It was not a question. It was the hard voice of my husband asking to be told what he did not want to know.

"It was a nightmare. If Chuza had known such a thing would happen, I am sure he would not have permitted me to come to Herod's birthday feast. Although I did not swoon or fall ill, which is more than I can say for poor Salome. The girl was sick all over the floor. She had to be removed from the hall, and I heard it was a whole week before she recovered from the shock."

We all breathed in unison. There were tears in Andreas's eyes. He knew what was coming; perhaps he had heard gossip in the marketplace, which he had wisely chosen not to relay to Yeshua. Why have knowledge of such violence when there was no way to address it?

"It was Yochanan the Immerser's head," Yohanna whispered, her lower lip quivering around his name. "Herod told Salome he had prepared a rare delicacy to honor her dancing, and the young girl smiled at the surprise of being honored. He had the platter placed in front of the girl, and she saw what was on it before we did. I was lower down in the hall and did not see at first; but her scream pierced me all the way through."

"His head?" Yeshua growled, getting to his feet, towering over us. "He presented Yochanan's *head* to the girl?"

"Yes," Yohanna knew there was no turning back. "He had been beheaded earlier that day by Herod's orders."

"What an abomination!" Yeshua's hands shook at his side. His body vibrated with anger so intense I felt I could see it. "To kill him was sin enough. To kill him for the service of a joke . . . to disrespect his body so . . ."

He could hardly speak. I rose, putting my arm around him as if I could still his trembling. But he shrugged off my embrace.

"Did you know this and keep it from me?" he accused Andreas. "Did you think me too peaceful? Too much of a lamb to hear of such violence?"

"I knew that Samuel and the others went to retrieve his body from Machaerus," Andreas admitted solemnly, his forehead gleaming with anxious sweat. The stout man refused to meet Yeshua's stare. "But I did not know that it was so mutilated."

"You knew," Yeshua said flatly.

I swallowed, tasting copper on my tongue. Blood.

"Yeshua . . ." I tried to speak.

He put out his hand to stop me. His nostrils were flared, his jaw locked. "Do not think I have come to bring peace! I have *not* come to bring peace, but a sword!"

He stormed away from us then, back into the chaos of the festival.

"What does he mean?" whispered Yohanna. "A sword?"

"He is upset," I explained. "And overdramatic. By morning he will be himself again. You will see."

I did not follow him, thinking it best to let his blood cool off in the forest. He usually came back from his brooding meditations cleansed of anger and frustration.

I found him some hours later when night had turned Nazareth into a sea of candlelight and smoke. He was standing next to the cisterns in the town square, watching the frantic activity.

According to Nazareth's custom, the villagers all brought the rabbi and his helpers bundled wood offerings on Tu B'av. The group of elderly men fed these sacrifices to a large fire while chanting psalms, the low hum of their recitations sounding just as much like the murmur of insects as they did the words of God.

"Look at them," he muttered, spotting me. "They think if they follow all their rules, they can escape sin. But their sin is not like dirt. It lies not in the uncleanliness of their clothes or the dust under their fingernails. Their vessel is not dirty, but what it contains is poison. The sin comes from within them. It cannot be washed away. They are rotten and diseased all the way through . . ."

"So you no longer agree with Yochanan? Some do not benefit from immersion?"

Perhaps it was not the best question to have asked him at that moment.

He made an angry clicking noise with his tongue. "You know that is not what I mean."

"Are you saying that some are beyond saving? Are those the ones you would slay? With your sword?" I had my hand on my stomach. The authority of the child was giving me strength.

"Herod did not *kill* Yochanan. He butchered him like swine to feed his hungry army. Herod served him up on a plate."

"What will you do? What does this change?" I questioned.

He glared at me, his nostrils flaring. A muscle twitched in his left temple.

"Will you kill Herod? Is that *the good* you mean to do? The good you told your mother about this night past?"

Yeshua opened his mouth and a small, guttural noise emerged. It could have been the start of a sob or a yell. But before I could draw him to me, press his head into my breast, lead him away to the nearest body of water where we could wash our hands, our heads, our feet, and our hearts of this sorrow, someone called his name from the other side of the square.

"Yeshua! My son!"

A small crowd was following Imah. At the center walked a young man, his eyes milky with blindness, his hand clutching a gnarled stick that he tapped on the ground in front of him.

"That's him! Yes! He can help!" Imah declared confidently as the crowd fell upon us and closed the circle.

"What is this ruckus?" A small rabbi with a long beard pushed through the crowd.

"This is my son, Rabboni," Imah nodded proudly. "Avram's nephew Binyamin traveled from Gadara when he heard that my son Yeshua was here. Binyamin has suffered blindness since birth and seeks healing."

The blind man nodded, his body bobbing with the movement. He clutched his stick to his concave chest.

The rabbi wrinkled his nose and looked over his shoulder at another man, tall and black-bearded, with the flinty eyes of a jackal. "Shall we allow it?"

"He is a charlatan come to draw circles in the sand and mutter nonsense for coins," the black-bearded man answered.

Yeshua spoke. "I do not require money. I am in the Lord's favor and do his work."

The rabbi's mouth flattened into a line. He tugged on his ceremonial scarf distractedly. A wave of disgruntlement passed through the group of men.

"Please, Rabboni," the blind man pleaded. "Let him put his hands on me."

Or I could lay my hands on you, I thought. *I will give you much more than sight. I will heal you enough to see the holiness in the ground, the birds, the sea, the trees.*

But now was not my moment to intervene.

"Fine," the rabbi snorted. "Do here what you have done in K'far Nahum," he said to my husband.

Yeshua rolled up the sleeves of his tunic. The air around us was charged with something like the buzzing of a thousand flies. His eyes were flat and black.

"Will you let me touch you?" Yeshua asked the blind man briskly.

"Yes. Yes." The man nodded eagerly.

Yeshua reached out and tilted the man's head up. The yellow light from the lamps the crowd was carrying made the man's face look like that of a demon. His cheeks were sharp and most of his teeth were chipped or missing. His eyes, when he opened them, looked like vacant holes.

"Ephatha! Be healed!" Yeshua spat into the man's face, using his thumb to press the spittle into his eyes.

The whole night shivered as though a tremor had gone through the ground. Everyone was silent.

Yeshua smiled. It would happen as it always did. The man would blink, rub his eyes, and exclaim, "Praise his name! I am made whole!"

But this time was different. I knew it before anyone else. Yeshua would not be able to heal the man. He was too angry. About Yochanan. About the real father he had abandoned who had also died. His was the anger of one who refused to acknowledge his shame.

Imah, too, was quick to assume that Yeshua's powers had worked. "He is healed!" she cried.

"Can you see?" the rabbi prodded.

"I . . . I . . ." The man blinked, his eyes fixed on the starry sky above us. "I . . ."

"What do you see?" Yeshua asked confidently.

"Only darkness . . . I see nothing," the man admitted. His lip quivered and tears appeared at the corner of his cloudy eyes. "I see nothing."

"Hush." Yeshua grasped his head so that they were face to face. "You see me?"

"No," the man whimpered.

"What?"

Imah was aghast. She swatted Yeshua as if he were a small child. "What? Your power deserts you now? In your own home?"

"Silence, woman!" he shouted, pushing her away.

"I thought so!" The rabbi was gleeful. His eyes sparkled with confirmation.

"Try it again! Try something different?" Imah suggested. "As I am your mother, do it for me."

Our friends had been drawn by the clamor. I spotted Yudas and Andreas struggling to push through the dense circle of villagers.

"Enough!" Yeshua threw his hands into the air. "Enough! I have not come to do the bidding of my mother." Yeshua's eyes flashed about him, as if daring someone to contradict him. He wanted a fight.

"Yeshua," I whispered. "You think *this* man is blind. It is *you* who are blind right now. You are blinded by rage. He has but a splinter in his vision. You have a beam in *your* eye."

"Hold your tongue!"

It was the first time he had ever been cruel to me, and I could tell that he hardly knew it was his wife who stood before him.

But it stung like a physical blow.

He ignored me and addressed the crowd: "I am not surprised my power fails me here. No prophet is accepted in his home." He glared at his mother then, fixing her with an icy stare. "Truly I tell you, I have not come just to heal. I have not come to make peace. I have come to turn a man against his brothers and a son against his mother."

His mother stared at him defiantly, refusing to look down in shame. Once again I recognized the deep, stolid power she emanated.

It was Yeshua who finally stormed away, leaving the blind man weeping and the villagers clamoring with confusion. He was gone for the rest of the night and when he came to get me in the morning, he did not meet my eye.

"Get up!" he commanded me. "Let us leave this awful place and never return."

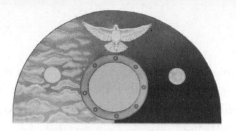

Thirty-Nine

He had to heal again. He had to prove to himself that he could still do it. He insisted on returning to K'far Nahum even though I urged him to travel north, to Samaria, to somewhere no one would know us. But he did not listen, and we arrived back at the sea to crowds already waiting for us.

Our days of anonymity were gone.

"Rabboni!" called out a woman, arriving with her family.

"Yeshua!" beseeched another.

"It is Elishah! Come to bring the rain!" A young man picked up his pace when he spotted us.

"Don't be surprised," answered Thoma. "Talk of your miracles has spread through the land. Everyone anticipates your arrival!"

But before Yeshua had time to respond, another swarm of people appeared on the crest of the next hill. A crowd approached us, pulsing across the wild grasses and groves like a wave that had surpassed the shore and was flooding the landscape.

"Rabbi! Rabbi!"

"Yochanan! It is Yochanan returned!"

"Help my sister! She is lame and cannot work!"

"What are we to do?" Adah implored, her children hanging from her arms. "We need to rest."

"Go to them, master! These are not the fools of Nazareth." Shimon threw out his arms to encompass the approaching masses like a priest standing before the temple. "*These* people believe in your words. *These* people know who you are."

These people. Even as I felt their pain, I felt something greater.

The pain was not merely ailments. Not poverty. Not just the Romans' violent rule.

It was the pain of living outside the garden. The pain of living apart from the plenty of the animals and the plants and the birds that were so very close. The anguish of living in cities run through with sewage and smoke and greed. Of trying to raise children in dark, mildewed houses, feeding them stale bread when just a walk away was a fertile, green world that could house and feed us endlessly.

Hadn't Moshe led us into the wilderness? Hadn't God provided for us when we shirked the yoke of empire and walked straight into the ocean?

It was the pain of that lost wilderness—the wilderness that still quivered like a green mirage below the deserts. It still wanted to spring forth, even when the groves had long ago been cut down to burn limestone into plaster for our ancestors. I could feel the wounded ache of that vast expanse, turned sterile so that our houses could be plastered white.

The vermillion water of the ocean pulsed at the horizon. Asking to be honored. Asking that we step into her and ask for healing as our ancestors had done on their way to the land of milk and honey.

The roots below our feet held the ground in place, humbly and anonymously performing the most important task: stability. The hillsides teamed with spiders and foxes and birds—beings who desperately wanted their brethren to return.

Shed your clothes, they implored. *Your dry wisdom. Come back to the forest.*

"You must go," I said to Yeshua softly. "Flee this crowd and come back when calm has returned. Go into the hills. To the river. No one yet recognizes you. I'll go into the city. Find me later on. But take Yudas with you."

Yudas wrapped an arm around Yeshua. "Come! We will seek peace in the hills."

Yeshua glanced at me. Which version of my husband was I looking at? The healer? The father of the child in my womb? My lover?

"Go!" I insisted, pushing him away.

"Miriam!"

But I shook my head and Yudas pulled him away from the approaching crowd.

"Where is he?" asked an old man. "I must have him heal my wife! She will give no children. He must open her womb!"

Andreas appeared with Salome. "Come with me. My family's home will give you board while Yeshua is gone."

I felt something tugging at me, as if a string in my skirts had unraveled and caught on the thorns in a bush. I kept glancing behind me to see if I was slowly unspooling the thread of my own soul. But I could see nothing.

If only they could reach out to each other for healing, I thought bitterly, *instead of always seeking it from my husband.*

• • •

Orpah, Shimon and Andreas's mother, was unhappy to see me. She eyed my belly and clicked her tongue derisively. "Begging from town to town and somehow you have managed to get fat!"

I was in no mood for jokes and sat down heavily on a bench placed against the wall. I could see through to the courtyard that joined Andreas's and Shimon's homes. Someone's child was sifting through pebbles under the shade of a fig tree.

"Mother!" Andreas scolded Orpah. "She is heavy with child and has narrowly escaped the mob. Give her food, rest, and *no* trouble."

My shoulders sagged. My face fell into my hands, and I breathed out slowly.

"Sit up, girl!" Orpah commanded. "Are you faint? This is no time for tantrums. You are no child."

I mustered my energy and sat up, leaning back into the wall, pulling aside my long hair so that my neck could rest against the cool stone.

"We were besieged," Andreas informed his mother

"There is talk . . . lots of talk," Orpah said dispassionately, rubbing her hands on her stained tunic. "He goes from town to town raising the dead from their tombs and making the demons do his bidding. He should expect to be mobbed, carrying on as he does."

"Hold your tongue," Andreas snapped. "Do not speak of the rabboni as if he is some scoundrel come to rob you of money and promise rain clouds."

"He leaves his pregnant wife to our care!" she shot back, mirroring her son's angry expression. "We are not blood. We have no duty to care for her. If he is not a charlatan, then he is *at least* a scoundrel."

"You liked him well enough when he stayed with us," Andreas grumbled.

"He is handsome and a good guest," Orpah admitted. It was *my* presence that had displeased her.

Andreas stormed back through the door, leaving me alone with his mother.

"You can help Ivah prepare the Sabbath meal," she said, refusing to meet my eye. "But make sure to wash your hands and feet first. Who knows where you have been and what you have touched?"

I felt dirty down to my bones. There was an impurity in me that a basin of water and a scrubbing stone would not remedy. I needed to wade deep into the Yarden River, letting the cold pierce my skin and the strong current wash away the hard, hot resentment that was beginning to constrict my heart.

I told him to go, I reminded myself. *He needs silence to return to himself.*

But I was still angry. It choked my breath and made the bread that Ivah offered me taste like dust.

• • •

I had not slept alone since our wedding. I tossed and turned, flinching when rough grass stuck into my back through the mattress's poorly woven cloth. I did not sleep—or, if I did, it was only for minutes at a time before I was wrenched awake by the sensation of falling.

But I *did* dream.

Now that I am old, I know that when these visions arrive it is best not to struggle against them. They bring me wisdom from within myself; worlds that have left behind no books, no ruins, no stories . . . worlds that only exist in my soul. But I did not yet understand that time is folded over itself. It overlaps in places so that, in some moments in our lives, we can see both forward and backward at once.

The cold of my dream was so intense that I felt it below my skin, needling into me.

"You will put an end to this," a man was saying. "You hear me? Put an end to this endless winter. I will not let you honor the old ones. We are not as beasts. We stand and walk. We store the grain so that we do not starve. And we will go further than that. We will surpass this cold. We will conquer death."

The man tightened the bindings around my wrists. I could sense the trees around us although I could not see them. They bore witness to this violence. I could feel their slow, woody intelligence in my mind, hear their roots absorbing this story. Before this, I know now, there was no murder among us. He would be the first to justify killing for the sake of something more.

Something without roots. Without breath. Without a face. Something imaginary and therefore deadly.

The man was fumbling with my blindfold. He ripped it away violently, taking a clump of my hair with it. But he kept my mouth strapped shut.

I recognized his face. It was long and aquiline, with a short dark beard. He had a notch in his forehead and eyes of two different colors.

"Show me you are afraid," he commanded. "Show me the fear that will honor the lord of the sun."

But I did not comply.

He moved away from me then. Struck flint flared, illuminating a curved blade that gleamed like the waning moon against the dark.

I am not afraid. I am angry. I am rage itself. And that rage will live beyond this body. My womb carries a child conceived on the full moon of the longest day. This will be a child of the trees and the animals. A child who will heal the seasons and end this age of ice. If you slay my child, you will slay the land itself. You will curse your people to their own destruction.

I spoke silently but he heard me through the power I had learned from my mother—the mother I called the lady of the dark waters. She had come to me wearing my own face, and she had taught me that my power came from a time before names, before words, before tongues. I called on the power of the deep in my curse. The power of coiled snakes and molten rock.

I stared up, willing him to drop the blade.

"The Lord will shine upon us," he continued. "His rays will illuminate our path, and his brightness will make full our grain. By him we will we harness the power of the waters that flood our lands. We need never fear hunger or cold again. We will banish the darkness of death."

What comes next feels too terrible to tell you, Leukas. But it happened. Of that I am sure. Most things that happen to women at the hands of men are too terrible to tell.

On the sandy shores of a forgotten lake, he took a sickle knife and slit me from my mouth down to my womb. He took the child from my womb and he held it in his hands, and the night was my only shroud.

He threw my unborn child onto the ice of that lake and scattered the pieces of me among the frozen reeds. And as the morning light appeared, unforgivingly bright, he bowed down to it. But when he looked up, he saw a hawk circling above him. The bird's wings blocked the sun again and again.

My son. My son. You could not be killed. You were a bird again. You were the world again. Nothing can stop me from giving birth to you.

"Let this sacrifice save us," intoned the man to the multitude that had gathered about him . . . men who I had grown up beside . . . women who had been my sisters. In their midst, I saw a tall man with flaxen hair, weeping. He wore the face of Yeshua. My beloved. But he had made no move to stop this abomination. This sacrifice. *Sacrifice.* Blood for blood. As if violence could change the tides of heat and cold across the land. As if blood could shift seasons longer than human lifetimes. As if death could be used to bargain for more *life*.

And yet that age of ice would thaw, obeying a pulse too vast and long and slow for men to comprehend. The heat would return. The waters would rise. Eventually it, too, would become a curse.

Someday these people would mop sweat from their brows, their bodies feverish, and they would long for cold. Where were the cliffs of ice? The clean, hard winds of winter? The snows of old would melt and their waters would flood the land.

Your eyes are wide now, Leukas. Does this sound like madness to you? It is not wise to believe in the strange dreams of an old woman. And yet you tell me that you believe Saul? You believe the visions of that man from Tarsus who claims to know my husband? Why is it that women's visions are lunacy, while men's are revelation? How is it the dark tale I would tell you is less real than the blinding light of Saul?

Of course he saw brightness. He pledged himself to it because he fears the dark. Saul fears the knowledge that arrives slowly, not from the heavens, but from the body. He fears his very flesh and would use the words of my own husband to praise the heavens above all else. But

Saul, too, will be born again and die many deaths under the sword of those he has inspired.

"Miriam! MIRIAM!"

Someone was shaking me by the shoulders. I gasped. Gradually, the dim outline of Ivah's face emerged out of the darkness. "Miriam. Are you sick?" she asked. "Lord have mercy on us!"

I was too wracked with anguish, too filled with my own death, to answer her immediately.

I was the slain woman on the lake's shores, her heart laid bare, eaten by crows. I was the woman with a curse still fresh on her lips, already mourning the land these men would unknowingly destroy. A land that now lay under the ocean, its hills and fields turned to silt. I was filled with the sense of a dire emergency. And with pain and anger. But I had none of the wisdom I do now.

"I must find my husband!" I struggled to rise to my feet, the woolen blanket knotted around my legs. "Where is he? Has anyone heard from him?"

"Be quiet, Miriam! Have respect!" Ivah forced me back down onto the mattress. The babe that was nestled in her arms woke and began to mewl. "While you were sleeping, Orpah fell ill. She is near death as you speak. The family is gathering and the rabbi has been sent for."

"What?" I was confused and suddenly awake. "Orpah is ill? She was well at dinner."

"Andreas found her collapsed in the courtyard. She had gone out to make sure the fires were out for the night. Sometimes it happens like that with vapors. They come suddenly . . ."

Ivah helped me to my feet. I pulled at my shawl, drawing it around my shift.

"Where is she now? May I go to her?"

A strange look passed over Ivah's face. The little boy reached up and tickled her chin. She turned her face from him. "Perhaps it is best you stay here for now. Are you well? Do you need food or drink?"

"I'm not hungry!" I snapped. "Let me go to Orpah. I have knowledge of the healing arts."

"It is not proper!" said Ivah, trying to bar me from leaving the storeroom. "You are with child!" Her boy wriggled out of her grasp as I pushed past her.

I flew through the house, stumbling over furniture and stone washing bowls.

Yiska was hovering at the door with Andreas. The husband and wife who now barely ever lived in the same home looked unnatural side by side.

She will die of fear, I suddenly knew, for I had seen an image of the woman slumped next to her bed, only a few years older than she was that night, her body chilled and stiff. *Her fear will squeeze her heart shut. But she is not wrong to fear. Perhaps I would do better to be afraid. To look at these men and to tremble. To run. To escape.*

"Miriam!" Andreas exclaimed, his eyes flashing.

There was no time for argument. "Where is your mother?"

"I told you she would come to finish what she began!" warned Yiska. "She has brought a stain into our home, and now we are cursed for it. Imah will die if we let her stay here any longer!"

Andreas slapped his wife so hard her skull snapped back and hit the doorframe. She cradled her head, whimpering. "Be quiet, woman, and if you speak again, I'll make sure you don't have a tongue to speak with!" he hissed venomously.

I grabbed him by the neck of his tunic. "Would you disrespect a woman who has brought your children into the world? Hear me when I say it is harder for a violent man like you to enter into the kingdom than it is for a camel to fit through the eye of a needle."

"Begone, devil!" cried Yiska. "Touch not my husband!"

Oh, I realized coldly. *She is afraid of me. The very one who would set her free.*

The young Miriam did not understand that it was her responsibility to earn the confidence of such women. Only then could they be coaxed into their power.

I did not understand much of anything in those days.

"Who goes there?" asked Shimon, appearing at the doorway. His eyes were bloodshot. He seemed smaller, as though his mother's illness had turned him back into a child.

"Let me heal your mother, Shimon!" I commanded.

"Rabbi Nahor will not allow a woman into the room with her . . ." he whispered, his hand rising to his chest as if reaching for his heart. He was vulnerable and exhausted.

"Where is my husband, Shimon? Did he flee into the hills or further down the shore?" I asked.

"I . . . I . . ." Shimon stuttered and looked away, unable to answer me or hold my gaze.

"Miriam," Andreas cut in. "We have no idea where Yeshua is, but we must bring him here this night."

"She can't find him, either," Shimon said darkly. "But she can do what Yeshua does. I have seen her do it before."

"Do you trust me now to heal your mother?"

Something flashed before me. Another face, another set of features. But it was so fast and the light was low—just the feeble glow from one lamp set into a niche in the wall—that I couldn't say for sure what I saw. His eyes were black lakes. Milky tears beading at his eyes. His parted lips revealed cracked front teeth.

"I will do it," I announced, taking charge now. "Bring me to her."

I followed the brothers as they led me to the back room. It was filled with fishermen, the Rabbi Nahor, but no women except for me and Orpah.

Orpah's face was bloated and red. Her hands clawed at the wattle of skin at her throat as if she couldn't breathe.

"Send her away!" the rabbi demanded. "I cannot purify your mother with *her* in the room!" He stepped in front of the mattress protectively.

"Out! Why did I ever think to call on you? You Pharisee! You snake!" Shimon roared at the rabbi. "Let her through! She'll do more than read words off a scroll!"

Rabbi Nahor was perplexed by Shimon's rage, but the other men looked at me expectantly.

In the past I had never been certain that the power would not desert me in my moment of need. Could I touch someone and remove their suffering? It seemed absurd. But suddenly I felt the certainty of it flood through me.

I had died before. I had lived inside whole lifetimes of pain. Who better to heal than someone who has been forced to heal herself—again and again? Each time I was born, I had to heal the rupture of my last life's violence. I had to stand up and say, *Yes. I will begin again.*

I knelt beside the mattress, feeling the heat radiating from Orpah's exhausted body. I knew the power was with me. It slept beside my child in my womb. It lived in my spirit like a tight, secret seed and blossomed each time I was born and named.

I pulled away the blankets unceremoniously.

"Agh!" Andreas cried, shielding his face.

Orpah lay in a soiled puddle of her own waste.

"Silence!" I demanded before crawling onto the dirty mattress with the wretched woman.

Orpah the crone. Orpah the angry mother of Shimon and Andreas. Orpah who disapproved of my very existence. What did I owe this woman? This family?

Unbidden, the image of my own mother, elegant and slender, standing by the tomb just days before her death, filled my mind. I could smell her expensive oils—lily and cedar—and feel the dry, gentle skin of her wrists brushing against my forehead as she combed my hair. I could see her swallowed by her own sickbed, her body slowly eaten from the inside by a pain that was without name or color or cure. *How I regret not healing you! Not touching you more! Oh Mother, to think you could still be here. Standing beside me.*

At the thought of her, my hands were immediately on fire. My fingers prickled and my palms itched.

It was effortless. I placed my hands on Orpah's hot cheeks, feeling my healing heat meet the heat of her illness. Blue and red. I could see the separate colors fuse as the flame of a candle will divide in two at the beck of the wind, dance separately, and then merge back into one fiery tongue when the air has stilled. Slowly I massaged her temples, pressing against the thin branches of her collarbones. Her fever dropped away from under my touch and her eyes sharpened, focusing on the ceiling above her.

But Orpah also healed *me*. I know now that it is always so with healer and invalid. She received that intense energy that had been building inside of me without a way of release. Without her help, I would have succumbed to my own fever and burned down to ash. For the first time I understood that illness and a healer's power are part of the same flame. If I was to keep my body whole—keep fever and madness at bay—I had to put my hands on the sick and help them. I had to release the fire in my hands so that I, too, would not burn up.

I felt light and strong. Orpah struggled to sit up, murmuring, "I have had a strange dream . . ."

"Mother!" Andreas and Shimon crowded close.

"How can this be?" muttered the rabbi, dumbfounded.

"Off of me! Do you want to crush my old bones?" she complained as she received her sons' affectionate embraces.

The sky, framed by a high window, was a fleshy pink, veined with indecisive clouds. I could hear a dove singing tenderness to its love. The sound rose sweetly without reply. Not even the wind tried to divert its pure melody as it curved into the room along with the light.

Perhaps the dove's song is for itself, I mused, standing up slowly, my hands on my thighs. *Does a song need to be received? Does beauty need a reason? Sometimes the seeds do not grow! And it is as God wills. The wind scatters them on stones. They are still perfectly seeds. Not flowers and trees but just the brief premonition of a plant . . . a child . . .*

My vision began to glimmer at the edges. The pale bedclothes swelled like waves before my eyes. I was about to lose control again. I swayed backward, one hand on my stomach and the other searching for the wall.

A seed. A child. An unborn child.

"Miriam. Are you well?" Shimon asked me just as my hand connected with the wall. The texture of the cold stones served to shock me back into this ordinary room.

"Yes. Yes. I am fine," I assured him, watching as the fisherman came back into focus.

Except that it was not the brawny, barrel-chested man I knew as Shimon. I saw the man from my vision carrying the sickle blade. The man ready to cut the child from my womb. But he was also a tall, bald man pushing a dagger into the long cedar box that held my beloved, my king. He was every man who had ever betrayed me, erased my truth, killed me, killed my children.

Was it the same man who orchestrated all this violence? No. It had been many different men. But they shared a similar darkness—the same monstrosity that had possessed the faces of the men ready to hurl stones at Ester all those years before.

Whether he knew it consciously or not, Shimon was laying a trap for my husband. The certainty tightened like a vice around my womb.

I felt it. It was that same fear that had run through me that day as a small child when I saw Ester weeping outside Bethany and understood clearly that men could kill.

Be afraid. Be strong. And move! There is still time!

"Miriam. What ails you?" Shimon asked. I could see the danger in his eyes. I would not forget my premonition. It was clear what I must do.

"Where are you going?" Andreas yelled as I stumbled out of the house.

But I did not say anything. My feet were bare, my sandals left carelessly back in the courtyard. I could feel the grit of the road biting into my soles. But I let the pain drive me. I ran faster.

Go! the still, small voice inside of me urged. *Take your beloved away from this place! Away from these men!*

• • •

A few donkeys grazed in the grove where we once had gathered. Salome was already tending the fire.

"Miriam!"

"Salome," I cried. "Do you know where Yudas and my husband have gone?"

Salome's eyes saw more than just my face. She nodded with understanding. "You must sit and breathe, Miriam," she whispered. "Wait for him here. In the woods. He will come. Do not follow him back into the city."

"I will not sit and wait for the worst to happen!" I said foolishly. "I must find my husband. We will leave . . . go somewhere else! To the river."

"You must be still and wait." Salome's eyes were closed now and the smoke from the fire rose up behind her, crowning her head with silvery flourishes like one of those Roman stories where the woman becomes a tree. I could feel her roots tied into the earth beneath us, pulling tighter still. The world was holding its breath as she spoke.

A single, flaming cinder landed on her cheek and left there a small, red mark. Salome made no sign that she felt the burn. "Miriam. Yeshua must decide what he wants. His purpose is both larger *and* smaller than he believes. But you cannot show him his truth. He must bring it forth from within himself. And if he does not—if you try to draw it out of him through force—it will kill him."

Yohan Ben-Zebedee, dressed only in a loincloth, returned from bathing in the nearby stream. "Miriam! I thought Andreas took you safely into K'far Nahum!"

"He did," I replied. "Where is my husband? Have you any word?"

"He is headed south toward the shore with Yudas and Philip," he answered, slipping his tunic over his head.

"No, Miriam!" Salome pleaded. "Let him sit with the ocean and then he will come to *you*."

"You have gone mad, Salome! Like the rest of them." The words were cruel and false. But they had been spoken and I would not take them back. Salome was so shocked that she loosed her grip and fell backward as though I had physically struck her.

Without another word I headed back into the forest, making my slow, heavy way to the shore.

Now I understand that I did a terrible thing that day. I betrayed another woman's wisdom. A wisdom so easily erased by this world. And when I denied her, I denied myself.

Forty

The sun's heat penetrated to my bones. My head throbbed and my feet were blistered. But I pressed on. I found them far down the beach where Philip and Thoma stood at the water's edge, cooling their ankles.

Yeshua sat apart, under the shadow of two sparse palms. Yudas was beside him, his brow wrinkled with worry.

I stumbled, utterly exhausted, as I approached them. But my husband did not rise to help me. He gazed on the low swell of waves blurring the horizon. The sorrow in his chest was almost visible. His shoulders were hunched around it. To deny people healing, to hide from their pain, went against his nature.

"We thought you were safe with Andreas," Yudas rose stiffly. "You look ill, Miriam. Are you ill?"

A gull landed on the stones nearby. It snapped its beak as if with impatience.

"Miriam!" Thoma called from the shore. Philip shielded his eyes from the glare of the sun.

"Yeshua," I began breathlessly. "There is something I must tell you . . ." I took his hands in mine.

He was real. I was real. But Shimon was also real, and I had seen the thirst for power in his eyes. He longed to control my husband. He could destroy him.

"What?" Yeshua finally turned to look at me, and I could see that his eyes were bloodshot from lack of sleep.

"I had a dream," I began, and already I could feel the impossibility of expressing what had been revealed to me, of what I had remembered from our past. He would simply have to believe. He would have to trust what I had seen.

"We have lived before. You have said it yourself. But we have made the same mistakes time and time again. We have taken everything from the earth and given everything to the world of men. It has been the death of us, Yeshua. Each time. And the death of our children, too. I have seen a danger deep in the past. A danger that is coming again."

"You look pale, Miriam," Yudas interjected. "You need water. And food."

I was too tired to care who heard me. "We must return to the forest to heal ourselves. We carry a heartbreak that will poison us and poison the land if we do not heal together."

Without wind or storm, the waves grew louder.

"Are you saying that you will abandon us?" Yudas asked, looking alarmed.

I ignored him. "Can you not feel the danger all around us, Yeshua? There are those who would use our healing powers for their own purposes. They will turn us against each other. They will turn us against the earth."

I could feel Philip behind me. Yudas was concerned.

"Are we not men?" Thoma scoffed. "The danger is everywhere. We could be devoured by a panther or cut down by the Romans tomorrow."

"There are enemies among us," I insisted, each word now clumsy. Incorrect. "We must go now, Yeshua. The grooves of this story are plowed deep into the earth. If we do not work against them, we will fall into a path that leads only toward sorrow."

I had never spoken so clearly before about my intuitions. But, as if I still slept and dreamt, nothing about it felt right.

"Is she ill . . . or drunk?" Philip asked, pressing a sweaty hand to my forehead. I pushed him away roughly. "You do not burn. But you could still be delirious with a fever that has not reached the head yet. . ." Thoma peered into my face, squinting as he searched for signs of illness.

"No!" I said forcefully. "*You* are drunk. All of you!"

"Silence, wife!" Yeshua jerked away from me, his eyes flashing.

"Has Miriam come to tempt us from our mission?" Thoma wondered.

It is painful to speak of these things. The shore smelled of dead fish and sweat and soiled clothes. The child in my belly suddenly felt uncomfortably heavy. The shadows of the palm trees converged above me as the sun dropped in the sky.

Had I been wiser, I would have known that this was the moment to let Yeshua defend me. But I was too filled with ancient rage from my dream. I could still feel the blade in my belly. "Yeshua, there are those among us who will betray you. One has betrayed us before. Even if he does not know it himself."

"Of whom do you speak?" Yeshua asked quietly.

"Shimon!" I spat. "You know it! In every life it has always been Shimon."

I can remember it all now like a scorched stone remembers the heat of fire. The memory is blackened into me. Even now I can see the line driven between my husband's brow, his shoulder muscles knotted.

When did I lose him?

Perhaps then.

Salome was correct, I think. Had I stayed in the forest, Yeshua would surely have sought me—his pregnant wife. Perhaps, had he slept another night under a sky full of summer stars, he too would have seen into the past as I had done. We had shared the same dream before. We could have run to the forests and shed our names, our clothes, our ancient sorrows. We could have asked to be let back into the garden.

I knew if we came naked, and came together, the earth would not deny us our happiness—and perhaps our happiness was what the earth needed most.

"Shimon?" he asked dumbly. "What do you mean?"

"I'm confused," Thoma interrupted. "What has Shimon done?"

Yeshua sprang to his feet, stretching his arms above his head. "Let us go to Shimon," he said—not to me, but to the men gathered around. "Let us find the others. We have been separated long enough. It is safe to go into the city now."

"Trust my visions," I urged him.

"Let us rest a while longer," suggested Yudas pensively. "Miriam could be right. Let us think and talk with each other more before we proceed."

"I am done with waiting," answered Yeshua decisively. "I have waited since Yochanan's murder. I waited to return to my father's house when I was young. And when I returned, I was too late! He was dead.

Would I let children die for lack of healing? Would I turn away from women burning with fever?"

And so we did not wait. We fell into footsteps on a path that led us both forward and backward into an old story, an old sorrow that we had known lifetime after lifetime.

• • •

The news of Yeshua's return spread throughout K'far Nahum. Men and women poured into the city, pushing each other into puddles of refuse. The air of the city was stagnant with disease, but Yeshua was coming to cure everyone of their ailments. Yet the more crowded the city became with people, the sicker the people would become. Why was it that only I could see this?

We walked through the gate and a group of women carried over a naked boy, covered in angry red pustules. Yeshua fell to his knees so that he could look directly into the child's eyes. The boy whimpered, struggling to cover his sore-covered face, and my own stomach clenched. Yeshua, too, could feel the hot knife of the boy's pain and shame.

Old fishermen crowded close to Yeshua, holding out their twisted hands. A widow scratched at an angry rash on her cheek. Feverish children appeared, their cheeks red and hot. There was a shocked murmur and the crowd parted. A leper staggered forward.

"We must not stop here, Yeshua," Philip insisted, looking around warily. "We must get you to a place where you can sit and truly take time with these people, in order to teach."

"He's right," I insisted. "These people will be easier to heal if we take them out of the city."

"Healing happens where it needs to happen," said Yeshua distractedly. He was focused on the small boy.

"You will be made whole," he whispered as he helped the dazed boy to his feet, his sores fading to pink scars before our eyes.

"Rabboni!" the boy cried out, and Yeshua hugged him to his chest, his own tears mixing with the boy's.

"He is the one we have waited for!" shouted a beautiful, dark woman to the crowd. She clutched her green shawl to her breast passionately, then leapt onto an overturned crate. "The Lord will raise up for you a prophet like me from among yourselves, from your own kinsmen! You are to heed him! I will put my words in his mouth, and he will reveal to them everything I say!"

A group of young men fell to their knees below the woman, more in awe of her beauty than in deference to Yeshua. "The Messiah!" they whispered.

A gray-haired woman scrambled through the crowd. "Help me. Help me! I have been bleeding and bleeding and it will not stop!"

"Mother. Your faith will heal you." With no thought of her unclean state, and despite audible gasps from the crowd, Yeshua drew the woman to him, pressing his forehead to hers.

"Ah!" She began to shake. I knew she could feel the heat of his healing entering into her.

Roman soldiers, dressed in full military attire, strutted forward to see who was stirring up trouble. "What is this? Scatter! Clear the gates at once!" They gleamed with metal and shimmering self-importance. One of them, wearing the distinctive helmet that identified him as a centurion, stepped forward, putting his hand to the sword at his belt.

"You speak to the servant of the Lord!" declared the beautiful woman. "He will vanquish your armies and return our land to us!"

"Do these fools think it wise to call someone the Messiah?" said a soldier.

"He does not call himself by that name!" I insisted. But no one heard me amid the pleading of the sick as they crowded all around us.

"The world will end," a man called out. "It is coming! What can we do?"

"Does he think he will save his people?" mocked the centurion to his fellow soldiers. "How many Galilean idiots have we already cut down? And each one has bled out just like a sheep! So much for being sent by God . . ."

"Yeshua, we must leave!" I urged him, drawing in close so that only he could hear.

"Miriam! Do you see them? Do you feel their suffering?" Yeshua implored, tears streaming from his eyes. "How can we turn them away?"

"Should we not lead them to the forest, back to the wilderness and a better way of life?" I asked, but the din of the crowd drowned out my voice.

We could heal a hundred, a thousand, ten thousand people a day for the rest of our lives and there would only be more and more heartache, more and more pain with each passing year. But I didn't understand how to explain it. What a shame that our deepest lessons take whole lifetimes to learn. Seldom are we ready to speak the truth when it is most needed.

Was not the earth the true healer? A night's sleep deep in the forest. A quiet day in the company of birds. River water. Bitter herbs. This was the slow medicine that healed us from the soles of our feet upward.

I was only just beginning to understand: the cause of this suffering was the way we lived—on top of the land instead of *inside* of it. The granaries and storerooms were the cause of their suffering . . . the armies and palaces . . . the cities themselves.

"Here! Let us move!" Thoma cried out. "Follow us to a place where my master can speak more freely."

"Keep clear of the gates!" the centurion declared loudly, no longer joking with his men. "Any sign of uprising will be met with strength and force! Zealots are unwelcome in K'far Nahum."

Zealots, I thought with confusion. We were not like those dagger-wielding troublemakers who believed they could murder the Romans. Since when had Yeshua's deeds and storytelling become insurrection?

"Yeshua!" I managed to grab his hand. "Come away! Now! We can heal. But not here!"

"Miriam is right," Philip shouted above the noise. "We must move to Shimon's home!"

But Yeshua was overcome. He had no space left to consider that healing might involve more than laying his hands on a feverish boy and declaring him well. I saw his fingers tremble with energy. He needed to cool down.

"Come, love." I tried my hardest to get through to him. But it was useless.

We were only paces from the gate. But the street leading into the market was packed to the walls. Women hushed their children. Men who had only ever been silenced by their own mothers closed their mouths and bowed their heads. When Yeshua started to walk down the street, people fell away to let him pass.

A boy broke away from the crowd. Covered in dirt, his hair was as thin and patchy as an old man's. Without even stopping, Yeshua scooped up the child and put him on his shoulders.

I walked behind him, concentrating on the confident set of his wide shoulders, the sure way he planted one foot in front of the next. The child had his hands in my husband's curls.

The crowd followed, their voices rising again with sorrow, celebration, and confusion.

When we reached Shimon's house, Ivah and Yiskah ushered us in. Yeshua let the boy down gently, searching out the tearful face of his mother in the crowd before releasing the child.

"Mama!" the boy yelped with glee when he saw her.

"Rabboni! He has been mute his whole life!" she cried out. "You have healed him!"

"Watch! He'll never shut up now! Soon you'll wish I left him as he was!" Yeshua joked as Yiskah pulled at his sleeve, trying to tug him inside.

Looking behind me, I saw that a soldier had followed us. He had removed his helmet, holding it in front of his narrow chest. His hair was flattened onto his pockmarked forehead.

As Yeshua ducked through the door, the soldier called out. "You tell *your* people what to do. But what about us? What shall *we* do?"

He was not baiting Yeshua. I could see it from the embarrassed flush on his round cheeks. I wondered what his fellow soldiers would think of his question?

Yeshua glanced over his shoulder. "Get out of our land! And don't hurt a single person," he said roughly. "Is that too much to ask?"

Something crumpled inside of the soldier. I could almost see his heart—the red, taut, muscle of it—collapsing down into something the size of a pomegranate seed. Pale and defeated, he put on his helmet and slunk away.

I followed Yeshua into Shimon's house, a burning dread rising in my throat. I could feel the close, stone walls shrinking to fit our exact dimensions.

"Come in. Come in," urged Orpah, returned to health. She ushered us into the communal room where a straw couch was covered in a dark blue cloth. Pillows had been flung on the ground.

"Mother, they have surrounded us and are trying to get in from all sides!" Yiska cried as she came into room. "What can we do?"

She was right. I could hear the cacophony threatening to burst through the windows. The very walls shook.

"Yeshua. You must understand that it will never stop. The more you heal, the more they will come. You will die before you can heal every last one of them! And it will all be for nothing. There will be more with each year that passes—until the whole world is ill. Tell stories instead. Teach. Show them how they may heal each other!"

"Would you ignore the people's suffering? That boy with a fever would surely have died."

"He lives in a dark, cold house with a father who beats his mother. He hasn't enough to eat. He will have another fever tomorrow, and he will die next week." I spoke quietly so that only he could listen.

"Miriam!" His eyes widened. "How do you know this?" But it was impossible to explain.

I still long to take us out of that house. To give us a field. A grove. Somewhere to speak. Somewhere to lay hands on each other. Perhaps we could still have escaped from sorrow.

How beautiful he looked, even then, his hair wild from the little boy's hands. Digging his right foot into the dirt floor impatiently. His whole body alive and tensed as if to dance or run or jump.

But as I was about to speak again, Andreas and Shimon came into the room, looking back at their mother.

"Isn't it a miracle, Shimon?" Andreas asked his brother. "My mother is up and providing for us when only this past night she was close to death!"

Shimon's face was warped with conflict. "Miriam healed my mother," he said, and I could tell he did not want to admit it. "She has done a great service."

Yeshua looked from brother to brother questioningly. Then he turned to me with that smile he saved only for our most intimate moments. *He has softened,* I thought. But I had misunderstood. "See, Miriam. Even you are compelled to heal! You cannot plan it. We must save those who we can save. It is a good thing!"

Andreas started to explain. "My mother was taken ill in the night, and just when we thought she would surely die, Miriam came. . ."

"They are lifting someone up onto the roof!" Thoma interrupted breathlessly, rushing into the room. "A paralytic man! He's been carried here on a bed all the way from Chorazin!"

Yeshua was already in movement, drawn to the source of suffering. "On the roof? Take me to him, Shimon. We will show them what my Father can do for the faithful."

We all scrambled after him, using the ladder accessible from the courtyard. I was last up, feeling a twang in my back. My breath was labored and shallow by the time I struggled over the edge of the roof and stood up.

A team of men had lifted a man onto the roof. Stretched out on a soiled mattress, his eyes were wet with tears, although the rest of his face was frozen and expressionless.

My hands warmed. I could heal him. I could step in front of my husband and stop this nonsense. I could show anyone that it was not just this man, this single man, who could save a life. A woman could do it. Then I would tell them the truth. That healing was *everywhere*. The kingdom was in every grain of sand, every mustard seed, every full moon. We need only open our eyes and our hearts to be filled with healing as thick and sweet and nourishing as honey.

I faltered.

"Master, my brother has been unable to move these past four years," pleaded a young man. "Please help him."

"Yeshua! Yeshua!" The roar came from below. I walked to the edge and looked out. It seemed the whole city had converged around Shimon's house. There were people backed up into the nearby streets and a few had climbed onto neighboring roofs. A girl let loose a red scarf that flailed in the wind like blood trying to find its way through water.

A great storm of humanity whirled around us on every side, and Yeshua stood in the eye of it. He sat down beside the paralyzed man and placed his hand on his forehead.

"It is done," he said almost instantly. There was no visible effort— no evidence that he was allowing a great power to work through him. It was a wonderful thing. But it was also terrible. No one saw how much the healing drained him. He needed to root back into himself before giving so much so quickly. He had left Nazareth knotted up in anger, disconnected from his wisdom.

Yeshua stood and offered the invalid a hand.

Haltingly, the man lifted his arm as if it were weighted. But when he saw that he could move easily, he grasped Yeshua's hand and sat up, giving a small, surprised cry. "I can . . . I can . . . I am made whole!"

Yeshua pulled the man upright by his hand and called out to the crowds. "See this man! His faith has healed him!"

The crowd cheered.

"Son of David!" a woman called out.

"Find us a home to seek refuge at once!" I demanded of the disciples.

And although he resented my authority, Shimon disappeared back into the house, heeding my command for once.

• • •

Shimon found shelter for us in the house of Mattiyahu, a tax collector who had attended Yeshua's meals during our last visit to K'far Nahum. He was wealthy and his home had enough rooms to house us all.

"We will stay here for a while, planning our healings carefully in advance," Shimon explained to Yeshua. "It will be easier that way."

Yeshua was too overwhelmed to answer. I knew that, although we had left the crowds behind, their voices still echoed in his head.

The large dining area was already full of men. As I sat down to eat, I was struck by how nauseating I found the smell of the rich meat. But I was distracted immediately by a familiar face.

"Miriam! You are huge!" My brother enveloped me in his arms, and for the first time in days my heart felt at ease.

"How did you find us?" I asked in disbelief. "We are in hiding!"

"Luck! I ran into Yudas in the streets."

"I will come sit with you shortly," Yeshua explained after embracing Lazaros. "I must pay my respects to our host!"

"Sit! Miriam," Yudas said kindly. "You must be exhausted."

I complied, putting a hand to my aching back, feeling the child stir within me. My body was not as resilient as I would have liked. I felt a burning in my pelvis as if a fire had been kindled there.

"Where are they?" I asked suddenly, peering around. "Where is Yohanna? And Salome?"

"Mattiyahu does not let women dine with the men," Yudas explained flatly. "I think the women are back in the hills, setting up camp."

"Then why am I allowed to dine here?"

"You are Yeshua's wife," Yudas said carefully. "He refused to eat without you."

"Is that all we are?" I shot back. "Only wives and sisters and daughters who cook but are not allowed at the table?"

Lazaros interrupted diplomatically. "When will the child come?"

"I . . ." The room spun as I looked down at my swollen stomach, my fingers gently pressing against the spot where I knew the child slept inside of me. "I am tired. Perhaps I am seven moons? Eight moons?"

"Father will be overjoyed," my brother answered.

I was struck by how much older he looked than when I had seen him last. His cheeks had hollowed out and his shoulders had broadened. He had the sleek beauty of a fox.

"Marta misses you and tires of my company," he confided. "All she can speak of is whom I should marry!"

I nodded, but I was not paying attention. Mattiyahu was gesturing toward me with his ring-covered hands. He was a strange man with small features and a lazy eye.

Lazaros, sensing my distracted state, spoke to Yudas in a lowered voice. "Answer me this. Does Yeshua know about the danger? It is said that Herod would see Yeshua dead. He would go so close to Herod? Even now?"

"Yeshua is not one for hiding away," Yudas offered. "I think he means to provoke Herod."

"In Yerusalem it is well-known that Herod thinks him another Yochanan. If not worse!" Lazaros was holding his cup. But he did not drink from it or look for more wine.

"All right. I've done my duty! Tell us the news, Lazaros!" A voice boomed from behind me. I felt a hand on my shoulder and looked to see that Yeshua had come to join us. "What is said about us?"

Lazaros's eyes brightened at the sight of his brother-in-law. "You won't believe any of it, Yeshua! I have heard it said that you are organizing an army."

"An army armed only with words and fish!" Yeshua laughed. "We are very dangerous indeed!" He drew close to me and I felt ragged need in his body. I felt that he and I should speak without words, flesh to flesh. Only then could we understand each other again. I could heal the wound that had been opened in Nazareth.

"It is said that you live on air alone and can call storm clouds to do your bidding! I will report back that I have found a well-groomed king instead of a starving ascetic!" Lazaros said, chuckling, before growing serious again. He leaned across the table and spoke more quietly. "You should know that our father is your staunchest supporter. He relays your parables to his students. All they speak of is the kingdom."

"The kingdom . . ." Yeshua's eyes were glassy. I reached out to brush a curl away from his cheek, checking for a fever. But he was chilly to the touch, almost cold. "And where is that kingdom? Buried in a field? Folded into bread? Some days it feels that it has been hidden from me . . ."

"I won't leave until I can see him!" Someone beyond the entrance was yelling at the servant boys who had crossed their arms and barred the entrance. "I know he is in here!" The voice belonged to a woman.

Yeshua squeezed my arm reflexively as if to draw strength from our connection. "Who are you turning away?" he asked Mattiyahu.

"Master . . ." Mattiyahu stood now, smiling with embarrassment. "Pay her no mind. She is a common harlot. I have told her she must seek you out some other time."

I saw the struggle that was his constant companion these days. A vein throbbed in his neck.

"Let her in!" Yeshua decided. "No one will be denied!"

The servant boys looked to Mattiyahu.

"You heard Yeshua!" Mattiyahu conceded, although his good eye narrowed with concern. "Let the woman in."

The boy stepped aside and the woman rushed into the room, flinging herself prostrate onto the ground, her hands out before her, palms up. Her graying hair was uncovered. She wore a faded tunic that I could tell had once been a fine thing—bright vermillion with embroidery at the neck and hem.

"Oh . . ." My mind did not understand yet, but my body did. My stomach churned. A metallic taste filled my mouth.

"Have mercy on me, Rabboni!" the woman cried.

"Peace, woman! What is wrong? What fills you with such darkness?" He bent down to touch her head in blessing, but she lowered herself further still, her hair cascading over his feet.

"I am a sinner!" The woman's voice was clotted with shame. She buried her face in the front of his tunic. "A sinner of the worst kind. I am unclean."

I recognized the voice. Where on our travels had we met before? On the river? In some market where I had bought fish?

"Can you heal her?" Shimon asked, an almost greedy expression on his face. "She is a prostitute. Can you take her sin away, Yeshua?"

"Hush!" Yeshua rebuked Shimon.

"Wait," I said, pressing my hands to the table in an effort to rise. "I know this woman."

And at the sound of my voice, the woman turned from Yeshua, revealing a face ravaged by despair. But I knew her almond-shaped eyes.

"Ester!" I cried out.

"Ester?" Lazaros echoed in confusion. And then he, too, was standing. "Ester!"

Here was the woman I had saved from stoning as a young child. Now she was a haggard prostitute? But she had escaped! How could this possibly be?

Every time I had imagined Ester in the intervening years, she had been safe and as fresh as the day of her wedding. I saw her in a garden of roses, holding hands with a kind man, enjoying a happiness I felt sure she deserved.

"Ester. It is Miriam. From Bethany. How did you come to be here?"

Her eyes narrowed as she looked at me. "I have traveled for some time to seek Yeshua," Ester said slowly. "I am from Tabariyyah."

"Ester. It is me. Miriam. The daughter of Nicodemus."

"I know you not."

"You do," I insisted. "I was sure you had escaped. I thought you had found your freedom."

"Freedom!" she laughed bitterly. "Freedom from my home! From the life I knew! If only you had let them kill me then. Instead, I have died slowly, year after year."

She knew me after all.

"Rise! Please rise!" Yeshua begged, trying to get Ester to her feet. "Do you need food? Wine?"

"I need to be made clean!" she exclaimed.

She was right, of course. I could feel the knowledge poisoning me. What could a woman without money and family do to make her way?

She could only sell her body back to the men who had ruined her life in the first place.

"Clean her, Rabboni!" Shimon demanded. "Take away her sin!"

"The sin is *ours!*" I could hold the words in no longer. "The sin is the world that punishes such a woman and forces her to feel shame. This woman has known terrible pain. It is *she* who must forgive *us!*"

But Ester remained stricken. "Help me!" she moaned, rocking back and forth. "Please!"

I watched my husband. He swayed gently as if he were a reed played by the wind. He looked at Shimon, at me, and then down at the sobbing Ester. The pearl of a tear glistened at the corner of his eye.

I felt the absence of my friends sharply in that moment. Had she been here, Adah would have put her soft arms around Ester. Salome had been a whore and would know the right things to say. Yohanna could speak to Ester's shame. A kindred shame had almost killed *her*.

And why did I not go to her? Why did I not run before the men and defend her as I had before?

Perhaps it is because, at last, I had begun to truly doubt myself. I had not truly been able to save Ester. Who was I to attempt it again? Is it worth saving someone for but a moment?

Thoma nudged Yohan Ben-Zebedee and snickered. Mattiyahu's mouth was curled into a knowing smile.

"I have been punished for my sins with sores of the body," Ester's voice rose above the men's laughter. "Take this from me, Rabboni, and it will be enough!"

"Even as you clean my feet with your tears, you yourself are cleansed!" Yeshua murmured through his own bewildered tears. "Get up! Rise!"

"Please!" Ester's tearful voice wavered. "Let me follow you, Yeshua. Let me wash your feet. Let me follow you on my knees."

"Go! Bathe in a stream. Leave this place and change your life!" High and strangled, the voice sounded as if it did not come from me. My knees felt like water beneath me. Was I about to faint?

"Miriam, do you not believe the words of Yeshua?" Shimon asked. "Why do you question him?"

"Because you believe, you are forgiven," said Yeshua. But he was rambling. Searching for words he did not have. "My Father heals you.

Through him you are made clean." As if fathers and their rituals of purity could offer this poor woman anything but more pain.

Something ripped inside of me then. A warmth spread down my thighs, and I knew I was going to be ill. I jerked forward, clutching my stomach.

Lazaros was the only one to notice what was happening. He ran to me as I began to faint. "Help us!" he was calling. "Help us! She is bleeding!"

I looked down at my brown skirt and saw that it was so. The bloom of my lifeblood was soaking through. My child's blood.

"Miriam!" Yeshua was there, his hands at my face as the darkness narrowed my vision.

But he could not save me. There are things that cannot be healed.

Blessed are the mothers, for theirs is the soil of the
*   earth.*
Blessed are the trees, for they will be embraced by winds
*   and water, stone and cloud.*
Blessed are the rivers, for they will lead us home.
Blessed are the fields that overflow with wildflowers
*   each spring.*
Blessed are the claps of thunder, for they will awaken
*   the desert from its dry slumber.*
Blessed are those with broken hearts. The raped. The
*   murdered. The insulted. The abused. The seeds*
*   that never grow.*
Blessed are the girls, for they know not what the sons of
*   men will do to them.*
Blessed are you who listen to this story.
Your reward will be that you hold my heart.
As I hold yours.

Forty-One

I do not remember the blood or the pain. I do not remember the small red face of my stillborn son. Nor do I remember my husband pounding his fists through the clay wall of Mattiyahu's dining room. I do not even remember him carrying me back into the woods and leaving me with the women.

I was consumed by a fever and slept for days, blindly sipping broth and milk as they were offered. It was only later that I heard he had gone deep into the desert to meditate. There he was tempted by devils, the men told me. He came back stronger. He came back ready to fulfill his mission.

But the devils were not in the desert. The devils were among us.

I was visited by ghosts. Dark women with arms as vast and soft as clouds . . . Midwives with indigo-stained faces, smelling like crushed rosemary . . . Sinewy women, bare-breasted, holding armfuls of wild wheat, their hair blowing in the wind . . . Girls with bloodless faces, their wide-open legs stained lily-red with their loss, hands cradling the open flower of their death, their battered wombs . . . Blue-lipped babes swaddled in fox fur, covered with eagle wings, coral necklaces wound around their tiny ankles, placed in burial caves alongside dead mothers, slipped into the chilly earth under grandmother sycamores.

Weep. Mourn. But know this, these ancestors told me. *Birth is the closest thing to death. Death is the closest thing to birth. Women have known this secret for thousands of years. Long ago your people buried their dead in the floors of their homes. They slept pressed against the bones of their lost children. They knew they were not truly lost. The dead are but seeds, waiting to grow again.*

Sometimes I saw my mother's face floating above me, her tears moistening my lips. Other times I was sure it was Marta's smooth hands pressing a damp cloth across my forehead. Most often it was Kemat I felt holding me in her arms.

And there were women who spoke with my own voice. They told me that, just as I had healed others, now I would heal myself.

When I was strong enough to push myself up on my elbows and peer out at the forest, I spotted a tall crone. Leaning against a pine, her hands clutched a tall metal distaff. There were dark blue lines painted down her forehead and chin. She held out a hand and I could see that a muscular black snake twined up her arm. I looked down at my own arms, and they too were covered in serpentine tattoos.

A great lion arrived. Not golden but red, and as brilliant as hammered bronze. I felt her heat as she lay down next to me on the grass mat, pressing her nose—soft and black as soil after a rainstorm—against my face. The vultures came. Their naked heads nuzzled my feet. And the wolves pawed a protective circle around these visitations. Their silken fur rippled like water at the edge of my vision.

And then the woman herself arrived. A woman who was not a woman. She was made of thunder, and she was as large and immovable as a mountain, as fluid and muscled as the ocean. Eyes glinting like onyx. Covered in feathers, in fur, in lustrous hair. In gems and scales. She was almost a tree. Almost a flower. Almost a whole forest. And her face kept changing. Sometimes it was the face of one who has lived for thousands of years.

Sometimes it was my own face.

Release, she said. *Let it come through you.*

She reached into me and massaged the darkness of my sex. She cradled my hips until the dead parts of my womb dislodged and gushed forth. She pulled me up and held me as I bled a river. It seemed the river ran until it grew clear and fresh—until it had consumed the whole clearing, the whole forest. It flowed all the way to the Galilean shore and into the water that held up the fishing boats.

Then she whispered, *Do not forget that you are always giving birth. If not to a son this time, then always to the river that floods its shores each year and nourishes the land.*

I turned to her, and she was the lion. The vultures. The leopards. The wolves. The silver, twisted olive trees.

And then she was gone, leaving me with a fever so complete my very skin felt it would burst and peel back from my bone.

I sank down into a deep dream, which arrived in my mind from low in my body.

I was standing on the top of a hill looking out at a barren landscape. Yeshua was standing beside me. He looked as he had when I'd first seen him on the rooftop: his hair was long and unkempt. He reached for me and squeezed the tips of my fingers in his hand.

"Where are we?" I asked.

He shook his head, similarly confused. "I recognize it not."

The sky above us was the tedious blue of a summer with no pause, no rain, no wind. The sun was closer than I had ever felt it. It was almost as if the ground could not properly absorb the glare. Fire danced through the sand and scorched the bottom of my feet.

"Look!" Yeshua spoke. "What is that there? A city?"

He was right. At the farthest limit of my sight, I spotted buildings. One stood above the rest, glittering like a great armored beetle.

"It can't be . . ." I whispered.

But it was.

"Yersualem," he realized, aghast.

I looked around, trying to understand.

This was not some distant land. This was our home—the land of milk and honey. But it was ravaged. The lush green farmland that had surrounded Bethany was desiccated. The wind carried no perfume of plants. A few palms were all that was left to protect the town from the ravages of heat.

No more animals. No more flowers. No more birds.

Yeshua was distraught, gripping my hand so hard that it hurt. "Who did this? What evil has been worked on this land?"

At that moment a sound like thunder began to pulse through the dry earth. Dust clouded the horizon. Yerusalem spat fire.

"No!" I gasped. The holy city was burning to the ground.

The noise belonged to horses. To armies. They unfurled. Men who had shaved the tops of their heads, their bald scalps reflecting the relentless sunlight. Men wearing brown robes. Red robes. They were not carrying weapons. No. They were carrying scrolls. Long sheets of paper.

"Who are these people?" Yeshua raged. "Why have they done this?"

One man, wearing white-and-red robes and a strange, tall hat, walked forward. He raised his hand as if to bless us.

"Our Father in heaven, hallowed be your name! Your kingdom come, your will be done!"

"No!" Yeshua yelled. "Not this!"

I woke in a cold sweat, groaning, clawing at Yohanna, who had been left to tend to me. She was not angry. Instead, she cried with joy, feeling the strong pulse in my neck. The fever was broken. I would live.

But it was too late. I wept for days. I was inconsolable and would take no food.

These trees will bear no fruit. And it is because of me. Because of him.

He did finally return, late one night when I was curled up in my cloak on the edge of camp. He knelt down next to me, gently brushing the hair away from my ear.

I could taste his sorrow. It was too much for me.

I pushed away his hand. "Do not touch me."

He lowered his head, got up, and left me again.

• • •

"You must live, Miriam. You must live for me."

The voice belonged to my brother. He had refused to leave the camp while I was ill. He now brought me honeyed milk to sip.

"Lazaros, will you help me?" My voice was cracked from disuse.

"Yes." He leaned close, his eyes as wide and dark as a doe's. "Anything."

"Take me away from here," I whispered. "Lazaros, take me home."

PART FOUR

The City

Forty-Two

Let me walk through the olive trees and the sycamores again. Let me breathe the fragrant almond blossoms. Let me bathe once more in the Yarden. Give me a moment to stand again at the shore. Be patient Leukas, as I kneel in the moss, feeling Yeshua's hand at my waist, his exhale as he kneels beside me and together we worship the forest that made for us each night a bed.

The forest. The sea. The hills. The streams. The river. He *is* these places.

The kingdom.

Forty-Three

Lazaros sent word ahead so that when we arrived, late on the third day after our departure, my father's home was filled with the smell of fragrant herbs and vegetables that had been simmered for a long time in a rich broth.

"He would have served you yesterday's bread and lentils!" Marta explained as she ushered us into the courtyard. "I came over immediately when I heard you were on your way."

"Good!" Lazaros clapped Marta on the back. "I'm starved!"

"You are always starved!" she complained, although her hand went up to ruffle his hair affectionately. "If I tried to match your hunger, you would eat even Amos out of his wealth. He comes to dinner every other night knowing we will serve him his favorite sweets! He has charmed all the serving girls. And I only just learned that on the nights he doesn't bother me, he's off dining with your old friend Yosseph!"

"It sounds like he needs a wife," I joked.

"Right you are!" Marta said, turning to me with easy laughter.

When I had seen her last, I had thought her soft. I had resented her womanly curves and her smug smile and thought her face overpainted. But now, after two years, I couldn't think of anyone more beautiful than my sister. Her skin had a golden glow and her lips were delicately pink. Even the kohl around her eyes was attractive, accentuating her long, thick lashes. She was stouter than my mother had been, with wider hips, but she moved in a light, graceful way that reminded me of the dancers I had seen during my travels in Galilee. Her hips swung from side to side and she walked on the balls of her feet, rolling into each step as if pushing into a soft bed of moss. Had she changed so much? Or was it that my eyes had at last learned to see what was beautiful in women? I was grateful when she embraced me in her strong arms. She smelled like cardamom and jasmine. She smelled like home.

"Look at you!" She pulled away, making a clucking noise. "You are still as thin as a child! I thought all your husband did was eat and drink. Has he not provided for you?"

I buried my head in the curve of her neck. "It is good to see you, Sister."

My reunion with my father was not as easy. His hair had gone completely white. He was proud and squared his shoulders to greet me, but when he smiled, I saw that his gums were inflamed and that his spine was beginning to curve inward. Two years. Enough time for a father to grow old. Enough time to gain and lose a world.

I could see in his eyes the questions he was struggling to keep quiet. Perhaps to keep these words from spilling forth, he kept forcing food and wine on me even after I had told him repeatedly that I was satisfied.

But I *did* eat and drink. I felt nourished for the first time in months. There was soft goat cheese and flaky pastries glazed with honey and sesame seeds. As I ate, my mind quickened. I laughed easily when Lazaros talked about my father's students.

"I am not sure who they are most eager to meet and interrogate, you or Yeshua! Father speaks of you more often and more highly than he does your husband. I think some of the stories he tells about you as a young girl are pure fiction."

"Is this true?" I asked, cocking my head.

My father smiled bashfully. "I only tell them what a quick study you were with scripture. You had memorized more Targums than most men my age by the time you had fourteen years!"

But the night ended early. Lazaros complained that the trip had left him exhausted. There was a spark in his eye, a telltale flush in his high cheeks, that told me he was lying. Someone waited for him somewhere in the night. *I should ask him about his heart,* I thought absentmindedly.

Marta and Atalyah cleaned up after the meal, hardly looking down as their hands swept crumbs into their skirts. They brushed past each other, passing platters and plates between them without making eye contact. They moved in such an organized fashion that it felt like I was watching a choreographed dance. I sat beside my father, my eyes on the glowing embers of the cooking fire instead of meeting his gaze.

A strange sense of detachment came over me. Were these people real? They had continued on with their lives without me. And I had continued mine, becoming a person who no longer fit into this home, this warmth, this easiness.

"Where is your husband, Miriam?" my father finally asked. There was no judgment in his voice, only curiosity. "Why is Yeshua not with you?"

I wanted to tell him: about the healings, the miscarriage, the dreams that had left me certain of other lifetimes.

I wanted to tell him, *Father, there is power in me. I have put my hands on people and healed their bodies. I have felt life stir and curl within my own womb. And I have seen it pass away.*

But as I turned to him, ready to unleash my sorrows and uncertainties, something made me stop.

He was looking at me with such kindness, a kindness he had not revealed during my childhood. This was the softening of age and distance. He could be sweet with me because he had not seen me for a long time. His eyes crinkled and his head inclined toward me. He was looking at me as if I was still a young girl, his prodigy, unstained by the woes of womanhood.

"Yeshua is avoiding Herod's men," I explained. "He is constantly traveling. I needed to rest. Yeshua knew how much I missed my family, so he suggested I come stay with you for a while. But don't worry. I'm sure he'll be here soon."

My father nodded. Everything was going according to plan. He was happy to hear all was well. "Good. Good. It is as I expected. I have many questions for him when he arrives. Rumors of his work have reached us here. It is high time I hear the stories from my son-in-law himself!"

He got up with some difficulty, bracing himself on the trunk of the olive tree that we sat below. Once up he offered me a hand, saying I must be tired after so many days spent on the road. But I waved him off, smiling sweetly, saying I would put the embers out. He patted my head and then paused, leaning down to kiss my forehead, before leaving me alone.

I breathed in deeply. It was winter, nearing the end of Shevat, but it had been an unusually dry year. There had been no rain to wash away the summer's layers of dust. The sun had set an hour earlier and a wind curled over the roof. Still, I did not feel cold.

I stared into the embers, realizing it had not been my father, my brother, or my sister I had been longing for. I had returned to Bethany to feel her close to me. If only her bones.

"Mother," I whispered into the night. "Mother. Where are you?"

• • •

I woke every morning half expecting Yeshua to have arrived overnight. Surely I would climb up onto the roof to greet the day and find him reciting the Shema alongside my father.

Did I want to him to appear? To follow me?

Yes. I believe I did. I wanted him to show me that he cared for me above all else, above his stories, his friends, his miracles.

Where are you? When will you return to me? I wondered as I took meandering walks through the fields, the hem of my dress picking up burrs.

My father was surprised that I did not want to attend the long dinners with his students. "I thought you would love to answer their questions. You were always so keen to demonstrate your scholarship." He straightened his heavy cloak. He was heading into Yerusalem for the day. It was overcast for the first time in months, and the flat, diffuse light drained all the color from his face.

I pulled my shawl tightly around my shoulders as I tried to explain myself. "I have dined with many men over the past two years! I have engaged them in debate and grown tired of it. I'd rather eat in the company of trees and birds."

He gave me a worried expression. "You have grown bitter, Miriam. Although you hide it well, I can see that your heart is heavy."

I turned from him, preparing for the questions I did not want to face.

Why are you childless after two years of marriage? Are you barren? What is the meaning of your husband's kingdom? Does he mean to overthrow the Romans? Who is the Father he speaks of?

But my father remained quiet, reaching out hesitantly and squeezing my arm before leaving. As he reached the gate, he turned back. "Go see your sister. I'm sure she needs help with the children."

I had forgotten that my sister, a woman who had borne children and withstood a difficult marriage, might also understand my pain.

• • •

The front door opened onto a large room fitted with scrolled couches and small divans covered in richly colored fabrics. Amos, gone quite bald, sat with his back to me, gesticulating to two older men. He was wider, more vegetable than when I had seen him last; hairy and dusty as something you might pull from the ground. He no longer looked like the man who had beat my sister all those years before. I wondered if something had changed. They all turned to see who it was when I walked in.

"Sometimes I forget your sister was pretty when we wed," Amos said, greeting me jovially, his eyes twinkling at his joke. "And then I see you."

The men chuckled at his comment.

"As you see me, know that I see you," I replied lightly.

"I heard your husband wrestled with demons in the desert!" An older man named Hezekiah said, laughing, his jowls shaking. "But by the look of his wife I'd bet he wrestled with a demon in his bridal bed."

"And have you heard the stories of me?" I asked as Atalyah appeared, hovering nervously by the doorway to lead me to my sister's rooms.

The men exchanged knowing glances.

"Then you know to be careful!" My tone was still playful, but I could feel my mouth harden.

"Good to see you haven't changed!" Amos called after me.

I spun on my heel and followed Atalyah, trying to calm my speeding heart. She led me through the courtyard to a room overlooking the house's garden. A large window let in light. There Marta stood at her upright Egyptian loom, her hands weaving the weft through the warp with the same kind of attention and grace I had seen on the faces of priests offering sacrifices to God. Each movement carried the weight of her ancestors who had completed the same stitches, the same gestures. As I drew closer, I could see that she was weaving with a dark crimson thread. Such fine wool must have cost Amos a fortune.

Underneath his rancor, his performance for friends, something had changed in the man. Why else would he be buying her such expensive materials?

"It is beautiful," I remarked. Was I speaking of the rich color or Marta herself? I tilted my head slightly and watched how the colorless light streaming in from the window glinted in her hennaed hair.

Marta smiled warmly. "It is byssus linen from Egypt. Feel how thick it is." She inclined her head toward the top of her loom where the cloth, the start of a cloak, was already complete.

I pinched the cloth and thought of how useful such a cloak would have been during my travels in Galilee. Yeshua and I could have spread it over us at night as protection against both the insects and the cold.

The thought of him sleeping beside me made me sigh. Time spent apart from my husband had the disconcerting effect of making him more real. I could feel the warmth of his body more sharply when I perceived the wound of absence. I turned away from Marta so she would not glimpse my turmoil.

"It is only the second time I have made such a cloak," she remarked placidly. I could not tell if she had noticed my upset.

"Yes," I struggled to keep my voice even. "It is an unusual loom."

"See, I have arranged another set of warp threads behind this first one?" She showed me the second layer hanging behind her work, each thread weighted down on the floor by a small stone. "The weft passes through one shed and then I work it through to the other side. The finished cloak will be without a seam."

"A seamless cloak! Mother would be proud." I turned back to Marta, smiling weakly. "I, on the other hand, have nothing to show for her years spent teaching me how to spin my thread and weave simple garments."

I had spent so much time listening to men that I had forgotten my sisters, my mothers, my friends. The lessons they had whispered to me over cooking fires, oil presses, and looms were lost. And now I was a woman without any useful knowledge; a boat without a sail on a stormy sea.

"Don't be foolish, Miriam." Marta had dropped her work, her hands now planted on her wide hips. She pursed her lips, eyebrows raised. I remembered this look always accompanied a chastisement when I was younger and instinctively bowed my head in shame.

"No! None of that simpering sadness. It does no one any good! Look up!" Marta grabbed my hand and tilted my chin up with her finger. Our faces were so close that I could taste the sweetness of her breath. "You are wiser than us all, Miriam, although we taunted you for it when we were younger. What has happened to make you doubt yourself?"

I buried my head in her shoulder, choking back my despair.

"Come now! Let it out!" Marta commanded me loudly in the voice of a woman who has had experience with young children.

The tears began to flow. My body shuddered.

"Good," Marta said. "If you keep the tears inside, it will make you sick."

She held me for a long time. I cried until my throat was dry, until my lips cracked, and my cheeks burned with salt. The dye in her shawl had stained her tunic when I finally pulled away from her shoulder, but she didn't seem to care.

She led me to a couch in front of the big window. A breeze carried the sweet smell of wet dirt up from the garden. Somewhere inside the winter, spring was gathering force, awakening the seeds hidden below. "Listen, Miriam. I believe you love your husband and he loves you. What sorrow separates the two of you?"

Without speaking, my hands cupped my empty womb through the heavy folds of my skirts.

"Ah!" Marta nodded knowingly. "I thought so. I felt it when I saw you last. You have carried a child."

"He died. He came too early."

"So it happens. Every day a woman loses a child. Or loses her own life giving birth." Marta stared deeply into my eyes. The dark reserves I perceived behind her gaze frightened me. "Men do not understand what a heavy burden it is to carry a life. To lose a life. That is why they must sacrifice goats and offer them to God. They offer blood up to God, but they do not know what it's like to bleed!"

"You have two children!" I protested. "You have brought two living sons into this world!"

Marta grabbed my hands and brought them to the curve of her own womb. "Do you think I do not know your pain!" She pressed my palms into her, and I could feel her warmth, the power that a woman carries low in her belly—not quite fire, not quite fever. A heat that can be used to create life or to burn it all down.

"You have lost children?" I asked.

"Oh, Miriam. Do you still think of me as a silly woman? Do you still scorn those who spend their time cooking and caring for children?"

"No!" I insisted fiercely, thinking of my friends. The friends I had been too dazed and mournful to bid farewell to.

Adah. Salome. Yohanna. Atarah. Ivah. When would I see them again?

Marta nodded and hugged me to her once more. "Miriam, I know your pain. This past spring I too felt a quickening in my womb. Although I was told by the midwife that I would never bear again after the long labor of my last son. It was a miracle."

"What?" I was dumbfounded.

Marta nodded. She pressed her hand over mine against my womb. "I conceived again. And then late in the summer I lost the child."

"I . . ." I could not speak.

"We were apart. But we are always together, you and I. Trust me when I say that you are blessed, Sister. You are blessed among women." Marta stood and lifted me up with her. The sun had finally broken free and the light that reached us carried a golden warmth. "All women are both blessed and cursed. And the child you carried and lost is also blessed. Worry not. Somewhere beyond this world our mother carries him. As she will one day carry us both."

• • •

The next morning when I woke, I looked down to see that I had bled through my linen shift. But for the first time since my miscarriage, I did not resent my blood. I took the stained cloth out into the fields and buried it in the fresh mud.

I resolved to tell no one and to not go into isolation. I would not travel to the mikvah to clean myself in the water. I looked up at the pink sky and spoke softly, feeling my voice carried upward by the first morning insects, dew glinting on their tiny, metallic wings. "Here is my blood. My body. My seed. My womb is never empty. It carries the world."

Forty-Four

"Go to him!" Lazaros suggested as he helped me carry the week's grain back from the market. "You have been home long enough."

"No." My reply was curt. Final.

"At least send him word," Lazaros needled me. "Why are you so hardheaded, Miriam?"

I did not answer, squinting against the morning light.

But he was right. I should have left then, fortified by my sister's wisdom. Yeshua and I had spent enough time apart to feel the sting of absence. Our reunion would have been sweet.

I can see now what might have been: I would have walked barefoot on my travel-toughened soles to Yeshua. I would have surprised the men eating old bread around a smoky fire.

"Don't you see?" I would say to him when I arrived after nightfall. "You have already lost the kingdom! The kingdom was the river, where we lived with the trees and the plants and the beasts. The kingdom was the children sitting in your lap as you told stories to toothless grandmothers. The kingdom was men and women washing side by side in the water after a night of lovemaking."

Every night, as his absence twisted my stomach tighter, I would tell myself that I must remain strong. I must not be the first to break. I would not grovel on the ground like Ester, asking for his forgiveness.

Oh, we were both so young and so proud. I imagine him then, sleeping with a stone for his pillow high in the rocky hills, resenting my absence, waiting for *me* to return to him.

I spent most of my time with Marta and her sons, helping with the cooking and weaving. Kernan, nine, was already too old to enjoy spending time with the women. A rigid sense of propriety gave a pained expression to his round face.

"Do you have an errand for me, Mother?" he would wheedle, looking for some reason to run off and find his friends.

"Don't bother me, Kernan." She would shoo him away. "I don't need you underfoot."

Her younger son, Samuel, barely four, was mischievous. He pulled my hair, dropped beetles into our laps. The children seemed to love their father as much as they did their mother, jumping up with joy when he arrived home, his hands behind his back hiding some treat or toy for them.

And Marta did not seem unhappy.

Could men change? Could a marriage that had begun so badly turn into something, if not passionate, at least livable? I hesitated to ask Marta how all this had happened. Why remind her of a time when she had been so very unhappy?

So the days passed. Long days spent weaving with Marta, caring for the children, walking back and forth across Bethany, paying visits to the other wealthy wives that Marta called her friends. Serayah still treated me like a little girl, barely addressing me at all. Tirzah offered to bathe my hair in scented oils and massaged my scalp, explaining that a woman who did not care for her hair lost her power. I'm not sure if the oils strengthened my hair or if it was her strong, plump hands holding my neck, pressing the fragile skin at my temples, telling my body that I could relax.

And there was young Naamah, just sixteen and married to Amos's nephew Laban, who was so beautiful with her thick dark lashes and big eyes that I thought she must be unreal, her face painted on by a Roman idolater fashioning a sculpture of a goddess. But when she opened her mouth and revealed a laugh like a goat's cry, I realized she *was* real.

Naamah welcomed us into her private mikvah where we took a leisurely bath. Marta and Naamah exchanged gossip while I stared at the tiled bottom, the green-and-blue pattern reminding me of the ornate floors in Yohannah's house. I let my hands drift in and out of the water, watching as each drop pulled something away from my hand and went back to join the water. I waded into the pool up to my waist, my shift billowing out around me, and stood still, letting the thin, wet breeze of early spring tickle across my parted lips.

After I had been home almost a month Marta told me she would be traveling with Amos up to Sephoris. "He has business, and I could do with a change in scenery. We won't be gone longer than a few days. Shall I get you something pretty? A bracelet? Some perfume?" She flicked her hand to her servant girl to show which clothes to pack in her traveling trunk.

I shook my head, wishing her safe travels. Inwardly I despaired. Time spent with my father had grown tense. Our unspoken words hummed as loudly as locusts whirring in the air. *Where was Yeshua? How long would I stay in Bethany? What of the child he had heard I was carrying?* Thus when Lazaros asked me to accompany him into Yerusalem, I jumped at the offer.

The walk to the city felt short after all my travels. Even the trees on the Mount of Olives seemed changed. Their twisted branches were hardly able to hold onto a handful of leaves. The city was baked into a tight, concentrated clamor of smoke and noise that pulsed on the skin of the land like a boil, and people squeezed past each other on the dusty road that led up to the gate.

"What lies within this city that drives men mad?" I mused to myself. "It cannot *just* be our Lord's word."

"It is that very question that drives men inside *and* drives them mad." Lazaros surprised me by answering. "The only secret is that there is *no* secret."

"When did you become so wise?" I said, laughing and slipping my arm through his elbow. He led me through the Fountain Gate, pushing past an entire family riding a beleaguered donkey. The beast's legs were bowing outward and his snout was flecked with pink spittle. I let my free hand graze his soft breast.

Blessed are the poor in spirit for theirs is the kingdom of heaven.

Lazaros wanted to visit his favorite barber on the far side of the city. The man's shop was open to the street with a porch that shielded his customers from the sun. I laughed when Lazaros called for Boaz, and a short, portly man without a hair on his head appeared.

"How are *you* the barber?"

Boaz laughed, patting his ample belly. "I have no hair now! But it is only so I can service my customers' vanity rather than my own."

I watched as my tall brother perched on a low stool and bent his head back. Boaz massaged his temples and began his work, every flourish of his plump hands creating an aura of ritual. I watched transfixed as he washed and oiled Lazaros's beard then unsheathed a razor and began to carefully remove my brother's stubble.

I could hear the goats and lambs, not far away in the temple's inner chamber, screaming as a less forgiving knife grazed their own throats.

I bid Lazaros goodbye, telling him to find me in the Upper Market when he was done. I wandered off, clutching the small satchel of my own money tied safely under the folds of my skirt. There was nothing I needed. Nothing that could be purchased at least. But I still let my eyes linger on displays of beautiful cloths in the Wool Weavers Square: bolts of vermillion with streaks of red so bold they looked like blood.

Why do we make markets? I mused. *Why do we erect buildings and homes that can crumble and burn? We would be safer sleeping underneath the sky's heavenly ceiling that cannot crumble.*

Climbing up the narrow-stepped streets I entered into another square and noticed that on an uncovered table a reedy old man with hair as yellow as his crooked teeth was setting out a collection of scrolls. Some he had purposely unfurled so that when I looked more closely, I could see the spidery inkings that were human words. My fingers brushed over the curls and dashes, and I wondered what I was touching.

Bird? Man? City? The Word of God?

"You can read Greek?" the man asked curiously.

I shook my head, fixing a haughty, cold expression on my face to hide my shame.

"These are in Aramaic . . ." He gestured toward a pile of scrolls at the far end of the table. "A collection of commentary from the Qumran Essenes."

"I cannot read at all," I admitted. "But the words are beautiful to behold."

"More beautiful when they come from a woman's mouth." He fixed me with icy blue eyes. "The written word is a dead thing. It cannot change to suit the times. A blessing that is written down very quickly becomes a curse."

A chill went through me. I glanced back down at the Greek scroll.

It was at that moment that I heard Yeshua's name and turned around, surprised.

A group of well-dressed young men were crowded at the other end of the square. One of them, wearing a pale yellow cloak, explained loudly, "They say there were thousands gathered and they didn't have more than five barley loaves and a handful of dried fish. But when they passed the baskets around, *everyone* was fed."

"I'm confused, Nathan," another man butted in. "How did this Yeshua feed them? What are you saying?"

"By the power of God he *multiplied* the food," the man called Nathan answered.

"These are children's stories," a slender man responded, leaning against the stone wall behind them, his arms crossed over his chest. "I have heard similar fictions. Some say he even turned water to wine at his own wedding!"

"His own wedding?" Nathan asked in disbelief. "I thought he only consorted with whores!"

"The whores are not sinful enough for his bed I heard," a man insisted. "I assure you, Rabbi Yeshua *is* married. But it is even worse, his wife is the Lady Miriam, the daughter of Nicodemus."

"Oh! Miriam of the seven devils! I've heard of *her* . . ." The slender man laughed cruelly. "I'm not surprised that a charlatan like Yeshua has chosen her for his consort."

I recognized one of the men as Lazaros's old friend Melech. He was no longer pudgy, hardly carrying any meat on his bones, but his face was small and boyish, just as I remembered.

"If it is true that Yeshua can raise a boy from his grave, then I don't care that he's mad," the slender man pushed back. "Have you met the man? Is it true that he calls himself the Messiah?"

"He says more than that," Melech insisted. "I have it from a friend who recently returned from Yericho that he calls himself the Son of God and that he is here to fulfill the prophecies. He insists the end of days is upon us. The Romans will soon be vanquished and our city returned to its rightful protectors."

"The Messiah? What nonsense! He would never claim such a thing," I clapped my hand over my mouth as soon as I had spoken, but the damage was done. The hood I had pulled up over my hair fell back from my face as the men turned to see who had spoken.

Melech blushed as he recognized me. "Miriam?"

"Yes, you fool," I said, letting all the anger flood through me. I strode up to the men and stuck my finger into Melech's chest. "Be careful who you insult. Those who can perform miracles can perform curses as well."

Melech shivered under my touch. Under the oil that he had smoothed into his hair, he smelled afraid. "Get the whore off of me!" he exclaimed.

Nathan tried to wrench me away, twisting my arm badly, but I dug my heels into the stone cobbles beneath me.

"My husband raises men from their graves. But who are you to think he can't also *put* them in their graves," I declared imperiously. "You play a dangerous game when you besmirch his name and mine."

"You play a dangerous game when you dare to provoke men like us," said the slender man.

"Well said, Adalya," Nathan snickered. "And where's your husband now?"

Melech seemed unnerved. Perhaps it was because he remembered the stories my brother had told. The strange spells of my youth. Hanan's story about the vultures. "Friends. Let us leave her be." Melech murmured, shivering.

"I'll leave her be after I've asked her to heal me," the man called Adalya laughed, grabbing at his crotch. "I've got a demon in me. Can you get it out?"

He grabbed my free hand and tried to shove it down his pants.

"Whore!" laughed Adalya, as I struggled to pull away.

I fell backward onto the hard cobbles. The men loomed over me.

The seller of scrolls watched. His mouth was a straight line, impassive. His hand lay flat on the table.

"If this Yeshua is really the Son of God, he will find a way to save her, won't he?" Adalya spat.

"It's a pity she's such a beauty," said Melech. "I wonder if her husband would still put up with her impertinence if she no longer had that pretty face." He pulled a short silver knife from under his robes. It glowed white in the midday sun. Nathan shoved him forward and the knife flashed.

There it was. Monstrosity. These boys, barely men, revealing what I had always known lurked behind their smooth, handsome faces. The cold, flayed face of violence.

"Miriam! Miriam! What's going on?" Lazaros was pushing through the crowd, tussling with Nathan and shoving him to the ground. He pulled me into his arms, away from the men.

"Lazaros, good friend," Melech tried. "Forgive us a little play. Your sister is badly behaved."

"Lazaros!" I cried, surprised by my own shock, my own meekness when confronted with violence.

Lazaros's beard was freshly clipped, his hair short and combed, but he was covered in dust and there was a scrape reddening across his left cheek.

"Miriam." He gripped my elbow. I could feel the intensity of his emotions vibrating through him. "What did these men do to you?"

"Do to *us*?" Adalya exclaimed. "*She* is the danger. You should take your whore sister for an exorcism."

I glared back at them, narrowing my eyes.

"They are fools. I am fine. Let us leave them!" I insisted. I had felt an immense power in me, the power to kill the men harming me, but I had been incapable of using it. Why couldn't I protect myself? *Am I unable to do harm? Even to those who mean me ill? Must I only ever heal?*

I watched as my brother squared his jaw and narrowed his eyes menacingly. "If I hear that you have touched any other woman in Yerusalem, I will make you pay," Lazaros declared. "And I am not as kind as my sister."

And, miraculously, the men were scared of my little brother. Some combination of his authority and his impressive height made them exchange looks and turn away, hurrying out of the market. Melech looked back once, grimacing, his eyes watery with regret. Did he want to apologize to Lazaros? It was no use.

"Lazaros!" I cried. I needed to assure myself that this was indeed my brother. Thus, I pinched his arm, hard.

"Ow! Stop! What?" His expression softened. "Heavens, Miriam! Are you whole? Did they touch you?"

"They did not violate me," I replied, looking my brother squarely in the eye. "But I believe I have you to thank for that."

"Must you always get into trouble? Let us go home before you manage to enrage the Romans, too. I have had enough brawling for one day."

As he pulled me out of the square, I looked back to where the men had stood and saw the small splotches of blood that had dripped from Nathan's knife.

"Lazaros . . ." I said, examining him and the torn sleeve of his tunic. "Did he cut you? Have you been hurt?"

"A scratch, nothing deep," he assured me as he brushed the scrape on his cheek. "Come on, Miriam. I would not be caught in the city after dark with such vile men on the loose."

We were silent the whole way out of the city. But once we were ascending the mount toward Bethany my breath came easily again. The dusk was peachy and slow. A light breeze disorganized the olive tree leaves above us as we finally reached the outskirts of town.

The city was bad for me. The stench, the noise, the chaos drowned out my intuition. But here, entering back into nature, I was returned to myself by the whispering of the trees. Yes, there were still voices. Of birds, leaves, mice, insects. But these voices carried neither anger nor abjection. They sang the blue song of the shadows merging with the sky.

Yeshua, I thought, imagining the roots of the olive trees stretching out many miles until they hovered below the soles of my husband's feet. I wanted to believe we were connected by the woody veins that held the earth together and sprang forth abundantly every spring, showing us that we were not wrong when we sensed that life did not end with death. Instead, it sank back into the dirt, grew invisibly, and returned after a season.

The dancing never stops, I realized. *It just goes underground.*

"What were they saying that provoked you?" Lazaros asked at last, breaking my reverie.

"They were telling lies about Yeshua," I admitted. "They say he calls himself the Son of God. That he claims he has come according to the prophets."

Lazaros's lips parted as if to speak.

"What?" I asked stupidly. "What are you keeping from me?"

He was a little boy again, his blush appearing purple in the watery light of dusk. "Enosh and Achim have recently come from Galilee and they said the same thing . . ." His voice was low, as if he did not want the trees to overhear.

"What?" I snapped. "Speak up!"

Lazaros flinched. "They tell me that Yeshua makes strange claims! He calls himself the Son of man . . . and my friends say his disciples swear by the signs. One of them told Enosh he saw Yeshua walk across the stormy waters of the sea."

Ice threaded through my veins. "It cannot be," I shook my head. "He would not do such things for show."

"He might if he was parted from you," Lazaros suggested.

"What are you talking about?" I asked hesitantly.

Lazaros stopped, taking my hand, pressing it between his big palms. "You are part of the same water, the same stream. I am not surprised he is doing such strange things without your guidance."

"Hold your tongue, Lazaros. I am angry and tired."

"I will hold my tongue if you promise not to hold *yours*. Speak up, Miriam! Claim your spot beside Yeshua. You are his equal in wisdom. I am sure of it." He gripped my hand so tightly that I winced.

"Lazaros, let's go home please," I begged him.

He did not release me. There was a faint heat his hands, radiating into my palms insistently.

"Miriam," he said once more. "Promise me you will send word to Yeshua?"

"I promise," I said.

Lazaros finally smiled, releasing his hold on me. We were silent for the rest of the walk home.

But I did not send for Yeshua that night. Or the next day.

And by then it was already too late.

Forty-Five

Marta invited me for supper, but when I arrived at her home she was busy overseeing the men's meal. Atalyah led me to a small room and handed me a silk-covered pillow. I curled up on it, peering out through the window. Once she was done with her wifely duties, Marta came to sit with me. She had her smallest son, Samuel, on her lap.

"Girl!" she scolded Atalyah. "It is as dark as a tomb in here! Bring us another lamp and some food before it gets cold."

Atalyah blushed. "Yes. I'm sorry, mistress."

"Samuel! Can you show your Aunt Miriam that you are grown up?" She smoothed back his downy black curls.

"Miriam!" he cooed sleepily.

I reached out to take the boy from his mother. Marta gladly handed him over. He was soft and heavy against my breast. The top of his head smelled like a patch of grass just after a rainstorm. His hand clenched around a long strand of my hair that he put it into his mouth, sucking.

"Samuel! Stop that disgusting behavior!" Marta exclaimed.

"It's fine . . . " I rocked him back and forth and eventually he lost interest in my hair.

"So I should tell you . . ." Marta said hesitantly, and I knew she was pained by whatever she was about to share.

"Yes?"

Samuel's head nestled against my heart. I rubbed the back of his neck absentmindedly.

"It is well-known in Galilee that Herod believes Yeshua is the return of Yochanan. Herod believes Yeshua is a danger to his rule." She bowed her head while she spoke.

"This is old news," I replied.

"No. Open your ears, Sister!" Marta snapped. "Herod has been angry in the past. But he means to act now. It is said he has sent his conternubias out to find Yeshua. And that your husband and his men spend most of their time in hiding. There is real danger now."

"In hiding?" I whispered. "Where?"

"It's said he's gone far north up into Gerasene."

I couldn't speak. I felt sick all of a sudden.

Atalyah arrived with two steaming bowls of vegetables. But the smell of spiced food was unappetizing.

"Samuel!" Marta cried as he lunged forward, sticking his hands into my bowl.

"It's all right," I explained. "I'm not hungry." I pulled the boy back into my lap, letting him wipe his hands on my skirt.

"He's calling himself the Son of God, Miriam." Marta chewed thoughtfully. "He did not seem a zealot when I met him last. At worst he seemed a drunkard. A child. At best a rabbi. But not a zealot . . . It strikes me as strange."

"It strikes me as gossip," I said angrily. "I don't believe a word of it."

"And yet you are here. Eating with me and my son and not with him." Marta's words were harsh, but her eyes were soft. "You were so happy at your wedding. I've never seen two people with more love between them. What has changed?"

"I love him still," I insisted. "I love him more now than I did on the day we wed."

"Then why are you here?" Marta asked.

• • •

It was a moonless night and the humidity gave the air an opaque quality that obscured the edges of the buildings and the tops of the trees. I was surprised when, having left Marta's, I rounded a corner to see Yosseph emerging through the haze. His hair was carefully combed and his eyes were bright as stones polished by the river.

"Miriam!" He recognized me before I had time to turn and hide. "What are you doing here?"

He looked older. His cheeks were sharp and he had grown a short beard. There was none of the boyish prettiness left in his features. His good looks had become severe.

"I was leaving my sister's," I explained flatly, knowing it was not an adequate explanation.

"Do you come with your husband?" he asked. "I am surprised I did not hear of his arrival. He is all anyone can talk of these days."

"I come alone," I whispered, noticing that Yosseph was holding, in his hands, the stiff black cap that signaled that he was now a member of the Sanhedrin. Around his shoulders was a striped shawl.

I couldn't help but imagine some ghost of myself standing beside him, married, holding two young children in my arms.

What if I had stayed in Bethany?

"Alone?" he nodded. "When did you arrive?"

"I must be going." I tried to brush past him, lowering my head so he wouldn't see the burning blush on my cheeks.

"Miriam!" He reached out and caught my arm. I stopped, looking up at him, knowing he would witness my mixture of sorrow and shame.

"What?"

"It is . . ." His words faltered.

"Yosseph," I said firmly. "I know you must hate me. But I cannot hold that hate tonight. Please let me go."

I turned and fled into the darkness, toward home.

Why do I feel so guilty? I thought as I neared the front gate, choking back tears. *Who do I feel that I have betrayed Yosseph? Yeshua? Myself?*

As I walked through the front door, I realized something was amiss. The dining room was empty, covered with untouched food that had long gone cold.

"Father?" I called anxiously.

Everyone was crowded in the hall: my father's peers from the Sanhedrin, his students, and Naomi, a servant woman reputed for her healing charms. Squat Beltis was pressed up against the wall, murmuring frantically in her mother tongue.

"Let me through!" I said, pushing past the swarm of people.

My father stood, blocking the door to Lazaros's room, his face ashen.

"Father!" I reached him. "What is it?"

"Miriam!" he cried. "It is your brother! He has fallen ill. I came home for dinner and he had collapsed in the courtyard. I could not rouse him . . ."

Oh. A shiver of foresight ran from the crown of my head down to my toes.

I pushed my way through those assembled, into my brother's bedroom.

The room was thick with incense smoke, and a lamp set on the chest at the foot of his bed sent out a circle of strangely dirty light. I could taste disease in the air.

My brother looked like a little boy again. His face was red and sweaty, and his fists clutched at the blankets. He was too tall for his bed, his feet hanging off the end. Rabbi Achan knelt at Lazaros's side, reciting prayers with his palms upraised.

"Get out of the way," I demanded.

"Miriam!" my father called from the door. "I beseech you! Let Achan finish his prayers."

But I did not listen and the rabbi got up wearily. "It is no use, Nicodemus. He is close to death."

"No!"

It could not be so. Lazaros had been well earlier. I would swear by it. My brother. My closest friend. My companion on the road to the river. We were both going to have families. Many children. We would sit together in our old age telling our grandchildren stories about our mother, our father, our childhood playing in the fields outside of Bethany.

I knelt down next to the bed, reaching out to touch his face, feeling the heat before I even made contact with his skin. He was on fire. His eyelashes fluttered, revealing that the whites of his eyes had darkened into a dirty yellow.

The smell was unmistakable. "He has a corruption of the blood," I said urgently. "How was he infected? Where did the poison enter?"

"Nothing but a scrape," Lazaros murmured with a thick tongue. I was the only one who could hear him amidst the clamor of conversations in the hallway.

My heart skipped a beat. I felt dizzy and my vision narrowed. My hands moved without volition, hovering over his neck, his chest, and his arms, searching for the source of the heat that was turning my brother to dust.

The scuffle in the city. I had thought it was just a scratch on his cheek. But there had been a struggle I had not seen properly. A knife. What had I missed?

I felt the heat radiating from his upper thigh. The heat of rot. I pulled up his shift.

The men at the door, including my father, let out a cry of shock.

"She is desecrating him! Get her off him!" my father's youngest student yelled.

Lazaros was right. It was *only* a scrape, hardly deep enough to merit a bandage. But it was deep enough. And Nathan's blade must have carried some impurity. The wound was swollen and putrid. A red finger of corruption led from the cut up into his groin.

"Oh . . ." The breath went out of me.

My brother, my brother. Why did I assume you would always be at my side? Always healthy and happy and whole.

"Work your magic on him!" one of the older rabbis urged. "Do what your husband is said to do!"

But I was chilled to my marrow. I laid my hands on my brother's chest and tried to summon the heat. A deep intuition rose in me. I remembered the boy outside of Nain, the boy who Yeshua had raised from mortal illness despite my protests. A blue pulse of light radiated from behind the burning body of my brother. He had already been claimed. Death had come for Lazaros.

"Why!" I cried aloud. "Why is this his time?"

I received no answer. No answer but a corona of blue around my brother, so pure and bright it could only come from inside a flash of lightning or a star.

I slapped my hands against my thighs and squeezed my eyes shut, struggling to summon the momentum of the river, the tenacity of tree roots beneath cobbled streets.

No. I must heal him.

But I could not heal my brother. Just as I could not heal my mother.

A deep voice, neither male nor female, reverberated inside my mind. *Everyone has their season. His season here is done. You cannot understand a story longer than this short life. Trust that death is wiser than you. Trust death when it claims a life.*

I clutched my brother, trying to summon what I knew would not come. I could not heal death. I could not go against the rightful tides of nature, even when they were terrible, even when they seemed wrong.

Lazaros struggled for another hour or so, trembling so hard that I could not still him even when I clutched him to my breast.

His death reminded me of the births I had witnessed. He was wracked with the same contractions that bring a soul into the world.

I suddenly recalled the words of Kemat, who long ago had told me that death was much like birth in that it is just as hard. Watching Lazaros, I now understood—our entrances and exits were not so different after all.

In the early morning hours, two weeks before Pesach, my brother Lazaros died.

Someone was howling like a hurt animal, a sound that swelled and rose and swelled until I thought it might burst the walls of our home. My father mourned for his son.

I was too stunned to cry or even speak. I held Lazaros for a long time afterward. I could feel him making that strange transition from flesh to wood to stone. His spirit had departed, but instead of making him lighter, it had left his body heavier.

I stood up at last and felt as if my own soul had vanished. I went outside into the garden. Overnight, winter had ended. The grass was green again. The flowers were forming in their buds. The dirt between my toes was wet and warm. Spring had arrived.

"No!" I wailed, sinking to my knees, trying to push the violets back into the ground, the green back into cold seeds. "No!"

Keep the spring from arriving. Let this season never come—if only to give me one more day with him! Give me back my brother!

• • •

Disbelief is always the beginning of grief. A loud vibration tolled in my ears, keeping me from hearing anything at all.

My fingers felt thick as Marta and I washed Lazaros's body. I sponged away the blood and puss from his leg, smoothed his freshly cut hair, and massaged his feet, which had turned heavy and purple right before his death. His legs were stiffening. My father brought us the proper oils: myrrh and aloe.

Was this why it was customary to wash the body? Not for the lost one's sake. But for ours. To teach our hands about death because our minds refused to believe in it. Every touch of my brother's cold hard flesh told us of our loss, made the knowledge of it physical and intimate.

We worked the oil into his elbows, his knees, and the soft skin under his chin. I smoothed aloe into the planes of his face, seeing my own features in his.

Brother. Wake up and I will tell you a story. I know that you are playing. I know that you are really asleep.

I wept. Marta wept. When I tried to swallow the tears back, my sister shook her head.

"No. You must weep for him, Miriam. Weep now, not later. It will hurt to hold it in."

The room filled so completely with incense smoke that we were suspended in a silvery ocean, our brother the boat that had kept us afloat.

Soon he smelled like freshly tilled earth, intimate furrows of dirt mixing with rain and pollen and seeds. He smelled like spices thrown on the fire that puff up their perfumes for a second before turning to ash. His lips turned gray but his face was smooth, as if he were sleeping.

My father, shaking so badly I was afraid that he too had a fever, tied Lazaros's hands and his feet with strips of linen. Then, with shaking hands, he drew the veil over his son's face, murmuring the necessary prayers as we rolled Lazaros from his soiled bedclothes onto his shroud. In so doing, he chanted, "Yitgadal v'yitkadash sh'mei raba b'alma di-v'ra chirutei, v'yamlich malchutei b'chayeichon uvyomeichon uvchayei d'chol beit yudeah, ba'agala uvizman kariv, v'im'ru: 'Amen.'" (Glorified and sanctified be God's great name throughout the world, which he has created according to his will. May he establish his kingdom in your lifetime and during your days, and within the life of the entire House of Yudeah, speedily and soon; and say, Amen.)

Again and again, he chanted, "May he establish his kingdom during your lifetime."

Men came in to help us move Lazaros's body onto an open litter they would carry to the rock-hewn tombs on the far edge of our land. Yosseph was among the men, but he would not meet my eye. He lifted one corner of the bier up onto his shoulders, using his free hand to squeeze my father's arm in condolence as they edged through the narrow doorway and headed into the open air. Achim and Enosh were there to lift up the body of their oldest friend, their faces squeezed and distorted by the tears they refused to release.

"Why couldn't I heal him?" I cried to my father, my own tears making my voice rasp. "Why?"

Did he look at me with anger? With disappointment? He grimaced, turning from me. "Don't ask me such things," he finally muttered.

Is this the kingdom you spoke of, Yeshua? I asked. *Is this the kingdom? How can it be the kingdom when it does not include Lazaros?*

Marta and I walked in front of the litter. The last time I had done such a thing I'd been a young girl confused by the performance of grief—the women kneeling in the dirt and taking up handfuls of dust that they rubbed on their faces and worked into their scalps.

But as the howling began again, I now understood. One young girl, wailing and trailing alongside the procession, caught sight of the litter and began to scratch at the front of her shift until it ripped open.

Who was Lazaros to this girl? I wondered. I had wasted so much time! I should have talked to him about all manner of things.

And I never would again.

The howl rose in my throat.

We knelt at the tomb. We rubbed the dust into our mouths so that when we swallowed, we could taste what Lazaros was slowly becoming. We had to take the dust and press it into our skin so that we remembered how close we always were to the dead. Every time our bare feet sank into the soil we were connecting with the layered, mixed remains of all the trees, flowers, brothers, mothers, and lovers that had once worked this land from above, planted their hands in the dirt, and said: "All go to the same place; all come from dust, and to dust all return."

I was choking on my own breath, gripping Marta's shoulder to stay upright.

I could heal birthing women. Cripples. Possessed people. But I could not heal my mother. And I could not heal my brother.

All else fell away. Why live? Why heal if I could not save my loved ones!

Oh God oh God oh God!

The men placed him on the farthest shelf in the tomb. The same one that my mother had lain on all those years before. I had been too young to consider the realities of rot and decay. The shelf was clean and bare now as if it had never housed another body.

They disappear from me. I cannot even remember her face. How soon until Lazaros disappears? Until he is only a name?

"Marta," I whispered, surprised by how strained my voice sounded. "Who removed mother after a year? Did father do it alone?"

Marta had a strangely stoic expression on her face as she watched the strongest men roll a boulder to close up the tomb's low, narrow entrance. "No. Father would have left her in there forever," she answered. "I did it."

She tilted her head, staring at me, her mouth turning down. The tears had streaked black lines of kohl on her cheek. She looked fearsome, powerful. "She was nothing but bones by then. Impossibly light. I picked up the shroud and cradled it. I remember thinking it was not much different than holding a small child."

• • •

Did time pass? Did we eat and sit together? Did people come to mourn with us?

All I remember is the wailing. My own; my body rocked by an emotion bigger than grief. Oceanic. I could hardly stand.

And my father wept, too. Every time I saw his face slick with tears it would loosen some part of me I thought did not exist. Oh . . . oh . . . oh! And I would be on my knees, hiding my face in my hands and pulling at my scalp, as if by tearing out my hair I could tear out the knowledge that my brother was dead.

Outside, the spring heat was transforming him into something else. Something other than my brother.

No. It wasn't grief, I finally realized. It was terror.

What comes next? What can possibly come after this? I trembled at the thought. I no longer understood the world.

Yet birdsong entered the house of mourning. These keen, questioning melodies drove into me the understanding that such music no longer had any attachment to human reason or purpose. The earth's purpose was bigger. Vaster and more terrible than I could possibly understand.

I did not eat. Or speak.

And then, on the third day, Yeshua arrived.

Forty-Six

He was here. I was sure of it.

The knowledge came from inside of me. A pressure between my eyes. The flip of my stomach. It wrenched me from my grief.

As I burst out of the front door into open air, I startled to hear a sharp scream greet me. Wheeling around, I caught sight of a hawk curving out of sight behind the roof of our house. My mind grew sharp and clear as it watched the tip of the bird's wing disappear.

But there was no more time to prepare. They arrived immediately, Marta leading the group, her strong, heavy strides kicking up yellow dust. Atalyah hurried to keep up, glancing over her hunched shoulder.

Yeshua had not come alone. He came with the sun itself, bright and insistent as sound. I could feel it reverberating in my skull, in the rhythms of my body.

He was flanked by Shimon and Andreas, with the rest following close behind: Mattiyahu, Philip, Yudas, the Ben-Zebedee brothers, Thoma, some young men I did not recognize and, much to my surprise, his brother Yakov.

Oh, he was familiar as sunlight on my skin, as morning birdsong. Yes, his hair and beard were longer. His skin was dark with sun. But he was the same wild man I had seen down on all fours, letting children ride on his shoulders. And there were tears brimming from his eyes. Eyes that were so red I knew that he had been weeping for days.

"Miriam!" His voice was thick with anguish. He ran to me immediately, crushing me in his strong, familiar arms. His tears wet my hair and I could feel him shaking. I breathed deeply his smell: river water and split cedar. My body began to soften. Why had I left him? Why had I ever been angry?

"Yeshua . . ." I breathed into his chest. "It happened so fast. And I couldn't do anything. I couldn't heal him."

He gripped me tight, pressing his hand into my back. "Miriam. I am here. I am here."

What I would give to seek solace in the arms of my husband one more time. How many days had I woken with the longing to take my grief to the temple of his body? His touch did not erase the loss of Lazaros. It warmed the loss. Gave it color. It made it feel possible to live with my sorrow.

Marta spoke up loudly. "Come inside. We don't want to attract a crowd. Come and I will serve everyone drink and food."

She was right. We were lucky no one had yet showed up. I wondered whether Yeshua was safer near the city, where fewer people knew of him?

"Miriam. I cannot bear it!" Thoma came to me immediately when we were in the courtyard and Marta was busy sending Beltis and Apphia off with directions. Always pale, he was grayer still. "I did not bid him farewell the last time I saw him."

"I . . ." I could not speak. I looked for Yeshua beside me. He was gazing back at me with the same intensity as when we had been wed in Kanna all those years before. I wanted to draw him to me, to massage the knotted muscles in his broad shoulders. To let him touch me, too, and bring me back into myself.

Thoma looked between us and backed away, intuiting our need for privacy.

"Why did you leave, Miriam?" There was no anger or accusation in Yeshua's voice. It was all hurt. "Why did you leave me? It has been strange without you. It has felt like I am without a center . . ."

Why did I leave? To come to Bethany and bring my brother into chaos? To put him in harm's way? Was Lazaros's death my fault? I felt my body begin to clench around the realization. I was going to be sick. This would kill me.

Where was Kemat? Where was my mother? I longed for them at that moment. Kemat could take both me and Yeshua into the safety of her slender arms. She could tell us a story about our sorrow, which would heal us.

There were tides that I could not see pulling me forward and backward, seasons that required small sacrifices so that the flowers and wheat could return each year. Slowly it was arriving in great, invisible waves. The understanding that I understood nothing. That my human life was not as important as the life of all the land, the seasons of weather creating and erasing rivers and fields and hills and mountains. There would be other kingdoms we would never live to see.

The most important wisdom is the wisdom that is painful. The wisdom that almost destroys the body as it arrives.

Lazaros's life was a single note in a cascade of birdsong. One brief, piercing call that served to welcome the morning and then was gone.

A cry that was almost animal came from my throat. I reached for my neck as if to strangle the sound. But Yeshua grasped my shoulders and steadied me.

"Yeshua," I put my hand to his cheek, drawing my finger along his bearded jaw. "If only I had called for you sooner. I am ashamed that it is Marta who called for you. If you had been here, maybe we could have healed him . . ."

"I am a fool who loses all those closest to him," Yeshua murmured, closing his eyes and leaning his face into my hand.

Steadied by love, my grief expanded. I no longer tried to press it down. I let it drift past the limits of my body. Past, even, the limits of a lifetime. I felt certain, suddenly, that Lazaros's death was important for some reason I would never be able to understand.

"Yeshua. I don't think we lose anything. Everything goes back to the earth . . ." I murmured. But my words were soft and uncertain. I didn't trust myself yet.

"Miriam. I fear I will lose everything. I have dreams that we are separated by dark waters and I am calling your name . . ." He spoke so fast he almost stumbled over his words.

"Yeshua," interrupted Marta. She spoke with steadiness and grit. "You should have been with us when we laid him in the tomb."

It was not an accusation. It was a fact. Marta reminded me of my mother that last night at the tombs. She had been burned down to her wick.

She continued, solemnly, as if reciting the words of scripture. "Three days ago my brother perished. And yet Miriam has been here over a month. If you had come but four days earlier, you could have healed Lazaros. You have healed men and women all over Galilee. And yet your own family you leave to rot in the ground."

"Marta!" I rose to my feet. "Enough!"

"It is true," Yeshua was kneeling at Marta's feet, looking up at her through a screen of fresh tears. He held his hand up beseechingly. "Everything you say is true."

In my mind's eye, I could see Yeshua coming back to Nazareth to find that his father had passed. Another vision: Yeshua leaving the river only to realize he had abandoned Yochanan to his death. His whole body was contorted with grief.

"Yeshua. No!" I was crying too. "Get up. Get up!"

"I sent for you seven days ago! Before Lazaros took ill!" Marta was almost yelling now. "Without Miriam's knowledge, I sent for you! If only you had come then, my brother would not be dead!"

This news shocked me, but I found that I could only say one thing. "Peace. Let us have peace. Let us go to the tomb. Let us honor him."

I took my husband's hand and pulled him up.

"Yes," he said grimly. "I must see where he lays. I must see my brother."

"Mistress! People outside the house! Many people!" Beltis squawked from the doorway to the courtyard. "They want to see! They want to see the mistress's husband!"

There were many voices. Men shouting. Children crying out. So his reputation *had* followed him here.

"It is right," I whispered, even as Yeshua rose, pulling me up with him. "You should see the tomb."

As we walked through the olive grove behind our home, a desire rose inside of me. A rootless desire. A human desire. *Bring them all back. Bring my mother back. Bring my brother back. Bring back Kemat. Bring me my lost child!*

Do not think I have outrun this flawed hope, Leukas. I feel the blade of this desire every day. Do not think my wisdom is comfortable. It fights against my very heart.

Bring back Bethany. Bring me back my home and my sister and my father. Bring Yeshua back. Bring him back to me.

The crowd found us easily. Achim. Enosh. Lazaros's friends. People from Bethany. Pilgrims staying at the local hostels. Men from

Yerushalem. Faces I recognized. Faces I did not. We numbered twenty, then thirty, then more.

My father had built up a small pile of stones in front of the boulder that closed the entrance to the tomb. The sight of them reminded me of his absence. He must be with the Sanhedrin on the Mount of Olives. He did not know that a crowd of strangers was standing in front of his son's tomb, looking at this intimate signature of his grief. The thought made me more frantic.

Yeshua still clutched my hand. Our combined pain seemed to register in the air itself. Dust sparkled in the shadows of the olive trees. A pale blue light suffused the clearing.

Yeshua's eyes were fixed on the tomb. He did not immediately speak.

Oh, Lazaros, I thought desperately. *Give me a sign. A bird. A flower. A storm. A sign that you have not disappeared from this place.*

"Miriam . . ." Yeshua said, turning to me confidentially. His eyes were dark and wet and childlike. "Miriam, do you think we can get the stones away? Can we push away the boulder?"

"Remove the stone?" I asked in disbelief. "Why?"

"Remove the stone?" Marta repeated loudly, having overheard me. "He will stink! He has been in there *three* days. Three *hot* days, Yeshua."

"Trust me," he said. "Trust me, please."

"Yeshua. What are you trying to do?" A feeling of dread was rising in my blood.

"Be quiet! You heard him!" Lazaros's friend Achim yelled. His round face was red with a desperation so intense it was on the verge of bursting the blood vessels in his cheeks. "We must remove the stones! Trust this man!"

A team of men came forward, immediately starting to dismantle my father's hard work. Achim was trembling almost too hard to help. Enosh, Thoma, and the Ben-Zebedee brothers did the bulk of the work. Together they pushed the final boulder back from the mouth of the tomb.

There was a pain in my womb as if my flesh was tying itself in a knot. "Yeshua . . ." I suddenly knew what it was he was going to do. "Yeshua. It cannot be done. It *should not* be done."

Marta drew close to me, and I could feel her trembling. "Miriam . . . what is he doing?"

I could feel him drawing energy from me. The soles of my feet tingled with it. I could feel a wire of pain piercing up through my spine.

Yeshua wanted to heal everyone. But he did not know how to do it. And I had none of the insight I share with you now. Only the clouded intuition that it was not as straightforward as my husband thought.

"Lazaros." Yeshua spoke the name as if he was right there. "Lazaros."

I shuddered. My blood changed direction. Every rhythm in my body suddenly opposed the warmth of the sun above me, the tides of the moon that hovered just below the horizon.

"No! Yeshua!" I was suddenly mad with certainty. I grabbed his cloak. "Do not do it!"

He dropped my hand and looked at me with complete brokenness. "Miriam. We have lost our child. What if we did not have to lose it all? What if we could have him back?"

"No!" The pain in my chest was almost unbearable. To deny myself my brother! To deny the miracle! "No, Yeshua. It is impossible. It cannot be done."

As he looked at the tomb's entrance, I heard a buzzing. Thousands of bees. A sandstorm churning through a forest.

He looked back at me once. The scar on his lip gleamed white. His eyes burned with passion. Passion for me. For my brother. For every suffering person who'd ever approached him with opened hands. "You would keep your brother dead? Miriam, let me bring our brother back. Let me give us our happiness. We can be whole."

"It is bigger than Lazaros," I said, choking on my words. "We must not bring Lazaros back to life, Yeshua."

I could see his breath coming fast and shallow. "It cannot be wrong to do such a thing for love," he whispered. "It cannot be wrong."

The crowd was growing uneasy, jostling closer so that we were crowded forward, closer to the tomb and closer to each other.

Oh, they would hate me. No one would understand.

Is this my burden? I wondered, the terror of the past three days rising like water in my throat. *To never be heard? Or understood?*

Yes. Yes. At least in this life. At least until now.

"Yeshua, he has been dead three days. Do not do it." I spoke so that everyone could hear me.

"Show us the Father's will, Yeshua!" Andreas responded. "Then all who are gathered will believe you have come to fulfill the prophecies."

"He can't raise anyone from the dead! He is a charlatan," grumbled an old grandmother holding a toddler to her breast. "Let us leave the body alone!"

"Elishah raised the dead!" a young boy called. "It is in the scripture!"

The young woman I remembered from Lazaros's funeral procession was there again, her eyes red and bleary from weeping. "Could not he who opened the eyes of the blind man have kept this man from dying?"

Yeshua glanced at her and his hand twitched. "Do not cry. Please. Your tears will be tears of joy soon."

"This death *is* natural, Yeshua!" I continued under the clamor of voices. "My heart is broken but I am not so foolish as to believe this death is the end of my brother. I am sure in my heart that we will be together again someday."

"Can you do it?" Marta asked Yeshua as he gazed into the tomb. "Can it be done?"

"We must believe in the glory of God. And he will do it for us . . . I know he will," he responded. Something had come into him. Fire that knew no check, no boundary.

Marta nodded passionately and her lips trembled. "I do believe. I do."

"Do you believe in me?" Yeshua raised his voice and turned to face the whole crowd. "Do you doubt in the Son of man?"

Son of man? I was too shocked by the strange phrase. How much had changed in my absence? "Yeshua. I beg you listen to me! Do not bring my brother back!"

But it was too late. Yeshua stepped up to the tomb's dark entrance. "Lazaros, come out!"

The world hummed. The crowd held its breath. Dust paused on each particular finger of sunlight, shimmering strangely and refusing to fall back down to the ground. But nothing happened.

Let it not work, I prayed. *Let it not work.*

But Yeshua's power was different from mine. It was a fire sparking in a dry wood . . . a heart opening and opening until it burst and could no longer hold anything at all . . . the sunlight that shines and shines until it bakes a land into desert. He needed my slow darkness, my understanding that the new moon was just as powerful as the sunrise. But I was stupefied by grief.

A pale shape stirred among the shadows.

The hawk again. Screaming relentlessly.

"Lazaros!" Yeshua called out and this time he spoke with surprise.

"Ahhhh!!!" Marta screamed and swooned, grasping at me so that I almost fell with her, pulled down by her sweaty hands.

He was still wrapped in his burial shroud, stumbling because his feet were bound together.

"Lazaros!" Yeshua cried out. He seemed more shocked than all of us. "Let us help him! Someone help me get off his graveclothes!"

Shimon and Yakov ran forward.

But what lay underneath the cloth? Lazaros had been rotting for three days.

They caught him in their arms and worked to untie his hands and feet and to draw away the linen blocking his face from view.

The face that they revealed belonged to my brother. My strong, handsome, living brother.

"Lazaros!" I ran to him.

How to explain it? The ecstatic, rising joy of my brother's return. The terrible knowledge of how wrong this was.

He was shaking, his hands held up to his face as if afraid it might fall off his skull.

"You see!" Yeshua's voice shook with relief and joy. "Father, I thank you that you have heard me! This for the benefit of the people standing here, that they may believe that you sent me! You have returned my brother!"

Lazaros's eyes were wide with fear. He scratched at my arms, his face distorted.

As the crowd rejoiced, he sank back down to his knees, weeping so hard that his tears wet the front of my shift.

"Brother, you are returned to us," I whispered in his ear.

"I am Lazaros," he moaned. "Lazaros."

I shivered, knowing he said this to remind himself of a name he had already left behind.

It was many hours before he could truly speak, and even then he refused to be parted from his shroud.

Forty-Seven

Lazaros. He looked the same except for a strange, indefinite quality that made his limbs appear longer, his face thinner. Something about his physicality had been fundamentally disturbed by his resurrection.

I must confess that, as I try to describe my brother to you, I have seen a black shadow flicker behind the flame of the candle between us.

Lazaros is closer to me now than he has been since he left for the Tin Islands, and that is only because I know that he is, for the second time, finally dead. His spirit is now loosed from the constraints of distance. Here he sits right beside me, and laments that his body has fallen so far from home. His bones will not go back to the ground to nourish the land of his mother and father.

Forgive an old woman's ruminations. Lazaros tells me to continue my story. He says it is time to lay it to rest . . .

• • •

By the time my father arrived home, Lazaros was seated at the table sipping wine from a large copper cup. Marta managed to corral Apphia and Beltis to prepare a meal on short notice. The men helped themselves greedily from the steaming bowls. It was warm enough that we all crowded into the courtyard under a sky stippled with stars.

Of course, my father had already heard the news in Yerusalem. As soon as Yeshua had called Lazaros out of the tomb, the gossip had blossomed outward from Bethany.

Rabbi Yeshua raises men from their graves!
Nicodemus's son died and on the third day he rose again!
But how could a man who has buried his parents, his wife, and his son believe the fantastical reports of pilgrims pouring into the city?

I expect my father pretended that he had misheard the rumors as he walked slowly home, removing his cap to let the last rays of sun warm the top of his head. It would be too painful to believe something so implausible.

But by the time he reached Bethany there was no denying the celebratory fervor that had consumed the entire village. People hugged Nicodemus, crying, saying they had seen the magic with their own eyes. Men ran ahead of him, toward our home, screaming, "The risen one! I will see Lazaros with my own eyes!"

And still I can see the doubt in my father's eyes as he came in the front door. He did not even bother to kneel next to the bowl and wash his hands. It was as if he was steeling himself to face Lazaros's death anew.

"Come in and sit, Father. There is food, and much to tell you." Marta had come to greet him with me. He looked back and forth between us without saying a word before following us into the courtyard.

"Father!" Lazaros knocked over the stool he had been sitting on as he stood up.

My father's knees gave way. He made a sound like a bird that has just broken through its shell, halfway between a whimper and a song.

Lazaros ran to him, grasping his elbows. "Father! I am here. It is me. I am returned to you."

I looked over my shoulder at the doorway that led into the darkened house. Something was on the cusp of happening. Was this the foreboding the lambs felt in the temple when they caught sight of the knife's shadow hovering above their necks?

What is the cost?

Yeshua sat beside me, but we did not touch. His nearness was sweet and strange. I could feel him breathing carefully. Once or twice our eyes met and I felt warmth begin to pool deep in my belly. I watched his strong, muscled calves slip from under his tunic as he shifted his weight, felt his heat, and remembered what it was like to feel him on top of me, to taste his sweat, to run my fingers down the ridge of his spine.

My father was overcome. He grasped Yeshua's hand, happy tears streaming down his face. "By God! By the book! All I have learned is nothing compared to your words and your work. I am an old man and thought I would never see a thing that changed my life. But you have done it. You have saved my son. You do the Lord's work!"

Yeshua shifted uncomfortably. "The Lord's work is all around, Father! Look to your daughter Marta's good cooking to see it revealed. Look to your daughter Miriam's wisdom."

Beltis manned the door but somehow people managed to make their way inside. Men and women streamed into the courtyard to see Lazaros. And children, as always, found their way to Yeshua.

A little girl, towing her mother behind her, pointed up to him and babbled incoherently. Yeshua smiled at the pair, producing a small shell from the folds of his cloak.

"You can hear the waves if you put your ear up to it," he explained, looking at ease for the first time since he had arrived. The mother mouthed her appreciation over the child's head.

"She has been sorrowful since her father passed," the mother explained to me. "And look, my daughter is smiling . . ."

Lilah, Yohanna's old friend, fainted when Lazaros leapt up to hug her, nearly bringing him down with her.

Achim and Enosh had their servants bring jar after jar of their finest wines.

Shimon was intimidated by this display of wealth. I could see him casting sidelong looks at Achim's unrestrained laughter and gold rings. The brash fisherman who was usually the loudest one at the table became reserved. He didn't touch his food. Philip, easily overwhelmed by crowds, got up and left, muttering something about needing to take a piss.

And Yudas watched Lazaros, his face twisted with an expression that was almost rage.

He sees his dead wife. His dead child. He resents that they are too far gone. He would have Yeshua go to them and raise them. It is bitterness I see in his face. Bitterness and longing.

Seeing this on Yudas's face made me recognize it within myself. *Why can Lazaros return but my mother is dust? What of my child?*

Marta hovered above us all like a maternal bird, removing empty dishes, passing around new loaves of bread, and ordering the servant girls to fetch more wine from the storeroom.

I kept my eyes on Lazaros. I was waiting for him to disappear.

He looked well enough in body. His cheeks were rosy. But there was something different about my brother. He flinched when a lamp was brought too close, as if the light hurt his eyes. He said practically nothing.

Where have you been, Brother?

When everyone had their fill of food and drink, there was a palpable shift in mood.

It was a dark night, foretelling the fourteen days it would take the moon to ripen into fullness and the fourteen days in which we would prepare for the Passover festivities. And yet it was unnaturally bright, as if some counterfeit moon was glowing just out of sight, causing the new leaves on the olive trees to appear silvery and the stars to blink against a sky that was more blue than dark. Even when the lamps sputtered it was still possible to make out the faces of everyone gathered.

"Tell us what you saw, Lazaros." Shimon finally asked the question we all had on our minds. "Where did you go for those three days in the tomb?"

Lazaros stared down into his hands. He wore his shroud in the Romans' toga style and his exposed shoulder looked impossibly sharp and thin.

Yeshua stiffened next to me. He, too, wanted to know what lay beyond death.

"Do they know how much doubt you hold?" I whispered to Yeshua. It was the first time I'd spoken to him since the meal began.

He shook his head slightly. "No. None of them know." He reached for my hand and squeezed tightly.

Lazaros finally spoke. "It was as if I was in a forest . . . or an ocean . . . with many different beasts. But I was also the beasts and the forest. It was as if I was constantly looking through many different pairs of eyes."

"What?" Thoma spluttered, spitting some wine down the front of his tunic. "Friend! Are you drunk?"

My father had gone very pale. How strange that it should be the son who knows death first.

"He's not drunk! He's resurrected, you fool!" Andreas whacked Thoma on the head playfully.

Yeshua was rapt. "You saw as if you were birds and beasts?"

Lazaros smiled hesitantly. "Yes . . . And I think I saw, in the midst of everything, a lion, and a bull, and a huge tawny eagle . . . and there was a person sitting there. And there was . . . a darkness like water or night. Maybe I saw two people. A maid holding a babe. Or was it a man?"

"He has reached Yeshua's kingdom!" Shimon exclaimed. His whole body vibrated with the news. "Tell us, Lazaros. Who was the man you saw?"

"The man?" He seemed addled, but not drunk. It was as if the effort of translating his experience was draining him of the ability to even sit upright. He was sinking into his cushion, leaning on my father who had put an arm around his shoulders. "Did I say a man?"

"Yes, you did," Shimon prompted. "Describe who you saw."

"Don't push my brother. Can't you see he is exhausted?" I snapped angrily. But Yeshua's hand squeezed mine as if to ask me to stop. He wanted to hear.

Lazaros frowned. "I don't know how to describe it. It felt like much longer than three days. I *saw* many things that are beyond belief. I *was* many things I can't describe."

Thoma sat with his mouth open. Philip had returned, hovering in the doorway. Yohan Ben-Zebedee's honey-colored eyes were wide. And Yakov looked like he might leap up, so overcome with nervous energy was he.

Tell us the secret! Tell us the secret!

The fools. The secret never comes from someone else.

"Did you see the prophets Moshe and Eliyahu?" Mattiyahu asked.

Yoses Ben-Zebedee rasped, "Was the man wearing shining white garments?"

"What man?" I asked. "I thought he said he saw a woman with a child?"

Lazaros gagged. I thought he might be sick. His hands shot up to cover his eyes.

"I saw . . . I saw . . . seven golden lampstands. And seven shining orbs. Every face of the moon. And someone. Not a man. But like a man . . . Or a woman wearing a shining robe with hair like white wool. This person had eyes of fire and held seven stars. The sun was behind them and the crescent moon at their feet. Out of their mouth came a sword. But the sword was . . . not a sword! It transformed into a head of grain. And the grain turned to liquid gold . . ."

"I knew it! It was just as we saw!" Yakov burst out. "It was as I saw on Mount Hermon. My brother has appeared to you as the Son of man."

Yeshua held up his hand. "Brother, you may interrupt *me* all you want. But let Lazaros speak . . ."

Lazaros frowned. I could see that he was trembling slightly. "The Son of man? It was almost a *woman*. She wore a mantle as black as ink. The mantle was the sky! Covered in golden stars. A dove came and landed on her shoulder. Actually, I think I *was* the dove . . ."

"Did you see Yeshua in the kingdom that comes after this life?" Shimon was desperate.

Oh, Shimon. I felt for him, even then. I understood that impulse: to know, to understand, to capture! The sense that there was something just out of grasp.

"Enough, Cephas!" Yeshua rebuked him, using an unfamiliar nickname. "No more about the kingdom. Look in front of you and you will find the kingdom."

I was watching Lazaros. He dropped his hands, sensing my gaze. The sight of me seemed to rattle something into place. "I saw Miriam! She was there with me always. Before now and once again in other lands. It seemed that we were as deer running through the forest. And other times I was sure we were inside the sky itself, held inside the smoothest, blackest water."

"Who was the man in your vision?" Shimon asked again.

Lazaros blushed with shame. "It was very hard to tell who I saw!" He looked at me nervously, pleading. Everyone was waiting expectantly. *Miriam,* his doleful eyes said. *Take me out of this place.*

"It was Yeshua," Lazaros said quietly, as if to test his own certainty.

I was not sure if he believed this himself, or if he was just happy that he could so easily please everyone. But he breathed a sigh of relief and repeated the name once again, "Yeshua! I saw Yeshua. All in white. Sitting in a seat that was also a giant hand. Clothed in white. I am sure it was my sister's husband I saw."

The disciples smiled with vindication, but Yeshua was paralyzed with shock, a perplexed smile frozen on his face.

"See!" Shimon declared. "We have been given enough signs to know."

"I told you," Yohan exclaimed, nodding vigorously. "We are not the only ones to have seen such magic." The men began to whoop and yell.

"What do they speak of?" I asked Yeshua, who was staring at the sputtering flame of the lamp that had been set on an old stump.

"I don't know, Miriam. They are drunk and cannot believe what they have seen today."

"It seems to me that they *more* than believe. They adore you as they would a king or a god."

"And does my wife adore me?" he asked gruffly.

I was burning to draw him to me in a kiss. I wanted to taste his words before they left his mouth, when they were tart with silence and intent, perfect as the seeds that grow under the red leathery shell of the pomegranate.

"Your wife loves a man, not a god," I insisted quietly.

"Let's go somewhere else, Miriam," he suggested, his voice low. "They have no need of us right now." He slipped back into the shadows. But as I went to follow, pausing at the door to slide on my sandals, I felt a hand at my elbow.

Lazaros stared at me with haunted eyes.

"What is it, Brother?" I asked.

"Miriam." He was breathless.

"Yes?" I said impatiently.

"You did not want me to come back. I see it now. You wanted me to stay dead."

"I . . ." The words faltered. I could not lie. How could I explain to him the awful conflict that still raged in my heart? The desperate need to have him back! The joy that he was here with me! And the dark certainty that it was *wrong*.

Tears welled up in his eyes and he gripped my arm even more tightly. "Why?" he pressed.

But I still could not answer.

Lazaros turned and left me, heading back to the eager crowd of men ready to resume their questions.

· · ·

Yeshua followed me through the gnarled trees, past the empty tomb, all the way to the stone wall that marked the edge of our land. He stepped silently, his bare feet sinking into the soft ground. His presence was thunder in the air, pressing each particle of dust and breath closer together. I could feel the dark burn of his eyes on me. And when I turned to look at him, one hand on the stones I had climbed over many times, the starlight turned him silver.

He has hair of white smoke, brilliant robes, and eyes of fire.

We did not talk or touch. But we moved in unison, clambering over the wall, running through the hills, and crushing wild thyme underfoot. The darkness pulled at us as we pushed forward. I felt it might slip off our skins, leaving us flayed, vulnerable: beings made of blood and breath, so insubstantial we could scatter in the invisible breeze. The watchtower emerged from the night as something blacker still, as if, when looking down into murky water, you sense a large presence passing below. The shadow of a huge fish. A being made terrible by its blurred edges, its indecisive shape.

Yeshua slowed his pace. He pulled me into his embrace. Lightly, he bit the skin of my shoulder. "You should fight to get away. I might eat you whole . . ."

Something yowled in the forest. An animal slipping away from danger.

"Can you feel it?" I asked, ignoring his play.

He moved his cheek against mine. The bristles of his beard tickled my face.

"Yes. I can."

"What is it?" I asked.

It was not danger exactly. The energy that permeated the landscape was more like hunger. Hollow. Open. Ravening.

Blood for blood, the thought suddenly struck me. *Our god told us to put blood on the door so that our son's blood would be safe. Blood should be spilled on this new moon night to nourish and ensure the return of her light. So that she can grow full again: moon of the harvest, the ripening springtime.*

Except that no blood had been spilled. Lazaros, the sacrifice, had been snatched away from the earth's open hands.

I was returned to my sense of dark foreboding. "Yeshua, I am afraid," I admitted, fearful even of my own admission of fear. "I am afraid that you have done the wrong thing. I am afraid we have offended God."

His eyes were black pools. "How could bringing back Lazaros be wrong? Why should we be denied happiness, Miriam? When I found you, I knew I could live fully. That wonders beyond my wildest imaginings were suddenly made possible . . ."

"I don't understand yet," I admitted. "But perhaps his death was necessary. Perhaps it was part of a longer story."

"A story where you are unhappy and suffer?" Yeshua shook me lightly, peering into my eyes. "Have faith, Miriam. Why should you suffer? Why must you pay for this?"

"I don't know yet. I don't understand . . ." But my words died as I softened into the sureness of his broad chest, his knee against the top of my thigh. "Perhaps I am wrong."

"It is no good to be parted from you, Miriam," he confessed gruffly. "I lose sight of myself. It has been a strange time . . . I won't be parted from you ever again. Even if it means we must eat dust and toil all our days."

An owl screeched above us, filling the open space that the absence of the moon had left behind. A small cloud no bigger than the wafted smoke from some shepherd's little fire passed over the brightest stars. All ebbed and flowed.

"Come with me," I said, pulling him into the tower.

Immediately a tumble of sticks and dust fell on our heads. I heard a cluck and a flutter of wings as some roosting bird shot up the staircase.

No one had been here in years. Maybe since my last visit, before my marriage.

It was like entering into a part of my mind that I had kept carefully hidden from myself. Each step resurrected an old childhood memory. Not the golden ones. But the mourning. The strange solitary pain. Standing at the foot of this abandoned tumble of stones, wishing I could become as vast as the night, as cold and staunch as the tower, instead of feeling the ache of losing my mother, losing Kemat.

The stairs were worse than I remembered, covered in moss and dirt and debris. But we were able to make it to the top of the tower. And the floor was, remarkably, still intact.

"You visited here when you were young," Yeshua said as he looked out through the large watch window facing the old vineyard. "I remember you speaking of it."

I came up behind him and rested my face against his shoulder, twining my arms around his waist, pressing my hands to the warmth of his chest.

"This is where I dreamt of you," I whispered. "This is where starlight and owls came to me and told me I should wait for a man. A strange, difficult lion of a man."

He laughed, putting his hands over mine, and drawing me closer.

"So this is it. Where I was born. From a virgin's dream?"

He caught my mouth in a hungry kiss and we sank to the floor. Our physical bodies reestablished an intimacy our minds had not yet reached. I could not get enough of his skin, his tense muscles pressing into the softness of my hips.

He put his hands between my legs, feeling my readiness.

"No." I grabbed his arm and shook my head. "Not tonight."

"Not tonight . . ." his words were strained and I could feel the speed of his heartbeat against me. I was struck again by the change in him. My fingers brushed the ribs in his chest I had never seen so visible. During our time apart he had grown thinner. There were new lines at the corner of his eyes that were not the fruit of laughter but of hard living and worry.

We both needed to heal each other. To put hands not on the lepers and the sick, but on each other. Only then would we become whole again: in body and in spirit.

But I was wracked with guilt. For letting Yeshua raise Lazaros. For trying to keep Yeshua from bringing Lazaros back. My heart was twisted by it. There would be no pleasure. I would not let myself feel it. I would not let myself heal.

"Yeshua," I said decisively. "I must return to you slowly. We will lie together tomorrow. Or the next night. Tonight I am tired."

But we did not understand that we had no time. We had no time at all.

Forty-Eight

We barely spoke. We held each other for a long time before falling asleep.

"We should always be close to water, I think," he mumbled, stroking my cheek with his thumb. "We will spend the feast days here but afterward let us leave this place—leave everyone—and go to live for a while on the seashore."

When I woke, he was gone.

I threw on my clothes, gathered my shawl around my shoulders, and pulled twigs from my hair.

I leaned out of the tower window, looking at the green tinge of spring flowing across the landscape. The first red anemones speckled the hills. The wind carried a buttery, tender smell that told me the almond trees were blooming. I walked back through the vineyard toward home, enjoying the sun's insistent rays on my face.

I'm sure I'll find him with the neighborhood children, playing some game in the street, I decided. *Or worse, he'll be arguing with the rabbi in the village synagogue.*

It wasn't until I made my way back up to the house that I finally started to worry. There was no one inside, no sign of my father or Lazaros or all the men I knew must have spent the night sleeping in the courtyard.

"Lazaros?!" I yelled, hurrying in and out of every room looking for a clue.

Something terrible had happened. Lazaros had fallen ill once again and died. Or maybe someone else had fallen in his place.

As I left the house and started up the road, I felt sure of tragedy. I shivered even though I was already sweating.

It wasn't until I had run through Bethany, up to the top of the hill that offered a view of the landscape and the city, that I ran into Enosh. He was flushed and bleary-eyed, as if he hadn't slept a wink, wearing the same embroidered tunic from the night before. I wondered if he had slept at all. He was coming from the direction of the city, heading back toward Bethany.

"What's going on?" I asked fervently. "Have you seen Lazaros? Is he well? Where is everyone?"

"Of course he's well!" he spluttered. He looked below my chin and blushed. I folded my arms over my chest, realizing I was still only wearing my shawl and shift, which made me completely underdressed to be outside of the privacy of my home.

"Then where is he?" I snapped. "Spit it out, boy, and don't gawk at me! Where is my brother?"

"Calm yourself, Miriam. He has gone into the city with your husband!" He frowned at my agitation.

"For the Tamid prayers?" I asked in confusion. "Why have they gone into the city?"

Enosh laughed. "For prayers? No! It was part of the plan from last night! Had you left already? I can't remember. I was quite drunk . . ."

"What plan . . ." My stomach dropped.

"Everyone has heard of Lazaros's resurrection. People are filled with the spirit." He was obviously parroting someone else's words. "All the men seemed to think it was a ripe time for some fun. Mess with those puppets of the high priest Caiaphas and send the city into a flurry. Everyone's here for the holiday . . ."

"What kind of trick? What was the plan?"

He chuckled. "You really don't know? I thought Yeshua would surely tell you."

"I don't," I insisted.

Enosh gestured back toward the town. "Everyone thinks Yeshua is the Messiah. So Shimon suggested it might be funny to play with the prophecies. Give all the pilgrims a good show!"

I groaned.

"Shimon got a pair of asses for Lazaros and Yeshua to ride into the city. The Risen One and the Messiah. Both dressed in white! You know the prophecy."

"Oh, people of Yerusalem! Look, your king is coming to you. He is righteous and victorious, yet he is humble, riding on a donkey," I repeated the scripture glumly.

How foolish they were! Like children playing with scripture they had overheard from their fathers. And Yeshua was the biggest fool of them all! I knew he loved to play. But playing with children was different from playing with grown men. Telling parables was different than acting them out. The stakes were much higher.

Enosh turned back toward the city. "I left them at the city gates. There were hundreds gathered. Proclaiming him the savior. They plan to go to the temple and cleanse it. Mattiyahu told me Yeshua has spoken of the temple's impurity for a long time. And I agree! Caiaphas has let the whole thing become distasteful."

All of this was news to me. It was mere hours before that I had lain in Yeshua's arms. He had said nothing of a plan. True, he had always been annoyed with the Pharisees and their rigid ideas about the scripture. But he had never suggested cleansing the temple.

What else have I missed?

I did not thank Enosh for his information or bid him farewell.

"Watch out, Miriam! It is madness in the city!"

I ran down the hill. The slow-moving masses of pilgrims grew thicker the closer I got to the city's gates. It shouldn't have surprised me that I heard his name of the lips of strangers. This had been happening all over Galilee. *Yeshua*. Perhaps the man still belonged to me. But his name was no longer mine.

"Hosanna to the son of David! Yeshua the rabbi of Nazareth is blessed! He comes in the name of the Lord. Hosanna in the highest heaven!"

"Did you see the boy? He was dead but a day ago! Cold in his tomb!"

I looked up at the city. The dense smoke reflected sunlight, burnished gold, the pale shimmer of the buildings through rising heat. I felt the walls of the city shrinking, beginning to crush me. The sky was heavy on my head. I thought of the story of Osiris. Saw the god grinning, stepping into the cedarwood box of my visions, delighting in its perfect dimensions. Stepping into his death.

Now I know that in every lifetime we are offered the same tragic grooves, again and again. It is easier to fall into the old story than it is to carve a new path. There are boxes in our lives. Traps that perfectly fit our flaws, our vanities, our worst inclinations. And I knew that day, spinning through the densely packed city streets, knocking over vendors' baskets of fruit and vegetables, that we had begun to move toward sorrow.

You see now? Yerusalem was the box.

Yeshua stepped inside of it . . . and found that it fit.

• • •

By the time I reached the temple, the men had already created chaos. Bodies crushed into me on either side; a mix of faces I recognized from Bethany. Pharisees, students with their striped shawls, pilgrims, followers I had seen swell our ranks in Galilee, pale-haired foreigners wearing drab, dirty cloaks. There was also the rabble of angry men who I was sure showed up anytime they thought there might be a riot against the Romans.

I could smell the burning fat as I elbowed past a family of dark-skinned pilgrims, holding their meager offerings of flowers and palm fronds, their eyes wide and confused.

"I'm sorry," I apologized, looking back at the youngest—a small, bright-eyed boy whose nose wrinkled at the smell of smoke and death. He hesitated as his mother tried to pull him along, working to slip inside of her ragged skirts.

"Imah, I don't want to go in!" he pleaded.

Out of the mouth of babes . . .

But then I was swept forward by the push of people trying to get inside the city.

It was remarkable that I managed to hear him above the mayhem. It was a testament to his volume. "Out! Out! You fools!"

I squirmed through the outer court, standing on my toes to try and see what was going on. A dove brushed my head from above, beating its wings so quickly it looked like a gray cloud trying desperately to return to the sky. A woman screamed as a goat ran past her, bleating.

"Den of robbers! Hypocrites! Out! Out!"

How was it that above the cries of animals, the songs, the praying, and the yelling, he could still be heard? "You've given our temple to *their* gods. The gods of money!"

A young man wearing the tefillin that marked him as a student of the Law was blocking my view. "He's mad! But maybe we need a madman?"

"He raised that man from the grave this past day! My sister saw it happen with her own eyes."

"Brood of vipers! Get out!"

I was close enough that I could see Yeshua, flanked by his disciples as well as by my brother, who was still clad only in his dirty shroud. "You have given my father's house to the Romans! You have forsaken our God for the god of money!"

He was a son of Galilee. Too big and too rough for this closed space. He flipped over a vendor's table, sending boxes of birds flying. One box bounced on the stones and burst open. But the bird, stunned, did not fly out. It fell onto the pavement, its wings at awkward angles, its beak opening and closing silently. A large man, struggling to get closer, stepped in front of me and crushed the bird underfoot.

"Look! The birds!" A little boy was tugging at his father's sleeve and pointing upward.

A cage of doves had exploded. Feathers the color of dust and metal rained down on us as the birds spiraled upward to freedom.

"Here. Take this!" Someone threw Yeshua a corded whip.

He bent down and picked it up, turning the leather-bound end over in his hands. For a second, I thought he was about to yell at the man who had given it to him.

"Stop! Stop this madness" A spindly man leapt from behind his table, attempting to grapple with Yeshua. Surprised, Yeshua leapt away, snapping the cord down on the vendor. Then Yeshua's eyes flashed, and he dropped the whip as if burned, looking down at his own hands with horror.

"Yeshua! Stop!" I tried to squeeze past two tall men. One of them clutched a large wooden box to his chest, which was making a metallic rattling noise. *Coins.* I realized they must be money changers fleeing Yeshua's wrath.

The biggest man looked me in the eye fearfully. "Get out while you can, woman! The Romans will be here soon and slaughter us all for rioting."

"Those weak-minded priests will have already sent them word," the other one added. "Caiaphas has no use for false prophets."

I was close enough to step into the open space that hovered around Yeshua as he stormed through the outer court upending tables and yelling, "Yah! Yah! Yatsah! Get out!"

I see it all now from the eyes of the doves still circling above the courtyard, unsure of their freedom. A crowd of people surged and closed and opened around one man. It reminded me of the ocean racing away from the touch of Moshe's stick. Surely the sea had overflowed some other shore to make room for his crossing. Yeshua was creating tides of people. Could he control how far the energy would travel? What shore would receive the overflow? The flood?

I elbowed my way past the men, trying to keep my eye on my husband. The man I had slept beside the night past was gone. He was a stranger to me now.

"Miriam!" Yudas's eyes were bright with worry. I reached out, clutching his hands in mine.

"What is this lunacy?" I asked frantically.

"Yeshua has spoken of taking the temple back from the Roman puppets . . ." Yudas explained.

Shimon and Mattiyahu were untying goats and kicking them into the crowd while a man cried, "Those are my year's wages! My whole year's wages!"

"Since when has Yeshua been concerned with the temple?" I asked.

Yudas frowned. He looked much older than he had when I had seen him last. "Much has changed since you left Miriam . . ."

"Master! They've sent soldiers!" shouted Yohan Ben-Zebedee. "We should get out now!"

A group of priests had stormed down the stairs from the inner sanctum and marched up to confront Yeshua. "How dare you disturb the peace during this holy week?" one of them exclaimed.

"How dare *you* destroy this temple!" Yeshua shouted.

"Destroy the temple?" the same priest questioned angrily. "It is *you* who desecrate this place with your violence!"

Yeshua stood tall, legs wide, with the power and stance of someone who had grown up doing hard physical labor, playing rough with his brothers, and tussling with animals. He radiated a vitality that made the priests seem unreal. They were mere scratches of black ink on paper. They were no match for the pure energy of his body.

"You fools! I tell you, if you burn this temple to the ground today, it will take me but three days to raise it up. It could be a pile of rubble and it would still be clean of Rome's foul money and your treachery!"

"Yeshua!" I screamed.

He heard me and his eye met mine.

Why did you leave me in the tower?

But before I could talk sense to my husband, Lazaros began shouting. "It is true! Hossanah in the highest! I saw this man sitting at the right hand of Our Father and he was wearing a shining raiment. He has come to be our Prince of Peace. I swear I saw that Yerusalem will rest on his shoulders."

Dressed only in his burial shroud, he seemed inhuman. An angel sent from above. His eyes burned with zeal. His lips were dark, as if stained with wine or blood.

The crowd began to chant as one. "It was written. He has risen. Hosannah in the highest!"

"Yeshua!" I cried again, though he was past hearing now.

But the birds heard. The rest of the cages exploded. The vendors yelled, diving after streaks of feather.

"He will burn this temple to the ground and he will raise it up again!" Lazaros prophecied.

A student standing near to the priests jumped in. "Men, you must believe him! This boy was raised from his grave by Rabbi Yeshua."

"You are all fools. They know nothing!" I yelled, pointing at my brother, knowing that I was denying my husband and my brother.

"Rejoice greatly, O daughters of Zion! Shout in triumph, O daughters of Yerusalem! Behold, your king is coming to you; he is just and endowed with salvation, humble and mounted on a donkey!" announced Yeshua, performing for the crowd.

I do not believe he truly meant it. By then he was flown through by chaos. The agent of some madness bigger than us both.

As the crowd roared, Shimon finally managed to get Yeshua's attention. "Away, master! We must go! They are coming now!"

I was thankful someone had spoken sense.

Yeshua spun around. Lazaros swayed on his uncertain feet for a moment, staring at the priests before following.

Children wailed, split up from their families. Sheep bleated, tasting terror on the air.

"Bring him back!" the priests shouted. "Hold him accountable!"

But we were gone.

When I caught up to Yeshua and the men, I was close to tears. Yeshua was between me and the world. It was impossible to imagine how I might equal the cries of an entire city. Perhaps I had saved the life of a bird or two.

Yeshua's feet hardly touched the ground. He strode forth with such exuberance that he appeared to be dancing; lifting his arms in the air, reaching out to tussle the hair of a child a mother was holding out for a blessing. "The day has come! The kingdom comes!" he cried out.

"The kingdom comes!" A group of children ran alongside him, boys and girls running barefoot. They echoed his cries, inspiring him into greater confidence.

A crowd swelled behind the disciples; pilgrims who had come to sacrifice and pray at the temple but found something more worthy of praise along the way.

The Messiah. The Prince of Peace. The Son of the Father. Why does he call himself these things?

"Yeshua! You must stop. You must rest," I urged him.

"It has begun, Miriam. I have received the signs and it will come to pass."

"Yeshua. What are you saying?" I fell into stride beside him finally, keeping my voice low.

He grabbed my hand and raised it to his mouth, pressing a burning kiss onto my knuckles. Even in the midst of this chaos, the touch of his lips vibrated in me, dimming the sounds and colors around us.

"My love. I will deliver to you back your city. This was just the start. Trust that I am beginning to understand my mission."

"It is not my city! I do not want it!" I replied breathlessly, trying to make him understand. "And *what* mission? What signs? You mean Lazaros's strange visions? Do not trust them, Yeshua. He hardly knows what he saw. He's still half in the grave . . ."

An old man had managed to elbow close enough to pull at Yeshua's cloak. "They say you brought the boy up out of his tomb! But *I* did not see it. How can I believe what I do not see?"

"I wager you still believe the moon will return to us even on those three nights a month she disappears?" I scoffed. "What a foolish question . . ."

But the old man ignored me.

"Yeshua. You need the dark," I insisted. "You must sleep and ask your dreams for help."

Yeshua was looking around as if he might spot an appropriate reply hovering above our heads. His gaze fixed on something in the distance. "Wonderous things have happened, Miriam. Things that should not be possible. I must trust in these signs."

"Unnatural things have happened, Yeshua!" I cried desperately. "Things that violate the seasons of life. You have acted against death! Let there be no more magic until we are sure they will heal more than they will harm!"

But if I did not hear my own voice thrumming in my ears, I would have thought myself mute. He made no sign of having heard me.

Yeshua stopped beside a spindly fig tree at the side of the path. Outwardly dormant, some green intelligence was yet pooling in its narrow trunk. Its leaves tentatively tasted the spring air, the five points curling inward protectively around the spine that led back into the branch. I thought I could just smell the tang of its rising sap.

"Stop and open your ears! Hear what I have to say!" Yeshua cried out to his followers, gesturing toward the tree. I let my fingers graze its bark. It was smooth to the touch . . . silver as moonlight.

"Listen to the rabbi!" Shimon commanded, waving his arms until he had gotten everyone's attention.

Yeshua came beside me and ran his hand down a branch. He reached up higher, taking one of the top branches and shaking it roughly.

"What are you doing?" I pulled at his arm.

"Do you see? This tree bears no fruit!"

Everyone was confused. However, the disciples, used to Yeshua's antics, smiled smugly in anticipation.

"It bears no figs," Yeshua said more quietly, just to me.

"Of course not," I responded just as quietly. "It is not the season for figs."

"In the kingdom of my father there are always figs!" he announced to the others.

"Yeshua, that is foolishness," I said, defying him now. "The kingdom has tides and seasons. Sometimes there are figs. Sometimes there are not. Sometimes the moon is full, sometimes she disappears in the sky." I was speaking quickly, so filled by a sense of urgency that I almost tripped over my words. "The harvest does not come every day."

"Master! I have some bread here!" a woman offered, holding up a little cloth bundle. "It would be my honor to share food with you."

But Yeshua ignored the offering. He was still bending the tree's branch so that its silver bark showed pale-veined cracks of strain.

He was playing to the crowd. To the small boy who pushed through to the front, calling out: "Rabboni! Why does the tree bear no figs?"

"It is not the season for figs." I spoke to the crowd now. "This tree is not barren. It sprouts figs in time with its season to do so."

"It is not the season?" Yeshua's eyes burned gold-white as the sun above us. "If my father says it is the season of fruit, then the trees will bring forth fruit!"

I slapped his hand away from the branch and it twanged up, releasing several leaves. "Stop!" I told him.

But he pushed me away and knocked hard on the slender trunk, proclaiming. "This tree will bear no more fruit!"

A rupturing pain exploded in my womb. I stumbled over and was sick into the sand. All that came up was water and bile, but my stomach convulsed several times before I could catch my breath again. I stumbled back upright, my vision blurred and bright. What I saw next was horrifying.

"Elishah!" cried a young man. "He is Elishah returned!"

It was as if lightning had shot down and burned through the tree, though the sky was blue and clear. The tree's leaves, tender and green only seconds before, had flecked away as ash. A long groove of bark had been peeled away to reveal a trunk as black and hard as obsidian. The young tree had been transformed into one dark, gnarled finger pointing up at the sky.

"No!" I screamed. I held out my hands, spreading my fingers wide as if I could feel the fig tree passing away as so much dust.

Forgive me. Forgive him. He knows not what he does.

Yeshua turned to the man who had questioned his abilities. "Truly I tell you, if you have faith and don't doubt, not only will you do what has been done to the fig tree, but even if you say to this mountain, 'Be lifted up and thrown into the sea,' it will be done. Whatever you ask for with faith, you will receive."

I reached out to clutch the blackened trunk. I was back in my dream from the night when, as a girl, I had started my monthly blood. Crucifixes had lined the roadside. The sky behind them was crimson with sunset.

What I saw now were no longer wooden beams fixed with human beings. The crosses had become withered, blackened trees.

I did not understand my vision then. But now that I live among people who worship trees, I see things I was blind to then. Trees nourish us. Provide us with shade. Their roots connect forests separated by whole countries. Trees pass down messages of tenderness and wisdom through the centuries. And we had already killed so many of them to build our cities and our homes.

"What is it?" Yudas broke me from my reverie. He was watching me closely.

"Doesn't he see?" I whispered. "This tree will be our curse."

Yudas was thoughtful. "Perhaps it is not so, Miriam. I have seen him perform strange magic in the past month. And no ill has come from his deeds yet."

But my anger was so big, so inhuman, I could not give it words.

My father had sent Yosseph ahead with news for Yeshua. "Good sir, Nicodemus bids me tell you that you should take shelter here and not return to the city immediately. Someone murdered one of the temple vendors during the riot and they are searching for him now. They mean to throw him into jail, and I am sure they will do the same with you if they find you."

Yeshua's brow was furrowed with concern. "Someone was killed? By whom?"

Yosseph shook his head stiffly. "It was no one here. I know the villain. His name is Barabbas. Yeshua Barabbas."

Barabbas. The name was as loud as thunder in my ears. *Bar Abbas. Son of the Father. The man was also named Yeshua! Son of the Father!*

A divine joke. I could not help myself. I began to laugh. The sound escalated out of my control, becoming higher and higher.

"Miriam is hysterical!" Lazaros exclaimed before turning to me. "Calm yourself! Let me take you away."

"There is your fruit, Yeshua!" I spat. "You kill a tree and *this* is your reward!"

I looked toward the horizon and I could not see the end of it. I could see an army of the dead. Dead women. Dead trees. Windswept, barren landscapes stretching far, far into the future.

Forty-Nine

My father descended on the house with five of his best students, eager to introduce them to his now infamous son-in-law.

"We shed our caps and shawls at the gates so that no one would know you were consorting with Pharisees," one of my father's students joked as everyone sat down to supper.

"And yet I see you have kept on your gold rings and expensive cloaks!" Yeshua retorted. "Don't bother taking off your caps if you are not ready yet to shed your belongings."

"Be careful, Azariah!" my father said, chuckling as the young man blushed. "Yeshua will catch you at every turn."

I looked from man to man, all of whom were congratulating each other, waiting for someone else to notice that everything was going wrong. Somehow I had ended up back in the life I had been trying to escape. Where were Salome, Adah, and all the other women? Where was the storytelling under the starry sky?

I needed silence to hear my own thoughts, and I retreated to the storeroom. Here I had helped Kemat when I was little, watching her string up herbs to dry in leafy bundles. Apphia and Beltis must be responsible for such things now. The musty smell of stoneware comforted me. *Ask the plant to heal you and to nourish you,* Kemat had instructed, a few dried sprigs in her slender palm. I pinched off a sprig of rosemary, enjoying the bright fragrance that erupted from my fingertips.

"Miriam . . ." Lazaros stood in the doorway, holding a lamp that circled his face with a yellow glow.

"What is wrong with you?" he asked quietly. "Why won't you join us?"

"I was going to see about more wine," I lied.

The very sight of Lazaros made my body tense with anxiety. I longed to hug him, to finally release all the grief and confusion. But how could he be here? How could he live again without consequence?

Lazaros was not fooled. "There's more than enough wine. You are hiding, Miriam."

"I just need a moment to breathe," I tried again. "The men will not miss me."

Lazaros glanced over his shoulder as if acknowledging some invisible presence. He frowned. Was it the lamplight or did he appear almost spectral? His face was long and gaunt, his edges indistinct, his eyes all black with no irises. "Miriam, I'm not sure if I'm alive. It feels like my spirit has become thin," he confessed.

"Lazaros, I don't know what happens when someone returns like this."

Lazaros looked very old then. Perhaps as old as he was when I'd seen him for the last time, his knotted hands curled around a wooden staff, his traveling cloak giving his skeletal frame the illusion of bulk.

"Listen, Sister. It seems I am alive. And Yeshua did such a thing. I believe he will do great wonders. I have seen him as a king of men." He was looking down at his own hands as he spoke, as if some confirmation would appear in their lines. "Yeshua will return our holy city to its rightful people."

Lazaros glanced over his shoulder again before nodding confidently. "Yes. Yeshua is the one who is spoken of in scripture."

I laughed then. A heartless bark. I was surprised by the coldness I felt. The paralyzing disbelief. "Then go! Dine with your savior! I'll wait until later when he transforms back into my husband."

"Your husband is a king among men," asserted Lazaros.

"He is a man among men," I said, exasperated now. "He is a man among trees, flowers, mountains, rivers, and birds, and it would be good if he remembered it."

Lazaros sighed and left.

I paced back and forth through the hallways, breathing in deeply through my nostrils.

A king among men. The words echoed.

I feared if I left the house I might not come back. When I passed my room, I saw that moonlight had spilled onto my bed like silver water. And, for just a second, I thought I saw someone sitting on the dark, far corner, past the shafts of light. This someone had narrow shoulders and a straight back.

I stood at the doorway, hardly breathing.

My mother.

A cloud passed over the moon. The puddle of light disappeared. The room was blue as if it were underwater.

I went in and sat on the bed where I had seen the shadowy figure.

"Mother. What must I do?" I was shocked when I said the words aloud.

My hand brushed something hard. Something that had been stuck between the straw stuffed mattress and the bed frame. I reached down and pulled it out.

In my hand was the small, black woman my mother had given me all those many years ago. The moonlight returned, burnishing her smooth surface, glinting along her pointed breasts, the tiny indents of her eyes.

"If he is a king, then I am his queen," I whispered, clutching the dark woman, peering into her face. "But queen of *what?*" For a second, the shifting moonlight made it seem as if the straight dash of her mouth curved into a smile.

I could feel tears burning in my throat.

The nightingale began to sing. An owl hooted.

Maybe I was queen of all things that sang. All things that spoke slowly, with green leaves and twisting trunks. Queen of nights with no center, when the moon hides behind a cloud and the dark penetrates even a shut eye.

And Yeshua? What was he king of? He was king of the kingdom. The king of the river. The king of the land. The forest. The starry sky.

I must help him understand his power. I felt like Isis, gathering the pieces of her murdered lover, putting him back together again so he could rule.

A smell curled in through the window. Dark and piquant. Some animal was digging in the dirt, releasing smells that had been trapped below the dried grass all winter. It reminded me of something.

Spikenard.

I was transported back to my childhood, learning scripture by heart next to my brother, Lazaros. A candle illuminated the deep furrow in my father's brow as he recited the sacred story of the prophet Samuel anointing King Saul: "Then Samuel took a flask of oil and poured it on his head and kissed him and said, 'Has not the Lord anointed you to be prince over his people Israel? And you shall reign over the people of the Lord, and you will save them from the hand of their surrounding enemies. And this shall be the sign to you that the Lord has anointed you to be prince over his heritage.'"

I rummaged through my old chests, throwing musty scarves and broken sandals over my shoulder. Had I lost it? I surprised myself when I pulled out the small, alabaster jar that Lemuel had gifted me so many years ago. It was filled with the precious oil used to anoint Israel's kings.

"I have been saving this for a king. Isn't that what I promised so many years ago?" I murmured out loud, feeling a huge snake-like energy beginning to uncoil inside of me. I imagined this must be what the trees felt when their sap began to rise.

"Mother. Am I right? Is this what I must do?"

Nothing but the quiet, insistent touch of the moonlight answered me. I could feel the light like cold water on my face, prickling down the center of my forehead.

And now I see it clearly. I, too, was anointed. Not by a man or a woman. But by the moon herself.

I clutched the jar to my chest as I entered back into the courtyard, heading straight to Yeshua.

Let me anoint him as my beloved. Let the oil be a spell of protection.

The whole world was rising to meet me. I could feel the air tightening around my flesh, stroking the length of my spine. Below my feet the steady drum of churning roots reverberated. Even the stars appeared to draw closer. The frog's song amplified until it was almost unbearable. Everything was a confirmation.

"Miriam!" Yeshua looked, up smiling with his whole body, his arms opening in welcome, his eyes sparkling. "Come sit beside me. Let us relax and drink together! There is much cause for celebration."

"Yeshua . . ." I said his name and imagined all his other names that I could no longer remember. The sun to my moon, the light to my dark. The green king. The lord of roots.

His face was a thousand faces—the face of every person he had ever healed. He carried their hearts within him. Although it was night, I could feel the glow of a red sunrise behind him. Even if he did not yet know it, he was ready for my blessing. The land's blessing.

If I could go back, I would say to myself, *Wait, Miriam. Take him out of the house before you do this. Take him into the trees and the safety of the night. Do not do this among men. Do not make it a human spectacle.* How many times have I wished I could have been my own mother, Leukas, gifting wisdom when it was most needed.

I did not speak as I knelt beside him, letting my curtain of loose hair fall around my face. I took the alabaster jar and slowly removed its top, releasing its keen, musky scent. The perfume rose like music up through my fingers and filled the air all about us. The smell of soil. The possibility of seeds and the decay of bones.

I knew that the power that had flowed through my hands when I touched the oil to Yeshua came only when the earth itself needed to be healed.

Slowly I raised the jar over his head. He exhaled slowly and he was years younger. Was this the boy Imah had scolded and loved? And yet the expression that flickered about his full lips was one of confidence.

I let the oil cover my hands and, with the same touch that I used to heal, I pressed my thumb to that tender spot between his eyes.

"Be the lord of the land again, the king of all the earth," I whispered softly so only he could hear. "Ask the land to support you and it will."

"What?" my father scoffed. "What are you doing, Miriam?"

"That is a year's worth of wages!" Thoma remarked astounded. "Wasted! You could have sold such costly oil to support our travels."

Yudas was the only one who understood. "Has she wasted the oil? Or has she anointed our king?"

Above me the sky was throbbing like a woman about to give birth. In the earth below us, bulbs and seeds were splitting through their tough shells. Green thoughts that uncurled and sent up their celebration.

For yours is the kingdom. The trees. The mountains. The valleys. The caves. The streams and glens. The birds and flowers . . .

And with that, I brought my eyes to his. It was done.

"Hail! Your king is anointed!" Andreas proclaimed in a honeyed voice, and the others laughed jovially, joining in the fun.

The aroma of spikenard had held the men in thrall. But now the spell was broken.

"Lord of the land?" my father scoffed. "What are you doing, Miriam?" he asked again.

Yeshua had been staring at me deeply, entranced throughout his anointing. But now his jaw clenched tight. "Miriam. Do you mock me?"

He did not understand his own kingdom after all.

Only Mattiyahu was not laughing. "Master! Does your wife show us the truth?"

There was moment when Yeshua could have remembered himself, the boy who had first spoken parables to the birds and foxes outside Nazareth, the boy who belonged to the hills and the streams, and perhaps it would have all been different. But it passed.

He laughed, his eyes suddenly brightening. "Yes! My wife has done a beautiful thing! Miriam has prepared me for my task. And for that she will always be remembered."

"What task?" My voice, which had left me during the ceremony, finally returned. "Saving the city? The city is doomed!"

Did my voice even make a sound? The men pretended I did not exist.

"Is it right that it should be her that anoints you?" Shimon asked. "Are we to listen to this woman? I need no signs to believe that this is my king. No woman."

I looked at the fisherman. He was the only one of them not reclining. He sat on a stool, his big hands folded in his lap, his eyes distrustful. He was completely sober, I realized. The only one of them to have a clear mind. What a dangerous thing. What did that mind want? What was it that Shimon really desired?

"Yes," Yeshua answered Shimon. "And I will make her whole, as if she too were a man, and then she will be able to enter into the kingdom."

"So you would make me your disciple and not your wife?" I spoke quietly. But he would not respond.

The jar fell from my hands and cracked, a thin line of oil escaping its container, running into the soil.

Fifty

Yeshua insisted on returning to the city for the next three days. He preached publicly. Told stories in the market squares. Made a big show of putting his hands on the sick who reached the pool of Siloam so drained from their pilgrimage that they could hardly hold themselves up in the water.

He came back to Bethany wearing flower crowns little children had woven for him. Smelling like the perfumed embraces of the feverish women who had asked him to please heal the pain in their hearts, their wombs, their spirits.

"Why does he do it?" my father despaired, worrying his shawl. He had returned home early, limping. When I saw that his feet were bothering him, I suggested he let me work some herbal oil into them. So he sat now, his eyes closed, with his swollen, gnarled feet in my lap.

I didn't answer, squinting down at his cracked skin. Such a task, body to body, grounded me. I could focus on the burr of bone on his big toe, press the thin blue skin pulsing below the notch of his ankle. I could forget my anger and my anxiety.

"You have healing in your hands," my father sighed, closing his eyes, the ridge between his brows relaxing for once.

Of course, I do! When did they forget that I, too, can do what Yeshua does?

"Some cloves. Ginger. Yarrow," I murmured to my father. "I will teach Apphia to make the oil and to use it on you."

My father was shaking his head. "Yes, the Romans have imprisoned that man Yeshua Barabbas. He's a good scapegoat for the riot. But that does not mean Yeshua is safe!"

506

My father's friends in the Sanhedrin stopped by later, hoping to catch a glimpse of Nicodemus's impertinent son-in-law.

"He makes a fool of us! Before Passover! Does he want Pilate to withhold Caiaphas's ritual vestments in retribution? Or worse?"

"He wants to reform us," my father argued. "To make us better Jews. He would revitalize the practices and rituals that have grown stagnant in the city!"

The men kept their eyes on the door. But Yeshua remained away until well past dark.

The first night I waited up for him. Filled with a prickling, feverish rage, I wanted him to arrive so I could yell at him. Tell him to stay out of the city.

Who was he to say he was the Messiah? It was vain. Worse, it was dangerous. The Romans would perceive it as a threat to their rule.

Oh, I was so angry! But I also longed to touch him. To breathe in his musky scent, press my face into his chest. These conflicting thoughts made me sick to my stomach.

I had wounded Yeshua more deeply than I had intended. Even when he returned with his men, he did not greet me, preferring to head straight to the courtyard for supper.

I retreated to my room, lying in the dark and feeling every part of me tingling with anticipation, my heartbeat refusing to calm. I put my hand up to my neck, feeling the insistent song of my blood. *What next? What next?*

One of us would have to bend. One of us would have to be the first to apologize. But it would not be me.

Miriam. Sometimes we must soften to encourage softness in others, I remember Kemat saying now. She had instructed that I apologize to Marta after a hair-pulling spat. *Your sister will love you better if you show her your love.*

Overwhelmed by the presence of men, I had forgotten the wisdom of my mothers.

Midnight came and went and still he did not come to bed.

I fell asleep, waking briefly when I felt him slip in beside me, careful to push the blanket up between us so that we would not accidentally touch.

In the morning when I woke, he was already gone.

And so it was the next night, and the next morning.

I felt more distance between us than when we had been physically separated by deserts and mountains. When we sat side by side at the evening meal, his whole body emanated a vigorous heat that I couldn't properly interpret.

Was it anger? Or pain? Was it both?

By the third night I was fed up. I gave orders to the servant girls about what wine to bring up from the storeroom and how slowly to cook the portion of goat someone had brought my father as a gift. But I did not stay to sit with the men and eat. Instead I put on a heavy woolen cloak and wound a scarf around my hair. The days were warming but the nights were still cool, the new water in the ground sending a dark, chilly thrill up through my bare feet. I so rarely wore sandals then, my feet toughened by two long years of walking through Galilee. Every step I took I was sure I was receiving some strange, wordless education that arrived, not from above or beyond, but from deep *below.*

And I let my feet lead me, distracting my mind by leaning my head back to look at the sky. It was a sheer lavender still filled with the muscular clouds that had generously offered shade during the heat of the day.

Every color seemed bodily. The moist soil was the same darkness as my husband's hair. The iris petals were the purpled lips of someone who had just sipped wine. The slow dusk did little to dim the red anemones that cropped up on the little hillocks that led up from the path.

Springtime—when the earth bleeds and we call it a bloom.

Each flower pierces through to above from below, I thought. *It is painful being born, I think.*

Squeezing my eyes shut, an afterimage of red flowers appeared in the darkness of my own mind.

"I was not expecting you."

I swung around to find Yosseph behind me.

He was dressed simply: a long, brown tunic tied loosely at his slim waist with a flaxen cord. A gold hoop sparkled at his ear.

He seemed the very essence of refinement—from his diamond-bright gaze to his well-oiled sandals. And there was the signature spice of the perfumes that provided him with his wealth: the herbal undertone of aloe and lily oil so fresh I could have sworn he held a handful of cut flowers behind his back.

Wealth and ease. Beauty for beauty's sake. Good food. Long, boring days arriving and departing in exactly the same way. I sighed

"Is there a reason you are outside my gate?" he asked, his tone almost warm.

"Oh!" I looked up, surprised to recognize the gate that led up to his lavish home. "I was walking to clear my mind. I did not mean to trouble you . . ."

"Trouble me?" Yosseph laughed dryly. "You have troubled me a long time, Miriam. I would not suddenly begin to worry about it now."

I was right, I concluded bitterly. *He hates me.*

"Go in peace, Yosseph. Have a pleasant night." I went to pull my scarf back up over my hair.

"Stop this, Miriam," he said gently. "Come inside with me and have a drink. Rest for a while. Then I will walk you back to your father's home."

I looked up at the house. His servants had already lit the lamps, and a honeyed glow emerged from the windows.

"Have some food. Rest your feet."

I followed him up the path and into the warm, still air of his home. When I paused to wash my feet at the doorway, my whole body crumpled. Tears already blurred my vision. But Yosseph shook his head, took my hand, and led me to the courtyard where he offered me a low, Roman-style stool.

"Sit," he commanded.

My head fell into my hands.

"Miriam," Yosseph said softly. "Why do you come to me with sorrow?"

I lifted my head and met his gaze. He was kneeling a proper distance away from me, the bowl between us.

Somewhere an owl hooted. Then there was the rustle of disturbed leaves as the bird's wings swept through Yosseph's garden.

"Yosseph. Do you ever look into the future and see sorrow? Do you ever have dreams that come to pass? Do you ever dream of lives that are not yours?"

He frowned, leaning closer as if he had not heard me.

"I look into the past and see what I have lost," he admitted, his eyes dropping to his hands.

"Will you tell me something?" I asked.

"I will try, Miriam."

I took a deep breath. The questions arrived like water rushing over a cliff's edge.

"Is he the Messiah? Am I a spiteful wife? Do I get in the way of his purpose? Sometimes I worry that I am blinded, that I do not understand."

The sky was dark now and the waxing moon showed up in a nearby bowl filled with rainwater. The golden orb rippled with a breeze, wavered, collapsed in on itself.

We were silent for a long time, staring at each other.

"Miriam, I am not a mystic. It is why you would not marry me."

I opened my mouth to speak but he raised a silencing finger.

"I know nothing of messiahs. But I have traveled widely. I have seen men. Powerful men. Squashed like flies. Brushed away, to death, like so much dust. I think, perhaps, you are your husband's only hope of survival."

I nodded as he continued.

"He flaunts his zeal in front of Pilate. And he has angered Herod. Pilate is seemlier than a man like Varus, but trust me, he is capable of crucifying two thousand Jews. Just four years ago he had a crowd of protestors bludgeoned to death."

"Yeshua is not a soldier," I said, thinking of those men surrounding him. "He leads no army."

"He *thinks* he is leading one," Yosseph explained. "And he doesn't understand the politics of Yerusalem. Yeshua is not a political man. He is a spiritual man. The distinction is important right now. Caiaphas has been playing a careful game. First he expelled us to the Mount of Olives so he would no longer have to answer to fellow Jews . . ."

Oh. I realized why I had come to Yosseph. It was for the same reason I had sought him so much as a young girl. I wanted information. Stories. Rumors. Knowledge. I wanted someone to explain the world of men to me.

"Miriam. You are the only one he will listen to. I am sure of it. He is surrounded by danger on all sides. He should leave—*you* should leave—as soon as possible."

I rose then, nodding. "Thank you, Yosseph."

"Don't thank me, Miriam," he said passionately as he led me to the door. "Heed my warning!"

But I did not seek out Yeshua.

I went to the tower.

Why isn't my power simple? Why isn't it as easy as it is for Yeshua? I raged at the indifferent stars spread out above Bethany. *Give me a sign! Anything! Show me what I must do!*

But all night the only thing I received was the insistent scream of the owls swooping through the rotted rafters, dropping down sometimes to snatch mice.

Where are you, God? I asked frantically, ripping away my dress and shift and offering my bare flesh up to the moonlight. I breathed heavily, trying to open myself up to clarity. *That cannot be you! You cannot be the owls!*

But of course, God was the owls. God was the night itself. The silence.

Now I know to listen for the birds.

If I had listened to their calls, watched the dart of their yellow eyes, I would have understood their message.

Go to him, Miriam! Wake him up! Go and save your husband!

Fifty-One

On the week of Pesach the number of pilgrims approaching Yerusalem tripled. Even the narrow roads of Bethany were thick with relatives coming to stay with their families for the holiday feast.

Our household, full of men, was not prepared to take on any more guests, so I was surprised when Lazaros burst into the house with a joyful cry. "She's here, Miriam!"

Salome came to me, wrapping me in her long arms. I sighed, my whole body relaxing as I smelled cooking smoke in her hair, the stone-beaten freshness of her clean dress.

"Why didn't I stay with you in K'far Nahum?" I mumbled into her shoulder, refusing to release her immediately. "Everything has gone so wrong."

She patted my back, steadying me. "I am here now. I had a dream of a hill. Birds above it. Great black vultures. I knew I must come to you."

Before I could ask her for more information, Marta arrived. She was covered in flour. Her hair, usually perfectly coiffed and covered by a delicate shawl, was curling out of a messy braid. Something had changed in the past two years. She wouldn't relegate the cooking to her servants any longer, choosing to do all the feast day preparations herself. "Who is it? Have you decided helping me is no longer important?" she asked me.

"Do you need help with cooking? Chores?" Salome offered. "Put me to work."

"Marta, this is my friend Salome," I added. "I met her at the river in Yochanan's camp."

"I don't care where you met her, as long as she helps," Marta snapped, dusting her hands off on the front of her dress.

"We must talk, I need your advice," I whispered to Salome, clutching her desperately.

Her blue eyes searched mine. She gripped my upper arms so hard I thought she might leave bruises behind.

"We will talk later. But I must confess . . . I have not come alone . . ." she glanced over her shoulder.

And then I saw her, having lagged behind, coming slowly down the path, fighting with a tall, sour-faced man who was carrying a worn satchel over his back that identified him as a fellow pilgrim. "My son? The Messiah? Heavens! What foolishness is this? Why? Yes, I am his mother. Why is it odd that I am his mother? Am I not as you imagined me?"

Salome frowned, tapping her chin thoughtfully with one finger. "I ran into her on the road. She recognized me from when we stayed in Nazareth and has refused to leave my side. Do you think Yeshua will be angry that she has come?"

For the first time in days I laughed. There was only one woman who could possibly make Yeshua angrier than me.

His mother.

She smiled brightly when she saw me, handsome under her sunburned cheeks and grizzled gray hair that poked out from under her dark blue headscarf.

"Daughter. Let me at him. Let me beat some sense into the boy. I have come to save him from himself."

And she had come. When no one had called for her. Alone . . . without her sons or younger children to protect her from brigands on the road. Without an ass to carry her weight. Wearing the same pair of sandals she had owned for the past twenty years.

"Imah!" I cried and opened my arms.

She ran to me and we held each other tightly, as if we really were mother and daughter.

• • •

Imah helped us prepare the meal, tending the lamb that was slowly cooking over the fire. The dripping fat sparked fragrantly when she turned the spit.

"When Yakov left . . . and left his wife to my care . . . I knew it had gone too far. Whatever it is that moves a man to live like an animal and walk the land, spitting in people's eyes and telling stories, I cannot understand. But I cannot stop it! He has always been a nuisance." She clicked her tongue with annoyance. "But convincing his brother to abandon his family! Leaving his poor wife to starve! When we have experienced grain shortages these past years . . . When the Romans are known to rape women who live without protection . . . He was leaving his children to die!"

Her voice swelled, filling the space around us.

"A man chased us out of our last inn," Salome confided when I went to check on her progress with the charoset. She slowly worked the dried dates, patiently adding in handfuls of crushed pistachios. "We left when it was still dark."

"What did she do?" I prodded.

"She yelled at a group of Galileans who were speaking of how Yeshua raised Lazaros from the dead . . ."

"Yes?"

Salome chuckled, wiping her hands off on her dirty tunic. "She declared they were all fools and asked them if they had ever been to a birth where a midwife blew the breath back into a blue-faced babe."

"What?"

"She said that mothers have always brought the dead back to life. And her son shouldn't let himself feel grand for having done such a thing. Of course, the men were furious and ran us out of the inn with a threat of violence."

I looked out the low window to where Yeshua's mother was scolding Marta's son Samuel about something. The boy did not cry like he would have had it been Marta scolding him. Instead he stood with his slim back straight, hands clasped below his round tummy, nodding in deference to the older woman.

"Safety at last!" A voice boomed from the front door. "And is that food I smell?" Shimon's hearty voice did not match his appearance. He was pale with exhaustion and worry.

Philip, too, looked undone by the crowds. He sank down onto a stool, letting out a low, pained groan. The men had come back from the city early. But Yeshua was not with them.

"What is wrong with you all?" I asked Yudas. He was looking up at the sky, his face so empty I thought he might have temporarily lost his mind.

"The Romans are everywhere today," he answered. "They are look-ing for any reason to arrest a Jew. Yeshua would have had us walk openly through the streets, declaring his message and healing. But even Shimon thought it was best we come back here."

Thanks be to Shimon. I looked at the burly fisherman, leaning against a tree, picking at the dry skin on his knuckles. He *did* love Yeshua. Would that love inspire Shimon to protect him?

"Where is he now?" I asked. "Where is Yeshua?"

"He is thinking things over, weighing the next move," Yudas said carefully, his eyes bidding me to ask more. "He went to walk in the fields. He said he had to speak to his Father."

"His Father," I said bitterly. "I see."

I snuck back into my room and curled up on my bed, massaging my chest, hoping that my fingers could finally reach my heart and remove the thorn of anger lodged there. *Mother,* I thought desperately. I wanted so badly for the power to come hot into my hands. I wanted to heal myself.

But instead, I fell into a dream.

• • •

I was in a river, thigh-deep in its waters. I looked to my side, watching as my white tunic floated away from me, answering the call of the cur-rent. The river receded into greenery, broken only by long fields filled with soil as black as the night sky. But the light was thick and flaxen, coming in at a slant from a setting sun. Palms on either shore leaned over the water, their fronds like fingers reaching out to each other. I looked down, seeing through brilliantly clear water that my toes were tucked between rosy stones, as rosy as the light warming my face, the bare skin of my neck. The water was just cool enough that it sent a shiver up the veins of my legs. I could feel its flicker and dance against my sex, washing me clean, waking up my own rhythms, my desires.

This was not the Yarden River. The current was fast. And yet it was familiar the way a mother's embrace is familiar. My body was not only *in* the river; it had been *made* by the river.

I caught sight of my hands.

Look at these old hands, Leukas.

There are waxy burns on my fingers and at my wrists, from cooking fires. This white scar is the only token I still have of my cat Azizi. He was a lovely, rust-colored tom who slept on my stomach every night, striking out with his claws only when he was feeling boisterous.

See. When I looked down, I saw *these* hands. These old, gnarled hands.

And when I reached up, I felt my face, familiar, but changed. My cheeks were papery, etched with a spidery scrawl. I ran my hand against the lines that radiated out from my lips.

"Miriam!" Yeshua's voice called across the water of my dream-river.

He was standing at the bank closest to me—his face, too, transformed by a map of crinkles and lines. His hands curled around a wooden staff. He was straight-backed, unbent by age, but his hair had gone completely white, his beard absorbing the last sunlight and glinting like spun gold. His eyes twinkled.

I had never found him more handsome.

"I thought you were just going to pick some herbs. But when you did not come back, I knew I would find you here . . ." He stepped carefully into the river, using his staff to test the rocky bottom before placing his foot forward.

"We made it." I said to him, with relief washing over me—so intense I thought it might sink me below the water. "We have lived a good life. A long life."

When he reached me, he slung his free arm around my shoulders and planted a kiss at my temple. "Made it, Miriam? Yes. I suppose we have." He laughed, leaning back his head.

A crane swept overhead, wings churning the air, its beak breaking through the humidity so that I could almost see ripples fanning out behind the bird.

"I mean. Here we are. Grown old together."

He gave me a questioning smile. "It has been a long time, hasn't it? I can remember you as you were when you first came to Yochanan's camp: a willow of a girl, tall and slender, with hands that moved like wings."

"And I you," I grinned, leaning into his familiar warmth. "You were a wild man, wearing only a loincloth. I desired you so intensely but could not admit it, even to myself."

He squeezed my arm. "And I desire you still, my love. You still drive me mad."

As the sun sank below the trees, its rays turned from gold to crimson: a vasculature of light that stretched out and upward as if to pump blood back into the sky. Somewhere far off a dog was barking, but the sound was mellowed by distance and the thickness of the air. It came to us like a long, sonorous greeting.

Goodbye day. Welcome night. Welcome stars and moon and darkness.

"How many children do we have, Yeshua?" I asked.

He shook his head. "You are acting strange tonight. Have you had a vision?"

"How many children?" I repeated my question.

It worked. He looked to his side, into the shadowy undergrowth of the trees on the farthest shore. "We have five children, Miriam. Five grown children and all five of them married and well. Your daughter and her husband, Khnemu, live with us. Don't you remember?"

"I do. I do." There were tears behind my eyes, rising in my throat. "And our first child?"

"A son," Yeshua brought his hand from my arm to my face, gently cupping my cheek, his own forehead knotted in worry. "Do you not remember Binyamin?"

"He yelled so much that first year I thought he would grow up to be an angry man. And now he is the gentlest being, hardly able to swat a gnat for fear that he might harm it." The words poured forth from me.

I could see my children. Seth, with his father's muscular build, his hair shorn close to the head, his smile cracking his face in half, already an old man in his own right, head tilted back as he let loose an infectious laugh. Binyamin, slender and small, his skin dark and smooth as a nut, his hair long, a narrow beauty to his face that reminded me of my mother. Leah, wide-hipped, beautiful, a babe at her breast, her hair so curly it could not be kept hidden below her shawl. Anah, small and dusky, with quick hands I could see moving in and out of a loom's warp, her eyes glassed over as if she were in a trance. Ah, yes. Anah was the heir to my visions. I saw her staring out at the fields, already entranced. And Elishah—handsome, outspoken Elishah—the scribe, always irked at the distance his learning had taken him from his illiterate parents, flanked by his own children: a glossy haired, pale-skinned brood that told me their mother must have come from the distant north.

"Yeshua." I turned into his chest, feeling his arms, still strong, encircling me.

"Yes," he breathed against my forehead, his lips touching my skin and sending a shiver down through my spine. The water lapped around us, pushing us closer together.

"Where are we?"

"My wife's gone mad!" he exclaimed to a pair of egrets swinging overhead. They followed the curve of the river until they disappeared.

He looked down at me again. He must have been at least seventy, but I could see that the power still lived in him, still burned in his hands.

"We have been here for the past thirty years!"

"Where is *here?*" I demanded.

"Home, Miriam. We are home."

I woke up to the sound of yelling.

• • •

"Woman! Why do you plague me?" His voice boomed through the house, penetrating the stone walls, rousing me so that I sat straight up, cold sweat slipping between my breasts, the taste of the dream-river still hovering below my tongue.

I gasped, remembering his words, my hand going to my stomach. Perhaps it *was* still possible. My womb *could* bear a child. Not just one child, but a whole family.

There were no prophecies I wanted to fulfill, I realized, except for the one that sprung from my own heart and told me about a small happiness that could still quietly, carefully, be reached. "We have to leave," I muttered to myself, getting up and slipping a dress over my shift. "We must leave tonight."

"Enough! If you have come here to chastise your son, then you are misguided!" Yeshua's voice resounded. "I am as much a Son of God as I am your son. To whom will you have me answer?"

"I thought the Lord detested the proud of heart! Am I wrong? Your pride is a disgrace! You have made your brother unclean with it!" Imah stood with her back to me in the courtyard. She was as solid as a thick sycamore trunk, its roots entangled with subterranean stones.

Yeshua's eyes were bright and sunken in his face. I could tell by the sharpness of his cheekbones, the tremble of his fists at his sides, that he hadn't eaten in days.

"Yeshua has given me freedom!" Yakov said contemptuously, glaring at his mother. "He has shown me the light of the kingdom."

"Freedom? Eh?" Imah cackled, her hands clutching her stomach, her shoulders shaking with mirth. The sound was as open and cataclysmic as thunder. She seemed more like Yeshua in this moment than he did himself.

"Why do you let her speak to you so? A woman!" Shimon complained from his spot in the shade of the old fig tree, the only disciple still seated, with a dish of food in front of him. He was gnawing on dried fruit, spitting out the seeds. "Women are not worthy of your audience. They are not worthy of life!"

"Silence!" Yeshua yelled. But I did not know to whom he spoke. His eyes darted from his brother to Shimon and then back to his mother. He saw me then, standing in the shadows of the doorway, and sighed loudly. "Did *you* bid her come? Did you promise her a bed to sleep in?" he asked me.

I went to Imah, putting my arm around her broad shoulders. "Why should I have to explain myself? Why is it strange to invite my mother for Pesach? Everyone else we know is pouring into the city at this very moment. Are you so surprised that your own mother, a good Jew, has come to sacrifice at the temple?"

I had to admit, there was something dangerous and beautiful about the way his body seemed a sheath for fire. His edges hummed, evaporating. I could see his heartbeat in his neck. It was less like looking at a human being than like looking at big weather: thunderclouds throwing mountain-size shadows across the landscape; lightning shredding the air, leaving treetops smoking; the surge of monsoon season coming down so fast, so hard, that caught in it, you were forced into supplication on the ground, your forehead in the mud, unable to breathe or rise.

"My mother?" he spat. "Whoever here does not hate their mother and their father as *I* do cannot call themselves my follower."

Imah flinched. She had finally been hurt.

Salome cried out in shock from the doorway to the storeroom. She was flanked by Marta and Atalyah. I, too, was appalled by his cruelty.

"Your real father? Yeshua! You drive a sword into your mother's heart," Imah replied. "Every day I mourn your father's death. Every day I say his name. Do you deny your father? The man who raised you and taught you a fine trade?"

But Yeshua was ready for her. He looked around at his disciples for support. "Do you deny *my* Father, the true Father?"

Philip gasped. Shimon nodded with approval. The Ben-Zebedee brothers were more apprehensive, exchanging looks of concern.

"Do you deny me, your wife?" I spoke loudly.

Yeshua grimaced, turning toward me. "I do not deny you, Miriam." It was painful for him to say. "But I cannot dine with my mother. If she will dine here, then we will go elsewhere for our Pesach meal."

"Miriam and her sister have slaved these past two days to feed all of us," Yudas interjected.

"Don't worry, Yudas," I spoke up. "Perhaps it will be better that the fine food is given to the fine guests. Go elsewhere for wine and bread. I expect you'll have no trouble. I've heard Yeshua can turn water to wine and pull bread out of thin air!"

"You would refuse your wife's cooking, her welcome?" Imah was furious.

"Away!" Yeshua swept his arms forward. "Let us leave this place."

Rallied by their master, the men picked up and began to shuffle out of the house.

No. He could not leave again. I went to Yeshua, reaching up to touch his face, but he flinched. "Forgive my sharp tongue. Stay. Talk with me. We will leave your mother in the care of Marta for now."

"Don't touch me!" he snapped.

I tried one last time to summon the power of my dream, the intensity of our love grown strong and old. "Where two can make peace, all manner of things are possible. I truly believe it. We will say to the mountain, 'Move!' And it will move."

"Don't speak to me of mountains, Miriam," he said, pulling away. "I am not here to make peace. I must finish what Yochanan began."

And I let him go, knowing deep inside of me that he was right.

Perhaps he *was* a god. How was I to know? But as Kemat had taught me so many years ago, gods could still make mistakes. This was no time for peace. I needed to fight.

Fifty-Two

"Yeshua will not dine with us?" my father asked.

"No, Father," answered Lazaros, flushed with excitement. "He will dine in the upper room of Enosh's home in Yerusalem . . . and I will go with him."

My father shrugged. He was not visibly upset. "I would think it safer for him to dine in Bethany tonight. Rabbi Huri believes that Caiaphas is dangerously angry. Pilate has put him in a tight spot, threatening not to release the ritual clothing. Every time Yeshua goes into the city and makes a scene, Caiaphas feels he is being made to look a fool. The Romans have been taunting the priests, claiming they have been bested by an illiterate peasant."

"Do they mean to arrest him?" I asked anxiously.

"What would they charge him with?" Lazaros was frowning. "He has not committed treason. He heals and teaches."

"But a man died when he incited that riot at the temple," I countered. "And there are many claiming that he is the Messiah."

My father finally spoke again, nodding slowly. "Barabbas will hang from the cross for that crime. We need not worry. It is true, Lazaros. The worst that could happen is that the Sanhedrin will try to question him and catch him in a falsehood that discredits his claims."

All of us standing there—my father, my brother, and me—shared the same blood. If I had the power to sense the invisible truth of things, to heal with my hands, then I had inherited it, in part, from my family. We shared the same deep, troubling ability to feel the future rushing toward the present moment.

Yet in that moment we were fools. Each of us worked to ignore the cold draft that had entered the hallway. How was it that all three of us managed in that moment to ignore our intuition?

Lazaros grinned brightly. "Save me some of the mutton stew. I doubt we will have a feast as sumptuous as the one the women have prepared here."

They grasped each other's arms and Lazaros took his leave. But he stopped before he turned the corner. "Come, Miriam. He misses you more deeply than you know. It will do him good to have you at his side."

At first I ignored this invitation. My husband had left in a cloud of anger. What good would it do to interrupt his group of men? They smiled condescendingly, forgetting that I had bested them in every argument, had healed the sick myself, had organized the care and feeding of the retinue of Yeshua's followers as they trekked all over Galilee.

Worse, I thought. *They have forgotten their own wives and daughters and mothers.*

This distaste kept me at my father's table. Inspired by the teachings that Yeshua no longer even followed, my father had done away with a woman's meal.

My father's cousin Dathan, an oily, supercilious fellow who had traveled from somewhere in Damascus to celebrate the holiday, put up a fuss. "I cannot relax and eat next to them!"

"Then do not relax," my father offered. I studied him hard. Where had this generosity been during my girlhood? True, he had let me sit at the table with his students, but only under the pretense that I act and pretend to be a man. Marta raised her hennaed eyebrows at me as if to say: *I won't question it! But I'll enjoy it!*

She insisted on serving everyone herself, sending the servants away to enjoy their own meal. Amos was on a trip and I thought she was glad to be celebrating with her family for once. A disgruntled Imah refused to sit down, following behind Marta and fretting about the wine. Oh, to savor it! Those moments that seem ordinary as they arrive. Surely they will continue for years to come! But we would never again sit down for a Passover meal together. Never be together again in such an easy way: my father, Lazaros, Marta, me.

But I was far from present.

"Go to him," Salome whispered into my ear. "He needs you."

She was right. I slipped away as Imah made my father laugh so loudly that I thought he must have spit out his food. I glanced back once when I was in the shadowy hallway and saw a sliver of my family, bathed in the generous mellow candlelight so that all their faces appeared smoother, younger.

I didn't belong. Not completely. But I had no reason to believe that I belonged at the men's dinner, either.

I stepped out into the cool night air, looking up at the full moon.

The light, almost wet, almost opaque, illuminated my dusty path so that at moments it seemed I was walking along a silver river that cut through the night.

A huddle of men at the city gate recognized my silhouette as a belonging to a woman and jeered as I passed.

The older I have gotten, the more uncomfortable cities have made me. Why live in a world made by men when the world made by God is so perfect? Why construct a ceiling when God's ceiling is studded with stars? Why build walls when we have trees and ivy and shadows to do the same work with less effort and more grace?

Cities are where men go to escape their best intentions.

I walked close to the stone walls, flattening myself against them whenever a group of people passed. It was the first time I had seen the market squares empty of vendors. And yet these open spaces rejected what the moon and the stars had to offer, choosing to buzz with a darkness that I swore came from below the stones, tinged red by the echo of fires and devastation.

All cities burn. All cities crumble. We build them up again and again. And again someone comes and turns them to rubble. If your temple is the ocean, it cannot wash away. If your temple is the mountain, it cannot burn. If your temple lives within you, you need not travel to find it.

I reached Enosh's rooms easily enough, knocking at the door and waiting. A servant boy opened it a sliver, frowning and shaking his head when he saw that I was a woman. "No! I do not know who you *think* is here. But he's not here. Go away!"

"Very convincing," I said, laughing. "What if I told you I am the wife of the person who is not here?"

The boy bit his lip. "Wait here."

"I will not." I was tired of the games, the passwords, the inscrutable talk of invisible kingdoms and absent fathers. I pushed into the anteroom easily.

I could hear the raucous bellows of festive men even before I reached the top of the stairs.

"Miriam!" Yeshua exclaimed. Gone was the anger. The frustration. The weariness. Yeshua was bright-eyed and joyful. He leapt up from the couch where he had been sitting between Shimon and Yakov. He came to me and swept me up in his arms.

"You're drunk," I whispered. "Stinking drunk."

"On a night like this, the crime is in *not* being drunk," he boomed so loudly that everyone heard. "You must catch up, Miriam! Here! Someone pour my wife a glass of the Cypriot wine."

I was so surprised by his good spirits that I let him lead me to the couch.

Shimon glared at me. I was confused. I knew I annoyed him. But this seemed unprovoked. "Have you come to spoil the fun?" he asked.

Now I understand, of course. I was his own wife, Ivah. His mother, Orpah. I stood in for those responsibilities that plagued him worse the longer he ignored them. I was all wives, all mothers.

"Hush, Cephas!" Yeshua laughed. "The fun cannot be spoiled."

"She wants to be a part of the mystery, just as we do!" chimed in Lazaros from where he was lounging on the rug.

"What mystery?" I asked hesitantly.

Yeshua was drunk enough that when he blushed it spread over his whole body, the skin of his neck turning scarlet. "I have told you all! There is *no* mystery greater than the one in front of you. I'm tired of your badgering."

"But Lazaros saw beyond life! He saw you seated at the right hand of the Lord. He saw you vanquishing the Romans and the lions all lying down at your feet!" Thoma lay on the floor, propping himself up on an elbow, his eyes blurry with drink. "You said there is nothing hidden that will not be revealed."

Yeshua's smile flattened. The dimple disappeared from his cheek. I knew then that he did not remember uttering the words. He had said many things to these men that he did not remember. Things that he himself did not understand.

"When was the last time you slept?" I whispered.

When he turned to me, his eyes were soft with love. "You! My dove, my perfect one. Have you seen the moon tonight? It is the only rival to your beauty!"

"Have you slept or taken something other than wine?" I insisted, unwilling to have the question evaded.

"Wine? Who has the wine?" he called out. "Bring it here so that I might pour my wife some more."

My cup sat at my feet, untouched, still filled to the brim. But Yeshua ignored it, immediately filling his own cup and that of Shimon's. Even Yudas playfully held out a piece of unleavened bread that Yeshua sprinkled a few drops of wine upon.

"Wine for everyone! To celebrate that we have made it this far. Out of Egypt and into the land of milk and honey."

"Master! Will you teach us now?" Yohan Ben-Zebedee exclaimed, slamming his cup down so hard that wine leapt up and out of it.

"Again with the teachings? Might I just be a man tonight?" Yeshua asked, sighing dramatically. "A man with no good advice!"

"We have followed you all over the countryside and into this perilous city," said Yoses Ben-Zebedee. "Don't we deserve to know what we saw up on Mount Hermon? The great wind and the light upon your face?"

The men were speaking a language I knew too well but had not yet heard from their lips. It was the language of power. Men's power. The same power wielded by Pilate, enjoying his own secular feast somewhere in the Antonia Fortress. The power that the Romans used to keep us in place. The same power they had wielded when they crucified two thousand Jews outside of Sepphoris before I was born. The power that inspired husbands and fathers to beat women into submission. The power of cities that kept us from the kingdom beyond the walls.

This was not the power that came when a woman screamed in pain and pleasure as the thin veil of her virginity ripped in two and she became her own temple, harboring the holiest of holies in her own womb. The power of earthquakes. Of childbirth. Of snakebites, wolf howls, and carrion birds. Angels that did not arrive beautifully. Angels that resembled death. Death that came loudly, darkly, and on time. It was not the power of weather.

"I . . ." Yeshua stuttered, his eyes unfocused momentarily. "I only disclose my mysteries to those who are worthy."

"Are we not worthy, master?" Philip asked. His face was gaunt. Adah would be worried to see him so drained.

"Shall I wash your feet with tears and rub precious oils on your head?" Andreas joked, exchanging a look with his brother Shimon. "Will I be worthy then?"

"Leave be, Andreas!" I stormed. "Do you think I have received some special knowledge?"

"Wait! Wait!" Thoma's voice was so high I almost mistook it for a woman's, but he leered like a man. "I *know* the mystery." The drunken youth grabbed his crotch. "Do not let the right hand know what the left hand is doing! Then there is no sin!"

Lazaros convulsed with laughter, clutching at his sides as if in pain.

"Be quiet!" Yeshua stomped his foot, frowning.

"Rabboni. Give them something." Shimon lowered his round chin and smiled as he would at a small child.

"Yeshua. Come back to Bethany," I pleaded.

"I am not returning to my mother. Damn that woman."

We'll go to the tower, I wanted to say. *I will tell you about the river. About our children and our shared life.* But it was useless to force my plea among these men.

"All right! A mystery!" Yeshua cried, jumping to his feet and clapping, ignoring me completely. "That's what you want?"

There was a collective bellow of approval: "Yes!"

"Tell us what it is to hear *him* speak to you."

"Why did Shimon and the Ben-Zebedee brothers get special treatment on Mount Hermon?"

Yeshua looked around and I could tell he was searching for something, anything, to tell them.

He should have told them that it was wrong to kill the fig tree. Wrong to bring back Lazaros. Tell them that it is not just men that mattered, but women, too. And plants and beasts and stones. And the water itself. He should have told them to go back to their wives. On their knees. To ask for forgiveness from their mothers and grandmothers! To abandon their homes and return to the forest by the river and live like animals.

I grasped at the seamless cloak of rich scarlet that Marta had labored over and gifted to my husband. "Tell them that you are a man, Yeshua! Not a god!"

But Yeshua only picked up a piece of bread and glass of wine.

"Here! This very moment is the kingdom! Can't you see it? It does not come! It does not pass. The kingdom is *now!*" Yeshua spoke as he gestured at the disciples. "We sit here together in love. And that is all, my friends. Love shared, brother to brother."

"And lover to lover," I added. "And mother to sister to son."

"Please be quiet, Miriam," Shimon groaned. "Let us listen to him."

"But I don't see the kingdom, Yeshua." Mattiyahu sounded frantic. "I've tried and tried!"

"Do you see this bread?" asked Yeshua, becoming more exasperated. "Do you look into your cup and see wine? If you look, you will find."

"Even I see only wine and bread," Shimon admitted. "Will you transform them?"

"I need not. They are already transformed by the greatest miracle of all."

"What miracle?" I asked.

"I eat bread, I drink wine. And they become *me*. They become my body, my blood!"

"What?" Thoma's narrow face blanched. "The wine is blood?"

But Yeshua did not understand the horror he had inspired in his disciples with such a statement. Blood held the possibility of impurity.

I saw Mattiyahu staring down into his own cup with distaste. "Master, I am confused."

But I understood the clumsy metaphor.

"You eat and drink to live," I explained, frustrated with the lot of them. "You are given gifts of abundance in each moment that nourish and sustain your life, your body. Even your blood."

"No, master. *I* understand!" Shimon stood, too, stepping in front of Yeshua, as if to act as his interpreter. I realized too late that this was a role he was comfortable playing, that he had been performing such translations more and more in the time I had been gone.

And, just like that, Yeshua let this man step in as his proxy.

"Our Lord works through Yeshua," Shimon declared grandly. "He has performed miraculous things. This bread and this wine are the blood and body of our master. He gives us the chance to taste his holiness and partake of his mysterious vision!"

Yeshua was frowning, but he did not immediately contradict Shimon.

"Must we drink the blood then? Will it make us unclean?"

"No!" Yeshua roared. "I am speaking of the kingdom! Not bread and wine. It could be a handful of olives or a fruit! The man that consumes the lion becomes the lion . . ." he was rambling. "Do you not see the gifts in front of you? The gifts of this very moment? Of this very body?"

"We must eat of your body?" Lazaros echoed, confused.

Yeshua was too drunk to articulate himself. But Shimon grew calmer the more agitated he became.

"Here, take Yeshua's bread and partake of his body," Shimon instructed, and the disciples reluctantly began to sip from the cup that Yakov passed to them.

"Yeshua. Will you not stop their foolishness?"

But he did not hear me.

"So now you steal my cup from me?" he joked with Shimon.

I rose slowly, allowing time for Yeshua to glance up and ask me to stay. But he did not.

At the door the young boy gave me a fearful look but did not say anything, letting me pass freely back out into the night.

But I was barely ten paces away when a voice called me back.

"Miriam!" It took me a second, squinting through the dense blue darkness, to recognize the thin, rangy frame of Yudas.

"Miriam!" he called again.

"What!" I flared. "Go back to your friends!"

"A word. Please!"

Yudas so rarely exhibited any real emotion, moving through life like a distracted ghost, that the tone of his voice made me pause. He had aged and become so thin that his face was almost a mask for a skull. He sounded truly worried.

"Miriam, Yeshua and the men have a plan . . . it was Shimon's idea, but Yeshua seemed to think it was the right course and they have asked me to do a thing." He could hardly string a sentence together. Was it the wine? I wasn't sure that I had ever seen him drunk. "I would say that it was foolish if any other man asked me . . . and at such a dangerous time! But I tell you, I have seen him do miraculous things. He walked on water; stopped a storm with the pressure of his hand. He brought your brother back from the dead! What if it is all true and Yeshua is the one we have been waiting for?"

"What are you asking?" I said, impatient to be on my way back to Bethany but trying not to sound unkind.

He tried to smile. A wan, empty smile. "Because you are his heart, Miriam. If he is truly holy, then you are holy, too. If he is to be king of men, then you are to be our queen."

The words caught me off guard.

"I despise this talk of kings and men and holiness," I snapped. "I will take no part in it."

"Miriam!" He reached out as if asking me to take his hands. "Tell me what to do! I cannot betray his word if he truly is the Messiah. It would damn me for eternity. But to speak before the Sanhedrin seems folly. Shimon says that Yeshua will confound them and take back the city. That this is how it all begins . . . It seems dangerous. But who am I to say? He has the protection of God on his side, and I am but a fool . . ."

A peal of laughter erupted from above us. The drunken chaos of the upper room had managed to slip out into the night. It bounced off the walls, echoing around us.

I knew I should respect Yudas's appeal. But he, too, was drunk, and I was tired of men needing my help. Certainly I would be blamed for ruining their plan in the morning if I intervened.

"I do not know, Yudas," I said flatly, stepping backward and away from him.

"No!" he cried out. "Tell me what do, Miriam."

"No! I'm done with this nonsense."

He stood there with his palms open, his eyes beseeching me to say anything at all. To stop him. To say, "Yudas, go back to Galilee and find another wife. Start your life again. You deserve to be happy."

But I was numb to his pain. I crossed my arms and lifted my chin defiantly. "Look to someone else for advice, Yudas. I will have no part in this plan."

I walked away without thought of looking back to memorize the face of my friend, the color of his eyes, the exact weight of the pain he carried in his bones.

And I think now that the moment I turned away from him, Yudas was already dead.

Fifty-Three

Lazaros woke me in the early morning hours, talking so fast that at first, deep in sleep, I thought I was listening to the drone of bees.

I could feel my brother's breath on my face, smell the sourness of the wine that darkened his lips. "What is it?" I sat up slowly. "Speak more slowly."

There were tears streaming down his face.

"Lazaros!" I cried in shock. "What plagues you?"

"It has all gone wrong," he wept. "And it is all my fault that they have done such a foolish thing! But no one will listen to me."

Fully awakened now, I grabbed his tunic fiercely. "Tell me at once what is going on, Lazaros! With no more tears."

"Remember when the men asked me what I saw when I was dead? And I told them, although I didn't really know what I had seen. And their questions led me to say things that were perhaps . . . not true. But I have been so confused!"

"This I *know*, Lazaros. The realm of death is beyond our understanding. But what does any of this have to do with tonight?"

"Yeshua and Shimon have conspired to bring down both the priesthood and to end the rule of the Romans . . . and it is all because of *my* visions that they feel so certain!" His whole body trembled. "Everyone was drunk, and it was decided we should act immediately. Yudas was reluctant. But Yeshua was insistent. None of them understand the danger!"

The loud, insistent drum of my own heartbeat filled my ears. "Lazaros?" I asked gravely, knowing suddenly as his sister that he had been holding something back. "What did you see in the tomb?"

"I saw terrible things, Miriam," he sobbed. "I saw all of time. And

I saw . . . you. More comes back each day and it makes me sick. I saw Yudea turned into a wasteland. The city on fire. I saw *you* on fire. And father dead! And all of those who we love dead! All dead!"

So death had given Lazaros dark prophecies of his own.

"When I first opened my eyes in the tomb, I saw only the darkness. I felt the linen confining my legs and my arms and I did not feel relieved. I felt . . . I felt . . . " Lazaros stuttered and trembled.

"Say it."

"I *despised* whomever had brought me back! I felt that I was about to arrive somewhere beautiful and new and then . . . I was snatched back into a life that no longer belonged to me. I did not want to be Lazaros anymore."

I stood up, pulling him to me, surprised at how light he felt, as if his bones were hollow.

"What trouble has this caused tonight?" I asked finally, a hand on both of his shoulders, trying to ground him. "Speak clearly. Where is Yeshua?"

"Shimon has convinced everyone that my visions mean that Yeshua is the Messiah and our victory against the Romans is assured. Yeshua will meet with the Sanhedrin this night and they will kneel at his feet as the temple crumbles. The Jews will finally be returned to their kingdom and their rightful city. And the Romans will fall under the weight of the temple ruins just like the Egyptians were swept away by the ocean that Moshe commanded."

"But this is madness!" I cried, shocked that they could believe in such a plan.

"Yudas has already been sent to ask the high priest if he will meet with Yeshua, even though everyone knows he is searching for a reason to hand Yeshua over to the Romans. And now everyone is drunk and asleep at Gethsemane. Yeshua is in a trance and will not answer to me. And Shimon won't hear a word I have to say. I have a terrible premonition, Miriam! But Yudas and the guards have yet to arrive, so perhaps there is still time."

He didn't need to say another word. I was running, my hand in his, flying through the streets.

Perhaps we were transformed into birds. The faster we ran, the less it seemed our feet brushed the earth. A wind came from behind us, driving under our cloaks, billowing out the fabric like wings. But as we neared the garden, the trees themselves told me the news I did not want to hear.

It has come to pass. He has been taken from this place.

The only one who remained when we reached the clearing was Shimon. For the first time since I had met him, his face was empty of any discernible emotion. The effect was uncanny: he seemed to be without features, his nose an inhuman block, his mouth slack, drooping open, his complexion fading into the silvers and blues of the olive trees behind him.

Slowly, as if he were asleep and speaking from a dream, he told us what we already knew. "Yudas came with the guards. But there were soldiers, too. It was different than we expected. We thought they would take him to the high priest. But they arrested him. Forcibly. And Yeshua worked no miracles. But that does not mean anything . . . God will keep his son safe."

"Will he keep *you* safe?" I took Shimon by his shoulders and shook him. I began shouting obscenities at him. I cannot remember now all that I said. But by the time Lazaros had managed to separate us, Shimon was sobbing. Whether from guilt or sadness or fear I could not tell and did not care to know.

• • •

In the hour before dawn, my father, with Yosseph at his side, met us back in Bethany. They had been up all night at an emergency session of the Sanhedrin at which Yeshua had been tried. Both men wore grave expressions and neither could meet my eye. I did not yet know what this meant. Or perhaps I refused to acknowledge it.

The morning arrived newborn. Yet we had been awake for an entire day and night—such a short time for so much to go wrong.

Atalyah went to fetch Imah. She sat silently as my father explained what had happened. Her expression was as impenetrable as rock.

"I still can't believe it. *Why* did he say such a thing . . ." My father was shaking his head, pounding his fist against his chest as if he could dislodge the answer to his question from within himself.

"It was a performance," Yosseph explained sadly. "The court held no real power. Caiaphas will do whatever Pilate wants. And then Pilate will do Herod's dirty work. The three men act as one . . . The priests seek to protect what power they still maintain. Their allegiance is to the Romans! Caiaphas was looking for anything that would give him the authority to hand Yeshua over to the Romans."

"And Yeshua gave it to them." My father's voice quivered, almost breaking. "I caught his eye with a look to say that he should remain quiet and let them tire themselves out. But . . ."

"What did he say?" My voice was strong. It seemed not to issue from my mouth, but from behind me.

"It was what he refused to say . . . refused to deny that is," Yosseph continued. "Caiaphas asked him again and again if he said he was the Son of God."

"He said he was?"

Yosseph and my father exchanged a grave look.

I closed my eyes, imagining how it had happened. I could see into the dark, drafty room lit by dirty lamps. The men were all shoved into this makeshift hall of judgment, with Yeshua standing in the midst of them, pacing back and forth like a trapped leopard. He was never at his wisest surrounded by men. Only in the forest, among women and children and trees, was he patient and tender enough to deliver real wisdom.

I heard Yeshua's voice as Yosseph's lips moved to answer me: "You say that I am."

Lazaros coughed. A dry, nervous sound. "What is the verdict?"

"Death," Yosseph whispered. "They will hand him over to Pilate in order to sentence him to death."

My father began to weep.

Imah slammed the table with both hands. "He has gone to his death then? It is finally happening? And you are surprised? The boy has been courting death since he was a child!"

And without a tear she stormed from the room.

• • •

I sought the safest place inside of me. Not my mind. Certainly not my heart. Not now.

I settled low. I sought protection in my own womb.

Still I can remember the fresh, almost fetal smell of spring that is not yet perfumed but holds space for the bud, the green promise of a scent that will come.

We went into Yerusalem. There was no choice but to get as close to the governor's palace as possible. My father assured us, before he left to seek more news, that this is where Pilate would exact his Roman justice. The sun had risen only an hour before and yet everyone had heard. Achim and Enosh met us at the city gates.

"It has come to pass. The kingdom is here. Yeshua will bring down the temple and then God will drive out the wicked . . ." A blind man practically sang his good news, blithely throwing about his walking stick so that I had to duck to avoid it hitting me in the face. A group of young women, weeping dramatically, were saying his name wrong: "Yeshu, Yeshu." They pushed past us with no sign that they recognized me or Lazaros.

How could he exist for these people?

Everyone streamed into the city, stepping on each other's feet.

I tried to spot Yohan Ben-Zebedee or Yudas, but the disciples were nowhere to be found.

"Keep moving," Salome instructed, talking to me like a child.

"Stand straight," Imah whispered into my ear at my other side. "Don't let any of them see your pain."

I let them escort me, walking as if in a dream, seeing dimly the dusty streets of my childhood when my feet had been too small, my body too light to even make a sound. Now our footprints would reverberate forever into an unimaginable future. I could feel the tremor of violence spreading out from this horrible moment.

As the streets grew narrow, so did our possibilities. I saw them dropping away behind us, forgotten . . . the stories of my life that would no longer happen.

"If he puts him to death, there will be a riot. If Pilate wants to control the crowds, it would be better to be merciful." Lazaros was talking to himself.

"Are you a fool, boy?" Imah grunted with disbelief. "Merciful? I don't think you know the same Romans that I do!"

"Imah, you are right," Achim agreed with Yeshua's mother. But I did not care, didn't even turn around to look at him. "A riot is *exactly* what Pilate wants. He's desperate for any opportunity to kill Jews and set an example."

"Do not say such things!" Lazaros pleaded. "You speak of my brother! Her son! Her husband!"

I could taste salt in my mouth, and when I swallowed there was the tang of iron behind it. Blood had already been spilled. I was sure of it. It stung my nostrils and I gagged against it.

"Will they stone him?"

"Not for treason! For treason it is always the cross."

It was easy to break free of Imah and Salome and push forward through the swarming throng of people struggling at the entrance to the courtyard. But I could not even get in, for people were packed as tightly as stones in a wall.

Push harder. Get to him. Words without a discrete origin washed through me. I tried to wiggle through the space between two men. "Move!"

One of the tall men swiveled around, looking up into the sky. "What a strange sign! A sign of evil! Perhaps he *is* the devil the priests think he is!"

High above the city, hovering in the sky directly above the court-yard, a group of vultures were circling. More vultures than I had ever seen together. Ten. Twenty. Thirty. Perhaps more. They circled tighter and tighter, black wings overlapping and merging into one as if to create the closed, dense circuit of a huge iris. The sky's eye peered down at me. An eye of birds.

Do not show me this, I begged. *Do not let me know this.*

Leukas, the Divine is terrible. It destroys you. When you see it at last, you will long to look away.

You will wake one night and it will be waiting in the darkness above your bed. A face without eyes. A mirror that reflects nothing but void. Fire the color of bones. And you will have to choose to journey through a fear so raw and violent it threatens to obliterate your very soul.

The vultures were the sign of a divine presence bigger even than weather. Higher, vaster than even the heavens. Deeper under the earth than even the worms had penetrated.

They would bear witness to this failure. The violence would spread like ink in water.

I still don't understand all that I saw that day and all that I know is still to come. The horror of it. Great smoky clouds would bloom up out of the ground. Men would slave to cover over the dirt with hard slabs of stone. Forests would turn into tombs. I saw sterile expanses without a single green shoot. A single smell. And everywhere I saw women aflame like candles. Eyes melting in their heads. Gaping holes where their breasts were sliced away.

I realized then that the kingdom *would* come. But only when every child was gone from the earth. The grass would come back. The trees would burst through stone and deserts. Rain would wash away our filth.

Oh Yeshua . . . The pain was a sword in my heart. *The kingdom will come. But it will not be a kingdom for us.*

The dark birds whirled in a tighter and tighter circle above me.

My mistake. Yeshua's mistake. It would not just destroy us. It would destroy all those to come. The realization rocked through me with such force that I felt my bones trembling. The crowd erupted in cheers as Pilate appeared on the steps in full ceremonial attire, his breastplate glinting.

"It is a miracle!" a woman cried out. "They have pardoned him! Pilate has pardoned Yeshua!"

"What?"

The woman continued to rejoice. "It is a Passover miracle! They have pardoned my brother-in-law! Pilate has pardoned Yeshua Barabbas of his crimes!"

Did I sink then? My knees were suddenly unable to support my weight. The vultures circled above me. To whom did that giant black eye belong to? What massive, impersonal entity was watching this unfold?

Why had we gone to the city? The sky would have saved us. The trees would have sheltered us. The birds would have let us pass. But our fellow men would not. They hungered for blood. The city always requires sacrifice.

• • •

My brother found me, held me, and for the first time I thought, *These are arms that have been folded under a shroud. These are a dead man's arms!*

No, I thought desperately. There was still time. The temple could crumble. The sky could turn black. The moon could cover the sun.

"The kingdom could still come," Lazaros said dumbly. He repeated it like a prayer. "The kingdom comes."

"It does . . . It does . . ." I moaned. He did not understand how ter-rifying those words were.

I did this to him, I thought. *I, too, am to blame.*

And then I was screaming in a language not yet born. Was I cursing myself? Or Yeshua? It was impossible to know. Lazaros had to pin my arms to my body. "She is going mad," he pleaded with Salome. "What can we do?"

Imah stepped forward and put her forehead to mine. Her breath tasted like bread. She sucked in my exhales and gave them back to me. Slowly I was strengthened by that wick of vitality that lived inside of her.

"We will follow him through the city," I said finally and Imah nod-ded, her forehead still against mine.

"We will follow him until the end," she echoed. "We will watch this and let it light a fire inside of us that will not be extinguished."

To the end, I thought with a pang of aguish. I stood as a flame stands on a candle that is about to burn out.

We knew it had begun when the yelling started. The jeering. The throng of onlookers running ahead to look back at the spectacle.

"Hold me," Salome said. She laced her arms around my waist.

"No," I protested stubbornly, pushing her away, pushing through people until I was closest to the road where he would pass.

The stones hummed, anticipating not only his steps but the steps of thousands more. Here they will walk for thousands of years, working the wound so deep that it will permanently scar the world. *Men and women will cut into this path again and again so that it may always bleed. Blood begets more blood. Honoring this death will create more death. This wound will be re-opened and celebrated when it needs to be healed.*

Let the heat come to my hands now. Let me put my hands on that moment. Let me close the wound.

The cheering started.

"Here he comes! The Son of God!"

Fifty-Four

Would you have me describe it as you have had countless others describe it to you? What perverse nature keeps drawing you to these details? The wounds on his back, the blood on his face, the cross on his back.

I will not dwell on the violence, Leukas. It does a disservice to his life: the beauty of his body, his laughter, his wisdom, his power, his anger, his clarity and vision, his vast and ancient heart.

I will not crucify my husband again to give you a better story.

You may hammer the nails in yourself.

• • •

One thing I will tell you. When Yeshua saw me, he stopped. We were so close we could have touched.

The soldiers urged him on, kicking at him. But he did not move.

He smiled lightly, as terribly as a child who has done something wrong and knows it. "Forgive me, Miriam," he whispered. "I did not know what I was doing."

• • •

I, too, needed forgiveness. I asked the birds that had begun their spring journey back to the land to forgive me. I asked the shrike to forgive me. I remember her exultant whoop and cry. I asked the mourning dove to forgive me and the one black crane that dissected the clear sky behind the cross. I asked the swallows to descend on my shame and cover it like a shroud of smoke. And the crickets in the grass, crushed underfoot by the crowd that followed the soldiers and Yeshua up the hill. I can still hear their dying pulse as our feet silenced them.

Will the bees ever forgive me? They hid in the spring flowers, making a contented, hungry buzz, unaware that the pollen they swallowed would be tinged with pain forever. The old wives say the honey was bitter that summer, that it tasted of chalk.

I know that it tasted of the guilt that bled from me like sweat. I could almost see it in the air: my shame and horror so potent and poisonous that it turned the wind an acrid yellow.

The hills were covered with a thousand red wounds. The anemones hemorrhaged out of the green. Each bloom reminded me that what lay below was not just soil, not just stones. It was the living, breathing body of the earth. And it bled.

Even here, far from Golgotha, I am denied the sweetness of spring. Never again will I wander the hills freshly furred with grass and feel renewal in my breast. All nectar turns to ash on my tongue.

I did not just lose my husband that day.

I lost a season. I lost flowers.

Above all, I asked Yeshua to forgive me.

He was washed away from me, down a river a thousand years long. His waters spilled onto the shore of some land I did not know.

It will be a long time until I reach the ocean of his love again.

• • •

"Do not take your eyes from him," Imah whispered into my ear on Golgotha. "Watch for the moment he goes."

I do not deserve to look at him, I thought. *This is my fault.*

The knowledge that I could have stopped Yudas, that I could have worked harder to remove him from his drunken friends, was going to kill me. Why had I fled to Bethany after my miscarriage? I suddenly couldn't remember. Wasted days. Wasted years.

He did not speak. But he held my eyes until the end.

We will not be together again for a long time. I knew it with a certainty that threatened to erase my mind. I swayed, and Salome steadied me.

I saw a thousand years spread out in front of me like a rug. Land rippling and pulsing as it grew cities. Whole peoples migrating up and down the length of rivers. I was going to be alone with this sorrow for an eternity.

"What good can come from this?" Salome whispered. "We must be wrong about everything . . ."

"I was wrong about everything," I answered her. "It is my fault."

Most of all, I remember Imah's breath in my ear and the knowledge that the arms holding me had once held Yeshua.

• • •

"Shut her up!" the soldiers pleaded.

Only then did I hear my own screams.

The women knew that we could not moan or sob.

When Imah howled it was not with sorrow. It was with rage.

That sound still lives in my soul. And if I relax too much it begins to rise. It is the music that makes me burn. And I expect I will hear it in the next life, too.

And we did not stop until the sun began to sink in the sky and Yosseph came with orders from Pilate to take his body down from the cross. I don't know what bribery it took, but he managed it elegantly, without inserting himself into our grief.

A small flock of warblers flew overhead, letting loose a cascade of farewell songs. They were heading home to their nests. The heat of the day dissipated until I could only feel it in my knees, grinding into the ground.

Where was the earthquake? The thunder? The voice of God? The fearful shrieking of an eagle come to announce the news?

He is gone. He has passed onward.

Yosseph, together with Lazaros and my father, wrapped his body in a linen sheet and placed him on a wooden pallet.

"Where are you taking him?" I wailed, scrambling after them.

"They are taking him to the tomb," Imah whispered. "We will go there to bathe him."

I nodded and let her lead me down the hill. I tried to imitate her stride, the straightness of her spine, the firm, grim set of her lips. She knew what it meant to wear a widow's face. She had lost her own beloved.

I came back to myself with a jolt, turning to see a soldier laughing, trying on the soiled, seamless cloak that had been flung from my husband before they began. The other soldier held out a coin, making an offer.

It is done, I thought. *I will never bear his child.*

I began to wail again.

"I know," Imah said. "Keep walking. I know."

• • •

"Whose tomb is this?" I asked. We had followed the men to a place just outside the city as the sky turned purple with twilight. My father lit a lamp so we could see the path, then handed me a satchel of expensive spices. Who had brought him such things?

"This my tomb, Miriam," Yosseph said quietly. "But the hour of my death has not yet come. So it will do better serving another."

I did not thank him. Did not say anything at all. I followed Imah and Salome into the darkness. Yosseph lit a torch for us.

Yeshua was laid on a low slab of stone. Imah unwound the linen and Salome helped her and I stood dumbly watching as the lamplight turned the white cloth gold.

"Untie his feet, Miriam," Salome instructed me.

I did not move.

"Miriam!" his mother commanded. "You *must* touch him. You must look at him."

What can I tell you about it?

That he looked as he had in life? That he did not seem dead?

But he *was* dead. The wound at his heart yawned open as a mouth. He was no longer warm, and when I peeled back the cloth and put my hands on his feet, I was shocked that he felt like a river stone, cold from the water. Yosseph had packed the linen cloth around his body with a fortune's worth of aloe and myrrh, but the costly herbs did little to disguise the smell of blood and shit. I was reminded of the birthing rooms I'd been in over the years; the sour funk of a body trying to release.

He was heavy and stiffening.

Imah watched me holding his arm, my fingers squeezing tighter and tighter, willing him to wake up. Willing him to live.

"He is still here, Miriam," she said. "Treat his body as you would if he was alive. Know that he is nearby."

Salome came to my side and touched my waist. "Honor him with your eyes. Look at him as you did in life. Your love for him has not passed away. Remember that."

I tried to look at each part of him discretely, tried to imagine I was circling a tree too big for my eyes to encompass all at once.

Here is the elbow. The hip bone. The neck. The arch of the foot.

It was only when we rolled him over to massage the herbs into his back and I took the nataph resin and began to carefully work it into the softness behind his knees that it hit me, finally, that my husband was truly gone.

It is a terrible thing to realize that the person you have loved is not just a body. That the body holds little of their essence.

Emptiness with substance opened in me. Emptiness many lifetimes thick. Emptiness that was so dense with suffering that it could not be filled or healed.

I knelt and rested my head on that stone slab and put my face against his calves, my hands gripping his thighs, feeling the strange newness of him. He had never been this still in life—not even when he slept. There was always a chord pulled tight deep inside, vibrating with some energy that found release in twitches, exhales, his arm reflexively reaching out and curling around me, his hand cupping my breast.

"Close his eyes," Imah instructed, but I shook my head.

She grabbed me and her touch finally communicated the depth of pain that her face did not.

"Look him in the face," she said. "You must witness this. Trust me. You must hold him in your heart forever. I will try. But there are already so many. Miriam, you are responsible for his memory."

And I saw them in her eyes. All the ones she had lost. A man with Yeshua's leonine nose and big smile. His father. The children as delicate and small as sun-wilted roses fallen from the bush. The sisters and brothers she had outlived.

I saw the distant blue outline of her parents; only the bright, dark intelligence of their eyes showing up clearly.

"Look at him."

His mouth was open and the scar on his upper lip glowed white.

All my life I had dreamed of his dead face. I had seen visions of this moment in my future and in my past. But none of it had prepared me for *this*. What good was such a vision if it did not prevent tragedy? What good was it to see his face now and feel its simple, open expression beginning to erase all that was good about him? All that was fresh and real and complicated.

I did not want to look at him. I closed my eyes.

Years later, I finally understood my despair. In the stories men tell about my husband, he does not wear his face. He wears a mask of death.

"Yeshua." I said his name, testing it on his body. I tried to meet his gaze, but there was nothing to meet. His eyes were as flat and blank as dust coating stones, tables, houses, after a wind has kicked up sand.

Still refusing to look at him, I passed my hand over his eyes to shut them and felt the tickle of his eyelashes against my palm.

And his nakedness. His beautiful, long body. The sturdy muscles of his thighs. His broad, hairy chest. It felt wrong for me to be clothed with him laid bare.

Sometimes I think that I wouldn't care if all his words were erased and forgotten. They are already twisted past their meaning. But his body. What I would give to have it back just for an hour. A day. To show everyone—to show *you*—that his greatest magic was not spoken or thought. It was lived. It was his eyes, his arms, his dancing feet. It was his hands slicing through the air as he told a story. The hunch of his big shoulders when he was thinking. The dark tuft of hair below his belly button. The fullness of his lips tasting wine.

We would never lie together again. Skin to skin.

"Curse me . . ." I said, but the words barely had edges. They stuck in my throat.

Did I condemn myself to loneliness in that moment? Or did it happen before, at the foot of the cross? I only know that a cold void flowered in my heart—a space that would only accept Yeshua and would stay empty as long as he was gone.

The worst part was that it had been months since we had lain together, months since I had been able to truly touch and see my husband, so foolishly naive to think that there would be time to look at him. To watch him as he took his meals. As he walked ahead of me on our journeys. To watch him sleeping beside me, a stray lock of hair across his forehead. As he held our first child in his strong arms.

"How did you do it? When your love died?" I asked Salome, and my voice was barely audible.

"Do not ask me such things, Miriam. How did I do it? I died. And then, at some point, later on, I was no longer dead. There is no path through this forest. There is only each second as it comes."

"Stay with him, and come out when you are ready," Imah told me, and I nodded without turning.

"Yeshua," I tried again.

I was choking on my own tears, climbing onto the stone with him, straddling his body, shaking his shoulders.

So close to him, I could finally feel the anger. An anger so intense it made me shudder. I slammed my fists down on his unyielding chest.

"You fool. You fool . . ."

Oh, I was yelling at myself. I wanted him to rise and pin my arms at my side.

"What are you doing, Miriam? Have you gone mad?" he would say.

I put my hands on my belly and I prayed. I prayed without words, without thought, without a name, summoning that part of me that endured from lifetime to lifetime.

Mother, I said. And I meant myself. I meant Kemat. The leopards. The vultures. The river. The olive trees. All my grandmothers. All the wavering blades of wild wheat in the field.

Bring him back to me. Bring him back to me. I don't care if it's wrong.

And I lay down on Yeshua's body, pressing my hands to his side, pressing my fingers into his wounds.

I felt it for a second. A vibration in my fingers. A stone of fever growing in my palms. But then it was gone. So it was true. He had always outmatched me in power. He could bring Lazaros back.

But I was not strong enough.

No matter how hard I tried, I could not bring Yeshua back.

When I walked outside, the night had finally arrived. Black and complete. Clouds covered the moon. The only shadows that remained belonged to the men.

I turned to my father and nodded.

"It is done."

Slowly, the men pushed a boulder in front of the tomb's mouth, the stone making a beleaguered sound as they rolled it over the ground. And I watched, unsure whether I was the one outside standing under the stars, or if I was the dead one they were shutting up inside.

• • •

What did I expect? That they had fled beyond the city?

The sight of the disciples camped out in the courtyard when I arrived back in Bethany made me want to be sick.

"Miriam!" Shimon approached me. "He has died. Everyone is speaking of it. They crucified him. What happened? Did the guards who did it fall down dead? What do we do? What comes next?"

I had never seen him so undone. His eyes were dilated, and his cheeks were red. Could he be drunk? Were they all drunk?

"Get out," I said flatly. "Get out of my home."

But Shimon did not listen. "I went to Caiaphas's house when they were trying him. I followed him, Miriam. Did he know that I followed him? That I did not desert him?"

It was too much. I was past rage. I had plunged into an ocean of despair and sorrow so vast that I was drowning. I ignored Shimon, looking around at who had stayed.

Yakov knelt next to the fire, rocking back and forth. Were the Ben-Zebedee brothers sleeping back-to-back under the fig tree? Everyone was here. All of them cowards, waiting in the safety of Bethany, while their master had died.

All but one.

I turned back to Shimon. "Where is he?"

"Who?" Shimon asked, his brows knitting together in confusion.

"Yudas." His name already felt like a bruise. Yudas, who I had betrayed just as badly as I had betrayed Yeshua when I washed my hands of their stupid plan.

"He is gone, Miriam," Andreas spoke. "When he realized they would kill Yeshua, he went into the fields and hanged himself."

I sank to my knees. The scream was silent, my mouth so open that my soul could have slipped out.

Oh, oh, oh. It was not just Yeshua I had forsaken. It was Yudas. It was my friends. It was my family. Everyone I had ever loved would be caught in this destruction.

The sky above me cared little for my shame. It was clear and perfectly blue.

Fifty-Five

My mind throbbed blackly no matter how hard I shut my eyes. Every beat of my heart repeated the unthinkable: *You are young with many years before you. You will long outlive this day. And at the end of your life, the time spent with him will amount to a grain of pollen.*

Three years. Years with months when we did not speak and boiled in our own anger. Months with days when we did not touch and chose not to drink each other's sweetness.

When Yeshua had tried to love me just a few nights prior, I had pushed him away, stupidly, saying, "Not yet. But soon."

There would be no soon. No time to come. We would never lie side by side, never join as one. I would never again feel his weight on top of me, his hands in my hair, his breath at my ear.

"I have been a fool," I whispered. It was the only thing I could bring myself to say.

• • •

Later I returned to the tomb. I did not sleep. I sat with my back to the huge boulder, feeling its rough texture grinding into my shoulders. I watched the garden take in the sunset's golds and reds and press it into the dark, slow wine of night. The shadows were so heavy and ponderous under the olive trees that they looked totally impenetrable, even more resistant than the boulder behind me.

The Romans had sent three soldiers. There was worry that someone might come and try to steal the body and stage some grand joke to throw in Pilate's face.

They were quiet when I arrived, but it didn't take them long to jeer.

"Lady!" The tallest one with a face so cleanly shaved it looked naked, called at me. "Tell us the truth of it."

"The truth?" another soldier scoffed. He was darker than the others, with leathery, weathered cheeks, but his hair where it peeked out from under his helmet was a shock of pale yellow. "What do you mean, Magnus? He's dead. That's proof enough that he's not their messiah."

Magnus, the tall soldier, gave a cruel laugh. "Hush, Nereus. If this rabbi *really* was special, his wife would know. Wouldn't she?"

Nereus's calloused face curled into a stupid grin. "Did you think your husband was a king?"

Magnus, the sharper of the three, snarled at Nereus, his blue eyes flashing. "Let her speak, Nereus. She knew the man well."

There was something in those chilly eyes. Curiosity. Fear. Longing. He was the same as all the other men. No different from Shimon or Yakov or Mattiyahu. Here was a man who had helped kill my husband, and yet he was still searching for meaning through Yeshua.

"I have nothing to give you," I said softly, understanding what it was that Magnus wanted.

"What's that?" Nereus scoffed even as Magnus leaned closer.

"I have nothing to give you. There is no wisdom here. Only death."

"Ah. Yes. That's it. He never told her anything." The short man nodded slowly, a smug smile spreading across his shiny, childlike face.

"Let her be," Nereus suggested. He was picking his ear with disinterest. "Her husband was no one."

"Enough," I whispered. "Enough. Go. Leave."

Magnus looking from Nereus to me, his hand at his hip, toying with the hilt of his sword. "They say he walked on water. Raised a man from the dead. I would have her tell us about it . . ."

"ENOUGH!" I was shuddering violently, could feel my skin becoming porous, drawing in the power of the garden around me: thorn and venom and shadow.

But Magnus stared at me as if the answer would arrive on my face. Written on my skin itself. "How did he heal then? How did he do it?"

Something brushed my right leg. Something muscled and warm.

"By Jupiter! What is it?" Nereus jumped with surprise.

Magnus frowned.

Without looking down, I took my hand and ran it along a pelt as smooth as water.

The leopard growled and it sent a vibration through the ground itself. I could feel the powerful animal humming with the potential for violence. His tail whipped back and forth, finally coming to curl around my ankles.

It had been years since I had seen the big cats that haunted my childhood.

"Magnus, she can charm animals!" the short man hissed, backing up slowly. "One of those Canaanite whores who learned their darkness from the hags to the north! We should leave."

"Are you afraid of a leopard?" Magnus snapped. "It is more likely it will eat *her* than us."

Oh, I could feel the cat as an extension of my own body, like my dark hair had rippled into the night until it connected with its approaching darkness.

But Magnus's diffidence wavered when he looked to his side and saw that another leopard had arrived, slipping by him, circling his legs, looking up with fangs bared, jaws open, the dark pink of its hungry throat beckoning.

"So help me gods, she has called them all!" the short one yelled. "There are more!"

Three more panthers emerged out of the shadows, announcing their presence first with the gem-like blinking of their eyes.

"I'm not staying for this," Nereus announced before slipping away. "This is the work of angry gods."

The short man did not need convincing. He left, almost running, making a grunting noise from the shadows when he stumbled over a root.

But Magnus stayed for a moment longer, breathing slowly and purposefully through his narrow nostrils.

"Who are you?" he asked. "Who was he?"

"No one," I said softly. "Now go."

And he did, looking over his shoulder twice, the intensity of his blue gaze almost burning me.

The leopards did not give chase. They paced the garden's border endlessly while one of them lay down at my feet. Exhausted, I let my back slide down the rock. The big cat nudged my thigh and put his heavy head in my lap.

"Oh." The weight and warmth reminded me of another head that had lain there but recently. My tears fell on his spotted pelt.

The leopard twisted his head and looked up at me, fixing me with his great yellow eyes, opening his fearsome mouth and letting a long gust of warm breath wash over my face. The tip of his whisker tickled my cheek.

"Yeshua," I said his name. But the cat blinked and did not respond.

"Where are you?" I asked again to the darkness.

Impossible to think of him inside of another life.

Impossible *not* to see him in every star, in every blade of grass. In the still, golden universe of the leopard's eyes.

The cats paced in front of me until dawn, when they departed with the night, melting back below the horizon.

The next night the soldiers did not return.

. . .

"Come with me to Nazareth," Imah said brusquely. There were the sounds of women going to fetch water and men saying the Shema from their own rooftops.

Miriam caught me early the second morning. I snuck back into the house, careful not to wake anyone, stole a piece of stale bread, and climbed up on the roof. But the bread was like a piece of rock that I could hardly even eat when I moistened it with my spit. I clasped it in my hand like a talisman.

The mellowness of dawn was still present in the blurred edges of the fields and trees, but the sun was already risen. I suddenly wished that I was like a flower and could draw all my sustenance from the sun's light and warmth. I wished that I could merely watch the colors wake up in the fields and appreciate the glory that I had been fed, rain falling every once in a while to wash me clean and wet my lips.

But the city glinting callously in the midst of the land reminded me that we humans were bound to something unnatural. A way of life that required cooking and killing and sacrifice. Required walls and rules and armies. We were always living against the seasons.

"You must eat. You must care for yourself."

Imah's voice did not surprise me. I didn't turn but watched out of the corner of my eye as she came to stand beside me, folding her arms across her chest, leaning back, looking at the clear sky, her eyes narrowing against the brightness.

"All right." It was all I could say. Words of substance were impossible. I could make no promises.

"Would you give the Romans another victim? Would you do their work for them?"

"I . . ." I stuttered, lifting the bread up before me and looking at it with new eyes.

I eat bread, I drink wine. And it becomes me. It becomes my body, my blood!

The words still carried the passion in his voice. A fresh wave of grief flooded through me.

What a terrible thing. To look out at the beautiful land, the bread in my hands, and realize this was his greatest teaching: now was the kingdom. Even the now of pain.

Oh my heart only wanted to love one person. One man. And the teaching was too big. Too painful. My heart was supposed to love all of it. Every moment. Momentous or insignificant. Every insect and particle of dust.

This was the kingdom. This very morning. Imah by my side. The farmers heading out to the fields with their sons. The women carrying pottery on their heads to the market.

This hard piece of bread. This ability to eat and drink.

This body of mine. Saltiness. Cramps and aches. Soft belly. Strong calves.

This was the kingdom and Yeshua was *not* in it.

All of this was the kingdom. And every painful day without him that followed after this would still be the kingdom.

A kingdom that needed no king. A kingdom that was larger, grander, stranger than men and women. Free of our sorrow, our love, our small, complicated stories.

"I will eat. I promise you. But I will not come to Nazareth. Not yet."

Imah nodded and then she surprised me; she finally began to cry. Her whole face crumpled inward, her hands going out in front of her to grasp the air. A shudder racked through her whole body; the ragged weeping of a mother who has been saving her tears since the day her son was born.

She spoke through her tears. "You knew him for who he was. That much I know. I am not sure anyone else truly knew him."

"I will tell the truth," I whispered. "But I fear no one will listen to me."

"They won't," Imah laughed. "But that doesn't mean you should stop speaking."

We hugged firmly before she left to return to her family who were still alive, still requiring care.

I watched her go, knowing full well in my heart that I would never go back to Nazareth.

Imah died three years later, the casualty of a Roman raid. A death perhaps as brutal as that of her son's. I would have no way of knowing. Did the soldiers know what woman fell beneath their sword?

But I did not know about her death then. It took me nearly twenty years to find out, the news coming to me from the lips of a man who did not know my true name, had no idea that my tears were for a woman I had loved. Not for a Mother of God.

The next night, fatigue made my feet heavy, but I could not sleep. I longed for dreamless hours that would dull the pain. But I took myself again to the tomb. My only companion was an owl that settled invisibly on a branch just past the outer edge of the garden. I heard him drop through the leaves, hooting triumphantly. The swollen note echoed in my own throat, as if to remind me that time *was* passing, even if nothing seemed to breathe or move or change.

"This is the kingdom," I said softly, looking at the darkness.

The owl hooted again. A series of questions. *Who? who? who?*

"This, this, this," I said, feeling my words move through me and into the world like an incantation.

The stars remained inscrutable and distant. Refusing to brighten. Something rustled in the woods, rooting for a burrow, or was it a mouse trying to escape the owl?

The night hummed smugly, teeming with crickets and bats and night birds. The sound grew louder and louder.

"I'm ready to go," I said. "Make my mind like the mind of a bird. Let me forget that I have edges."

It was a powerful prayer. A dangerous prayer. I wasn't sure if I meant it. What I meant was that I found my mind and my body to be a prison. I wanted to dissolve into deep time. To fly out of my birdcage body like the doves I had released in the temple.

No more hands. No more arms. No more thighs or womb. No more breasts or belly.

Slowly I tried to forget myself. To forget the body that had touched him, loved him, and was now made sick by his absence.

No more bones. No more lungs or breath. No more heart.

Like water in water, I was floating. The wind pushed through the night air like blood through my own veins. At once I was expansive and extremely small: an ocean, an iota of ash, pulsing between omniscience and nonexistence.

What would it mean to erase myself? Would I be erasing *him,* too?

No more tongue . . . I began. *No more lips. No more voice.*

A waft of dark musk rippled through the garden. An animal used to hunting in the darkness was padding softly across the grass.

Ah. I smiled, feeling myself about to disappear. *The answer to my prayer. The leopards will come to deliver me. They will eat me and turn me into grace and fur.*

I felt the warmth of a body exhaling as it settled beside me.

"Miriam."

Time stopped.

"Miriam."

I had no choice but to open my eyes.

He was almost touching me, his hand hovering above my thigh, the apprehension in his eyes telling me he would not touch me without my permission.

He was wearing the same old, blue tunic he always wore, with the rip at the neck that I had tried to get him to let me mend a dozen times. His color was restored, his forehead smoothed of worry. He looked as handsome as he had on our wedding day, only his eyes appeared older, deeper. They mirrored my own disbelief.

"How are you here?" My hands were trembling. I could not touch him. "How is this possible?"

"I . . ." Tears bloomed at the corners of his eyes.

"Where did you come from?" I repeated, trying to keep my voice steady.

"I don't know. Oh, Miriam." He was sobbing. His huge body was shaking uncontrollably as he leaned over his knees, grasping them, rocking back and forth. "What have I done? How could it all end so quickly?"

"What were you thinking?" I whispered, hardly trusting my own voice. "What was *I* thinking? I have lost you, Yeshua. I have let you slip from my fingers."

His lips quivered. I thought he might dissolve. His eyes were haunted when he finally met my gaze again.

"I was wrong about everything. Wrong about the Father. Wrong to bring Lazaros back. Wrong about the temple and my ability to face the Romans. Wrong about Shimon and Andreas and Philip and Yakov and Thoma . . . They understand nothing, will understand less as the years pass. They will be driven by power now."

"Of course," I said, nodding. "They are men. And you were not here for men. Don't you see now? You were here for the hills, the birds, the mountains. For the mustard seeds! The lilies! For yourself! For our children! For me!"

"Yes, I was here for you." He finally broke the distance between us, his hand shimmering blue in the darkness, clamping down on mine, squeezing my fingers.

I gasped. His touch was firm and strong.

"It was my fault, too," I whispered, bringing his hand closer to me, letting my lips graze the place where the nails should have driven through. But the veins were unbroken and the skin of his palm was smooth.

"It is my fault that I left you alone with fools," I began. "That I turned from you in anger. That I did not seek out your love and let it heal us both after I lost the child."

"The child . . ." A strange look passed over his face and he glanced behind him. The owl hooted again and he startled, laughing when he realized it was just a bird.

"Leave it, Yeshua. There is no time. It is long past us. This life is already spent."

The darkness tightened. The stars were heavier in the sky. Time pressed in on us. Down on us. Thousands of years. Lifetimes spent apart.

"Spent. Yes. Gone," he moaned in frustration.

"We had a chance to heal old wounds this time, Yeshua. And we failed. That is no small thing. I fear this will cause much pain."

How could I explain my dreams? Burning hillsides. Mountains gutted. Oceans as thick and black as rancid oil. Smoke covering entire countries. My people scattered. Their homeland destroyed. Men dragging women into squares and tying them to giant piles of wood and setting them alight. Floods swallowing cities with such speed that there was no sign there had ever been anything there at all. Whole landscapes parched past color.

"I know. Do not think that I have not seen the cities on fire. The death and the suffering. Do not think I have not heard my name on the lips of murderers. I am in hell, Miriam. Or perhaps I am the cause of hell."

His face was so close to mine. I could taste his breath.

"Yeshua . . ."

He reached up, his fingertips burning my cheek. "Do I dream?"

"Do I?" I turned the question back on him.

"I don't know, Miriam. I'm not sure how long we have."

"Not long enough," I whispered.

With no warning he pulled me into his lap, crushing his chest to mine, burying his face against my shoulder, pressing his big hands into my shoulder blades.

His heart beat a frantic rhythm against my breast.

"How can I do it?" he whispered huskily, tightening his embrace. "How can I move on? There is more to be done. I cannot bear to leave you."

But I did not answer him with words. Words would do us no good anymore.

Instead I nudged my face against his until he sat up and we were looking at each other, our eyes wet and bright, memorizing the other's face, slowly letting our lips brush. It was as sweet as the first time. When we kissed, I felt my entire being concentrated into the point of union.

Come to me one last time. I don't care if it is a dream.

We undressed slowly and I pressed my hand against his chest. There was no more wound.

It did not need to show on his body. The wound was in the world. It was bigger than us.

He tried to push me back into the soft moss, hungry to touch me, to cover me, but I held up my hand and made him pause. "Let me look at you."

And so, the last time I saw my husband's body it was beautiful. It was whole.

This. This. This . . .

. . . When we were done, we lay tangled together under the stars and I marveled that they had multiplied: the heavens experiencing their own springtime, each star the brilliant bloom of a secret seeded in some long-ago season.

"How long will it be until I see you again?" I whispered into his neck, my hand playing with the coarse hair of his chest, looking up at the line of his jaw, trying to burn it into me.

"It will be a long time, I think," he said, confident now. His body emanated an intense heat. This was the same heat the earth absorbs from the sun and uses to push new growth up out of the soil.

"A long time," I answered. "Many lives."

"Many lives," he echoed me. "But someday we will have to heal this."

I did not truly understand him, but I nodded anyway, relishing the tide of his breath against me.

"I will look for you, Miriam. Always." His arm curled around me tightly. "Our kingdom will come again. Someday. We will be simple people with small lives. We will walk softly, and fate will never hear our steps."

He rolled over, leaning on his arm, his heavy lashes hooding his eyes, his lips parted. He brought his fingers to my collarbone and traced the line of my neck, pressing his fingers to my cheek. His touch burned.

"How are you here, Yeshua?" I asked one last time.

"You tell *me*, Miriam. You brought me back."

Fifty-Six

I woke with my face pressed to the ground. The fresh dew on the grass chilled me. Slowly I sat up, my joints stiff, shaking out sticks and dust from the sleeves of my tunic.

I was still dressed. There was no imprint of a sleeping body. No footsteps leading into the garden. No sign of Yeshua at all.

The sky above me reddened, turning the foliage russet and gold.

It had been a dream.

Every bone in my body ached. I could hardly open my eyes. The beauty of the dawn was an offense to my sorrow. I could not bear to let it touch me.

But as I reached the edge of the garden, I looked back.

The boulder had been rolled away from the tomb.

Holding my breath, I went inside, my whole body shaking so hard I thought I would break apart.

The rising sunlight streamed onto the stone table.

The tomb was empty except for a soiled shroud.

. . .

"Where have you put him? Where have you taken his body?" I burst furiously into the courtyard with the morning sun.

The men were still sleeping, curled up under the fig trees. The sun hit Thoma's sallow face. He snored softly.

Yakov lifted himself up on his elbow, his cloak falling off his shoulders. He grumbled, going back to sleep.

Shimon was awake, stoking the embers of yesterday's cooking fire. He motioned me over to him, his finger up to his lips telling me to be quiet. "What is it, Miriam? Speak softly. Everyone has been up for days. Let them sleep."

"Someone has played a terrible joke," I hissed. "Was it you? Did you do it while I slept? Or did you pay someone? Is this another of your pranks? The first one went so well!"

"What joke?" Shimon dropped a piece of bread from his mouth, his leathery forehead wrinkling. He threw the heel of bread into the fire and looked at me intently. "What did we do while you slept?"

"His body!" I screamed. "Where have you put his body?"

"Is someone here?" Yohan rolled over, rubbing his eyes.

"It's nothing," Shimon answered. "Go back to sleep."

The look on Shimon's face when he turned back to me confirmed one thing: he was just as surprised as I was, his jaw dropping, eyes going wide and clear.

"Who did it?" The tears made my voice tremble. "Who took his body?"

"I don't know what trick you speak of," Shimon whispered angrily. "But we have been here all night. No one has come or gone."

"His body is gone," my voice faltered. He was telling the truth. He knew nothing.

Shimon eyed me warily. "You have not slept in days, Miriam, and have had little to no drink or food. Tell us slowly what you have imagined."

It was too much. Too much to have Yeshua and again to lose him. To come back and find them all asleep. I needed someone else to come and see, to tell me it was true. "I had a dream. And in it Yeshua was there as if alive again . . ."

"So you dreamt. You speak to me of dreams." Even as he spoke, Shimon was standing, picking up his wool cloak.

"Yes. I dreamed. But when I woke, the boulder had been rolled away and . . . the tomb was empty."

Finally Shimon grasped what I was saying. He made a whistling noise as he exhaled.

If not Shimon—if not the disciples—who had done this thing? Was it the zealots trying still to prove that there had been a messiah? The Romans stealing his corpse so they could further desecrate it?

"Show me," Shimon said solemnly.

The disciples stirred as we stepped over their sleeping bodies. But no one else rose to come with us.

Perhaps it was right that it was the two of us going to see the tomb. The two who had failed Yeshua the most. I, who had closed my heart to him. And Shimon, who had led him into the city.

Shimon let me walk ahead. I did not trust myself as we approached the garden. The trees looked ordinary in the daylight, silvery trunks below a growing fan of leaves. The day was already hot and I knew by how the air resisted our movement that there would be no breeze. The tomb was empty.

Shimon ran in front of me then, his cry sounding through the trees. "He is gone!" Shimon cried out again.

I knelt there, my palms up to the sky, listening as the morning doves and their silken tongues sliced through the humidity with their songs.

Shimon came out, holding the shroud in both of his hands like it was a child. He looked from it to me, and I could see the tears in his eyes. "I was not mistaken," he said. "I was not wrong! He was the Son of God. It has been proven. It is as David said, 'For you will not abandon my soul to Sheol, nor will you allow your holy one to undergo decay.'"

"No," I said softly. "You are wrong, Shimon. It was a mistake. This does not undo the pain of it."

"It does! He is risen from here, Miriam," Shimon argued. "He lives again as only a Son of God can live again." But he was overcome by the strangeness of it all. He sank to his knees in front of me, holding out the dirty shroud for me to see.

I needed no proof that Yeshua was gone from this place. My body pulsed with the wound of his absence. But it was different from Lazaros's return. I did not feel that Yeshua had been poured back into his body.

"If he is risen from this place, it is not to fulfill your prophecies, Shimon," I declared firmly, trying to make him see his error. "It has served some other purpose that we do not yet understand."

"Oh!" he exclaimed, his face brightening, dropping the shroud and reaching for my hands. "*You* have seen him. I know it. You have hidden it from us. But he has come to you!"

I could not lie. Even if I did not know the truth of what I said.

"I . . . I saw him here. It was as a dream, and he seemed alive." I admitted finally.

Shimon's face reflected my own grief. A spidery vein had broken on his ruddy cheek. His eyes were swollen with trapped tears. "What do we do, Miriam?" he asked me. "He loved you the best. He told you hidden things. What did he say when he came to you? What is the meaning of his death? Of his rising?"

"I will not tell you anything of his words," I whispered. "He spoke to me as a bridegroom speaks to his bride."

"You lie!" He was weeping. "Teach me as he taught you, Miriam. I am lost without him. You did the things that he did. You healed. Teach me! I am lost."

So many lost opportunities. Moments that I look back on and hold with tender hands, thinking: *If only I had known. If only I had done differently. What would it have meant to step into the role as their teacher? Could I have changed what happened next?*

If ever I witnessed a true miracle, it was Shimon in front of that empty tomb, imploring my help, asking me that I teach him, lead him.

I could have stood slowly, steadying his hand in mine, undoing his anger and said, "Shimon. We must forget this violence and go back to Yeshua's wisdom. We must not let the tragedy obscure the simplicity of his love."

But I did no such thing.

I was repulsed by this fisherman. I could see the shadow of his past lives behind his sun-toughened face. This man had laughed at me life after life. In some he had killed me. He had always been a part of my undoing.

And I could see his future faces also. Tall hats and shining robes. Buildings so ornate they must be built for kings.

"I am lost, Miriam," he cried. But I had already turned from him.

I left him, sobbing, staring after me, framed by the darkness of the tomb.

• • •

Salome was tentative. She entered into the tower's little round room, stepping over the debris and stones, and set a bowl down in front of me. It was a pottage of lentils and onions, still steaming. "We are all bewildered, Miriam. We do not know what to think. Yeshua has died. But his body does not decay. It does not rest in his tomb. What should we do?"

"The men should go back to their wives. They should fish and provide food for their children."

Salome nodded. My friend's cheeks were gray, the veins at her temple casting a blue sheen around her eyes, and her blonde hair had gone white. "Your life has ended, Miriam. But you have not ended. Trust me. Women have a special skill. They can give birth to themselves. They can begin a new life."

"Every dream I had included him . . ." I confessed.

"Whatever happens next, you must dream for them, Miriam. For us. For Adah and Atarah and Yohanna. Or the men will do something foolish. You know it."

"No," I said forcefully. "I have nothing left. If the men stay, Pilate will surely have them killed. They should go back to Galilee. There is no sense in this. There is no teaching."

"And what of you?" Salome pressed me. She knelt at my side, her hand hovering at my shoulder, not daring to actually touch me.

"I do not know, Salome. I doubt Pilate worries about me. I will stay here, in this tower."

"I will not leave you," she promised. "Not until you can tell me how you will live again."

"I will not live again."

She stood to her full height, crossing her arms across her flat chest. "Eat, Miriam. Sleep. Dream."

My father came later that night, imploring me to come home. And still I refused.

A week after Yeshua's execution, the disciples scattered, afraid that they would meet the same fate as their master. Even my father stayed home, avoiding Yerusalem. Pilate was looking for someone to blame. Who had stolen the Galilean's body?

Andreas and Philip came calling that last night. "Come out, Miriam. We know you're in there. Tell us that you saw him! Tell us what happened at the tomb? Miriam. For God's sake. Speak to us!"

Finally I came out to the window of the tower, my eyes raw from crying and lack of sleep.

Philip hung back nervously. Andreas was right below the window, staring up at me.

"Miriam, come tell us what you have seen," Andreas implored me, reaching one of his short arms up as if I could drop down a gem of wisdom into his open hand.

"I have seen nothing," I said flatly.

"You saw him at the tomb!" Philip insisted. "Please, Miriam! Has he returned to us?"

"He will not return to me. He is gone."

"Miriam, you were his wife!" Andreas thumped the stone of the tower with his fist.

"I am nobody's wife," I said slowly, beginning to vibrate with the horror of what I said.

Something was rising in me. Erasing the last traces of my maidenhood. This was my spirit that had existed before the garden. Before the flood. Before mankind.

Was this what Salome meant?

I could feel myself emerging as a terrifying being from the ashes of my life. This could not possibly be the daughter of Nicodemus and Hadassah. The girl grown in Bethany, raised alongside Lazaros and Marta. This was a snake. A hornet. Cords of molten rock veining an exploded mountain.

"What do you mean you are nobody's wife?" Andreas implored. "Miriam, we are confused. We are terrified."

"I am no one's wife," I said coldly. "Don't call me Miriam."

"What?" Andreas asked, totally dumbfounded. "Then who are you?"

I felt every one of my lifetimes stacked below me like the stones of the watchtower. Every tragedy. Every love. Every birth and death. And above me were the lives to come, as numerous as the stars glittering in the night sky. I was bigger than Miriam. I was many Miriams building toward some greater height. A height I could not yet see.

"Migdal," I said calmly. "I am the tower."

The laughter that emerged was the laughter of revelation. It thrummed through me. But I was weeping, too. Holding myself. Clutching my shoulders.

"Leave her," Philip said, and he pulled Andreas away, back into the darkness. "She has gone mad."

But I did not care. I finally knew my own name. A name that was bigger than one birth, one life, one love. A name that would pull me out of the ashes.

• • •

I could not stay in my father's house. Marta welcomed Salome and me into her home, giving us one of her rooms to share. I tried to live quietly, carefully, making each small task its own world.

"Let me cook," I suggested, and cooking became a ritual. I would hold the cucumbers tenderly, slicing them so thin they were as translucent as glass. Each spice added to the soup was pinched and sprinkled with utmost delicacy. Salome helped me with my tasks, rubbing between my shoulders sometimes, squeezing my arm. Each inhale was a lifetime, each exhale a dreamless sleep that lasted centuries. I could only bear the grief by living moment to moment without any sense of memory or selfhood.

"I will come out of this," I promised Salome late one night when we lay side by side in the bed. "There is something bigger. I'm sure of it. I just don't understand yet."

Her pale eyes gleamed like moonstones in the dark. I could hear her swallowing, thinking. "Take as long as you need, Miriam. I will not leave your side."

• • •

When Amos had his friends over, I tried to stay out of the way. But one evening, chillier than usual, Marta sent me to fetch blankets from an old chest just off the house's main room. As I shook out the blanket, closing my eyes against the dust, I overheard voices.

"Two men who were with him in K'far Nahum. Yes. They say he walked with them on the road to Emmaus."

"I don't believe it."

"Do you believe the soldiers who fled from the empty tomb, chased by angels? Professional butchers scared senseless. *I* believe that."

"They weren't angels! I heard it was leopards."

"Seven leopards. Angels. What's the difference? I would have fled, too."

I stopped what I was doing, clutching the musty blanket to my chest. The voices knifed through my stupor, jolting me back into myself. Immediately a thick clot of grief lodged in my throat.

"I say his men stole the body. It would be typical of the Galileans to pull a stunt like that."

The sound of a man breaking something open on a hard surface. A nut. Someone chewing loudly.

"I heard he fishes with them and breaks bread."

"With whom?" The other man's voice was measured, soft.

"His men. His disciples. He has come to them in Galilee."

I could smell lilies, incense, the dense, sharp smell of balsam perfume. I imagined the men behind the voices: their hair oiled back, richly embroidered vests worn over silken tunics.

"Who told you this, Clopas?"

"A man who studied with him. The one they call Cephas, the Rock."

Something twisted in my stomach. Suddenly, without willing it, I was dropping the blanket with a soft thud, walking up the length of the dark hallway.

"It is true. Cephas, also called Shimon, and Yeshua's brother Yakov, have returned. They have been hosting secret dinners where they share the mysteries of their teacher."

I burst into the room just as Marta backed in, followed by Atalyah and Salome bearing trays of food.

"*Who* has seen him?" I demanded.

The men were surprised.

"Who is this, Marta?" The older man called Clopas stood up indignantly.

Marta ignored Clopas. "Miriam. Did you find the blankets? We will surely need them tonight. The wind is picking up."

I felt light-headed. "*Who* has seen him?" I repeated.

"Miriam!" Salome ran to me, letting me lean into her.

"Marta! How could I have forgotten? The prophet was your brother-in-law!" exclaimed Clopas.

"Tell us all you know! Is it true your husband rose from the dead?" asked the younger man.

"Yes," Clopas agreed jovially. "Tell us, Miriam! Does he live? Will you invite him here to dine with us?"

At first I thought it was the nausea of anger. The discomfort of grief. But too late I realized the sensation was totally physical.

Something lurched in my stomach and I doubled over. I was sick all over Salome's feet.

"Good god! She's ill!" Clopas cried out in revulsion.

"Get her to my room," Marta instructed Salome. The two of them slung my arms around their shoulders and pulled me toward the open doorway. But I still struggled, calling out, "Where is he? Who has seen him? Why hasn't he come to me?"

They got me into bed. I was sick again, this time into a bowl Salome held before me.

I clutched at my friend's wrists. "Tell me Salome. Is it true? You must tell me. Has he been seen?"

Marta crossed her plump arms over her chest. "Miriam . . ." my sister began slowly, thinking about her words. "It is true. Many men claim to have seen Yeshua."

"Many men . . ." I muttered, tasting bile on my lips.

Salome leaned in, brushing some hair away from my sweaty face. "It is not just strangers, Miriam. Thoma has seen him. He says he put his fingers in Yeshua's wounds."

"Many other men claim to have seen him, Miriam," Marta added. "There is talk all over Yudea . . ."

Had this been my doing? Had I truly brought him back? And if I *had,* why was my husband not with me?

All I had received was a dream, and on my lips, the taste of what I had lost. Yeshua had seemed real. But the dream had not lasted. He was not with me now in my heartbreak.

I was utterly alone.

The cramping wracked my body again, but this time it was so violent, so total, I thought I might lose consciousness. I was sick again, the smell sour as death, my hands shaking at my face. "How can he return to Shimon and not to me?" I wailed.

Marta and Salome held me still, their warmth anchoring me to the world, to my body.

"Miriam, be strong!" Salome's blue eyes had hardened to flinty gray.

"No!" I screamed and Marta tried to hush me. "No. I don't know what comes next. I don't understand."

It was hours until they could calm me enough to sleep.

• • •

The sickness did not pass. I laid in bed, vomiting intermittently. Did days come and go? It was hard to tell. The certainty I had felt at the tower dimmed.

It was dusk when I finally came back to myself. Marta had left the window open. The sweetness of ripening fruit and newly opened flowers carried in on the breeze made me queasy.

But along with these footsteps a different smell wafted in: the bitter, clean perfume of aloe and galbanum. Moonlight on black water. A line of smoke against a white wall.

Yosseph.

"Miriam." His voice was gentle but closed. A clear effort to repress any emotion. "Miriam. I must speak with you."

I sat up slowly, my joints stiff with disuse.

"Good. Now I need you to listen to me." Yosseph had forgone the stool and was sitting on the bed, very close to me.

His hair and his beard were short, his eyes unreadable. He was wearing a cloak and tunic of such a dark blue it looked almost black.

He watched me without blinking and I stared back, unhindered by any sense of self.

Yosseph. Handsome as a night heron. Sleek, slender, made for flying through dusk shadows, dropping down into moving waters, feet entering into the current without a sound. Yosseph, who smelled expensive but moved as lightly as someone who did not understand the weight of a coin. A man who slipped in and out of Pilate's palace and convinced the tyrant to give me back my husband's body.

When had he become so foreign to me? My friend, my child's heart, my almost betrothed.

"Yosseph?" my voice was breathless. A question.

"Miriam. Do you know why you are sick?"

My lips were thick, "I don't understand any of it, Yosseph. I thought I did. But perhaps I am wrong."

"You're not ill, Miriam. You're pregnant."

I was weightless. And I was heavier than the world. "It's impossible."

Yosseph didn't say anything. Instead, his eyes drifted to the window, turning dark blue as they reflected the night. A few leaves of a nearby bush growing just beyond the ledge danced like silver fishes, illuminated by the glow of his lamp.

"It . . . it cannot be," I continued. "We had been apart so long. There was no moment when it could have happened."

Saying it aloud was a release.

"Miriam. Trust me. It is so."

"How do you know this?" My hands lay palm up, open on the blanket between us.

He looked uncomfortable. When he spoke, his voice was constricted. "I was told this in a dream. Yeshua came to me in a dream and told me that you were bearing a child."

"No." I shook my head, trying to clear the clouds from my vision, the sense that Yosseph's words were coming to me across a great distance. "He did not come to you."

"He did," Yosseph said, nodding, the tears slowly beginning their descent down his cheeks. "He looked younger, wearing a fine, embroidered mantle and a blue tunic. His hair was short."

"Oh!" *Our wedding day.*

The memory was so sweet, so sharp that it made me cry out. Suddenly I could see Yeshua perfectly, his cheeks ruddy from joy and drink, gems sparkling at his hands, the golden threads woven into his bridal mantle refracting the sun as he was carried in on the litter by his friends and family. It was the only time I had ever seen him deign to dress in such finery.

Of course Yosseph had not been there to see this. How could he know?

"He was nervous, pacing, trying to speak all at once. We were somewhere misty and green. A riverbank? He kept saying it had all gone wrong. But that you would need protection."

"And you believe this dream?" I asked, breathlessly.

To my surprise Yosseph smiled wryly. "Yes, Miriam. I believe it. But that does not matter. The question is, do *you?*"

• • •

The owls woke me. Three of them. Hooting insistently.

I obeyed immediately. I rose and climbed right out of the window, my bare feet landing softly on the twigs and moss below. A gust of air flew back into my face as the birds departed.

I walked until I was far from the house, down the hill, over the road, and into the fields beyond, clear of tree branches.

The moon was full again. Impossibly. Everything was achieving ripeness. The crickets and frogs hummed in the taller grasses just beyond the edge of the field. The figs and dates and pears were imitating the moon, growing fleshy and sweet. The soil between my toes was springy, wet, alive.

"How can this be?" I asked, raising my hands to the moon.

The world did not need to utter a word.

Every new blade of grass, every slender sapling, every grape curving the vine down to the ground with its weight was my answer.

How naive I had been to think he had abandoned me.

He had come back.

I placed my hands on my belly, weeping, feeling I might burst with joy, with sorrow, with awe, with terror.

I did not need to press my fingers to Yeshua's wounds.

His body lived on within me.

Fifty-Seven

It had been twelve weeks since Yeshua's death and I had not bled once. In the midst of my grief and the rumors of his resurrection, this had passed unnoticed. But as summer reached its ripeness—the days growing hotter, the skies cleaned of all clouds—my breasts grew heavy. My vision was clear and particular, the flight of butterflies etching lines across my eyes, the color of a flower in a distant garden blinking as brightly as a flame. Something was clenching and unclenching low in my stomach, making itself at home.

It was undeniable. I was pregnant.

I told Marta and Salome later that night when we went to pick herbs in her garden. "You see, we did not lie together except afterward. As in a dream." I tried to explain the miracle of it. The impossibility.

Marta laughed and laughed. "Oh, Miriam. You are a blessed woman among women. Blessedly simple! You *would* insist on such a thing. A woman can get pregnant in many strange ways."

But Salome was solemn, crushing a handful of mint leaves in her fist. The smell they released was cool and sober. "Miriam. The child you bear is blessed."

Marta's arms were around me. Despite her teasing, she too was crying. Hot tears coated my cheeks as she pressed her face to mine.

"What will this child do?" I asked breathlessly, gazing into Salome's eyes over Marta's shoulder.

Salome answered softly. "Only you can say, Miriam. Bless this moment. The magic here is strong. Use it well."

It took me a moment to forget my mind. I spoke from my body instead. "May he perform mighty deeds. May he destroy cities and proud men, men who kill women, who abuse babes and girls and animals and trees and even . . ." my voice faltered " . . . even stones. Let him bring down the rulers from their thrones who care only for men and not for the earth. Let him show us that when we are hungry the forest will always fill our stomach; when we are thirsty the rivers will flow forth readily."

Marta was kneeling beside Salome. They had been on the ground to pick the mint but now their position seemed to be one of deference. The two women had clasped hands. Marta's plump lower lip was quivering.

I looked from them to the moon and finished my prayer.

"May he heal this wound. This tragedy. Please let him heal me."

"It is so," Marta said and, for a second I saw her and Salome as much older women with skin as black as ink. I saw them as young girls with red hair, wearing sheer shifts soaked through with water.

I saw them as wolves. As leopards. Lions. Heavy-shouldered cows.

You see, we had been together like this many times before. The three of us. Not always human. But always women. Always sending our prayers down into the soil and up to the great, waxing moon.

• • •

"Miriam," Lazaros touched my shoulder gently. "We must speak of the child. You are beginning to show."

He was right. I was nearing my fifth month and every morning I woke and remembered that other pregnancy, my hot, swollen feet pounding the long roads through Galilee. My prayers no longer held any relation to those I had recited with my father as a child. They were small and personal. Pebbles thrown into the river. Words murmured over the cooking fire and sung into a puddle of rainwater.

Let me get through today. Tomorrow. Let me keep you.

"Let me show," I said simply "There is no shame in it. I am . . . a married woman."

"You are a widow," he wasted no time in saying. "And you are carrying the child of a man many believe was no ordinary man. If Yeshua's followers hear that you are carrying his child, there will be uproar. And they grow in number every day as Shimon and Yakov spread their wild stories and host their secret dinners. The child will be seen as an heir of the Messiah. A son of a god."

"Let there be uproar," I said bitterly, digging the toe of my sandal into the dirt between us. "I do not care."

"Miriam. If Herod hears that Yeshua leaves behind an heir . . . If Pilate hears . . . they will surely kill the child. And you."

Now it was my turn to stop walking, looking closely into my brother's face twisted in worry. "What do you mean?"

"Many believe Yeshua was the Son of God. And so the child in your womb would surely be Divine."

I laughed and laughed.

"Be quiet!" hissed Lazaros. "We have risked much even walking so publicly tonight. I only wanted to speak to you about how we may protect you and the child."

I read his mind. "You think that I should leave Bethany."

Lazaros ran his hand through his hair nervously. "We must get you north. Out of danger. At least until the child is safely delivered. Then you may return."

"No," I said firmly, gravely. "I traveled before and lost a child. It nearly killed me. I will not move from this place. This is my home."

Lazaros groaned in exasperation. But I would not change my mind.

I had been born in Bethany. My mother's bones lay nearby. My husband had died here and here he had come to me again. My son would be born here.

• • •

How did I know I was carrying a son?

I knew because each morning that I walked the dewy fields outside Bethany a hawk circled overhead. I understood him perfectly. He was saying to me, *You have given birth to animals before. Birthed a son with a hawk's head. An elephant son with a broken tooth. A wounded boar. But soon you will bear a different kind of son.*

A son who looks like a man. But has the heart of a fish. The strength of a bear.

A king of animals and *men. A king who will heal the land.*

His name came to me one dawn, when I was still half-asleep. A whisper of breeze through reeds. A watery sound.

It is not a name that I will speak to you tonight. It is a name like a seed.

And someday it will emerge from the ground. Green and ready.

• • •

I also dreamed of Yeshua. It was as if his seed, rooted more deeply in my womb with every passing day, was giving me access to his lost life.

I could see a brood of young boys, all with the same golden-brown shoulders and wild curly hair, running down a grassy slope and sliding into a swollen stream. The bigger one caught his brother in a headlock, wrestling him into the water. A group of girls on the opposite bank screeched in mock terror. One of them with dark waves of hair, lifting her skirts and running into the water, beat Yakov on the back, demanding he let Yeshua go.

Laughter swelled as Yeshua burst free of the water, pushing his brother back and beating his chest playfully.

I saw him slipping out of his home early in the morning, hiking barefoot to the crest of the nearby hill, echoing the dove's song with his own voice, jumping easily over the crumbling stone walls, pausing to watch the dew on the grasses glisten like a field of gems. He would reach the rock ledge by sunrise, getting so still and so silent that birds came and roosted in his hair, nuzzled their beaks into his open palms. His hair was freshly cut by his mother's deft hands, leaving the back of his neck bare. I could see his smooth chin and cheeks, the rosy, boyish swell of his lower lip. He didn't have his scar yet. It was still to come.

Older. A handsome youth with a short, dark beard, still unused to his new height, a little loose in the joints, laughing too loudly, slamming his fist on a wooden table so forcefully that a cup jumped and spilled wine down an older man's tunic. That older man rising like a storm cloud, grabbing Yeshua by the collar of his homespun tunic, and punching him firmly in the stomach, again and again and again. Yeshua falling backward, still laughing, refusing to let his mirth be spoiled by the man's violence.

I would wake from these dreams breathing hard as if I had run a long distance. I would look over at the sleeping Salome, thankful for her company, for her bony back and gentle snores, the almost floral scent her dormant body exuded.

Keep Yeshua alive in these memories. Keep him always a child. Keep us apart so that we may always be about to arrive to each other.

In my favorite of these dreams, he was grown, almost the man I had first seen in Bethany. Long, wild, unbrushed hair, skin darkened by the sun, wearing nothing but a simple loincloth. He was standing on the banks of the Yarden at dusk, completely alone.

As the light purpled the trees, the sky, the black of his hair, he began to walk into the water. At the last moment, he would always look back, his wide grin disarming me, his eyes warm and familiar and playful. His hand reaching out, toward me.

Join me.

I was always weeping when I awoke.

• • •

"Stay in your room," Lazaros had commanded me when the men arrived. "Or go out to the tower. Stay away from their prying eyes."

"I will do no such thing."

"Miriam . . ." Salome pleaded, sharing a knowing glance with my brother. "We must."

"Go to Marta's," Lazaros instructed us. "Leave the house if you must. Whatever you do, stay out of sight."

But my curiosity was too intense. "I'll just spy on them from the storeroom," I explained.

"Wine please!" We heard my father command Beltis. She scurried past me, giving me a wide-eyed look that told me she had not been expecting this many guests.

I knew them before their familiar voices boomed, before I heard the characteristic high laughter of Thoma, the loud grumbling of the Ben-Zebedee brothers. When I glanced around the corner, I saw that all of them—including the men who had joined Yeshua after I left in K'far Nahum—were gathered at the table, with my father in the middle, frowning, his hands gently cradling his small, stone cup.

Shimon. Thoma. Yakov. Andreas. Philip. Mattiyahu. A young man whose name I thought was Bar Talmai.

Beltis whipped by, clutching a jug of wine. Apphia followed, a simpleminded expression on her wide face.

"You come to me with demands; am I correct?" my father asked wryly as Beltis circled the table, filling each man's cup and blushing if the man looked up and leered at her.

"I come to you as a follower of Yeshua," announced Shimon. "I come to you in the hopes that you will help us spread our mission."

Shimon was dressed in a linen tunic of a rich cerulean blue, his beard and hair obviously cut by a barber in Yerusalem. It had only been eight or nine months and there was nothing of the fisherman left in him. Even his brother Andreas appeared strangely refined, his graying curls oiled away from his ears, his mouth pinched in a performance of dour importance.

Yakov, on the other hand, had gone toward the other extreme. His hair was so knotted and wild, grown out past his shoulders, that he either slept in the woods every night or had carefully manufactured his derelict appearance. It was in contrast to his blinding white tunic, belted only with a flaxen cord. He looked like a poor imitation of one of the Qumran Essenes.

"You are spreading your mission just fine in Yerusalem," my father remarked placidly. But I could see from my hiding spot that his eyes were shrewd and protected. He did not feel safe with these men.

"True, our meals are popular," Thoma explained. "But Pilate threatens us at all sides."

His voice was deeper than when I had last heard it, as if he had finally passed over the threshold into manhood.

"Pilate cares little about your meals. He cares about the resurrected Yeshua. And as far as I can see, the Messiah has not walked into the city and revealed himself to the Romans." Lazaros spoke, still standing, leaning against the wall with his arms crossed tightly across his chest. I was surprised by his petulance. He must have run into the disciples in the past few months, although he had never mentioned it to me.

Shimon continued his petition. "We wish to send men out as emissaries of his teachings. The news of Yeshua's resurrection must reach the blue-eyed fiends in the north, those gentiles who are willing to save themselves, the whore islands where the witches practice their dark arts. We must baptize those past the Paropamisadae Mountains. Our savior has given us the fire we need to speak to strangers."

The language was totally foreign to me. Baptisms? Yeshua hadn't practiced such immersions in years. Not since he had been a talmid of Yochanan. Spread his message? To gentiles? Their savior?

What *was* Yeshua's message? He had hardly reached it when he died, I thought. Or perhaps it was so simple it could not be called a message.

Love and good food. Living off the land, in the land. Bathing in the river. Family and friends sitting out under the stars, around a fire, sharing stories. Riddles that inspired good-natured arguments. Healing the ill. Entering each crystalline moment so intensely that it could expand into an entire world. A kingdom.

I laughed, muffling the sound with the back of my hand.

"Why have you come to me?" my father said, adjusting his robe. "I have no issue with your groups. But you must have noticed that I have chosen not to associate myself with them." Shimon had pulled his stool too close to him, leaning forward with his big forearms on the table, his fingers intertwined under his chin.

"We need funds. To pay for more than just a room. Our meals have expanded, and we can no longer all fit in such a small space at once. We need a place where we can live and host our mysteries."

"Our messengers must be sent out with provisions," added Yohan. "Food and sturdy sandals. Heavy woolen cloaks for those heading to the north."

"Cloaks! Money! Did he tell you to ask for material goods when he appeared to you?" I was done hiding, stepping into the light of the room, revealing myself to the men. "Did he tell you to turn his message into a profit?"

Thoma gasped. Andreas swore under his breath. And Lazaros cried out, "Miriam! I told you to stay. . ."

Shimon was the only one who kept his face relatively composed. "So you bear a child?"

"Is it Yeshua's child?" Mattiyahu asked no one in particular.

"Who else would it belong to?" Yakov said, staring at my belly. My urge was to cover myself with my hands, draw my cloak around my form.

I didn't even bother answering the question. I glared at Shimon. "He came to you?"

"Yeshua has spoken to me privately," Shimon finally asserted, refusing to meet my eye and looking grandly around at the others gathered. "He has given me charge of his students and teachings."

"What was his purpose in speaking to you?" my father asked quietly, choosing to ignore Shimon's claim to Yeshua's spiritual inheritance. "What mysteries did he reveal to you alone?"

Shimon was startled. My father had always been an accommodating host, asking careful questions of Yeshua and hardly ever directly arguing with any of the disciples. He had let the disciples stay overlong after Yeshua's execution, supplying them with food and drink.

But Yeshua was gone now. Nicodemus was no longer a fellow follower of Yeshua. He was my father.

"Yes, Cephas," my brother called out. "I would like to hear."

"I . . ." he started, his cheeks reddening. "He said I would inherit his teachings. He would build his kingdom upon my work and give me the keys. I should perform the secret mystery of transformation with the bread and the wine and remember the pain he suffered for us."

"Ah, yes." I nodded. "The pain he suffered. So that you could all be important men. Men with a mission." The anger was not so frenzied as it had been in the days after the crucifixion. It had transformed into something sharper, chilly as a knife. "He died for you, did he not, Shimon? Did he tell you that?"

"Do you think I am lying about Yeshua?" Shimon was shouting, as if he had been waiting to be questioned. He half got up from the table, his nostrils flaring, his whole face beet red now. *There* was the fisherman below the finery and delusions of importance.

"Yes," I said it simply. "You are lying."

The men all began to speak at once. Shimon stayed standing, breathing heavily, glaring at me.

My father's voice rang clear through the commotion. "Did Yeshua tell you that Miriam would bear his child?"

Shimon's mouth opened. But he did not speak.

Until that moment I had not known for certain that he was lying, but still, I had no proof.

To be honest, I did not understand why Yeshua had appeared to these men. But I *did* believe that he had come to Thoma, to those men heading to Emmaus. Yet I remained suspicious of Shimon.

You would not put such a man in charge, I thought. But as I watched Shimon, something shattered in his dark, hooded eyes.

"You believe yourself to be his heir, but you are wrong," I said firmly. "You inherit nothing."

"Miriam!" Salome was behind me, speaking urgently, her hands at my waist. "Let us go, Miriam. These men are not our business."

But I would not stop staring at Shimon. He was growing pale, his hands trembling, the blood vessels at his temples bulging as if they would burst. "We have all inherited his mission. We have inherited his body that we eat as a sacrament. We break bread and drink wine, and our savior is within us," he said. Yakov rose, putting his hand on Shimon's shoulder in support.

I laughed and laughed. And it was no longer a girl's laugh. No longer bells. No longer birdsong. At some point I had developed the thunder of an old woman's laugh. The raven's declarative cry.

"Shut her up!" Thoma urged.

"The whore does not carry his child," Andreas chimed in, surprising me. "How far along is she? Seven months? She has whored herself with the Romans. She has slept with those who murdered Yeshua!"

The *whore*. The word first bloomed from Andreas's mouth. But now it is not just one voice calling me such. It has blossomed into a garden of voices. Whore. Harlot. Prostitute. Anything but his lover and wife. Anything but Yeshua's equal in spirit and mind and heart.

Mattiyahu turned to Yohan Ben-Zebedee. "Are we to treat her as an adversary? The one Yeshua loved best? It does not seem right."

"Enough!" My father rose to his feet and slammed both of his fists down on the table. His face was transformed into the forbidding man of my childhood. "I will not entertain brigands and thieves in my house who have come to destroy my daughter's good name."

"Let them stay for this, Father." I caught my breath, putting my hand on my lower back for support, massaging the curve there.

I looked at them all in turn, and I could feel myself growing in stature. The collective wisdom of my many lives surged up through my ankles, through the full moon of my womb.

And they were afraid. I could taste the sourness of it in the air.

"You may think you eat his body. But his body lives on within me. You may try to partake in the blood mysteries when you drink wine. But your own wife is closer to them when she bleeds every month."

Philip cried out in shock.

"Yes, Philip," I said. "Find Adah. Ask her about her blood. Worship it."

Andreas was about to begin shouting again, but I raised my hand.

"Do you feel it, Andreas? Do you feel the crushing weight of your suffering? It is waiting for you. In this life. In the next life."

I knew that my words were more than words. They were the air itself, closing like a cold vice around his barrel chest.

"I do not know how it will come to pass, but someday, in some life, every one of you shall fall under the sword of your own deeds. You have seeded a violence here that will haunt you longer than this life's body and name."

Shimon was the only one who spoke then. "You are unlike him," he sneered. "He would never speak with such vengeance."

"You are right." My words were revelation both to me and my audience. "I'd rather be hated than loved and misunderstood. I *am* unlike him; I am alive."

I swept out of the room without looking behind me.

Did my words penetrate? I still do not know. The stories they have spread are full of falsehoods.

What I *do* know is that for eight months I had managed to keep my pregnancy a secret from everyone but my closest family and Yosseph. I had stayed close to home, preferring to wander the fields and gardens behind our house than reveal my secret to the gossiping town. But within three days of the disciples' visit, everyone in Yerusalem knew that Miriam, Yeshua's widow, was pregnant with a holy child. Which of them betrayed me to the Romans? I do not care. My rage, still planted deep in me and never properly healed, says it was Shimon. But they all resented me. It could easily have been Thoma or Andreas.

While Pilate tolerated the disciples, he would not tolerate this. Herod made it known that there could be no possibility of the prophet's nonsense continuing. Another Son of God was too dangerous. It was not long before the rumor reached us in Bethany that Roman soldiers would be sent out soon with one mission.

To slaughter any newborn child.

And still I refused to leave.

• • •

All that was left of autumn was light, lingering in the yellow of the bleached grasses, the dry leaves, the thin strip of dawn pushing up from below the horizon, struggling to lift the grayness of the sky. But the sky was swollen with the rainy season that had not yet decided to begin. Perhaps we had another week before winter would start in earnest.

We needed the water. Dust flew off the hills in such giant waves when the winds came through that I thought they might totally dissolve in the flatness of the desert. The bark on the olive trees cracked.

Nightfall. Two and half weeks had passed since the news of Pilate's fury had reached Bethany. My father was so besieged in Yerusalem that he had temporarily relinquished his place in the Sanhedrin, preferring to stay home and make sure I was safe. Salome had agreed to help look after Marta's children earlier on, so it was just the two of us in the room he used as a study.

"Father, you should not worry," I told him. "The child would be born well past Herod's violence. I am not due for another two or three weeks. I will hide in the tombs when the soldiers come. No one will find me."

He sighed and turned from me.

I went to the tower, where a lemony glow illuminated the square window.

Was it the last sunlight, already sunk below the horizon, sending up its last red rays, that played the trick, or was it a glance into the future? Suddenly the entire town was red, consumed by a ravenous fire—a billow of dense, black smoke rising up into the sky. I almost screamed, my hands rising to my mouth in shock, the babe somersaulting in my stomach. I blinked and it was gone. But something else caught my eye. I hardly had time to catch my breath when I realized what I was watching.

Yosseph approached with long, elegant strides. A striped cloak rippled out behind him, his hair sleek and black, his slender face pale amidst the shadowy trunks and long gray branches rattling their brittle leaves. But he was not alone. As the group drew closer, I recognized the two figures walking at his side: Marta, the sway of her hips hardly disguised by her blue cloak, and the painfully precise steps of Salome.

When they got to the tower none of them paused to look up and acknowledge me. They ducked their heads to enter and were up the crumbling stairs and by my side in mere seconds. Yosseph placed his hands lightly on the ledge, an opal ring on his left hand reflecting the same indeterminate color of the dusk beyond the window. He kept his eyes fixed on Bethany in the distance, his mouth slightly downturned. Salome stood at my side, her hands clasped at her waist. She tugged at her fingers with worry.

A warmth came from behind and Marta was enveloping me in her embrace, wrapping her arms around my shoulder, nestling her chin into my neck. I took Marta for granted in that moment. My beautiful, pugnacious, competent sister.

She stood behind me so I cannot remember her face clearly, but because of that she has never truly disappeared. Vision fades. But the presence remains. I feel her shadowing me along with my mother, with Kemat, Salome, Adah. With Yohanna, with Ivah, Yeshua's mother. These women speak through me and hold me up.

It has taken me my whole life to understand why it is impossible to turn around and see them. It is because they *are* me.

But Yosseph I could see and smell intensely.

Perhaps it was the late stage of my pregnancy, a state that was like the intensity of drunkenness without any of the fog, but I felt more aware of Yosseph than I ever had as a young girl. I could sense the slow, purposeful energy that pulsed through him. It was so different from the uncontrollable fire of Yeshua. His profile, watching the heavy, purple clouds gradually fade into the uniform black of night, was as sharp and elegant as if it had been cut with a knife.

"We must go, Miriam."

I inhaled slowly through my nose, feeling the child within me. Humming, turning, a being with its own blood and spirit. I was brimming with life. Filled with birds, with rain, with storms, with song. How could I speak? A word could hardly explain this feeling.

"Tonight, Miriam. There is no more time. I have a spy in Pilate's private circle and he has warned me that they will send out the first raids tonight."

"They will not find me here in the tower," I said.

"You are wrong, Miriam," Marta explained. She placed her hand over the strong beat of my heart. "The disciples call you 'the Tower' to anyone in Yerusalem who will listen. This is exactly where the soldiers will come to find you."

"I will not leave this place without planting Yeshua's body in the ground," I whispered, despising the tremble in my voice. "I cannot leave without knowing where he is."

"Miriam, you must go!" Salome whispered urgently. "You must live for Yeshua."

"You will come with me if I go?" I asked.

Salome smiled tightly. "I will come eventually, friend. I will find you."

I turned to Yosseph. There was a war of emotions in his eye. Was it grief? Melancholy? Anger?

"How will I leave alone then?" I asked. "I am near to giving birth and cannot walk far."

"I will take you, Miriam," Yosseph said without hesitation. His fingers curled around my forearm gently. "I will take you out of this place."

Oh. Yes. I slowly realized that something huge was shifting inside of me. The story of my life widened into many stories.

Yosseph. We, too, had shared a life together; many lives in fact. There were stories in my blood that I did not understand. There were places I had yet to remember. Places I had yet to go.

It felt like dying to leave Bethany. To leave my mother's tomb. And his empty tomb. The last place he had held me. But I finally felt the urgency my family had been trying to communicate to me for weeks. The soldiers were on the road already. And their blades were sharpened.

"Yes, Yosseph," I finally said, my eyes brimming with tears. "Take me to Egypt." Where else was there to go?

• • •

My father and Lazaros were ready for us with an ass saddled with a week's worth of provisions.

"You will travel as man and wife," my father explained, his voice husky with feeling. He could hardly meet my eye. His hands trembled as he patted the beast's side anxiously. "Say you are from Galilee. Anywhere but Bethany."

Yosseph nodded stoically, accepting the old, brown cloak Lazaros had worn when he traveled to visit me in Galilee. As he fixed it around his shoulders, I tried to imagine him as a common peasant. A farmer. A fisherman.

It was impossible.

"Do not argue with anyone, Miriam," Lazaros added, bracing my arms, pulling me to him, my pregnant stomach keeping us from fully embracing. "I know it is hard for you to hold your tongue."

Salome came to me and pressed my hands between hers. "Pretend to be someone else," she whispered. "Wear someone else's face. If you believe it, others will see it."

Suddenly I remembered the old whore from the inn in Yericho. Her dark eyes and knowing smile. "Yes, I will!" I promised my friend, trying hard not to cry, not to feel the distance when we were still close, still touching. "Promise you will come to me."

"Yes," she looked down, unable to meet my gaze. "Yes, Miriam. I will travel to you."

She was lying. I could tell. But I didn't care. I needed her words to keep me moving.

Salome would survive. She had done it all her life, against every odd. She would change her name and disappear back into the world, doing what she had just advised me to do: wear another's face.

I placed my hand against the ass, feeling its steady breathing, and I remembered leaving with Lazaros only a few short years before, heading for the Yarden River.

A different river lay ahead this time. The river of Kemat's stories. The river of my dreams.

It happened too quickly: Lazaros and Yosseph were helping to lift me up onto the animal and I was looking over my shoulder at my childhood home, which was receding into the darkness of the night.

"Lazaros!" I cried, and I suddenly felt like a young girl. My heart was pounding in my chest. I reached out desperately and his hands caught mine. He stared up at me, smiling sadly, his long curls falling back from his face. His features had retained that unearthly, exaggerated quality that I had first noticed after his resurrection.

"Brother," I whispered. "Come with me. Please!"

"It is too dangerous, Miriam. We cannot be seen together."

"We must go, Miriam," Yosseph said gruffly, tightening his grip on the rope attached to the ass's neck.

Marta was standing in the doorway, haloed by lamplight. "He is right! Go!"

"Go!" my father urged, his face catching the light cast from inside the open door. He was as gray as winter rain. "Our long goodbyes are meaningless if they get you killed!"

"Father!" I could hardly speak. "Father . . ."

"No words, Miriam," he shook his head. "I will hold your child in my arms. Next year perhaps. Do not weep."

We both knew he was lying, as Salome had lied before him. As Yosseph began to lead the ass into the inky darkness, I turned and cried out once more. "I will see you again. In the kingdom!"

We turned at the next house and my family disappeared.

I would never see my father again. He would never hold my child. He would die of the flux many years before the siege of Yerusalem, thankfully succumbing to a more natural death than that of the sword. Marta was not so lucky: the victim of one of the zealot's riots, a passerby caught in the midst of a violence she did not own.

I would never see Bethany again. Never sit under the olive and sycamore figs that had raised me like a mother and father. Never again would I walk to the tomb where my mother had been laid to rest.

They cannot die in my heart. And Bethany cannot burn. For I have never seen them dead. Never seen the ashes of my hometown.

They live in me. And now that I have told you my story, Leukas, they live in you as well.

Hold my family well. Love them. Do not let them disappear.

Fifty-Eight

We had only traveled an hour when it happened. It was such a strange sensation that at first I thought the water had originated from the body of the ass below me, instead of issuing forth from my own womb. Heat spread down my legs, warming my thighs. A cramp twisted my belly so intensely that I thought I might fall off the animal. But I tightened my knees and breathed deeply.

"Miriam!" Yosseph stopped on the moonlit road. "What is it? Are you in pain?"

"Ahhh!" The sound I made was ragged. "No!"

"Miriam!" He rushed to me, reaching up and struggling to pull my swollen body up and off the ass.

"Never mind!" I protested as the cramp passed and I could breathe easily again. "We must continue now."

"How fast does it usually happen?" he asked as the realization dawned.

Not this fast.

"You are not squeamish?" I said instead of answering his question, surprised that he was still standing beside me, his hand clutching my soiled skirts.

"I do not care, Miriam!" he insisted. "I was born of a woman. I should understand my beginnings. But we must get you a place to rest for the night. You cannot ride in this condition."

The darkness was impenetrable except for a twinkling of lights in the distance. They looked like stars that had wandered too far from the sky and found themselves impossibly nestled between the swelling hills.

A small village. Where were we? We couldn't be more than a few miles from Bethany.

Something extraordinary was happening to my vision; I could no longer focus on one detail. Everything appeared infinitely intricate: the shape of my fingers gripping the donkey's short wiry mane, each individual strand of its hair, the blue shape of Yosseph walking with his back to me. I could smell the pungent aroma of his sweat, which he could usually keep disguised underneath his rich perfumes.

Hot stones, I thought, breathing in deeply through my nose. *The still, placid water of a lake holding a reflection of the full moon. Crushed berries.*

"Miriam!" Yosseph interrupted my reverie, speaking firmly. "We must find you a bed here. It is too dangerous to go further." I was surprised to see that we had arrived at a small cluster of lights. Before us was the rubble of a stone gate.

"We are still so close to Bethany," I protested. "Why not just turn around?"

Yosseph grimaced. But true to his character he did not grow angry. "No. We cannot. Here, we are safe. No one knows our faces. And please do not argue. The child agrees with me."

He was right. The minute after he had spoken, I had to cry out again from the pain, leaning over the donkey's neck to steady myself, pressing my forehead into the curve of his neck.

The town was subdued at this late hour. A few men made their way through the wide dirt roads. I was struck by the sounds of life that issued from the houses closest to the road: the muffled laugh of a woman and then a swell of chattering. Children. Several of them. A small, high window was illuminated in a home that we passed by, and I watched a man's profile appear just as he said something to someone out of sight. He waited a second before leaning his head back, chuckling at his own joke.

"There is an inn on the farthest side of Bet Lehem," Yosseph explained to me. "I've stayed there once before on my travels. We will go there."

I did not answer, focusing instead on the animal between my thighs: the wet sparkle of her eyes as she looked back at me when Yosseph paused to get his bearings.

What a burden I am to you, I thought. *Thank you for your service. Perhaps someday, somewhere else, you will ride* me.

The inn was hardly an inn; but it *was* loud. A squat, one-story building with a stone step cracked down the middle from some violence I couldn't immediately imagine. Yosseph bid me stay on the ass as he went up and knocked loudly on the door.

But no one came.

"Curses!" he swore to himself, running his hand through his hair and glancing back at me.

"Yosseph. Stop! Let's go."

One more time he knocked: a loud rap that I thought must have bruised his knuckles.

"Who is it?" A cackle came from the nearest window, and I heard shuffling before the door slammed outward, nearly hitting Yosseph in the face. He jumped backward, down from the broken step.

A man wider than he was tall, with a swollen mushroom of a nose, blinked up at us. I could see a dark hallway behind him and another couple, their arms around each other, further back in the depths of the house.

"Please! Do you have a stable where we can keep our donkey for the night?" he asked, surprising me.

"No! A room! We want a room!" I pleaded.

The drunk innkeeper stared blearily up at me. "What is that you want?"

"A stable. That is all. Lodgings for our beast."

The man peered at us with increasing distrust. "Bandits will steal your animal. Bring him inside with you. Everyone else does. Buy a room."

I opened my mouth to agree, but Yosseph squeezed my thigh.

"All we want is a stable. We will pay handsomely." He reached under his cloak, digging into the pouch of coins I knew he kept in a purse tied close to his heart. The coins glinted as he held them up to the squat man.

"You want to sleep with your ass?" the man laughed, but he didn't take the coins. "Then go! The stables are empty."

He was still chortling as he pointed us around the side of the establishment.

"Why are you doing this, Yosseph?" The pain was robbing me of all gentleness. All decorum.

"We are close to Yerusalem, Miriam." He spoke with a clip, his words as brisk as his steps. "All it takes is one greedy informant to run out and find soldiers. And then you and your child will be slaughtered before my eyes. We are safer in secret. No one will look for us in the stable."

I groaned in response, leaning forward and clutching the donkey's mane.

The stable was unlit and open to the night air. One traveler had been brave enough to leave his donkey. And I realized it must be fresher than the sweaty crush of bodies inside the inn. Maybe Yosseph's intuition was correct on more than one account. It *would* be safer in the stable. And quieter. My senses were so magnified that I didn't think I could bear the chaos and voices of other people.

I used my hands to grope along the rough wall, finding a soft mound of hay and peat in the corner. Each wave of pain marked a widening of my womb's door.

Pain drives us into the body. Each twist of my womb pushed me down into my belly. I closed my eyes, seeing pulsing purple-and-blue spots dance across the undersides of my eyelids.

An ocean of sensation. Sweat prickling up from my armpits. My groin. A thousand hot, desert-baked years. Feeling my mind squeezed from my head downward. Into my roiling stomach. Into my fingers curling around the hay. My spine flattening into dust under the weight of the baby.

All this, and it had only been a second.

The distortion of time reminded me of that distant, unspeakable moment in Yerusalem when I had last seen Yeshua alive.

"What do I do, Miriam?" Yosseph was next to me. I could feel the heat of his body.

"I don't know!" I screamed. "Oh, I don't know!"

I had been at births. I had set the bricks. Mixed the plasters and rubbed them onto women's stomachs. I had reached inside the slick sexes of other women and felt the hot muscle of the womb preparing to exhale and release. But it was different to do it yourself. I could not jump across these wide expanses of pain. I would fall down the chasm of one instant.

"AHHH!" I screamed. The screaming helped. It brought my center back up into my lungs for one second. And then I was plummeting again. Down into the cramping.

I screamed again. And again. My eyes squeezed shut.

"Miriam! What can I do?"

Dying must be very easy compared to this, I remember thinking. Although it was a thought without words.

To give birth I had to return to the intelligence of my animal lives. Go into the forest. Find the safety of shadows. Get low to the ground. And let pain open a door in you that will never close. A door that gives birth to life and to death. A door from which a child will flow. Blood will flow. Waste will flow. Darkness. Pleasure.

"I am going to die!" I screamed again and again. "I am going to die!" And I was not wrong.

How did he know to get behind me? To hoist me up by the arms and force me into a squatting position. The closeness of his body was almost unbearable. I arched my back and yelled, feeling the tendons of my knees straining to bear my weight.

"No! You will not die!" Yosseph insisted. "You will do this, Miriam. You were born to do this!"

We were alone with the donkey in the darkness. The smell of musty hay and blood. How did he know to rock me back and forth? He pressed into the very center of my palms with his finger. Massaged in a circular motion the root of my spine.

"Stop!" I yelled out, hunching over. I gagged and pushed my face into the dirt, tasting dust and fur and grass.

Keep going, came the rumble of my mothers. Voices from the desert. From the valleys. The black soil. Women with yellow eyes wearing eagle wings. Red ochre smeared across their blackened cheeks. I could see them. I could feel the vibration of their voices opening me so wide that my bowels would surely fall out of me. A groaning, heaving chorus of mothers. *You are only here because hundreds of women did this. You are only one woman in a long line of women. Keep the blood moving.*

"Ahhhh!!!" I screamed for them. I screamed *with* them.

Birth screams rupture time. They go forward and backward. I sent my scream forward. To my great-granddaughter. It has yet to reach her. But I know it will.

Again and again I howled as my insides twisted.

Yosseph pulled me back up, steadied my knees. "Do this, Miriam. Do this for him."

If I could have spoken, I would have told him that I was not just doing this for Yeshua. I was doing this for every woman who would ever be born and would ever give birth. Just as they had done it for me and *would* do it for me, again and again.

It was as if a hand had reached inside me and begun to pull apart my hip bones. I could feel fingers prying open my belly. Unlocking the very structure of my body.

I had seen my mother die. My brother die. My husband die. Washed his body. Lost his body. I had lost my own child. But none of that came close to *this*.

"Oh!" I moaned finally when there was no energy left to even breathe. I couldn't tell you how long it had been. It could have been minutes or an entire day.

"He is coming!" Yosseph cried out.

Push! said my mother.

Push! said Kemat.

Push! said Marta.

Push! said Salome and Adah and Yohanna and Atarah and Ivah.

Push! said Imah.

A world blooming through a mote of dust. Thunder rolling out of thin air.

"He is here. He is here."

Life expanded and separated. I opened my eyes blindly in the darkness, convinced that I no longer had a body. I had released my own heart.

What does it feel like to give birth to life?

It feels like losing a life. And then holding it in your hands.

"Look at him!" Yosseph held up my son up to me. Shiny and purple with blood in the darkness. Squalling like a hungry bird. "Look at your child!"

I died when I saw my son.

What I mean to say is that one life ended and another began. The life where I loved Yeshua was over. The loving of this new life would be bigger, harder.

Welcome, the women's voices said. *Welcome home. You are one of us now!*

"Imah!" Yosseph whispered softly as my eyes closed and I descended into a stupefied slumber. "Miriam! You are a mother!"

• • •

I slept. Although it was deeper than sleep.

Do you swim? Have you ever rested in the water, the breath in your lungs keeping you afloat, gazing up at the flat sky above you until you are not sure you have ever been human?

You are water. Water in water, looking at water. Cradled by a color, a coolness outside of time.

That is what it felt like. Although I knew the babe was at my breast suckling. I could feel the clench of his tiny mouth.

I floated. It was the sensation of being held. I think the only other time I ever felt such security was when, as a child, Kemat let me sleep next to her. Curled to her side, my head pressed into her slender neck, breathing in her dreams, I was certain of the world's softness and beauty.

"Let her sleep."

"She is well. Look at the color in her cheeks."

"And the babe is healthy, too."

The voices entered in slowly. Men's voices. Strange accents that could hardly fit around my own language.

"I must ask you to leave," came Yosseph's soft plea. "She is only recently delivered. Let us be."

The birth had so drained me that I hardly even cared. Let men and women walk around me, gawk at me all they wanted! I would never care about such things again. As long as I had my child with me. As long as I could sleep.

A man with a gravelly voice spoke. "We have traveled very far to see our lady. We will wait until she rises."

"What do you mean?" Yosseph asked cautiously.

I was fully awake now, but kept my eyes closed.

A silken voice answered: "Isn't it strange that none of us knew each other? That we met in an inn only a day's walk from here? But each of us has followed the stars to this town. I, myself, have traveled across the sea from the land you call Ibernia."

"I have traveled from Ethiopia," the gravelly voice offered.

"I have done trade in the state of Sheba," Yosseph offered. "I traveled down the Nile, but my work has not taken me far north. Although I've heard tell of Ibernia."

"Near the Tin Islands," said another man. "Where you will one day rest. I have seen it."

"Who are you?" I spoke as I sat up. The baby cried out and I looked down in shock.

My son. A shock of downy black hair. The tiny seashells of his balled-up fists, his eyes squeezed shut, mouth open, screaming. His loudness was the very song of aliveness.

"My lady!"

The three men bowed when I turned to see them. Yosseph had lit a lamp and it bathed them in a dim, orange glow. Fire beings. The light glinted off the bald head of a dark-skinned man. His slender hands were pressed into the soil in front of him.

"How could you allow men in here?" I asked, turning to Yosseph. "Who are these strangers?"

Yosseph's hair was tangled and there was blood smeared down the front of his tunic. Some had dried in a streak across his cheeks. But the grime had the odd effect of making him appear younger. More vital. His eyes widened at my question. He opened his mouth slowly, almost gaping at me.

"We are each a king in our own land," the silken-voiced man answered, sitting up and revealing a fiery red beard that obscured most of his pale face. His nose was dissected by an angry red scar, and his eyes were the color of ice. "Although the Romans would not call us kings."

The youngest man, with a tanned face and long black mustache, smiled widely. "We call ourselves kings. But we do not yet have the right to rule."

"What do you mean?" I whispered, looking down at my child, his tiny red lips latched to my nipple again. I felt no shame that these men looked upon me.

Perhaps it was because they did not look at me with lust or revulsion or curiosity. No. In all of their eyes was reverence.

The Ethiopian held out a glittering box in his hands. "We have all dreamed that our lady would come to us and anoint us. She would come to give birth to a son and bless the land."

The red-bearded king spoke now with the grave intensity of prophecy. "A great sign appeared in heaven. A fire drake. A woman clothed in sunlight with the moon under her feet."

The young king broke in. "With twelve stars on her head. And she was pregnant. Crying out in agony and pain as she gave birth."

"That is how we knew we were close," the Ethiopian king explained. "The stars led us to this town. But your cries told us where you would be. It was then that we knew our dreams were true. That we had come to the right place."

"Have you come for my child?" I asked fiercely. "You cannot have him. He will be nobody's king, nobody's messiah. I swear it."

I clutched my child to me tightly and he squealed, his tiny hand brushing my throat.

Keep him safe. Keep him unknown.

I would die for this child. Again and again. But I would not let *him* die for anyone.

The kings all laughed, exchanging knowing looks. "No."

Yosseph was also perplexed. "Then why have you come? What has drawn you here?"

"Her," said the Hibernian king. "We have come for her blessing."

"Please." The Ethiopian king opened the box to reveal three stone jars. Carefully he placed the jars on the floor and removed their waxy stoppers.

"Oh . . ." I sighed.

Myrrh. Frankincense. Spikenard. The smell of ritual. The smell of grief.

"Anoint us that we may rule," the young king pleaded. "That we may rule for you and for the land."

My son cried out again, his eyes fluttering open. We stared at each other.

"Do you promise to protect the trees and the rivers? The stones and the roots?" I did not look at them as I spoke, continuing to gaze into the black depths of my child's eyes.

"We promise."

"Do you promise to remember your mothers? And your mother's mothers? Do you promise to honor your human ancestors and your beast ancestors?"

"We promise."

"Do you promise to tell stories about me and my child? Do you promise to remember us even when our names have been changed and forgotten?"

"We promise."

I had done this before. I was sure of it. The oil on my fingers felt familiar. These men had come to remind me of who I was.

Queen of heaven. Tower of light. Anointer of kings.

I felt all the women behind me. My mother and Kemat at my shoulders. My past lives vibrating in my hands, heating up my palms as I carefully marked the men's foreheads.

"Let it be so."

The flame brightened. The red-bearded man cried out. Tears were in all their eyes. "Hail mother. Hail queen. Full of grace."

"Be with us when we perish and at the hour when we are born again."

The last thing they did was address Yosseph. "Hail, servant of queens. Servant of kings."

"Why do you say this?" Yosseph asked of them, his hands open, tears washing away the blood on his cheeks.

"You will come to my land someday," the black-bearded king said quietly, certainly, to Yosseph. "And you will die there and be born there. You will serve many kings in that land. And you will serve one mother. One queen. Always."

Yosseph was suddenly an old, old man with skin as thin and white as snow melting on a hot stone. With blue eyes and a hawkish nose. I felt certain it was a glimpse into the distant future, many lifetimes away.

"Yosseph," I asked then with the kings watching. "Will you be this child's father?"

"Yes, of course!" He knelt beside me, his whole body trembling, reaching out to brush the inky fluff of hair on the babe's head. "He is my beloved son."

We were never married. But in that moment, both us covered in afterbirth, surrounded by the stink of the donkey with the kings bowing before us, and starlight streaming in through a hole in the roof, we were at last husband and wife.

Fifty-Nine

We named him Yudah, meaning "to give thanks."

Yudeah. The land of his birth. The land lost to him.

And when we reached Egypt, I brought my son to the great river and bathed him in its water.

I washed away Yeshua, his father. His miraculous conception. His uncertain beginnings. It was a baptism of forgetting.

"Be safe. Be loved," I whispered to my son, his eyelashes clumped with pearls of water, his little lips opened in an *O* of surprise. I anointed his forehead with the black river silt, pressing a mother's charm into his body.

"Be happy. Be nobody. Be a passerby."

Epilogue

Gallia Comata 72 CE

The young woman, her face streaked with dust and tears, disappeared. The river disappeared.

And yet, for a moment, the hut was filled with people.

A hunched man wearing a prayer shawl with a grizzled, gray beard had Miriam's nose. The tall, statuesque figure must have been Miriam's mother. Salome was there, recognizable by her willowy frame and long white hair. Marta was closest to Leukas, kneeling at his side, looking up at him with a face so soft and open he thought he might weep. A woman in the corner stared at him with slender almond-shaped eyes and he knew it was Kemat. Lazaros stood at the door with Yosseph. Both wore blue cloaks and carried sturdy wooden staffs.

And there was Yeshua behind Miriam. A big man with a head of wild curls. A square jaw. Eyes that were almost too large for his face, wide and aflame. But he was not looking at Leukas. The man was gazing at Miriam. Miriam, the crone with white hair and a face mapped with wrinkles. His hand lightly brushed the papery skin of her cheek, and she turned her face into his touch.

This *is the resurrection,* he realized. *She has brought them all back to life. Right here. For me.*

The candle between them sputtered out. Morning light streamed in through the window, turning the puddle of melted fat on the table between them gold.

When Leukas looked up again, they were gone. Only Miriam remained.

Dust sparkled in the air. The cold of morning snaked inside, curling around his feet.

Outside, someone was cooking. A thick, salty aroma reached him. Sera had come back. She was singing something in a foreign tongue. He listened as she offered up tendrils of song to the coming dawn. And dawn it was. Light was pouring into the small hut. Pale, clean, newborn light.

Light that was too clean. Too cold. He longed to return to the heat of Galilee, the humid air of the river.

Take me back to Bethany, he longed to say, although he had never been there.

Somewhere a turtledove churned the air with its muffled song. The mournful sound told him that the world Miriam had given to him no longer existed.

Only one question remained. "Where is your son? Where is Yudah?"

Nothing changed in her expression, but her eyes appeared to contract and shatter like a glass ornament thrown to the floor.

"I will not speak of him. His story is not mine to tell."

"Does he live?" Leukas sensed warning like a physical presence in the room, thickening the air.

Miriam, too, was undergoing some change, almost in element, appearing as cold and stiff as the white cliffs he had traveled through to reach this cold country.

"That is all. That is the story."

She would protect her son to the end.

He nodded. He could taste the salt on his lips. How long had it been since he had cried last? Years. "What should I do?" Leukas asked. "What do I do with this story?" The pressure between his eyes was almost too much to bear.

"I do not know." Miriam's eyes sparkled. "All I know is that I have given you my family and my heart. I have given you Bethany. My sister. My mother. My father. My brother. I have given you Yosseph and Kemat. And I have given you my beloved Yeshua."

"I do not know how to write it as you told it," Leukas admitted. "Who could understand it?"

Suddenly, for one last moment, they were all there again. In the hut. Surrounding him, watching him. Asking him to hold their memory.

Marta. Lazaros. Nicodemus. Hadassah. Kemat. Yohanna. Salome. Imah. Yiskah. Ivah. Yudas. Yael. Adah. Yosseph. Yeshua.

Miriam reached out then, and she touched him. Her hands burned like fire against his cheek. The pressure between his eyes melted and he felt a liquid, golden calm descend into him like he had never before known. "Do not worry about who will understand. It will serve to awaken those who are ready. My story is made of soil and water and wind and pain. It lives in people's breath. It is held in the body. Someday it will not just be written down. It will be told, woman to woman. It will be sung."

She turned from him then and swept from the hut, picking up a basket from beside the doorway. He followed after, but as he broke out into the soft, pink morning, she was already far ahead, across the fields.

He watched her go, her hand trailing the tall, dried grasses, picking something and putting it into her basket. The rosy light caught the silver in her hair, turning it almost red.

Sera was sitting on the ground near the cooking fire, twisting grasses into a braid.

"Will she come back?" he asked.

"Yes," Sera smiled. "She always comes back."

Acknowledgments

Thank you to my female ancestors. Perdita Finn. Patricia Havens. Nellie Havens. Molly Finn. Elizabeth Laycock. Ellen Laycock. Thank you to my more-than-human mothers of the land of the Munsee Lenape. Overlook Mountain. Lewis Hollow. Tivoli Bays. Mount Tremper. Cooper Lake. The Ashokan Reservoir. The mountain lions and black bears. The honey fungi and chanterelles. The lichen-laced glacial erratics and spotted salamanders. The crickets and tree frogs. The coyotes and blue herons.

Thank you to my family. To my father, Clark Strand, who early on invited me to the table with adults to talk scriptural exegesis and theology. To my brother Jonah for the laughter and companionship. To my cousins Adam and Daniel Finn for music and mirth. To Michal Seligman and Mark Finn, my other set of parents. Thank you to Alana Seligman, Dana Seligman, Talia Seligman, and Noam Seligman for opening your homes and hearts to me in Israel and introducing me to the landscape that I would spend so many years writing inside. Thank you to Lucinda Finn for your belief in me as a writer. Thank you to the animal kin that guided this book into being: Sebastian, Rosamund, Sputnick, Oliver, Rumi, and Fujiyama. And thank you to my canine companion Baba Ghanoush for overseeing the final edits.

My best writing happens in the caffeinated clamor of coffee shops. *The Madonna Secret* was written thanks to the strong coffee and warm welcome of Rough Draft in Kingston, Bread Alone in Woodstock, and The Pines in Mount Tremper, all in the Hudson Valley of New York. Thank you to the early and crucial creative input of several trusted readers: Diana Rowan Rockefeller, Marion Albers, Hannah Sparaganah, Perdita Finn, Clark Strand, Alicia Encisio Litschi, and Robert Burke Warren.

I am deeply grateful for my editor Richard Grossinger. His belief in this book has been key in bringing it into the world. Thank you to my agent Anne Marie O'Farrell for supporting *The Madonna Secret* so early on. And many thanks to the wonderful team at Inner Traditions.

Gratitude to the rivers and bodies of water of the Hudson Valley that flowed through me into the vasculature of Second Temple Period Palestine. The Hudson River. The Battenkill River. The Millstream. The Esopus Stream. The Beaverkill. The Rondout Creek. And thank you to the time I spent in Israel, walking the same paths, following the same rivers that my characters would someday tread.

Thank you to the many friends whose love and support made this book possible: Marion Albers, Sabin Bailey, Seraphina Mallon Breiman, Polly Paton Brown, Daniela Decaro, Edith Lerner, Karen Morissey, Kristen Mounsy, Mary Evelyn Pritchard, Ilana Silber, Hannah Sparaganah, Michael Steward, Emily Rose Theobald, and Fiona Saxman.

This book would not be possible without the dedicated study and scholarship of a great many people. I would like to honor Bruce Chilton, John Dominic Crossan, Anne Baring, Jules Cashford, Marcus Borg, Simon Schama, Aryeh Kaplan, Jacob Neusner, Elaine Pagels, Willis Barstone, Marvin Meyer, Karen Armstrong, Michael Haag, Margaret Starbird, Susan Haskins, Riane Eisler, William G. Dever, Bart D. Erhman, Stephen Mitchell, and Rabbi Joseph Telushkin.

Thank you to my grandmothers for whom I wrote this book: Patricia Finn, Nellie Havens, Molly Finn, Lois Walker, and Andrea Sender.

Lastly, I want to thank my gray cat Sebastian whose unexpected death inspired me to begin this book many moons ago.